Great Mother

Robert Grant

NT Publishing Company
P.O. Box 43572
Louisville, KY 40253-0572
www.NTPublishingCompany.com

This book is also available as an eBook.

DEDICATION

This book is dedicated to the next generation of medicine.

OTHER TITLES BY ROBERT GRANT

ACKNOWLEDGMENTS

The cover design is by Tatiana Vila.

www.viladesign.net

COMING SOON

Sovereigns' Refuge

BULK PURCHASES

We will gladly provide copies of this book at a discounted price for bulk purchases. Send a request to Robert@NTPublishingCompany.com

PROLOGUE

Somewhere in a remote part of the Himalayas is a small monastery. It was carefully designed by ancient craftsmen skilled in the art of feng shui. Clever engineers positioned it on a small ledge halfway up the face of a mountain.

They took advantage of the mountain's perpetual misty cloud cover to keep it hidden from the world. Miles of bewildering canyons make it inaccessible to all except the initiated. Indistinguishable from the rock from which it is carved, only a few know of its existence. The resident monks call it Sovereigns' Refuge.

It is a place lost to time, as if time does not exist. Still, on this day two cloaked figures quietly stand on the east terrace watching the morning sun peek between two misty mountains.

It is a woman's voice that breaks the silence.

"It is time."

CHAPTER 1

Twice already the jury reported they were unable to reach a unanimous decision and both times the Judge sent them back for further deliberations. A hung jury is like a tie. Nobody is ever satisfied with a tie. Especially, a man like Wilbur Goth.

Goth is one of the richest men in the world and is accustomed to getting what he wants. He did not want a hung jury. Laying a heavy hand on my shoulder he told me that a win in a case like this could launch a young lawyer's career. What he didn't have to say is a loss would ruin me.

I needed that not guilty verdict as much as Goth did, but after five days of deliberations, the Judge was on the verge of declaring a mistrial, which could lead to a new trial. Goth didn't want the prosecutor to get a second bite at the apple. He wanted finality.

The Judge had cleared the courtroom while she considered the matter, so I returned to my office to await her decision, but with each passing minute, I grew less confident in the outcome.

Gaia, the firm's documents clerk, stuck her head in my office door and asked, "Have you heard anything yet, Mr. Li?"

I shook my head.

"Don't look so glum," she said with a broad smile. "You'll spoil that handsome face."

Her compliment didn't feel like a come-on. Gaia has a way about her. No matter what dark place my thoughts wander into, she always manages to lead me out. It's less about what she says and more about a strange light that radiates from her. It's as if I can see her spirit.

She is tall, maybe 6'2", dressed in a sky blue button down shirt and a black skirt just shy of indecent. Her long dark hair is woven into an intricate braid that falls straight down the center of her back. She tied the end of the braid with semi precious blue stones that match her blue eyes.

It's hard to be grumpy when she's around, so I flashed her my best smile. Funny thing about a smile, it always seems to work a strange alchemy on my mood and on the moods of everyone around me. It's as if a jolt of happiness runs through anyone who is lucky enough to come into contact with it.

"That's more like it," she said.

The smile was interrupted by the theme song from my favorite 1950's legal drama. I checked my mobile and saw it was a call from the Judge's secretary. The anxiety returned with a vengeance and I hesitated for just a moment.

"Go ahead, answer it," said Gaia.

I put on my game face and said, "Hello, this is Grant Li."

"Mr. Li, this is Judge Flint's secretary," said the young man on the other end of the air wave. "The Judge wants everyone back in court in thirty minutes."

"Do we have a verdict?" I asked.

I couldn't help but wince at the desperate tone in my voice.

He paused before answering, "I really can't say, Mr. Li."

"Thanks, I'm on my way," I said.

I dropped the phone in my pants pocket and slung a briefcase over a shoulder. I took a calming breath and reminded myself, good or bad, this was about to come to a head.

"Good luck, Mr. Li," said Gaia.

"Thank you," I said.

As she turned to leave, I asked, "Is he in his office?"

She nodded and scurried off to get some work done in the firm's file room.

John Biggs is a senior partner in the law firm. His legendary skill as a tenacious litigator is the reason I chose this particular firm. I wanted to mentor with one of the best, but lately our relationship had been strained, because John was upset that Wilbur Goth chose me to defend him.

More than once, he shook his head and said, "Why would he want someone barely out of law school to defend him against serious criminal charges? It makes no sense."

John has the big corner office and makes the big bucks, while my tiny office overlooks the pigeon infested HVAC unit perched on the adjoining rooftop. While Pathogen is based in Louisville, it is an international company with an army of lawyers all over the world representing them.

John is the company's local counsel and Wilbur Goth is the CEO. I didn't want to admit it, but John was right. Clients like Pathogen do not want a young associate attorney to defend them against serious felony charges.

John would want to know that the jury was back in the courtroom, so I headed down the hall to deliver the news. His secretary, Helen Gloria, usually guards the door to his office, but she was in the break room arguing with her tearful teenage daughter.

While most of the attorneys in the firm fear Helen, clearly her daughter does not. Helen has been known to send more than one young associate away from John's doors with his tail tucked between his legs. She is one of those women who look soft on the surface, but when you cross them, they cut you to shreds with a tongue as sharp as a Samurai sword.

Helen's daughter looked like a younger version of Helen. They were both medium height brunettes with big brown doe eyes. Their body types were soft and curvy. Mom was dressed in a white blouse and blue skirt. Her daughter wore a plain white t-shirt and blue jeans.

"I promise you I will be there, Laurie," said Helen.

"Mom, you never do what you say you're going to do," said Laurie. "Why should I trust you?"

Helen's shoulders slumped just enough to tell me that Laurie had hit a raw nerve and her half-hearted response confirmed she was losing ground.

"I'm doing the best I can," said Helen.

"No you're not, Mom," said Laurie. "You give everything you have to this job and to that tyrant you work for. There's nothing left for me."

"Show some respect, young lady," said Helen.

"Really, Mom?" said Laurie with a level of sarcasm only a teenage girl can muster. "How about you show me some respect for a change? Isn't that what we're really talking about here?"

Helen's sob was all the response I heard as I moved out of earshot and closer to John's office. It's amazing how much of a conversation you can catch just walking by an open door. In this instance, it was enough to make me think twice about ever having a teenage daughter of my own. Not that there is much chance of that since I'm currently separated from my wife, Cynthia.

Still, Laurie had made a valid point and I felt a rush of compassion for her. There are rumors about John and his secretary that are fueled by their behavior toward each other. Rarely does an office romance end well, and in this instance, it was clearly putting a strain on her relationship with her daughter. Besides, John is a known womanizer. They deserve better.

Helen is in her mid-thirties and a few years younger than John's oldest daughter. Twice married, he has a second family. His son is about the same age as Laurie, and the last I heard, they are both juniors at duPont Manual High School.

I must admit, it was a relief to move out of range of the mother-daughter battle because it sounded to me like it was going to get much uglier before it got any better. However, my relief was short lived, since I found John in his office arguing with a teenager of his own.

John is soft and gray. If I had to guess, he was born conservative. He was dressed in gray slacks and a blue blazer worn over a light blue shirt loaded with enough starch that it could stand on its own.

At first blush, he looks like a pushover, maybe a minor clerk, but certainly not a high-powered lawyer, which is exactly what he wants his enemies to think. John's son must take after his mother. He is tall, thin and blessed with runway model good looks. However, I could see he was tough like his father.

"Richard, I have a law practice to run and you're upset because I missed a football game," said John.

"Yeah right, Dad, it was just a football game," said Richard. "It doesn't matter that I scored the game winning touchdown, because it's all about you and your stupid clients."

"If it wasn't for clients like Pathogen, you wouldn't have the luxury of playing football instead of working after school like I did when I was your age," said John.

"I play football because you're never home," said Richard. "You don't get it, Dad. What I really need is a father. Do you know where I can find one?"

"That was unnecessary," said John.

"For once can you put me before Wilbur Goth?" asked Richard.

John cut his eyes toward me and said, "Speaking of Wilbur Goth, do we have good news, Grant?"

I shrugged.

"The judge's office called," I said. "She wants us back in court."

"Is this the Goth trial?" asked Richard.

I nodded.

"It figures…the man I hate most in this world will most likely dodge justice and it's all on you, Grant Li," said Richard as he stormed past me.

John scowled, but let him leave without another word.

"Did you inform the client?" asked John.

I shook my head.

"Not yet," I answered.

John raised a bushy eyebrow. His disapproval of me was getting old.

"I just got the message and wanted to make sure you were the first to know," I said.

John gave me a begrudging nod and said, "I'll call him myself."

"Suit yourself," I said.

"Let me know how it goes," said John.

I had a feeling he was conflicted about the outcome. It wouldn't surprise me a bit to learn John wanted a guilty verdict against his biggest client just to see me fail.

"Will do," I said and turned to leave.

"Grant, you better not lose this," said John.

I looked him in eye and instead of telling him I could do without the added pressure, I simply said, "Roger that."

It's six blocks from our office to Federal Court. I prefer to walk, but usually drive when I'm loaded with files. Not that it's much help since there is nowhere to park close by thanks to the car bombing of a Federal building in Oklahoma City back in 1995. In this instance, a lightweight brief case hung from a shoulder and my hands were free of files, so I walked. Besides, I needed to clear my head.

Pathogen is the world's biggest pharmaceutical company. Last year they developed a drug called Gutchriem that is now routinely prescribed by physicians all over the world for acid reflux and other intestinal disorders. It didn't take long before patients using the drug started getting sick.

In an unusual move, the prosecutor, Zeke Kruthers, brought Federal fraud charges directly against the CEO, Wilber Goth, alleging the public was intentionally deceived about the drug's risks. In typical Goth fashion, he went on the attack, using Pathogen's public relations machine to portray the case as a witch hunt that was less about the law and more about a young prosecutor's political ambitions.

It was still early spring, but unseasonably hot and humid in the Ohio Valley. The river is flanked on both sides by knobs that trap pollution, pollen, and heat which hang over the city like an oppressive blanket of smog that is hell bent on suffocating the residents. I thought about the health advisory issued earlier in the day by Louisville Metro Air Pollution Control District and second guessed the decision to walk.

Unfortunately, it was too late to turn back, so instead, I picked up the pace and breezed past the wig shops and other merchants struggling to make a living on a dying inner city street. By the time I reached the courthouse steps, my crisp white shirt had melted into my skin.

A blast of cool air greeted me at the metal detectors located just inside the door. I dropped the brief case, car keys, cell phone, and suit jacket onto the conveyor belt and stepped through the detector. It was manned by a United States Marshall, named Mark Fritz, who served with my Uncle Jim in Afghanistan.

"Good luck, Grant," said Mark.

"Thanks Mark," I said as I collected my things. "It's been a tough trial."

"Aren't they all?" he said.

"No kidding," I said. "It's our way of settling disputes in a civilized society without resorting to bloodshed, but if you ask me, they are no less savage."

"I don't know about that, Grant," said Mark. "I've seen savagery and it can scar a man for life."

Mark was right, comparing our justice system to war is foolish. I nodded and headed down the hall.

While State Court is always filled with a mass of broken humanity, the Federal Court Building feels like a mausoleum. The old marble floors are polished to a sheen, but the brass doors that once led to the post office, social security administration, and other federal offices are closed and locked. Foot traffic is limited to the few individuals on official court business, and at the moment, it was my solitary footsteps echoing along the corridor leading to the elevators.

As I exited the elevator, I checked the time and was pleased to see I had eight minutes to spare. If I was lucky, I would get a chance to sit in an empty courtroom for a few minutes before everyone arrives. It's a small pleasure that also gives me a chance to focus my thoughts on the task at hand.

This particular courtroom has a special feel to. It is old school, spacious and full of rich woodwork that I find comforting. Maybe it's because of the natural materials. I love the woods, and while I don't condone cutting down trees to fulfill man's vanity, the polished wood makes me feel like I belong there.

The double doors leading into the courtroom are at least ten feet tall and made of polished oak trimmed in brass. The brass is etched with the scales of justice on one door and a blindfolded lady liberty on the other. They are perfectly balanced on their hinges and easily swing outward.

As hoped, the room was empty so I made my way to the bar, eased through the swinging gate and took a seat at the defense table. This is the only time I can relax in court and I needed it to mentally prepare myself for what was about to happen.

Taking a lesson from martial arts, I've learned that what happens in the mind shapes the events of our lives. I took a deep breath, relaxed and envisioned the foreman reading a not guilty verdict.

It was working pretty good until the curse of modern life disturbed the peaceful moment. Where ever we go, our cell phones follow us like a little puppy demanding our constant attention, but not nearly as cute.

I wanted to ignore it, but you never know when it's going to be an important call and this wasn't just any ringtone, it was Mom's long term care nurse, so I took the call.

"Is everything okay, Roxanne," I said.

"Hi Grant, it's Roxanne," she said.

"How's Mom?" I asked.

"There's an emergency, you need to get here right away," said Roxanne.
"What's happened?" I asked.
The call dropped. I tried to reconnect with her, but she didn't pick up.

CHAPTER 2

I owe Mom's nursing home a lot of money and their collection efforts have been getting more aggressive. Lately, I've been busy with the trial and ignored their calls, but they've never been cold enough to fake a medical emergency to reach me.

Mom's life could be in danger. If it really is a medical emergency, I will never forgive myself if I'm not there. On the other hand, I need to be here for the verdict. Torn in two directions, I sat frozen in my seat, struggling with an impossible situation.

I don't know how much time passed before the doors swung open and the prosecutor, Zeke Kruthers walked into the courtroom. Zeke can't be more than 5'6" and is shaped like a teddy bear. He is pushing forty and balding at the crown. What Zeke lacks in physical strength is made up with a force of will that leaves you thinking he is 6'4" and packed with muscle.

Zeke nodded respectfully in my direction and then took a seat at the prosecutor's table. I hadn't noticed before, but there was an envelope at his seat. He picked it up and turned it over in his hands, before setting it down again just as Goth entered the courtroom.

Goth is medium height and round. Not fat exactly, just round. Most people's heads are more oval than round, but not Goth's. His head is round and a size too big for the rest of him. Everything else is curved. His hips and thighs are soft and rounded, like a woman's, but that's as far as the softness goes.

Goth is edgy and dark of spirit with a head of orange hair that contrasts sharply with the black suits he always wears. I suspect there may have been a fool or two in his past who tried to call him Pumpkin Head and lived to regret it. I know that is the nickname that comes to mind when I think of him.

He extended an ice cold hand that I took for a brief moment and then quickly released.

"Let's get this over with," said Goth. "I have a meeting tomorrow morning in London."

"You seem confident of the outcome," I said.

"I'm the master of my fate," he said.

"Right now the jury seems to be struggling with your fate and the Judge is on the verge of calling this a mistrial," I said.

"You won't escape justice with a mistrial," said Zeke. "If necessary, we will retry this case."

Goth glared at the prosecutor.

"There won't be a mistrial," said Goth.

I didn't know whether he was blustering or if he knew something that I didn't know. He certainly had the resources to tamper with the outcome of a trial, but that is unthinkable and I pushed it out my mind.

Zeke turned away from Goth's glare and picked up the envelope, but then set it aside when the bailiff entered from a side door near the bench.

"All rise," said the bailiff.

Judge Sarah Flint entered the courtroom and took a seat at the bench. Federal Judges are appointed for life and Judge Flint wears the deep lines cut into her face as a living testament to a long career on the bench. She has a reputation as a brilliant jurist who is both fair and tough. Judge Flint has little patience for fools and liars.

She took a long hard look at Goth and said, "Gentlemen, the jury foreman reports we have verdict. Let's bring in the jury."

A side door opened and the jury filed into the courtroom. I studied them carefully for any sign of their decision. One juror in particular caught my attention. She was a twenty-something mother who spent a lot of time during the trial shaking her head and glaring at Goth, except now, she was smiling in his direction. I hoped this sudden switch in body language meant we had a favorable verdict.

Once the jury was seated, the Judge asked, "Mr. Foreman, has the jury reached a decision?"

The Foreman stood and answered, "Yes, your honor."

"Bailiff will you bring the verdict to the bench?" said the Judge.

The bailiff accepted a folded piece of paper from the Foreman and handed it to the Judge. She read it and then cast a hard look at Goth, before handing it back to the bailiff, who then returned it to the Foreman.

"Please read the verdict, Mr. Foreman," said Judge Flint in a hard tone.

The Foreman looked at Goth and then at the Judge. He swallowed hard, took a deep breath and then read.

"We the jury, find the Defendant, Wilbur Goth, not guilty of all charges," said the Foreman.

"Ladies and Gentlemen, thank you for your honorable service in this matter," said the Judge. "Our freedom as a nation is dependent on the honest faithful service of men and women who sacrifice their time and families to dispense justice."

It sounded like a lecture to me, rather than a heartfelt expression of gratitude and the looks on the faces of many of the jurors told me they felt the same way.

"Mr. Goth, you have been found not guilty by a jury of your peers and are free to go," said Judge Flint.

She slammed the gavel hard and brusquely left the courtroom. Not once during the trial had she used the gavel, but I wasn't about to let her antics spoil this for me.

I raised a victory fist and said, "Yes!"

I have to admit, this was one of those shining moments that we get to experience from time to time. In these rare moments, all is right with the world. Everything is perfect and possible. I was on top of the world and it felt damn good.

Goth patted me on the back and said, "Thank you for a job well done, Grant."

I shook his hand and said, "Congratulations!"

"I should be congratulating you," said Goth.

"Thank you," I said.

There was something odd in his eyes that I couldn't quite put a finger on. It was almost predatory, but then it quickly disappeared.

"You deserve everything that will come from this," he said.

Before I could say anything else, Zeke Kruthers stormed out of the courtroom. Goth watched him leave with a look of complete contempt on his face. When the door shut behind Zeke, Goth turned his attention back to me and I thought I saw remnants of that contempt in his eyes, but then he smiled and left without another word. I remembered Mom and the nursing home, so I didn't waste any time gathering my things and following Goth out the door.

When I was eight years old, all Dad ever talked about was buying a new Harley, but couldn't bring himself to do it. Instead, he would shake his head and tell Mom he had a family to think about. She had ideas of her own. Mom scrimped and saved for it anyway and on his thirtieth birthday she fulfilled Dad's dream.

Mom woke me early that morning and whispered that it was a special day. She led me down the hall to the bedroom where Dad was snoring softly. Together we pounced on him while singing happy birthday. Dad growled at us for waking him, but his eyes were shining and filled with love.

After our early morning celebration, Mom told him she was having car trouble and asked if he would take me to school. We followed him to the garage and watched as he lifted the overhead door. Instead of his car, a new Harley was sitting in his parking space. I've never seen Dad so surprised as he was in that moment.

After dropping me off at school my parents decided to take the Harley out for a maiden ride. I never saw Dad again thanks to a hit-and-run driver. Mom...well, she lay in a crumbled heap at the bottom of a ditch for several hours before a passerby discovered her. They waited an hour for an ambulance that never showed.

The Good-Samaritan finally gave up and carried her to his car, put her broken body in the back seat and drove her to the hospital himself. Nobody knows for sure whether his good deed or the wreck caused her paralysis from the neck down, but she's been that way ever since.

With Dad gone and Mom unable to care for a child, Uncle Jim raised me, but he almost didn't get the chance. Some know-it-all social worker wanted to place me in foster care. She kept telling the Judge I needed the positive influence of a woman in my life. The social worker didn't like the fact that Uncle Jim had lived all over the world, mostly on military bases, and she was suspicious that he had never married. She was convinced that a single man knew nothing about raising a son.

That social worker picked the wrong man to attack, because Uncle Jim knows a few things about winning a fight. The Marine Corps trained him for some hush-

hush special ops unit that he never talks about. A legal battle is no different than any other fight and Uncle Jim put up a tough fight. He convinced the Judge that it was in my best interests to be with him. As far as I'm concerned, the Judge made the right decision. What kind of crazy person would think foster care is better than a loving family member?

Taking care of Mom has been tough. When the insurance ran out, the doctors lost interest. I was glad because I hated the hospital. Uncle Jim brought Mom home and set her up in her old bedroom. Every day after school, I sat by her side and prayed until bedtime. I was taught that God always answers our prayers, and with the faith of a child, I prayed for God to heal her.

Days turned into weeks, then months. When I lost interest in everything else, including Ch'ing's martial arts classes, Uncle Jim decided it was time for an intervention, so he sat me down and we had a long talk.

"Grant, I know you've been praying a lot for your mother," he said.

"Yes, sir," I said with a small nod of the head.

He patted me on the shoulder and said, "She's in my prayers as well."

"Why hasn't God answered our prayers?" I asked.

"It's a funny thing about prayers," said Uncle Jim. "They are always heard and answered. It's up to us to be patient and to keep our eyes and ears open."

"I asked God to make her like she used to be," I said.

"Do you believe she will be?" he asked.

"Yes, sir," I answered.

"Then God has heard your prayers and he will take the appropriate action in his own time," said Uncle Jim.

"I don't want to wait," I said.

He squeezed my shoulder as he said, "I know, Grant. There's something else you should know about faith."

"What's that, sir?" I asked.

"An important part of faith is having the courage to trust that things will work out for the best in end," he answered.

"Yes, sir," I said. "Will it be okay if I keep praying?"

"Yes, it will be okay," said Uncle Jim. "In the meantime, it's our job to take care of ourselves and leave it to God to work out the details. Do you understand what I'm saying, Grant?"

"I'm not sure," I answered.

"Taking care of your mother seemed like the right thing to do at first, but now I see it's a job best left to a nurse," said Uncle Jim.

"I can do it," I said.

"I know you can, but it takes a lot of time and it's a job for a grown-up…a professional," he said.

I tried my best to keep the sadness locked inside, but it would have none of it.

"I ca…ca…can…dddd…do it," I sobbed.

I can count the number of hugs Uncle Jim has given me on one hand. This was hands down his best effort.

When he finally pulled himself together again, he said, "I know son, but it's time to give you your childhood back. You should be playing with your friends and doing fun stuff, like martial arts with Chi'ng."

A few days later we drove Mom to Shady Days. In the years that followed a day never went by without me saying a prayer for her and hoping it would be the day she made a full recovery. That was twenty years ago.

CHAPTER 3

Shady Days is located in a historic sanatorium that was built in 1912 following an outbreak of the white plague. Uncle Jim chose it because he thought Mom would like the hilltop view of the Ohio River. Other than a central tower constructed of white stone that is now stained by years of smog, the four story building is covered with red brick and ivy. One of the unusual features of the building's architecture is the way it curves to follow the ridgeline.

When antibiotic treatments proved effective for tuberculosis, the sanatorium was closed. After sitting empty for years, like a forgotten ghost haunting the hillside, the owners of Shady Days bought the property and converted it to an adult long-term care facility.

While the outside of the building looks antique, they spared no expense giving the inside a polished new look. The living quarters are designed like luxury apartments, complete with a comfortable living room and eat-in kitchen where residents can make themselves a snack at any hour. Since Mom is bedridden, the living room and kitchen are used by her only visitors, me and Uncle Jim.

All that fanciness makes it expensive keeping Mom there. I haven't opened a bill lately, but the last time I checked, I owe Shady Days nearly $200,000.00. I don't have the money and don't know where I'll get it. Between my wife's extravagant spending and the high costs of getting Mom the care she needs, I'm on the verge of bankruptcy.

A few months back, I worked out a payment plan with their administrative director, Alexi Minted, but after John cut my monthly bonuses I missed a few payments. When I confronted him about it, he claimed the firm's profits were down and he had to reduce attorney bonuses.

We both know that's a bunch of bull. John got a young woman in trouble and had to pay her off. Instead of using his own money to pay for his sins, he used mine.

Some of Mom's functioning comes and goes, so she has both good days and bad. The worst are the days she stops breathing and they have to put her on a respirator to keep her alive. Those are the days I fear the most. Since Roxanne didn't take my return call, I had no way of knowing whether this was one of those days or if the nursing home had stooped to an all-time low to get their money.

Fortunately, the facility isn't far from my downtown office and I expected to have an answer soon. I took River Road, a scenic byway that provides spectacular views of the Ohio River. On most days you can catch a glimpse of Louisville's small sailing community out on the water. The sailboats share the river with an authentic steam power paddle wheel and barges running coal up and down the river. The paddle wheel gives the river a whimsical, out-of-time, Mark Twain mystique.

These days my only transportation is an old pickup truck Dad left me. I kept it for sentimental reasons, but even though it is fighting a losing a battle with rust and rips off an occasional noisy backfire, I have grown fond of it.

As much as Louisville wants to be a big city, it is really a small town with loads of southern friendliness. Most folks are pleased to see you and Ginger is no exception. She mans the front desk at Shady Days and we've been on a first name basis for years.

Ginger is fifty, plump, and warm. She loves talking to people and when the administration tried to give her a promotion with more money and responsibility, but less contact with people, she rebelled.

She was wearing a classic white nurses outfit, complete with the little white hat. If it wasn't so conservative, I would have thought she found it at a costume store. All of that white contrasted with her auburn hair and pink skin tone.

Ginger is a sweet person, but scatterbrained. Sometimes it's hard to get her to focus.

"Oh, I'm glad you're finally here, Grant," said Ginger.

"What's the emergency?" I asked.

Ginger looked around and then whispered, "It's not right."

"What's not right?" I asked.

Her eyes darted in two different directions at once as she whispered loud enough to be heard halfway down the hall, "Shhh…keep it down, would you?"

I lowered my voice, "What do you mean…it's not right?"

"I can't say," she said.

This was going nowhere, so I asked instead, "Where is she?"

"Intensive care," she answered.

I've never had a panic attack that I know of, but this had to be one. It felt like three hundred pound gorilla was jumping up and down on my chest. I tried to grab my heart, but all I got was a hand full of shirt.

"Are you okay, Grant," said Ginger. "You don't look so good."

Mom has been there before and even though she's a survivor, it doesn't get any easier. Each time, I fear this might be the one she can't win. Remembering my martial arts training, I replaced the picture in my mind of Mom dying alone in a hospital bed with an image of her sitting up in bed, brushing her hair. It was the picture of her perfect health. It helped.

Sometimes we get off track, but all it takes is a moment or two to set ourselves in the right direction, with the right frame of mind. When my hands finally stopped shaking, I thanked Ginger and headed to intensive care.

As I turned toward the elevators, Ginger said one last time, "It aint' right. There's nothing right about it."

The medical wing of the facility looks and feels just like a hospital. I'm not sure I like that since hospitals trigger such painful memories for me. On the other hand, it is reassuring to know they are equipped to respond to Mom's medical needs.

The intensive care unit is small, but seems to have all the latest medical gadgets. I found Mom surrounded by a doctor and two nurses working to resuscitate her. The panic attack returned, but this time the room felt oppressively hot. I removed my suit jacket and looked for a place to sit. The only option was a short stool on wheels tucked away in the corner of the room which I gratefully took. The key to a calm mind in a crisis is to center yourself in the eye of the storm, but it can't be found outside of yourself. It resides in your center like a calm pool of water radiating peace. That's where I went to calm myself and when I opened my eyes again, I could watch Mom's medical team work with far less anxiety.

Mom was lying on her back. Roxanne tilted Mom's head back slightly and lifted her chin. The doctor stacked his hands, one on top of the other, in the middle of her chest. Using his body weight, he pushed hard and fast. After about a minute, he paused while the second nurse pinched Mom's nose and did several rescue breaths before dropping her ear to Mom's mouth.

The nurse looked up at the doctor and said, "She's breathing."

"We're not out of the woods yet," said the doctor. "I want to know what caused this. Put her on saline and draw some blood."

The nurses scrambled in two different directions to comply with his orders. The doctor was in his early thirties, medium height, sandy blond hair, green eyes, and physically fit. He wore thick glasses, blue jeans, sneakers and a lab coat with a pocket protector filled with ink pens and a penlight. He was both handsome and a total nerd at the same time. His nametag identified him as Dr. Michaels.

"Who are you?" he asked.

"I'm her son, Grant Li," I answered as I extended my hand. "What is wrong with my mother?"

He took my hand in a firm grip and answered, "We don't know yet. You shouldn't be here."

"I'll stay out the way, but I'm not leaving her side," I said.

"Suit yourself," he said.

"What happened?" I asked.

"The nurse was feeding her and she started choking," he answered.

"What did she feed her?" I asked.

"One of her favorites, apple sauce," he answered.

"You wouldn't think she would choke on apple sauce," I said.

"I agree," he said.

"Anything else?" I asked.

"Sweet green tea," he answered.

"What happened then?" I asked.

"While the nurse was checking for obstructions, your mother broke into a cold sweat," said Dr. Michaels.

I felt a chill because I had heard this before.

"Was that followed by shaking?" I asked.

Dr. Michaels' eyes widened.

"How did you know that?" he asked.

"When the shaking stopped, so did her breathing," I said.

He nodded.

"How could you possible know this?" he asked.

My hands were shaking when I asked, "Is she taking Gutchriem?"

"Yes," he answered.

"When was her last dose?" I asked.

He checked the chart and then gave me a long appraising look before answering.

"It was fifteen minutes before she was fed," he answered.

"We need to get that drug out of her system," I said.

"It is a harmless heartburn treatment," said Dr. Michaels. "It couldn't have possibly caused this."

"Listen to me very carefully, doctor," I said. "I just spent two weeks in trial listening to evidence that Gutchriem causes those very symptoms."

Dr. Michaels slid his glasses down an inch and studied me over the top of them.

"What exactly do you do for a living?" he asked.

"I'm an attorney," I answered.

He let out a barely audible groan.

"These symptoms are not listed as possible side effects of Gutchriem," he said.

"No they're not, but there have been twelve deaths since this drug was approved by the FDA," I said. "I do not want my mother to be number thirteen."

"Thirteen," he repeated.

"Can you pump her stomach?" I asked.

He nodded.

"I need to call the poison control center first," he said.

Roxanne walked into the room and said, "Do you want me to make the call, Doctor?"

I raised my voice, "Do it now, Dr. Michaels! There is no known antidote and time is of the essence. We have to get that drug out of her stomach before any more of it enters her blood stream. Her life depends upon it."

Dr. Michaels nodded and turned to answer Roxanne, "Never mind, let's pump her now. Have you ever done a gastric lavage, nurse?"

She shook her head.

"Let's begin with intubation," said Dr. Michaels.

Roxanne nodded before grabbing a silver device shaped like a water pistol. She tilted Mom's head back, inserted the device in her mouth and then worked a plastic tube into her throat.

I must have looked a bit pale, because she said, "This protects her trachea."

"Would you rather wait outside?" asked Dr. Michaels.

I shook my head.

"I want her in left lateral decubitus position," said the doctor.

Roxanne tilted Mom to the left and stuffed a pillow under her right side. Then she titled her head slight to the left.

"Give her a bite block in case she wakes up," said Dr. Michaels.

Roxanne added something that looks like an infant's pacifier to Mom's mouth. Dr. Michaels took blue tubing and measured from the bite block to her stomach before marking the spot with a sharpie. While he was bent over her, he placed an ear close to her mouth and listened.

He nodded in satisfaction and then began feeding the tubing through an opening in the bite block, before connecting it to a port in the hand pump that Roxanne had set near Mom's head. A second port in the pump was connected to a plastic bag on the floor.

Dr. Michaels pulled the handle of the pump back and then released it a couple of times to confirm the flow of stomach content to the bag on floor. He added some charcoal to the pump and connected a bag of water hanging from an I.V. Stand. He double checked his connections and then began pumping until nothing else came out of Mom's stomach. Roxanne removed the tubing and the pillow.

I was surprised at their speed and efficiency. The entire procedure only took a couple of minutes from start to finish.

Afterwards Dr. Michaels pulled me aside and said, "I will continue to monitor your mother's condition."

"Thanks, I'd like to see her as soon as wakes up," I said.

"We can do that," he said.

"Thank you for listening to me," I said.

"I hope you're right about this," said Dr. Michaels.

"Do you plan to run more tests?" I asked.

"Yes, I want to be sure we didn't miss anything," he answered.

"Will you let me know as soon as you have the results?" I asked.

"Yes, of course," he answered. "By the way, is your trial over?"

The trial was the last thing I wanted to talk about. I was emotionally drained and physically exhausted, but tried not to let it show to much as I nodded.

"What was the outcome?" he asked.

"We got a favorable verdict," I answered.

"Good, that will be one less dangerous drug we have to worry about," said Dr. Michaels.

Then it hit me. Gutchriem nearly killed Mom and today's verdict ensures that it will remain on the market.

I excused myself, but Roxanne stopped me in the hall. She's my age, 5'6", curly brown hair, and green eyes. She was wearing blue scrubs with a wet spot on her chest from the sweat she worked up during Mom's emergency. I've known Roxanne since high school and she didn't look happy.

"I'm really sorry about everything, Grant," said Roxanne.

"No need to apologize for saving Mom's life," I said.

"It's all in a day's work and you're welcome," said Roxanne.

"I don't know what would have happened if you hadn't called me," I said.

"Yeah, it's fortunate you know so much about Gutchriem," she said. "Did you talk to Alexi?'

"The director?" I asked.

"Yes," she answered.

"No, I haven't," I said. "Does she want to speak with me?"

"Yes, that's why I called earlier," said Roxanne. "You should talk to her right away. It's important. Oh, and Grant, did I tell you I'm really sorry."

I found Alexi sitting at her desk. Even though she can't be more than thirty-eight, her retro afro looked like it was styled in the late sixties. Other than the hair, she was all 21st century style with a sharp grey business suit, white blouse, and designer glasses.

"Come in and sit down," said Alexi. "I have something to tell you."

"Look I know I owe you a lot of money, but I'll figure something out," I said.

"The Board of Directors has made a decision," she said.

"I don't understand," I said. "A decision about what?"

"Ms. Li can't stay here any longer," said Alexi.

"You can't just put her on the street," I said. "It could kill her."

"Your account will be turned over to our attorneys for collection," she said.

"Please, just give me a little more time," I begged.

"I'm sorry, Grant, but it's too late for that," she said.

I wanted to be angry with Alexi, but she looked like she had the weight of the world on her shoulders. I ran a hand through my hair and tried to think of some way to stop this, but came up with nothing. I needed time to figure this out.

"How long do I have?" I asked.

"They want her out now," she said.

"She almost died a few minutes ago," I said. "Give her time to stabilize while I make other arrangements."

"You have a month," said Alexi.

CHAPTER 4

Change is inevitable, but I'm no different than most people who fear and resist it. Maturity is defined by a man's willingness to take full responsibility for his life. Blaming other people for our problems is immature and leads to a miserable existence.

It was time to make some changes in my life, beginning with taking care of Mom. The only way I can effectively do that is find a way to pay my debts. As a starting point, I need to use the win in Goth's high profile case to leverage a bigger paycheck, so I headed straight to the office to discuss it with John.

Unfortunately, his office was empty and I didn't want to put this off another day since Shady Days didn't leave me much time. I considered picking up the phone, but if John didn't answer, then I would have to leave a message and I wanted to discuss this face-to-face without giving him a chance to prepare. John works late every day, and since it was still early, I figured I could catch him before he left for the day.

I decided to wait in my office until he returned and was surprised to find a bottle of the rarest bourbon in Kentucky sitting on my desk with a note of gratitude from Goth. It's like liquid gold if you're lucky enough to get your hands on it. They distill it in a batch so small it's damn near impossible to get unless you have serious money and connections. I had neither.

As I stared at the bottle, a call came in from Eric. We've been friends for as long as I can remember, but it was rare for him to call in the middle of the work day.

"Hey, what's up," I said.

"Dude, I can tell you are stone sober," he said. "There is no possible excuse you can give for not celebrating right now."

"It's not five o'clock yet," I said.

"Winners get a pass on that stupid five o'clock rule," he said.

"How did you know we won?" I asked.

"It's all over the news, including you running from the camera like you're afraid of it, or something," said Eric.

When I left for Shady Days, I found Goth talking to the press on the courthouse steps. He tried to wave me over, but I told him I had a personal emergency to tend to.

"I had somewhere else I had I be," I said.

"Why would you pass an opportunity like that…didn't they teach you anything in law school about the power of free publicity?" asked Eric.

Instead of answering his question, I asked one of my own, "What's the press saying about the trial?"

"That you're a rising star who just won the biggest trial of the year," answered Eric.

"I don't know about that," I said. "What about that double murder trial a few months back?"

"Pathetic," said Eric.

"Look I'm just saying," I said.

"How did I end up with such a lame best friend?" asked Eric.

He paused to take a swig of whatever he was drinking, but not long enough for me to answer.

"Everybody knows a celebrity trial trumps double murder," said Eric. "Besides your little dog and pony show included twelve deaths. Goth is practically a serial killer and you got him off scot-free. Damn, I've never been more proud of you."

Eric's ramblings were intended to be funny, but after watching Mom fight for her life, they hit a raw nerve and I needed to change the subject.

"Something has happened," I said.

"Damn right something has happened," said Eric. "Get your butt over here and have a celebratory drink with me."

"Yeah, umm…I got something important to take care of first," I said.

"Geez, you're hopeless," said Eric. "I'll expect you in an hour. Anything longer and I will personally hunt you down and drag you to a good time."

"Ummm…okay," I said.

"This is important, Grant," said Eric. "You have to get better at celebrating the good things in your life and this one is epic. Don't you dare let this slip away without paying homage to the gods of victory."

The call dropped without another word.

Eric is right. It's time to celebrate. I broke the seal on the bourbon and poured myself a drink. You don't rush twenty three year old bourbon, so I swirled the glass and watched the amber liquid roll along its sides. Next, I warmed it with both hands before sticking my nose over the rim and inhaling deeply. I enjoyed the distinctive scent of the oak barrel. It smelled a little like caramel to me. There was another scent that was a little more difficult to identify, maybe vanilla.

Finally, I sipped just enough to cover my tongue and left it there for a moment before letting it roll down my throat. The bourbon was smooth…both soft and full-bodied. I let out a contented sigh.

Today's victory would be the first of many. In the meantime, I would develop a winning campaign to convince Shady Days to keep Mom. It's the only home she's known for the last twenty years and I don't want her to start over in a new facility.

As I mellowed with the drink, I stretched my legs and brought my feet to rest on the desk. It was at that very moment John appeared in the doorway.

He sniffed the air and said, "Your office smells like cheap booze. Are you drunk?"

His comment took me completely off guard. I had a bad feeling about the direction of this conversation and shifted slightly in my chair.

"Umm…no, of course not" I said. "I just poured one…but…umm…no, I'm not drunk."

John suddenly seemed angry and cut me off.

"This is not acceptable behavior for an attorney in this firm," said John. "I have to say that I'm extremely disappointed in you."

"It's just a celebratory drink," I said.

"If you had bothered to read the HR manual, then you would know that there is a zero tolerance for drugs and alcohol on the premises," said John.

I sat the whisky on the edge of desk, but when I dropped my feet to the floor the drink tumbled into my lap. There wasn't much left anyway, so I just left it. I was more concerned about John. His attitude was annoying and to control the rising irritation, I took a long and deep breath. It helped

Ch'ing says irritation ages us and if it becomes chronic, then it kills us. He taught me to relax in a difficult situation.

"Take a deep breath," Ch'ing had said. "Breathe all the way down to your toes. If you can learn to do that, then your irritation will evaporate."

Ch'ing is a martial arts teacher who appeared out of nowhere the day of my parent's motorcycle crash. You might say he helped shaped me into the man I've become. John was behaving like a bully and Ch'ing taught me to show a bully polite respect, but never fear.

"Sorry about that," I said. "It's a gift from Goth."

"You mean a gift from Mr. Goth, don't you," he snapped.

A uniformed officer appeared in the doorway next to John and asked, "Which one of you is Grant Li?"

"I am," I answered.

He handed me a summons and said, "You've been served."

It was a petition for dissolution of marriage. I moved out a couple of months earlier when my wife told me she was in love with another woman. I held out hope that we would find a solution to this problem. Clearly, she saw things differently and was headed in another direction. This was the end of a short and painful marriage.

Most guys that know about her sexual orientation snicker behind my back, like I'm not man enough to satisfy her. Or worse, they ask if I ever got a chance to be with the two of them. When I tell them no, I didn't even know it was going on, they quietly shake their heads, like I'm even less of a man because of that too.

John was red faced, "Somebody has served you with papers in this office."

"My wife," I said. "It's a divorce petition."

He rolled his eyes.

My mobile rang. I checked to see if it was Dr. Michaels calling with an update on Mom, but it was Eric. I declined the call and silenced the ringer so there wouldn't be any further interruptions. John glared at me, but said nothing about the call. Instead he went on the attack about the trial.

"Explain to me why I heard about the outcome of a trial involving this firm's biggest client on the news instead of from you," he said.

"I had a call from Mom's nursing home," I said.

"When?" he asked.

"While we were waiting for the verdict," I answered.

"You took a personal call in the presence of a client while in court," he said.

"Ummm, yeah I guess I did," I answered.

"You guess," he said.

"I did," I said.

John's scowl was growing.

"We expect more professionalism from our attorneys than that," he barked.

"It was an emergency," I said.

"Your personal life is a shambles and it's beginning to affect your judgment," said John.

"How can you say that?" I demanded. "I've worked sixteen hour days, seven days a week for months on this case. If anything has suffered, it's been my personal life."

I detected an ever-so-slight shake of his head.

"That is the minimum effort necessary if you want to get ahead in this profession," said John.

"I won a favorable verdict for a high profile client in a case with national interest," I said. "How's that for getting ahead?"

"It was hardly a slam dunk, since you barely avoided a hung jury," said John.

"Maybe, but I won," I said.

"You won nothing," said John. "The firm won this case. Do you really think you could have done this alone…without the support of the firm and all of its resources?"

"Maybe so, but I was the guy Goth chose to be in court with him throughout the trial," I said.

"It was your first trial," said John. "What exactly did you do to earn the job?"

"Look, I don't know why Goth wants me, but he does and I won," I said. "Now we need to talk about my salary."

His lips tightened into a thin line as he said, "You already earn more than any other young attorney with your level of experience."

"That may be, but I have bills I can't pay without a raise," I said. "I want my salary doubled."

"Doubled?" said John.

I nodded.

John went on the attack once again.

"I think you overestimate your value to this firm," he said.

"What do you mean?" I asked.

"You are a worker bee," he said.

I ignored an incoming text message from Eric and wished I could ignore the implications of what John had just said.

"Excuse me," I said. "I'm not sure what you mean by that."

"Each year we hire a group of young attorneys to increase our billables," he said.

"I don't understand," I said. "We work long hours in the hopes of someday making partner."

"Have you noticed that most are gone before their one year anniversary with the firm?" said John.

I had noticed that and nodded.

"We don't intend to make any of you a partner," said John. "Instead, we pay you a small salary and then bill the clients for all of your long hours and hard work. We earn a huge profit off of your hard work and then wait for you to burn out. You drop like flies, but it makes no difference to us since there's plenty more young attorneys where you came from."

"That explains a lot," I said.

John shrugged.

"It's just good business," he said.

"Now I understand why you have been so upset that Goth insisted I handle his case," I said.

It was John's turn to nod his head.

"It would be disastrous if you lost the attorney Goth wants in his corner," I said.

John scowled at me, but said nothing. He was beginning to show signs that he was losing his composure.

"I guess that means I'm more than just a worker bee," I said.

"This law firm is a business," said John. "Pathogen accounts for 60% of our revenue stream. Our survival is tied to Pathogen and I will protect this firm at all costs."

"What are you saying?" I asked.

"I will not allow you to steal this firm's clients," said John.

"Who said anything about stealing clients?" I asked. "I just want a raise."

Helen appeared behind John in the doorway and said, "Mr. Biggs, you have a call."

"Take a message," said John.

"He says it's urgent," said Helen.

John glared at her and snapped, "Who says it's urgent?"

"Mr. Kruthers with the United States Attorney's Office," she said.

John whipped his head in my direction and asked, "Do you know what this is about, Grant?"

I shook my head.

"I'll take the call in my office," he said to Helen.

Eric messaged me to get my butt over there before he ran out of liquor. I wasn't ready to join him for a drink and didn't want to get into a debate with him about it, so I ignored the message and turned my phone off. The salary discussion with John was unresolved. I need that raise, and even though I promised Eric I would stop by for a victory drink, I wasn't leaving the office until John agreed to it.

I know a raise alone won't accomplish the goal of keeping Mom at Shady Days without finding a way to convince the Board to give me another chance. If I could find the money to bring her account up to date, then I had a fighting chance, but it wasn't going to be easy.

Our assets are virtually non-existent. My wife collected credit cards like some women collect shoes. Every one of them is maxed out and I'm way too young to have amassed any significant retirement. I have nothing of value to sell. All I have is my law degree and a willingness to work hard.

Then it occurred to me, I had one other asset. I had Goth. I poured myself another glass of the whisky, and this time, I defiantly threw it back like it was rock gut. Once the burning in my throat subsided, I mindfully folded the divorce papers and then stuffed them into my hip pocket. I figured it was where they belonged…right there with all the other crap.

I headed down the hall in search of a raise. I didn't see John, but I did pass Richard and Laurie in the hall debating who had the worse parents. Like typical teenagers, they ignored me. When I turned back to say something to them about their rude behavior, I crashed into a short, balding man wearing an Italian designer suit that must have set him back at least eight grand. He went sliding across the marble floor like an air hockey puck before coming to a rest in front of John's office.

Richard and Laurie were snickering behind me as I helped Mr. Suit to his feet and offered my apologies. He glared at the giggling teenagers and then rushed off toward the main entrance with the kids strolling casually behind him.

John's door was ajar and I reached out to knock, when I first sensed something was terribly wrong. There was an odd gurgling sound coming from inside his office, but it was the smell of urine and feces that stopped me dead in my tracks.

I cautiously peered around the corner and into the room. John was dangling by the neck from a hideous fleur-de-lis chandelier in the center of the room. His swollen tongue protruded from a face bloated with blood that couldn't escape because of the knotted red power tie squeezing tightly against his jugular vein. His limbs convulsed one last time before he went deadly still.

Hoping the loud crack wasn't what I thought it was, I rushed to release him from the gallows. Once I had him on the floor, I fumbled to loosen the knot and then checked his pulse. I didn't feel one, but since I'm not trained for that, doubt filled my mind. Maybe he was still alive.

"Why did you do this to yourself?" I asked.

John didn't answer. Instead, I heard a shrill scream coming from the doorway. It was his secretary, Helen. She held her cheeks in hand and released a second scream.

I turned toward her with an extended hand and said, "Call 9-1-1."

Helen dug her cell out of a pocket and called the police, but instead of requesting an ambulance, she repeatedly stabbed an accusatory finger at me and told them that John had been murdered.

She looked at me with hate-filled eyes and said, "They're coming for you."

"What have you done?" I said.

"I hope you get the electric chair for this," spate Helen with more venom then I ever imagined she had inside of her.

I should have stayed and sorted this out with the police, but I had already been through so much in the last few hours. My nerves were raw. My lunch was threatening to come up and I couldn't stop my hands from shaking.

I needed time to think and regroup. I told myself I was doing the right thing under the circumstances as I scrambled for the door, but I knew I was lying to myself.

CHAPTER 5

Friends provide insight and comfort in a crisis. I definitely needed some of that, as well as the drink Eric offered earlier, so I headed to his house. He lives to the east of Louisville, in Prospect, an affluent community overlooking the Ohio River.

Most of the residents work as professionals in Louisville. Each evening they endure rush hour traffic to escape to the quiet comfort of home and family. Most take pride in their homes and are known to gossip about a poorly tended lawn.

They drive luxury cars like Mercedes, Lexus, and BMW. Dad's old Ford doesn't fit in with all of the fancy imports, but no one ever seems to pay it much mind. They probably assume it belongs to a handyman hired by one of the neighbors.

I don't remember much about the drive. I was still in shock over the disastrous turn of events and must have been a couple of blocks past Eric's house before I realized there weren't any parking spaces on the street. Homeowners in this neighborhood have big garages to park their vehicles and these quiet suburban streets are usually empty. I scoured the area and was lucky enough to find a space two and a half blocks away I could squeeze into.

As I approached his house on foot, I noticed music was blasting from out back. Figuring I'd find Eric near the music, I followed it to the rear of the house and opened the eight foot privacy gate. The place was packed.

Eric's back yard is designed for entertaining. Every inch is utilized as living space with curved paths, fountains, koi ponds, and various sitting areas situated around the yard. Each area has a different theme. My favorite is the Zen garden, but there's also a tropical beach, backwoods campfire, and Parisian café, among others.

Standing at the edge of the swimming pool was an exquisitely shaped brunette with The Eye of Providence tattooed on her lower back. I couldn't see the front, but her backside was flawless in a Barbie Doll sort of way. She wore one of those

26

flesh toned bikinis that give the illusion of nudity. It did a wonderful job of complementing her figure. Her flawless legs lead the eye upward toward a tight little behind, while waves of soft dark brown hair fall gracefully onto her broad swimmer's shoulders.

As if the eye couldn't possibly convey all that she is, her musical laughter sliced through the party chatter and found its way to a dusty room deep in my mind where long forgotten memories were laid to rest. It was disconcerting.

I reluctantly pulled my eyes from the woman and appraised her companion. He was a few inches taller than her and several shades darker. Whereas her skin tone was olive, he was chocolate. His frame was packed with tightly compacted muscle that rippled in unison with their flirtatious back-and-forth banter.

He touched her lightly on the arm and flashed an eye-crinkling smile just before leaning in to whisper something in her ear. She pushed him away, but softened the rejection with a light-hearted laugh that, once again, sounded strangely familiar.

He answered the laugh with flared nostrils and a gentle push of his own. She rolled with it and counter-grabbed his upper arm in a surprising move that unbalanced him. He managed to drag her with him as the two of them tumbled into the water, making a huge splash that reached a group relaxing in lounge chairs.

When they surfaced, I saw her face for the first time. I couldn't believe it was Ginny, and found myself torn between the urge to run away and a strange need to watch her every move. Once again, he leaned in to whisper something to her, but her eyes suddenly opened wide in alarm. She had caught sight of me for the first time.

She let out a little squeak before pushing him away and scrambling from the pool. Once out of the water, she looked wildly about for a towel, before giving up and turning for the house.

Her flight was interrupted when a throaty voice called to her, "Are you okay, Ginny?"

Eric's wife, Kinsey, rose from a white wicker chair and walked toward her. She is tall like Eric and thin as a model. In fact, she did a short stint of modeling in New York before returning home to marry Eric.

If it wasn't for the boob job, her most prominent feature would be her large boney joints. She picked-up the boobs in New York and likes to refer to them as evidence of her misspent youth. Her strawberry blond hair frames a long face filled with freckles.

She is one of those people who could easily slide into unattractiveness, but has always made the most of what she has. Kinsey owns her sensuality, and because of it, she turns heads when she walks into a room.

It was the first time I had seen Ginny since high school. It had been ten long years and I couldn't stop looking at her. Once an awkward plain-jane, she had grown into a beautiful woman.

Ginny has an aristocratic high bridged nose set between wide cheekbones. Her slightly flushed face narrows into a high forehead. I even spotted a few freckles on her broad shoulders. Believe it or not, the eyes are her best feature. They are the color of a tropical sea and filled with intelligence.

Of all the people I could have seen after a crazy day filled with anxiety and change, none would have been better for my spirits than Ginny. A page had indeed turned and the new chapter held more promise than I could ever have imagined.

She stopped in her tracks at the sound of Kinsey's voice, but did not change directions. Her body was still pointed toward the house when she glanced backward over a shoulder. Her eyes darted in my direction before quickly returning to Kinsey. Clearly, she was torn. Exhaling, she finally gave up her escape and turned in Kinsey's direction, but not before she flashed a hard defiant look at me.

Her decision had been made. There was something new in her eyes. It was grit. This wasn't the same awkward teenager from my past. Ginny had grown into a strong young woman.

Kinsey looked at me and frowned before repeating her question, "Is everything okay, Ginny?"

She looked like she was about to answer her old friend, but I cut her off.

"Ginny," I said.

It was hardly more than a whisper, but she heard me. Her eyes softened as she took a tentative step in my direction. I was equally timid as I matched her step. She was unsure of herself and it was my fault because I had ignored her for years. It was on me to close the gap between us, and if possible, repair what had been broken.

I took another step and then another. Before I knew it, we stood toe-to-toe on a strange new battlefield. I reached out and brushed aside a rebellious curl that had fallen across her face and was dripping water in a steady stream along the inside curve of her cheek.

She parted her lips and instead of speaking, she licked the last errant drop as it rolled past the corner of her mouth. I don't know why, but that simple act opened a conduit to my inner smile. It first came out as a contented sigh, but then grew into a full blown smile, eyes and all.

The smile was contagious and spread wide across Ginny's face and deep into that place which is only revealed in the eyes.

"Hello, Grant," said Ginny.

"It feels really good to see you again," I said.

"Yes, it does feel good," she agreed.

"God, I've missed you," I said.

Ginny inhaled sharply and looked like she was about to say something, but was interrupted by Eric.

"Well, well, well…if it isn't the man of the hour with a beautiful woman," said Eric.

I glanced over my shoulder and the first thing I noticed was a cheesy gold chain hanging around his muscular neck. If he wanted attention, it was working. The chain looked like something you'd see in a 1970's disco.

Eric is tall, lean, and well proportioned. I'm a couple of inches shorter than Eric and more muscular. My face, hands, and body are square. His blond hair and blue eyed Viking good looks drive chicks crazy. Not that they don't love my brown almond eyes and dark hair. At the moment, Eric's eyes were glued to Ginny.

"Welcome to the victory party," said Eric.

"Who are all these people?" I asked.

"Just fifty of your closest friends," said Eric with a grin.

"Right, I haven't seen half of them since high school and the other half I definitely don't know," I said.

"Dude, you work all the time," said Eric. "That doesn't leave a lot of time for nurturing friendships. I had to dig deep."

Kinsey spoke up and said, "Babe, Ginny's here!"

Eric's phone rang. He ignored it. Instead, he looked at Ginny and poured the charm on.

"Wow!" said Eric. "How did I miss you coming in…it's a pleasure to have you back in town."

Eric was on a roll.

Instead of waiting for an answer, he pointed toward me and said, "I take it you're not with this scoundrel. Good thing too! Grant, you remember Ginny from high school. She went away to college in California and then skyrocketed in the fashion industry as a designer. She and Kinsey have stayed in touch all this time, but this is the first time since graduation she has returned to Louisville."

Ginny visibly stiffened and narrowed her eyes to tiny slits. High school had been painful for her. I was surprised she had changed so much. In high school she was Kinsey's nerdy best friend, Virginia. She wore thick glasses and hardly ever spoke. Her hair was always pulled tightly back into a severe bun. Her clothes hung loosely on her without showing any sign she was making the transition from child to woman.

Throughout high school, I felt a strange mix of mortification and longing whenever I was near Ginny, so I avoided her at all costs and never spoke to her. Not even our best friends knew the reason why I behaved this way or the painful secret we shared.

I was trying to think of something to say to make her feel better when someone put hands over my eyes and whispered, "Guess who?"

Geez, I knew immediately who it was…Cindy, the cheerleader I dated off and on throughout high school. What was she doing here? It was like a class reunion!

Instead of answering her question, I reached up and peeled her hands off. She slipped around and positioned herself between me and Ginny.

"Congratulations, Grant," she said. "You've become an instant celebrity. Look at all these people who came tonight just to rub elbows with the likes of you and here I thought you would never amount to much of anything at all. Nothing like winning your first case for a rich client to get your name all over the news. Although, seeing you run from the camera was just priceless."

Cindy got all of that out without taking a single breath. I figured she had been rehearsing it in her head for hours.

Ginny was a head taller than Cindy, who couldn't have been more than 5'2". I looked over the top of Cindy's blond head and into Ginny's hard gaze. This couldn't have been more awkward.

I thought it would be easier to look at Cindy instead of Ginny, but when I turned my attention back to my ex-girlfriend, she was looking at me like I was food and she was ravenously hungry. She was still cute as a button in a Betty Boop sort of way, with bright blue eyes, a little upturned nose, and girlish features that belied her real age, but I had zero interest in her.

"God, don't you look yummy," said Cindy.

Did she really think I was going to respond to that? I figured it was time to nip this one in the bud.

"We're having a private conversation here, so do you mind giving us some privacy, Cindy?" I said.

Cindy's expression shifted from her best cheerleader smile to an unpleasant scowl in an instant. She cut her eyes to Eric, but all she got from him was a shrug.

Her eyes narrowed for the briefest moment before she caught herself and rolled them upward along with both hands, palms facing the sky, like a snarky little teeny bopper.

"Try not to suck all the joy out of your little victory party, Grant," said Cindy. "You never know, it may be your last one."

She laid a hand on Ginny's arm and said with an exaggerated shake of her head, "Good luck with that girlfriend."

Ginny's eyes flared, "I'm not your girlfriend."

Cindy ignored her and was already off flirting with the nearest cute guy. Ginny looked like she wanted to pull every last hair out of Cindy's head.

Eric shook his head at Cindy and silently mouthed the word "chicks."

Kinsey gave Ginny a big hug, "I'm so glad you're here. Now, let's go inside and find you a towel."

We watched them scurry off to the house. Eric turned his attention back to me and frowned.

"Dude, you don't look like someone who is on top of the world," said Eric.

"A lot has happened since the verdict," I said.

"Let's go inside and get you a drink," he said.

"Yeah, I need one," I said

"Geez, we'll make it a double of my very best and then you can tell me all about it," he said.

CHAPTER 6

Kinsey insists on buying local, so the party was stocked with beer, wine and bourbon from the region. Eric poured a half tumbler of bourbon from a new Louisville distiller, dropped a couple of ice cubes in it, and then gave it a swirl before shoving it into my hand with a bottoms up command.

He was sipping from a bottle of beer. The company was established in 1905 by a group of entrepreneurs who banded together to fight a monopoly that had a strangle hold on the beer market in Louisville. Eric loves David and Goliath stories. It has become a tradition for him to repeat, "Go little guy," whenever he opens a beer, and this night was no exception.

"Are you trying to get me drunk?" I asked.

"Yep, you got a problem with that?" he said.

I shook my head, but said, "I'm not that kind of girl."

"You mind if us girls join you," asked Kinsey.

She and Ginny had slipped up behind us carrying two bottles of a Sauvignon Blanc from an area winery. Kinsey poured Ginny a glass of wine, which she immediately turned up and emptied.

Eric raised an eyebrow and quipped, "I didn't know we were doing shots."

"I'm just trying to relax," said Ginny.

"Girl, you keep that up and everyone will be stepping over your relaxed self in the middle of my kitchen floor," said Eric.

"I have a big day tomorrow, maybe I should slow down a bit," agreed Ginny.

He grabbed a couple of bottles of beer and the bourbon before heading out back where we settled into comfortable eco-friendly chairs arranged around a fire pit. Eric took a swig of beer and let out a belch that would have made any ten year old proud.

Kinsey rolled her eyes, but said nothing about her husband's social lapse. It may have been the wine going to her head, but Ginny giggled.

"Now that I've restored peace and stability to my gut, tell us what happened today to spoil your shining moment," said Eric.

I felt suddenly shy around Ginny and wasn't happy about revealing my problems to her. My eyes darted in her direction and then to my feet that were restlessly shifting back-and-forth at the foot of my chair.

Ginny looked incredibly sad as she said, "I'll leave if you prefer."

That was the last thing I wanted, so I sat up straight and then leaned in toward her as I said, "Please don't leave. I just don't want you to think…"

I couldn't say it out loud, but Cindy was right about one thing. In my finest hour, I was a failure.

"Whatever it is, Grant, it won't change my opinion of you," said Ginny.

"That I'm a jerk, who treated you badly," I said.

"No, I don't think that at all," she said.

I was relieved she didn't feel that way about me. Ginny had my attention now, so I leaned in a little closer and looked into her eyes for any sign of deception.

"Then what is it you think of me?" I asked.

"I think you are destined for greatness," said Ginny.

I was like man dying of thirst who fell upon an oasis in the desert. My wife, Cynthia, tortured me with her criticisms. I don't believe she thought I deserved to be anything more that a low level nobody. Hearing Ginny's words of encouragement refreshed my dying self-esteem.

I wanted to hug and thank her for what she had just given me, except we were interrupted by an old teammate from our high school football team, Jerry Flayer. The last ten years had aged him twenty. He looked beaten, as if life had slapped him around and then dared him to hang around for more.

"Hey Grant, I just wanted to congratulate you before I left," he said.

"Ummm, thanks Jerry," I said.

He reached across his face and absent-mindedly scratched his jaw line just below the ear. Jerry looked like he had more to say and wasn't certain if he should. Whatever it was, I doubted I was going to like it much, but waited for it, all the same.

"I've got to tell you old friend that I have mixed feelings about this," said Jerry.

"Why's that?" I asked.

"I don't know if you heard, but I lost my sister last year," he said.

"Yes, I heard, Jerry, and I sorry for your loss," I said.

He chewed on the bottom of his lip for a moment before blurting out, "There was a medicine that might have saved her, but she couldn't afford it. It costs $1,700.00 per pill and she needed a lot of pills."

"I had no idea," I said. "Wasn't there any insurance?"

"She lost it a couple of years back," answered Jerry.

"I'm sorry," I said.

"Here's the rub," said Jerry. "Six months before she got sick, the medicine cost eight dollars apiece. Then Pathogen bought the exclusive rights and increased the price."

I nearly spit out a sip of whiskey. It took a moment before I got it under control enough to speak.

"Pathogen?" I asked.

Jerry nodded. That simple action seemed to open a floodgate of emotion.

"They ki...ki...killed my sister with their greed," he choked out between sobs.

Ginny popped up and gave Jerry a comforting hug as he sobbed on her shoulder. The rest of us followed her lead and did the best we could to comfort an old friend.

He wiped the tears on the back of his hand and with big sad eyes said, "I'm happy for you, but I hate those people. Maybe you're fighting on the wrong side of this war."

After Jerry left, we sat together in silence for a few minutes. The quiet moment was broken by Eric's phone. Instead of answering the call, he grabbed the bottle of wine and leaned over to refill Ginny's glass, spilling the last few drops. His hand was shaking and that's not something you see very often.

Kinsey chewed on her lower lip as Eric sat back stiffly in his chair. They exchanged a glance. Finally, Eric nodded slightly at Kinsey, who shifted her gaze to me. She took a deep breath and the corners of her mouth turned slightly upward just before she spoke.

"Grant, please don't take it personal, but we all know somebody who has been hurt by Pathogen," said Kinsey.

I slumped in my seat. The story about Jerry's sister had gotten under my skin and I didn't know what to make of it.

Eric jumped in with exaggerated light heartedness and said, "Hey what can you do, right. It's the way of the world, so tell us about the rest of your day."

I hesitated.

Ginny placed a reassuring hand on my shoulder and said, "Please, Grant, we'll listen without judgment."

"Isn't that what friends are for?" added Kinsey.

Yes, that is exactly what friends are for, so I told them everything that had happened to me before arriving at the party. They sat and listened to the whole story without a single interruption.

"That's a lot to take in, Grant," said Kinsey.

"Dude, no wonder you aren't your usual sparkly self," said Eric.

"Me sparkly?" I said.

"Are you sure your boss killed himself and wasn't murdered?" said Eric.

"Who would kill him?" I asked

"Well, according to his secretary, you," said Eric.

My best friend has moments when his humor is inappropriate and this was definitely one of them. Kinsey jumped in for damage control.

"We know you wouldn't do something like that, but the police will be questioning you about this, so you might want to give some thought to who would want John dead," said Kinsey.

"He's made a lot of enemies," I said.

"Did you see anything out of the ordinary?" asked Kinsey.

I shook my head, but then remembered the guy I knocked down in the hall, Mr. Suit.

"There's the guy I bumped into outside of John's office," I said.

"Have you ever seen him before?" asked Kinsey.

I shook my head.

"Do you think he killed your boss?" asked Eric.

I shrugged.

"Hanging someone in a busy law office doesn't sound like the best way to commit murder," said Kinsey.

"There's a good way?" I asked.

"The logistics are just too much of a challenge," said Eric.

"Logistics…really, you sound like you plan murders all the time," I said.

"I mean, he was hanging from the chandelier," said Kinsey.

"Exactly, how would you get him up there without him screaming his head off loud enough to sound the alarm," said Eric.

"Suicide is far more likely," said Kinsey.

"Do you have any idea why he would want to kill himself?" asked Kinsey.

"Not a clue," I answered.

"Did he seem depressed?" asked Eric.

"No, he was his usual arrogant self," I answered.

Ginny had been quiet during the discussion about John and we all were a bit startled when she spoke.

"Have you heard back from your mom's doctor?" asked Ginny.

"No, I haven't," I answered.

"You think her episode today was caused by this drug manufactured by Pathogen," said Ginny.

I nodded.

"It was the same exact symptoms discussed in Court," I said.

"Could it be something else?" she asked.

I shrugged.

"They're running tests on her and may know something more when the results come in," I said.

"Will the results be in before she…umm…before she leaves the facility?" asked Ginny.

"I don't know," I answered. "Her doctor didn't say how long it will take to get the results back."

"I haven't heard one word of blame from you," said Ginny.

"It's on me to find a solution," I said. "Blame is for control freaks and the immature."

"Isn't that sort of what lawyers do...play the blame game?" asked Kinsey.

"Blaming somebody else for our problems has never made much sense to me," I said.

"So, what are you going to do about it?" said Ginny.

"I need to make some changes, but I'm still trying to figure that out," I answered."

"Ummm, one more thing, Grant," said Ginny.

"What is it?" I asked.

"How do you feel about the divorce?" she asked.

I searched her eyes for some clue as to the reason she asked the question, but all I saw was someone who was worried about me.

"Relieved," I said. "I feel like I'm finally waking from a really bad nightmare."

CHAPTER 7

Kinsey's eyes darted back and forth between me and Ginny. She looked like there was something she desperately wanted to say, but couldn't get it out. So instead she squeezed Eric's hand hard enough he winched and only managed to escape her clutches when his phone rang.

He excused himself, and as he walked away, we heard him say, "This better be important."

"Whatever it is, just go ahead and say it, Kinsey," said Ginny.

"What happened between you two that has made you act like fools toward each other all these years?" asked Kinsey.

It was the last thing I wanted to talk about, but maybe Kinsey was right. Maybe, just maybe, it was time to air it out.

"I've never told a soul," I said.

I looked at Ginny and what I saw in her eyes was a glimmer of hope. She gave me a nod, as if to encourage me to tell it.

I took a calming breath. Since I wasn't exactly sure where to begin, I pictured what happened in my mind all those years ago.

"It's one of my earliest memories, but I remember every detail like it happened yesterday," I said.

"We were just kids, maybe five years old," said Ginny.

"I'm not sure where to begin," I said.

"I find it's best to not overthink it," said Kinsey. "Begin your story with the first syllable that slides off your tongue and then let momentum take over."

That made sense to me, so I began just like that, and before I knew it, the telling transported me back in time...at least in my mind, anyway.

"It was a wild and unpredictable chase," I began. "Our prey suddenly changed directions and landed within reach. I stretched my tiny hand toward its powdery wings, but jerked to a stop when Ginny pleaded, "Don't scare it away, Grant.""

We had chased it around the yard for the better part of an hour, giggling each

35

time we had it cornered and then shouting when it made its escape. We were finally close enough to claim our victory and now she didn't want me to touch it. Geez!

I wanted to see what it felt like to hold it in my hand, but more than that, I didn't want to disappoint her. Not sure what to do, I shuffled my feet in the fresh cut grass. I could feel the blades between my toes, but not much on soles hardened from a summer of running barefoot throughout the neighborhood.

She gently squeezed my hand. I looked up from my grass stained feet and into her innocent eyes. They shifted between green and blue like a tropical sea. She was about my height, a little over three feet. She wore white shorts, a little pink top, and no shoes. Her dark hair was pulled back into a pony tail that dangled in soft curves to the middle of her back.

Her olive skin was tanned from the summer sun. She once told me the spattering of freckles on her nose and shoulders were a gift from her daddy. She was adorable and I was hopelessly in love with her.

Standing in a little patch of sun next to the creek, we watched the butterfly move from the flower to a cattail. Smiling she changed the subject. "Boys and girls are different," she said.

"Huh..," was all I said.

"Her eyes were big and innocent. "I saw a baby getting his stinky diaper changed," she said crinkling her nose. "He was different."

I had no idea what she was talking about. "Different," I said.

She pointed at the cattail and said, "Boy."

I said nothing, so she pointed at the flower and said, "Girl."

She waited expectantly. I still didn't know what she was talking about.

"Oh silly, let me show you," she said.

Grabbing the elastic waistband, she yanked her shorts to her ankles and stepped out of them.

"Now your turn," she coaxed.

I shrugged and pulled my shorts down. She giggled and pointed. I looked down, but didn't see anything unusual.

A dark shadow loomed over us and something hard smacked me across the mouth, knocking me to the ground. I landed on a sharp stone and pain shot through my tailbone. Stars danced in front me as I gasped to catch a breath.

Two fat women loomed above me and then began moving together until there was just one. When I could finally breathe again, I gingerly touched my throbbing lip. I tasted something salty and saw blood on my finger.

The fat woman's lip was curled upward exposing yellow teeth. Her face got bigger and I felt a weight on my legs, pinning them to the ground. She planted her hands next to my ears.

I didn't like the look in her eyes, so I focused on a big vein throbbing in her neck. It made me think of the snake with big sharp teeth I saw on television the night before. I was pretty sure she had one crawling inside of her, and it scared me. When she opened her mouth I expected it to crawl out and bite me. Instead, the pungent scent of garlic blasted me. I crinkled my nose. Yuck, I hate garlic.

"You nasty little boy," hissed the fat woman.

I was confused and scared but managed to mumble, "I don't know what you mean?"

She grabbed my ear and twisted it hard. "You're a nasty boy who can't keep his pants on," she said. "Outside even, where everyone can see. What's wrong with you, boy? Didn't your mother teach you anything?"

My ear hurt badly from the twisting she gave it and I desperately wanted the safety of my mother's arms.

"I think I hear my mother calling," I cried.

"So you're a liar as well," she said as she inched her face closer.

The movement shifted more weight to my legs and my knees were starting to hurt. I tried to squirm free but couldn't budge her. A wave of hopelessness washed over me.

"What do you want?" I asked.

"I'm going to make certain you never do this again," she hissed.

She even sounded like a snake. I shuddered.

"I didn't…I didn't do nothing," I said.

"Nothing…nothing, he says," she snarled. "You think hurting my little girl is nothing. You're a nasty little boy like all the rest of them."

I didn't hurt Ginny. Maybe she thought I hurt the butterfly.

"I…I didn't…didn't hurt the butterfly," I stammered.

It didn't seem possible, but her face screwed up into a tighter ball of anger.

"You…you insolent little brat," she sputtered spraying a little garlic flavored spittle on my face.

I moved my hand to wipe the nasty stuff from my face, but she grabbed my wrist and slammed it back to the ground.

"How dare you raise a hand to me," she screamed. "I'm going to beat the devil out of you."

She raised a menacing hand to her ear and poised it for the first blow.

"Beat me," I said in voice that was barely audible.

Something warm and wet drizzled to the small of my back. The sour smell of pee was strong and I was afraid she would get even angrier if it got on her clothes.

"No…no please," I begged. "I didn't do nothing."

A small hand grasped the fat's woman's fist and I heard Ginny's voice plead, "Mama…mama, please don't hurt him."

Her mother's head whipped in Ginny's direction.

"How dare you interfere with me," the fat woman said. "So you want to protect this nasty little boy. Then you'll get the first beating."

I was relieved when she climbed off me, but it was short lived as I watched her snap a limb from a tree and strip its branches. She ran her fingertips along its length and then shifted her attention to me.

Slowly her eyes traveled downward and stopped. The tip of her tongue moistened her lips. I didn't like the way she looked at me at all and reached for my pants, but they weren't at my ankles. Abruptly, she pulled her eyes from me and turned toward Ginny.

"Someday you will thank me for this," she said.

"Mama, please, don't," begged Ginny.

The corners of the Fat Lady's lips spread wide into a cruel smile.

"I'll beat the wickedness out you," she hissed.

With that, she tore into Ginny with a vengeance. It was brutal. Her screams pierced the quiet little neighborhood. The thing that scared me the most was the way her mother's smile got a little bigger with each blow.

I wanted to make her stop, but I couldn't move. I wanted to protect Ginny, but I was afraid the woman would turn the switch on me. The best I was able to manage was to wrap my arms around my knees, as I rocked back and forth, whining in a voice only I could hear.

"Please stop," I pleaded.

"You'll not speak to that nasty little boy again," her mother hissed. "Do you understand me?"

"Yes mama," sobbed Ginny. "I promise."

My stomach was feeling hot and then I threw up all over myself. As I was wiping the vomit from my chin, the beating stopped, but not before angry red welts swelled across Ginny's backside.

Her mother was breathing heavy from the exertion. There was an odd glow to her face, as if she had enjoyed herself.

When she finally caught her breath, she said to Ginny, "Get your pants and go to your room while I deal with this nasty little half-breed."

"Yes, mama," said Ginny.

"When I'm finished here, I better find you on your knees in prayer," said her mother. "Say ten Hail Mary's and ten Our Father's as your penance. When you're done with that, beg God for forgiveness, and pray he does not to send you straight to eternal fire and brimstone for your sins."

Ginny nodded and then limped in the direction of her house. She only stopped and looked back once. Her eyes met mine. They looked so sad before she turned and disappeared into the house. I'm pretty sure it broke my heart, because I've never been able to truly love anyone else.

There wasn't any time for sadness that day. Terror washed through me when I tore my eyes from Ginny and looked into the body of hate that was her mother. Taking a menacing step toward me, she raised the switch.

I shrank from her and tried to make myself as small as I could. Closing my eyes, I waited for the first blow. Instead of the swish of the switch, I actually did hear my mother calling me for dinner.

Relieved that I hopefully wouldn't get the beating after all, I jumped up to run home, but she grabbed my arm and pulled me close and hissed.

"You think you've escaped your punishment," she said. "I'm sure you'll get much worse from your mother after I tell her about the terrible things you did today."

I tried to pull away, hoping the ordeal was over. It wasn't and my hope evaporated in an instant. The image of her beating Ginny flashed through my mind, and then was replaced with a picture of my mom standing over me with a switch. I felt a chill run up my spine and shuddered.

"Please don't tell Mom," I pleaded.

"The boy's afraid of his mother," she said. "That's good. I can use that."

She thought for a moment and then said, "If you don't want your mother to know her son is a nasty little boy, then you'll do exactly what I tell you. Is that understood?"

I didn't answer right away, so she squeezed my arm and glared at me. I wanted to tell her she was hurting me, but knew it would please her. Instead, I nodded my head.

"Promise you will never speak to my daughter again," said the Fat Lady.

I hesitated because that just wasn't something I could do. I loved being with Ginny. She was my best friend.

"Promise me," snapped her mother.

"Okay, okay, I promise," I said.

"If you ever come near my daughter again, I'll make sure your mother gives you the beating of your life," she said.

"I won't," I promised.

"May God have mercy on your miserable soul," she said.

With that she finally released me and I fled for home. I should have been happy I escaped without a beating, but I wasn't. I kept my promise, and never spoke to Ginny again…until today.

CHAPTER 8

My vision was turned inward toward the painful memory and it wasn't until I finished that I saw the tears streaming down Ginny's face. She gave me the strangest look, but said nothing.

"This explains a lot," said Kinsey. "You do know, Grant, that you can't spend your life victimized by the past. Especially something that happened when you were five years old. Ginny's mom caught the two of you playing a game of show-n-tell. Big deal, it's normal childhood curiosity. It certainly doesn't make you a bad person, or as she put it, a nasty little boy. I've met her mom, and no offense Ginny, but she is obviously the sick one."

I had never considered that her mother might be wrong. She had scared me half to death and I never wanted to feel that kind of terror again. So I did exactly what she told me to do, I stayed away from Ginny. Except, it didn't work.

"There's more," I said.

"What do you mean, more?" asked Kinsey.

"For months I had nightmares where I re-lived that horrible experience," I said. "I awoke every night to my own screams. Terrified, I refused to go back to sleep or to tell my parents the details of the nightmare for fear they would learn that it wasn't just a nightmare, that it really happened. They couldn't know I was a nasty little boy, because they might not want me anymore. The exhaustion caught up with us. At their wits end, they took me to see a doctor."

"Did it help?" asked Kinsey.

I shook my head.

"She was a bad person," I said. "She locked me in a hospital room and tortured me with electroshock treatments once a day for nearly a month."

"Oh, Grant," said Kinsey.

"I learned a lot from Sadistic Doctor," I said.

"What could you possible learn from that?" asked Kinsey.

"I learned to keep my nightmares to myself," I answered. "I learned to keep the screams inside. I learned to keep the people I love at a distance."

"I'm so sorry," said Ginny.

She looked like all of the guilt and shame buried deep inside of her had found its way to the surface. It hadn't occurred to me that her memories might also carry a load of negative emotion.

I started to tell her she had nothing to apologize for, but she abruptly got up and rushed into the house. I should have followed her, helped her, but I didn't. Instead, I just sat there and watched her walk away.

When I turned back to Kinsey, I saw a conflicted face. Her eyes shifted between compassion and anger. Without a word, she got up, gave me a hug and hurried after her friend.

I was alone.

The party continued all around me, but I didn't join in. Instead, I turned my attention inward...following the breath...relaxing tension wherever I found it...emptying myself, just like Ch'ing taught me.

I don't know how long I floated in the great void, but it was Eric's voice that pulled me out of the meditation. I opened my eyes and saw him standing on the deck in front of the French doors that lead into the rear of the house. His face was pale and drawn.

He waved toward the open door. I was halfway between the void and the real world, giving the scene an otherworldly hue. Like an autumn leaf, I caught the updraft from Eric's wave and floated past him into the house.

"My office," was all he said.

Eric keeps a small home office off the living room. While he has corporate offices nearby, he prefers to work remotely. Eric also likes to brag that he can run his company from anywhere in the world with a laptop and a cell phone. The truth is, while Eric works hard, Kinsey is the brains behind their success.

Following her modeling stint in New York, Kinsey returned to school. She attended the local community college for two years before enrolling at the University. After graduating with honors from a tough business program, she set out to build a first rate business.

At that time, Eric was working as a bouncer in a biker bar. Kinsey wanted more for them and it was her idea to start a security company. Thanks to her marketing skills, the business grew rapidly. Today, it is wildly successful and earns them a good living.

Eric closed the office door behind us. I settled into a comfortable oversized chair and watched quietly as he combed fingers through his blond hair. He didn't say anything for several minutes and then finally opened his mouth to speak, but stopped short. His hands were trembling.

"Something has happened," I said. "The phone...it was the call you took earlier. What has happened, Eric?"

"Ch'ing is missing," he answered.

Ch'ing has been our martial arts teacher and mentor since we were both eight years old. Calling him our teacher doesn't begin to describe the depth and reach of our relationship. He teaches us in the old way. Today, most dojos are businesses, but our relationship with Ch'ing is not a financial transaction.

We are tied together by bonds far greater than a tuition payment. It is a family bond that is stronger than any family I've ever been around. I couldn't imagine loosing Ch'ing.

"What do you mean…missing?" I asked.

"He didn't show up for class today," answered Eric.

To my knowledge, Ch'ing has never missed a class. He loves teaching, and as far as I know, has never been sick a day in his life.

"That's not possible," I said.

"I know," said Eric.

Ch'ing is eccentric. I wanted this to be just another oddity in the world of Ch'ing, but my gut wasn't buying this superficial explanation. I knew deep down that something very bad had happened to him, and I needed to help him.

Eric looked lost and afraid. I had never seen him like that and wanted to reassure him, but I felt fear in the pit of my stomach like nothing I've ever experienced.

"Have you tried to call him?" I asked.

"No answer," said Eric.

"Has anyone stopped by his house?" I asked.

"I sent one of my guys over," he answered.

I waited for him to tell me more, but he lost his focus for a moment.

"What did he find?" I asked.

"Ch'ing's door was ajar," answered Eric. "The house has been trashed."

I couldn't imagine Ch'ing's house being trashed. His home is like a Zen garden with the elegance that flows naturally from simplicity. Everything has its place and is in perfect order at all times. More importantly, it is a peaceful retreat from the chaos of the outside world.

"Why would it be trashed?" I asked.

"There are signs that he was taken by force," said Eric.

This day was getting crazier and crazier. There's no way anybody could have taken Ch'ing by force. He's like superhuman or something. He is a martial arts master…the greatest that has ever been.

"There has to be some other explanation," I said.

Eric shrugged.

"Let's hope," said Eric. "In the meantime, the only way we'll get any answers is to find him."

Even though we had known him most of our lives, in many respects Ch'ing was still a mystery to us. Other than the monastery in Tibet, he never spoke of his past. He had appeared out of nowhere, and didn't seem to have any family that we knew of. Nor did he ever mention other people, let alone, any enemies.

"Did you call the police?" I asked.

He shook his head.

"You know how they are about missing persons," he said.

"I'll call Rose," I said. "Maybe she can help."

He nodded.

Rose is a detective with Louisville Metro Police Department. She and my Uncle Jim lived together when I was growing up, so she's like a second mother to me. She didn't take their breakup well and I can't have a conversation with her without listening to a monologue of complaints against Uncle Jim. I love them both and hate being in the middle of their problems.

Eric was looking lost and even though I was feeling like the biblical Job, I walked over to him and laid my hand on his shoulder. I stood toe-to-toe with him and held his gaze until he found himself again. I didn't step away until I could see in his eyes that he was back.

"We need to search his home," said Eric.

"I don't know if that's a good idea," I said.

"Most abductions end badly," said Eric. "There might not be much time left to find him."

"If you're right about the abduction, then his house is a crime scene," I said

"His house is the only place we have right now to look for clues," said Eric.

"Let me talk to Rose first," I said.

"You said that before," said Eric.

Eric knows me well and he knows that calling Rose wouldn't be easy for me.

"Call her now, Grant," said Eric.

I sighed.

Eric nodded.

He was right. This couldn't wait. It had to be done now. So, I dug into my pocket for the phone, but when I pulled it out the screen was blank. For a moment, I thought the battery was dead, but then I remembered turning it off at the office. I sighed once again and hit the power button.

When it booted up, I was surprised to see I had seven missed calls and eleven unread text messages. My impulse was to check the messages before I made the call, but Eric was growing restless, so instead, I dialed Rose's number and braced myself.

She didn't pick up, so I left her a voice message before hanging up.

"Let's give her a few minutes to call back," I said.

Eric grunted, but said nothing.

"Can you think of anyone else who might know where he is?" I asked.

"We can call around and talk to his other students," said Eric.

"Anyone else?" I asked.

He shook his head.

"Do you have a student list that we can divide up?" I asked.

Eric thought for a moment and then started toward his desk, when someone rapped on his office door.

"Come in," said Eric.

The door opened and a woman with the most beautiful chocolate complexion I had ever seen stepped inside. She gave me a little wave and then turned her attention to Eric. I didn't have a clue who she was.

"I'm sorry to intruded, but can I have a couple of minutes of your time," she asked Eric.

He looked like he might say no, but then thought better of it, and said instead, "What's on your mind, Ebonie?"

"There's a guy out by the pool who is creeping all the girls out," she said. "He's getting drunk and grabby. Do you mind saying something to him?"

Eric sighed.

"There's one at every party," he said. "Give me a minute to take care of this,

Grant."

"Congratulations, Grant," said Ebonie.

She looked familiar and she seemed to know me, but I was having trouble placing her. It was her beautiful smile that I finally recognized, but she had changed. The young woman standing before me was half the size of the girl I knew in high school. Ebonie was now slim and fit.

"Thank you," I said. "By the way, whatever you're doing, keep it up. You look great."

"Thanks, but it's nothing," she said. "I discovered I like leafy green vegetables and the gym."

"I wouldn't call it nothing, because it's working," I said.

"Yeah, let's hear it for super foods," she said with a smile.

I followed them out of the office, but wasn't interested in Mr. Grabby. I knew Eric could handle it. Instead, I wanted to check on Ginny and make sure she was okay.

I expected to find her somewhere in the house with Kinsey, but didn't see her. I was thirsty, so I made my way into the kitchen to grab a bottled water. I had been monopolized by Eric, Kinsey and Ginny since I'd arrived at the party and now that I was standing alone in the kitchen I became a beacon for well-wishers wanting to congratulate me for my success in court.

When the last of them patted me on the back and finished telling me how happy they were for me, I let out a sigh of relief and thought again about Ginny. I wanted to make sure she was okay after re-living that terrible day so long ago.

The backside of Eric's house is a wall of glass that provides a view of the pool and yard. I glanced out the window and was surprised to see Ginny talking to some guy. I knew most of the people at the party, but not this one. He was good looking in a hippie sort of way, wearing jeans, sandals, and a Bob Marley t-shirt. His skin tone was brown, but the hair was blond and his eyes were blue. He wore his long hair pulled back into a ponytail.

Pony Tail leaned in and touched her arm to emphasize a point. I expected her to lean away from him, but she didn't. Instead, she threw her arms around him and held him tight.

I turned away from the spectacle she was making of herself and downed the water. Thinking I could use something stronger, I went in search of the bourbon when I ran into Kinsey.

There was still a touch of anger in her face, but mostly I saw concern.

"Are you okay, Grant?" she asked.

"Yeah, sure," I answered.

Her eyes softened a bit.

"That must have been really difficult for you," she said. "I saw how you looked at her earlier and it's exactly how you've always looked at her."

"If you're talking about Ginny, you're mistaken," I said.

Kinsey's eyes widened and then just as quickly narrowed.

"What's this about, Grant?" asked Kinsey.

"She's like all the rest," I said with a touch of bitterness.

"The rest of what?" asked Kinsey with an edge to her voice.

"Women, the rest of the women," I said.

"You've had a bad day, Grant, and for the moment, I'm going to cut you just a little slack, since you've forgotten that I'm also a woman," said Kinsey.

She was right. It was a terrible generalization and I'm better than that…she's better than that.

I tried to apologize.

"I'm sorry, it's just…" I said.

"You're an idiot who doesn't know anything about women," said Kinsey.

"I know they can't be trusted," I snapped.

"Really, Grant, and why is that?" asked Kinsey.

"My wife for one…she cheated on me with another woman," I said.

"You married a lesbian and now you're shocked it didn't work out," said Kinsey. "Have you considered for a moment that embracing her true nature is the most honest thing she could have done, or, are you too caught up in your own drama?"

"You may be right about Cynthia, but that doesn't explain why Ginny is out there right now hanging all over some surfer dude," I said pointing over my shoulder.

Kinsey looked past me and said, "I don't see her."

I turned and looked out the window. Ginny was nowhere in sight.

"She was there a minute ago," I said.

"I don't know what you saw, but there is one thing I know beyond a shadow of a doubt," said Kinsey.

"What's that?" I demanded.

"Ginny loves you and she always has," said Kinsey.

CHAPTER 9

Ginny loves me. It doesn't seem possible considering the way I've treated her all these years. Kinsey must be mistaken. I was about to ask her if Ginny ever actually told her that she loved me, but we were interrupted by Eric.

"All right, the drunk with wandering hands turned out to be Kim Massinkil's date," said Eric. "It was their first. What do you think the odds are on a second date?"

"Is it under control?" asked Kinsey.

"He's sitting on the front porch waiting for a ride," answered Eric.

"While you grab Ch'ing's student list, I want to talk to Ginny for a few minutes," I said.

"No can do, Dude," said Eric.

"You don't have a list?" I asked.

"Yeah, I have a list, but talking to Ginny will be a challenge," said Eric.

"Why is that?" I asked.

"She left with a hippie dude," answered Eric.

I cut my eyes to Kinsey, but resisted the temptation to say I told you so. From the look on her face, I'd say she was using her powers of mental telepathy to shut her husband's mouth, but he wasn't listening.

"Let me guess, he had a Bahamas tan, blond ponytail and was wearing a Bob Marley t-shirt," I said.

Eric cleared his throat before answering, "Yeah, something like that. Is there a problem?"

"Nope," I answered.

Kinsey tried to step in and soften this latest news, "Grant, you shouldn't..."

I cut her off and said, "We have more important things to focus on right now, like finding Ch'ing."

"Has something happened to Ch'ing?" asked Kinsey.

"He's missing," said Eric.

"His place was busted up," I said.

"Have you heard back from Rose?" asked Eric.

"You called Rose?" asked Kinsey.

"Yes, I called Rose and no I haven't heard back from her," I answered.

As if on cue, my phone rang and it sent me pocket diving once again. It was the prosecutor, Zeke Kruthers, calling.

"Is it her?" asked Eric.

I shook my head.

"No, but I have to take it," I answered. "Can you grab that student list while I see what he wants?"

"Sure thing," said Eric. "Let's make some calls, Babe."

"Mr. Kruthers," I said.

"We need to talk," he said.

"I don't have my calendar with me," I said. "Can you call the office Monday morning to schedule an appointment?"

"This won't wait," he said. "Can you meet for a beer?"

"Umm, well, we kind of have an emergency here," I said.

"Whatever your emergency is, this will trump it," he said. "All I need from you is the time it takes to drink one beer."

"Are you buying?" I asked.

"Yeah, sure," he answered.

"Where did you have in mind?" I asked.

"Do you know Ed's Tavern down on the river?" he asked.

"The dive bar on Harrods Creek?" I asked.

"That's the one," he said. "Meet me there in fifteen."

I found Eric in his office and told him that I had to meet Kruthers for a few minutes, but would be back to help with the search for Ch'ing. The few stragglers at the party who hadn't congratulated me yet, caught me on the way out the door. I thanked them as quickly as I could without being rude and then I was on the road again.

My phone rang just as I pulled into the gravel parking lot of the bar. I would have let it go to voice mail, but it was Uncle Jim.

"Geez, I thought you were in jail or something," said Uncle Jim.

"Why would you think that?" I asked.

"Detective Lambers stopped by the house and was asking questions about you," said Uncle Jim. "Do you remember him?"

I remembered him all right. I had heard the story a million times, but had learned long ago it's best to go with it.

"Isn't he Rose's ex-husband?" I asked.

"Sure is," said Uncle Jim. "Can you believe it, he still holds a grudge because he thinks I stole Rose from him?"

I sighed. Here we go. When it comes to assigning blame for their busted relationship, Uncle Jim could be as bad as Rose when he gets on a roll. It's best to nip it in the bud, if I can.

"Unbelievable," I said. "Everybody knows Rose chose you because you're the better man. What did Lambers want?"

"Said he's working homicide these days," said Uncle Jim. "Who'd you kill,

Son?"

I know it was intended to be a joke, but given the day I'd had, it didn't sit well with me.

"John Biggs hung himself today," I said.

"What do you mean, he hung himself?" asked Uncle Jim.

"I mean he tied the end of his red power tie onto the chandelier and kicked a chair supporting his feet halfway across the room," I answered.

"Geez, what would make him want to go and do a fool thing like that?" said Uncle Jim.

"Beats me," I said.

"You'd think he'd be happy and in a mood to celebrate following your big jury verdict," said Uncle Jim.

"You'd think," I agreed.

"Congratulations, by the way," said Uncle Jim.

"Thanks," I said.

"You don't sound too happy about winning your first big case," said Uncle Jim.

"I'm happy about the win," I said.

"Well, cheer up then," he said.

"I'm sorry, but it's been a tough day," I said.

"What else has happened that's big enough to tarnish your milestone victory?" he asked.

"Geez, where do I begin…umm…well let's see…Cynthia filed for divorce," I said.

There was dead silence. It lasted long enough I thought the call might have dropped, but Uncle Jim finally spoke again.

"How do you feel about it?" he asked.

"Happy to be moving on with my life," I answered.

"That was a bad fit from the start," he said.

In my mind's eye, I could see him shaking his head as he said it.

"Yeah, she likes girls and I'm a boy," I said.

"Good riddance if you ask me," he said. "What has really got you upset, Son?"

"Shady Days is evicting Mom," I said.

"What?" said Uncle Jim. "I don't understand how they can do that."

"Cynthia has a spending problem," I said. "I'm broke and don't have the money to pay Shady Days."

"Spending problem…like I said, good riddance," said Uncle Jim. "Do you want me to drop by Shady Days and talk to Alexi about the bill?"

"No, I spoke with her earlier," I said. "I'll think of something."

"When do they want her out?" asked Uncle Jim.

"End of the month," I answered.

"Geez, that doesn't give us much time," he said.

Uncle Jim loves his sister and I know he'll do whatever he can to help, but a military pension hasn't exactly left him financially flush.

"Tell me about it," I said.

"Grant, I know you love your Mom and wouldn't do anything to put her at risk," said Uncle Jim.

"I'll fix this," I said. "Did Lambers leave a card?"

"Yep, got it right here," answered Uncle Jim.

"Can you take a picture and text it to me?" I asked.

"Seriously," said Uncle Jim. "You want me to do what now?"

Uncle Jim hasn't wholeheartedly embraced the full line of features on his new smartphone. I needed to try something different.

"Can you text me the number?" I asked.

"And you will read it like all the other text messages I sent you today," he snarked.

I sighed. Uncle Jim gets testy when I don't respond immediately to his calls and messages.

"I turned my phone off earlier for a meeting and forgot to turn it back on," I said.

"Humph," said Uncle Jim.

"The number," I said.

"I'll text it to you," he said and hung up.

I figured it would be a while before I got the text, so I headed inside. Ed's Tavern isn't much more than a shack at water's edge. It's one of those neighborhood watering holes that owes its survival to outside customers. In this instance, it's a combination of bike nights and boater happy hours.

The boaters come in from a day on the river wearing swim suits and flip flops. The bikers enjoy the river views from the saddles of their motorcycles as they parade up and down River Road. Inside, they rub elbows with area residents and add their spending dollars to the locals hard earned paychecks.

The bar never changes. I'm pretty sure the last coat of paint was applied in the 1950's when the place first opened. It is dark and dirty on the inside, with maybe twenty-five tables jammed together in a space better suited for half that. Everyone else spills outside to sit at the worm eaten picnic tables and rusted-out cast iron tables dotting the riverbank.

I found Zeke sitting at a picnic table that was pulled off to the side and offered the greatest amount of privacy. I was accustomed to seeing him in a cheap government issued business suit, and it took a few before I spotted him wearing a pair of crisp new blue jeans and a canary yellow polo shirt.

He waved me over and pointed to a full bottle of beer sweating on the table. We shook hands and I sat in front of the beer.

"What's so important?" I asked.

His eyes darted around the crowd before he answered in a voice barely above a whisper.

"Keep it down, would you?" he said.

I nodded in response and couldn't help but think, how's this for keeping it down.

"Geez, Grant, what are you doing showing up in a place like this wearing a business suit?" he asked.

"I haven't been home yet," I said.

He shook his head and said, "One of the things I like about government work is we keep normal hours."

I absent-mindedly tapped the beer bottle, but I think he took it as a reminder he only had one beer to say his peace. I was actually thinking about the arguments my wife and I had over the long hours spent at the office.

"Long hours have their costs and rewards," I said.

"Congratulations, by the way," said Zeke. "I'm sorry I stormed out today without telling you that."

"Thanks, but I don't think that's why you called me here," I said.

He looked around again before speaking.

"Did you put that envelope on my table today?" he asked.

"No, I didn't," I answered.

"Look, if you did, I won't report you," he said.

"Report me to who and for what?" I asked.

"It's a game changer," he said.

"What are you talking about, Zeke?" I asked.

"I told you, the envelope," he answered.

"As I said, I didn't put it there, and if I did, I would say so," I said.

"All right, don't go postal on me," he said.

"What's in the envelope?" I asked.

"I can't tell you," he said.

"Then why did you bring it up?" I asked.

"Because it involves your client," he said.

"Goth?" I asked.

"Pathogen," he answered.

"In what way?" I asked.

"I can't tell you," he answered.

"Look this is going nowhere really fast and you asked for this meeting," I said.

"I was sure you left the envelope," said Zeke.

I opened my mouth to protest once again, but he held up his hand.

"If you had left it, then we could talk about the contents," said Zeke.

"What difference does that make?" I said.

"This complicates things," he said.

I wanted to know how it complicates things, but I was finally getting the picture that even though Zeke wanted to discuss it, he can't. I figured there had to be a legal or ethical barrier, that wouldn't exist if I was the source, but I couldn't imagine what it was.

"There's more," he said.

"Just get on with it and say what it is you want to say," I said.

"It involves your law firm, particularly, John Biggs," he said.

I felt a chill run my spine.

"Did you speak to Biggs today?" I asked.

He nodded.

"What did you talk about?" I asked.

"The contents of the envelope," answered Zeke.

"Seriously, Zeke, if you could discuss it with John, then why not me?" I asked.

"Because it involves him directly," said Zeke.

It was time to shift the tone of the conversation.

"Did you know he hung himself?" I asked.

The blood drained from Zeke's face. When he spoke again, his hands were shaking.

"I didn't know he would go and kill himself," he said.

"What did you say to him that would cause him to hang himself?" I said.

"I told him there would be new indictments," he answered.

"For what?" I asked.

"I can't say," answered Zeke.

"What can you say?" I asked.

"Investigate your father's death," he said.

"What is that supposed to mean?" I asked.

"Look, I'm really sorry, but that's all I can say," he said.

"Then we're done here," I said.

"Just one more thing, Grant," said Zeke.

"What?" I asked.

"I'm really scared of these people," he said.

"You're scared of who?" I asked.

"Watch your back, Grant," he said.

Zeke rose from the table and left without another word.

CHAPTER 10

I have to say, the entire conversation with Zeke baffled me. He was acting like he was genuinely spooked and I didn't have any idea what it was about, except it involved Pathogen and John Biggs.

Oh, and then there was that business about my father's death. That was twenty years ago and he was killed in a motorcycle wreck. What in the world could he be talking about?

I pulled my phone out to call Eric about Ch'ing and saw the messages and missed calls from earlier. Since I still had a half a beer I decided to take a few minutes to go through them.

The first voice message was from a partner at the law firm. It was short and to the point.

"Grant, this is Bill Pulver. In light of John Biggs' death, you should take a leave of absence until this matter is cleared up."

A leave of absence means no pay. I need that job to take care of Mom. What am I going to do now? I took a swig of beer and gazed out over the water hoping I might get the perfect answer in a flash of insight, but nothing came to my rescue.

The next voice message was from Uncle Jim. It was a no frills message.

"Call me," he said.

I took a draw off the beer and checked the time. It was earlier in the day and we've since spoken, so I listened to the next message. It was Roxanne from Shady Days.

"Grant, I'm leaving my shift and wanted to let you know that I've been with your mother all day," said Roxanne. "She's still not awake. Thoughts and prayers. Oh, one more thing. I heard about your trial. Congrats."

It meant a lot to me that Roxanne took the time to sit with Mom today and to give me an update. I know that isn't part of her job description. She did it because she's a good person and it's the right thing to do.

I didn't want Mom to be alone, but visiting hours were about up and I still needed to help Eric find Ch'ing. So, I promised myself I'd stop by tomorrow for a visit. I drank the last of the beer and slapped at a mosquito.

"Blood sucking vampire," I grumbled.

The next message was from Goth. It wasn't much.

"This is Wilbur Goth. I need to speak with you."

I figured I'd call him back later. Right now I had too much on my plate. There was a duplicate message from Uncle Jim to call and one from Eric demanding I come have a celebratory drink with my best friend. The final message was from Detective Lambers to call him regarding the death of John Biggs.

I slapped at another mosquito and started on the text messages. There wasn't much there. It was a bunch of call-me messages from Uncle Jim and Eric. I deleted them and was about to stuff the phone into my pocket, when it rang. It was Rose calling me back.

Caller ID has pretty much eliminated the old school tradition of saying hello and waiting for the caller to identify themselves.

"Hi Rose," I said.

"I heard about your verdict today," she said. "Congratulations."

"Thanks," I said.

"Your Uncle Jim must be very proud of you," said Rose. "I know I am."

Geez, here we go. I cleared my throat while I tried to think of a way to distract her from Uncle Jim. As it turned out, it wasn't necessary.

"You should be out celebrating with your friends and co-workers, instead of calling a washed-up old broad like me," said Rose

The washed-up old broad reference was a slippery slope into fifteen minutes of what went wrong between her and Uncle Jim, so I ignored it, and instead, focused like a laser beam on the purpose of the call.

"Ch'ing is missing," I said. "We don't know how long he's been gone, but his place is torn apart and it's giving us the willies."

"Other than the condition of the place, is there any blood or other signs of violence?" she asked.

"I haven't gone through it yet," I answered. "We wanted to clear it with you first."

She exhaled loud enough I could hear it over the phone.

"Let's you and I have a look together," she said.

"I'm just leaving Ed's Tavern," I said. "I can meet you there in ten."

"It'll take me a few minutes longer," she said. "Don't go inside without me."

"Thanks, Rose," I said. "I'll see you there in a few."

I made one last call to Eric to let him know the plan.

"Dude, where are you?" he asked.

"I'm leaving Ed's Tavern now," I said.

"You're such a slacker," he said. "If I didn't know you better, I might think you let today's win go to your head."

"I may be sitting on the river bank, but I'm not pulling a Huck Finn on you," I said.

"More like Tom Sawyer," he said. "You snookered me into making all the phone calls."

"Any luck?" I asked.

"No one knows anything about Ch'ing's whereabouts," said Eric. "Any luck with Rose?"

"She's on her way right now to meet us at Ch'ing's place," I said.

"That's what I'm talking about," said Eric. "I'll see you there in a few."

Ch'ing's home is upriver a couple of miles from Ed's Tavern. It's an old Victorian with attached bait shop. He meticulously restored the house from old photographs to its original glory and converted the bait shop into a dojo. The place comes complete with a boat ramp where he keeps his kayak and sailboat moored. Sometimes I think he confuses Louisville with Cape Cod.

I studied the mansion from one of the parking spaces in front of the dojo. Eric's men had pulled the front door shut, but I could see into the windows. Ch'ing doesn't use blinds or curtains to close out the light. His place is ordinarily full of life, but today it looked abandoned.

The wrap around covered porch extends the full length of both sides and the front of the house forming a horseshoe. Like many Victorians, it is asymmetrical with a four-story turret on the left and a three-story dormer on the right.

The siding is painted a medium shade of grey and the rust trim matches the slate roofing material. The decorative trim adds cream highlights to mix. There is no lawn to speak of. Instead, the lush yard is filled with a variety of mature trees, shrubs and colorful wild flowers.

It wasn't long before Eric pulled into the space next to me. He was driving a black paneled truck with the name of his company, Cotungin & Company Security Specialists, painted in orange script on the side.

Eric was wearing his combat face, jaw set tight and eyes unwavering. He loves to fight and I've watched many of his opponents falter when they face his ferocity for the first time. Still, it was highly unlikely he would see any action today.

Neither of us spoke. Instead, we sat quietly and watched the place for any sign of trouble. Rose arrived just as we both started to lose patience and began formulating mental excuses to justify going in without her.

"I can see I got here just in time," said Rose. "Another minute longer and the two of you would already be inside."

Rose knows us well. She gave both of us a big hug. Eric got an additional disapproving tsk for the length of his hair as she tugged at one of the sandy blond locks curled over his collar. Neither of us minded her mothering behavior and if the situation hadn't been so serious we might have enjoyed a little lighthearted back-and-forth banter.

She handed us disposable gloves and said, "Put these on, but refrain from touching anything until we have some idea about what's going on here."

We both nodded in agreement.

She led us to the big storefront window and had a look through the glass into the dojo. It appeared undisturbed, so we headed to front door of the house. There was no sign of forced entry.

Rose used her thumb and forefinger to turn the knob and push the door open. She stood in the doorway and scanned the room. Eric and I stood behind her, shifting our feet like a couple of racehorses loading the gate for a big stakes race.

Much to our dismay, she took her time surveying the room. We couldn't see a thing and knew better than to rush her. Instead, we had to settle for craning our necks in the hopes of catching a glimpse beyond the door.

Finally, she stepped inside and made room for us to follow, but held a hand up to slow our break from the gate. Taking her cue, we entered in our best ninja mode, slowly, with all five senses engaged.

The entry hall never fails to take my breath away. It is twenty feet wide and reaches the length of the house. At the far end is a large bay window overlooking the Ohio River.

To the right is a wide staircase made of polished mahogany that curves upward to the second floor. Matching mahogany wainscoting lines the lower half of the wall. Dark inlays in a triangular pattern form a border around the outer perimeter of the polished mahogany floor. Intricately carved columns lead into the western wing of the house.

The central table had been overturned and the area rug was cluttered with a spilled vase of white lilies that had been cut fresh when the day began. A message had been spray painted on the wall that read, "It has begun." Underneath the message was a symbol similar to an ouroboros, except instead of a snake swallowing its own tail, this was a snake and a bird forming a circle and swallowing each other's tail. An unfamiliar plant was painted on the rest of the wall.

"Have either of you seen this mural before?" asked Rose.

We shook our heads.

"It looks like gang graffiti," said Rose.

We slowly made our way through the remaining rooms in the house. There was no blood. Nothing was broken, but Ch'ing's thing were scattered everywhere. The one thing that caught my eye was an old black and white photograph of Ch'ing standing outside of a monastery carved into the side of a cliff. It was lying in the middle of a mess of papers on his office floor. I had never seen it before.

"Do you think somebody took him?" asked Eric.

"The place has been vandalized, but I don't see any evidence of violence," said Rose. "If somebody tried to take him against this will, Ch'ing would put up a fight."

I swept my arm around the room, "You have to admit, this doesn't look good."

Rose shook her head.

"They could have broken in when he wasn't here," she said. "Did he mention a trip?"

"Kinsey and I have been calling his students and none of them know anything about his whereabouts," said Eric

"Is there anyone else?" she asked.

"I could ask Uncle Jim," I said.

Rose's face tightened, but she didn't start one of her tirades about him.

"Do you think they were searching for something?" I asked.

"That's possible," she said. "Can you tell if anything is missing?"

We shook our heads.

"What can we do?" asked Eric.

"Keep asking around and calling his phone," she said. "I'll keep an eye out, but other than possibly filing a report for the vandalism, there's nothing I can do right now. If he doesn't show up in a few days, then we'll do a missing person."

"Thanks for helping," said Eric.

"There's one other thing," I said.

"What's that?" asked Rose.

"John Biggs hung himself today," I said.

"I heard," said Rose.

"Lambers wants to interview me about it," I said.

"That's news to me," said Rose.

"Do I need an attorney?" I asked.

"As an attorney you know the smart thing is to have representation at any interview where you are a person of interest," said Rose.

I nodded.

"Is there any doubt that it was a suicide?" asked Rose.

"Not in my mind, but John's secretary thinks different," I said.

"It's your call, Grant, but I'll see what I can find out for you," she said.

CHAPTER 11

Detective Lambers doesn't try to hide his dislike of Uncle Jim. Instead, he will tell anyone who is willing to listen. His tune sounds like the lyrics of a bad country and western song that goes something like, I hate him because he did me wrong.

I could wait for Rose to put out feelers with Lambers or I could consult with an attorney, but I didn't feel like waiting. On the heels of good fortune, this day had turned into something ugly. It would eventually turn again, but I didn't want to wait. Instead, I wanted to take constructive steps to resolve some of these problems and Detective Lambers seemed to be as good as any place to start.

Besides, I saw no value in making assumptions about his intentions. If I'm not careful, my mind will easily slip into a dark place that believes this hateful man is out to get me. I'm a twenty-first century Taoist and Ch'ing would never let me get away with such sloppy thinking.

Ch'ing focuses on the facts. He only considers data acquired directly from his senses and carves away any assumptions. One of his favorite internal arts is called Marrow Washing Chi Kung. While it has a physical component, the internal aspect of the practice contains the hidden secrets of the art. It is used to scrub the mind of self-deception. Ch'ing insists it is the shortest path to clarity.

I could certainly use a little clarity at the moment, so I returned Detective Lambers call. It went straight to voice mail. What now I thought to myself? The prospect of sitting alone in my little apartment didn't appeal to me. I had a moment where I wished I had taken Eric up on his offer of dinner, but dismissed it because I wasn't a bit hungry. While I awaited his return call, I needed to focus my attention on accomplishing another positive task.

My thoughts turned to the leave of absence from work. I didn't have any illusions about what it means. There was no longer a place for me at the firm. I had been let go. It didn't seem a bit fair to me, but then I had learned early on that lawyers don't care much about what seems fair.

Law schools flood the market each year with fresh eager faces hoping to make a mark for themselves. A young lawyer works long hours to get a toehold into the legal market. Being a lawyer may sound glamorous, but it's a competitive profession where you have to get your hands dirty to get ahead of the rest of the pack.

Attorneys learn to criticize everything, including each other. It creates a mindset that infiltrates our personal lives as well. I learned in my marriage it is not easy to sustain a relationship when you're busy attacking others. Most young lawyers give up the practice once they get a taste of these harsh realities, but it doesn't bother the law firms much since they have a steady supply of replacements.

I decided it was time to return to the office to pick up my personal belongings and headed that way. It was a little after nine when I pulled up to the building. We're on the thirty second floor and ordinarily there would be a few lights still shining through the windows, but on this night the office was dark and ominous.

I still had a key card to the building, but I wasn't sure if it worked. I had never been on a leave of absence before and a part of me felt like a thief sneaking into someone's home. The security camera pointing straight at my face didn't help relieve the angst I was feeling. My hand shook slightly as I slid the card into the slot for the garage overhead.

A wave of relief washed over me when the door began rising, but it turned to confusion when a car roared out and damn near side swiped me as soon as the door was high enough for it to pass through. They were obviously in a hurry. It didn't help my growing anxiety one bit, and I had to resist the temptation to just forget the whole thing and go home.

The garage was mostly empty. A lone car was parked in an area where the lights were burned out. It reminded me of a tombstone standing watch on a dark night. I was accustomed to leaving the building at a late hour, but being here under these circumstances was creepy. I managed to pull it together enough to slip the battered old truck into my assigned parking space.

I never lock the truck, because I figure no one would want to steal it, but this time, I did lock it. Stuffing the keys into my pocket, I headed toward the elevator, but stopped when I thought I heard someone calling out from the direction of the tombstone. When I turned toward the sound, there was no one there.

I changed my mind about taking the elevator and chose the stairs instead. I wanted to keep moving and being trapped in a box hanging from a cable did not appeal to me at the moment.

Since I was parked on lower level two, it was a thirty four story climb, but I had done it many times before as part of my training for mountain climbing trips out west. A busy lawyer has to find ways to incorporate fitness training into his daily routine if he hopes to stay on his game.

I hoped the physical exertion would help clear my spooked head. A sour smell in the stairwell door did little to alleviate my anxiety. I noticed a puddle of fresh urine with a faint hint of steam still rising from it. Why do people urinate in stairwells? I reconsidered the elevator, but couldn't get past the uneasiness I felt about it, and began the ascent.

It could have been the stress-filled day, but the climb seemed unusually difficult. I had to stop several times to rest. It might have been my imagination, but I thought I heard footsteps in the stairwell below. Each time I stopped the steps below continued like an extended echo before coming to an abrupt stop. Someone seemed to be following me and trying to avoid discovery.

The thought of someone stalking me was creepy enough, but under the circumstances, it was nerve wracking. Maybe I was being paranoid, but I kept thinking about Kruthers telling me he was afraid of these people. He was spooked and it spooked me. I had a few questions I wanted to ask this stalker, so I devised a strategy to catch whoever it was.

After climbing four more flights of stairs, I opened the door leading to the twenty-fifth floor, but didn't step through the threshold. Instead, I quietly crept further up the stairs until I was out of view and waited. I expected the stalker to rush up the stairs, but that didn't happen. In fact, nothing happened at all.

It's possible that my pursuer didn't take the bait, but I convinced myself instead that the whole thing was nothing but my imagination. Scolding myself for getting spooked over nothing, I finished the climb and slipped into my old office. It is never a good idea to ignore our instincts.

The office foyer is intended to impress. The marble flooring is polished to a high sheen. Matching Doric columns and a fresco of the Parthenon is calculated to give the impression that Socrates resides within its walls. To me, it's a little over the top. The first time I stepped into the place I half expected to see everyone dressed in togas and sandals.

Ordinarily, there are number of young attorneys working late on projects dumped on them at the last minute and a night shift of clerical staff working diligently to meet the next day's deadlines, but not on this night. On this night, the offices were all empty. As far as I could tell, there wasn't a soul working. Everyone was probably sent home in deference to John's death. The place felt like a mausoleum.

This is the home office of Biggs, Scranton & Pulver, a multi-state firm with over 250 attorneys. The firm services large corporations with deep pockets and ties to Louisville. Pathogen's home office is in Louisville and it is the richest of all of the firm's clients.

Like most big companies, they are a target for scam artists looking to make a quick buck, which is good for the firm because it keeps a large portion of the attorneys busy defending frivolous law suits. John was right about one thing, losing Pathogen's business would definitely hurt the firm. Cutbacks would follow and more than one attorney would lose their job.

There are two routes to my office. Curiosity caused me to chose the route that would take me past John's office, where I found crime scene tape barring entry. I thought about what Kruthers told me earlier and decided to have a look around to see if there was any clue as to why John killed himself. I squeezed past the yellow tape and wormed my way into his office.

Even though the place appeared to be empty, something told me to close the door behind me. Rather than turn the lights on, I used the flashlight app on my phone. I'm not sure what I expected to see, but it wasn't this.

John's office looked intact except for the obvious mess indicating a crime scene, complete with mangled chandelier and chalk outline of dead body. I thought they only did that in the movies. It sure looked like the police were treating this like a homicide rather than a suicide.

There was a stack of files on the corner of his desk that I quickly rifled through. None of them looked suspicious. There was nothing else on the desk. The desk drawers were locked. Unless I was willing to force them open, there was nothing left for me to do in this room. I just couldn't see myself breaking into John's desk.

I did one last scan of the room for anything that might shed some light on the mystery of John's death, but saw nothing out of the ordinary. I was turning to leave when I felt something under my shoe. As bent to pick up a wadded piece of paper, the doorknob turned and the office door slowly opened. Panicked, I slipped the paper into my pocket and squatted behind the desk for cover.

My mind was racing for a cover story, but I couldn't think of a plausible excuse for being in John's office. I don't know whether it's true or not, but everybody knows a criminal returns to the scene of the crime. If I was caught here, it would make me look very guilty.

I waited breathlessly for the lights to come on, but they didn't. The only light in the room came from a full moon shining through the window. Now that my eyes had adjusted, it seemed way too bright at the moment. I risked peeking around the edge of the desk and caught a glimpse of the door just before it closed shut.

I crept over to the door and listened for a few minutes, before I decided I could risk opening it and taking a peek. The hall was empty and I slipped out. I didn't want to push my luck and thought about leaving, but I needed to do what I came for and was about to head down the hall to my office when Detective Lambers stepped in front of me.

He was gaunt. The man I remember had let himself go soft, but not this man. He was too thin and the slack skin along his jaw line made him look older than he really is. There was nothing slack about his eyes. While they were surrounded by shadow, the eyes burned with intensity. I can't be sure of their color since all I really noticed is they were bloodshot, as if he hadn't slept well recently.

He was dressed in grey slacks, a navy blue blazer that could use a trip to the dry cleaners, and a sky blue mixed cotton poly shirt that was wrinkled despite claims of being permanent press. A blue and white tie was hanging loose around an open collar that revealed a tuff of chest hair.

"Couldn't resist returning to the scene of the crime, could you?" asked Lambers.

"Geez, where did you come from?" I asked.

"Why did you kill him?" demanded Lambers.

"I didn't kill him and you know it," I said.

"I know a murderer when I see one," he said.

"You know only a deep-seated grudge and you're letting it cloud your judgment," I said.

"I have an eye witness that places you at the scene," he said.

"I work here," I said.

"Not anymore," said Lambers.

"Are you behind that?" I asked.

"I'm going to make sure you spend a lot of time in prison," he said.

"John Biggs committed suicide and if you continue to harass me, I will press charges," I said.

"Are you threatening me," he said.

"The problem with having a big mouth like yours is everybody knows your business," I said. "What that means for you is everybody knows you hate my Uncle Jim and you hate me because of him."

"Helen Gloria overheard you arguing with Biggs, just before you killed him," he said.

"We were discussing a raise when Helen interrupted us to tell John he had a call from Zeke Kruthers," I said.

"She saw you kill him," said Lambers.

"She saw me try to save his life," I said.

"What are doing here?" he demanded.

"I came to pick up my personal belongs," I said.

"Not in Biggs' office," he said.

"Kruthers told me he delivered some bad news to John just before he killed himself, but he wouldn't tell me what it was," I said. "I was hoping to find an explanation for John's suicide"

"You violated a crime scene," said Lambers. "I should arrest your right now for obstruction of justice."

"I've never seen a man kill himself before," I said. "I needed an explanation."

"I know you killed him and I'm going to prove it," he said.

He turned and left. I shook my head and headed down the hall to my office. By no means is it a fancy corner office like John's, but it had been home to me for several years. Unlike John's office, it had been ransacked and was a total mess. One odd thing I noticed was the bottle of bourbon was gone and in its place was an empty bottle. I wondered about that, but it was time to pack and leave, except I needed a box.

I found a single box in the copy room. There was some trash in the bottom that I would have thrown away, but I couldn't find the trash can that usually sits next to the copier. I let out a sigh and carried the box, trash and all to my office with the intention of cleaning it out before I put my things in it, but when I got there the trash can from my office was gone too. I could have dumped it onto the floor, but instead, I made quick work of tossing my stuff on top of the trash and headed out.

I managed to get out of the building without further incident. Once I was on the road again, I decided I needed to stop somewhere and have a good stiff drink. It seemed like the best idea I had all day.

CHAPTER 12

My head throbbed to the beat of a rap song crackling from an old clock radio salvaged from my parents' attic. Like a scratched record, the same two annoying lines repeated again and again.

"I'm a man of Tao, naked and wild. I can make you howl, naked and wild."

Something had to be done about that throbbing. Either I needed more tequila or the radio needed to die. Since making a decision was totally out of the question, I decided to do both. First, I hit the mute button, but it didn't work. Frustrated, I stabbed it a second and then a third time. It must have been possessed, because it kept playing.

That's when a brilliant idea leaked through the alcohol haze and I yanked the cord out of the wall. The music played on. Just as I was about to take a swing at the radio, a bright light dialed the headache up to max.

I put a pillow over my face and groaned, "Just kill me now."

It didn't help. The pillow stank from last night's sins and the radio continued tormenting me. I groaned and tossed the pillow to the floor. Then I grabbed the radio and smashed it against the wall. It couldn't have gotten much worse, but it did.

"Have you lost your mind, Grant?"

It was a chick's raspy voice, sounding like she'd smoked one too many unfiltered Camels. The voice belonged to a tall brunette with nearly two inches of dirty blond roots and chipped red nail polish. She was standing in my bathroom doorway.

There was something familiar about this woman, but I couldn't place her. She was also a little scary thanks to a tattoo of Eve holding a snake in one hand and a half-eaten apple in the other. Her face was hard-worn, as if she had seen some tough times. I thought she might look older than she actually was. I have a habit of giving strangers nicknames and tagged her Eve.

She cleared her throat expectantly, so I mumbled the first thing that came to mind, "The music woke me."

She blinked a couple of times. I wasn't sure if she was adjusting to the light, or if she was trying to decide if she should ask about the radio.

"What music?" she finally asked.

Now I was confused, so I asked a question of my own, "You didn't hear the radio?"

"No, I sure heard you though," she said. "You were dreaming…all curled up into a ball and begging someone to please stop."

The disgusted look on her face did not help with my sour stomach or pounding headache.

"It's pathetic for a grown man to act that way, if you ask me," she added.

I let out a groan. For years, my nightmares have been filled with the Fat Lady. I've tried everything I can think of to rid myself of them and failed. It was bad enough that I have to re-live that horrible experience on a nightly basis, but this judgmental behavior from the likes of her is something I won't tolerate.

I was about to ask her to leave when she shifted to another tactic.

"Do you want to pick up where we left off last night?" she asked.

I had no idea what happened last night and I hoped we didn't sleep together, but I sure wasn't going to let it happen now. Besides my head felt as if last night's tequila had taken root and a large, festering agave was growing in it. I fought back an eruption of stomach acid burning its way past my heart and half way up my esophagus, before I finally managed to choke it back down.

She was nearly to the bed when I blurted out, "I have a headache."

She froze in place and fixed a glassy stare at the center of my forehead, as if she could see into my head.

"Really?" she asked. "You have a headache. I can't believe you just said that to me. It sounds like something I would say to my husband."

Even though it was the truth, I also hated saying it. Cynthia often used the same excuse. I heard it often enough from her that I stopped asking.

That wasn't the worst of it. Cynthia revealed her true nature on those occasions she tried to negotiate an exchange for something she wanted from me. As you can imagine, it didn't go well when I pointed out she was trying to turn a trick with her husband.

After a couple of months she told me I was emotionally bankrupt and demanded a divorce. It was just like her to make it my fault. She said she needed more from a partner than I could give. Go figure. She emptied our bank account and moved her girlfriend into the house.

Eve was looking a bit impatient as she crossed her arms over her flat chest. I didn't know what she expected me to say. I sure didn't want to talk about headaches or spouses. If anyone was due an explanation, it had to be me. Geez, she was a married woman standing in my bedroom.

I shrugged.

"The headache is real, but you have a husband at home," I said. "Maybe you should spend some time with him. I'm really not interested in married women."

"Yea, that's what you said last night," she said.

My hands were shaking. I wasn't sure if it was caused by an overdose of tequila, or the nightmarish day I had yesterday.

"I'm still not interested," I said.

Maybe I should have been more diplomatic, because it started to get ugly at this point.

"Look at you," said Eve. "You're a mess. You live above a hookah bar. I thought you were some kind of hot shot lawyer."

She was right about the apartment. It wasn't much. Two small rooms above a hookah bar in a busy section of the Highlands, an old neighborhood with a young look thanks to an influx of hipster energy. The larger of the two rooms was divided by a laminated countertop into a kitchen and living room. The initials of a prior tenant were carved into the countertop and judging by the burn marks, it was once used as an ash tray.

Two mismatched thrift store bar stools lined the bar. One was solid enough, but the other was a menace. I kept meaning to throw it out before someone got hurt and sued me for what little I had. Not that I entertained guests in the place.

The half-eaten pizza and empty tequila bottle was just the tip of the mound of trash. A stack of unopened mail lay in a pile of dust at the end of a beat up old coffee table. Several of the envelopes were marked "final notice." I should have opened the mail and paid a few bills, but I really got distracted with the big case I was working on for Goth.

The only thing of value in the place was a dusty antique sword with strange markings standing alone in the corner like a silent sentry. It was a gift from Ch'ing. With a twinkle in his eye he told me it was older than the hills, and a priceless piece of junk. I felt a stab of panic remembering that he was missing. I needed to get it together and find out what was going on.

At the end of the kitchen counter was an open door leading into a small windowless bedroom. On the floor was a king sized mattress that took up most of the room. That's where I was at the moment. The only light in the room came from a bare light bulb in the small bathroom. It provided backlighting for Eve. The truth is I would have preferred something closer to total darkness.

I sighed. I couldn't remember ever waking up with a stranger before, and didn't know how to handle it. What I did know for sure, it was time to get rid of her, but first I asked her about last night.

"For the last six months I watched you come into my bar and order the same thing," she said. "It was the most expensive bourbon in the place and never diluted with a mixer or ice."

She swept her arm around my apartment and shook her head in disbelief.

"You have that right mix of bad boy and good guy that is so delicious," she said. "There is danger lurking behind your smooth lawyer façade. I could tell you were some kind of bad ass, but I could also see a lost little boy in there too. It made you especially hot!"

"It was always the same," she continued. "You would sit at the bar and sip your one drink, while the hottest chicks in the place hit on you. Once you finished your whiskey, you would excuse yourself and go to the men's room. From there you would quietly slip out the door without saying goodbye to anyone."

"I thought you might be gay or something," she said. "What a waste that would be. I always wanted to turn a gay guy. So, last night when you started ordering shots of tequila, I saw an opportunity and decided to take it. You were interested at first, but then you noticed my ring and chilled. So, I made some adjustments."

I raised an eyebrow and asked, "Adjustments?"

"I told you my husband died in a motorcycle wreck a few months ago and I wasn't ready to take my ring off," she answered. "You got all sappy and told me about your dad."

"But why would you lie like that," I asked.

She narrowed her eyes and said, "Because I can."

I didn't remember any of this and I didn't like her lies.

"How did we get back here?" I asked.

"Seriously…it didn't take much once you were good and drunk," answered Eve. "I let you call me Ginny and bent over every once in a while so you could peek down my shirt. We closed the deal when I followed you into the men's room. Men are so easy to manipulate."

I didn't like being manipulated and the last thing I needed was a jealous husband.

As an afterthought she asked, "Who's Ginny by the way?"

I wasn't about to discuss Ginny with this woman and decided to keep the discussion focused on her.

"Won't your husband want to know where you spent the night?" I asked.

"I'll tell him I couldn't sleep after work and went to my sister's for coffee," she said. "He's so stupid. He believes whatever I tell him."

The lies reminded me of Cynthia. I did not need another liar in my life. I was trying to figure out how to get rid of her when my phone vibrated. The call was from Eric. Getting rid of her was going to be an unpleasant task. I dislike being rude, especially to women. I don't usually take calls when I'm with someone, but it was a welcomed diversion.

"It's very early," I said.

"He lives," said Eric. "Glad you survived the night."

"What do you know about last night?" I asked.

"Only that you didn't go home after we finished searching Ch'ing's place," answered Eric. "You were seriously wasted dude and wouldn't tell me where you were. I've never seen you so paranoid. You kept jabbering some nonsense about a stalker cop, Ginny, and a kiss."

"I didn't kiss Ginny last night," I said. "You're tripping man."

"I was afraid of that," he said.

Eve was ransacking the room, all the while cursing her stupidity. I have no idea what she was looking for. The place was a mess before she started, but somehow she still managed to make it worse.

"How do you find anything in this mess?" she growled.

"I hear a chick's voice," said Eric. "Dude, you're holding out on me. Did you take Ginny home? It's about time you found someone like that. I have to say…you stayed with Cynthia way too long! What was that skanky stripper's name? You know…the one she left you for…Chasity…Candy?"

"Candida…and no I didn't bring Ginny home with me," I said.

"Unbelievable…Candida…how fitting she chose a STD for a stage name," said Eric. "It's not Ginny…bummer. Well…anyway, I'm glad you got some action last night, but if it had been me, I would have poured my energy into Ginny. That girl is special!"

Eve said a little too loudly, "You're a loser, Grant."

She slammed the door on her way out for added emphasis.

"Dude, she's really pissed," said Eric.

"Yeah, the perfect ending to a really bad night," I said wryly.

"There's nothing you can to do about the angry chick, but move forward, Grant," said Eric.

Speaking of moving forward, I asked, "Is there any news on Ch'ing?"

"No, but I've got my best guys on it," answered Eric.

"I'm worried," I said.

"Yeah, me too," said Eric.

"Stay on it," I said.

"Roger that," he said. "Oh, I almost forgot why I called. I've got a job for you."

"I don't want a job, Eric. I'm moving to Bhutan."

"Yeah right, you're broke," he said. "Let me help you out, Grant. I have a job for you."

I was suspicious.

"What kind of job?" I asked.

"Padma Ganesha needs protection," replied Eric.

"You're joking right," I said. "I'm not a bodyguard, Eric. I'm a lawyer."

"Grant, you're an unemployed lawyer," said Eric.

"How did you know they let me go?" I asked.

"Drunk talk," said Eric. "I couldn't shut you up."

"I wonder who else I called?" I said.

"Who knows," said Eric. "Anyway, Dude, you need the money and maybe it's time for a change. Besides, who knows where this could lead."

I wondered why Eric needed me to guard someone and asked, "You're the professional. Why don't you do this?"

"I would, but they asked for you," said Eric. "It's a lot of money and could keep you occupied while we get the rest of this mess sorted out."

"Asked for me…really…and who would that be?" I asked.

"You know better than to ask that question, Grant," said Eric. "I would tell you, but then I'd have to kill you."

"Geez, you can be so incredibly corny sometimes," I said. "How about cutting the crap and telling me why the winner of the Nobel Peace prize needs a body guard?"

"Who knows, buddy," said Eric. "It'll pay a few bills and might even buy you a plane ticket to Katmandu. He is speaking today at the Center."

"I thought Padma Ganesha never did speaking engagements," I said.

"Yeah, I know," said Eric. "He surprised everyone when he accepted. The sponsor is Emerald Allure, Inc. It's part of their lecture series, Ideas to Change the World."

"Emerald Allure…isn't that Ginny's company and don't they make high-end women's clothing?" I asked.

"Sexy clothing seems like a good place to start world change to me," snickered

Eric. "I find it uplifting."

I ignored Eric's sophomoric joke and searched my memory for details about Padma Ganesha. A few years ago he wrote a best-selling book about the happiest place on Earth. The inhabitants are totally at ease with themselves and the world around them. There is no hatred in their hearts. Their minds are free from worry. They live simple and honest lives, giving much and expecting little. It is a place of peace and prosperity.

It is also a place where people live long lives. The natives credit their longevity to a magical pool of water they call the "Bubbling Well".

Padma's book stayed on top of the best seller list for one hundred and thirty-six weeks. Although he never gave the place a name, the media took to calling it "Shangri La." His fans hounded him for the location of the Bubbling Well, but he steadfastly refused to reveal it.

I thought about Mom's unpaid bill and asked, "What do I have to do?"

"You should dress in black," replied Eric. "Keep it casual."

"What…no uniform boss man?" I quipped.

Eric sighed.

"Amateur," he said. "I'll send over a shirt that identifies you as security staff. Be at the Center by 6:00 p.m. Use the back stage entrance off 7th Street. Ask for Tiny at the security desk."

"Let me guess," I said. "Tiny is 6'8", weighs 350 pounds, wears a pony tail, and is covered with tattoos."

"With a face only a mother could love," said Eric. "He's a real character. This is his night job. His day job is leader of the outlaw motorcycle gang, Dragon Gate. You'll like him, Grant."

"Does Tiny have a last name?" I asked.

"If he does, I've never heard it," answered Eric.

CHAPTER 13

After ending the call with Eric, I sat on the edge of the dirty mattress and took a long hard look at myself. The apartment smelled like a toxic waste dump. I scanned the filth scattered around the room and only saw a place where chaos reigns. I had made a mess of my life.

Eve was toxic. The tequila was toxic. They were poison to me. I shook my head in the hope of ridding myself of a specter lurking in the shadows of my mind. Despair was at hand, threatening to take over.

I couldn't go on like this. It was time for change. I desperately needed to clean up and restore order to my mangled life. It was time to rid myself of the toxins, but where should I begin, I wondered.

Ch'ing likes to say that the place to begin is with a simple practice right where you are, so that's what I did. I closed my eyes, inhaled deeply and released the toxins. I repeated this simple formula over and over again with the absolute faith that it was working until peace filed my mind and there was no long any room for despair.

I sat in meditation until I knew with absolute certainty what I needed to do next. The details of a plan took shape in my mind and when it was fully fleshed out, I opened my eyes and began.

I took some niacin and washed it down with a couple of quarts of distilled water, before heading to the gym, where I found an empty aerobics room and did Tai Chi until my clothes were drenched in sweat. Then I headed to the steam room.

There was no one else taking a steam bath, so I settled down on the center of the top bench and closed my eyes. The heat washed over me in waves that melted away the last vestiges of crud. I had one thought and only one thought…restore me.

There was momentary draft of cold air and then the bench creaked next me. I heard a familiar voice.

"Well, here we are," said Goth.

He was the absolute last person I ever expected to see in the gym steam room.

"What are you doing here?" I asked.

He peered at me with dark inscrutable eyes.

"Having a steam bath, what else?" he finally answered.

"I got your message," I said.

His eyes flared hot with anger at the reminder that I had ignored him. Then they quickly went cold again as he found a way to suppress it. He waited.

"What is it you want to discuss?" I asked.

"Nasty business, Biggs killing himself like that," he said.

I nodded.

"What do you know about it?" he asked.

"I found him hanging from the chandelier in his office, but not in time to save his life," I said.

"You spoke to him?" asked Goth.

"Yes, earlier when I told him about the verdict," I said.

"Did you discuss anything else?" he asked.

"I asked for a raise," I said.

He nodded as if he was checking items off a mental list. Many times I have seen attorneys do the same thing during depositions.

"Anything else," he said.

I shook my head.

"Did he give you any hint why he did it?" asked Goth.

"None," I answered.

"Why do you think he did it?" he asked.

Something told me not to share my conversation with Kruthers.

"I really don't know," I said.

He nodded thoughtfully.

"It's unfortunate that the firm let you go," he said.

"I didn't deserve it," I said.

His eyes got that predatory look I had seen before.

"Not to worry," he said. "There may be something for you to do for me. I'll be in touch."

He then abruptly got up and left the steam room without another word.

Once I had enough heat, I took a cold shower before heading over to Shady Days to see Mom. There was something important I needed to tell her.

Ginger waved me over as soon as I stepped into the building. Without a word, she walked around her desk and gave me a warm hug.

"How is she?" I asked.

She shook her head.

"Ms. Li still isn't awake," she said. "Let's assume the best. We heal ourselves, and to do it right, we need plenty of rest."

"You're right about the rest," I said. "I won't stay too long."

"She's strong," said Ginger.

I nodded.

"Is she still in ICU?" I asked.

She shook her head.

"The Doctor moved her back to her room," said Ginger.

"Would you tell the Doctor I want an update on her condition?" I asked.

Ginger had been less than her usual chatty self and more focused than usual. I guess it was a bit too much to ask for, because she suddenly resumed her usual behavior.

"Oh, you know how those Doctors are, Grant," said Ginger. "Getting one to think about anything other than their next big purchase isn't easy. Why Dr. Michaels was just saying that he is looking at vacation homes in Bermuda. Like you really have to own a home just to visit a place."

She shook her head and continued mumbling to herself as I headed off to Mom's room.

The door was open and noise from a television rerun could be heard inside. Part of Mom's therapy is to leave it on for several hours a day to keep her mind stimulated. The curtains were open wide and the midday light was flooding in. I turned the television off and sat in the rocker next to her bed.

Her eyes were closed, but I could see her chest rising and falling with each breath. Her hair was pulled back, making her already gaunt face look just a little thinner. I took her boney hand in mine and held it as I rocked the chair ever so slightly.

I'm not sure how long we sat like that, maybe an hour or so, before I was able to tell her that I needed to sell her house to pay the nursing home bill. I didn't know if she could hear me or not, but I wanted to tell her in person. Her home was the last place she had known happiness…it was the last place I had known happiness. It was time to move on with our lives.

I gave her hand another squeeze, promised I would soon return and then left. That was the hard part. Now I needed to swing by the house and tell Cynthia it's time for her to leave.

There was a Subaru Outback in the driveway behind my Benz, so I parked on the street. I figured it belonged to her lover. When she didn't answer the third knock I dug into my pocket for the house key, but before I could use it, the door jerked open.

"What are you doing here, Grant?" demanded Cynthia.

"You need to gather your things and leave," I said.

I could see from the look on her face that my answer surprised her, but it didn't take her long to regroup and return to her usual bully self.

"I filed for a divorce or haven't you heard yet?" she asked.

"The sheriff delivered your message," I said.

"Good, then you know that I've asked for the house," she said.

"This house doesn't belong to you," I said.

"We'll see about that, my attorney says…"

I interrupted her.

"I'm selling the house," I said. "I'll be listing it with a realtor when I leave here."

"You can't just do that," said Cynthia.

"Really, when did you get a law degree, Cynthia," I said.

"The judge will decide who gets this house," she said.

"No he won't," I said.

"I'm calling the police," she said.

I waited.

"I'm calling them now," she said and pulled her phone from a pocket.

"Go ahead," I said. "They will tell you to call your attorney and then leave."

She hesitated.

"I'm calling my attorney," she said.

"Go ahead," I said.

This time she actually hit the call button. I waited.

"This is Cynthia Li," she said. "Let me speak to Ms. Kingsport."

"If you are lucky enough to get through to her, tell her the house is deeded jointly to my parents," I said. "This is Mom's house and you are trespassing."

Cynthia's eyes opened wide in disbelief. There was a certain amount of satisfaction seeing her go slack jaw with shock. Without another word, I turned and left.

What happened next wasn't part of the plan. Ginny grew up around the corner from me. Not once after the incident with her mother did I venture down their street. Her mother still lives around the corner from Mom's house, and as I walked away from Cynthia, I surprised even myself when I turned toward Ginny's old house.

I stood on the sidewalk and stared at it for the longest time. Overgrown shrubs blocked much of the narrow sidewalk and obscured the front of the house. There were no lights on or signs of life inside.

It was a hot muggy day and all the other homes along the street were buttoned up tight with air conditioners running full blast. Her house was the only exception. The front door was open, allowing fresh air to flow into the house through an ornamental security door with no glass, just a screen for bugs.

Using the butterflies in my stomach to galvanize myself, I walked up the front steps and onto a small porch. I paused for a moment and considered turning back. My hand reached for the door of its own accord and knocked.

"In the kitchen," called out her mother in a heavily accented voice. "I'm baking and my hands are full. Come on in."

I'm not sure what I expected, but it wasn't that. I took a deep breath and stepped over the threshold.

The inside looked like a mother's house. It was neat and orderly. Scattered around the living room were photographs taken at various stages of life. A scrap quilt patterned as a crucifix was draped over the back of the sofa. The agony of Jesus was the focal point. Facing the corner sat a straight backed chair made from dark hardwood. An open Bible rested in the seat. The house was filled with a familiar aroma.

The kitchen was around the corner to the right. The oven door was standing open. A plump middle aged Spanish woman with a loose strand of graying hair draped over the right side of her face was turning toward the counter top with a sheet of cookies. My knees weakened.

"I made your favorite...hot almond cookies," she said. "Don't they smell delicious? Would you..."

Her chattering stopped abruptly and the smile evaporated. She narrowed her eyes and glared at me over the top of her glasses.

"You...you...you're that abomination...the bastard son of mixed parents," she stuttered. "What are you doing in my house?"

"I knocked," I said. "You invited me in."

Maria tilted her head slightly, planted her fists onto her ample hips and glared at me.

"I thought it was my daughter coming to visit," she said.

"I have something I want to tell you," I said.

Maria barked, "I don't care what you have to tell me. Get out of my house you nasty little boy...out!"

"I'm not a little boy anymore and I'm not afraid of you," I said. "You're a hateful woman and from this day forward I will gladly leave you behind to wallow in your own misery."

The last thing I heard as I stepped out the door was her prayer, "Hail Mary, full of grace..."

CHAPTER 14

The Center is located in downtown Louisville on the Ohio River at water's edge. While not far from the apartment, it was too far to walk on a hot day, so I headed out in dad's old truck. Traffic was bumper to bumper on Main Street. Horns were honking. People were partying in the streets. Their hands were stuffed with super-sized beers and foot long hot dogs.

Street vendors were selling t-shirts that read, "Immortality Is Only Kinky the First Time." It was a festive carnival atmosphere. I wondered if these people really believed they were going to learn the secret of immortality, or if it was just another reason to get rowdy.

Even though the event didn't begin until 7:00 p.m., the Center parking garage was already jammed packed when I arrived a few minutes before six. I made my way to the rooftop where I spotted one last empty space at the end of a row.

Before I could park, a green Porsche whipped around the corner heading in the wrong direction and straight at me. A brunette with wavy hair blowing in the wind was behind the wheel. A phone was stuck in her ear. She was focused on her conversation and did not see me.

I hit the brakes hard enough that I was jerked forward and smashed into the steering wheel. A sharp pain shot through my sternum as the Porsche slipped into the last spot.

The chick was completely oblivious. I leaned out of the window intending to give her a hard time about what she'd just done, but stopped short when I heard her shouting into the phone.

"I'm sorry you feel that way," she said.

When she turned and dropped the phone into her purse I got a good look at her face for the first time. It was Ginny. She opened the door and gracefully swung her legs out of the Porsche. I forgot the pain in my sternum. I forgot she stole my parking space. I forgot she nearly crashed into me. Damn, if I didn't forget to breathe.

Then to my utter amazement her grace evaporated into a spell of clumsiness as she awkwardly dropped her car keys onto the pavement. When she bent over to pick them up I heard the unmistakable sound of tearing fabric.

"You've got to be kidding me!" she said.

Still oblivious to my presence she tried looking over her shoulder for the torn fabric. When that didn't work she twisted at the waist. Finally, she bent over and tried to peer up her dress.

When she looked up for the first time, she saw me watching her from the truck. Her jaw dropped as we made eye contact and I smiled.

"Your dress is torn," I said.

Her beautiful eyes narrowed slightly. I tried again.

"You need some help with it?" I asked.

She mumbled something I couldn't make out. Turning on a heel she stomped off in the direction of the stairwell. For the first time, I could see the rip down the small of her back revealing a glimpse of her tattoo.

"A Porsche," I muttered. "I'm sure she was real impressed with my truck."

Since Ginny had taken the last available parking space, I reluctantly parked the pickup in front of a no parking sign at the end of the row. There was a good chance it would be impounded. At that point, I just didn't care.

It was the first time I had ever been back stage. I expected security to be tight at all of the entrances, but there was literally no one attending the door. I quietly surveyed my surroundings. To the right was a small vending area with several empty tables. To the left was a security office. Straight ahead was a corridor with a sign posted at the entrance that read, "Authorized Personnel Only." I didn't see Tiny anywhere.

I returned my attention to the security office. The overhead light was on, but the view into the room was obscured by a smoked glass window. I could barely make out the outline of a desk surrounded by security monitors. No one was sitting in the desk chair. The office looked empty to me. I figured Tiny was making his rounds, but since the door to the office stood wide open I decided to just have a peek inside.

As I moved closer to the office door I smelled it for the second time in the last twenty-four hours…a strange combination of coffee, rust, and shit. I froze in place, listening for any sound that would explain the now familiar odors. The last few drops of a fresh pot gurgled from a coffee maker. I heard nothing else, so I peeked cautiously inside the door.

A mountain of a man, obviously Tiny, was lying in a pool of blood. His meaty hands were grasping at the hilt of a combat knife that had been buried in his chest. I rushed to his side and dropped to my knees. Tiny's head rolled in my direction. His pupils were large and unfocused. Blood trickled from the side of his mouth. He tried to speak, stopped, and then gurgled something that sounded like "Mung."

I wiped his mouth with my shirt tail and laid my hands on top his to stop him from pulling the knife out.

"Don't," I said. "Just hang on. I'll get help."

I dug into my pocket and pulled out my phone. It squirted from my blood soaked hand and landed on the floor a few feet away. A thin stream of blood squirted from the edge of the wound.

"Damn," I cursed.

I needed both hands to stop the loss of blood. Tiny needed medical attention fast. How was I going to get help? I had to make that call. Tiny's life depended on it. Trying to keep pressure on the wound with one hand, I stretched the other hand toward the phone. Just as my fingertips reached it, a foot came out of nowhere and kicked it across the room. The phone bounced off a metal file cabinet and spun out of reach on the other side of Tiny.

In the corner my eye, I saw a sandaled heel pivot and point in my direction. I instinctively rolled under a back kick that would have crushed my chest and slammed hard into the attacker's supporting leg. The maneuver worked. His knee gave way and he crumbled to the ground.

I thought I had him, but quick as a cat, he popped to his feet. I lurched at him with blood soaked hands, but missed. The miss cost me dearly. I never saw the foot that slammed into my ribs or the hand that grabbed my throat a second later. Before I could retaliate, his knee pinned my arm to the floor. This guy was fast.

Instinct is to pull away, but Ch'ing had trained me well. Instead of trying to yank my arm away from him, I rolled in the direction of the pinned arm and slammed a palm into the back of his elbow. It worked. He grunted in pain and released my throat as he tried to tumble away from me.

I followed close behind, but he caught his balance and I caught his fist in my sore ribs. Grimacing in pain, my hand clutched at a cracked rib. It was instinctive, but the wrong move because it gave him a chance to roll to his feet and flee the room.

I wanted to follow him, but scrambled back to Tiny instead. His pupils were fully dilated. The bleeding had stopped. I checked his pulse. It confirmed what I already knew. Tiny was dead. My second death in two days. What was happening? People around me were dropping like flies.

There was nothing I could do for Tiny, but I could do something about his killer. Determined to catch him, I pulled the knife from Tiny's chest and scrambled after the killer. I didn't make it far before I slipped on the blood soaked floor and crashed head first into the door jam. The blow brought me to my knees, stars dancing before my eyes, and then I blacked out.

I'm not sure how long I was out. When I came to I remember gingerly touching my brow and feeling something wet. I looked at my finger tips and saw blood. I vaguely remember thinking I needed a doctor. I stuck a hand into my pocket to call one, but couldn't find the phone.

I was disoriented. It was the sight of Tiny's body that brought it all back. I pulled myself together as best I could, grabbed my phone and the knife before staggering out of the office. I headed for the door marked "Authorized Personnel Only" which opened into a long corridor. I was pretty sure it was the direction the killer took thanks to the blood stains on the floor, but the trail he left didn't last for long.

The passageway was lined with doors. As I rushed down the hallway, I looked for something that would tell me which way the killer might have headed. There were more doors on the left, the N.E. Stairs, and an elevator. The elevator did not appear to be moving.

I peeked into the stairwell, but didn't hear any footsteps. I was about to turn back when a small bit of blood dripped at my feet. Another drop followed, but this one splattered on my wrist. I looked upward and caught a glimpse of crimson fabric. The monk was on the landing above me, waiting for my next move.

Rather than rush in and try to chase him down, I decided on stealth. Ch'ing taught me that the secret to moving with stealth is balance. The key to balanced movement is to never move a weighted foot. You must take all the weight off a foot before you move it.

As quietly as I could, I stepped into the stairwell and let the door close behind me. Still as a tree, I waited to see what the monk did next. He didn't budge, so I inched toward the first step as quietly as I could. I stopped and waited again. Everything looked good, so I started up the stairs. One by one, I slowly climbed the steps. All the while, my neck stretched to catch a peek of the monk before he saw me.

Laying in a crumpled mess on the landing was the monk's discarded robe. It was damp with fresh blood. Disappointment washed over me. I nudged the robe with a toe and saw a slice in it. Tiny must have gotten in some blows and gone down fighting.

I didn't get a good look at the killer's face. Without the robe to distinguish him from everyone else, I had little hope of finding him. He could be anyone. There were over three thousand people at the Center to hear Padma reveal his big secret. Finding the killer in that crowd was definitely beyond my skill level.

Besides, I didn't know whether he used the stairwell to dump his disguise, or if he took the stairs to a different floor. The Center is a big place and Tiny's murderer could be anywhere. Capturing Tiny's killer would have to be left to the police. It was time to call them, but first I wanted to wash the blood from my hands.

I didn't have any trouble finding a bathroom, but I was preoccupied and didn't pay much attention to the sign on the door. I wish I had. Instead, I rushed in, set the knife next to the sink and began cleaning up.

As the blood swirled down the drain, I thought about the statement I would give to the police. That is when it hit me. I had made another huge mistake. I was in the ladies room. It is also the exact moment the door opened and Ginny walked in.

She took one look at me and froze before the door closed behind her. At first there was an odd confused look on her face, but then it changed to concern.

"Oh my god, Grant, is that blood?" she asked.

I don't know what I expected from her, but after last night I knew she was a player. More to the point, despite what Kinsey said about her, I figured she didn't care one way or the other about me. I wasn't sure what to think about her concerned behavior.

"I was just cleaning up," I answered. "I guess I missed some."

She fumbled in the purse hanging on her shoulder and said, "Let's get you a doctor."

"I'm okay," I said. "It's not my blood."

Her concern shifted to confusion and then to shock.

"What do you mean it's not your blood?" she asked.

I didn't like the direction this was headed and said, "It belongs to someone else."

I was about to explain what happened when she noticed the knife. She started to say something and then snapped her mouth shut. It was her eyes that instantly concerned me the most. They were filled with terror. I had seen the same look in the eyes of witnesses I badgered during cross-examination. I hated it.

Ginny took a cautious step back. When I extended a hand in her direction, her eyes widened in alarm and then she fled the room.

"Not good," I muttered.

I'm ashamed to say, I considered fleeing. I wish I could say I decided to do the right thing instead of running, but the truth is I wanted to protect myself. I knew if she called the police and told them about the bloody knife, they would lock me in the deepest hole they had. Therefore, I went after her. It wasn't until much later that I realized I had forgotten the murder weapon.

Once out of the bathroom, I scanned the hall for her. She was nowhere in sight. I couldn't understand how she managed to disappear so quickly. She could be anywhere. I took a moment to weigh my options, but what I did instead was feel sorry for myself. I had done nothing wrong, but everything that could possibly go wrong, had gone wrong. First John and now this! What else could go wrong, I thought. The answer is plenty and it did.

When I regained my composure, I noticed an unmarked door standing open. I was pretty sure it was closed earlier and decided to take a look inside. There were several rows of alternating stage lights hanging from the ceiling separated by sliding curtains and open moveable wall partitions. A simple podium was the only stage prop. I could hear the buzz of the audience's conversation. Somehow I had managed to find the stage.

That's when I remembered I was there to protect Padma. I had a job to do and that was what I needed to take my mind off myself.

I didn't have a clue what to do next. There was one thing I knew for sure…I had no training as a body guard and there was a killer on the loose. Ch'ing would tell me to listen, not just with my ears, but with my whole being. Sighing, I wondered what that meant and decided the only thing to do was wait and see what happened next.

I chose a position out of the way, but with a strategic view of the podium and audience. The audience was an odd crowd…a cross section of America. For example, a hippie chick in the front row sat next to man in a conservative business suit. The rest of the crowd was equally incongruent.

Leaning lightly against the wall, I felt something poke me in the back and looked over my shoulder. It was a bank of light switches for the stage lights.

When I turned around again, the guy Ginny left the party with last night was on the opposite side of the stage watching me! What was Pony Tail he doing here and why did he have a gun tucked into his jeans?

CHAPTER 15

The audience erupted into applause as Ginny walked across the stage. Her step had lost its spring and her eyes were noticeably puffy. At first it puzzled me to see her on stage, but then I remembered she was the CEO of the program sponsor, Emerald Allure, Inc. Despite the bombshell good looks and the hot clothes, Ginny feels like the girl-next-door. It's easy to forget she is a rich and powerful woman…the kind of person who can summon the police. I figured she had them searching the premises for me now.

At least I would have help finding Tiny's killer. I turned my attention to Pony Tail. He was at Eric's party and now here. To make matters worse, he might be the master of disguise, so I couldn't be certain where else he would show up. The best way to be invisible is to appear ordinary. While Tibetan monks aren't a common sight in Louisville, that disguise was a stroke of genius today. Tiny must have thought he was with Padma.

If Tiny had read Padma's book, then he would have known that Buddhists believe all life is precious. They won't even dig a hole without carefully sifting the earthworms from the soil and moving them to safety. Tiny would not have felt threatened by a Tibetan monk. I figured he never saw it coming.

If Pony Tail was the killer, he must have changed into the hippie clothes after he ditched the robe. It was a perfect disguise to blend in with this peace and love crowd. Still, I couldn't be certain he wasn't another body guard like me hired to protect Padma. I decided to keep a close eye on him.

The gun concerned me, but he made no move for it. Instead his eyes were locked onto Ginny. The way he watched her every move bothered me. What were they talking about last night at Eric's party and what is he doing here?

Ginny stood before the packed house. She was focused on the audience and did not acknowledge me or Pony Tail. Given her reaction to the bloody knife a few minutes earlier, I wasn't sure what to expect from her. Was she going to cancel the event while the police searched for the murderer…searched for me? The buzz from the audience slowly subsided until you could have heard a pin drop in the place. Everyone waited, including me.

Slowly Ginny began to smile. It seemed to radiate from her whole being. I was certain you could feel the smile in her touch and when she began to speak, you could hear it in her voice. This is not what I expected at all!

"Hello. My name is Virginia Bardough, but my friends call me Ginny. So, please call me Ginny. I want to thank you for joining us at this session of Ideas to Change the World. These presentations are offered to you on faith. Not blind faith, but absolute faith in you."

"We hold the sincere belief that each of you has everything you need to have an impact on the world," she said. "Sometimes all it takes to get things going is a little reminder of what could be. So without further fanfare, we would like to present a remarkable man who inspires us with his simple message."

Ginny paused for dramatic effect before saying, "We are sovereign."

Her shining eyes surveyed the audience. One by one she pointed to individuals in the audience and repeated, "You are sovereign."

The audience was riveted to their seats by the spell she had cast.

She scanned the crowd before adding, "No one has the right to interfere with a sovereign's decisions. You decide how to live your life."

Ginny owned the audience.

"Now that I have your attention, ladies and gentlemen, please give Padma Ganesha a warm welcome," she said.

The crowd erupted into cheers and applause as a small round man in Tibetan Buddhist's crimson robes waddled onto the stage. His tiny hands were held high above his head with the palms facing the audience. He took a few steps and stopped. A smile stretched across his round boyish face. Bowing he brought his hands to his heart. The audience went wild. The little guy was like a rock star.

Padma repeatedly bowed to the audience. After five minutes of standing ovation, he finally moved prayer hands to his left shoulder and tilted his head to the side as if saying, "Give it a rest folks." The crowd roared with laughter at his good natured gesture and began to quiet down.

He took a step toward the podium, paused as if he had seen it for the first time, and then a sly grin tweaked the corners of his mouth. Taking the last few steps in its direction, he slipped behind the podium and disappeared. Well sort of. He was much wider than the podium, but the top of his head was barely visible.

If it wasn't for the extra three inches the green cowboy boots gave him, he may not have made it to the top. Seriously…green cowboy boots! The combination of red and green made him look like a chubby little Christmas elf.

An awkward silence descended over the audience before it was broken by a lady in the front row who said, "You'd think somebody would have thought of this."

As if on cue, Padma peeked around the side of the podium like a child playing a game of peek-a-boo. A few in the audience laughed nervously. Most were quiet.

The ensuing silence was broken by an outrageously long and noisy fart. Padma let out a sigh of relief. The audience shifted uncomfortably in their seats.

You could have heard a pin drop before an old man in the front row busted out with laughter. Padma turned to me and winked through thick black rimmed glasses. As I stood there in shock, he stepped away from the podium and began speaking in a singsong voice.

"Hello again dear friends," he said. "Are you ready to learn the secret of a long life?"

Mr. Giggles in the front row said, "Damn right I am."

The crowd applauded.

Padma pointed to Mr. Giggles.

"If you could live forever, what would you do differently?" asked Padma.

Mr. Giggles didn't hesitate.

"I'd live life without regret," he answered.

"What is it you regret my friend," asked Padma.

"I did what I was told instead of doing what I wanted," answered Mr. Giggles.

Padma leaned toward Mr. Giggles and in a conspiratorial tone asked, "Do you want to hear a secret?"

Thirty two hundred hungry souls eagerly leaned forward in their seats. They came from all over the world to learn the secret of happiness and long life.

Padma gave them a relaxed peaceful smile and said, "The secret is…"

I felt a sudden chill. Pony Tail reached for his gun. Without thinking, I hit the light switches and bolted toward the podium.

"Gun, everybody down!" I shouted.

The handgun exploded. I ignored the ringing in my ears and tried to adjust my eyes to the sudden change in lighting. I suddenly felt Pony Tail to my right and turned him so that I had his back. Knowing I needed to disarm him quickly, I hooked his throat with my left hand and tilted his head until his back was bent like a bow.

Once his balance was broken, I owned him. I slid my right hand down his shooting arm. Something was wrong. There was no gun and the arm was soft. It was definitely not Pony Tail's arm.

The stage area was filled with the smell of gunpowder and fear. Still, I caught a whiff of a vaguely familiar scent and buried a nose in my captive's hair. It was not a man's smell. Nor was it perfumed. It was natural and real. This had to be Ginny. I decided to hold on to her.

A second shot was fired. The first shot must have shocked the audience. The second woke them from their stunned silence. Shrill screams and fearful shouts of escape filled the hall.

My first instinct was to get Ginny to safety. Thinking of Padma, I resisted the temptation to rush to an exit. It was also my job to protect him.

As my eyes slowly adjusted to the limited light cast from the emergency exits, I scanned the area for Padma. He wasn't on the stage. Where could he be? Beyond the stage, I saw shadowy shapes moving toward the auditorium exits. The shooter seemed to have disappeared into the shadows. Ginny was tense, taking shallow breaths, but she didn't try to get away from me.

People were stampeding the exits. It was starting to get ugly. The mood of the peace and love crowd had changed dramatically. Panic was growing and the shrieking intensified as people fought their way to safety.

I whispered to Ginny, "We need to get out of here before the gunman finds us in the dark. Come with me. Try to move quietly."

She didn't budge. Since I couldn't see her expression in the dark, I wondered if she heard me over the screams. Maybe she panicked. Finally, her head nodded slightly. Good, I thought, she's calm. I took her firmly by the elbow and we maneuvered through the stage curtains. An exit sign above the double doors glowed in the dark. We headed toward it.

Just as we reached the door, I heard footsteps behind us. Without looking back, we hurried out the door and took the stairs to the parking garage. The door opened behind us and someone followed us down the stairs.

We burst into the parking garage and rushed to the concrete steps leading to the rooftop. There were four flights to climb before we reached the top level. My breathing was ragged and the broken ribs were killing me. Ginny showed no signs of exhaustion.

We sprinted toward the truck. Ginny quickly surveyed the rust bucket before allowing herself a small smile.

"Maybe we should take my car," she said.

I turned to the Porsche and my pulse quickened. Damn, I wanted to drive that car more than anything and despite the situation, could hardly contain my excitement. I nodded in agreement.

At that instant, the stairwell door burst open and clanged against the wall. I immediately turned toward it and dropped to a crouch. There was a flash of crimson and for a moment I thought it was the killer before I finally recognized Padma's smiling face.

He headed toward us at a turtle's pace. I'd forgotten all about my charge...some bodyguard I turned out to be.

"Are you injured?" I asked.

Padma's gaze dropped to my ribs before answering with a smile, "No."

I followed his eyes. There was fresh blood on my shirt mixed in with Tiny's dried blood. I was about to explain the blood when Ginny took a step back.

"Oh my god Grant, you've been shot!" she said.

CHAPTER 16

Great! On top of everything else, now I've been shot. I could walk away right now and be done with it. All I have to do is climb into the truck and head back to that dump I call home. It may not be much, but it provides a safe haven where I can pick up the pieces of my shattered life while this broken body heals itself.

Yet, I knew I was already in too deep, and whatever this was, I would have to see it through to the end. Besides, I'd never be able to look Ch'ing in the eye again if I quit...assuming we find him.

I took a mental step back to evaluate this growing catastrophe. John is dead and a cop with a score to settle with my family is trying to pin it on me. Someone dressed as a monk stabbed Tiny to death and then broke my ribs, but since I was careless enough to leave the murder weapon in the Ladies room covered in Tiny's blood and my fingerprints, Detective Lambers will think I killed him. He's going to love that.

That loud sigh I heard was coming from me. I had messed up big time. Instead of chasing after Tiny's killer, I should have called the police and reported the murder. I didn't do the right thing because I wasn't ready to face another barrage of questions from Detective Lambers.

Tiny's murder would only increase scrutiny of the circumstances surrounding John's death. I needed evidence proving John had a motive to kill himself, but my only lead comes from a spooked prosecutor who is keeping what he knows close to his chest. Now I would have to prove my innocence in two deaths....so much for innocent until proven guilty.

On top of everything, I was completely confused by Ginny. She magically reappears in my life and then I see her flirting with a man who has since wounded me while trying to kill Padma. Ginny disappeared from the party without a saying a word to anyone, but when I next saw her in the parking lot, she totally blew me off. Afterwards, she flipped-out when she saw me with a bloody knife...as if I was a psycho killer or something.

I could feel Padma waiting for a decision and searched his face for answers. The only thing I saw in his eyes was infinite compassion. They contained no boundaries, no limits, and it felt as if I was pulled me into a bottomless well.

I shook my head and willed myself back to the present. Here I stand in a parking garage with a monk, who I'm supposed to protect because I got fired from my real job. It should have been an easy task, but no, a gun-toting hippie wants to kill him. I couldn't imagine why anyone would want to kill such a gentle man, but there was one thing I knew for sure, there was a killer on the loose and whatever was going on could probably get me killed too.

The killer was still out there somewhere and needed to be apprehended before he hurt someone else. Or worse, tracked us down and hurt one of us. Every second was critical and I didn't hear any police sirens rushing to our aid. Where were the cops?

One of my favorite law school professors, Laurence Filmore, once told a room full of first year law students that the police have no duty to protect us. We were discussing a wrongful death case filed by the parents of a teenage girl who was brutally raped and murdered after the police failed to respond to a 9-1-1 emergency call. The Supreme Court ruled in favor of the police and threw out the grieving family's lawsuit. They said it was law enforcement's job to investigate crime and apprehend criminals, not protect individual citizens.

I knew we were on our own. It was my job to protect Padma, and I would get no help from the police. Still, Pony Tail was on the loose and it was their job to apprehend him. It was unlikely this ordeal would be over anytime soon. While I wasn't feeling very optimistic about it, I hoped we could work together on this. It was time to call the cops even though they would have plenty of hard questions for me.

My phone was grimy with dried blood and didn't open when I swiped a finger across the screen. Resisting the temptation to fling it across the garage, I wiped it on the front of my shirt, but that only made it worse.

"Should I call an ambulance?" asked Ginny.

She was staring at a bullet hole in my shirt. I was pretty sure it was just a scratch, so I shook my head.

"No, did you call the police earlier?" I asked.

Ginny held my gaze. Her eyes were clear and calm. I could feel her searching for confirmation that she made the right choice. After a long moment, she shook her head.

"No, I didn't," she answered. "What do you think we should do?"

"Do you trust me?" I asked.

She gave me another long appraising look before answering, "Yes."

I felt relieved. It was less likely she would call the police if she trusted me. Trust is a critical component in a relationship. Without it, there isn't much chance for it.

"Then let's call the police," I said.

Ginny nodded and reached into her purse, but before she could locate her phone, we were startled by the sound of screaming tires and she spilled the purse onto the garage floor. Someone was speeding up the ramp and headed in our direction. Given the shooting, people should be in a hurry to get out of the garage. This guy was racing to the rooftop. Nothing good was going to come of this.

"We need to get out of here," I shouted.

Ginny had squatted down to gather up her things. I looked at the two seats in the Porsche and sighed. Trying to hide my disappointment, I grabbed Ginny's arm and pulled her up.

I did my best to build a sense of urgency into Padma, but the man moved like a turtle. I had a feeling if he didn't get a move on, we would live to regret it. Maybe everything was starting to get to me, but that's no excuse for the rising irritation I felt.

I was about to bark at Padma when he winked at me and said, "The way of long life is slow and easy."

I blinked. That sounded exactly like something Ch'ing would say. Padma held my gaze with calm eyes. It felt to me like he reached into the center of my being and stilled my soul. Only Ch'ing has ever been able to do that. It occurred to me that Padma may know something about Ch'ing's whereabouts, but that would have to wait for later.

Once I got Ginny and Padma to the truck, the mercurial little guy shifted gears and now sounded like a twelve year old as he clapped his hands and called out in his high pitched voice, "Shotgun! Shotgun! I call shotgun!"

Padma slipped in front of Ginny as she reached for the door handle, climbed into the truck, and closed the door in her face. The little turtle can move when he wants to. Instead of being upset by Padma's rude behavior, Ginny's shoulders were shaking with barely contained laughter. I was instantly caught off guard by her unexpected sense of humor. I helped Ginny climb into the truck from the driver's side and slipped in next to her feeling a lot better about her.

She smelled delicious, like fresh baked bread. To take my mind off her yummy smell, I took one last look at the Porsche before starting the truck and shifting into reverse. We were nearly out when a black SUV roared around the corner and sped toward us. This maniac wanted to smash us into the concrete wall!

I slammed it into first gear and gunned the truck back into the parking spot. The SUV clipped the corner of the truck and went spinning into the Porsche. The crash echoed through the garage like thunder.

Ginny's beautiful car was a crumbled wreck. A billowing cloud of smoke drifted in our direction. I couldn't see the driver through the tinted windows, but suspected it might be Pony Tail. I had all I was going to take from this creep.

"Wait here," I said.

As I opened the door to investigate, the SUV's driver side window lowered and a gun barrel peeped out.

"Duck," I screamed.

The garage exploded in gunfire. Shattered glass sprayed across the back of my neck. I backed the truck out without looking and then gunned the engine down the ramp. We raced out of the garage and turned right on 7th Street. It was a block to River Road, where we made a right. I accelerated past the YUM Center and headed east toward Prospect. I kept checking the rearview mirror for the SUV and didn't see any sign of it. I sped out of town along River Road. I needed to get somewhere safe where I could lay low and think.

"Where are we going?" asked Ginny.

"We need to lose the SUV," I answered. "I'm headed to my Uncle's house. He will know what to do next."

The truck has a standard transmission mounted on the floor. Ginny's left thigh was squeezed next to the shifter. Each time I changed gears my wrist brushed her leg. It triggered thoughts of tearing fabric in the parking lot. I glanced down. The short dress was hiked up and revealed damn near all of her legs.

I willed my eyes up. They came to rest on her cleavage, which didn't help much with the distraction problem, so I locked my eyes forward on the road ahead.

Thinking it would help to shift my focus, I opened my mouth to ask Padma why someone wanted him dead, but nothing came out. My throat was dry. I tried to swallow, but nothing happened. As I struggled to find my voice, Ginny turned toward Padma. She studied him closely before asking the question for me.

In response, he laughed and jiggled like a department store Santa. Ginny looked at him like he'd lost his mind. The laughter finally stopped. The jiggling took a bit longer. She waited patiently.

Finally, he said, "What makes you think someone wants to kill me?"

"You were about to reveal a big secret just before someone fired two shots at you," she answered. "They want you dead for some reason."

Padma ripped off a long noisy fart and said, "Life and death are two sides of the same coin."

Ginny opened her mouth and then closed it again. To our utter amazement, Padma began singing a popular teenybopper hit. A silly little song popularized by a half-naked pre-pubescent girl. It was something about lost innocence.

An incoming call interrupted his song. I tried to dig the phone out of my jeans pocket without straightening my legs, but the pants were too tight. Cursing under my breath, I stretched and finally managed to get hold of it, but by the time I got it out of my pocket, the ringing had stopped. The missed call was from Eric.

I considered waiting until we arrived at Uncle Jim's place to return Eric's call, but the phone went off again. I figured it must be important and answered it.

"There's trouble dude," said Eric.

"The last twenty four hours have been nothing but trouble," I replied.

"Are you sitting down because it just got worse?" asked Eric.

"What is it now?"

"I just got a call from a friend with LMPD," answered Eric. "They are under pressure to bring you in, Grant. You've made some powerful enemies."

"It will have to wait," I said. "Any news on Ch'ing?"

"Not a thing," answered Eric.

"Stay at it," I said. "In the meantime, I'm headed to Uncle Jim's."

"Good idea," said Eric. "Maybe he can call in a few favors from his friends on the force. Wait a minute, Grant. Something just occurred to me, the lecture can't be over yet. What's going on?"

"Too much to tell you over the phone," I answered. "Ginny and Padma are with me."

Eric groaned.

"I got a feeling I'm not going to like this," he said.

"There was another murder," I said.

There was a long pause before Eric finally said, "Geez, another one! What happened?"

"It was Tiny," I answered. "I'm sorry, Eric. I'll fill you in on the details later."

"Damn…I got him that job," said Eric. "There's some crazy shit going down.

Do you think there is a connection to John's death?"

"It would have seemed like a stretch before, but now I don't know what to think about all of this," I answered.

"You can't put the cops off much longer," said Eric. "If you delay too long, it will look like you've got something to hide."

He was right, of course. I couldn't put them off much longer. Sooner or later, they would find me and if they did, it was unlikely my word would be enough. The pressure was on to find proof of my innocence for two deaths, and I needed it fast.

If I learned anything as a trial lawyer, I learned that you never know where the answers to a problem might turn up. I remembered something that was bugging me about this job.

"Eric, you said this morning they wanted me to guard Padma," I said. "Who are they?"

"I don't know," answered Eric. "Someone else took the call. I thought it was odd myself. I'll have one of my people look into it. Have you asked Padma?"

I hate it when I miss the obvious.

"Good idea," I said sheepishly.

After I ended the call with Eric, I intended to ask Padma about the security job, but happened to glance in the rear view mirror. There was a black SUV coming up fast!

CHAPTER 17

I hoped it wasn't the same SUV that tried to run us over in the parking garage, but of course the passenger side head lamp was smashed in and there were streaks of green paint on its front bumper. I just wished I knew who I was dealing with. There were a lot of unanswered questions, but right now I needed to do something about the SUV.

There were several options. I could try to lose them in traffic, but River Road doesn't have much traffic to speak of, unless you include the occasional biker enjoying his favorite scenic byway. I didn't think the old truck would outrun the SUV, so that was out.

In the movies, they run traffic lights or make last minute turns, but neither would work here since there are very few traffic signals and a last minute turn would most likely end up in the river. Trying to lose them just wasn't a good option.

We could stop and confront them, but the last time I tried to do that they shot at me. I did have a .357 magnum under the seat of the truck, but a wild-west shoot out in a residential area did not seem like the best option. The last encounter we had with them was in an isolated area of a parking garage. It's possible they would be less likely to shoot at us on a public road, but I didn't want to risk it. There were homes along this street and I didn't want an innocent bystander to get hurt.

We could set a trap. I liked the sound of that option best. I just needed to figure out how to do it and we were less than ten minutes from Uncle's Jim's house. Since they didn't know where we were headed, I could use that to our advantage.

Uncle Jim is an ex-marine sniper who knows how to set a trap better than anyone, so I called and told him we were being chased by some maniac in a SUV and asked for his help. I knew I could trust him with my life and he didn't let me down. He told me to get everyone to his house as soon as possible.

I kept an eye on the SUV as we made our way into Prospect. I wasn't sure what Uncle Jim had in mind for them, but I was about to find out. It was only a few more blocks until we reached his street. The SUV followed close behind as we turned into his upscale subdivision, but stopped short when I made the last turn onto Uncle Jim's quiet cul-de-sac.

Uncle Jim lives in a red brick two story on the cusp of the circle. As I pulled into his driveway, I felt a little uneasy about leading the SUV to my Uncle's home, but Uncle Jim knows what he is doing. We found him sitting on his covered porch dressed in his usual faded jeans and Harley t-shirt. His bare feet were crossed at the ankle and his right hand held a smoldering Cuban cigar. Don't ask me where he gets them. Lying across his lap was a hunting rifle intended for large game.

A hand carved staff he uses when an old injury is acting up was leaning against the brick wall. He managed to escape the Gulf War unharmed, but fell rock climbing in the Red River Gorge a few years back. He survived the fall, but broke his back and lost an eye. The doctors said he would never walk again. Of course, Uncle Jim proved them wrong.

Thanks to a lean muscular frame, he looks younger than his age. His hair is more pepper than salt, with only a touch of a receding hairline. He wears an eye patch over the missing socket like a proud pirate. The remaining blue-grey eye was locked onto the SUV idling on the street corner. It reminded me of a dangerous beast that couldn't make up its mind whether it should venture into the cul-de-sac or not.

Uncle Jim waited. The tension was thick. I wondered what would happen next. Of all the things I imagined, it sure wasn't what happened. A splash of rainbow descended from the heavens, squawking "Death from Above" and splattered bird shit all over the SUV's windshield. It was Dad's crazy macaw. That's all it took for the mighty beast to tuck tail and run. Of course, the sight of Uncle Jim's high-powered rifle might have had something to do with it too.

I suspected we weren't finished with the SUV, but it was a welcome relief to see it leave. Uncle Jim flashed his Cheshire cat grin and shouted Generalissimo. I stuck my left arm out the window and waved.

Ginny poked me in the side. Pain from the broken rib shot through me like a jolt of madness, but I liked her touch all the same.

"Generalissimo," she said with a broad smile.

"He says I might be a reincarnated Civil War general...he just can't figure out which one," I said sheepishly. "He's partial to Grant."

"Grant or Lee," she murmured. "But isn't your last name spelled Li?"

My mom's family is a distant relative of U.S. Grant on her mother's side. She and Uncle Jim have different fathers. He is lily white in a Nordic sort of way and every bit the Viking. My mom is half African-American.

Dad was Chinese and always said we were related to a famous internal martial artist who lived a ridiculously long life. It was someone named Li Ching-Yun that the New York Times reported to have lived to be 256. I think my dad believed the crazy long life nonsense to be true just because it was in the newspaper. This very interesting bloodline explains my somewhat exotic, foreign look.

I was about to explain the nuances of my mixed heritage to Ginny, but was distracted by a flash of color and loud screech.

"Aaawk, Grant's a peckerwood."

It was dad's macaw with his usual greeting. The bird flew across the hood of the truck, up the windshield, and landed on the top. Hanging upside down he stuck his head in the driver's side window and looked around.

"I love you too bird," I grumbled.

He cocked his head at me.

"Aaawk, get a life," said Bird.

"Dad loved this bird," I said. "He belongs to me now, but I'm pretty sure he hates me."

"Aaawk, I belong to no one," squawked Bird. "Hate will be the death of us all."

Ginny looked mystified.

"Did he just respond to what you said?" asked Ginny. "I thought birds only mimic speech."

"Aaawk, such a pretty girl," said Bird.

Ginny cooed.

"Oh such a flirt," she said. "I like him."

"Aaawk, give us a kiss," squawked Bird.

"How cute, he just winked at me," said Ginny. "What's his name?"

"Bird," I answered.

"No really," said Ginny. "What's his name?"

"Dad always called him, Bird," I said. "I've never heard him called anything else."

"Humph," said Ginny.

Clearly she wasn't satisfied.

"Aaawk, my name is Senor Juan Ponce de Leon," said Bird.

Ginny asked, "Did he just say he is Ponce de Leon?"

"Aaawk, the one and only, pretty girl," said Bird.

"It's news to me," I said.

Uncle Jim limped over to the truck.

He handed Bird a peanut and said, "That's enough, Bird."

Then he opened the truck door, pulled me out, and gave me a bear hug. I winced as pain shot through my ribs. Uncle Jim doesn't miss anything and noticed when I stiffened from his embrace. He leaned back until I was at arm's length and looked me in the eyes to make sure we were good.

Satisfied, he looked me up and down, only pausing a moment to take in the blood stains. He knew I was there for a reason, but waited for me to begin an explanation.

"We should talk before we call the police," I said.

He nodded his head and then shifted his one-eyed gaze to Ginny. A slow easy smile spread across his face.

"Don't pay any attention to that crazy fluff of feathers," he said. "I'm Jim."

"Aaawk, not crazy," said Bird.

Uncle Jim took a lazy swipe at Bird, who flew off squawking, "Aaawk, PETA alert! Someone call 9-1-1."

Ginny smiled at Uncle Jim and said, "I think you hurt his feelings. I'm Ginny."

"Don't let him fool you," said Uncle Jim. "That bird is tough as nails. Girl, you look just like your father."

If Ginny was surprised that Uncle Jim knew her father she didn't let on.

Instead, she said, "Well except for my dark hair, green eyes, and assorted girl parts."

Uncle Jim flashed a wolfish grin and said, "Your girl parts are welcome in my home. Who's your friend there?"

"This is Padma Ganesha," said Ginny. "He's my guest. I invited him to America to talk about his book. He was speaking tonight at the Center when someone tried to kill him. I think he was just about to reveal a secret about living a long life when it happened. We barely escaped with our lives thanks to Grant."

If Uncle Jim was surprised by any of this, he didn't show it.

Instead he gave Padma a long appraising look before saying, "I just lit the grill. Come out back and have a bite to eat. Grant, come inside for a moment, so I can look at that injury. Then, we can talk about your adventure over a cold drink."

We went inside where he cleaned the shallow gash with peroxide, and then protected it with gauze secured with first aid tape. I told everyone it was just a scratch, but it was a little more serious than that.

Uncle Jim is fond of telling people he has everything he needs in his own back yard. He is most proud of a 1970's style barbeque pit he built himself. Every evening the barbeque sends puffs of smoke into the sky as he grills burgers and sips cold beer. Its distinctive smell is a like a call to prayer for friends and neighbors, who religiously heed the summons.

Folks wander in from all four corners of the neighborhood. Gathering around the grill, they talk about the day's events and watch meat sizzle over hot coals. Later they sit in Adirondack chairs grouped under an ancient oak tree and watch the setting sun paint the clouds coral and blue. These are simple salt of the earth people sharing simple pleasures. There are no fences separating them. They move freely from yard to yard, house to house. It is a community in its truest sense.

As promised, Uncle Jim led us to the back yard where we settled into comfortable chairs and watched a squirrel gather acorns for the winter. Up and down the tree he went, never venturing onto the low hanging branch with the bug zapper. The distinctive sound of the zapper's grim work was balanced by the refreshing sound of bubbling water coming from Harrods Creek bordering the rear of the property.

The creek deepens enough at its mouth to provide a safe haven to area boaters who like to idle and party before emptying into the Ohio River. However, at this location it looks more like a mountain stream as it runs white over large flat rocks. This familiar scene calmed my nerves and the day's events began to feel surreal.

Uncle Jim disappeared into the house and then returned a few minutes later with tall glasses of bourbon and coke. He flashed his trademark confident smile and told Ginny it was for medicinal purposes only. She returned his smile, saying she could use all the medicine she could get.

Uncle Jim looked at me and winked.

"Grant", he said, "this one's a keeper."

Ginny beamed at Uncle Jim. I took another sip of the bourbon and relaxed into the scene playing out before me.

We sat quietly for a few minutes and listened to the evening's sounds. It felt good to not talk for a while, but then Uncle Jim spoke up. It was the last thing I wanted to talk about.

"Grant, you want to tell me what's going on?" asked Uncle Jim.

I stiffened and felt the first twinges of a headache.

Rubbing my temples I said slowly, "I don't know where to start."

"Do you remember calling me last night?" he asked. "You must have been about halfway through a bottle of tequila. You said you had won a big case for Wilbur Goth yesterday, but it didn't sound like much of a celebration. Instead, you got yourself fired. Your boss hung himself. Ch'ing is missing and you were chased here by gangsters with guns. Does that about cover it?"

"Actually, there's more, but I don't feel like talking about it right now," I answered.

"Last night you said you said you were going to take some time off and search for Ch'ing in the Himalayas," said Uncle Jim. "Please tell me that was just crazy drunk talk. Ch'ing can take care of himself. You need to focus on your current predicament."

"Aaawk, lawyers get to lie and cheat for a living," squawked Bird. "Why do you want to give that up just to hang out in a drafty old monastery?"

"Bird, you're supposed to be guarding the perimeter," said Uncle Jim.

"Aaawk, eyes and ears on it," said Bird. "The perimeter is secured, sir."

I shook my head at Bird. He actually saluted Uncle Jim.

"Things can turn on a dime," I said. "Now, I may be the one who needs a criminal defense attorney."

"Your enemies have given you the gift of change," said Padma.

I had a flashback of Ch'ing teaching us an internal martial arts called, Baguazhang. The student is encouraged to overcome their natural resistance to change. High-level fighting techniques can be found in the transition moves, if the student has the courage to embrace change.

Ch'ing liked to spar ten-on-one and was always the last man standing. He moved like a whirling dervish teaching hidden techniques as he laid waste to all ten opponents. When the session was over, he'd look at our bodies on the floor and tell us we needed to do a better job of embracing change. We'd ask him how to do that, but he'd just shake his head and tell us to keep our feet moving next time.

Uncle Jim pulled me back from my reverie with a question.

"Do we need to talk to someone about representing you?" he asked.

"It would be best," I answered. "Lambers is dogging me over John's death and now there's...."

"You would never do such a thing!" said Ginny.

"No, but my word won't mean much under the circumstances," I said. "I need proof of my innocence or I'm in for a rough time."

"What kind of proof?" asked Ginny.

"I'm not sure, but Zeke Kruthers may hold the key," I answered.

"Isn't he the prosecutor you went up against in the Goth trial?" asked Uncle Jim.

I nodded.

"What's he have to do with John's death?" asked Uncle Jim.

I shook my head.

I filled them in on my meeting with Zeke at Ed's tavern.

"Do you have any idea what was in that envelope?" asked Ginny.

"Not a clue," I said.

"But you think it upset John enough he took his own life?" asked Uncle Jim.

"That's what Kruthers seems to think," I answered.

Uncle Jim knows me well.

"You think Kruthers is right, don't you?" asked Uncle Jim.

I nodded grimly.

"Do you think this has anything to do with the murder at the Center?" asked Ginny.

I thought about the hug she gave Pony Tail and shrugged.

"Wait a minute…you mentioned a gunman earlier, but you didn't say anything about someone getting killed at the Center," said Uncle Jim.

"A security guard was stabbed," I said. "He was a friend of Eric's. A biker named Tiny."

"The leader of the Dragons," asked Uncle Jim.

I nodded.

"I had a run in with the murderer," I said. "He broke a couple of my ribs and then escaped."

"The Dragons will be out for blood," said Uncle Jim. "To bad he got away."

"I wished I had caught him," I said. "It all happened so fast. I went after him with the murder weapon. My prints are all over it."

"That's not good," said Uncle Jim in his best deadpan voice.

At this point, I don't think anything I said could have fazed him.

"This is bad, very bad," I said.

"We need to find the murderer," said Uncle Jim. "What did he look like?"

I shrugged.

"I didn't get a good look at his face," I said. "He wore a hooded monk's robe. I just saw a monk. They all look the same to me."

Padma snorted.

"Ch'ing will not be happy to hear you weren't more observant than that," said Uncle Jim. "Have you called the police?"

"I know I should talk to them about all of this, but I would prefer to get proof of my innocence first," I answered.

Uncle Jim nodded.

"What were you doing at the Center?" he asked.

"Working as a bodyguard," I answered.

He looked astonished.

"Bodyguard…who were you protecting?" he asked.

"Padma," I answered.

Uncle Jim raised an eyebrow.

"I am a simple monk," said Padma. "I have no need for a bodyguard."

"You didn't request protection," asked Uncle Jim.

Padma shook his head.

"Eric hired me," I said. "The strange thing about it is that his client specifically asked for me."

"Who are they and why you?" asked Uncle Jim.

I shrugged and turned to Ginny.

"Since your company sponsored this event, maybe you know something about the security arrangements," I asked.

She shook her head.

I sighed.

"Eric is looking into it," I said. "We should know something soon."

There was a flutter of feathers as Bird landed softly on Padma's shoulders. Bird looked lovingly at Padma and then gently rubbed his beak against the monk's cheek. Padma welcomed the comforting gesture, but looked like he was exhausted and fading fast.

In a tired voice he said, "It was a long journey from Bhutan and I must rest now."

Uncle Jim turned to Padma and asked, "Do you have any enemies?"

"Enemy...friend...two sides of the same coin," answered Padma.

The corners of Uncle Jim's mouth tightened, "You don't give straight answers to simple questions, do you? Why is that?"

Bird inched closer to Padma's cheek and glared at Uncle Jim. Padma reached up and gently smoothed his ruffled feathers, stroking from the back of the neck downward to the tip of his tail.

"Easy my friend," whispered Padma.

Ginny reached out and placed a soothing hand on Uncle Jim's forearm.

"Padma came all the way from Bhutan at my request," she said. "He planned to reveal an ancient secret. Someone tried to stop him."

"What secret?" asked Uncle Jim.

Padma smiled gently before answering, "Something that will change everything."

Uncle Jim shook his head, "You're not going to tell us, are you?"

"Now is not the time," replied Padma. "Be patient. Events must run their course."

"Run their course...people are dead and they're trying to kill us," I growled.

Uncle Jim looked thoughtful and nodded toward the house.

"Padma, you can use the bedroom at the end of the hall," said Uncle Jim. "I'll show you the way. I better call a few friends at the station and see what I can find out. Just sit tight until we figure out what to do next."

Bird stayed glued to Padma's shoulder as he followed Uncle Jim into the house. In the fading light, he looked like a strange two headed beast.

CHAPTER 18

According to Ch'ing, at the end of each day, the immortals gather in the coral colored clouds to party. He promised I would see them when my heart is ready. I never watch a sunset without hoping for a glimpse of Dad. This sunset was different. On this evening, I watched the coral hues gather around Ginny.

As the color faded in the heavens, the last of the restless birds settled in for the night. Frogs began their nightly mating ritual, croaking to each other on the banks of Harrods Creek. Crickets marked territory with dueling chirps and the bug zapper fried insects unlucky enough to be lured into its purple glow. After all that had happened, it felt surreal to be sitting at Uncle Jim's like it was any other day.

When the first star appeared low in the sky, Ginny turned her glass and swallowed the last of the highball. She looked hesitant and when she finally spoke, it was tentative.

"Do you mind if I ask you a question?" she said.

This question usually triggered a red flag for me, but not this time. I wanted us to open up with each other...I wanted to open myself to her.

"I don't mind," I answered.

"Do you regret that you listened to my mom and stayed away from me?" she asked.

It took a bit before I could formulate an answer without giving in to the great sadness that I lived with everyday. Still, my eyes burned with tears, but I didn't try to hide them from her.

"Yes, I regret it," I said. "The hardest thing I've ever done was watch her beat you without lifting a hand to stop it and then watch you walk out of my life."

"We were just little kids," said Ginny.

"I should have done something to stop her," I said.

"This isn't on you, Grant," said Ginny. "It's all my fault."

"What do you mean?' I asked.

"I was curious," she said. "I started the whole thing.'

I wasn't following her meaning at first, but then it hit me. She started the game of show-n-tell, but I didn't blame her. I never once blamed her. I always blamed myself for not standing up to her mother, for not protecting Ginny from her mother. It's true I was afraid of her mother, but all those years I stayed away, not because I was afraid of her mother, but because I wanted to protect Ginny.

"No one is to blame," I said.

There was confusion in Ginny's eyes, that quickly shifted to hope.

"Assigning blame has never solved anything," agreed Ginny. "We need to stop living in the past and move forward with our lives."

That's exactly what I was thinking and nodded.

"I visited your mother today," I said.

Ginny's hands flew to her mouth. Her brow was pinched and her eyes were filled with alarm. I waited until she recovered from the shock and understanding replaced the alarm.

"You wanted closure, didn't you?" she asked.

I nodded.

"I needed to let her know that she can't stop me from speaking to you, ever again," I said.

"How did it go?" she asked.

"About like you would expect," I said with a wry smile.

"She is a difficult person," said Ginny.

"Your mother was baking when I arrived," I said. "She was expecting to see you at her door, not me."

The amusement in her eyes disappeared. It was replaced with something dark and terrible. Her gaze dropped to her lap. I couldn't see her face to read it, but I sensed she needed comforting. It wasn't my thing, but something drew me to her side.

After a false start, I put a stiff arm around her. Unsure what to expect in return, I was relieved when she buried her face in my chest. She started to cry. I wanted to say something comforting, but nothing came to mind. Instead, I stroked her hair and just held tight until she stopped.

"I think she means well, but she's a nightmare," said Ginny.

After my talk with Kinsey, I wasn't sure her mother meant well. She seemed backward and filled with hate. Ginny's mother was religious in a way that bordered on fanatical. After hearing about the backward way the Taliban treated women in Afghanistan, I sometimes think of people like her mother as America's Taliban.

"Dad was nothing like Mom," said Ginny. "Dad was warm and loving. When she started one of her tirades, he would find a gentle way to diffuse her anger. Soon we would all be laughing and making plans to do something silly. He was a shining light on a dark night."

I remembered the gossip when Ginny's dad disappeared. Some said he ran away with another woman and just left his family to fend for themselves.

"What happened to your dad?" I asked.

"I don't know all of the details, but they argued about a trip to the Amazon Rainforest," she said. "Mother didn't want him to go. Before he left, he told me he had to do something that would change everything. He promised me he wouldn't be gone long, but he lied. I never saw him again."

"Do you have any idea what happened?" I asked.

"They say his plane crashed somewhere over the jungle," she answered. "The day we got the news my mother beat me with one of Dad's belts because my shorts showed too much leg. It was a hot day, but I changed into long pants and sleeves to appease her."

The beating I witnessed was not an isolated incident. Ginny's mother is abusive and she had been left alone with her. The realization that I could have helped brought the tears back. I resisted the urge to hide them, and instead, just let them have their way with me.

At least I had Uncle Jim and Ch'ing after I lost my parents. I couldn't imagine what it was like for her...alone with someone like that. To take my mind off her mother, I took a deep breath and tried to clear my head. Instead, I got a whiff of her intoxicating scent.

"It must have been tough after he left," I said.

She nodded.

"I wanted to placate her, so I dressed conservatively during my high school years," said Ginny. "You might even say, old fashioned. It didn't work. She got worse, instead of better. Eventually, I just lost myself."

"Old fashioned...you've definitely changed," I said. "How did that happen?"

Ginny bit her lip. She looked torn...as if she wasn't quite sure she could trust me. Finally, she made up her mind and answered.

"You know, I never had a date in high school," she said. "Instead, I poured myself into books and it paid off with scholarships. When it was time for college, I picked a school as far away from my mother as possible. I figured it would be harder for her to get to me in California."

"As soon as I got to Stanford, I set out to reinvent myself...to find myself," said Ginny. "I didn't have much money, so I started redesigning my old clothes and everyone started noticing."

"The other co-eds loved them and wanted to know where I bought them," she said. "They were trust-fund kids. I was embarrassed and didn't want to tell them the truth about my circumstances, so I avoided their questions. At least for a while, but they wouldn't stop pestering me until I finally confessed."

"I thought that would be the end of our friendships, but they were really cool about it," said Ginny. "In fact, they were so impressed with my talent; they begged me to redesign their designer clothes. It surprised me. I didn't take them seriously until they offered to pay me."

"My designs were all the rage on campus," said Ginny. "Thanks to the power of social media, it spread like a virus to other campuses. Before long, I was running a small, but thriving business."

"By my junior year at Stanford, the business had grown to the point that I employed over a hundred workers, mostly women," she said. "Emerald Allure had arrived and me...well I found myself."

"Sounds like you're mother actually helped you in a back-handed sort of way," I said.

Ginny frowned, "I suppose so, but if it wasn't for Marguerite, I don't think I would have survived."

"Who's Marguerite?" I asked.

"She was my nanny," answered Ginny. "Mother wanted a good Hispanic woman to keep me on the straight and narrow while she was at work. I think she assumed Marguerite was Catholic, but she wasn't. Marguerite followed a more ancient path. Instead of bible study, she taught me to open my mind to the mystery of nature."

"The mystery of nature," I murmured. "That's a subject Ch'ing often talked about."

Ginny's smile was gentle. Her voice was soft.

"Marguerite was compassionate, like Dad," she said. "She also provided a soothing buffer from my mother's episodes."

"What happened to her?" I asked.

"I don't know," said Ginny. "We've stayed in touch and planned to meet for lunch yesterday, but she never showed. That's not like her at all."

"Odd, Ch'ing disappeared yesterday too," I said.

"Do you think there is a connection?" she asked.

I shrugged.

"You are very lucky to have both Uncle Jim and Ch'ing in your life," she said.

"He and Uncle Jim like to slap each other on the back and tell me what a good job they did raising me," I said. "Despite my present circumstances, I tend to agree."

Nodding toward the house she said, "I like your Uncle Jim. He's good people."

"He's always been there for me," I said. "I have been blessed to have him in my life."

"He seems worried about you," she said.

"He thinks I've lost my way," I said.

"Have you?" she asked.

"It's possible," I answered.

"What do you meant?' she asked.

I felt like she could be trusted, so I told her the truth.

"I hope I don't sound like an egomaniac, but I've always felt like there is an important role I have to play in the course of world events," I said.

She looked surprised, but quickly recovered.

"That's exactly how I feel, but I thought I was just compensating for my home life," she said.

"Are you satisfied with the direction you've taken in your life?" I asked.

She took a few breaths to give it some thought, before answering.

"As you have no doubt gathered, I stumbled into my line of work," she said.

"Me too," I said.

"I was undecided about a major at Stanford," she said. "When the clothes started selling, I knew I needed business skills, so I started taking business classes."

"Clearly, you have a talent for business," I said.

"Talent is good, but I believe a person needs a worthy life goal," she said.

"Have you found yours?" I asked.

She shook her head.

"Not exactly," she answered. "I have worthy goals, but haven't found the big one yet."

"What do you mean?" I asked.

"I'm working to restore balance as best I can," she said.

"In what way?" I asked.

"Take for example, the corporate glass ceiling," she said. "I hire desperate women and give them the skills they need to succeed. I help them find their purpose…their focus. They have the opportunity to rise in my company based solely upon their performance."

"That is certainly a worthy goal," I agreed. "Do you have any idea what the big one might be?"

She shook her head.

"It's elusive," she said. "Sometimes I wake in the middle of the night with the feeling that it is nearby, but I can't quite get a picture of it."

"I know what you mean," I said.

"You're a successful attorney," she said. "Is your destiny tied to the law?"

"I'm not sure," I said. "Lately, I've gotten a look at the business side of a law practice and it's not as noble as I'd like, but like you, I stumbled into it and am trying to use it as a vehicle for something bigger."

"How did you stumble into it?" she asked.

"For as long as I can remember, I wanted to be a writer," I said. "I imagined writing great books that lived forever in the imagination of readers."

Ginny looked surprised at my answer.

"Then why did you go to law school?" she asked.

"Uncle Jim wanted me to go to college, but he didn't have the money to pay for it," I answered. "When I was offered a scholarship to play football at West Point he was thrilled. He took to calling me General Li…sometimes General Grant. Later, it was just Generalissimo, but he always said it with pride."

"I heard him call you that," she said. "I like it."

"Thing was…I didn't want to play football anymore and I sure didn't want to disappoint him," I said.

"How did you get out of that bind?" she asked.

"Badly…I'll never forget the day I told him I wasn't going to take the scholarship," I said. "Uncle Jim looked so damn disappointed. He sat there at the kitchen table looking tired and beaten. I had never seen him like that. To his credit, he shook it off and asked me what I planned to do with my life."

"I told him I still planned to go to college and had even thought about going to law school," I said. "He lit up like a Christmas tree, slapped me on the back and told me he was proud of me."

"It was true I planned to go to college, but I don't know why I said that about law school," I said. "The thought never crossed my mind. Afterwards, he kept going on and on about law school and I didn't have the heart to tell him it was a weird slip of the tongue."

Ginny looked thoughtful and said, "You did it for him and still became a rock star lawyer."

"It was important to him and that's what love does," I said.

"Love puts another before self," she said. "So many people seem to get that backwards."

Light shot up my spine and exploded in my head like a Fourth of July display. Despite the evening's heat, I massaged the goose bumps on my arms.

"Yes, but we can never sacrifice the prime directive to live our own lives on our own terms," I said.

Ginny nodded in agreement.

"Rock star lawyer," I said. "Besides Uncle Jim, you might just be my first and only groupie."

"Do you have room for anyone else?" she asked.

I was about to tell her that there is plenty of room in my life for her, but we were interrupted by Uncle Jim.

"What are you two love birds talking about?" asked Uncle Jim.

"The mysteries of life and love," answered Ginny.

"Good luck with that," said Uncle Jim. "Speaking of problems, we have something more immediate at hand that requires our attention."

"Let me guess," I said. "The police have a witness and they are planning to charge me with John's murder."

Uncle Jim looked surprised.

"How did you know?" he asked.

I shrugged.

"I bet it's John's secretary," I said.

"They didn't say," he replied. "We need to clear this up as quickly as possible. It's always best to nip things like this in the bud."

"I'm trying," I said. "I even rummaged through John's office to see if I could find out why he killed himself."

"What did you find?"

"Nothing," I answered. "All I found was a slip of paper."

"What did it say?" asked Uncle Jim.

I smacked my forehead.

"I never read it," I said. "Lambers showed up and drilled me with questions."

I shoved my hands into my pockets, but all I felt was my phone. Of course it wouldn't be there, because I was wearing different pants. The slip of paper was still in my suit trousers. I needed to see what was written on that paper.

CHAPTER 19

Ginny refused to be left behind. To my dismay, she insisted on seeing where I lived. I have to admit I was not looking forward to showing her my crappy apartment and tried every excuse I could think of to avoid it. None of them worked. I learned she can be very strong willed and must confess that I caved in when it became apparent she intended to get her way.

To soften the blow, I took the long route through Cherokee Park. It was designed in the late 1800's by Frederick Law Olmstead after he finished work on New York's Central Park. As you can imagine, it's a world class park and unlike my apartment, it is beautiful. I hoped it would fill Ginny's mind with nature's images and leave very little room for hookah bars and beat up second hand furniture.

Once inside of the apartment, she stood in the middle of the room and took it all in. After what seemed like a ridiculously long inspection she finally spoke.

"Living above a hookah bar does have a certain charm," she said.

In that moment, I knew I loved her all over again. The place was a dump and we both knew it. She was trying to alleviate my embarrassment and that meant a lot to me.

Relieved I said, "When I left Cynthia, I needed to find a place to stay. This was never intended to be more than temporary."

"Where do you see yourself?" she asked.

I wanted to tell her I saw myself married to her with a house full of kids living the fairy tale of happily ever after, but couldn't bring myself to say something that corny out loud.

"A home should…"

I was interrupted by a harsh male voice coming from the doorway behind me.

"He doesn't give a shit about marriage," he said.

Standing at the threshold was a big hairy guy with the Harley Davidson logo tattooed across his chest. He was wearing dirty jeans and a black leather vest worn over bare skin. A pack of Marlboro's jutted from his jean's pocket. The vest displayed the colors of Dragon's Gate motorcycle club. His black motorcycle boots showed signs of heavy wear at the heels and toes.

Huge hands hung at his sides, opening and closing spasmodically. His finger nails were outlined with black grease. Hard eyes glared at me from a weather beaten face. He was a rough looking man wearing an unhappy expression. This did not bode well.

"Who are you?" I asked.

"I'm your worst nightmare," he growled.

"Maybe, but a man who doesn't know his enemy is doomed to a life of regret…assuming he manages to survive his ignorance," I said.

He sneered.

"What kind of stupid fool are you anyway?" he asked.

"I'm the guy who may have to decide whether you live or die," I answered calmly.

Doubt flashed in his eyes and then passed quickly. His right hand swept to his low back, but I didn't wait to find out what kind of weapon he had. Instead, I closed the gap between us in an instant and jabbed him in the solar plexus. The air left his lungs and he crumbled to the ground desperately trying to catch his breath.

I rolled him over and removed a 9mm jammed down the crack of his ass. I didn't stop there and quickly found the knife hidden in his inner vest pocket and the snubbed nose revolver stashed in his boot. Once I was satisfied he was disarmed, I sat him up, and rubbed his back behind the heart until he calmed himself and found some air.

"Let's try this one more time," I said. "Who are you?" I asked.

"My name is Gil," he answered.

"Why are you here Gil?" I asked.

"Because you slept with my wife last night," he answered.

"Why do you think that?" I asked.

"Because she came home without her wedding ring," he answered.

The big lug started to sob. I comforted him as best I could until the sobbing finally stopped.

"Look Gil, I didn't…"

I was interrupted by Ginny, who held a gold wedding band in her hand.

"What is engraved inside of her ring?" she asked.

"True love," he answered.

Ginny handed him the ring and then turned to me.

"The one thing I can't tolerate is a liar," she said.

Then she walked out. Gil stood up, brushed himself off and followed her. But he stopped for a moment, turned, and looked at me with big sad eyes, before shaking his head and walking away with more dignity than I could have mustered under the circumstances. I was stunned to say the least.

It took a few minutes for me to process what had just happened. When I finally realized that Ginny didn't understand that I had never slept with Eve, I started after her, but the minute my foot stepped outside the door I was slammed faced down onto the ground and my arms were pinned behind my back. I felt a knee jam into my spinal cord as handcuffs were roughly slapped onto my wrists.

When I tried to get a look at my assailant, he pressed my face into the floor and barked for me to stay still as all hell broke loose around me. Armed men stormed the stairs and poured into the hallway. Doors were opened and then slammed shut as they yelled things like "clear" to each other. I realized I was in the middle of a full-on swat team raid. This could not be good.

They packed me into a paddy wagon with four armed guards and hauled me downtown to Louisville Metro Police headquarters. I was left alone for about an hour before the interrogation began. I have to say, it's a lot easier to ask the questions, than to answer them. The interrogation was grueling. They came at me in waves... men, women, young and old with assorted titles from the CDC, Homeland Security, and Louisville Metro Police.

I couldn't understand why I was being treated like a terrorist. Of course, no one would explain why the CDC and Homeland Security were interested in a homicide. Instead, they poked me with needles, drawing several vials of blood, which seemed weird, and repeatedly threatened to throw me into prison. When that didn't work, they offered me leniency if I told them everything. That was easy since I knew nothing. I had nothing to hide, but I was concerned about my prints on Tiny's murder weapon.

It would have been smarter to hold my tongue until I had an attorney present. Even I had enough sense to know that I couldn't represent myself, but I really wanted to help find the killer. So, I held nothing back.

Still they weren't satisfied, so they threw me a curve ball when Rose entered the room. It sent me reeling into the past.

***

I flashed back to myself sitting in the third row of Sister Mary John's class. Her thin frame was swallowed in a nun's traditional black habit. During the first week of school she told us she was married to Jesus, but I didn't believe her. Because of her hawkish nose and shrill voice, I was certain she was the Wicked Witch of the West and who would want to marry her? Definitely not Jesus, who I'd been taught was some kind of superhero.

With a spooky air of mystery she told us, "God knows all things. That means you don't have any secrets from God. He knows when you've been good or bad."

Danny's hand shot up. Danny's hand was always shooting up.

"Is God Santa Claus?" asked Danny.

She sighed.

"Daniel, wait until you are called upon before you speak," said Sister Mary John. "God is more than Santa Claus. This means that God is omniscient."

She paused dramatically, as if she had revealed a great secret to us that needed time to sink in.

Then she added, "He is also omnipotent. Does anyone know what that means?"

We stared at her with blank faces. Even Danny's hand stayed down. She sighed once again.

"It means God is all powerful," she said. "He can do whatever he wants, whenever he wants."

Danny's hand shot up once more.

"Does that mean he leaps tall buildings like Superman?" asked Danny.

"God does not leap over buildings," said Sister Mary John. "He uses his power to create. God created everything, even you Daniel. Last but not least, God is Omnipresent. That means God is everywhere at the same time. God is even in each one of you."

I thought if God is in me, then maybe I have super powers too. Maybe I can be smart like Einstein or a superhero someday. As I sat there pondering this amazing realization, Sister Mary John's class was interrupted by a knock. Her eyes shot daggers toward the door and then quickly softened. The principal stood in the doorway apologizing for interrupting her class. She then asked Sister Mary John to excuse me from class.

I was being called to the principal's office. I had never been to her office. As everybody knows, only the bad kids are sent there. I went from superhero to scared little boy in seconds. I was terrified. It got worse when I saw the police woman with her.

Every one of my misdeeds ran through my mind. Maybe the Fat Lady told the policeman I was a nasty little boy and they were taking me to jail. I didn't want to go to jail. My legs didn't seem to work so good as I shuffled toward the police woman. I kept my eyes on the floor, not daring to look into her face.

"Grant, look at me," said the police woman.

When I looked into her face, she didn't look angry. Instead, I only saw sadness. When she spoke it was with a gentle voice. She told me her name was Rose and she had some bad news…my mother was hurt and in the hospital, but my dad was in heaven now.

***

Rose Bloom had been that young police woman and was now in her mid-forties. She had aged well. Her auburn hair shared space with a few streaks of grey at the temples, and her grey eyes were framed by a faint hint of crow's feet, but she was still a beautiful woman. She no longer wore a patrolman's uniform. Instead she was dressed in jeans and a navy blue sport jacket over a white blouse.

Rose looked grief stricken and angry, which didn't quite mesh with the situation, unless I was missing something. It occurred to me that she almost seemed to be in shock, but was making a tremendous effort to keep it together. It didn't make any sense. She was her normal self yesterday when we searched Ch'ing's house.

"Has Ch'ing showed up yet?" she asked.

"Not yet," I answered. "Rose, I didn't kill Tiny."

"Why were you at the Center?" asked Rose.

Here we go again. I had been over this dozens of times already.

"Eric called and offered me a job," I said.

"You had just won a big trial for Wilbur Goth," said Rose. "Why would you take a job the next day as a bodyguard?"

"I was placed on a leave of absence pending an investigation into John's death, so despite the win yesterday, I'm currently unemployed," I answered.

"Do you have any bodyguard experience?" she asked.

"No, I don't," I answered.

"Then why did he send you?" she asked.

"I asked him that and he said they specifically asked for me," I answered.

"Who asked for you?" said Rose.

"I asked Eric that too, but he doesn't know," I answered. "Someone else at his company took the call. He's looking into it."

"Let's go over the shooting," she said.

I ran through it once again, telling her everything I remembered about it.

The door opened and Detective Lambers walked into the room. He moved off to my left and glared at me without speaking.

"I've been expecting you, Lambers," I said.

"That's Detective Lambers, punk," he said.

"What you are is a man who isn't fit to wear a badge," I said.

He came for me. Rose pulled him from my throat and then two uniformed officers removed him from the room.

"Seriously Rose, he needs to get some help," I said.

She sighed and ran her finger tips through her hair.

"This is important, Grant, what aren't you telling us?" asked Rose.

"We've been over this dozens of times already," I answered. "I saw Pony Tail reach for his weapon. I killed the lights. There were two shots fired. I was hit. I fled with Ginny. Padma followed us. There was a second shooting in the parking lot. We drove to Uncle Jim's. The SUV followed us, but left when they saw Uncle Jim armed with a hunting rifle."

"What did you see after the lights were turned off?" asked Rose

I shook my head.

"What was the audience doing?" asked Rose.

Funny thing about memory, we have a tendency to focus on the things we think are important. Those are the things we recall the easiest. Everything else is forgotten. Except, nothing is ever really forgotten. It is stored away and ignored, but never really forgotten.

"They were fighting to get to the exits, but there was a logjam at the doors," I said. "They were pounding on the doors. It was if they had been locked inside, but that's not possible."

The blood drained from Rose's face. She sat across from me in shocked silence, not breathing. It seemed like an eternity before she caught her breath.

"The doors were closed," I repeated. "They couldn't get them open."

Rose's hands were trembling. Her eyes haunted. I placed a reassuring palm over her shaking hand. She broke down.

Between sobs she repeated over and over, "Oh my God...my baby...my poor baby."

It seemed to be confirming something she already knew. Had something happened to Kim? How was she involved in all of this? Before her breakup with Uncle Jim, Rose and her daughter, Kim, lived with us for several years.

Kim was like a sister to me and if she had been injured during the shooting at the Center, I would never forgive myself. I should have called the police when I found Tiny's body.

"Has something happened to Kim?" I asked.

"The Center...she was at the Center..."

The door to the interrogation room clanged open and a deep voice bellowed,

"Get her out of here…now!"

Two burly men with buzz cuts stormed in, grabbed Rose under the arms and drug her from the room. I expected the door to close behind them, but instead a tall grey haired man with cold blue eyes stepped into the room. He was dressed in a military uniform. I didn't know how to read the soldier's rank, but his chest sported an impressive collection of medals.

Mr. Medals strode across the room in two strides and then stopped within inches. He was well within my personal space which would have made most people uncomfortable. Since I'm comfortable with close range combat, it didn't bother me. Arm's reach just means I have less of a gap to bridge when the fight starts.

I guessed his height to be six four or five. In my seated position, it was a bit of a strain to tilt my head up and look him in the eye, but I did and I wished I hadn't.

The room suddenly felt cold. Goose bumps appeared on my arms. As hard as I tried I couldn't stop shivering. It probably only lasted ten seconds, but it seemed much longer. Stillness followed. I didn't dare blink. This man had seen so much death, it had become who he is.

Finally, Mr. Medals asked, "Where is she?"

It was the last thing I expected. What did he want with Ginny? Even if I knew, I wouldn't have told him. So instead of answering I continued my vigil.

Very deliberately, Mr. Medals opened a manila folder, removed a photograph and slid it across the table. I guess I expected him to say something, but he didn't.

I cut my eyes to the photograph and saw a man wearing a wife beater, combat boots and military style trousers. He posed in front of a dust covered Humvee with muscular arms folded across his chest. I guessed him to be about 5'8". His brown hair was cropped short and a combat hardened face was partially obscured by aviator glasses.

Shrugging my shoulders I deliberately pushed the photograph back to him and waited. It was getting easier to look into death's face without feeling sick to my stomach.

He studied me closely. Maybe he saw something, I don't know, but he tapped the photo with his forefinger as if to say, "Look again."

Something was vaguely familiar about the soldier in the photo, but I couldn't get my head around it. My mind grasped at fleeting images that flashed through it at lightning speed, like those subliminal messages encoded in video that they tried to outlaw years ago because of its alarming ability to brainwash us all.

I was really close to putting my finger on it when Mr. Medal's fist slammed the table and he shouted, "Where is she, boy?"

She? He seemed to be referring to the photograph of the soldier. It was then that I realized the soldier was a woman.

My dad was Chinese and mother was mulatto. Most people don't have a clue about my ethnicity. They just think I am exotic. I was only one-quarter African-American, but calling me boy was enough to piss me off. It made me hot enough I was willing do something stupid, like kick this jerk's ass.

That was exactly what I was about to do when an authoritative voice ordered, "Stop right there."

My unwavering gaze was locked unto Mr. Medals, but his eyes faltered for the first time. It was a small victory, but one I desperately needed under the circumstances. There are pivotal moments in a life when everything seems to turn on a dime. This was one such moment. Mr. Medals released me and turned to the voice.

CHAPTER 20

It was an orator's voice, powerful enough to carry to the back of an auditorium without assistance from a microphone. Deep and rich, it commanded one minute and seduced the next. I knew it well. The saving voice belonged to Laurence Filmore, my criminal law professor.

He was a tall man with a full head of white hair that draped his proud face like a lion's mane. He was dressed in a bright Hawaiian shirt covered with pink pineapples, Bermuda shorts, and lime green flip flops. At the moment he didn't look much like an attorney, but it was the weekend, after all. Come to think of it, he didn't look like he'd just come from church services either.

Despite the lack of a proper lawyer costume, Filmore filled the room with his presence. It was more than charisma, although he had that in abundance. This man commanded respect.

In addition to teaching young men and women to be effective litigators, he was Louisville's top criminal defense attorney. His success was legendary. He never lost a case. The very mention of his name causes law enforcement officials to cringe.

Law hadn't always been his career path. Following his graduation from the Naval Academy he rose to the rank of admiral. He brought his skills to bear in two wars, but shifted gears when his son was wrongfully convicted of a brutal rape and sentenced to fifteen years in prison thanks to a forced confession.

Filmore earned his law degree from Georgetown University during a tour of duty in Washington, D.C. The Navy wasn't willing to let him go and when he insisted on practicing law, President Bush convinced him to remain in the naval reserves.

Filmore and I became friends thanks to a program the law school called "Dining with a Professor." Each of the law school professors would invite a small group of students to their homes once a month and cook dinner for us. I selected Filmore because he reminded me of Uncle Jim. In fact, it turned out Uncle Jim had served under him on some secret mission during the Gulf War. Their history created a bridge that helped facilitate our relationship.

Mr. Medals knew who stood before him. I could see it in his eyes. It was also evident that he was weighing his options and not liking the outcome of any of them.

"Stand down," ordered Filmore.

Mr. Medals' jaw tightened. There was a flash of defiance in his eyes that Filmore moved to quash.

"You will not ask my client another question until I've had an opportunity to speak with him in private," said Filmore.

"You are interfering with my investigation," growled Mr. Medals.

"This young man is a murder suspect and you just tried to provoke him into a fist fight," said Filmore. "You're a Marine Colonel and you answer to me. This isn't Bagdad. Step away from my client."

"I was testing him," said Mr. Medals.

"You were trying to entrap him," said Filmore.

"I wanted to know if he really has the skills to survive an encounter with her," said Mr. Medals.

"Who is she?" asked Filmore.

"This investigation is classified, Admiral," answered Mr. Medals.

"Then, you're done here," said Filmore. "That's a direct order."

Mr. Medals deflated with a sharp hiss. His eyes scanned from side to side a couple of times as he quickly processed Filmore's order. When he spoke again, his tone was less combative…softer.

"There are other prints on the murder weapon," said Mr. Medals.

"The killer's prints…they belong to Pony Tail," I said.

Mr. Medals shook his head and pointed at the photograph on the table.

Filmore calmly walked to the table and picked up the photo. Recognition flickered in his eyes. His shoulders dropped a fraction of an inch and for the first time since his dramatic arrival he seemed unbalanced…less sure of himself.

"Kim Slotter was awarded the Congressional Medal of Honor for God's sake," said Filmore. "How could this happen?"

It wasn't so much a question directed at Mr. Medals. Instead, it seemed to be a private thought that somehow had managed to find voice. One of those slips of tongue that leaves us wondering if we really said that out loud. The problem was that Filmore never made mistakes. It was as if the photograph had put him in a place where he lost himself.

"Private sector," answered Mr. Medals with a hint of distaste as if that explained everything.

Filmore looked up from the photograph. The trance was broken, but he looked less commanding…more collaborative. Even though he knew me well, he studied me like a potential enemy. My life was in his hands and he appeared to be compromised. It scared me.

He was looking at me, but his next question was directed to Mr. Medals.

"She's one of yours, Colonel," said Filmore. "You trained her?"

"Yes, she's the best I've seen," said Mr. Medals. "This man could not have survived a knife fight with her."

"You've lost your objectivity in this investigation," said Filmore. "Stand down."

"I have to find her," repeated Mr. Medals. "It's a matter of national security."

"You're only protecting one of your own," said Filmore. "How is that a matter of national security?"

Mr. Medals shook his head and said, "That's classified."

"I am your superior officer," barked Filmore. "You will answer my question."

Mr. Medals cut his eyes to me.

"Not in front of the civilian," he said.

Filmore turned sharply toward the door.

"Follow me, Colonel," said Filmore.

They left me alone to ponder this strange turn of events. I had assumed Tiny's killer was Pony Tail, but it was Slotter. Before Rose was dragged from the room in tears, she was about to tell me something about Kim…it had to do with the Center.

Then, I thought about the swat team and the interrogation. The physicians from the CDC kept asking how I was feeling and whether I noticed any unusual odors at the Center. I told them I didn't smell anything other than gun powder. Why did they ask that and why was the CDC involved in a murder investigation?

Then, there was the full blown physical exam they put me through. It went way beyond the collection of evidence. Geez, they wore hazmat suits for heaven's sake, like I was hazardous or something.

Filmore's return interrupted my thoughts, but when I noticed his pale face and trembling hands, my fears returned with a vengeance. I desperately wanted to know what Mr. Medals told him and started to ask, but he shook his head. The police station had too many eyes and ears.

Motioning me to follow, he led me out of the building and to his black Cadillac parked in front of LMPD headquarters. I couldn't believe we were just walking out of there after all they put me through. Judging by the sun, it was early evening. I had been interrogated for nearly twenty-four hours and was exhausted, but ecstatic. I really thought they were going to lock me up and throw away the key.

Filmore didn't speak until we pulled into Uncle Jim's driveway.

"You need to be very careful, Grant," said Filmore.

"What is going on?" I asked.

"Something very dangerous," he answered. "That's all I can tell you. Try to get some rest. You look like crap. One more thing, stay out of the city."

His intention was clear. I was dismissed. Uncle Jim was waiting for me at the door, looking like a worried parent, so I thanked Filmore for his help and went to face my uncle.

I expected him to drill me with questions, but instead Uncle Jim pointed to the sofa and handed me a pillow. Grateful, I curled up on the couch and closed my eyes. I remember thinking too much had happened over the last couple of days and sleep would be impossible, but I did sleep. As I drifted off, the last thing I thought of was the Colt 45 tucked in Uncle Jim's belt. It was a comforting end to an insane day.

The smell of fresh coffee woke me from a nightmare. It wasn't the familiar one involving the Fat Lady. Maybe that demon had finally been laid to rest. This one was a new one and it was far worse. It involved mass murder, but thankfully, I couldn't remember the details.

I peeked out of the corner of my eye and into a ray of light shining through the living room window. It was morning. My back was stiff from the soft cushions, but I was safe in Uncle Jim's house. A hand moved toward me, blocking the glare.

"Have you started having those dreams again?" asked Uncle Jim.

He offered a cup of coffee.

"This was something new," I murmured. "Maybe I've graduated to new terrors. How long was I out?"

"You slept about fourteen hours. It's Monday morning. Come join us for some breakfast."

"Us?" I asked.

"Padma showed up a few of hours before you," answered Uncle Jim. "It was kind of weird. I didn't hear a car drop him off. I'm not sure how he got here. When I asked him about it, he said he took a ride on a magic carpet."

"Showed up…didn't I leave him here Saturday night?" I asked.

"He slipped out of the house," said Uncle Jim. "I didn't even know he was gone."

Uncle Jim looked thoroughly disgusted with himself. Given his background in the Special Forces, I could understand why it bothered him that a monk was able to slip by him undetected.

I rubbed the sleep from my eyes and followed him into the kitchen. Padma was sitting at the table drinking coffee. The guy never stops smiling. Geez, you'd think he would have to give his cheeks a rest once in a while.

Sausage gravy was bubbling on the stove. Bird was perched at his favorite spot on top of the refrigerator. The smell of homemade biscuits drifted from the oven. Jars of jelly and sorghum molasses sat in the center of the table. It was a comforting scene.

"Aaawk, the jailbird is free," said Bird. "Did you make any new friends in the slammer? I'm surprised you can sit down."

"Hush bird," said Uncle Jim.

Oddly, it made me feel better. It was familiar. Bird gives me a hard time and Uncle Jim calls him out on it. You might call it a family tradition.

"Merry morning!" greeted Padma.

I'm not much of a morning person, but it felt good to be home. As Uncle Jim topped our cups with hot coffee, I had to smile at Padma's mug. There was a silhouette of a dancer with her leg hooked around a pole. He turned it so I could read the other side where it said, "Support a Single Mom."

"Good morning Padma," I said. "That's an interesting coffee mug."

His smiled widened.

"Isn't it lovely?" he asked.

"Ummm, yes it is," I answered. "Where did you get it?"

Padma nodded toward Uncle Jim.

"It was a gift from my doctor," said Uncle Jim.

I choked on my coffee. The spray made a huge mess. Sadly, a stream of it hit Bird, sending him squawking across the room in a flash of red, blue and yellow. He was very upset. Oh, the joy of revenge!

"She worked as a dancer to pay her way through medical school, and yes, she was a single mom," said Uncle Jim.

After I cleaned the mess, Uncle Jim filled mismatched plates with hot buttermilk biscuits and then poured sausage gravy over them. He sat a pitcher of orange juice and a gallon of whole milk in the center of the table. I rarely eat breakfast, but my stomach rumbled approval.

We finished our breakfast in silence. Uncle Jim was thoughtful. Padma was inscrutable. Bird focused on his morning bath and shooting me dirty looks every couple of minutes. I'm pretty sure I heard him grumble something about never getting the stains out of his feathers.

After the last dish was washed and put away, I excused myself and stepped outside for some fresh air. I needed time to think. Too much had happened too fast. The door squeaked opened behind me and Uncle Jim stepped out. He draped his arm across my shoulders and stood quietly next to me. I had a memory of him doing the same thing after my dad was killed. It was comforting.

A woodpecker searched for breakfast in the oak tree. Together, we scanned the ancient tree for a glimpse of him. Uncle Jim was a marine sniper. Even with one eye, he could see better than most.

He spotted the woodpecker first and said, "Do you see him, Grant? Look about half way up the tree, to the right. He's sitting about a third of the way out, on that branch."

Thanks to his directions, I found the woodpecker and said, "Yes, I see him now."

"I know it's corny, but I call him Woody," said Uncle Jim. "Bird hates him. He says all that knocking gives him a headache."

"He's such a drama queen," I said.

"Aaawk. Bird's a king. All hail the king."

I thought Bird was still inside. He must have slipped out with Uncle Jim. A few comebacks came to mind, but I didn't want to fuel Bird's foul disposition. Instead, I just watched Woody do his thing.

Padma appeared at my side. Funny, I was sure he didn't come out with Uncle Jim and I didn't hear the noisy door hinged. How does he keep doing these things? And the way he looks at me…it feels as if he can see into all of my dark places.

As if he had read my mind, Padma said, "You stand at the eight gates."

Eight gates…I've heard that expression before. Then, I had a flashback of myself standing on this very porch when I was eight years old. I was alone and crying. Earlier that day, a police woman had told me my dad had been killed in a hit-and-run motorcycle accident.

Then, I heard a voice. It was gentle and kind. It came from a man who wasn't much bigger than me. He told me his name was Ch'ing and that it is okay to be sad. He said sadness is one of the eight gates of change and, someday, I would stand at all eight gates. I didn't understand any of that, but he had gotten my attention when he had asked me if I wanted to learn Kung Fu.

I was brought back to the present by a ring from my cell. I glanced at the screen and saw it was an unknown caller. I never take those calls, but something told me I should this time. I'm glad I did. It was Ginny's voice I heard, but what she said sent a chill up my spine.

"I'm so scared, Grant. They have me. Please help."

CHAPTER 21

A man fights many battles in his lifetime, but the only one that really matters is the fight for something he is afraid to lose. It doesn't matter whether it's a person, thing, or the cherished notions he holds about himself. All that really matters is how he handles the fear.

Fear causes him to settle for less than he deserves. Settling for second best is never a viable option in an enlightened life. It is a darkness of spirit that reduces him to less than he is...a shadow of his true nature. Settling is a compromise with fear that never works out for the best in the end, because the purpose of life is to express his true nature.

Never chose the safe path when it requires you to choose something other than your true nature. Fear must be faced head-on with the determination to give it your best shot and enough resolve to accept whatever outcome fate holds for you.

Ch'ing taught me to remain calm in the face of danger by centering myself in the present. Hours of full contact sparring made it an absolute necessity. He would attack on multiple levels at blistering speed...hands, feet, hips, shoulders, elbows flying everywhere, seemingly, at the same time until the pain of the blows got my full attention.

All of those hours of training fell away at the sound of Ginny's plea for help. Before I could answer, I heard another voice...an icy cold voice. It sent a cold fear down into the pit of my stomach. The voice told me Ginny is as good as dead if I even think of calling the police. The voice told me to wait for further instructions that must be followed without exception or she will die a slow and painful death.

My knees buckled and I gripped the phone like it was some sort of lifeline. Once again, I felt the crippling terror of losing someone I love. There had been too much loss, already. Fear had arrived full force into my life.

I had to rescue her, but I was frozen in place by the terrible news I had just received. It was Padma who came to my rescue.

"Come sit with me, Grant," he said softly. "It is time for meditation."

Padma led us down the bank of Harrods Creek to a large flat rock at water's edge where he gracefully dropped into a perfectly balanced sitting position. Even though his back was ramrod straight, he didn't look stiff. Instead, he seemed completely relaxed. For such a heavy-set man, he was amazingly nimble.

In sharp contrast to Padma, I was bent like a bow...rigid and filled with anxiety. The phone call from Ginny had ended abruptly. My repeated call backs dropped without a single ring. I desperately wanted to know where she was and who had her. If Ginny was taken by Slotter, then she was in grave danger. The not-knowing was unbearable.

"Grant, it's time to get out of your head and come to your senses," said Padma.

I felt a flash of anger and said a little too harshly, "What the hell does that mean?"

My anger didn't last. It was instantly swallowed by the kindness in his eyes and just evaporated. I knew what he meant. It was time to quiet my worried thoughts and focus on the present moment. I really did try, but failed miserably. The last couple of days had been a nightmare that continued to plague me. My thoughts refused to be silenced.

With a graceful sweep of his arm Padma asked, "What do you see?"

I half-heartedly glanced around me and mumbled something about a creek. Like any good teacher, he enthusiastically praised my correct answer. I knew he was pulling my leg, but the silliness of his praise somehow managed to hook me. So, I took another look.

When the spring rains pour heavy, Harrods Creek is a wide stream full of boulders and white water. On this summer day, it carried less water and flowed more gently around the rocks with only a touch of white.

The far shore was lined with dogwoods, redbuds, and a sycamore or two. Twenty-feet downstream, a bushy-tailed red fox slipped quietly down the bank and took a sip of water. Two baby foxes followed close behind.

It is a rare treat to see a fox and a miracle to see a family enjoying one of the simple pleasures in life. The kids were more interested in play than water. They chased each other through the tall grass, darting back and forth in a joyful game of tag. Oddly, the fox family paid no attention to us until a splash sent them scurrying back into the safety of the woods.

The splash came from a small eddy behind the flat rock I was sitting on. A tail fin was sticking vertically out of the water. I had never seen anything like it. How does a fish do that?

Curious, I reached down and grabbed hold with my thumb and forefinger. You'd think the alarmed fish would dart away. But it didn't. So, I gave a little tug. Something pulled back, even harder. My competitive nature took over and I tugged back. The fish came out of the water, slipped through my fingers with a splash and swam away.

I thought that was the end of it, but an angry water moccasin popped its head out of the water and glared at me for ruining its meal. I jumped out of my skin. Snakes scare me and water moccasins are one of Kentucky's most poisonous varieties. Padma just laughed his ass off as I jumped to another rock.

"Real funny," I grumbled. "I hate snakes."

"You and Indiana Jones," giggled Padma.

Comparing me to Indiana Jones was a stretch, but it somehow made me feel better and I smiled for the first time that morning.

"Oh, you've found your humor," said Padma. "That's good. Connecting with your inner smile is what meditation is all about. If you can do that 24/7, especially during a crisis, then you will have discovered the secret of life."

His comments surprised me, so I said, "That's it...that's the meditation lesson. I thought we were going to sit in lotus posture and chant a mystical phrase or something."

Padma's only response was to do that laughing Santa thing he does. It was annoying at first, but suddenly I got it. A huge load lifted and light poured through me. Before long, I was laughing like Santa myself.

When the laughter subsided, he suggested I take a moment to acknowledge the healing that had just taken place and to never forget the difference it can make in one's life. I can't explain it, but I suddenly had this overwhelming sense of energy and felt invincible. All of my senses were heightened and I knew with great certainty that I could save Ginny.

"Anxiety is toxic," he said. "Never let it rule you."

I wanted to kiss him, but settled for a much manlier bear hug. The unmistakable thunder of Harley Davidson motorcycles interrupted our embrace and we made our way back to the house.

Six hogs thundered toward us in a staggered formation. There wasn't a rice burner in the group. The lead chopper flew a black flag with a red dragon, its left claw squeezed blood from a beating heart and the right supported a big set of testicles. The dragon image was also inlaid into the chopper's paint job, flowing from the front fender to the rear. A small bell dangled from the bike's frame, just inches from the asphalt, as a warning to the road gremlins that they weren't to mess with this bike.

The solo saddle made it clear that this biker always road alone. The wide seat was filled with an even wider ass supporting a gut that hung way over the gas tank. The biker's belly was covered with a tattoo of the red dragon except its claws stretched from his chest down into his dirty jeans. Long greasy salt and pepper hair was pulled back into a French braid. Mr. Braid's long beard was divided into two similar braids that were tied off with chrome pony tail holders.

The next two bikes were less flashy...a couple of black Harley Low Riders with lots of chrome. The riders, however, were a different story. It was two chicks as different as night and day. The blond wore her hair man short and spiked at crazy angles. She wore no makeup and her only adornment was a hand full of huge silver rings that, when taken as a whole, formed the shape of a dragon. In fact, it looked like a set of fancy brass knuckles.

This chick looked like she could put a hurting on someone. Her thick muscular biceps would have made any body-builder proud. Obviously, she spent a lot of time in the gym. In fact, the closer I looked the more convinced I became she was a body builder herself. Ms. Amazon's shoulders, back, chest, and thighs were massive, like her biceps. She was a big girl, but there wasn't an ounce of fat on her. Odd, but she had this massive chest and no tits.

A thick black leather sweat band displayed a hot pink dragon centered on her forehead. Just below the dragon, wrap-around sun glasses rested on the bridge of her nose. Both nostrils were pierced with pink studs. A wife beater was stretched tight across her chest. It was stenciled with hot pink lettering that proclaimed: "I'm a Survivor Motherfucker." A Susan G. Komen pink ribbon made it clear she was a breast cancer survivor.

Her faded jeans were held up by a thick black leather belt with an antique silver dragon buckle. The jeans were ripped at both knees and mid-thigh on the left. Strapped to the right thigh was a black handled commando knife. Her wardrobe was completed with square-toed black engineer boots.

The other chick was hot in a scary kind of way, all dressed in black like Cat Woman. This one had no need to confirm she was female. In fact, she wasn't wearing a shirt. Her double D's just barely squeezed into a black leather vest that looked as if it could burst at any moment.

She wore tight-fitting black leather pants that displayed a prominent camel toe. If there was any doubt about her role, a black leather whip with multiple tails tucked into her thigh-high dominatrix boots, made it clear she was the one who dealt out the punishment.

Ms. Dom's witchy black hair blew wild in the wind and partially obscured her freakish white face. For an instant it formed a tai chi pattern that most people call the yin-yang symbol. She wore no eye protection, unless you want to count black makeup painted in a jagged pattern around her green eyes. If there was any warmth in her wide Cheshire cat smile, it was lost in blood red lips that stood out in sharp contrast to her pale face.

Close behind Ms. Dom was a gorilla clinging to a set of ape hangers. These are tall handlebars that extend above the biker's head, giving the impression that he is hanging from a tree. He was the only rider wearing a helmet…a simple black brain bucket with stickers pasted all over it. He was still too far away to read them, but the red dragon pasted on the forehead was unmistakable.

There was no hair showing below the tiny helmet except for a mustache and goatee, unless you want to count the bushy unibrow. His brow was pinched tight and both corners of his eyes were pierced. King Kong had a square face and no neck. A thick tuft of reddish hair pushed its way through the neck of his Harley Davidson t-shirt.

The next rider in line rode hands-free. In fact, he was arched backwards over the rear wheel with his arms spread wide palms facing the sun. "Ole' George" was painted on the tank of his vintage Harley Davidson Pan Head.

Ole' George wore a crumpled black Fedora. I don't have a clue how he kept it from blowing away. Maybe the hat was just too intimidated to cross him. His rugged face was cut with four parallel lines rising from the corners of his mouth…one set to his nostrils and the other to his cheek bones.

Despite the hot weather, his raw boned frame was covered with multiple layers of clothing. It was nothing fancy…a blue jean vest with club patches, flannel shirt open to the navel, and a black Grateful Dead t-shirt. I don't consider myself a Deadhead, but for some reason I instantly heard a few lines of their song "Built to Last" play in my head.

The final biker was Eve's husband, Gil. Shit. This time he brought his gang with him. The bikers pulled to a stop in front of the house and shut down their hogs. The rumble of Screaming Eagle pipes was replaced by engineer boots crunching loose gravel. They spread out like hunters driving their prey to the kill. A beat-down seemed imminent, but I refused to be cowed. Instead, I waited…relaxed and ready to fight, if necessary. It was the smallest of the bikers who broke the silence.

In a gravelly voice Ole' George said, "You the motherfucker that killed Tiny?"

CHAPTER 22

Dragon Gate Motorcycle Club was formed after World War II by a couple of fighter pilots. They were joined by other servicemen who got a taste of the world in their fight against the evil empire and still weren't ready to settle down. Like the cowboy migration in the 1800's, they mounted their iron horses and hit the trail. Their only goal was to explore the land of the free and home of the brave.

The club had its ups and downs over the years. In the 1960's an over-zealous prosecutor looking to advance his political career fabricated a case against one of their members. It resulted in a high profile prosecution that was, eventually, withdrawn for lack of evidence. It left a bitter taste in their mouths.

The incident also created a public perception that motorcycle clubs are infested with violent criminals. Hollywood made a few movies about bikers that reinforced the public perception that they are dangerous outlaws.

Of course, some bikers really are thugs who do nothing to dispel the outlaw myth. Instead, they use it to intimidate others and very few are willing to show them any disrespect. Of all the biker clubs, Dragon Gate had the worst reputation. The menacing group that now surrounded me certainly lived up to it.

The ragtag group of bikers standing in front of me thought that I had killed the president of their motorcycle club. If not handled well, somebody was going to get hurt, and it would likely be me.

Most martial arts make a show of being hard, strong, and fast. By contrast, Tai Chi is calm, centered, and peaceful. It is a mystery to most people how something so peaceful-looking can be used for self-defense purposes. Yet, in ancient China, it was revered as one of the most effective fighting styles. So what is the secret?

I first learned the secret of Tai Chi on my sixteenth birthday when Ch'ing tossed me the keys to his car and said, "Let's try out that new learner's permit."

I jumped at the opportunity to get a driving lesson. A license is everything to a teenage boy. Without one, dating is impossible.

Thinking we'd start slow, I asked, "Are we going to stay in the neighborhood?"

"Head to the Interstate," he answered.

I felt my stomach flop. I'm not sure what I expected, but Ch'ing told me to relax and not overreact.

"Just point it between the lines, Grant," said Ch'ing. "If you remember to make small adjustments, then you'll be okay."

Gulping, I backed down the driveway and did what he said. I figured he'd offer more driving instruction, but instead, he talked about his life in the monastery.

"Once a year, the old monks descend the mountain with food, wine, and medicine," Ch'ing said. "First, they tend to the sick. Afterwards, they throw a huge party for the villagers, entertaining them with stories and martial arts demonstrations."

"I wish I could watch them do Kung Fu," I said. "Ch'ing, what is the ultimate martial art?"

Without hesitation he answered, "Tai Chi."

"Yea, right," I said. "It's so slow. How could anyone fight with that stuff? I mean, it's for old men, isn't it?"

He didn't answer. Instead, he said we needed gas and told me to take the next exit. Ch'ing went inside to pay as I began pumping fuel into his old convertible Cadillac.

For the first time, I gave our surroundings a good look. It was a very rough area. The streets were empty. All the other businesses looked closed. Most of the buildings in the immediate area were boarded. Vacant structures were covered in gang graffiti. The convenience store windows were covered with bars. I realized this was a very scary place.

As I surveyed my surroundings, I saw something move in the shadows. I couldn't quite make it out at first. Slowly, a sinister figure emerged and took shape. His face was hidden by a hooded sweatshirt. He paused for what seemed like an eternity, and then began to move in my direction.

I did not like the looks of this at all. I felt my heart start pounding and I couldn't catch my breath. My blood pressure increased a notch with each menacing step. By the time he stopped a few feet in front of me, I was in a full blown fight or flight state.

Time slowed. Sweat trickled down the small of my back. He shifted his feet and mumbled something unintelligible. It was a strange garbled sound. I wasn't even sure it was speech. So much information can be gained about a person in just a few sentences. If you listen carefully, you can read their intentions. I learned nothing from the garbled sounds coming from him. I was frozen. I waited.

I tried to see his face…read his eyes and expression. Even at close range, his face was still obscured. He was like a shadow and it totally creeped me out. He spoke again. I still didn't understand him. This time I responded, but my voice cracked before coming out high and sharp. Damn, I didn't mean to do that.

He snorted in disgust and reached for his pocket. He was going for a weapon. My only chance was to hit him hard and fast. I was a split second away from attacking when I heard Ch'ing's warm friendly voice.

"What can we do for you friend?" asked Ch'ing.

Ch'ing had appeared out of nowhere. He quietly sided up to the stranger and put his arm around him. His manner was friendly. The embrace was warm. He used the connection to trap the mugger's arm against his body. The hand reaching for the weapon was immobilized in the thug's pocket. Ch'ing's smile never wavered. His kindness was genuine. His control of the situation was absolute.

The shadow turned to look at Ch'ing. For the first time, I could see the mugger's face. It quickly shifted from hatred to shock and confusion. Ch'ing's appearance had been so unexpected. His lighthearted and friendly demeanor was equally astonishing.

As I processed this unexpected turn of events, I witnessed the most amazing transformation. Slowly, the mugger's face changed until it mirrored Ch'ing's warmth and friendliness. He visibly relaxed. His eyes began to twinkle just like my teacher's. Ch'ing repeated his question. This time more softly.

"What can we do to help you friend?" asked Ch'ing.

After handing him a couple of cigarettes, Ch'ing gave him a pat on the back and sent him off into the night.

His parting words were, "Be careful my friend. It can be dangerous out there."

We climbed into the car and started for home. Neither of us spoke for a while. I was thinking about what could have happened and my hands started shaking.

I needed to talk about it so I asked Ch'ing, "What happened back there?"

"Tai Chi lesson," he answered.

"Lesson?" I asked.

"It's easy to hurt people," said Ch'ing. "That takes little skill. The greater skill is to diffuse aggression without causing harm. The best way to do that is to win the fight before it begins. Nip it in the bud, to quote your great American philosopher, Barney Fife."

"I don't understand," I said. "That wasn't a fight."

He looked at me and said softly, "Then, why are your hands still shaking."

I thought I had hidden it. I should have known better. Ch'ing doesn't miss anything. I knew better than to give him a bullshit answer.

"I thought he was going to kill me," I said. "It scared me."

Ch'ing patted me on the shoulder.

"You did good," said Ch'ing. "You stood in the face of danger and didn't overreact."

More honesty from me.

"The truth is I was about to punch him when you appeared out of nowhere," I said.

"The better strategy is to embrace rather than destroy," replied Ch'ing.

"How do I do that?" I asked.

"Join energy at the onset of conflict," said Ch'ing.

"Huh?"

"Never run from conflict," said Ch'ing. "Enter a dangerous situation and lead the attacker to safety. That is true martial mastery. Anything else falls short of the objective of an enlightened master."

That's exactly what Ch'ing did. If I had not seen it for myself, I would have thought he was talking about an unrealistic philosophy.

"Can you teach me Tai Chi?" I asked.

"Tai Chi is for living," said Ch'ing. "It is about balance. The symbol people call the yin-yang symbol is a graphic representation of Tai Chi. It depicts opposites in balance. Opposites need each other. Light does not exist except in relationship to dark. Good and evil define one another. Grant, did you think that young man at the gas station was evil?"

"I thought he was bad guy," I confessed.

Ch'ing pressed, "Do you wish there was no bad in the world, Grant?"

I answered without thinking.

"Yes, I do," I said. "Then, we would have a perfect world, don't you think?"

Ch'ing shook his head.

"Good and bad define each other," said Ch'ing. "If bad ceases to exist, then, so does good. When good and bad are out of balance, our life is filled with turmoil. The goal is to embrace life as it is. It does no good wishing things were different. If you can manage this, then you will be able to smile in the face of danger."

I was brought back to the present by a low growl. Ole' George was waiting for an answer to his question. He thought I was Tiny's killer. As I looked into his eyes, I saw his pain. I know what it feels like to lose a loved one. I didn't know if he would believe me, but it was time to tell him what happened.

"I found Tiny in a pool of blood," I said. "I did everything I could to save him, but...I'm sorry you lost your friend, man."

Ole' George studied me long and hard before reaching around to his low back. Remembering Ch'ing's lesson, I resisted the temptation to spring for his throat. It was the right decision. Ole' George pulled out a bottle of bourbon, slowly opened it, took a long draw, and then, offered the whiskey to me.

Even though I had just had breakfast, it somehow seemed to fit the moment, so solemnly I took a drink. It was the strangest communion I ever shared.

Bourbon burns as it slides down the throat, but the whiskey he offered burns more softly than most. It is smooth, very smooth whiskey. Instead of fighting the burn, I embraced it and let it send my thoughts back to race days at the horse track with Dad.

He loved the track, but not because he was gambler. Dad loved the horses. For me, a day at the track was a day filled with the smell of bourbon, cigars, and horse manure. It was something we did together and bourbon always reminded me of those happy days.

After the burn subsided and I returned to the present moment, I handed the bottle back to Ole' George. Just when I thought the day couldn't get any weirder, my hand touched Ole George's and he said, "It's a good day to die."

And that's when the phone finally rang.

CHAPTER 23

Disrespecting a Dragon is never a good idea, but the most important thing at that moment was the phone call. Tiny was dead. Ginny might end up that way too, if I didn't take the call.

I looked at Ole' George and said, "I'm sorry your friend is dead, but I am taking this call. It's a matter of life or death."

As I dug a hand into my pocket, the biker scowled and spat an ugly green mess at my feet. That wasn't the reaction I hoped for, but now he was starting to piss me off.

"Someone I care about was abducted," I said. "I think it was Tiny's killer who took her."

I didn't wait for his permission. Instead, I answered the phone hoping to hear Ginny's voice. I was disappointed. It was the same voice that had forced its way onto the line earlier. Androgynous, is the best description of the voice I heard...not masculine or feminine...neutral.

"They're going to kill you, you know," said the caller.

"Maybe," I said.

"It would save me the trouble of doing it myself, but I need to talk to you first."

"I'm not talking to you until I know Ginny is okay," I said.

"Patience grasshopper," said the caller.

"Do you still have Ginny?" I demanded.

"There's an abandoned warehouse on West Market near the Shawnee Expressway," said the voice. "Bring the monk and be there in an hour. If you're one minute late...she dies. If you call the police, she dies."

"If you hurt her, I will kill you," I said.

The caller paused.

"If you want this pretty little thing to live, find a way to stay alive," said the caller.

That was it. The call abruptly ended. Sometime during the brief call the Dragons had pulled weapons and moved a step closer. Ole' George was pointing a .44 Magnum at me. Why do the little guys always carry the biggest guns? It was almost as big as him. He was maybe 5'7" and couldn't have weighed more than 130 pounds, soaking wet.

Ms. Dom brandished the cat o' nines. The crack of her whip added a surreal sound to the scene. The Amazon held her knife commando-style. Mr. Braids was pointing a Glock at my chest. The tip of the barrel was all I could see of the gun in King Kong's massive hands.

I needed to convince them I wasn't Tiny's killer, but, when I opened my mouth to speak, Ole' George shook his head and pulled the .44's hammer. That's when a red dot appeared on the first knuckle of his forefinger. Someone had him dead in his sights, and I knew that someone had to be Uncle Jim.

Ole' George saw it and muttered, "What the…"

The laser dot quickly moved to Ole' George's heart and, then, to his right eye. But, it didn't rest there. In a flash, it moved to King Kong's forehead and, then, to Amazon's chest. The red dot never stopped. It continued dancing from target to target.

"Uncle Jim was a marine sniper," I said casually. "If you lay down your weapons he might be willing to tell you about the time he snuck into Pakistan and singlehandedly took out an Al-Qaeda cell."

Surprisingly, it was Ms. Dom who showed the first signs of submission. I guess she figured a whip wasn't much use against a sniper rifle. Or maybe, she had a streak of sub deep inside of her that was dying to get out. Either way, Ole' George was having none of it.

He glared at me and said in a voice loud enough for Uncle Jim to hear, "Man, I ain't leaving nothing on the table. I'm gonna use every bit until there ain't nothing left of me. Not a damn thing for any of you fucking buzzards. One minute Ole' George will be here and then poof I'll be gone. That's cuz I'll be all used up. So, just try to shoot me motherfucker before I put a golf ball size hole in pretty boy's chest."

Let me tell you what folks…Ole' George is one crazy dude. I knew at that moment, beyond a shadow of a doubt, he was going to get a bunch of us killed.

Just when it seemed like my death was imminent, I was granted a reprieve. It was the sound of a Harley that provided a moment of respite. It's like biker catnip. They can't seem to get enough of it. No matter what they are doing, they pause and turn their attention toward an approaching bike.

Unlike the bikers, I never once took my eyes off Ole' George. Ch'ing had taught me well and I knew better than to let anything distract me from a threat. It wasn't until the rider pulled into my field of vision that I recognized the bike.

Eric is one of those guys who wear a smile like it's their favorite pair of jeans. Comfortable, may be the best way to describe it. He wasn't smiling as he backed the Road King next to the other motorcycles, dropped the kick stand and dismounted.

Ch'ing did his best to teach Eric that fighting is never the solution to a problem, but Eric loves a good fight. A few years ago, he was confronted by four muggers as he and Kinsey were leaving a bar. Eric grinned and said something to Kinsey about how much fun it was going to be. When she rolled her eyes and yawned, the muggers fled.

I figured this situation was going to escalate now that Eric was here, but he surprised me. Instead of displaying his usual macho attitude, he walked straight to Ole' George, placed himself between me and the gun, and gave him a warm hug.

Ole' George laid his head on Eric's chest and began crying. At first it was just a tear slipping down his cheek, but then it turned to sobs. Eric didn't say a word. He just held him.

When Ole' George was cried out, Eric finally said, "I can't imagine the pain of losing the love of your life, my friend."

That started another round of tears. Not just for Ole' George, but all of the biker's had tears in their eyes. It only lasted a minute or so before King Kong realized he was crying in front of strangers. Looking thoroughly embarrassed, he wiped his eyes with the back of his gun hand and pulled himself together. One by one the others did the same.

"You all need to put your weapons away," said Eric.

Ole' George nodded and slipped the Dirty Harry cannon into his waistband. I've never understood why someone would want to point the barrel of a gun toward their junk. The rest of the bikers followed his lead and stashed their weapons in various nooks and crannies.

"Tell me, my friend, why you were pointing that cannon at Grant," said Eric.

"A friend on the force told me his prints were on the murder weapon, his and some chick's," said Ole' George.

The Amazon jabbed her thumb at me and said, "He doesn't think a chick could ever take Tiny out, so, it had to be him. Especially, since he was trained by the same guy who taught you to fight."

"The chick's name is Kim Slotter," I said. "She's ex-special forces and a serious bad-ass."

I pulled up my shirt and pointed to the knife wound. "It's just a scratch, but she cut me when I found her in Tiny's office," I said. "Same with the bullet wound next to it. There was a shooting at the Center and I caught a bullet."

"Show them the truck," said Uncle Jim.

I had no idea Uncle Jim was right behind me. For a guy with a cane, he can move like a cat when he needs to. The truck had been parked on the street in front of my apartment when the swat team arrested me, but there it sat in the driveway. The back glass was shattered and the tail gate sported three bullet holes.

"There was a second shooting in the parking garage at the Center," I said.

Nodding in Padma's direction, I continued, "Somebody wants us dead. It's starting to look like they may have hired Slotter to do the job. Ginny was kidnapped and they are holding her hostage at a warehouse out by the Shawnee Parkway. If Padma and I don't get there soon, they are going to kill Ginny."

Gil spoke up for the first time and asked, "Is she the one who gave me the ring and then walked out on you?"

"Yes, that's her," I answered.

"I like her and am not going to let someone hurt her," said Gil. "She may have just saved your life. Let him go, George."

Ole' George nodded.

"Okay, but Slotter is mine," said Ole' George. "I'll show the bitch what a bad ass is."

I pulled Eric aside and said, "This guy is a loose cannon. He could get Ginny killed."

"I know Grant, but you'll never convince him to stay behind," said Eric. "Let's find a way to make him an asset."

"I got a bad feeling about this, Eric," I said.

"Ah, don't sweat it man," said Eric. "It'll be fun. So, what's the plan, buddy?"

I didn't have a plan, so, what I said was, "We're going to do whatever it takes to rescue Ginny."

Eric grinned at me and said, "I like it."

"We could use the bikers as a diversion," I said.

"Now we're getting somewhere," said Eric. "While the bad guys focus on the bikers, Uncle Jim can position himself at a strategic location with his sniper rifle."

"Time is not on our side right now," said Uncle Jim. "It's time to move out. Grant, I need to speak with you for a minute before we leave?"

As the bikers rode off in a thunder with Eric trailing them, Uncle Jim pulled me aside.

Looking a little uncomfortable, he said, "I just wanted to say, I love you, son. Be safe."

This was so unexpected. I know he loves me, but he's never actually said it. I was choked up and tried to respond, but he waved it off as he walked away.

I was still recovering from the shock as Uncle Jim backed his classic 1963 Corvette Sting Ray out of the garage. It's the model with the split rear window and it's in pristine condition. He had it painted a beautiful candy apple red and usually only takes it out for an occasional Sunday drive or other special occasions. I guess he figured this was a special occasion.

Padma's eyes bugged out of his head when he saw the car.

Uncle Jim smiled and asked, "Padma, do you want to ride with me?"

"Slotter is expecting me and Padma," I said. "He has to ride with me."

It might be the only time I've seen Padma show disappointment as Bird hopped from his shoulder and took his spot in the passenger seat. That surprised all of us, and I think Uncle Jim was about to tell him to get out of his car when Bird glared at him. Bird's glare is not something you take lightly and Uncle Jim knew it. So he shrugged, fired up the 360 horse power V-8 and followed the bikes out of the neighborhood.

Time was running out on Ginny. Padma and I hurried to the truck, but when I turned the key, nothing happened. I tried again and still nothing. The truck was dead in the water. Shit, we had no way to get there.

CHAPTER 24

Dad's truck was dead. If I didn't get us to the warehouse soon, Ginny would be too. I couldn't believe it. The old rust bucket wasn't pretty, but had always been reliable. Eric thought I was crazy, but I had trusted it during my travels across the country. Not once had it ever let me down. The last road trip was to Glacier National Park for a backpacking trip a few weeks earlier.

"That does not sound good, Master Li," said Padma in his ridiculously cheerful voice.

If I hadn't been in shock about the truck and filled with worry about Ginny's safety, I might have taken a moment to wonder why he called me that, but I was too busy feeling tested like the biblical Job. How many setbacks can a man endure before he loses faith in himself? I guess that's the question we all have to answer for ourselves.

"Focus on the challenge before you," said Padma. "What's the solution?"

The truck needed repairs, but there wasn't time. We were at the end of the sidewalk and needed to leave immediately. I knew what I had to do. My mind was racing for some other option, and there was one, but it was the last thing I wanted to do. On the verge of panic, an image of Ginny popped into my mind. I pictured her scared and hurt. I had made my decision.

"Come with me," I said.

We hurried to the back of the house and stood in front of the garage. Taking a deep breath, I raised the overhead door. The inside was neat and orderly. This was Uncle Jim's man cave and he ran a tight ship. Everything had its place.

In the corner, hidden by an old bed sheet covered with faded yellow daisies, was the thing I hated most in this world. Padma patted me on the shoulder and gave me a little nudge in its direction. I wasn't sure I could do this.

My feet didn't want to move, but I willed myself forward until we stood next to it. I could feel the blood pounding in my temples as I reached for the sheet and tossed it to the floor. There she was. For the first time in years, I looked at the motorcycle that had killed Dad.

Glancing at my clenched fists, Padma said, "You look like you want to hurt someone."

I relaxed my hands and answered in a hoarse whisper, "This was Dad's bike."

Padma eyed the bike.

"It is pristine," he said.

I choked. The damn thing took my parents from me and it didn't have a scratch on it. They were thrown head-first into a culvert. The bike landed in a pile of leaves.

"After the funeral, Uncle Jim rolled it into this corner," I said. "It hasn't been moved since. Ch'ing brought me in here once. We silently stood in this very spot for a long while...just looking. After I cried myself out, he patted me on the shoulder and told me this magnificent machine would save me some day. I can't imagine how. I hate this bike."

"Love and hate are opposite sides of the same coin," said Padma.

Maybe Ch'ing was right, after all. The thing I hated most in the world would carry me back to something that had been missing for many years in my life...love. After all these years, I realized I still loved the little girl who had now grown into a beautiful woman.

Resigned, I swung my leg over the saddle and settled in. Surprisingly, it felt comfortable. It was a big bike and I expected it to be heavy and clumsy. It wasn't. Instead, it was beautifully balanced.

"Let's see if she'll start after all these years," I said.

Taking a deep breath, I hit the starter. The engine churned without firing. I lifted my thumb from the start button.

"Damn," I muttered under my breath.

Padma patted me on the shoulder and said, "Try again."

This was my chance to redeem myself...to heal old wounds left festering too long. I wasn't about to let Ginny down...again. I wanted redemption. Failure was not an option.

My determination calmed me and, for some reason, I knew the bike would start. The engine fired on the next try. The rumble of the old Harley's pipes was like a victory shout.

I grinned at Padma and said, "Climb on. We can still make it to the warehouse in time if we hurry. Let's find out what this bitch wants with us and get Ginny home safely."

Padma didn't hesitate. He hiked up his robe, swung his leg over the back and settled in behind me. It was kind of weird having him back there, but I tried not to think about it too much. Instead, I focused on backing the hog out of the garage and off we rode to rescue Ginny.

It's a twenty minute drive across town from the east end to the west end and we had eighteen minutes to get there. It was no time to worry about a speeding ticket, but a traffic stop would be disastrous. We had no time to spare and the risk was necessary. I trusted my instincts to slow down, if necessary. So, we flew down I-71 toward the west end, like a bat out of hell.

The west end's ghettos are the source of Louisville's reputation as one of the most dangerous places in the country to live. Like most ghettos, there isn't much of a police presence. The natives are left to fend for themselves and extreme poverty brings out the worst in people.

The area is near a port that services barges running up and down the Ohio

River between the steel mills of the northeast and the Gulf of Mexico to the southwest. As a result of the fading steel industry and the general economic downturn in this area, many of the warehouses are empty. Finding a particular warehouse might not be easy.

It was Padma who solved the problem. He pointed toward a huge building with decayed red brick. Faded paint announced it was once the home of the best damn bourbon in Kentucky. It had a few broken windows and rust was overtaking the paint. Someone had cut the chain lock and the entry gate was standing open.

Weeds pushed through the cracked asphalt parking lot. I maneuvered the bike around the potholes and loose gravel. The lot was empty, so we circled around to the back.

It's hard to believe, but the rear of the building was in worse shape than the front. Chunks of brick had crumbled from the façade and lay in pieces among the weeds. What was left of the wall was covered in gang graffiti. A rusted eight foot chain link fence with razor wire at the top ran the property line. Someone had pulled it open in several places to gain access to the property.

A black SUV was parked next to the loading docks. Uncle Jim and the Dragons were nowhere in sight. I rolled to a stop about twenty yards from the SUV and killed the engine. Tinted windows hid the driver from view. There wasn't any sound except a creaking door and the occasional rustle of leaves in the undergrowth along the fence line. Someone had written "ENDGAME" on the door using firehouse red spray paint.

I dropped the kickstand and we dismounted. Three of the SUV's doors opened, but no one got out. There was nothing to do but wait.

Finally, after what seemed like an eternity, three men climbed out of the SUV and headed in our direction. Ginny was not with them. The driver was a big man with a thick neck, barrel chest, and huge muscular arms. Shrek was wearing camouflage pants, a wife beater, and combat boots. His head was shaved and every inch of visible skin was covered in strange tattoos.

The man who'd been riding shotgun was much smaller with cold eyes and a hard face filled with contempt. He was hairy. His unruly black hair hung low on his forehead like a sheep dog. He wore faded jeans and a Hawaiian shirt opened at the neck exposing a big tuft of curly black hair. Bizarrely, Mr. Hawaiian Tropic's white sneakers looked like they were fresh out of the box.

The third man had an ugly, jagged scar running from the corner of the mouth to his ear lobe. Scarface was wearing black jeans, black polo shirt, and black combat boots. He was about six feet tall with a tight, compact frame. His hair was cut in a 1950's flat-top style. There was an airborne symbol tattooed onto his muscular forearm.

They stopped about three paces in front of us and spread out. Scarface was in the center. Mr. Hawaiian Tropic was to his right and Shrek took up position on the other side. Mr. Hawaiian Tropic leered at Padma. Shrek's jaw twitched. Scarface tried to stare me down. I resisted the temptation to break the silence and waited for him to speak first.

It took a couple of minutes before Scarface finally asked, "You come alone?"

I nodded in Padma's direction and asked, "Where's Ginny?"

I was starting to think that Scarface wasn't going to respond, but then, he raised his hand and motioned someone in the SUV to come forward. The fourth door opened and two women climbed out.

Ginny was gagged with a red ball connected to a black leather strap that was secured at the back of her head. Her hands were tied in front with white plastic zip ties. There was a trickle of blood from a cut somewhere above the hairline. I noticed a tear in her dress. She was subdued…maybe in shock.

I knew these guys played rough and I couldn't believe I had left my gun under the seat of the truck. There's nothing like bringing your fists to a gun fight. The odds were not good, but thankfully, Ch'ing had trained me well. I set my jaw in anticipation of the fight to come.

When I noticed the deference Scarface gave the woman standing next to Ginny, I took a closer look. The hair was longer and the clothes were more feminine, but it was Slotter. No question about it.

"Your Harley is an old man's bike," said Slotter. "I prefer my Ducati."

I suddenly felt the need to defend Dad's bike, but resisted because I knew that Slotter was obviously baiting me. She wanted to know if I could be easily provoked into an emotional outburst. One of the keys to a successful negotiation is patience. I waited to see if she would need to fill the silence. She did.

"That's an antique," she said. "A mint condition Heritage Classic Softail. Doesn't look like it has been ridden much. Are you an owner instead of a rider?"

I didn't answer, so she said, "You are one of those pussies who always plays it safe…watching from a safe distance while other people live their lives. I bet you'd enjoy watching me do your girlfriend while you two-finger that little wanger of yours. What do you say to a little girl-on-girl action?"

She cut her eyes to Padma and said, "You probably prefer the company of men. Is this teddy bear your biker bitch?"

Ginny crinkled her nose like she had just stepped into a construction crew's port-of-potty on a hot summer day. I wasn't sure if it was the idea of being raped by Slotter or the thought of seeing me with another man. But, I was glad she was showing signs of life.

We needed to get off this subject, so I finally spoke, "Did you go to all this trouble getting us here just to taunt us?"

"Glad to hear you're not a mute too," said Slotter.

From the corner of my eye, I caught a glimpse of movement on the warehouse rooftop. Hopefully, it was Uncle Jim and not one of Slotter's men.

"You got what you wanted," I said. "Let her go."

"Actually, I wanted all three of you here," said Slotter. "So thanks for cooperating and bringing me the monk."

I had no idea why she wanted all three of us. Sooner or later I knew she would get to the point, so I waited.

"Where is he, Padma," she asked.

Padma seemed to understand but, didn't answer Slotter.

"Who are you talking about?" I asked.

Slotter nodded toward Ginny.

"Why Barbie Doll's father of course."

CHAPTER 25

We are born into violence. Like a newborn forced from the womb and slapped on the ass, Ginny let loose a muffled wail that even the ball gag couldn't entirely suppress. Since she couldn't ask the question, I asked it for her.

"Is Ginny's father alive?" I asked.

That's pretty much when all hell broke loose. The Dragons stormed around the corner of the building, but it was nothing like a cavalry charge. Instead of a tight military formation, they were weaving in and out like amusement park bumper cars. I couldn't make much sense of the keystone cop strategy until the bikers suddenly scattered and came at us from multiple directions. They were trying to surround Slotter.

This was going to end badly and I wanted to get Ginny out of the line of fire. Slotter's men froze and nervously tracked the bikers' movements. I looked for a chance to rescue her. It wasn't going to be easy. Slotter's grip tightened on Ginny's upper arm and the barrel of her gun was pointed at my chest.

"You'll be the first one to die, pretty boy," shouted Slotter. "Wave 'em off."

"This isn't my doing," I said. "They're acting on their own and you brought this on yourself when you killed Tiny."

She was only confused for a moment before saying, "You must mean the fat-ass security guard at the Center."

I nodded.

"He was their president," I said.

"That wasn't me," she said with a shrug and a smirk.

"Right," I said.

"I guess that makes you the low hanging fruit," she said. "You're the easiest problem to deal with, so I might as well kill you now."

Suddenly, gunfire flashed from the rooftop and Slotter's weapon clattered to the ground. She had been well-trained. Instead of confusion, she reacted immediately by turning toward the rooftop and pulling Ginny in front of her to serve as a human shield. She pulled another gun from her waistband and jammed the barrel into Ginny's ear.

"Show yourself or I blow her brains out," shouted Slotter.

A man rose near the roof's edge. I expected to see Uncle Jim with his hands in the air, but instead of an eye patch I saw a long blond ponytail hanging midway down the back of a Bob Marley t-shirt. Geez it was Pony Tail. This guy seems to be everywhere.

"Both of you," demanded Slotter.

Uncle Jim slowly stood up next to Pony Tail. His sniper rifle was held high above his head. He looked thoroughly disgusted with himself.

"Toss the rifle," said Slotter.

Uncle Jim complied with Slotter's demand and threw his gun over the side of the building. As the rifle fell toward the ground, Slotter swept her gun toward Uncle Jim and was taking aim when a flash of color streaked past.

Bird gave no advance warning unless you want to count a squawk about death from above as he slashed the back of Slotter's head. She let go of Ginny while she desperately tried to snatch Bird out of the air.

That was the opening I was waiting for, but Scarface moved a split-second before me. I thought he was going to block my path to Slotter, but instead he grabbed Bird and began shaking him.

"Aaawk, do I look like shake n' bake to you," screamed Bird.

Scarface stopped shaking for a moment and looked at Bird like he was some kind of alien. Then, he grabbed Bird's head with one hand and his body with the other as if he was going to wring his neck. I wouldn't have believed Padma could move that swiftly, but in the blink of an eye, he closed the gap between them and did some weird two finger typewriting thing over Scarface's body.

The thug appeared more annoyed than concerned by Padma's martial display. He snorted and rolled his eyes just before his limbs began shaking. The shakes only lasted a moment before his eyes rolled completely back, displaying nothing but white.

Scarface was a big man, but it seemed like the life had been sucked out him. He shrunk a size or two before collapsing in on himself and slowly crumbling to the ground. His death grip on Bird held and the foul mouth macaw disappeared somewhere under Scarface's massive body. I knew Bird could not possibly have survived that.

Slotter shrieked like a girl when Scarface collapsed. She swung her shooting hand in Padma's direction and would have blown a hole in his chest, but Ms. Dom caught her forearm with the whip and gave it a yank as she rode past her.

If it were anybody but Slotter, she would have been pulled to the ground and drug behind the bike like a bunch of wedding day tin cans. Her gun clattered to the ground, but Slotter managed to coil her arm around the whip a few rounds and give a yank. The Harley wobbled and changed course.

Ms. Dom tumbled from the wayward Harley just before it crashed into the side of the warehouse and exploded into flames. Amazon Chick broke rank and rushed to the aid of Ms. Dom, who lay in a crumbled heap of leather on the broken asphalt. The flames from the burning bike reached the building and it lit up like a match. Uncle Jim would soon be engulfed in flames.

Ginny took advantage of the distraction by inching back and creating space between her and Slotter. I had been so focused on Slotter that I didn't notice the bikers had closed ranks and dismounted.

I wanted to put more distance between the two groups and Ole' George provided the means when he reached for his gun. Somehow he managed to dislodge the bottle of bourbon and it shattered at his feet. That's when all the shooting really got started.

There's nothing like the sound of gunfire to make a man painfully aware that he isn't carrying a firearm. I'd like to tell you it makes me a bigger man than the bad guys with guns, but it just made me feel stupid and vulnerable.

While my attention was on the blazing building, Slotter must have scooped her gun up because, once again, it was pointing at my chest. I knew I was about to die. I watched helplessly as her trigger finger squeezed. Time slowed. I saw the bullet leave the gun barrel. It would have killed me, but Ginny dove into its path and took the bullet intended for me.

Maybe it was rage or maybe I had nothing left to lose. Either way, something shifted inside me. The space between seeing what needed to be done and taking action disappeared. While Slotter stood in shock, I closed the gap between us and disarmed her with the simplest of moves. In one continuous action the gun was out of her hand and in mine. I wasted no time in pointing it at her face and would have pulled the trigger, but I was knocked to the ground.

I fell facing Ginny. She lay in a puddle of blood a few feet from me. Her eyes were closed, and I saw no signs of respiration. She was pale, very pale. I stretched a bloody hand in her direction, but she was just out of my reach. I wanted to get up and go to her, but there was a disconnection between thought and action.

I felt tired and was about to close my eyes when I heard sirens. I can't be sure, but I may have heard a scream come from the burning building. The sounds seemed so far away.

Faint red and blue shadows told me fire and police were already here. Rose was the first officer I saw. She was rushing in our direction. I was thinking how glad I was she would be the one to help Ginny, when I noticed her lips were moving. She was speaking but I couldn't quite make out the words, so I focused as hard as I could to read her lips.

I can't be sure, but it looked like she was saying, "You fucking bitch, you killed my daughter."

That's when I saw the gun in her hand...the one she shoved into Slotter's belly before pulling the trigger. As Slotter sunk to her knees, other uniformed policemen rushed in and disarmed Rose. They were gentle with her and held her as she quietly sobbed.

The last thing I saw before everything went black was Mr. Medals. He intercepted Slotter's gurney just before it reached an ambulance. Words were spoken. He flashed some sort of identification to the medics and then soldiers loaded Slotter onto a military helicopter.

I came to in a hospital room. A flat panel television hanging on the wall was tuned to CNN. The sound was turned down, but I could see a graphic reporting a tragedy in Kentucky. It said a gas leak killed 3,212 people gathered to hear Padma Ganesha speak about the happiest place on Earth.

A toilet flushed and Eric walked out of the bathroom. All of the events of the last few days came flooding back to me. I was overwhelmed with anger and sadness. Ginny, Uncle Jim, Bird, all gone.

"Hey buddy," said Eric. "I knew it would take more than a bullet in the back to keep you down."

I nodded toward the television and said, "That's not what happened."

The smile left Eric's face and was replaced with a pinched brow. He opened his mouth to speak, but then changed his mind and bit his lip instead. It wasn't like Eric to not speak his mind, but what was there to say. My whole world had been turned upside down in one fell-swoop and I had no idea why.

"Grant, we've all been so worried about you," said Eric.

In that moment, I made up my mind that someone would pay for my loss, but that's not what I said to Eric.

"I'll be fine," I said.

"That's the spirit," said Eric.

"We need to find out why they took Slotter," I said. "I'm sure it's connected to the mass murder at the Center."

Eric sat in the side chair and began rubbing his hands up and down his pant legs. He stood up and glanced around the room, without focusing on anything in particular, before looking at me and sitting down again.

I knew I had been shot and only God knows what pain medicine was coursing through my body, but Eric sure was acting weird. Then it hit me. I hadn't seen him at the warehouse when all the shooting was going on.

"I needed your help during this fight, where were you?" I asked.

He sat there for the longest time without answering.

Finally, he said, "She's upstairs in ICU."

"Really...that's a shock," I said. "I thought I saw them whisk her away to some secret location. I need to see her Eric. Get me up there."

"There's someone you need to see first," said Eric. "I'll be right back."

"Is it Uncle Jim?" I asked. "Is Bird with him?"

"I'm sorry," said Eric as he stepped out the door.

I felt myself deflate again. They were gone. Slotter had taken everything from me. They were all dead...every one of them. There was nothing left for me. I was all alone again, just like I'd always feared. Well, I was tired of coping with loss. I was going to do something about this. I needed to get upstairs and wasn't about to wait on Eric. Slotter was going to pay now.

I pulled the IV from my arm and rolled sideways enough to get my feet on the floor. The last thing I remember thinking was that the A/C must be broken.

I heard a familiar voice, but couldn't quite place it. It was hard work, but I managed to open my eyes. The face finally connected to the voice. It was Professor Filmore, my attorney.

"He's finally awake," said Filmore.

I heard a second voice, less familiar. It took a moment, but I finally connected it to Mr. Medals.

"You need to make him understand," said Mr. Medals. "If not then..."

Filmore made a small cutting motion with his hand that stopped Mr. Medals from finishing his sentence. I didn't like the implicit threat in Mr. Medals' voice. I figured he wanted to protect Slotter, and if I didn't cooperate with Mr. Medals, then what? I wanted to keep things light, but my voice was little higher than normal when I spoke.

"Got myself shot, Admiral," I said.

He managed a half-hearted smile that wasn't consistent with the shake of his head. It was odd. I couldn't imagine Filmore displaying such openly conflicted body language.

"This is a tough situation you're in," said the Admiral.

I don't know about you, but that's not what I wanted to hear from my attorney. He should have told me that he had worked his legal magic and that I could rest easy. Besides, why was he with the Mr. Medals? I did not like it one bit.

"Have you cleared me of the charges?" I asked.

"That depends on you," said Filmore.

"Either the charges are dropped, or not," I said. "Which is it?"

"The gas leak explanation for what occurred at the Center is necessary for national security," said Filmore. "There are nuances to this cover story that protect you. Without it, you will be the prime suspect for Tiny's murder and for the murders of everyone at the Center."

"What about Slotter," I asked.

"She plays a vital role in our plans for national security," said Mr. Medals. "You do not."

I knew I was screwed if I openly opposed them, so I said, "I understand."

Filmore raised an eyebrow, but said nothing. He motioned Mr. Medals toward the door and led him out of the room. I waited a few minutes for them to clear the area and, then, swung my feet to the floor. This time I would hold it together long-enough to repay Slotter for what she did to me.

I blocked the pain. I blocked everything that stood in my way. My sole focus was on taking one step at a time. Little by little, step by step, I made my way down the hall to the elevator and to the intensive care unit.

Once I reached ICU, I assumed she would be protected in a guarded room, but saw no guards. My next thought was they may be in the room with her, so I cautiously stuck my head in a few doors, but none of them was Slotter's room. I was beginning to doubt I'd find her, but continued looking.

Finally, I saw a nurse dressed in blue scrubs hovering over a patient who might be her. I was about to duck around the corner and wait for the nurse to leave when I noticed he was wearing sandals. There was something familiar about those sandals, and while I searched my memory, I let my eyes drift over the rest of the nurse's body. The blond ponytail gave him away.

I should have kept my mouth shut. What did I care if Pony Tail wanted revenge against Slotter. I couldn't, of course. Such was the pain of my loss.

"Take your hands off her," I said. "She's mine."

When he turned to face me, I think what surprised me the most was how open Pony Tail seemed. There was nothing adversarial about him. He wasn't guarded. He didn't look like he was buried under the weight of many secrets. He seemed authentic. His smile was real. Go figure.

Pony Tail took a step to the side, and with a graceful sweep of the arm, invited me to claim my prize. A part of me wanted to remain cautious, to expect some kind of trick, but I didn't listen to that voice. If I had, who knows what dark turn the moment might have taken. Instead, my feet led me to Ginny's side. Her cheeks were rosy. Her chest rose and fell with a strong breath. And then her eyes opened.

CHAPTER 26

An instant turns into the tragedy of a lifetime when a bullet tears a pinky sized hole into the forehead of the woman you love. It is especially painful when you've spent a lifetime ignoring her. I allowed a single tear to follow the path of least resistance to the corner of my mouth, before wiping it with the tip of the tongue. Savoring the slight burn from the salt, I thought about the kind of man who treats a woman the way I've treated her. It wasn't flattering. There were reasons, of course, but I knew they didn't justify my behavior. I deserved all the pain it caused me, but I wasn't so sure about the joy that came from seeing her still alive.

I tried to remember if I've ever shed tears of joy. No luck there. It's not as if my life has been bankrupt of happiness. I've had my moments. Maybe not enough of them by my reckoning, but some. If I was going to be honest with myself, it's possible I've had more than my share of tragedy, but a life without joy would indeed be a miserable existence.

I've been such a idiot, but there's one thing I know for sure, I've been given a second chance and I'm going to do better. Ginny is alive. I don't know how, but she is alive. Somehow she survived the gun shot and still looks radiant. By comparison, I feel like I've been kicked by an ornery mule.

Ginny doesn't need the clothes her company designs to make her beautiful. Even in a flimsy hospital gown, she is stunning. Tall and athletic, her flawless legs led the eye upward toward a tight little behind, while waves of soft dark brown hair fell gracefully onto her broad swimmer's shoulders spotted with a few freckles despite her olive skin tone.

Her eyes sparkle with life. Even though I've known her as long as I can remember, I find their color difficult to pinpoint. It is an unusual shade of blue or green that is best described as the color of a tropical sea.

The rest of Ginny's face is equally magnificent. She has an aristocratic high bridged nose set between wide cheekbones that narrow into a high forehead. It is a beautiful face that is enhanced with the flush of radiant good health. You might even say all true beauty is a reflection of good health.

As happy as I was to see her like this, I thought I might be hallucinating. The last time I saw her she was lying in a pool of her own blood, pale and lifeless. Yet now I find her in a hospital bed, the model of good health. How the hell is that possible?

"You're alive," said Ginny.

I shook my head as if that would wipe away any illusions. Still, there was no mistaking her musical voice. It was time to test the waters.

"You died," I murmured.

"I knew Slotter was going to pull the trigger before she did," said Ginny. "Everything happened so slowly. When the hammer fell I only had one thought…deflect that bullet. I knew, without a doubt, I could do it…but I failed."

Kim Slotter was a war hero gone bad. She had kidnapped Ginny and held her at an abandoned warehouse in the wrong end of town. I took a ragtag group and tried to rescue her, but the heroic deed went south and we were shot by the bad guys.

"You succeeded in deflecting the bullet, but that shot was intended for me, not you," I said.

Ginny absentmindedly massaged the spot just above her heart. Without thinking I mirrored her movement and felt the bandages covering the exit wound. I was lucky. If the bullet had been slightly lower it would have killed me.

"You're wounded," she said. "I failed."

She thought only of protecting me and damn near got herself killed doing it. Without thinking, I gathered her into my arms and held her tight.

I had never done anything so rash in my life and had a moment where I thought maybe I had overstepped a boundary between us. The moment of doubt passed when Ginny melted into me like she had been there a thousand times before.

"You did not fail," I said. "It wasn't Slotter who did this to me. I was shot in the back by one of her minions."

The brush with death opened my eyes to a few things. Introspection has an annoying way of doing that. The thing that hurt the most as we lay together in an expanding puddle of blood was the regret.

I couldn't understand why I had ignored Ginny all of those years. None of the reasons that once seemed adequate withstood the test of final judgment as we faced death together.

After the wave of grief passed, I wiped the tears from her shoulder and reminded myself that somehow she was miraculously alive and well. The grief was replaced with self-doubt. She couldn't still be alive. I must be dreaming, or worse, experiencing a psychotic break.

Neither was acceptable and I was thinking of giving myself a good hard pinch, when our tender moment was interrupted by a disapproving voice.

"What do you think you're doing?"

A young nurse with a fake smile plastered across her face stormed into the room. Her dirty blond hair had been hastily smoothed back, leaving a few stubborn strands that refused to comply. Instead, they curled around a flushed cheek, as testament to her refusal to follow the straight and narrow. On the opposite side of her face, a streak of dark mascara ran a quarter-inch from the corner of her left eye.

She was dressed in rumpled surgical scrubs and the buttons on her top were out of alignment. She smelled of sweat from a quick tryst in some dark corner of the hospital.

Her name tag identified her as Nurse Nightshade. She was trying hard to be perky, but failed miserably. I had the sense Nurse Nightshade was trained to be upbeat, but it didn't come naturally to her. It was obvious she wasn't pleased with me.

"This patient is in critical condition," she said coldly. "I'm going to change her bandage and afterwards you need to leave so she can get some rest."

For someone charged with patient care, she was shockingly unobservant. She hadn't once looked at Ginny and seemed content to glare at me instead.

I nodded toward Ginny. Nurse Nightshade followed my eyes. At first she didn't seem to register what was in front of her, but when it finally sunk in that Ginny was the model of good health, she muffled a small scream with her hand.

"That's impossible," gasped Nurse Nightshade. "She's at death's door and Doctor Wiemp doesn't expect her to make it through the night."

It irked me that she gave more weight to what the Doctor said than what her own eyes revealed about Ginny's condition. Clearly, she was not at death's door. Ginny was alive and well.

I wanted to point this out to her, but resisted the temptation.

Instead I asked, "How do you explain it then...a miracle maybe?"

Nurse Nightshade ignored my question. Instead she made the sign of the cross, as if that would somehow protect her from something she didn't understand. I can't be certain, but I think I also heard her whisper something about God's own miracle.

I wasn't serious about the miracle comment, but that didn't seem to matter much to her. Once she completed the religious rituals, her nurses' training took over and she busied herself with Ginny's bandage.

At first she seemed hesitant, as if she feared what lay beneath it. Her fear didn't last long before she made up her mind to do her job and began to slowly remove the blood crusted dressing.

While she fussed with the bandage, I turned to ask Pony Tail what he knew about Ginny's condition, but he was nowhere in sight. Weird, I thought. He had been dressed in nurse's scrubs and hovering over Ginny when I walked into the room a few minutes earlier. I sure didn't hear him leave.

"Maybe the other nurse knows what happened to Ginny," I said to Nurse Nightshade.

Her attention was on the bandage and I wasn't sure if she heard me at first. I was about to repeat it when she finally answered.

"I'm the only one working this shift," she said.

"There was a male nurse in here a few minutes ago," I said.

Since she ignored me, I added a description of Pony Tail to give her memory a boost.

"He's in his mid-twenties, medium height, brown skin, and blond hair," I said.

I still didn't get a response from her, so I lamely continued with the description in the hopes something would register with her.

"He wears his hair long, but tied back in a ponytail," I said. "You can't miss him."

Nurse Nightshade was rude, but she was also working so I didn't take it personally. Besides, her focus was on carefully removing Ginny's bandages and I didn't want to distract her. It almost felt random when she finally responded with a shake of her head.

"There's no one like that here," she said.

I gave up on Pony Tail and chalked it up as one more strange mystery to follow-up at a later time.

While the nurse fussed with the bandages I took a moment to look around the room. Hospital rooms are places where I put on horse blinders, since it's best not to see too much. The rooms tend to be stark and filled with unpleasant odors. For the most part, Ginny's room was no exception. However, it did have one interesting feature that drew my eye.

An odd picture hung on the wall next to the bathroom. Most art work in hospital rooms is virtually invisible, but this one caught my eye. It was a wreath, but I saw something odd hidden in its design. I could very clearly see a snake eating a bird. It appeared to be the same symbol vandals painted on Ch'ing's wall.

Ch'ing is my martial arts teacher who mysteriously disappeared a few days ago. When we searched his house for him, we found it had been vandalized. For some unknown reason, they had spray painted the snake eating bird symbol on the wall along with the message, "It has begun."

Nurse Nightshade removed the last of the bandages and gasped. Since she was obstructing my view, I craned my neck to see around her, but still couldn't see a thing.

I wasn't sure what to expect. I know I saw Slotter blow a hole in her forehead and a sick part of me wanted that hole to be there, so I wouldn't have to face the possibility I was crazy. The rest of me wanted Ginny's forehead to be as smooth as a baby's butt.

When Nurse Nightshade finally shifted positions, what I saw was a bit of dried blood that she wiped away. Where there was once a hole the size of my little finger, now there was only smooth healthy skin. There was no evidence Ginny had suffered an injury.

I was relieved for sure, but now I doubted my memory of the events at the warehouse. Was Ginny really taken by an ex-special forces renegade and held hostage in a warehouse in West Louisville?

A group of us went to rescue her, but all hell broke loose. I was shot. Ginny was shot. The only family I had left was trapped on the roof of a burning building. I don't know how Uncle Jim could have survived those flames. Oh…and my crazy macaw, Bird, went down underneath a tank of a man.

The only person I care about who managed to get through it unharmed was my best friend, Eric. When I awoke in the hospital, I found him sitting at my bedside. It should have been comforting, but Eric was behaving strangely. He seemed worried about more than recent events, but wouldn't say what it was.

Then it got even weirder when my attorney, showed up with a Marine Colonel in tow. The Colonel is in charge of some hush-hush military investigation involving Slotter, the special forces renegade who shot Ginny.

They offered me a deal to avoid prosecution for two murders I didn't commit. One of the dead men was my boss, John Biggs, who was found hanging from the chandelier in his posh corner office after he got a call from a federal prosecutor.

I'm a lawyer, by the way. At least I was before the firm placed me on unpaid leave. A spendthrift spouse and strangling medical bills for my mother's long term healthcare have left me broke. So, I took a job working as a body guard for a monk named Padma Ganesha.

He wrote a bestselling book about the happiest place on Earth. Ginny somehow persuaded him to travel to Louisville and speak at a lecture series called, "Ideas to Change the World." It was held in an auditorium on Louisville's waterfront called, the Center. When I arrived, I found the security guard with a knife buried in his chest.

The evening went from bad to worse after Pony Tail started shooting. Thirty-two hundred peace loving hippies fought their way to the exits, only to find themselves locked inside. They are all dead now. According to the news reports, there was a gas leak, but I was told by the Marine Colonel the gas leak is a cover story.

For some reason, the military wanted to cover up the truth and offered me immunity to keep quiet about what really happened. The deal was a huge insult to my intelligence. Even though I was in no mood to allow myself to be controlled by some military goon, I went along with it to get rid of them.

As soon as the Colonel left my room, I slipped out in the hopes of finding Slotter in the intensive care unit recovering from her own gunshot wounds. Following Slotter's arrest, a police detective stuck a pistol in her belly and pulled the trigger. The Jack Ruby moment was motivated by vengeance for the death of the detective's daughter at the Center.

Slotter had made a few enemies and we all wanted her dead, but it was beginning to look like she was under the protection of the same Colonel who was trying to hush up what really happened at the Center.

Instead of Slotter, I found Ginny alive and well in the intensive care unit. I thought for sure she was dead and now I was beginning to doubt my own memory of what happened. It was inconceivable that she took a bullet to the head and survived, let alone healed so quickly. At least it was inconceivable to a sane person.

I shook off the self-doubt. Something was amiss, but if Ginny survived by some unknown miracle, then maybe, just maybe, Uncle Jim and Bird also survived. I could only hope, but for now I wanted to focus on what was right in front of me. Ginny was alive and that was huge.

Neither the nurse nor I knew what to say in response to the sight of her perfectly healed wound. It was Ginny who broke the silence.

"My father is still alive and I'm going to find him," said Ginny. "Will you help me, Grant?"

Ginny's father had disappeared years ago. For some reason, Slotter thought he was still alive and that's why she kidnapped Ginny. In some weird way, it must have given Ginny hope. I didn't think for a minute the man was still alive after all this time, but I wanted to be with Ginny and she wanted to search for him.

"Of course I will," I answered. "Where do you want to begin?"

"Brazil…he was last seen boarding a small plane for a tour of the Amazon Rainforest," answered Ginny without hesitation. "We'll begin there."

"That's a long time for someone to be missing," I said.

"I've never given up hope that my father is alive," she said. "One of the many reasons I opened a factory in Brazil was to pick up where the police left off with their investigation into his disappearance."

"What did they tell you?" I asked.

"Only that he charted a small plane and it never returned," she said.

"Where was it chartered?" I asked.

"Manaus, at the mouth of the Amazon," she answered.

"The Amazon Rainforest is huge," I said. "Do you know where he was headed?"

She shrugged.

"Nobody seems to know," said Ginny.

Something was bothering me about this story, but I couldn't quite put my finger on it. There were pieces of the puzzle missing and I had a nagging feeling I knew something about them.

"Do they know where the plane went down?" I asked.

"No," answered Ginny. "They spent a few days looking for the wreckage, but soon gave up when it couldn't be spotted from the air."

"Do you have plan?" I asked.

She nodded, but before she could answer, the nurse hit the emergency call button.

"You don't just walk out of ICU," barked Nurse Nightshade. "You're not going anywhere until Dr. Wiemp releases you."

Ginny stiffened. She looked like she was about to give the nurse a piece of her mind. I don't know about Ginny, but I don't like to be told what I can or can't do, especially by a stranger.

Still, no good ever comes from an unnecessary confrontation over something that is easily resolved. It was time for diplomacy, but before I could speak, Ginny snapped at the nurse.

"I'm not your prisoner," said Ginny.

Nurse Nightshade puffed her flat chest out as far as it would go.

"Rules are rules," she said. "You have to see the Doctor first."

"Not if she doesn't want to," I said. "As you can see, she's in perfect health."

The nurse shook her head.

"Who are you and what are you doing in my ICU outside of visiting hours?" she demanded.

Her attitude stunned me. It was time to kick it up a notch, so I extended my hand to her.

"My name is Grant Li, Attorney-at-Law," I said. "This woman does not need your permission to leave. Surely it's not your intention to hold her against her will."

Nurse Nightshade shrank from the extended hand, as if it held a poisonous snake. She opened her mouth to speak, but then abruptly shut it again. I think she was accustomed to patients following orders and our rebellion unbalanced her.

Between my martial arts training and law practice, I know a fighter when I see one. Nurse Nightshade was a fighter and wasn't about to lose a conflict with a couple of patients. She shifted her focus to the hospital gown I wore and somehow managed to regain her sense of power.

"You are a patient in this hospital and there is blood seeping from your bandages," said the nurse. "Let's get you back to your room before you hurt yourself."

I wasn't feeling my best and the bed rest she offered was tempting, but her tone annoyed me. I was about to say something I might regret when I heard footsteps outside of the door.

An arrogant voice barked a little too loudly, "This better be a real emergency."

A wave of relief passed over Nurse Nightshade's face. She could now pass the torch to someone else and that somebody happened to be wearing a name tag that identified him as, Jonathan Wiemp, M.D.

Dr. Wiemp was tall, but seemed much shorter thanks to a pronounced stoop. In addition to the stoop, he had a sag in the back of his neck that reminded me of a cartoon vulture I had seen one Saturday morning years ago.

In sharp contrast to an exceptionally pointed chin, he had a wide forehead with four rows of deep wrinkles spread across it. Thinning hair and grayish skin, gave him a haggard look.

It didn't get any better as you moved downward. A pot belly pushed the waist band of his slacks to the max. I didn't get a sense that the doctor took very good care of himself.

I guessed he was much younger than he appeared, but his clothes didn't help him look his age. They were old fashioned and added to his antique appearance. From the faded bow tie, to the heavily worn wing tip shoes, he looked like he had been wearing the same outfit since 1958.

Nurse Nightshade must have seen something different in Dr. Wiemp, because she never once took her doe eyed gaze from him. On the other hand, Dr. Wiemp hardly looked at her. My feelings about her softened considerably when I realized it would eventually end badly for her.

"This patient wants to leave, Doctor," said the nurse.

Dr. Wiemp scowled over the top of black rimmed glasses at Ginny. Leaving was not part of his prognosis. He expected her to be dead by morning. I saw something else in his face. This arrogant man disliked being wrong and found her recovery insulting.

"No one is leaving," said Dr. Wiemp in a raspy voice that told me he was a heavy smoker.

I had one of those random moments we all have from time to time. For some odd reason, Dr. Wiemp's statement reminded me of the title to Jim Morrison's biography, "No One Here Gets Out Alive." The disturbing comparison was all I needed to abandon diplomacy and shift into full blown lawyer mode.

"Unless you step aside and allow her to leave, you will be prosecuted to the fullest extent of the law for false imprisonment," I said to Dr. Wiemp.

He looked me up and down before digging a hand into his pocket and pulling out a smartphone. He punched in a call and waited impatiently.

"We have a problem," he said into the phone. "Send security."

"Has everyone gone completely insane?" asked Ginny.

"This is ridiculous," I agreed. "We're leaving."

I took Ginny's hand and gently pulled her to her feet. At first, she submitted, but then looked down at her clothes. I followed her eyes. She was wearing one of those awful hospital gowns that invariably expose the patient's behind. In most instances, it's a behind I'd rather not look at, but as Ginny cut a path to the closet I enjoyed a lingering look at a backside that was flawless in a Barbie doll sort of way.

I had seen her in a bikini a few days earlier and hungered for more. I watched as she stuffed her things into a bag and grabbed my hand again.

As we headed to the door, I caught a glimpse of the nurse's hateful glare. She quickly cut her jealous eyes to Dr. Wiemp, who was standing in the door blocking our way. He didn't show any signs of yielding.

I looked straight into his eyes and with dead calm said, "You need to step aside, now."

Dr. Wiemp's arrogance seemed to dissipate. For the first time, he was unsure of himself. His eyes faltered and his gaze dropped to his feet as he stepped aside. I led Ginny into the hall where we ran smack into two huge security guards.

Dr. Wiemp's arrogance returned as he barked, "Take this man to the psychological services unit and put him in restraints."

Of all the things he could have said, Dr. Wiemp managed to say the only thing that could send me over the edge. Raw terror pushed me into berserker mode. In keeping with my training, I savagely attacked the biggest guard first, delivering multiple blows to his vital points within the first three seconds.

He was out cold and on his way to the ground when I disarmed the second security guard and pressed the 45 to his temple. I would have pulled the trigger too, but I heard something in Ginny's voice that pulled me from the brink.

"Oh, my God!" said Ginny. "Grant, no…please don't!"

Her voice saved the guard's life and it saved me from doing something that would have haunted me for the rest of my life. In the face of what might have been my hands started shaking uncontrollably. When I turned to Ginny, I was crushed by what I saw in her eyes. I wanted to explain and took a deep breath to gather myself, but felt something stab me in the neck and then I was out cold.

CHAPTER 27

My throat was dry. I tried to swallow. Nothing happened. Panicked, I tried again and again without success. I was suffocating. That would end it for sure.

"He's waking up," said a man with a kind voice.

A woman with a hard edge to her voice said, "Good, prep him for his therapy session."

"Are you sure he can handle it?" asked the man. "He's not very strong."

"If you want to keep your job nurse, you will never presume to question me again," snarled the woman.

"Yes doctor," he said.

The woman scared me. Still, a part of me was curious about the nurse. His voice was kind. I wanted to open my eyes so I could get a look at him, but they were clinched tight and refused to budge.

Everything was dark. I heard footsteps. A door opened and shut.

The man said, "Don't be afraid young man, it will be over soon."

He loosened the straps restraining my arms and rubbed my wrists to get the circulation going. The massage moved to my legs. The doctor's hands were different from his. Hers were hard and cold, but his were gentle and warm.

"Can we walk today?" he asked.

I wanted to answer him, but couldn't. It wasn't safe. Better to stay inside…away from people, especially the Fat Lady. I needed to stay away from her. She wanted to hurt me. It was her fault I was in this terrible place where bad people hurt me. There wasn't anyone I could trust.

Strong arms moved me from the warm hospital bed to a cold gurney.

"Should we open our eyes today?" asked the man.

I vigorously shook my head. I didn't want to see the terrible things they were about to do to me.

The nurse used his fingers to comb my hair back. When he finished, he paused a moment before pushing the gurney out the door and down the hall toward the therapy room. At least that's what they called it. After the first therapy session it was the "Bad Place" to me.

The Bad Place smelled like burnt hair and pee. I shivered from the cold…and the fear. The doctor ordered me to be still. Her voice echoed slightly in the cavernous room. I knew what she would do to me if I didn't comply and willed myself still. I hoped the goose bumps had the good sense to cooperate too.

I resisted the urge to scream as Sadistic Doctor strapped me to a cold narrow table. Next she taped electrodes to my forehead and ordered me to open my mouth wide, but then didn't give me a chance to comply before roughly jamming a mouth plug between my teeth.

"The meds interfere with the therapy, so we'll skip them," she said. "You are a broken little boy who needs the full treatment. Still, I don't have any hope that it will work for the likes of you."

That's what she always said right before she sent electricity jolting through me. The doctor said it wouldn't hurt, but it did. It hurt so bad I wanted to die…tried to die, but death never came. Instead, I'd shake real bad and then pass out. I know that's what I did, because she told me. It made her mad when I didn't stay awake, but I didn't care.

I awoke in a cold sweat. Slowly, I opened my eyes and looked around. The room was different…more modern than before, but I knew I was back there again. This time I wanted to see my tormentors…to look them in the eye and let them see I was unafraid.

The door opened and a determined looking woman stepped inside. I caught a glimpse of Dr. Wiemp in the hall. He was talking in low tones to a short, balding man wearing an Italian designer suit that must have cost a small fortune.

It was a different suit, but I'd recognize Mr. Suit anywhere. I bumped into him in the hallway of my law office and sent him sliding across the polished marble floor like an air hockey puck. Moments later, I discovered my boss gasping for his last breath while hanging by the neck from a tacky chandelier. What was he doing here?

The door closed and a shadow filled its place. The dark woman was topped with witchy black hair and matching circles around her eyes. She had tried to fill the deep craggy lines in her face with makeup, and then tried to offset the paleness with rouge painted on her cheeks and lips. The end result was hideous.

She wore the same sensible shoes I remembered from twenty years ago….square toed, black patent leather, laced up and tied with a perfect little bow. Dark pantyhose covered chicken legs sticking out of the bottom of a straight black skirt that hung exactly two inches below the knee.

Her white lab coat was the only thing she wore that wasn't black. Even it was somehow dominated by the top of the black pen sticking out of her pocket and the black and chrome stethoscope hanging around her neck. The name tag pinned to her lab coat identified her as "Doctor." I would have added the word, "Sadistic," but that's just my opinion.

Sadistic Doctor had aged thirty in the last twenty, but it was still the same hateful face I saw gloating over me. I was back in hell, but this time I was a full-grown man. Stronger than before and I wasn't about to show this bitch any fear.

"I always knew you'd be back," said Sadistic Doctor. "We never finished your treatment plan and look what it got us…two innocent men savagely attacked."

All the rage buried inside of me came to the surface. I wanted to hurt her like she once hurt me. The only thing that kept me from her throat was the restraints tied to my wrists and ankles. Restraints or not, I tried to break free.

"He has learned to rattle the cage," she mocked.

I glared at her and said, "I'm not a helpless little boy anymore."

Something in my eyes gave her a moment's pause. As she pondered what she saw, the door opened and Mr. Suit walked into the room. Sadistic Doctor reluctantly pulled her cold eyes from her prey and gave the intruder a slight nod of recognition.

There was a subtle change in her demeanor, as well. Mr. Suit's body language told me he was accustomed to being in charge and the scowl on Sadistic Doctor's face was all I needed to know she didn't like it one bit. He made a dismissive movement with his hand. She looked as if she might argue the point with him, but then seemed to think better of it and left the room in a huff.

"Who are you?" I asked.

For a moment, it looked like he might tell me, but then he gave a small shake of the head and changed the subject.

"I want to assure you," said Mr. Suit, "that we will keep you here as long as necessary."

"You won't be able to hold me more than seventy-two hours," I said. "When I get out, you will regret this."

He smirked.

"How do you know we haven't already kept you strapped to that table for weeks?" he asked.

That gave me reason to pause. I had no way of knowing how long they had kept me drugged and unconscious. There should have been a quick hearing before a Judge, but I sure didn't remember one.

"What do you want from me?" I asked.

"First, we want you to return the confidential files you stole from us," he answered.

I didn't expect that answer and had no idea what he was talking about. I didn't have what Mr. Suit wanted, but maybe I could use this to my advantage. I wasn't exactly sure how, but I decided to string him along for the time being.

"I'm not sure what you're talking about," I said.

Mr. Suit stroked his power tie. It looked to me like he was choosing his next words very carefully.

"We know you have our property," he said. "If you return it, we will reward you. If you keep it, then we will hurt you until you break. Once you are broken, you will give us our property and the only reward you'll get is all the pain you needlessly suffered."

His threats didn't scare me. I had endured electroshock treatments as a small boy and figured I could handle them now.

I now knew that these files were the real reason I was tied to this hospital bed and they were willing to torture me to recover them. It was time to find out what else I could learn from Mr. Suit.

"You said the first thing you wanted was your confidential files," I said. "What else do you want?"

"We want to know where he is hiding," said Mr. Suit.

This was the second time in the last few days that the bad guys used extreme measures to find someone. The last time it happened, Kim Slotter, was looking for Ginny's father. That did not end well.

"Who are you talking about?" I asked.

"Your little girlfriend's father," he answered.

I wasn't sure how her father was connected to all of this, but the bad guys seemed to be willing to do anything to find him. Warfare is about deception. It's best to keep your enemies guessing as long as possible. I decided to play dumb and keep Mr. Suit guessing about me. Besides, I didn't want these people to ever think they could use Ginny as leverage against me.

"I'm a married man," I said.

"Don't play me, Mr. Li," he said. "We both know your marriage has tanked and now you're seeing Virginia Bardough."

"She's an old friend," I said. "She's certainly not my girlfriend. Other than a few days ago, I hadn't seen her for years."

"Where's her father?" demanded Mr. Suit.

"He's dead," I answered. "Why are you searching for a dead man?"

Before he could answer, the door burst open and Eric stormed in.

Pushing Mr. Suit aside, he said, "Get out of the way fat boy. I'm taking Grant and we're leaving this God forsaken place."

Eric and I have been friends since we were kids running barefoot all summer. We went to the same school, played football, and even studied martial arts together. We were more like brothers than anything and always had each other's backs. Boy was I ever glad to see him.

If Mr. Suit was surprised to see Eric storm into the room, he didn't show it. Instead, he puffed out his chest and demanded that Eric leave immediately or he would have him arrested.

In response to the threat, Eric quickly closed the gap between them and crushed Mr. Suit with a hard right hand to the jaw. Mr. Suit had one of those square chins you see on tough guys in Hollywood films. The jaw shattered like cheap glass and his arrogant eyes rolled back an instant before he crumbled unconscious to the floor.

Eric loves a good fight, but the easy victory over Mr. Suit hardly qualified. Still, the way Eric gloated over his limp body reminded me of Muhammad Ali towering over Sonny Liston. For some reason he seemed to take special pleasure in kicking Mr. Suit's butt. I have to admit, it felt good to see that happen, but I think it would have been better if it had been the Sadistic Doctor instead…woman or not.

When it dawned on Eric that Mr. Suit was hardly worth gloating over, he turned to me and said, "Damn, don't you look freaky…all strapped down and submissive like."

He must of seen I was in no mood for jokes, because he quickly added, "The straps look tight, but you could stand to do some work on the submissive part."

"Unstrap me," I growled.

"Awe, lighten up dude," said Eric.

It is hard to be upset with Eric for long. His good nature is genuine and he wears it on his sleeve like a proud trademark. Take his shit eating grin, for example. It says in no uncertain terms he could care less what you think of him.

In addition to his winning smile, it doesn't hurt that Eric is blessed with classic

Hollywood good looks and a male stripper's body. Chicks love him. Frankly, I can't see what all the fuss is about, but that might just be me.

Eric is one of those friendly fun loving guys that everybody loves. When you couple his winning personality with pretty-boy good looks, it's not hard to understand why he's usually surrounded by a crowd of groupies...mostly female.

Even though women of all ages are forever hitting on me, I'm no ladies man. Casual is just not my thing. I'm looking for depth and that isn't as easy to find as you might think. So many of these women just seem to be looking for one thing and it's not my heart.

Their approach varies in the details, but the thrust of it is always the same. They open with a lame line like, "I always wanted to get me a big hunk of yummy chocolate, like you," and then it goes downhill from there.

Hell, I'm not even full blooded African-American. You might say I'm an all American mutt...a mix of several diverse blood lines, including Chinese, African-American, and a good measure of U.S. Grant...the dead President on the fifty dollar bill.

I sighed. Eric grinned.

"Let's get you home where you're free to engage in all kinds of kinkiness," he said.

"Not my thing," I said.

"I'm just trying to help a friend get over a bad marriage," he said.

"What I need right now is to get out this place," I said.

"That we can do," said Eric.

"I'm not leaving without Ginny," I said. "Let's go get her."

Eric's demeanor changed radically. Suddenly, everything in the room was more interesting than me. He was hiding something and I was in no mood to pry it out of him.

"What is it now, Eric?" I asked.

He recognized my tone of voice and abandoned his usual irreverent attitude. He cleared his throat, started to speak, stopped, and then cleared it a second time as if he missed an obstruction the first time around.

Finally, he mumbled, "Umm...she's gone, Grant, and I don't think she wants you to follow."

CHAPTER 28

Eric released the straps securing me to the hospital bed, but refused to say anything else about Ginny. On the one hand, I was grateful for the rescue, but he had been behaving strangely lately and it was beginning to take a toll on our friendship.

In addition to whatever he was hiding about Ginny, there was the bungled rescue attempt. When I needed his help, he didn't show-up. As a result, Uncle Jim was trapped in a burning building, Ginny and I were shot, and Bird was smashed underneath a tank of a guy. I was starting to have some nagging doubts about him.

"Where were you?" I demanded.

Eric looked a bit sheepish as he answered, "It took us a while to find you."

"We didn't have any trouble finding it," I accused.

He stared at me long and hard as if he wanted to be sure he said and did the right thing.

"One minute you were in a hospital bed and the next you were gone," he said. "We figured you had to be somewhere in the building, but didn't have clue where that might be. They kept you off the grid, so it was a bitch finding you in this place. In fact, if it wasn't for the information Ginny gave us you'd still be strapped to that table."

I was so upset, I wasn't really listening.

All I heard was, "Ginny gave us the information we needed to find you."

"That makes no sense," I said. "Ginny, was bound and gagged. How could she have helped?"

Eric didn't answer right away. He was clearly thinking something through. Finally, the pinch in his brow relaxed a notch or two. When he finally spoke, it was with the thing he loves faking the most in life…sincerity.

"Dude, you've lost your mind," said Eric.

I have always appreciated Eric's lighthearted sense of humor, but not this time. I needed some straight answers.

"You damn near got me killed at the warehouse," I accused. "Where the hell were you?"

Judging by the change of expression, he must have realized we were talking about two different things.

"Oh, you're talking about that cluster fuck," said Eric. "Ole' George led us to the wrong warehouse. I had a bad feeling about it and shouldn't have followed the Dragons. You realize, don't you, that the West End is a wasteland of abandoned buildings?"

I knew he was right about the West End. It is a mess of a place, but Eric is a natural leader, not a follower and I couldn't understand why he would follow a ragtag group of bikers who live on the edge of the law.

"Since when do you follow anything other than your own gut?" I asked.

Eric shook his head.

"Yeah, I know," he said. "I'm sorry man. It never works out well when I ignore my instincts. Following the Dragons was a bad idea. I've been replaying the whole thing in my head. Maybe I could have kept you from catching a bullet if I'd only followed my intuition."

I could see the pain in his face. Eric blamed himself. I didn't need to keep punishing him, since he was completing that task himself. I figured I should say something to help him get through this, but I was struggling with my own shit, and besides, I didn't know what to say.

When my silence lasted long enough to make us both feel uncomfortable, Eric started talking again.

"When we finally found the right warehouse, I thought I'd find a way to flank the bad guys, but ran into one obstacle after another," said Eric. "By the time I got to the fight, it was over."

I knew without a shadow of a doubt Eric would never miss a good fight. I was about to tell him to forget it, when he started talking again.

"The police were swarming the place and the two of you were being loaded into an ambulance," he said. "While I missed the whole damn thing, I did manage to get Uncle Jim out of that building."

"He's alive," I gasped.

"Yep and still kicking," grinned Eric. "I'm pleased to report he's as mean as ever."

"You saved Uncle Jim?" I asked.

"Well, I don't want to brag, but it was pretty damn heroic, if I do say so myself," said Eric.

"Tell me my humble friend, was he still on the roof when you found him?" I asked.

"I'm glad you have finally taken notice of my finer qualities," said Eric with a grin. "Yes, he was still on the roof. You know how he is...once a marine sniper, always a marine sniper."

"He took a high position with his rifle," I said. "It was a good plan. He can shoot the eye out of the Jack of Diamonds at ½ mile with that damn rifle, but Slotter spotted him. She's good. I don't think anyone else would have seen him. Anyway, Slotter threatened to shoot Ginny, so Uncle Jim tossed his weapon to the ground. That's pretty much when all hell broke loose."

"He wasn't alone up there," said Eric.

"Yea, I know," I said. "Pony Tail was up there too. That guy seems to be everywhere."

"It was the damnedest thing," said Eric. "I thought they were fighting at first, but now I'm not so sure."

"What did you see?" I asked.

"The smoke obscured everything," answered Eric. "But I got a glimpse of your surfer dude with Uncle Jim. At least, he sure looked an awful lot like your description of Pony Tail. At first, I thought he had Uncle Jim down and was pummeling him, but when the smoke drifted it looked more like he was helping him."

"That's weird, because I found him hovering over Ginny," I said. "At first I thought he was trying to hurt her, but now I think maybe he did something to help her."

"There's something else you need to know, Grant," said Eric. "Uncle Jim claims Pony Tail gave him medicine. He says it cured him."

"Cured him from what?" I asked.

"Everything," he answered.

Years ago, Uncle Jim fell rock climbing in the Red River Gorge. He broke his back in the fall. The doctors said he'd never walk again. Uncle Jim proved them wrong, but he uses a cane from time to time when the pain becomes too intense.

"You mean his back too?" I asked.

Eric nodded.

"That's not all," said Eric. "He swears he feels like a teenager again."

"Teenager," I said absently mindedly.

"Yea, the old goat claims the medicine has given him his mojo back," said Eric. "Geez, some players just don't know when to leave the field."

"If he's telling the truth, then that might explain why Ginny made such a miraculous recovery after I found Pony Tail hovering over her in ICU," I said.

"It seems like crazy talk to me," said Eric.

"I need to see Uncle Jim," I said. "Can you take me to him?"

"Piece of cake, Dude," said Eric. "He's down the hall negotiating your release with hospital administration."

"These people are acting like I'm their prisoner or something," I said. "Let's go see if he needs any help."

Eric led me to the patient discharge office where we found Uncle Jim glaring at a middle aged woman with scarlet colored big hair that could only have come from a bottle. Her hefty jowls were quivering like a disturbed bowl of Jell-O. I think maybe she had something important to say, but couldn't quite get it out.

Uncle Jim is a serious badass. The Marine Corps trained him for a hush-hush special ops unit that he never talks about. His job was to assassinate bad guys for Uncle Sam and I'm pretty sure he was damn good at it. Scarlet was way out of her league.

He was wearing his usual faded jeans and Harley t-shirt. To keep his fashion statement fresh and interesting, Uncle Jim likes to alternate between square toed biker boots and Jesus sandals. Today it was sandals.

Thanks to a lean muscular frame, he looks much younger than his true age. His hair is more pepper than salt, with only a touch of a receding hairline. He lost an eye in a rock climbing accident and wears a patch like a proud pirate.

He leaned in toward Scarlet and fixed his one eye on her two.

"On whose orders is he being held?" demanded Uncle Jim.

He didn't give her a chance to answer before adding, "And don't say the doctor's. There is something shady going on here and we both know it."

I imagine Scarlet was a seasoned administrator with years of experience dealing with the disgruntled public. She looked pretty damn tough to me, but she had met her match.

Uncle Jim knows how to win a fight. It doesn't matter if it's against the Taliban or a skilled public relations expert. He is relentless and she was beginning to crack under the pressure.

"Aaawk, tell us the truth toots and we'll let you go unharmed," squawked Bird.

I was shocked to see that my foul mouth macaw was still alive. I don't know how I could have missed him standing there on Scarlet's file cabinet with his colorful feathers all in a ruffle, but I did. The last time I saw him, he went down underneath a huge man. I thought he had been squashed like a bug.

Dad had adored the bird for some strange reason. Me, well I think Bird is obnoxious and wasn't real happy when he was left to my care. Fortunately, he and Uncle Jim seem to get along pretty good, so I let my uncle take care of him most of the time. Despite our issues, I was happy to see Bird alive.

Uncle Jim has a way of dropping his chin a fraction of an inch and clenching his jaw when he doesn't approve of something. If you know what to look for, then you can see a little quiver in his jaw line just below the ear lobe. That's exactly what I saw him do in response to Bird's silly threat.

Scarlet seemed surprised by Bird's coherent speech, but it might have been too much to expect her to actually answer him. Instead she kept her eyes squarely on the bigger threat, Uncle Jim, while half-heartedly mumbling something about no pets allowed in the hospital.

Uncle Jim turned to me and winked. I nodded toward the door.

"Never mind, Uncle Jim," I said. "It doesn't matter who wants to hold him prisoner here because he's leaving with me."

Scarlet bristled, but looked relieved to see Uncle Jim turn toward the door. I doubt she knew who I was and no one else tried to stop us as we left the building. Once outside, Uncle Jim lit up like a Christmas tree.

"Grant, aren't you a sight for sore eyes," said Uncle Jim. "It's good to see you, son."

I thought I'd lost him to the flames and I'm pretty sure that explains the wave of emotion I was desperately trying to hold back. Since I couldn't seem to find my voice, I gave Uncle Jim a bear hug instead.

"Aaawk, group hug," squawked Bird as he landed gently on my shoulder and cradled us with his colorful wings.

I have never felt closer to Bird then I did in that moment.

"I'm glad you're alive," I said.

"Aaawk, thanks Peckerwood, but what about that one eyed monster horning in on our hug," squawked Bird.

"Awe, I'm gonna live forever," said Uncle Jim, "but if you keep calling me one eyed monster, then your life expectancy will be considerably shorter."

"Yea, I wanted to talk to you about that," I said. "What happened on the roof?"

"It was the damnedest thing," he said. "The building caught fire and the blaze went viral. I was trapped by the inferno and choking on the foulest black smoke I've ever encountered. My pants caught fire and burned me pretty good before I put it out."

"To make matters worse, the flames were closing in," he said. "If I didn't move quickly, then I'd never get out of there alive, except my damn legs wouldn't move. I really thought I might be a goner."

I've heard Uncle Jim tell many stories of his harrowing escapes over the years. He's like a big cat with nine lives. Somehow he always finds a way to survive. Still, we had a little tradition. When he reached the critical point in his story, he would pause, tilt his head slightly, and wait for me to ask the question.

"How did you manage to get out of that one, Uncle Jim," I asked.

He smiled a crooked smile and with a twinkle in his eye said, "The hippie helped me."

"Are you talking about the guy up on the roof with you...the one with his blond hair pulled back into a pony tail?" I asked.

"That's him," he answered.

"This guy has been popping up everywhere," I said. "What was he doing on the roof?"

"Damn if I know," answered Uncle Jim. "I didn't even know he was up there with me, until Slotter ordered us to throw our guns off the roof. I thought I moved quietly, but that guy is a ghost."

"How did he help you?" I asked.

"He gave me a pinch of herb and asked if I knew how to use snuff," he answered.

"What was it?" I asked.

"I don't know," he answered.

"Why would you put something up your nose without knowing what it was?" I asked.

Uncle Jim looked slightly embarrassed.

"I'm not sure," he said. "But maybe it was his eyes."

I was stunned. Uncle Jim was as tough and practical as they come. He isn't the type of guy who ever would say out loud that another guy's eyes affected him, let alone trust him enough to inhale an unknown substance.

It could have been the way I was looking at him, but Uncle Jim seemed eager to add, "It smelled like sunshine."

"Sunshine," I repeated incredulously.

He nodded.

"I felt a wave of intense pleasure when I inhaled it," said Uncle Jim. "It was better than sex."

"Better than sex," I repeated.

Uncle Jim winked.

"Intense pleasure," I added.

Uncle Jim giggled like a school girl. I'm pretty sure that was a first.

"Then the most amazing thing happened," said Uncle Jim.

Uncle Jim just stood there looking at me with the goofiest shit eating grin I'd ever seen on his face.

"Are you going to tell me about this amazing thing that happened next?" I asked.

I didn't think his smile could get any bigger, but it did.

"I'm glad you finally asked," he said. "It healed me."

"Healed you," I said.

He nodded. I waited for further explanation. It didn't come.

"What did it heal?" I asked.

"Everything," he said.

"Eric mentioned something about that," I said.

"The burns, my bad back...everything, except for growing back my missing eye," he said.

"Well that would be asking for a lot," I said. "It would make this whole story unbelievable, don't you think?"

"He told me there is a way to do that too, but it will have to wait until we have more time," he said.

"Grow a missing eye back," I said.

Uncle Jim nodded.

"Did he happen to tell you how that is possible?" I asked.

Uncle Jim shook his head.

"And you believe him," I said.

Uncle Jim grinned.

"Did he say when he would perform this miracle cure?" I asked.

"Nope," said Uncle Jim. "He said he had been called back to Amazonia, but would return when he could.

"Amazonia," I repeated.

Uncle Jim said, "Yep. Then he disappeared into the smoke."

"Are you telling me he vanished into thin air...like a damn ghost or something?" I asked.

Uncle Jim plastered an exaggerated hurt look on his face and said, "Somehow I don't think you believe me."

I gave Uncle Jim a long hard look, but he didn't show any signs of wavering on this, so I turned to Eric and asked, "Can you shed any light on this?"

Eric shook his head.

"I couldn't see clearly through all the smoke, but I saw Pony Tail hovering over him," said Eric. "When the smoke shifted, I lost sight of both of them for a few minutes. After it cleared again, Pony Tail was gone and Uncle Jim was walking toward me."

"I knew we didn't have much time and needed to get off the roof as fast as possible," said Uncle Jim.

"I tried to lead him out the way I had come in, but the path was blocked by flames," said Eric.

"Aaawk, these knuckleheads would be dead if it wasn't for me," said Bird.

"I thought you were squashed underneath that tank of a man," I said.

Bird held his wings like a body builder flexing cantaloupe sized biceps.

"Aaawk, with guns like these, baby, there will never be a chance anyone will squash me like a bug," said Bird.

Uncle Jim snorted, but when Bird glared at him he thought better of it and changed his attitude.

"It's true Bird guided us out of there," said Uncle Jim. "He rose above the inferno like a majestic phoenix and led us to safety."

I can't say for sure, but I think I heard Bird purr like a kitten and bat his eyelashes. He can be impossible when his ego is allowed to run unchecked. It was time to change the subject.

"I'd have never thought that old warehouse would go up in flames so easily...or expected a Harley to explode on impact," I said. "Did the biker chick survive her last second tumble from the bike?"

"Yea, but she's pretty damn bitter about the broken hip," said Eric. "She says it's an old lady injury."

"Were any of the other Dragons injured?" I asked.

I was talking about the Dragon Gate Motorcycle Club. It was their President, Tiny, who was stabbed in the chest at the Center. They were out for revenge and tagged along on our mission to rescue Ginny.

"Ole George was shot in the ass," said Eric. "If the rest of them weren't so scared of him, they might enjoy giving him some grief over taking one in the ass. Instead, they are waiting on him hand and foot."

"Was anyone else shot?" I asked.

"Just you," said Uncle Jim.

"Was Ginny shot?" I asked.

Eric looked at me like I might be a little crazy after all and said, "You were there, Dude."

"Between the eyes," said Uncle Jim.

"Aaawk, it wasn't pretty," said Bird.

"So, I'm not crazy," I said.

Eric let out a little sigh of exasperation. Uncle Jim raised an eyebrow. It was the one over the patch. He only raised the one over the patch for seriously stupid comments.

Bird chimed in, "Aaawk, bat shit crazy if you ask me."

"When I found her in the hospital room, she was perfectly healthy," I said. "How is that possible?"

Uncle Jim and Eric gave each other a knowing look, but said nothing. They just waited, as if I was a small child that couldn't quite keep up.

"Do you think Pony Tail had anything to do with it?" I asked.

The three of them stared at me like I might have been dropped on my head at birth, but it was necessary to treat me in a politically sensitive manner. I'm not sure we've ever been politically sensitive with each other. It was weird.

"He must have used the magic herb on her," said Uncle Jim. "We need to find him."

It felt like I had fallen down Alice's rabbit hole. Uncle Jim was a tough minded old marine. Magic was not something he believed in. Somehow this hippie had gotten under his skin.

"I need to find Ginny," I said.

Eric became very interested in his shoes. "Give it up, Grant," said Eric. "I told you. She's gone."

I was about to snap at him, but caught myself before I said something regretful.

Instead, I counted two breaths. It helped immensely, since I couldn't stay mad at Eric for long. He was a good friend. If he couldn't tell me, then he had a good reason. Besides, I knew where she went and had already decided to go after her.

"Eric, I'm not sure what she said to you to get this level of loyalty, but I'm catching the first plane to Rio de Janeiro," I said. "You can come with or stay. It's your choice."

CHAPTER 29

Eric didn't ask why I thought Ginny was in Brazil. In fact, he didn't bat an eye at my plan to search for her in the Rainforest. This confirmed what I already knew, bolstered by Slotter's belief that her father is still alive, Ginny plans to search the Amazon Rainforest for him.

It bothered me that Pony Tail is also traveling to Brazil. He keeps popping up wherever Ginny happens to be and I don't like it one bit. Eric made it pretty clear Ginny was pissed at me and I feared it had something to do with Pony Tail.

I tried to convince myself that I wasn't jealous of Pony Tail, but I knew I was lying to myself. It didn't help that I had treated Ginny badly for years and knew very little about the life she had built for herself. Those thoughts just added guilt and regret to the jealous feelings I was desperately trying to deny.

Even though Uncle Jim was now Pony Tail's greatest fan, I didn't trust him. How could I trust someone who tried to kill Padma? Geez, this guy shot me. I wasn't buying this crap about him being some kind of healer. Still, there was a part of me that wanted Pony Tail to be a healer. If he really did heal Uncle Jim then I couldn't help but wonder if he couldn't work his miracles on Mom.

I needed to find this guy and get some answers. Hopefully, I could do that sooner, rather than later. The clock was ticking on Mom's eviction from Shady Days and I wasn't convinced I could sell her house in time to pay the bill and stop them from putting her out. Particularly, since my wife was threatening to get a court order to stop the sale even though Mom could die without the medical supervision they provide.

Eric accepted the offer to travel to Brazil, but not without a friendly dig or two. He patted me on the head saying I had the relationship I.Q. of a middle-schooler. On top of that, my best friend had the nerve to tell me I couldn't be left alone with a beautiful woman, like I needed a babysitter or something.

Eric knows my boundaries well enough and I was about to give him hell for crossing them when he quickly switched the discussion to Brazil's reputation for tiny bikinis. With his trademark shit eating grin, he whispered loud enough to be heard in an auditorium that Brazilian thongs are just the right size to titillate a man's imagination. I was worried about Ginny and not particularly interested in talking about bikinis, but the distraction worked well enough I didn't give him a hard time about his disrespectful behavior toward me.

There's something else that was bothering me. Ginny is afraid of me. I had seen it in her eyes twice now. The first time was when she found me in the women's bathroom cleaning blood off myself. I know it sounds awful, but I got blood all over myself when I was trying to save a man's life.

This last time was different. I know I overreacted, but I couldn't let them send back to the psyche ward. The worst part of it is I think I understand why Ginny feels this way. She suffered from years of abuse at the hand of her violent mother. I understand it because I also suffered because of her mother. I got daily shock treatments from Sadistic Doctor because of her mother. Ginny's mother had wreaked havoc in our lives, and until we stop taking it personally, the effects of her mother's abuse will continue to rob us of the life we are meant to have together.

We invited Uncle Jim to travel with us to Brazil, but he was acting mysterious and all he would say about it was he needed to follow-up on something. I was curious, but learned long ago to stay out of his private affairs. The man had his secrets and it was pointless to pry into them.

Of course, Bird was damn pissed he wasn't invited to come with us. There was no reasoning with him. Especially, when we told him he'd have to travel in a crate as cargo. He was outraged that birds couldn't fly first class, and spent considerable time grumbling about the value of diversity.

Eventually he gave up his bitching, but not before saying, "Aaawk, why the hell would I want to get on a damn airplane anyway. I got my own wings, baby."

"Yes you do," I agreed.

To reinforce our sensitivity to his plight, we nodded in unison. It's best to not piss Bird off too much. He relaxed a notch or two, so it was working, but to make certain we got the point he flexed his biceps body builder style and added a final comment.

"Aaawk, this bird is a bad ass in the air!"

There wasn't much response to that except for a snarky comeback or two that came to mind, but I sure wasn't willing to set him off again and since Bird was in no mood for a ribbing, I focused instead on getting us tickets. I used the latest travel app on my phone to make the purchase.

There was a tense moment when the app took its sweet time spitting out a flight confirmation. I was sure it was going to report my credit card had been summarily rejected thanks to my wife's spending problems. However, it was eventually approved and after hastily packing a carryon bag, we rushed to the airport.

People stared as we boarded the plane for Rio de Janeiro. Maybe I was a little self-conscious, but I hadn't showered or shaved for days and had to fight the temptation to sniff my pits. I only won that battle because I figured it would just draw more attention to us.

I had to shake my head and grin at Eric as he bounded to our seats and claimed the window. I wanted that window seat, but yielded it to him as gracefully as I could. I had more important things on my mind and he was my best friend, after all.

We managed to settle into our seats without anyone sniffing the air distastefully or demanding to be moved to a new seat. There was a long flight ahead of us and for the first time, I allowed myself to consider the daunting task ahead, but before I descended too far into despair, Eric jolted me back with an elbow to my sore ribs.

Leaning over us was a flight attendant with close cropped brown hair, big boobs, and a touch of light pink lipstick. Her green eyes were filled with warmth and I sensed she was quick to see the humor in ordinary things.

"Sir, you have the seat next to the emergency exit," she said.

I cut my eyes to the emergency door and nodded.

She leaned in a little closer and dropped her voice an octave, "In the unlikely event of an emergency can you open that door and assist the other passengers off the plane."

I nodded once again.

She squeezed my bicep and said, "Whatever you're worrying about will work out for the best."

Before I could thank her, she winked and sashayed off.

Eric elbowed me yet again and said, "There you go, Dude, words of wisdom from the in-flight nurse."

I raised an eyebrow, but said nothing.

"Geez you're so damn uptight," said Eric with a sigh. "The Tao keeps throwing beautiful women at you, 'cuz it knows what you need. You just gotta learn to relax and flow with it."

He's right about the women. They're always throwing themselves at me. I don't think they do it because I'm more attractive than the next guy. Instead, I think they sense I'm not interested in casual hook-ups.

It's like they have a radar for men like me who hunger for happily ever after. All I ever wanted was to be loved, and since they want the same thing, it draws them to me like flies to cow patties.

Eric was waiting for a response, so I said, "I'm here to help Ginny, not hook-up with a flight attendant."

He shook his head and said, "A fool on a fool's mission, my friend."

"Speaking of missions, have you had any luck finding Ch'ing?" I asked.

Eric shook his head.

I didn't press him for details. We were both upset by the disappearance of our martial arts teacher a few days earlier. It was very odd since Ch'ing never went anywhere. He was always there for us and when he didn't' show up at the dojo for class, Eric sent someone to investigate. Much to our dismay, Ch'ing's front door was standing open and his home was trashed leading us to fear the worst.

Eric turned toward the window and acted like he was settling in for a nap, but I think he just wanted to hide his tears.

I let him be and returned to my worries. How the hell am I going to find Ginny in the vastness of the Amazon Rainforest? I'm generally an optimist, but was beginning to think this was a seriously ill-conceived venture. Maybe Eric is right. I'm on a fool's mission.

Overwhelmed with a growing sense of impending doom, I searched on my smartphone for Ginny's company, Emerald Allure, to see what I could learn. I knew she had a factory somewhere in Brazil and I figured that would be her base of operations while she searched the rainforest for her father.

A few days earlier, Ginny had told me the story of how she got her start in the clothing business. Like many things in life, it was happenstance, but she had the vision to build it into one of the world's fastest growing companies.

The thing I admire most about her is the commitment to building a company with heart. While other companies exploit the poor, she finds ways to empower her employees.

Earlier, I had downloaded information about Brazil from the State Department's website. The thing that struck me the hardest was the country's involvement in the slave trade. It was a disheartening read about the many ways the desperate are exploited.

For example, unethical companies use bonded labor to clear trees in the Rainforest. The trees are used to manufacture charcoal for barbeque grills in the United States. The Rainforest is home to a wide diversity of plant and animal life. Once stripped of plant life, the naked land offers the creatures little refuge.

These companies go into the slums of Rio de Janeiro and promise the desperately poor a better life. Instead of a life-upgrade, they get long hours, unsafe conditions, and little or no pay. The slavers think nothing of exploiting the poor's only possession, their hope.

The recruits acquire debts for travel and living expense that they never pay off. They are prisoners of a lie and the vast jungle serves as their prison bars.

After reading about the charcoal industry, I vowed to never use it again. Not that I owned a grill or even a backyard for that matter, but it was the principle of the thing.

Ginny's company is different. Emerald Allure hires the poor, gives them good pay, health benefits and safe working conditions. It is more like collaboration than a traditional employment relationship. It may be a drop in the bucket, but she is trying her best to make a change.

While I admire her commitment to change, I'm not sure what to think about this obsessive search for her father after twenty years in the jungle. Even if it were true, which I seriously doubt, the Amazon Rainforest is vast…over two million square miles. I wonder how she expects to find him in all of that wilderness.

Stranger still, both Slotter and Mr. Suit are looking for her father as well. I don't know what they want with him, but they are willing to use violence. Ginny is in grave danger. I need to find her fast and it isn't going to be easy.

I also need to find Pony Tail. This business about him curing Uncle Jim and Ginny seems suspicious to me, but I want to keep an open mind because Mom needs help.

A wave of hopelessness tried to push its way into my mind, but I pushed back. This is not the time to give in to despair. Somehow, I will find Pony Tail and learn more about this medicine, but first I need to complete my mission and find Ginny. Failure is not an option.

With a sigh, I decided to get some rest. As my eyelids closed, I opened the door to the inner eye and pictured Ch'ing standing before us. He's short, a pinch shy of 5'4", and can't weigh more than a buck twenty soaking wet. His size and coloring suggests he is originally from Southeast Asia, but since he deflects all questions about his origins, no one knows for sure where he actually came from.

Ch'ing wears his black hair in a long braid that hangs below the shoulder blades. Sparse whiskers and smooth skin make him look more like a teenager than a grown man. I sometimes think of him as an older brother, until I look into his ancient eyes and see a man who knows eternity as well as you might know your favorite television show. Ch'ing is timeless.

"Well, what do you two hooligans know about gathering energy?" he once asked.

I looked at Eric for an answer, but his blank face told me that he was just as clueless as me about Ch'ing's question. At the time, we were no older than ten and I'm pretty sure that we had an overabundance of energy. At least that's what the nuns at catholic school told us.

"Aaawk, it won't do you any good to try sandbagging us, because we have ways to make you talk," squawked Bird.

Bird's favorite torture is to drag his claws across a pane of glass. When we were kids, the screeching sent our hands to ears, followed by rounds of belly-laughs. The funny thing is, it really works, because after the laughter died down, we would spout whatever came to mind just to get him to stop and Ch'ing almost always approved of these spontaneous answers.

"I always feel full of energy after school," I said.

"Good!" said Ch'ing. "Why do you think that is?"

"I don't know, maybe it's because I'm happy to be free again," I answered.

"That's right!" said Ch'ing. "When someone forces us to do something we don't want to do, it causes tension, and tension robs us of our Chi."

"What's tension?" asked Eric.

"Awe, very good question Master Eric," said Ch'ing.

We always liked it when Ch'ing called us Master. It made us feel grown-up and important.

"For example, the way you boys just puffed your chest out is good tension, " said Ch'ing.

"Is there bad tension?" asked Eric.

"I'm glad you asked," said Ch'ing. "You are such an intelligent young man."

He rubbed his eight chin whiskers and looked up toward the left. Ch'ing always did that when he was thinking up an exercise for us. Some of those exercises were fun, but others we didn't like too much.

"I know you boys don't want a lecture from me, so let's give you a way to experience tension firsthand," said Ch'ing.

We might have groaned just a little.

"I'm glad you two agree," he said with a twinkle in his eye. "Here's what I want you to do. Hold your hands about chest high, palms facing downward."

As always, he demonstrated exactly what he expected us to do. We looked at each other, shrugged, and did as instructed.

"Well done!" said Ch'ing. "How did I get so lucky as to have the Tao send me two brilliant young students?"

We suspected he was pulling our legs, but praise from Ch'ing wasn't something we ever took lightly.

"Now, take a deep breath and squeeze your fists, as hard, and as long as you can," said Ch'ing. "Come on boys. No slacking. Really squeeze hard."

As usual, Eric and I made a competition of it, determined to hold it longer than the other. It's harder than it looks. We were both sweating in a matter of minutes and soon quit.

"I beat you," said Eric.

"No, I beat you," I said.

"Aaawk, nobody wins," said Bird. "It's a tie and ties are lame."

Ch'ing was smiling as he smoothed out his skimpy mustache.

"Why did you give up so easily?" he asked.

"It's hard," I grumbled.

"Yeah, it's way harder than it looks," said Eric.

"That squeezing is one example of tension," said Ch'ing. "It's hard because it drains us of energy really fast. It is a waste of energy and Taoist like us don't like to waste energy."

"You mean we shouldn't squeeze so hard," I asked.

"I mean, the first lesson of Chi Kung is to stop wasting energy," said Ch'ing.

"How do we do that?" asked Eric.

"You begin by relaxing any muscles, including your noggin, that aren't required for the task at hand," said Ch'ing.

I'm pretty sure all Ch'ing saw was two boys with blank faces, because he looked us up and down and then shook his head with exaggerated sadness.

"Think of it like a cat," said Ch'ing. "They lay around sleeping all day, but as soon as that mouse tries to sneak out and steal a meal, the cat pounces."

To add emphasis, he snapped his fingers just when the cat pounces.

"Relax and gather energy," said Ch'ing. "When you spring into action, do it completely and without hesitation. Act without tension, because tension slows you down and divides you against yourself."

The Captain interrupted the trip into the past with a message about turbulence and seat belts. Eric stirred, but his eyes never opened. Instead, he went back to snoring softly with the left side of his face smashed against the window.

I closed my eyes again and rested for a few minutes. Gradually, my breathing deepened until it reached the soles of my feet. Breath carries oxygen to every cell of our bodies. It exchanges nutrients for waste products and then eliminates them with every exhalation. It was comforting to know that my breath does this without any effort on my part.

When it was time, I slowly and methodically searched for tension. It wasn't hard to find. There was a lot of tension in my body. Wherever I found it, I replaced it with a smile. My inner smile slowly worked its magic dissolving tension and replacing it with contentment. It was going to be a long flight. I was in no hurry and permitted myself to sink deeper into a delicious, relaxed state.

I must have fallen asleep, because I woke from a dream filled nap as the plane began its final descent into Rio. The view was spectacular. Sugar Loaf Mountain stood at the gateway to the city like a rounded pyramid that had seen better days. Then there was the iconic statute of Christ welcoming travelers to the city with open arms.

They say the statute is one of the Seven Wonders of the World, but for me it was just a reminder of too many hours spent attending long boring Masses. In addition to Sunday services, we began school each morning with church. That left only Saturday mornings to rest my weary spirit from the somber ritual.

Unfortunately, when I served as an altar boy I always seemed to get assigned to Saturday morning Mass. Seven days a week is way too much religion for anybody, especially a kid who spends church service plotting his escape. I wanted to run barefoot in the grass, not kneel at the foot of the altar.

Galeão International Airport came into view below. I wondered what the architect had in mind when he designed it as circle split into halves. It seemed to symbolize division.

In contrast, I remembered an image from a weird dream I had just before I woke. I was in an eight sided chamber lined with stone. In the center of the room was a pool of water. "Water's Edge" was written above the pool in an ancient script. In sharp contrast to the fragmented life I was struggling to put back together, the chamber filled me with a soothing sense of wholeness

Padma was in my dream and I asked him, "What is Water's Edge?"

"There is an ancient pool of water deep in the jungle," he answered. "Many years ago a temple was built around it. We call this place Water's Edge."

"Why would anyone build a temple around a pool of water?" I asked.

Padma's eyes glistened as he answered, "It is the water of life. From this pool springs eternal life."

"You can't be serious," I said. "Are you telling me this is the mythical Fountain of Youth?"

"Open your mind," said Padma.

I figured I was more open-minded than the next guy and was about to argue the point when the plane touched down and rattled me out of the dream.

As we came to a stop I remembered something Ch'ing once said about immortality. All of eternity is contained in the present moment. The past and the future are illusions. Living in the past is a sickness because it was never really the way we remember. Hurrying headlong from the present moment into an uncertain future is likewise an illness to be avoided at all costs. Immortality is living your life fully in the present and in such a manner that others want you to live forever.

Whenever we found ourselves surrounded by people in a rush, Ch'ing encouraged us to slow down and pay attention to everything around us. As usual, he had an exercise to demonstrate his point.

Holding our arms out to the side, he had us spin clockwise until the world around us became a blur. This blur is what people experience when they rush about. In their haste, they fail to focus on the things right in front of them. They ignore the reality at their feet. Ch'ing called it a state of ignorance. He encouraged us to find our center and become the eye in the middle of the storm that sees clearly.

Because of this conditioning, Eric and I were able to wait patiently as our fellow passengers rushed to escape the flying tin can. Once the others were off the plane, we made our way into the airport terminal. I was surprised that it was a modern facility. For some reason, I had expected it to be more primitive...more third world.

Everyone else moved as a herd toward baggage claim. Since Eric and I hadn't checked our bags, we split from the crowd and made our way to ground transportation where we found a crowd of travelers milling around. There wasn't a single bus or taxi within sight and the restless crowd was growing by the minute.

Eric and I had been friends long enough that sometimes we behave like an old married couple. There isn't any need for forced conversation between us. If we have something to say, we say it. Otherwise, we keep to our thoughts. This was one of our quiet moments.

My thoughts were interrupted by an unknown caller on my cell phone. Thanks to a growing stack of bills at home, I usually ignored these calls, but my gut told me this one was important and so I reluctantly took it.

"This is Grant Li," I said.

"Is this Grant Li?" asked a woman.

I resisted the temptation to snap at her for not listening and instead answered politely, "Yes, it is. Who is this?"

She ignored my question and stuck to her script.

"Mr. Li, I am calling on behalf of the Shady Days Adult Care Center," she said.

My mother has been a resident at Shady Days facility since the motorcycle crash that left her a quadriplegic and killed my father twenty years earlier. Recently, she took a turn for the worse after a bad drug reaction.

To make matters worse, they are evicting her at the end of the month. Since the doctor has to put her on life support from time to time, this turn of events has put her life at risk.

"Is my mother okay?" I asked.

"Mr. Li, we are calling to tell you that the insurance company has denied your claim," she said.

The insurance ran out years ago, so I knew for sure she was reading from a script.

"Can you please tell me whether my mother is okay?" I said.

"Mr. Li, we have you down as the responsible party," said Ms. Nobody.

I finally snapped at her.

"Does my mother need anything?" I shouted.

"Mr. Li, the balance on the account is $332,456.22," she said. "I can take your credit card information now. Do you have it ready?"

I was stunned.

"Mr. Li, what is your card number?" she asked.

I hung up on her. Between the ravages of divorce and losing my job, I was broke. I had no idea what I was going to do. I just knew I had to do something and do it soon.

"Breathe," said Eric.

My friend was staring intently into my eyes. He didn't know what was happening, but he knew the call upset me. I needed help and he was there for me. Eric was pulling me back into the present.

"Bill collector," I said as if that explained it all.

"Just take a deep breath," he said.

That was as good a place as any to start, so I gulped down a big bite of air. Once I let that one out, I took another, and then another, until finally, I settled back into the present moment.

"What just happened?" asked Eric.

"I'm in trouble," I said.

"I know," he said. "But you don't have to face it alone."

Eric and I had been friends for a long time, but there were parts of my life that I didn't share with him. I always figured a man doesn't burden others with personal matters. These things must be faced alone. Maybe that's a mistake. Maybe it's time to open my life.

I was about to unburden myself when a lone bus rolled in and came to a stop in front of us. Even though we didn't have a clue where it was headed, it was the only option available to us, so we climbed aboard.

The crowd squeezed in and when the bus couldn't possibly hold another body, the driver shut the door and pulled away. I was afforded a view out a small slice of a window and gratefully took it since the next best option was to stare down the huge backside of a woman with a 1960's style beehive hairdo.

I absent-mindedly gazed out the window of the bus and was shocked to see Ginny displayed on a giant digital billboard. She held the rainforest in her arms like a mother holding a newborn child for the first time. Her eyes were filled with the wonder of precious new life.

I have to confess she looked like the Madonna holding baby Jesus, but it didn't make me feel a bit better. Instead, I thought of my own mother lying wasted in a hospital bed desperate for a cure.

The last good memory of my mother was the morning of the motorcycle crash. It was my dad's birthday and we were together for the last time. Mom's gift to my dad was the Harley he always dreamed of owning. After dropping me off at school, my parents took the Harley out for a maiden ride. I never saw my father again thanks to a hit and run driver.

Mom survived the crash, but is a quadriplegic. The doctors tried to strip away our hope by telling us there is no cure and the best we can do is make her last few months comfortable. That was twenty years ago, but I've never given up hope that they would someday find a way to heal her broken body.

My rumination about Mom was interrupted when the bus suddenly swerved to the right squeezing me between Eric and the Beehive. An explosion sent glass flying everywhere. The scent of burning rubber was followed by a crash that jerked us forward. It slammed my forehead hard enough into the back of the forward seat that I saw stars.

My head was pounding, or at least that's what I thought at first. I was trying to shake off the effects of the blow, when I saw hands pounding on the window. The bus was surrounded by an angry mob.

"Grant, we need to get out of here," said Eric.

I nodded in agreement. The bus was beginning to feel like a death trap. The other passengers were still in shock, but some were beginning to stir. I feared they would soon panic and wanted out before they stampeded the doors. Squeezing out of my seat, I began elbowing a path to the door.

We were nearly to the front of the bus when a man sprung from his seat and drove a shoulder into my already sore ribs. They had taken a beating over the last few days and I was determined to protect them at all costs. I instinctively slammed a knee into his face and watched him crumble to the floor.

Eric nodded toward the door and said something to the bus driver in Portuguese. The driver responded by pointing to a 70's model car burning in the street and shook his head.

A line of helmeted police rushed to the fire where they clashed with unarmed men. A police baton ripped open a teenager's face from the corner of his eye to his ear lobe. The poor guy staggered too close to the fire and the flame ignited his shirt. Panicked, he ran in the general direction of the bus.

"Oh hell no," I shouted as I drove my foot through the door.

A woman running past the bus toward the burning kid was caught by the door and knocked to the ground. Pain shot through my ribs as I jumped over her crumbled body.

Eric followed me out of the bus and squatted next to her. He gently placed his hands on a wound oozing blood from the back of her head. Her eyes flickered open and she murmured something to him. After exchanging a few words, he helped her to her feet.

Concerned I asked, "Is the wound serious?"

"The cut will heal," answered Eric. "Her wounded mind is more serious. She told me a group of policeman assaulted her daughter. The authorities denied it. The police said the girl was working for a local drug dealer and they were only trying to get information from her."

Eric waived his arm toward the angry mob.

"These people are upset, so they took to the streets in peaceful protest of police corruption," said Eric. "Things got out of control when the police used tear gas and the demonstration quickly turned into a riot."

The woman was mumbling something to herself as she picked at an imaginary wound on her forearm. She seemed lost to herself. I couldn't imagine the pain she felt. A stone whizzed past my head and smashed into the side of the bus.

"Speaking of the riot, we better get out of here," I said.

Eric led me into a shantytown filled with poorly constructed buildings pieced together from scraps of wood, cinder block and chicken wire.

"What is this place?" I asked.

"Favela," he answered.

"Huh?" Was my brilliant response.

"It's a Brazilian ghetto," said Eric.

"I was under the impression Rio is a rich modern city," I said.

"Like most places in the world it's sharply divided between rich and poor," said Eric. "In this land, there are very few in the middle."

"Where did all of these poor people come from?" I asked.

Eric shrugged.

"Many here are native people who lost their ancestral homes in the rainforest to logging and mining interests," he said.

As we circled around the crowd, Eric's phone chimed.

"I'm not sure what to make of this, but you're not going to like it," said Eric.

"The last few days have been hell for me," I said. "I was served with a petition for dissolution of marriage, lost my job, saw two people die horrible deaths, got shot…twice, watched Ginny get shot, and was nearly locked up in the loony bin. On top of all of that, they want to throw Mom out of the nursing home. I'm guessing whatever you have, will be more of the same."

Eric shook his head.

"Geez Dude, when you put that way, it sounds kind of like you've hit a rough spell," he said.

I gave him my best glare and asked, "What's up?"

"We found out who was behind your gig at the Center," he said.

Shortly after my employment was terminated from the law firm, an unknown person hired me as a bodyguard for a famous monk who was speaking at the Center. Things didn't go well. A security guard was murdered, I was shot, and thirty two hundred people in the audience died.

I figured whoever hired me was behind this nightmare and said a little impatiently, "So are you going to tell me, or what."

"It was Ginny," he said.

"Ginny?" I asked.

"Well...more precisely, it was her company, Emerald Allure," he said.

"A company that designs upscale clothing for women hired me to guard a monk in Louisville on a speaking engagement," I said.

Eric nodded.

"Was it Ginny personally?" I asked.

He shook his head.

"No, it was Victor Branco, her head of security," he said.

"It's time you tell me where Ginny is," I demanded.

"She's in Brazil," he said. "Your instincts were right, but she's not here in Rio. She's in Manaus at the gateway to the Amazon Rainforest."

"Why the hell didn't you tell me that sooner?" I asked.

"Because Ginny asked me not to and because I wanted to do a little partying in Rio, maybe add a few bikinis to my collection," said Eric.

"Your collection," I said.

"Seriously dude, you don't think I wear them, do you?" asked Eric.

I shrugged my shoulders.

"Beats me," I said.

Eric gave me his best hurt look. He even stuck his lower lip out to add a little pout to enhance the overall affect.

"Where is Victor Branco?" I asked.

"Manaus," answered Eric.

"Then we need to get to Manaus," I said.

"Yep."

CHAPTER 30

In sharp contrast to the lack of transportation at the Rio airport, there was a string of eager taxi drivers hustling to make a buck at the Manaus terminal. They were backed into parking slots with the trunk lids open, urging us with a wave to load our bags into their vehicle. None seemed to notice we carried no luggage.

A pear shaped guy leaped with surprising agility from a three wheeler hugging the curb in a no parking zone and huffed in our direction. The other drivers were wearing white short-sleeve shirts and tan slacks, but this guy stood out in pink polyester yoga pants stretched to the max across his broad ass and a canary yellow t-shirt that sagged in all the wrong places. He had a likeable round face, large mouth and tiny white teeth.

"Hello, my friends, I am Paulo," he said. "Welcome to Amazonia."

His cab was part motor scooter and part car. It was barely wide enough in the front to support Paulo's ample derriere, but could easily seat two in the rear. It was white with a black convertible top that provided shade from the equatorial sun.

Paulo must have seen the doubt on my face because he said, "Not to worry my friends. I have the best rates in Manaus thanks to the vastly superior gas mileage I get from this most amazing and very safe machine."

Eric poked me in the ribs and said, "Come on, Dude, live on the edge for a change."

I shrugged and we climbed into the back of the cab. The inside had the same hard plastic seats you'd find in a golf cart, but Paulo had softened them for his customers with colorful hand sewn cushions. A small wind chime, hand crafted into the shapes of endangered jungle critters, dangled from the rear view mirror. It provided musical accompaniment to Paulo's incessant chattering about Manaus.

"Where to my friends?" asked Paulo.

"Emerald Allure," I said.

"Are you rich Americans here to shop in the free trade zone?" he asked.

I shook my head.

"Yes, we go to the free trade zone," said Paulo answering his own question. "Scenic route today, my friends?"

"No," I answered.

"Yes, I want to see the real Manaus," said Eric.

"Very good choice, my friend, we take the scenic route and I show rich American shoppers the real Manaus," said Paulo.

The road leading out of the airport cut through green space dotted with occasional industrial buildings. There were patches of wind farms adjacent to the factories where huge blades reminiscent of airplane propellers spun atop a single mast to generate an alternative source of energy.

It was in the low nineties and humid. A bank of clouds riding the southeast trade winds rolled in from the east, serving as a reminder that this city had been carved out of the jungle and it's true nature is wet and primitive.

"Did you know, my friends, that Manaus is named after the Mother of the Gods?" asked Paulo.

I pulled my eyes from the roadside scenery and met his gaze in the rear view mirror. He didn't expect or wait for an answer. Paulo is one of those people who just like to talk.

"This beautiful city was once considered the Paris of the Tropics," he said. "You been there...to Paris, France?"

I shook my head.

"Well, this is a city of romance," he said. "We have many pretty people who live here."

So far, I had only met Paulo and he wasn't my type.

The cab turned down an umbrella lined street filled with shops, restaurants and open markets displaying colorful fruits and vegetables. Two small girls, about seven years old, squatted next to an anaconda that was thicker by far than their skinny legs. One controlled the head while the other pinned the tail to the ground. A scruffy medium sized dog with shaggy black hair squatted nearby with a bored expression on his face.

These four story buildings were old, but most were well-maintained. They were painted with bright tropical pinks, yellows, and lime greens. The food smelled amazing and my stomach growled in appreciation.

"We have festivals in Manaus...many festivals," he said. "We love to fiesta, and you my friends, have arrived just in time to enjoy the boat parade."

Paulo made several more turns before pulling to a stop in front of a modern six story building displaying a bold sign that announced, "Welcome to Emerald City." He left the taxi running and followed us inside the building while chattering something about wanting to say hello to his cousin.

The revolving door cast us into an open area with hardwood floors softened by an occasional area rug. The colorful artwork was framed in the same distressed wood as the flooring and molding. Organic is the word that best describes the gateway to Ginny's offices.

A dark haired receptionist sat at a small table that looked like it was better suited for a coffee shop. Still, it somehow fit the space perfectly.

Her white blouse was unbuttoned far enough to reveal a deep cleavage that led my eyes downward. Once they started down that slippery slope, I couldn't seem to stop them. Just below the table top was a bit of olive green fabric that qualified as a mini-skirt.

Further down were bare legs crossed at the shins. She had at least five inches of spiked heels as a base. Her thighs opened just enough that I could see she was freshly waxed, before chastely closing again as she rose from her chair.

Paulo's huge backside moved into my field of vision as he wrapped his arms around the receptionist and gave her a platonic hug. When she broke the hug he spoke to her in rapid Portuguese before introducing her as his cousin, Aida, and us as his new best friends from Kentucky, USA.

Aida quickly scanned our left hands, taking note of Eric's wedding band. The disappointment in her eyes was clearly evident. Her predatory gaze shifted to my empty hand. Once she determined I was available, she moved in for the kill.

"Well aren't you just a hunk," she said to me in perfect English.

Thinking I might capitalize on the flirt, I flashed my best engaging smile.

"We are friends of Virginia Bardough and would like to speak with her for a few minutes, if she's available," I said.

Her eyes traveled down to my jeans, where they paused a beat.

"Sorry gorgeous, but she's not here," said Aida.

"Are you expecting her anytime soon?" I asked.

Aida shook her head and then said suggestively, "Maybe someone else can help you."

I ignored her invitation and asked, "Ginny's here in Manaus, isn't she?"

Aida froze for just an instant, and then did a bobble headed dance between a shake and a nod. Her conflicted body language left me confused and uncertain about what to do next.

Eric spoke up and asked the obvious question, "Is Victor Branco available?"

A touch of fear briefly flashed across Aida's face. Before she could formulate an answer to Eric's question, her phone buzzed. I could see a slight tremor in her hand as she reached for the handset.

Aida took a small breath to bolster herself, but her greeting was stifled before it ever got started. Instead she listened attentively to the voice on the other end. It was loud enough that I could hear it, but not loud enough to make out the words. There's one thing I can say for sure, it was a man's voice and it was demanding.

"Yes sir, I will tell them," said Aida.

She lowered the handset into the cradle like it was something she feared breaking, but really wanted to smash into a thousand pieces. When she returned her attention to me, it was different. It reminded me of the way someone looks at a sick patient they are visiting in a hospital.

"Mr. Branco can meet with you in the morning," she said. "In the meantime, relax and enjoy our festival. The Procissao Fluvial de Sao Pedro is one of my favorites. It's like your Macy's Thanksgiving Day Parade, but on water."

She dropped her voice an octave and added, "Look for me."

We thanked her and had turned to leave when I saw a door behind Aida open a few inches. An eye peeped out at us for the briefest moment and then the door silently closed once again.

As soon as we stepped outside of the building, Paulo turned to us and said, "Victor Franco is a very bad man…very bad indeed, my friends. Be careful with that one."

"Why do you say that?" I asked.

He opened his mouth to speak and then shut it again. Instead, he cut his eyes toward one of the windows above us, gave a little shutter, and then shook his head.

"Hurry, let's get you inside of my limousine," he said.

Eric jabbed me in the ribs with an elbow, but didn't need to say more. The laughter in his eyes said it all as we climbed into Paulo's limo.

"Where to next my friends...are we ready to do that shopping now?" asked Paulo.

"No shopping," said Eric.

"Can you recommend a hotel near the water?" I asked.

"Only the very finest for my rich American friends," said Paulo.

"No, something more modest," I said.

"We want a place that is clean, but with historical character," said Eric.

"I have the perfect hotel for you," said Paulo. "My cousin will make sure you get the finest and most spacious room overlooking the water."

Paulo caught my eye in the rearview mirror and winked.

"Rooms...we will need two," I said.

"As you wish," he said.

Paulo drove us past the big resorts that looked like they had been cloned from the same template used by developers all around the world. Sitting off alone at water's edge was a historic three story Spanish colonial with a gold dome and high arched windows. The stucco was painted a discreet sandstone and trimmed in white. A monkey hung from the second story balcony screaming obscenities at us between bites of a juicy mango he possessively clutched with his right foot. It was the perfect hotel for us.

After we checked into our rooms, I walked down to the beach to watch the boats parade along the river. Eric decided to skip the parade in lieu of a nap.

I spotted an empty lounge chair by the water and settled in with a fruity drink made of acai berries and rum. It was served up in a hurricane glass with a wedge of lime and the choice of a straw or a long handled pink spoon. The drink was thick and slushy enough I decided to use the spoon instead of the straw.

The boats came in all sizes and shapes. Some were decorated like floats, but others were not. More than a few were good sized party boats loaded on two levels with passengers dancing to live salsa music. Even the river dolphins enjoyed the party. Their lively antics seemed to follow the sexy Latin beat.

Between the alcohol and the events of the last few days, I began to drift off. The last boat I saw before I closed my eyes carried a large banner with a white skull sporting large orange eyes, black nose and a mouth full of horse teeth.

I'm not sure how long I slept, but it was the shrill voice of Dad's macaw that woke me.

"Aaawk, wake up peckerwood," said Bird. "You have a date with destiny."

It must have been a dream because the foul mouth bird was nowhere in sight. The sun had set and twilight fell across the empty river. A band played to a fiesta somewhere off in the distant night. The party had moved to the streets.

My stomach rumbled for food. I decided to forego hotel fare and headed instead into the thick of things in search of a place to eat with local character. The savory aroma of street food pulled me into the older part of the city.

People were dancing in the streets, each dressed in a uniquely bizarre costume lending a Mardi Gras atmosphere to the place. As I weaved through the crowd of drunks, I saw a young girl with vacant eyes and a sad demeanor standing in the center of an alley.

Despite the heat, she wore a hooded cloak that covered everything except her hands, feet and face. Those areas were covered with white powder accented by streaks of red, like smeared blood. It gave her a creepy voodoo look.

Just as I was about to turn away, Voodoo Girl collapsed. Without giving it a second thought, I rushed toward her, but a police officer stepped from the shadows and blocked my path. I froze in my tracks.

He was covered from head to toe in navy blue swat clothing. Swat Cop wore a riot helmet, dark glasses, and the remainder of his face was covered with a mask. I'm pretty sure he was wearing body armor as well. The outfit looked unbearably hot to me, but I didn't see any signs of perspiration on him.

I expected Swat Cop to do something to help Voodoo Girl, but he ignored her and instead raised his weapon and pointed it in my face. For the first time, I wondered whether he was a real cop or not. I didn't see any indentifying markings for the Manaus Police Department and he seemed undisciplined to me…more like a common crook than a well-trained policeman.

As I wondered whether this might just be a mugging, a young woman wearing a wife beater and faded blue jeans appeared from the shadows. There was a snake tattooed around her right bicep. Wife Beater seemed to look right through me. I don't think I saw her blink once and was beginning to think she might be blind, but then she cut his eyes to Swat Cop and spoke.

"Bring him," said Wife Beater.

Criminals are just people who are too lazy to work. So, when they commit a crime, they want it to be easy. They do not want the crime to be anything like work and they certainly don't want to get caught.

If the crime begins at a location where there might be witnesses, one of the first things a criminal tries to do is convince the victim to go with them to a more remote location. Once they isolate the victim, then the criminal can do anything they want without worrying about getting caught. Never leave a public place and go with a criminal to a more isolated location.

I raised my hands in the air and said, "Hey, you can have my money, but I'm not going anywhere with you."

Swat Cop jammed the gun in my belly and Wife Beater asked, "Do you hear those fireworks?"

I nodded.

"No one will notice if he pulls the trigger," said Wife Beater. "The gun shot will blend in with the sounds of the fireworks. You'll just be another dead asshole on the streets of Manaus. Do you understand?"

I let out a deflated sigh and murmured, "Not good."

"Understand?" asked Wife Beater more forcefully.

I nodded.

Swat Cop spun me around and pushed hard into my mid-back with the barrel of his gun. I took the first step toward crime scene number two.

As if on cue, Voodoo Girl popped up and joined the group. It was now clear that her sudden collapse had been a ruse to lure me into their trap, but I had no idea what they wanted with me.

We made our way down to the Amazon where they had a small boat tied to the tangled roots of an uprooted tree that had washed ashore with the rest of the driftwood. Wife Beater reached behind herself and produced a coil of rough rope made from a stiff natural fiber. She handed it to Swat Cop who tightly bound my hands. When I tested the knots, I was rewarded with tortuous pain from the prickly fibers ripping into my skin.

Voodoo Girl leaned ever so slightly in my direction and sniffed as a drop of blood fell to the river bank. Her dark hunger sent a chill up my spine. It only lasted a moment before she once again became a blank page empty of human emotion. The thought of her drinking blood like a real life vampire feeding off unsuspecting tourists gave me the creeps.

Swat Cop said something to me in an unfamiliar language. I answered in English, telling him I didn't understand him. The fake policeman pointed his gun at me. I calmly stood my ground. Swat Cop snarled and pressed the barrel against my temple. I remained silent.

The cop waited and then pulled the hammer back. I felt sweat trickle down to the small of my back. Oddly, his hand trembled. I also noticed his breath wheezed, heavy and labored.

I could smell fear, but wasn't sure if it was mine or if it was his. The tremble seemed to piss him off and he pressed the cold steel deeper into my flesh. I figured I was as good as dead. There was nothing to do but wait.

My senses heightened. I swear I felt the river's life force. It seemed I was part of something bigger...a force of life that permeates all things. It reminded me of music I heard long ago. A piece from Mozart, I think, but I couldn't quite place it.

Finally, Wife Beater said something in the same strange language. Swat Cop grunted and lowered the hammer. With a small wave of the barrel, he pointed in the direction of the boat and I climbed in. I shook my head. I did not have time for this shit.

As the others climbed aboard, I felt something moving against my leg. I casually slapped at it, expecting an insect. Something hissed at me. I peered into the darkness. There was something there, but I couldn't quite make it out until the moon passed through the clouds and a beam of light revealed a huge snake.

Instinctively I sprang backward and fell over the side of the boat and into the river. Disoriented in the dark water, I struggled to find my footing and slipped under the surface a second time.

A strong hand grabbed me by the collar and yanked me back into the boat. Wife Beater's face was inches from mine. I held my breath to avoid the foul stench of her breath. It reminded me of a burnt match...full of sulfur. She scowled for a moment before allowing herself a small smile.

I nervously glanced in the snake's direction. The anaconda's lidless eyes stared back...its forked tongue flickering in and out. I suppressed a childish urge to stick mine out as well. I could be mistaken, but I'm pretty sure I saw the damn thing smirk.

Swat Cop took the helm, gunned the engine and launched us toward the center of the Amazon where black water meets brown water, but the two refuse to mix. We steered past a group of fishing boats lit up with lanterns. The fisherman used the light to sort through the days catch. As best I could tell, the river had generously provided a rich bounty, but there was something gut wrenching about seeing the fish gasp for their last breath.

Once we moved away from their lights, everything was black…the sky, the water and my mood. These people were taking me away from Manaus. To where and for what, I didn't know.

The boat ride went on for what seemed like hours. The river was crowded with drifting trees and plants we maneuvered around. I couldn't quite figure out why they were still green until I saw huge chunks of river bank, plants and all, avalanche into the river.

Creepy snake or not, exhaustion caught up with me and I slipped in and out of a restless sleep filled with nightmarish images. The only hope came from a pair of playful river dolphins tracking our progress. They seemed to smile encouragement at me and I liked them all the more when the snake shrunk from them. Still, I can't be sure if I didn't dream that part too.

I lost all track of time and couldn't say for sure, but figured we had floated down the river for most of the night before the boat was beached just before dawn.

In the predawn light I saw a group of heron fishing near the bank. Their food supply was so plentiful they would grab a fish in their beaks and then inspect the variety of their catch before making a snap decision whether they wanted to eat it or throw it back.

There was something else moving in the water among the heron that I couldn't quite make out at first. It wasn't until one of the crocodiles lifted its snout wide and then abruptly snapped it shut on an unsuspecting fish that I figured it out. I couldn't help but wonder why the crocodiles left the heron alone. Fishing side by side, the two creatures made for very strange companions.

We made a wide berth around the crocodiles on our way to the shore. Once we were on the bank, Voodoo Girl led us into the jungle. There was no apparent trail. Still, we moved at a blistering pace through the dense foliage. She seemed to follow an unseen path of least resistance. We continued to travel at a brutal pace. Foot sore and weary, I focused on my breath.

Ch'ing's voice echoed from the past telling me, "Just breathe. Take one breath at a time. Nothing else matters."

It helped. I felt a sense of well-being spread to the deepest parts of my inner self. Despite the desperate circumstance, I began to feel calm within minutes of the hike. The trail does that to me. An old forest is a peaceful place. It tends to its own needs, free of human manipulation. It's like a cathedral where the hand of God is within reach.

Finally, Voodoo Girl stopped next to a mountain stream. She scanned the surrounding jungle. Satisfied, she dropped to her knees and slowly bent toward the water. I expected her to scoop it with her hands, but she began lapping it up like a cat. No one else moved toward the stream until she had her fill.

Then one at a time, they drank. I was the last. When my turn finally came, I gratefully dropped to my knees and scooped a handful of cool water. In the moonlight I could see the stream was clear, like glass.

I heard the flutter of wings. A bat swooped in, nabbed a small fish, and abruptly changed course to avoid a head on collision with me. I know bats aren't the evil creatures portrayed in Dracula movies, but it's hard not to get little freaked out when I see one swoop in at eye level.

When I finished, I turned toward the others and was greeted by the anaconda's cold eyes. I recoiled and shifted my gaze to Voodoo Girl. She looked at me like food. No relief there.

After we drank from the stream, I thought we would rest for a while, but Voodoo Girl resumed her brutal pace into the depths of the jungle. There was a sense of urgency, as if she was in a hurry to get to a safe place.

She never stopped scanning our surroundings and sniffing the air. I wondered what she feared might be lurking in the jungle. Although I saw no outward signs of danger, I could feel unseen eyes watching. Someone or something was following us.

We were deep into the wilderness when the temperature began to drop. I heard a deep rumble that sounded like a lion from an old Tarzan movie. Of course there are no lions in the Amazon rainforest, but there are Jaguars. Then I saw the unmistakable flash of lightening and it began to rain.

Suddenly, the anaconda whipped its head to the side. Voodoo Girl froze. Swat Cop rapidly scanned the surrounding bush. There was a wild animal look in his eyes. Wife Beater dropped into a crouch. The anaconda slithered off her shoulders and disappeared into the forest.

Swat Cop raised his gun in my direction and shouted, "Die gringo devil."

Having guns pointed in my face was becoming annoyingly familiar. I heard the twang almost the same instant that an arrow pierced his throat and silenced him. Swat Cop crumbled to his knees without firing a shot.

Voodoo Girl hissed. For the first time I saw her teeth. My God, it looked like a cat's mouth. She sprung toward the cover of the jungle but a dart in the neck stopped her cold.

Wife Beater was flat on the ground. Damned if she wasn't slithering like a snake, moving in the same direction as the anaconda. A spear between the shoulder blades pinned her to the ground where she lay in pool of dark blood.

They were all dead. Only I remained standing. The forest began to close in on me. There was a flash of lightening. Faces slowly emerged from the shifting shadows.

Painted warriors carrying Stone Age weapons surrounded me. Other than a few feathers and beads, they were naked. They were also huge. I estimated they were nearly seven feet tall and packed with muscle.

Naked or not, these Amazons looked deadly, even the women...correction, especially the women. When you meet a tiger in the jungle, you don't check its private parts to see whether it is male or female. It's a tiger and you better respect it because all tigers, regardless of gender, are dangerous.

These naked giants had just killed three people. Would they kill me too? No one spoke. We waited.

Finally, an ageless man broke the circle of warriors and moved toward me. I say ageless, not because he was elderly. In fact he looked to be in his mid-twenties. My assessment had more to do with the way he carried himself. It spoke volumes. This man was wise. It was the kind of wisdom that comes from years of experience and it made him seem ancient. Like he was an old soul.

He was shorter than the others, maybe six and a half feet tall, give or take an inch or two. The spear in his left hand was at least a foot taller. He may have been shorter than the others, but he had a bigger presence.

Coal black hair flowed down his back and reached just below his shoulder blades. His head was perfectly symmetrical, like the letter "O" and crowned with yellow and green feathers. The only other thing he wore were strips of white fabric wrapped around his lower legs and blue fabric around his biceps. His brown skin was painted red on the right side of his body and black on the left.

The warrior stopped inches from me and peered into my eyes. I figured he invaded my personal space for a good reason, so I returned his gaze in search of my own answers. What I found were surprisingly kind eyes. This man was a gentle soul.

Whatever he was looking for, he found. In one swift movement, he unsheathed his knife and cut the rope from my hands. As I rubbed circulation back into my wrists, the warrior gracefully swept his arm toward the others and spoke for the first time in perfect English.

"We are the Guardians," he said.

They bowed their heads in unison.

He placed his hand over his heart and said, "I am called Teekal."

"My name is Grant," I said.

Teekal placed his hand over my heart and said, "Welcome to the gateway, Grant."

One by one, the rest of the group stepped forward and introduced themselves in a similar manner. I'm normally good with names, but theirs were so unusual I quickly gave up trying to remember them. When the introductions were completed, Teekal motioned me to follow him deeper into the jungle.

I pointed in the opposite direction.

"Thank you for your help, but I have to get back to Manaus," I said. "Can someone show me the way back to the river?"

"What you seek is in this direction," said Teekal.

Without another word he led the group of warriors into the jungle. I briefly considered blazing my own trail in the opposite direction, but I was far from home and hopelessly lost. There was also a part of me that knew I could trust them, so without further hesitation, I followed the Guardians to an uncertain outcome.

The rain was falling steadily, but I was accustomed to hiking in the rain. Still, it wasn't easy to keep up with them. The Guardians moved at a blistering pace in the dark jungle and somehow blended in as if they were protected by a space age cloaking device.

At first I wanted to slow down and carefully pick my way through the darkness, but I knew they would have gone off and left me there if I had. Instead, I had to use my intuition like it had never been used before, trusting that each blind step was exactly where it needed to be.

Focused on each step, I was completely immersed in the here and now. Time disappeared. For the duration of the hike, there was nowhere else but here.

As my awareness heightened, I sensed something was shadowing our movements. I couldn't see or hear it, but I felt it all the same. The warriors showed no signs of concern. These people belonged to the jungle.

When I thought I couldn't take another step, we finally stopped. One of the women took my hand and led me to an open-air dwelling that I hadn't even realized we'd come to. It blended well with the forest and was nearly invisible. Inside I heard the sounds of sleep. She pointed in the direction of an empty hammock. I gratefully collapsed into it and fell immediately into a deep sleep.

CHAPTER 31

I awoke to the touch of a warm body cuddled next to me. It was still night, but the jungle was glowing softly with moonlight. Some of the light managed to penetrate the shelter, revealing the faint outlines of six other hammocks stuffed with sleeping bodies.

I didn't know this place and tried to remember how I got here. The initial confusion passed and yesterday's events flooded my mind. Not sure what to make of it, I thought of getting up and sorting it all out, but the need for sleep won out and I closed my eyes once again.

Without clocks, I had no way of knowing how long I slept before a nagging bladder interrupted a sexy dream where I saw Ginny standing at the edge of my bed. Her eyes were soft and luminous. Neither of us spoke. She reached behind and slowly unzipped her black cocktail dress. As it began to slide down her shoulder, I awoke from the dream with a full bladder screaming for release.

I didn't want to get up. Instead I lay there thinking about Ginny. She was in trouble. I could feel it. I needed to help her…to rescue her, but had no way of knowing how to find her in the vast Rainforest.

My bladder refused to be ignored. I started to groan, but stopped. No sense in waking the others. Instead, I slowly opened my eyes. A beam of moonlight cut across the shelter. I was alone in the hammock. Whoever was sleeping next to me earlier had left.

As I reluctantly swung my feet to the ground, it occurred to me that I was in a primitive place without the luxury of a bathroom down the hall. I would have to make my way by moonlight to the edge of the jungle before I could relieve the pressure on my bladder.

With a sigh, I tiptoed into the night. When I reached the tree line, I counted another twenty paces before stopping next to a chest high bush with leaves as big as watermelons to pee. Not that anyone else was awake, but I figured the broad leaves would insure privacy while I tended to business.

I'm an experienced backpacker and have spent many nights in the backcountry. Unlike some of my city dwelling friends, I find the forest's night sounds soothing. The symphony of sound I heard as I tended to nature was unique to the Amazon

Rainforest.

For the first time since I arrived, I could relax and let the forest's music carry me where it would, but it was short lived. The music abruptly stopped. The jungle became deathly still. As I stood there shaking the last few drops, I was suddenly knocked to the ground. Somebody had ambushed me.

A hundred razor sharp teeth glinted in the moonlight. The attacker hissed. Holy cow, not somebody, but something and it was huge. All I could see was a field of white and too many teeth to count.

The strike came fast. I was groggy from the blow and flat on my back. A heavy weight pressed me into the earth. Not much time or room for a maneuver. Instinctively, I shifted my head at the last second. Teeth sank into my left shoulder.

I tried to lift my right arm, but something heavy pinned it against my chest. That's not good. My left hand flew to the source of pain. I punched it. The teeth sunk deeper. It hurt like hell. I tried to pry it off, but it was bigger than my hand. We started rolling. I couldn't quite get a grip on it.

I felt a sharp pain in my ribs. Damn, it was squeezing the breath out of me. I pushed back. It squeezed tighter. I was strong. It was stronger. Where did all the oxygen go? It was hard to breathe. I tried to shout, but nothing came out except a muffled moan.

I panicked. In my fumbling to get a hold of it, I felt something soft. It was the corner of an eye. The squeezing intensified. Desperate, I shoved a finger in as far as I could. The eye popped out. The bite released and the ambusher tried to pull away, but I pressed its head firmly against my shoulder.

I was pissed now and shouted, "Die…die…die a painful death…die…die…"

It rolled us across the jungle floor. Something sharp, maybe a rock, jabbed into my hip. Still, I held firm and began rotating my finger inside of its head. I felt a shock. It ran from my finger and pulsated throughout my body. When it hit my head I saw white light and then everything went dark.

I tried to claw myself out of the darkness, but the weight of it was too much. Finally, I accepted the inevitable and relaxed. So this is how it ends, a grave less death in the middle of the jungle, far from home, without friends or family to see me off.

I was surrounded by darkness and expected to see a light that I could move toward, but it never appeared. There was only darkness and it seemed to extend forever into eternity.

I don't know how much time passed before I heard a voice. It was a welcomed break from the nothingness. The crushing weight was gone and I could breathe again. The voice came louder. It was a woman I heard and she was speaking soothingly, like you would to a wounded animal.

"Open your eyes," she said.

It seemed like a good idea and I wanted to open them, but there was a disconnect between desire and action.

"Aaawk, open your eyes peckerwood," squawked Bird.

I thought it was weird how I kept hearing my dad's macaw way out here in the middle of nowhere. I chalked it up to snake venom and tried to go back to sleep.

A man whispered, "The serpent is dead."

Another voice, "It is him."

When I realized these people weren't going to let me rest, I opened my eyes and focused on the face leaning over me. It was soft and feminine, framed by long black hair. I could see compassion in her luminous brown eyes. There was something else in them too…ancient wisdom, I thought weirdly.

I'm pretty sure she had been the one in my bed earlier. She was tall like the others and packed with muscle. Her hips and breasts were round and proportionate to each other in a classic hourglass way. She was nude and in the light of the full moon, I could see that her brown skin was flawless.

There was a self-possessed air about her that seemed regal to me. At first I assumed she was a leader, but when I shifted my gaze to the small crowd that formed behind her, I could see they were not followers. None of them showed any sign they were the subjects of a master.

"How extraordinary," I whispered. "Each and every one of you is clearly in charge of yourself."

"As it should be," she said. "Do you remember me?"

I nodded.

"You were in the hammock with me earlier," I answered.

She smiled. "Yes, but we met earlier," she said.

It took a moment, but I remembered seeing her with the warriors who rescued me from the freaks. The face paint had been washed away, but it was her. I nodded.

"I'm sorry I don't remember your name," I said.

"My name is Layah," she said. "Let us help you with your injuries."

Gentle hands cleaned my wounds. I intended to nod in assent, but felt a sharp pain and grimaced instead.

A man handed me a cup saying, "Drink."

When I raised an eyebrow, he grinned and said, "Great Mother."

I had no idea what he meant. I sniffed and found it to be pleasantly aromatic. It smelled faintly of the jungle around us and what I imagine sunshine would smell like if it had a smell.

He put his hand to his mouth and tilted his head back. I took a sip. It was neither hot nor cold and tasted odd. It wasn't odd in a bad way…but rather odd because it was beyond my experience. It seemed to be sweet, sour, salty, and bitter all at the same time.

My body's reaction to the sip was surprising. I instantly craved the rest of the liquid and drank it down without hesitation.

"Rest now," said Layah.

The remainder of the night was uneventful. The next morning I felt rested, but extremely weird. I tingled, as if unimpeded electrical current flowed through me. It wasn't unpleasant…just unusual.

I remembered the snake bite and checked my shoulder. There was no sign of injury. How could that be? The damn anaconda ripped out a huge hunk of flesh.

I also cracked another rib in last night's battle with the snake. That made two cracked ribs over the last few days, the other coming from a hard kick delivered by Slotter, the psycho ex-Special Forces chick, disguised as a Tibetan monk. I gently pressed against both ribs. There was no pain…nothing.

I checked my gunshot wounds. The first was nothing more than a scratch that I received while guarding Padma. He is one of those unassuming people you'd never think could become a celebrity, but when he wrote a book about paradise the world fell in love with his ideas about peace and happiness.

At the time, I wasn't sure why anybody thought he needed a bodyguard. As it turned out, things got crazy when he tried to reveal the secret of long life to an auditorium full of fans hungry for something meaningful. Instead of Padma's description of a land of peace and plenty, gunshot blasts filled the auditorium.

A lot of people died, but not from bullet wounds. The official reason given for their deaths was an accidental gas leak, but it sure looked like they were locked inside to me. I don't think it was an accident.

The second gunshot wound was far more serious. I took a bullet in the back trying to rescue Ginny from Slotter, the Special Forces chick who broke my rib.

Despite all of that, I felt great. I was the walking wounded when I arrived in Brazil. Now there wasn't a sore bone in my body. The Guardians gave me medicine that worked wonders on my injuries and I needed to know what else it could heal.

Was this the medicine Pony Tail had given to Ginny and Uncle Jim? If so, could it be used to help my mother? She has been a prisoner of her bed for twenty years, a paraplegic, robbed of the life she was meant to have by a hit-and-run driver. No matter how slim the chance, I needed to explore the possibility this medicine could heal her.

For now though, my rumbling stomach reminded me it had been more than twenty-four hours since I last had something to eat. I tried to swallow, but my throat was parched. I didn't know if it was meal time for the Guardians, but I needed food and water.

I looked around for signs of food, but the shelter was empty except for a beam of sunlight splitting the space. A cool breeze drifted across my skin. Other than goose bumps, I was naked. I arrived fully clothed and had no memory of undressing.

I scanned the room for my clothes. They were nowhere in sight. The only thing I could use to cover myself was a basket. The thought of hiding behind a basket seemed silly around a bunch of naked people, so I abandoned the idea.

As I was about to step into the light, I suddenly stopped. My entire body was shaking. I couldn't remember being this scared, except maybe when I was a kid and the Fat Lady caught me playing a game of show me yours with her daughter, Ginny. Some wounds seem to resist healing.

Public nudity is definitely not my thing. It took every ounce of courage I had to leave the shelter, but I did it. Squaring my shoulders, I abandoned the shadows and stepped into the morning light.

I stood in a small clearing surrounded by a group of open aired lodges. The roofs were constructed from palms and connected together to form a ring around a central fire pit. The location of the four cardinal points were marked on the edge of the pit. The overall effect was a circle within a circle.

Looking out from the center of the circle was a twenty foot clear space buffering the lodges from the surrounding jungle. I imagine it also provided light and security for the Guardians.

The small village reminded me of a scene from an old movie and I half expected to see a feral man-ape swinging from limb to limb in the treetops. I could almost hear his voice calling to the jungle, "aweuaauaawe."

I was starting to feel comfortable, when I saw a one-eyed snake. My blood ran cold. It was huge...the biggest damn snake I've ever seen...at least a hundred feet long.

"Aaawk, don't be afraid," squawked Bird. "It's as dead as a doornail."

"I had no idea they got that big," I muttered.

"There are giants among us," said a woman's voice.

"Must be something in the water," I said.

"Aaawk, we grow 'em big around here, for sure," said Bird.

"Yes," said the woman.

"The damn thing almost killed me," I said.

"This was once a great serpent," she said. "Now she belongs to you."

I tore my eyes from the beast. Standing close enough that our hips almost touched was Layah. On her shoulder, sat Dad's macaw. As long as I can remember the only name he ever had was Bird. Except lately, he had taken to calling himself, Ponce.

"I don't understand," I said.

"You survived a battle with a powerful enemy," she said. "The serpent's spirit is now a part of you."

"A part of me?" I murmured.

She nodded.

"Aaawk, are you going to say hello or just keep pretending I'm not here," squawked Bird.

Bird was a hemisphere away in Louisville. Since he had to be some kind of hallucination, I ignored him. On the other hand, the snake was as real as it gets.

I've always hated snakes. I'm not exactly sure why, but I was raised on the biblical story of Eve's temptation and her fall from grace. Thanks to the serpent's lies, paradise was lost and mankind was left to toil and suffer. It was unthinkable that I was the serpent.

"What if I don't want a snake's spirit inside of me?" I asked.

"Where is the me that is separate from the serpent?" asked Layah.

"You sound like a friend of mine," I said with a laugh.

"Your friend must be very wise," giggled Layah.

"Aaawk, I'm the smartest bird that ever was or ever will be, Toots," said Bird.

Layah stroked the side of Bird's ample beak and said in soothing tone of voice, "Why you're not a bird at all, Ponce."

"If Bird isn't really a bird, then what is he?" I asked.

Bird leaned slowly in my direction as if he intended to reveal a great secret and then suddenly bit the tip of my nose. It hurt like hell and I'm pretty sure he drew blood.

"Aaawk, if you want to see my true nature, peckerwood, then open your eyes," said Bird. "Or at least pay attention to the clues."

I covered my nose to protect it from a second assault and said, "Stop that, Bird."

"No need to get violent, Ponce," said Layah. "I think Grant was talking about someone else."

I checked my nose for signs of blood and was relieved to find it clean.

"I was talking about Ch'ing," I grumbled.

"Aaawk, Ch'ing, Ch'ing, always Ch'ing," said Bird. "It's about time this peckerwood gave me a little respect too."

I swatted at Bird, but he managed to duck at the last minute. I could be mistaken, but I think he hissed at me. Then again, it could be I only imagined I heard a hiss when I got an unobstructed look at the one eyed snakeskin when he ducked.

"The serpent is a deceiver," I said. "That's not something I want inside of me."

"Are you open-minded?" asked Layah.

"I like to believe so," I answered.

"Aaawk, open-minded my ass," said Bird. I bet your wife would have a different opinion on that subject."

Layah raised an eyebrow, but didn't ask Bird what he meant.

Instead she said to me, "If you're open-minded, then guard against assumptions about the serpent. Kundalini is the path to freedom."

"What do you mean?" I asked.

"There is latent energy stored at the base of the spine, like a sleeping serpent coiled around the sacrum," answered Layah. "It is called, Kundalini. When it awakens, it spirals up the spine, energizing each aspect of your life. In the process, you become the person you were destined to be."

Bird ripped a noisy fart and screeched, "Aaawk, I got your sacral energy right here. Take a deep breath and feel the power of this bird."

"Really Bird?" I said.

Surprisingly, Bird looked a little embarrassed by his own behavior. That had to be a first. As I turned my attention back to Layah, I couldn't help but wonder if it wasn't the end-times.

"Aaawk, that's exactly what it is," said Bird.

I wasn't sure if he was still talking about the power of his fart or the end-times. I decided to ignore him. I mean…really…as if he could actually read my mind.

"Kundalini sounds something like the energy work I practice," I said to Layah. "We call it Chi Kung."

"Don't get caught up in terminology," said Layah. "It makes no difference what we call it, the life force is the same."

"It's not just terminology," I said. "We collect and store energy in our lower abdomen, a place we call the Tan Tien. It sounds to me like your practice draws energy from that area."

"Truth lies in the common ground, but it can also be found in our differences," said Layah.

"It seems to me that the two practices are very different," I said. "Maybe I could see the common ground better if I knew a little more about your practice. You said something about awakening Kundalini. How is that accomplished?"

Layah flashed a radiant smile and said, "Ahhh…you're listening. Good. You begin at the beginning, of course. The first aim of meditation is to quiet the mind's incessant chatter. This is best accomplished by opening the mind until it quiets of its own accord. I like to think of it like opening a window and letting a cool breeze clear the air inside of the room."

I looked around and noted that none of the buildings in this tiny village had windows. In fact they had no doors or walls for that matter. They were completely open.

"You do air it out," I said cutting my eyes to Bird.

"The best practice is to remember what is good for the inside is also good on the outside," said Layah. "It reconciles the incongruent aspects of life."

"What do you mean?" I asked.

People are often divided against themselves," said Layah. "They say they want one thing, but do the opposite. When the mind is faced with an incongruity, such as a paradoxical problem, it's best to reconcile that or else the mind will grab hold of the first thing that makes any sense."

Bird fluttered off with a squawk.

I was not only having trouble with the idea that part of me was a snake, it was pretty damn weird having a spiritual discussion in the nude. On top of that, the snake skin drying in the sun added to the bizarre scene. It seemed primitive to me...almost barbaric and not spiritual at all.

I was uncomfortable being around someone stripped of outer clothing. Likewise, the snake was stripped of everything on the inside that makes up a living creature. How that had anything to do with me was unclear...and trying to sort it out gave me the first hint of a headache.

"What purpose does saving the skin serve?" I asked.

"This one is special," said Layah.

"How is it special?" I asked.

She seemed to search my face for something before answering.

"This creature is more than a dangerous beast," she said. "You might say it is supernatural."

I took another look at the huge snake and to my chagrin began shaking. It embarrassed me. I tried to control it and failed.

"It must be a chill," I said.

Layah wrapped me in a warm hug.

"You are very brave," she said softly.

At six feet, I was at least a head shorter then her. Still, my face shouldn't have ended up between her breasts like it did. I told myself she coaxed it there in a motherly way, but my reaction was not familial.

My response to her touch mortified me. What is even worse, it attracted the attention of a group of women. I hadn't thought they were paying any attention to us, since they were circling the fire, hand in hand, while chanting in a strange tongue. It embarrassed me when they stopped and openly stared. The tallest one whispered something to the others and they all began giggling like school girls.

A man I recognized from the night before smiled and waved me over. He was roughly the same height as Layah, maybe a tad shorter at 6'7". Like her, his skin was smooth and unblemished. His smiling face was wrinkle free, but his eyes also seemed ancient. By ancient I don't mean tired. Instead, they were infinitely wise. We've all heard the term "Old Soul" before, but he really fit the bill.

Layah gave me a little push in his direction. Smiling, I walked over to join him near the fire.

"That's a little embarrassing," I said.

It hardly seemed possible, but his smile widened a bit more.

In a voice we usually reserve for small children, he asked, "What do you find embarrassing?"

I opened my mouth to answer, but nothing came out. How do you explain "embarrassment" to someone who is so obviously comfortable in their own skin? It was as if we spoke a different emotional language. I wasn't certain yet, but I think I liked his language better.

I shrugged and said, "I'm Grant. I think we met last night. Isn't your name Teekal."

A wide grin filled his face.

"Yes, I'm Teekal," he said. "You must be hungry."

He offered me a wooden bowl filled with creamy porridge. Unfamiliar fruit, nuts, and seeds were stirred in. I expected it to be bland, but it was delicious. In fact, it was the best thing I've ever eaten. A mug of rich dark roasted cowboy coffee and cocoa followed. Yummmm!

"Good," he said.

I nodded. He waited as I ate and drank the food he provided. Even though we didn't speak during the meal, it didn't feel awkward and I wasn't hurried.

After I swallowed the last bite, he asked if I wanted more. Good food has a way of arousing greed, but not this meal. I was satisfied on many levels and declined his offer. What I wanted instead, were answers.

"Why do you call yourself the Guardians?" I asked.

"It's who we are," he answered. "We guard the gateway."

"The gateway to what?" I asked.

"Paradise," he answered.

I looked around. This remote part of the Amazon Rainforest was beautiful and you could call it "Paradise," but I sensed he was talking about something else, something more mysterious and hidden from view. I wanted to ask more about it, but my gut told me a direct approach would only push it further out of view. It was time for a new line of questions.

"Do you know what happened to my clothes?" I asked.

He scrunched up his nose in distaste and said, "Smell bad."

Nodding toward the fire he added, "I burned them."

"Damn," I murmured.

"Come, you smell bad too and we have just what is needed to fix it," he said.

He turned and walked toward a path leading into the jungle. I stuck my nose in my armpit and breathed deeply. He was right. I smelled ripe and hoped he didn't plan to burn me too.

I had a vision of myself being slow cooked over an open fire. I didn't think I would be very appetizing and I had to laugh out loud. He looked over his shoulder at me and grinned. I trusted him.

He led us down to a stream and we waded into the center. It was an easy walk since the stream flowed across a sheet of bedrock that curved up the north bank like a breaking wave forming a rock shelter. The opposite bank was lined with a wide variety of flowers, some as big as your head, mixed with ferns, palms, and broad leaf plants.

I wasn't familiar with the vegetation, but overall it reminded me of the bank of the many streams and rivers I had paddled over the years. The only exception was the wide variety of tropical flowers that were home to an astonishing number of butterflies. The most interesting flower looked like a set of large red painted hooker lips. I had never seen anything like it.

The water was never much deeper than just below my knees. Still, I continuously scanned it for fish. I wasn't interested in catching them for food; instead I couldn't get images of man eating piranha out of my mind. Each time I saw a fish, I tensed up thinking it might try to take a bite out of me.

After I saw a snake, I immediately stopped worrying about the fish and my ample imagination ran wild with the dangers of snake bites. It was fueled by a guy I met on a backpacking trip a few years earlier who told me he had spent years in the back country only to be bitten by a snake in his own back yard. With a disgusted expression he told me the anti-venom cost him $28,000.00 dollars a dose.

I didn't want to believe the medicine actually cost that much, but given the way the healthcare industry has run amuck, I'm sure he was telling the truth. In any event, I sure didn't want to test it. Of course, I knew the chance of getting to a hospital in time from this remote location was virtually nil. I was really getting tired of snakes.

In the corner of my eye I saw a flash of movement and turned just in time to see a dragon faced toad, nearly as big as a dinner plate, leap from the bank and splash into a pool next to a fallen log.

Even though I was experienced in the backcountry, I don't remember ever being so skittish about the wildlife. It was time to take it down a notch, so I took a deep breath and focused on the beauty that surrounded me. It helped. Once I started paying attention to how good the cool water felt, I began to calm down. I liked this place.

After a short walk, we came to a confluence of two streams. Teekal headed up the second stream which led into a bowl shaped area formed by rock shelters on three sides. A twenty foot water fall emptied into a swimming hole filled with frolicking swimmers.

The fourth side of the bowl was dominated by a beach filled with coral colored sand where sunbathers were stretched out napping or engaged in various forms of play.

There was steam rising on the backside of the beach that I initially mistook as smoke. Upon closer examination, I saw about twenty people soaking in a hot spring. The bathers smiled and waved me in. What the hell, I thought. I figured a bath would feel great. So, I waded into the hot water.

At its deepest point, it rose to my chest. It was there that I came to a rest. It felt wonderful. The water was fragrant, a little like rosemary and a second scent I couldn't quite pinpoint, but was hauntingly familiar. It was calming to the mind and soothing to the skin. No wonder everyone in the hot springs looked so mellow.

The waterfall crowd was more playful. They laughed and frolicked with each other. There was no indication they felt self-conscious about their nudity. In fact, no one seemed to give it a second thought. I didn't see any aggressive behavior in their play. They seemed so different than the warriors who had killed so efficiently the night before. I never heard a cross word spoken. Their laughter penetrated deeply. It was music to my soul.

Folks moved back and forth from the hot springs to the waterfall, alternating hot and cold. Feeling hot, I decided to switch pools. The waterfall was cold and refreshing. I began to laugh, slowly at first, and then uncontrollably. It felt so good to be alive.

I spent the next few hours going back and forth between the two pools. I smiled and chatted with them from time to time, but mostly I communed with my inner self.

The sun had reached its apex and begun its descent toward the western horizon when I noticed everyone had left. I was beginning to feel whole again. Like Congressional pork that piggy backs onto a new bill, the urgency to find Ginny attached itself to my sense of well-being.

I resolved to ask to be guided out of the jungle first thing in the morning.

CHAPTER 32

Ham sized chunks of flesh sizzled over an open pit at the center of the village. The meat looked unfamiliar, but smelled delicious. For some reason, I had pegged these people as vegetarians and wondered what manner of beast they were barbequing. When my eyes fell on the snake skin curing in the sun, I began to suspect we were having slow roasted Anaconda for dinner. Ughhh…

The villagers wandered in with decorative baskets filled with fruit, vegetables, and flat bread. The food was set on low tables arranged around the central fire pit. Garlands of pink and white flowers softened the setting and gave the evening meal a festive feel.

There were a few odd pets, but I hesitate to call them that. No one acted as if they owned them. It seemed more like they just wanted to hang out with the Guardians and each other. For example, a playful monkey with orange hair and black eyes trimmed in white rode around the camp on the back of Jaguar. The big cat didn't seem to mind when the monkey tugged on his whiskers and ears. In fact, I'm pretty sure I heard him purring.

There were many other creatures that were so colorful and exotic the place felt a little like nature's art gallery. One of my favorites was a little guy that looked like a mix between a caterpillar and bright blue cotton candy.

He had a voracious appetite and could easily consume several times his weight in a short time. Not surprisingly, his favorite food was a blue leaf vine that climbed many of the trees near the Guardian's swimming hole.

I was deep in the Amazon Rainforest and didn't have a clue how to find my way home. It felt wonderful to be lost in this wild place. It occurred to me that these primitive people were far more civilized than anyone at home. In fact, I felt more at home here than I did at home.

People watching is one of my favorite pastimes. This was the first time the entire community was gathered together in my presence. They were as interesting as any group of people I have ever encountered, but something bothered me about them that I couldn't quite put a finger on at first. Then it hit me. There was no diversity in this crowd.

While I wouldn't go so far as to say they all looked alike, what was clearly evident was they were all young and beautiful. Not one of them showed any sign of being older than twenty-five. In fact, the more I thought about it, they all appeared to be in their mid-twenties.

There were no children, teenagers, middle aged adults, or seniors. How could that be, I wondered. Absent foul play, it seemed impossible.

Likewise, none of them were overweight, handicapped, or had any visible scars. They were all brown skinned, healthy and gorgeous. Each and every one of them was physically fit and attractive. Not a single exception. I had never seen anything like it and couldn't make any sense of it.

Finally, and maybe more importantly, they all seemed cheerful and well-adjusted. If I hadn't seen them wipe out my creepy captors in a blink of an eye, I would say they didn't have a violent bone in any of their beautiful bodies.

There was a loving gentleness between them that I had rarely seen between two people, let alone an entire group of thirty or more. It was a beautiful thing to witness and as I watched it, something deep inside of me shifted. I could feel it and it felt right, as if I had been out of focus and suddenly I could see everything more clearly.

That's when I felt something else that was even more remarkable. It was like I had a big goofy grin that was as much on the inside as the outside. This inner smile can best be described as contentment. I felt as if everything was as it should be. The world was the way it needed to be and I was right with it…perfect just as I am.

A smiling woman approached and handed me a stone carved mug of herbal tea.

"You have a beautiful smile," she said. "It radiates from your true nature."

"Thank you," I said. "This place brings out the best in me. I like it here."

After we introduced ourselves, I pointed toward the meat sizzling over the fire pit and raised an eyebrow.

"We rarely eat meat and when we do, it's in small quantities, but this is a special occasion," she said.

"What's the occasion?" I asked.

"We are celebrating the end of an era," she answered.

I raised my mug and offered a simple toast.

"To new beginnings," I said.

After she excused herself, I stood alone in a beam of the waning sunlight and enjoyed the bliss rippling through me like gentle waves kissing the shore. The moment of peace was interrupted by a big commotion at the edge of the village. It wasn't a negative buzz. Instead, everyone seemed excited and happy.

I looked in the direction of the commotion, but my view was partially blocked by the Guardians. I couldn't quite make out what was going on. A woman obstructing the view moved slightly and I caught a glimpse of a man walking into the village.

Except for the lack of a battle axe, the newcomer looked like central casting's version of a Viking warrior. This man had fought and won a few battles in his lifetime. It showed in the way he carried himself.

In addition to the fighter's body language, there was deep intelligence in his eyes. This guy was formidable. He was smart, tall, muscular, and did I mention, very blond. I guessed him to be about my age, maybe twenty-eight or so.

Unlike the Guardians, Mr. Viking was fully clothed. In this place it seemed wrong somehow. He was wearing something that looked like homemade chaps and a vest. The bottoms of his feet were protected with sandals fashioned from some sort of rough rope similar to the rope that my captors had used to bind my wrists.

Layah bounded in his direction and took a flying leap into his arms. Given she was nearly seven feet tall and packed with muscle, it was no small feat that he actually caught this Amazon Woman in mid-air and pressed her high over his head.

The other Guardians showered him with greetings, hugs, and kisses. Once the love fest was over, his expression shifted to something far more serious. The Guardians grew silent as he spoke in a language I didn't understand.

When Mr. Viking finished speaking, everyone scattered. There was a bustle of activity as they returned one by one with faces painted for war and weapons in hand. Without a word, they moved quietly into the forest.

I didn't have a clue what had just happened and didn't know whether I should stay put or follow them. I needed to find Ginny. My gut told me time was running out for her. It was also clear that I couldn't do it alone, so I followed them.

We ran silently through the thick foliage for nearly an hour without a break. The big Viking must have been near the front of the group because I hadn't seen him since we started. There were a few questions I wanted to ask, but couldn't figure out a diplomatic way to do it. Besides, the pace was blistering and I was focused on keeping up with everyone else.

Finally, we took a break and I found a spot to rest on a bed of hooker's green moss within arm's reach of a bubbling brook. I leaned back and rested my eyes. I must have dozed because someone woke me with a shake. Startled, I opened my eyes to see Layah offering me food and water.

"You must keep up your strength," she said.

I took her offering and munched quietly on something that tasted like a cross between a fruit cake and a granola bar, only better. The big Viking walked by and I figured it was a good time to ask a few questions.

I pointed toward Mr. Viking and asked, "Who is he?"

"I think you would call him my husband," she answered.

That surprised me, because none of these people behaved like the married people I knew. Instead, they treated everyone in the group with a level of love and respect, the likes of which I had never seen before.

I wanted to ask more about the Viking, but for now, that would have to wait. I had other, more pressing questions I wanted to ask.

"Where are we going?" I asked.

Before Layah could answer my question, the group stood on some unspoken command. Layah gave me a little shake of the head and rose with them. Without another word, we continued the journey. My questions would have to wait.

I didn't have a clue how I was going to find Ginny in this vast place. My only lead was in Manaus. I needed to return to her factory and speak with her security chief, Victor Branco, since he was somehow connected to the events at the Center.

We ran in silence for another hour before coming to a halt. There was a brief discussion between Layah and the Big Viking. Layah nodded before trotting off ahead. I slid over to Teekal and asked him where she was going.

"To find a weakness," he whispered.

I wanted to ask more questions, but he put a finger to his lips and shook his head. There was nothing to do, but wait. Which is exactly what we did for about thirty minutes, when Layah returned.

There was another whispered discussion, before the group began to move quietly in the direction Layah had traveled. Teekal motioned for me to remain, but that only lasted for a couple of minutes before I began to feel restless and decided to follow anyway.

I figured it would be easy to catch up with them, but the warriors had vanished. Initially, I followed their example and moved as quietly as I could through the jungle, but once I realized they were nowhere in sight, the likelihood I'd get lost filled me with panic. The Amazon Rainforest is huge, over two million square miles, and I was a stranger here.

By the time I stumbled through the undergrowth and into a small clearing, I was nearly as loud as a freight train. I knew I had made a huge mistake in not listening to Teekal when I found myself looking down the barrel of a gun.

CHAPTER 33

Lately everyone wanted to point a damn gun at me, and sadly, I was getting used to it. The handgun was held thug style, as if it was her habit to intimidate as much as kill. Hard eyes delivered a chilling message that didn't need to be spoken. It seemed unlikely she could say it anyway, since her jaw was clamped tight around a pitiless mouth. There wasn't a bit of softness in her face that I could see.

She wore camo pants, combat boots, and a purple sequined tube top. A tie-dyed bandana with the peace sign in the center of her forehead completed her cartoonish appearance.

There was something that wasn't quite right about Camo Girl that I couldn't quite put a finger on. She appeared to be hard to the core, but it didn't fit. My years of martial arts training told me she was no fighter. In another world she could have been a Victoria Secrets model. If it wasn't for the 9mm and hard expression, it would have been hard to take her seriously.

Still, there was no doubt in my mind that she had lived a hard and violent life. The disturbing thing was I knew that unless something happened real fast, I was destined for a violent ending.

I raised hands in the universal sign of surrender and said, "Easy, I'm just looking for my friends."

Camo Girl said nothing. It never occurred to me until that moment that she didn't speak English. In fact, for the first time I began to wonder how the Guardians, who lived in an isolated village deep in the Amazon jungle, spoke English like it was their own.

Her coal black hair was pulled back tight, heightening her high cheekbones and almond shaped eyes. She wore it as a long braid pulled over her shoulder where it was left to fall in a curve around her ample breast.

I did a double take when it moved. About the time I was sure it was only my imagination, it twitched like a cat's tail. You know your life has taken a strange turn when you begin to assume that just because something is odd, it has a supernatural explanation, like maybe Camo Girl was part jungle cat.

"Would you please stop that?" she said.

As I wondered what the hell she was talking about, a face popped over her shoulder. I sure as hell didn't expect to see my best friend Eric, but that's who appeared from the bushes. Being Eric, he couldn't resist tugging on her pig tail like a school boy.

"I was just messing with Grant," he said.

"You know this guy?" she asked.

"Yeah, you can put the gun down," he said. "This is the rascal I've been looking for."

"What took you so long?" I asked.

"Ingrate," he said. "The party woke me from my siesta," said Eric. "You've got to love a place that parties in the streets. I was ravenous for some fun. You've been a real drag lately, my friend, with the divorce, arrest, electroshock therapy, and all the other nasty messes you've managed to get yourself into lately. I'm just saying."

"I'm sorry to disappoint you," I said. "The last few days haven't been that bad. What about the damsel in distress?"

"Well it is true I love a good rescue and fight," said Eric. "But we both know that didn't work out too well, since you had to go and get yourself shot during the rescue attempt."

"It wasn't one of my finer moments," I said. "How did you find me in the middle of this jungle...and don't tell me it's the outdoorsman in you since we both know you're a city boy to the core?"

Eric flashed a big toothy grin and then answered, "I was thinking more along the lines of badass survivalist."

"Right, when was the last time you slept on anything other than a king sized mattress?" I asked.

He curled an arm around Camo Girl's waist and said, "You mean other than the bed of leaves just last night?"

I gave him my best disgusted look.

"What are you saying?" I demanded.

"I'm saying it can get mighty cold in this jungle," he said with exaggerated innocence.

"You're not admitting to cheating on your wife, are you?" I asked.

"You have a wife?" asked Camo Girl.

"Damn right he does," I said.

She considered for an instant turning the gun on Eric, but instead, plopped her fists on her hips, pinched her brow and waited for an answer.

"Ummm, yea I do, but we have an understanding," he said.

"What kind of understanding?" she asked.

"We are...let me see," he said. How do I say this? You might say we are open-minded."

"Open-minded?" she asked.

"Yea, what do you mean...open-minded?" I asked.

"We have a don't ask don't tell policy that serves us well," he said. "Besides, after what I witnessed girl, you've got no room to complain."

Her eyes went from hard to sultry in an instant. She gave Eric a wink and added emphasis by slowly running the tip of her tongue the full circumference of her lips.

Eric gave her one of his long appraising looks before saying, "I like the way you think, girl."

His eyes were fixated on her tits, which were trying their best to escape the undersized tube top, but he spoke to me.

"Do you see, Grant?" he said. "It's like I'm always trying to tell you…no one is all bad."

"I don't know anything about a don't ask don't tell policy," I said. "You're married and I happen to care about Kinsey."

"Grant, I love you, but this is none of your business," he said. "What happens under our roof is your business. Stay out of this."

He was right of course, so I shrugged and cut my eyes to Camo Girl as a way to escape his angry stare-down.

"You hunks want to do a threesome?" asked Camo Girl. "There's something about the jungle that gets me wet as hell."

I'm pretty sure I looked exactly the way I felt…appalled. Eric busted a gut.

"Some other time, babe," said Eric. "That's not why I followed you into this God forsaken jungle."

"You followed her here?" I asked.

Eric nodded.

"Can't you think with something other than your…"

Eric interrupted before I could finish.

"Nice," he said. "You had disappeared without a trace. The only lead I had was Victor Branco, but I didn't have a clue what he looked like. I needed a plan, so I decided the only thing to do was get a drink and enjoy the carnival."

"That's a brilliant plan," I said.

Eric grinned.

"I find that I have all kinds of brilliant ideas over cocktails, don't you?" he asked.

We have this glare we use with each other when we detect bullshit. I used it on him, so Eric cut the bullshit short and continued with his story.

"I was sitting at the bar of a little hole-in-the wall enjoying an amazingly good fruity libation as the freaks paraded down the street when I noticed this chick at a nearby table looking like a total badass," said Eric.

"That would be me," said Camo Girl flashing her best badass expression.

For the first time, I realized there was a spark of mischief gleaming through Camo Girl's hard façade.

"She was talking in low tones to a dandy, who must have been in his early 40's," said Eric. "I couldn't hear any of their conversation, but she stood up, spat in his face and said loud enough for everyone in the bar to hear, "Fuck you, Victor Branco.""

Eric was wearing one of those smug I told you so looks. He waited for me to tell him I thought his plan was brilliant, but I decided to hold out for more of his story first.

Eric wasn't fooled one bit by my strategy. He knew he had me, but he continued with his tale anyway.

"The guy grabbed her by the wrist and pulled her across his lap where he delivered the first of many hard slaps to her ass," he said.

I cut my eyes to Camo Girl expecting to see outrage on her face. Her eyes were indeed smoldering, but I suspect it was lust instead of outrage.

"This chick never let out a whimper," said Eric. "Instead she delivered her own brand of abuse in the form of a not stop stream of the foulest curses I've ever heard. She said unspeakable things that involved his entire family."

Eric paused for dramatic effect before continuing.

"Let me tell you, Dude, it was both shocking and a huge turn on," said Eric.

Eric pointed toward Camo Girl and shook his head.

"She was breathing hard and I was about to step in between them and do the gentlemanly thing, when I realized she wasn't distressed at all...she was enjoying it," he said. "In fact she climaxed right there in the middle of the bar."

He shook his head in amazement.

"No one else in the bar paid a bit of attention to them," he said.. "I'm wiping the sweat from my brow as Victor lays some cash on the table and splits. All I could think was welcome to Brazil."

"You let him leave without asking about Ginny," I said.

It wasn't the first time I was completely exasperated with Eric. He was in the same room with our best lead to find Ginny and he does nothing. Instead, he let Victor leave, just like that.

"I wasn't sure whether she was a hooker or if Victor was just paying the check," said Eric. "What I did know for sure was I needed to have a conversation with this woman."

"Some conversation," said Camo Girl. "He said in a voice loud enough for half the bar to hear that he was next."

Eric flashed his trademark confident grin and said, "They don't call me Mr. Discreet for nothing."

"Does that work...telling a stranger you want them for sex?" I asked.

"When will you men ever get it through your empty heads, that women love sex as much, if not more, than you do," said Camo Girl. "Now that we earn our own money, we no longer have to pretend to be chaste just to secure a husband. Besides, who would want one...husbands make for lazy lovers. I should know. I've had four."

"Eric is someone's husband and his beautiful wife is a good friend of mine," I said to Camo Girl. "I don't get this open marriage crap, but I know one thing for sure, I don't want to see her hurt by the likes of you."

We glared at each other before Eric slapped me on the back and said, "Rest easy, my friend. I would never do anything to hurt Kinsey. I love her with all my sappy heart. Don't you want to hear what I found out about Victor?"

Damn right I wanted to hear about Victor Branco and was reminding Eric that Ginny's security chief was our best hope if we ever hoped to find her, when we heard something crashing through the forest and it was headed straight for us. It was loud and sounded big.

Camo Girl raised her gun and pointed it in the direction of the stampede. Whatever it was, it was moving fast. I dropped to a crouch in anticipation of the fight to come. Of all the things that could have burst through the foliage, the last thing I expected to see was Ginny fall face first at our feet.

I jumped between Ginny and the gun.

"Don't shoot!" I shouted.

CHAPTER 34

Ginny lay sprawled in front of us looking tired, dirty and lost. She was the most beautiful woman I had ever laid eyes on and I wanted to give her refuge...to hold her...to comfort her.

Without thinking I moved toward her, but she shrank from me. I froze. Something was wrong. She didn't seem herself. She didn't seem to see me. I looked more closely. It was more than dirt on her face; Ginny had a nasty black eye.

Concerned, I spoke her name ever so softly, but I don't think she heard me. Camo Girl brushed past me and knelt at Ginny's feet. Taking her hands, she spoke to Ginny in a soothing way. It wasn't speech so much, but more like she was humming a lullaby. A small light of recognition sparked in Ginny's eyes.

The Guardians stepped from the shadows of the jungle and formed a half circle around the two women. They began chanting, softly at first, and then more loudly in a strange ancient tongue that sounded something like Sanskrit.

My mind was running a million miles a minute. Were the Guardians chasing Ginny? Had they hurt her? I shook my head and discarded these theories before they could take root. The most likely explanation was they had just rescued her from something horrible.

The jungle began to shimmer. At first, I thought it might be the wind, but decided it was something altogether different that made the foliage around us dance ever so gracefully to the rhythm of the ancient song.

What I did know for sure was the air was filled with an electric current that drew the hair from our bodies. Not just the little hairs on our arms, but also the longer hair from our head was swaying like a snake charmer's mark.

The only time I had experienced anything like it was during a camping trip in the Red River Gorge. It was my fifth day in the backcountry and I was lying in a hammock staring out over the canyon. It was quiet and peaceful...just the break I needed from the stress of a busy law practice.

There wasn't a cloud in the sky, but I heard the rumble of distant thunder. If you've ever been camping, then you know that rain is a curse to campers. I laid there as long as I could as the wind picked up and dark clouds rolled in from the west.

Like most people, I know when to get out of the rain. I planned to let the storm get as close as possible, before seeking shelter in my tent. When the first of the lightening tore the fabric of the sky nearby, I got a wild idea. It had been a day full of wild ideas, like sunbathing nude.

It's not like me to get naked outdoors. I had tried it once when I was five years old and was caught in the act by Ginny's mother. She so traumatized me that I swore I'd never do it again. I kept that vow for over twenty years. Still, I hadn't seen a soul in five days and figured the backcountry was empty. Besides, it was a hot day and my clothes were sticky with sweat and dirt from the trail.

The wilderness worked a strange alchemy on me. It was enough of a change that I acted on the impulse and stretched out in the sun without a stitch of clothing. I liked it enough that my clothes were still laying in a pile in the tent.

As the wind picked up, I remembered the tent wasn't staked because of the rocky ground. I imagined it lifting off and flying across the canyon, like Dorothy's little house in the Wizard of Oz.

All of my gear, including every stitch of clothing was in the tent. Damn if my hiking boots weren't in there too. I didn't want to risk losing all of my stuff, but for some strange reason, I had a compelling need to feel the rain on my naked skin.

It was twelve miles to the trailhead. I couldn't imagine hiking all that distance naked and barefooted. Even worse, what would people think when I finally made it back to civilization with bloody feet and a sunburned bare bottom.

I was torn. The sensible part of me wanted to use my body weight to anchor the tent and belongings against the force of the rising wind. The adventurous side wanted to experience the storm, naked and exposed, like a primal man.

I'm not sure how long the debate lasted because time gets weird when you're alone in the backcountry. What I know for sure is I chose the storm over my things thanks to a moment of clarity. I wasn't going to let things deprive me of this experience.

So, I stood on a rock in the middle of a huge thunder storm. The wind was blowing hard. Lightening crackled all around me. I could feel the electricity in the air as I hooted and hollered in joyous victory over the tent full of things.

I was hit by lightning that day. Thor's energy coursed through my body at the speed of light and was gone in the blink of an eye. All that was left was the metallic taste of cold steel and a completely different view of life and death.

The Guardian's mystical chant filled the air with the taste of cold steel. Steam rose from our skin and enveloped us in a foggy cloud.

The chant descended along the same path it rose. It slowed and softened, first to a whisper, and then to silence. When it was over, Ginny found her way back to the here and now. This simple act somehow pulled her from the dark place she was in.

At first, she looked bewildered, as if she couldn't imagine how she came to be in this place. Then her eyes found me.

Her lips moved. It was only a whisper.

"Grant, is that really you?" she asked.

Just as I was about to throw my arms around her someone grabbed my right wrist and yanked hard. Instinctively, I countered with an arm bar. Slamming him roughly to the ground, I jammed a knee into his lower back and pinned him face first into the dirt.

Ginny let out a yelp.

"No, Grant," she said.

I looked at her and then back at the man on the ground. For the first time, I got a good look at his face and let out a gasp. It was Pony Tail.

Since this crazy adventure began, Pony Tail had appeared at key moments...usually when something bad was about to happen. I didn't like the site of him one bit. Of course, my intense dislike for him might also have something to do with seeing him behave so intimately toward Ginny a few days earlier.

Then there was the shooting at the Center. He pulled a handgun from his pants and tried to kill us. Damn if he didn't hit me with one of those shots, but I was lucky enough to escape with only a scratch.

Yep, I would say I had some pretty damn good reasons to dislike this guy, but I also had to admit there were a few things about him that didn't add up. Like for instance, there was this business about him being a healer. He might have saved Uncle Jim's life.

Come to think of it, I found him hovering over Ginny in the hospital and now she was protecting him. I didn't like this one bit, but was about to do as she asked and let him up, when I realized there couldn't be a plausible reason why he was here in this remote part of the Amazon Rainforest with Ginny, so I shifted tactics.

"Who are you?" I growled.

He didn't answer. I waited. Just when I thought it would never come, I noticed he had a clump of dirt jammed into his mouth. It's possible he couldn't speak because I had his face pinned to the Earth.

I thought about giving him room to spit out the dirt, but a part of me wasn't willing to be reasonable. I took pleasure in knowing I was in total control, and if I was honest with myself, I also wanted to punish him for all of the trespasses I was sure he had committed against me.

Ginny had other ideas.

"Please, let him up Grant," she said.

I wanted to give her whatever she asked for...to never say no to her, but feeling that way about someone was new to me, and must admit, it was causing some discomfort. For now, I had issues with her request.

"This guy tried to kill us," I said.

Unbelievably, Ginny shook her head. She was there for God's sake. I have a tendency to get a little stressed when I'm torn between something I really want and something I fear.

So I added in a voice that was too whiney for my satisfaction, "He shot me at the Center, Ginny."

In a tone of voice we usually reserve for the severely impaired, Ginny said, "If you let my brother up and give him a chance to spit that clump of dirt out of his mouth, then maybe he could explain to you what really happened at the Center."

Pony Tail is Ginny's brother! I couldn't believe it. I tried to think, but my head was spinning.

Finally, I hissed, "That's impossible. He's an assassin."

"My brother is not an assassin," she said. "He was protecting me."

"What do you mean protecting you?" I asked.

Ginny said, "Let him up. We will explain everything."

I didn't move.

She tried again, "Grant, my father sent him."

Ginny's father was dead and it was time for her to face reality.

"I know you want to believe he is still alive, Ginny, but your father is gone and you have no siblings," I said.

Ginny glared at me, and then puffed out her chest, as if she planned to give me a blast of shit that would blow me half way back to Kentucky, but it didn't come. Instead her eyes shifted to something over my shoulder and every drop of blood seemed to drain from her face.

I couldn't imagine what it might be, but I sure didn't expect to hear a deep voice say, "It's okay, Grant, you're both here now."

The voice was vaguely familiar. I sifted through millions of bits of information in an instant before it hit me. Turning slowly I fixed my gaze on the big Viking.

His eyes were wet and shinning. One by one, the stream of tears made their way down the line of his nose, then curving along his upper lip and finally changing direction to make the turn around the corner of the mouth before dripping to the soil at his feet.

Ginny stood transfixed before him, a ghost made flesh. Neither spoke for a time. It was Ginny who broke the silence.

"Daddy...is that you?" asked Ginny.

The big Viking nodded and opened his arms to embrace her.

"Yes, Lil Froggy," he said.

"Oh my God, it is you," she said.

There was no hesitation left. Ginny rushed into his arms and held him tight. It was her turn to sob, and sob she did.

I crouched awkwardly on Pony Tail for another half second before getting up and pulling him to his feet. We glared at each other as he spit out the clod of dirt and wiped his mouth with the back of his hand. When he was finished, he pushed past me to join Ginny and her dad in a group cry-hug.

CHAPTER 35

The hike back to the village was slower and more relaxed than earlier. No one seemed concerned that nightfall was coming to the jungle. I was relieved we found Ginny, but was also worried about her. She was convinced she had found her father, but I didn't believe it was him. None of this was adding up.

I wanted to talk some sense into her, but she stayed close to him, cheerfully chattering non-stop about her life since his disappearance twenty years earlier. I didn't get a sense he was a bad guy. In fact, much like the rest of the villagers, he seemed to be a decent human being.

Still, there is no way in hell he could possibly be her father. Ginny's father would be a middle-aged man by now. Instead the Viking looked like he was our age. I wasn't ready to accept that this twenty-something man could possibly be her father. It defied logic.

To complicate matters, it wasn't just him. All of the Guardians looked to be twenty-something and that isn't the only odd thing about them. They claim to guard the gateway to paradise. I'm not sure what they mean by that, but the one thing I could say for certain about them is they are the most pleasant group of people I've ever had the pleasure of knowing.

"Why so quiet, Dude?" asked Eric.

In response, I showed him the most exaggerated glum face I could muster. Eric flashed teeth bleached so white they look fake. When he spoke again, it was with exaggerated cheerfulness.

"Where's the happy-go-lucky guy we all know and love?" asked Eric.

I nodded toward Mr. Viking and asked, "Do you believe this guy is really her father?"

Eric pinched his brow and then told Camo Girl to follow the rest of the group. Once she was gone, he grabbed my upper arm and pulled me to the side to give the Guardians behind us room to pass.

When the last of them was out of site, he asked, "Have you forgotten, Grant?"

At first, I didn't have a clue what he meant, but then it came in a flash. When we were kids running the streets barefooted, we sometimes pretended we were Indian trackers. We got very good at moving undetected around the neighborhood and made a game of sneaking up on people.

We saw some things we shouldn't have seen. Like Mrs. Sims kissing the cable guy. Later we saw her husband sobbing alone in the garage. Embarrassed for him, we tiptoed away without a sound. The next day, we were stunned to hear he passed away from a mysterious illness. That was the official G-rated story for us kids, but we overheard the real story. Mr. Sims stuffed a potato in the tail pipe of his car and closed the garage door.

Of course the Sims tragedy isn't what Eric was asking me to remember. No, we saw other things during our forays into the wilds of suburban Louisville and one of those things is relevant to this story.

One evening, as the sun touched the horizon, we saw Ginny's parents arguing in the fading light. They were an odd couple. She was dark, short, and fat. He was tall, fit, and very blond. The top of her head just barely reached his chest. More importantly, she was mean spirited and fought dirty, while he was calm and reasonable.

"What kind of man are you?" asked Ginny's mom.

"I'm the kind of man who does the right thing," he said.

"You've lost your mind, Bill," she said sarcastically.

"Maria, try to understand, this is necessary," he said.

"It's not necessary for you to leave your family on some fool's mission," she said.

"I have to go back to Brazil," he said. "There's too much at stake."

"Do you really think some jungle weed is going to make a difference?" asked Maria.

"There may be no limit to what it will cure," he said. "It could make the world a better place."

"The world can go fuck itself," growled Maria. "All I care about is my family."

"You can't be that selfish," said Bill.

Maria jabbed her husband in the chest with a stiff finger and said, "You heard those FBI people."

Bill shook his head, "How can a healing plant be a dangerous narcotic?"

"If the government says it's bad, like heroin, then we don't want anything to do with it," she said.

"That shaman cured me with it," he said. "It's nothing like heroin. It's not destructive at all. It feels wholesome, like perfect health."

She rolled her eyes and said, "Perfect health my ass. Bill, just tell them everything."

Ginny's father shook his head.

"If I do, then they don't need us anymore," he said. "There is a lot at stake, Maria. These people are capable of anything."

"Find another way," she pleaded. "Don't go back to that damn jungle."

He ran his hand through his hair and said, "There's no other way."

"Don't leave us here alone," she said.

With a heavy sigh he said, "I'm going. For all of our sakes, I'm going and it's too dangerous to take you along."

She stomped off to the house and slammed the door behind her.

The last thing I heard her say was, "Go to hell then."

As we slipped away I remember thinking Ginny's dad looked so sad. I didn't like her mother one bit. Of course, that wasn't the first time I had seen her red faced and angry.

Yes, we had seen some things while skulking around the neighborhood like little cold war spies.

"Eric, I remember what Ginny's dad said, but we both know if he was alive, he'd be a middle aged man by now," I said.

"I know it defies logic, but you need to open your mind," said Eric. "If not your mind, then at least open your eyes. You'd have to be blind to not see that he is her father."

In response, I clinched my jaw and glared at him. Eric shook his head sadly.

"Dude, you've been a real drag lately," said Eric. "Sometimes you act like a little old woman. I'm just saying."

I knew he was right. I had plenty of excuses for my behavior, but excuses are the mainstay of failures and I sure as hell wasn't ready to include myself in that group. I had been off balance lately thanks to a series of events that challenged my assumptions. It was time to pull myself together.

That's exactly when Pony Tail slipped up so quietly it startled me. It bothered me that I wasn't paying better attention to my surroundings. I had been trained better than that, but then again, maybe there was a reason for it. Ch'ing once told me we stumble from time to time for no apparent reason other than to keep us humble.

"I don't really like guns much," he said

I figured he was bullshitting me since he shot me a few days ago. Or, had it been longer than that. I had one of those weird moments, when time gets all fuzzy. I couldn't say for sure how long it had been since he shot me, since I didn't know how long they had kept me drugged in the loony bin.

I tried my best to shake off the time warp and said, "Maybe you should have thought of that before you pulled a gun on me."

He shrugged.

"I saved your life," said Pony Tail.

I shook my head.

"You tried to kill me," I said.

Pony Tail slid his index finger across his throat with a dramatic flourish.

"You were about to get your throat slit," he said.

I swallowed hard. It was purely a reflex action, but I hated to show weakness to this guy. I tried to deflect attention from it by using my best tough guy voice.

"What are you saying?" I demanded.

The tough guy act didn't work. My voice raised an octave, rather than drop one, like I intended. To his credit he noticed it, but instead of taking advantage, he softened his tone a bit more. The guy was trying to put me at ease.

"I saw a someone behind you with a knife," he said. "Scorned lover, maybe?"

"Impossible," I said.

Pony Tail raised an eyebrow. The scorned lover comment was ridiculous, but he may be right about the rest of it. I had forgotten that I sensed someone behind me and was about to turn around when he pulled the gun and the shooting started. It occurred to me he might be telling the truth, but I had more questions.

"What were you doing back stage?" I asked.

"We had information that they were going to make a move for my sister," he said. "I was there to protect her."

"Ginny?" I asked.

He nodded.

"Who were you protecting her from?" I asked.

"Much will be revealed very soon," interrupted Layah. "Come, we are almost there."

"None of this makes a bit of sense," I grumbled.

She gave me a gentle pat on the shoulder and said, "Patience Grasshopper."

The reference to my favorite classic television show was a surprise. Under other circumstances it may have felt dismissive, but Layah's face was filled with kindness.

"We're not far now," she said.

"Come on, Dude," said Eric. "When all else fails, follow the naked babe."

"It always comes back to that," I said with a shake of the head.

Eric stopped in his tracks, folded his arms across his chest, and with the most offended expression he could muster said, "Such disrespect…and coming from the hypocrite who has seen fit to liberate his boys from underwear prison, no less."

Somehow I'd forgotten I was naked. In this place it seemed natural, like the Garden of Eden before the fall. I had been such a prude before and was pondering this huge change when we broke through the dense foliage and stepped into a small village.

"Yeah, I guess I've gone native," I said.

Eric slapped me on the back and said, "It's about time, my friend."

He didn't wait for a response, but instead called out to Camo Girl, who had been flirting outrageously with Teekal, to come explore this cool place with him. They split together without another word.

I thought it would be a good time to talk to Ginny, and found her near the central fire chatting with Layah. As I approached, I couldn't help but notice her eyes were focused below the waist. In the face of her frank appraisal, my newfound casualness about nudity suddenly evaporated. I was exposed to her once again.

It was useless to wish for clothes, but I wished for them anyway and couldn't seem to stop myself from looking anywhere but directly at her. When it became too much, I let it go and gave her my undivided attention.

The hunger in Ginny's eyes was a huge turn on. Her breath caught in her throat when my body responded in a predictable way. Getting turned-on in public was way beyond my comfort level, but I didn't know how to stop it.

"Well, aren't you full of surprises," said Ginny in a husky voice.

I wanted her, but I didn't want to show it to everybody. Desperately I searched for a way out, a safe retreat, but the glow in her eyes pulled me forward, toward her.

"Ginny…" I said, but then again, it may have been just a croak. It's hard to say for sure.

She began speaking at the same time, but left me standing there stunned when her eyes rolled back and she collapsed midway through the first syllable. Layah didn't miss a beat and took charge, sounding an awful lot like an emergency room nurse.

"Ginny needs rest and medicine," said Layah.

I snapped out of the trance I was in and gathered her in my arms. Layah pointed to one of the shelters, where I laid her in a bed of red and yellow feathers.

They stripped her clothes and someone fed them to the fire. Teekal applied a paste to her wounds and then they covered her with a soft blanket with a subtle design woven into the fabric. It depicted a snake swallowing a bird's tail and the bird swallowing the snake's tail.

When she briefly regained consciousness, she was given a few sips from a delicate bowl that appeared to be carved from rosewood. There were faint markings on the rim that I resolved to check out at the first opportunity, but for now, I was concerned with Ginny's recovery.

I hovered around her feeling scared and helpless. Her sleep was restless. Each time she awoke briefly from her rest, she was given another sip from the bowl.

I stayed with her all day and through the night. At one point or another, I think all of the Guardians looked in on her, but the Viking and Pony Tail stayed the longest. Finally, she rested peacefully.

By morning, the black eye and the sores were gone. I was relieved she looked like herself again. I can't say the same for myself. When she finally awoke, I was at her side.

"How do you feel Ginny?" I asked.

"I feel great, but you look like hell, Grant," she answered.

I nodded and asked, "What happened to you?"

Ginny searched my face for a moment before she said, "After Dr. Wiemp gave you the sedative, they quickly loaded you onto a gurney and rolled it away. I started to follow, but got a call from one of my investigators. She had information that my father was alive and being held captive by a group of dangerous radicals. There wasn't much time and I needed to get on a flight as soon as possible."

"You left me," I said.

"I felt bad about that," she said. "I kept telling myself you were in good hands, but I knew that was a lie so I called Uncle Jim and told him where you were."

"How did you get away from Dr. Wiemp and his goons?" I asked.

"Everyone was focused on you," she answered. "I moved away from the noise to better hear the phone. When the call was over, I found that I had wandered around the corner and was standing in front of the elevator. The door opened, I got on it, and never looked back."

I opened my mouth to ask her a question, but she quickly added, "I'm sorry I ditched you, Grant. There is no good excuse."

"I guess we're even," I said.

When we were kids, Ginny's mother caught us with our pants down. We weren't doing anything other than being curious about the differences between boys and girls, but her mother had an intense reaction. Under threat of force, she made me promise to never speak to Ginny again.

It was the hardest thing I ever had to do. Ginny was my best friend, and I loved her as only a five year old can, but I kept the promise. It cost me in ways I could never have predicted, since the fear and lost landed me in Sadistic Doctor's hateful hands.

Wiping a tear from her cheek, Ginny said, "It had nothing to do with our past. Finding my father has been a lifetime obsession."

"Of course it didn't," I said. "I'm sorry I brought it up. That's a long time to keep searching for a missing person. What made you think he was alive all these years?"

Ginny chewed on her lower lip as she thought about her answer. It was something I had seen her do as a child many times.

"I am connected to my father," she said. "Maybe it's because of my mother's illness. I'm not sure. What I do know for sure is I could feel him…feel his life force, if you will. He was…is still alive. I knew this with an absolute certainty, even when everyone else had given up."

"This man you met today…he's our age Ginny," I said. "Your father would be a middle aged man right now."

Ginny's eyes flashed angry then softened.

"I know it's weird," she said. "I don't understand it, but he is my father," she said.

It was time for a graceful retreat, so I asked, "How did you end up deep in the jungle, injured and alone?"

"I was abducted," she said.

"Was it Slotter?" I asked.

She shook her head.

"Who then?" I asked.

She shrugged.

"Any theories?" I asked.

"I have a few ideas, but who knows if I'm right," she answered.

"What are they?" I asked.

"My company is committed to social reform in Latin America and I've made some enemies," she said.

"I thought you sold designer clothing to rich people," I said.

"We do, but unlike our competitors, our clothes are not manufactured in third world sweatshops," said Ginny.

"What are you trying to reform?" I asked.

"Our focus is on Latin women," she said. "They are treated like property here."

I nodded my head in agreement.

"I was reading about the slave trade on the flight over," I said. "It is disturbing."

"The problem is deep-seated," she said. "South America's machismo culture is male orientated and women are expected to submit to their will and whim. Many are slaves, but even in the best case scenario, they are hardly more than servants to be used by the men in their lives."

"So how do you plan to change these attitudes?" I asked.

"Part of the problem is economics," answered Ginny. "Men control the money and women are financially dependent on them for survival. This gives the men too much power over their lives. I give them good paying jobs so these women have money of their own."

"I can see where having their own money would be a game changer," I said. "Still, it sounds to me like these are the kind of men who would just take it away from them."

"Sometimes they do," she said. "This isn't an easy or overnight process. It takes time. Attitudes must change, so I also train them to be decision makers and managers. Slowly, they are learning how to be in charge of their own lives."

I thought about Ch'ing's teachings on living an authentic life. We come into this world fresh and free, but it doesn't take long for well-meaning people to bully us into conformity.

Each time we concede, we abdicate a little more of our sovereignty. Eventually, we become so disempowered we are little more than slaves. The Taoist path offers one way to reverse this process and live a self-directed life where we are our own masters.

"That sounds like practical Taoism to me," I said.

"I don't know much about Taoism," said Ginny. "For me, Ch'ing was just a sweet guy who taught you boys martial arts. I was more influenced by Marguerite's teaching. Nature was her classroom. We looked at what folks would call Mother Nature and we also looked inside at our own nature. The aim was to live an authentic life. She emphasized things like living independently in a co-dependent world."

"That could also sum up the heart of Ch'ing's teachings," I said. "People like to talk about freedom, but when push comes to shove, they follow the herd. He encouraged us to resist the herd instinct."

"Some follow, while others fight to maintain control over the followers," said Ginny.

"I bet there are some who don't support your efforts to help Hispanic women become more independent and self-reliant," I said.

"There are a group of angry men who think these reforms are the devil's work," said Ginny.

"You think they are behind this?" I asked.

"I don't know for sure, but my instincts tell me they are," she answered.

"Why don't you tell me what happened," I said.

She nodded and began her story.

"After getting the call about my father, I went straight to the hotel where I quickly packed a bag and headed to the airport" said Ginny. "I got as far as the parking garage when I heard footsteps behind me. For some reason it made me nervous, so I picked the pace up, but whoever was behind me broke into a run. I panicked and turned to face the stalker, but all I saw was a fist. The creep punched me hard in the face."

Without thinking I reached out and touched the spot on her face where a nasty bruise had been just a few hours earlier.

"The blow knocked me out cold," said Ginny. "When I awoke I was laying on my side. I tried to roll over to get circulation back into my arm, but thumped my knee. There was little room to move. To make matters worse, I had a pounding headache."

"It was pitch black," said Ginny. "I didn't have a clue where I was or how I got there. I heard a familiar sound, but couldn't quite place it at first. It took a minute to figure out it was road noise. I was in the trunk of a car and it was hot."

"It was several hours before we stopped," said Ginny. "I could hear the car door open and then gas flowing into the tank. I started yelling and pounding on the inside of the trunk. No one seemed to hear me."

"We stopped many more times, but the trunk was never opened," continued Ginny. "I had no idea whether it was night or day. I fell in and out of a restless sleep. Time disappeared. I could no longer feel my arms and legs. My clothes were soaked with sweat. The trunk stank of urine and motor oil. Hope slipped away."

"When light finally poured back into the trunk, I was barely conscious," said Ginny. Someone pulled me out and dropped me to the ground. I heard voices but couldn't comprehend what was being said. The language was familiar, but the words just jumbled in my head."

Ginny paused for a breath and to gather her thoughts before returning to the narrative. She crinkled her nose, looked at me and then shook it off.

"I smelled something like a burnt match and opened my eyes," said Ginny. "A gruesome face contorted with hate leered at me. Why are you doing this, I asked. The bastard sneered and told me I was about to learn my value. He said I was too old to get top price, but he should be able to sell me to one of the lesser whore houses for a few pesos."

Ginny shivered slightly and again paused in the telling of her story. Before she resumed, I saw something flash across her face that looked to me like a moment of realization.

"You don't have to do this," I said gently.

She gave me a sad little smile and went on with her story anyway.

"The thought of being a sex slave in a third world brothel was not my idea of a good time," said Ginny. "I laid there shivering in the dirt, wishing I could just die. I didn't see any way out."

"It was then I heard another voice," said Ginny. "It was a much kinder voice that whispered to me. It told me to be brave, because help was on the way."

"At first I thought the voice was only in my head," said Ginny. "I figured it was like a mirage, or something, but he told me he was real. When he said to look to the right, I saw him standing there with a three toed sloth draped across his shoulders. I could be wrong, but they looked like they had been smoking some really good weed. Their kind faces were filled with sparkling eyes and shit-eating grins. Strangely, it filled me with hope. "

"The sloth wasn't the only odd thing about him," said Ginny. "He was naked except for a shiny gold medallion around his neck. The medallion looked oddly familiar. It depicted a snake eating a bird and the bird simultaneously eating the snake. His lips never moved, but I distinctly heard him tell me not to worry. Then I blacked out."

"When I recovered consciousness, I was bouncing in the back of a pickup truck," said Ginny. "I have to tell you, it was a huge relief to be out of the trunk. I was beginning to think things might be looking up, when I saw a flash of lightening and heard the rumble of thunder. The sky opened and the rain came hard. The temperature dropped. I was cold and miserable. The only upside came when I opened my mouth and got a few drops of water to drink."

"When the rain finally stopped, the sun came out with a vengeance," said Ginny. "I tried to position myself to minimize exposure, but there was only one way I could lay without irritating the sores spots. I was pretty sure they were infected. Despite the brutal heat, I was cold and shivering. I knew I was running a high fever. On the positive side, I figured I'd be long dead before we made it to the brothels and that was oddly comforting."

"I don't know how many days we traveled through swamp land and forest," said Ginny. "The road was rough, barely a trail. When we got stuck in the mud, Match Breath first checked the ropes that bound my hands and feet, and then left me in the bed of the truck while he walked off."

"I figured he went to get others. It was the first time I was left alone and I didn't want to waste it. I needed to find a way to escape, but first I had to find a way to cut the ropes. I had limited mobility and couldn't see what he had tied me to. I tried to feel it, but that didn't work either."

"I didn't know how much time I had and every second was vital. Fighting back a wave of panic, I chose to replace it with a sense of urgency instead. I took a deep calming breath and saw the solution right in front of me."

"At each of the four corners of the truck bed was a metal eye-hook. The edges looked sharp enough to cut the rope if I worked it back and forth long enough. I figured it would be a slow process, but it was my only chance. I said a little prayer of gratitude and got started."

"I didn't know if it was a good plan or not, but it was all I had. I started with enthusiasm, but my resolve was challenged when the ropes didn't cut easily. Several hours later I was still trying to cut the rope and on the verge of giving up, but the fear of being a sex slave kept me going. My hopes were dashed when Match Breath returned hours later and I was still tied to the truck."

"He had brought several more men with him, two teenage boys and an old man. The boys acted shy and didn't look at me. The old man was a different matter. As they pushed the truck out of the mud, I showed him the ropes."

"Even though the old man was taller than Match Breath, he lowered himself to the smaller man's level and asked what I was doing tied to the back of his truck. Match Breath raised his chin and sneered. The old man rose to his full height, but I'll never know what he intended to say because Match Breath pulled a pistol from his pocket and shot the old man in the chest."

"The boys left the old man bleeding next to a mud hole and fled into the forest. Match Breath calmly started the truck and drove off at a leisurely pace."

"Then the terrain changed from swampland and became more mountainous. The truck started up a steep hill and I slid to the back slamming against the tailgate. It clanged open and I rolled out the back. I expected the truck to stop but it didn't. Instead, it ground its way up and over the hill. I rolled myself into the bushes and waited. I expected to hear the truck stop and the asshole come looking for me, but it never happened."

"After a while, I started laughing. It was hesitant at first, but quickly overwhelmed me until it bordered on hysteria. That's when it turned to tears…gut wrenching tears."

"When the last of the sobs subsided, I took stock of my situation. I had a bruised shoulder from the fall, but I was alive. All of the hard work on the ropes had finally paid off and the bindings around my wrist gave way to the weight of my body on the uphill grade. I fumbled with the remaining rope around my ankles."

"Once my feet were free, I took a moment to rub circulation into my joints. My biggest concern was the possibility Match Breath would return for me. I had to move deeper into the jungle to be safe. I was also lost. I could wander aimlessly in the forest or I could head back into the swamp and try to find those boys. I imagined snakes and other foul creatures in the swamp. There had to be another alternative. I heard running water and thirst made my decision for me."

"My legs were weak, but I managed to hobble in the direction of the stream. The water was surprisingly cool and crystal clear. After a long drink, I stripped my clothes and let the stream wash away the ordeal. It might have been the best bath I've ever taken. Even though I knew the nightmare wasn't over, I finally had a chance."

"After resting, I decided to follow the stream. I knew it would empty into a larger river where there was a greater likelihood I would find help. After going so long without water, I also wanted to stay close to a source."

"It was good to move again. Regardless of the outcome, I was once again in control of my own destiny."

"As I maneuvered through the thick vegetation, my mind wandered. After all of my effort to protect the rainforest, it was odd that it now threatened me. Lost in thought, I failed to pay close attention to my surroundings. When I heard voices, I dropped to a crouch and peered through the foliage."

"It was Match Breath again. He wasn't alone this time. He and another man were moving in my direction. The new guy had a snake tattooed on his right arm. His face was hard and cruel. He stopped and sniffed the air. His eyes narrowed and he pointed in my direction. Shit. I was screwed again. What now, I wondered?"

"I was about to run, when a man with a blond ponytail appeared out of nowhere. He hit Match Breath hard in the mouth with his left hand, while he simultaneously sliced the other guy's throat with a commando knife held in the other. Despite the hard blow, Match Breath recovered enough to make a grab for the knife, but it was quickly buried deep in his gut. Both men crumbled to the ground."

"It was over in an instant. I didn't know whether I should cheer or run for my life, so I ran. I ran even though I had a nagging feeling I had seen that distinctive blond ponytail somewhere before. The last words I heard before I disappeared into the bush was, I'm your brother."

CHAPTER 36

I had a thousand and one questions for Ginny, but it had been a long sleepless night. Exhaustion finally had her way with me and I closed my eyes a couple of hours before dawn. The story of Ginny's harrowing car trip south of the equator wove its way through my dreams and yet I still slept soundly knowing she was safe.

When I finally opened them again to a new day, Ginny was bent close whispering something in my ear that I couldn't quite make out. Layah stood behind her with a leather bound book held high over her head. The morning sun peaked above the book like lady liberty's torch lighting the way for all seeking a new life in the land of the free and home of the brave.

Ignoring the book, Ginny said to Layah, "I'd like to see my father now."

"Soon," said Layah. "Ginny, this journal was kept by your father and he asked me to give it to you. It will explain much."

"Thank you, but why doesn't he just give it to me himself," said Ginny.

"He wanted to, but was called away on assignment," said Layah.

Ginny pressed her lips together, but a small hiss escaped all the same. She looked pretty damn pissed to me and I thought she might say something harsh to Layah, but she somehow managed to keep her disappointment in check.

"After all this time, I hoped we would have some time together," said Ginny in a tight voice.

"Please don't be too disappointed in him," said Layah in soothing tone. "It is a mission critical task that couldn't wait."

With furrowed brow, Ginny muttered, "Mission...humph," but she said nothing more.

"You must have a lot of questions for him," said Layah. "The journal will answer many of them. Afterwards, I will fill in as many gaps as I can. The rest will have to wait for your father's return."

Ginny absent mindedly stroked the book as she considered it. She took a deep breath and released the tension held in her shoulders. The hard expression softened as her curiosity replaced disappointment.

She opened her father's diary to the first page and read the inscription in a voice that was almost a whisper, "To my beloved Ginny, on this her 9th birthday."

Ginny managed to choke back a sob, but she couldn't prevent her eyes from filling with tears. It took a few minutes, but she finally bowed her head and began reading. I imagined she was searching for answers to all of her questions.

I'm not sure how much time passed before the others left for the hot spring. I declined their invitation, content to stay and watch Ginny read.

She never once looked up from the book and I waited, quiet as a church mouse, for her to finish. It gave me time to reflect on all she had been through. Her ordeal revealed much about her character. She was truly something special and I felt privileged to know her.

I must have dozed off, because when I opened my eyes again, Ginny was sitting at my feet. Her expression was complex. On the one hand, there was an air of serenity I had never seen in her face. On the other, she seemed dangerous, as if she was coiled for a strike. Without speaking, she handed me her father's journal. Curious, I opened the book to the first page and began to read.

My Little Froggy, I miss you very much and wish with all my heart I could be with you. I am setting pen to paper so you will know it is no small matter that keeps me from you. Once you have read this account, you will understand that I have stayed in this remote place, not for selfish reasons of my own, but instead, to protect you.

To begin, I want you to know that this story is so incredible that I have decided it would be best if I tell it as it happened and avoid any commentary that might taint its objective telling.

The world is full of suffering. When I entered the job market after college, I wanted to have a positive impact on people's lives. I believed beyond a shadow of doubt that I was destined to eradicate human suffering. So, I took a position as a research scientist with the world's largest pharmaceutical company, Pathogen.

Little did I know, I had stepped onto a stage at the center of a great drama that will thrust us all into a whirlwind of change. Perhaps it's best I didn't know, because I may have faltered at the starting gate if I had even a glimpse of where it would lead and the personal price I would pay.

I hadn't been with the company long before I was assigned to a team of scientists searching for the cure of a dreadful virus. A few weeks earlier, a team of explorers from National Geographic found the doors to a cold war era Soviet laboratory standing wide open. In the wake of budgetary cuts, security personnel had been re-assigned and looters ransacked the unguarded building.

It was believed that the facility was used by the Soviets to develop bio-weapons during the cold war, but of course the Russian government vehemently denied it. We were told the Soviets used the lab to develop a virus called "Deathblow." When exposed to the virus, our lab rats died a painful death within minutes of exposure. It was horrible.

Intelligence sources reported the virus had fallen into the hands of radical terrorist groups. It was our mission to find a cure before it was used as a weapon against innocent people. We were in a race against time and worked around the clock to find a vaccine.

Our search for a treatment frustrated us. We failed many times and were close to giving up hope. If it wasn't for Pathogen's CEO, Wilbur Goth, we would have quit many times. He is the most determined man I have ever known. Each time we tried to give up, he told us to keep looking because there's a cure for everything. I was proud to model my life after him.

Unlike Goth, we had little faith. In the end, his spirited pep talks didn't last long. When we were certain all hope was lost, something horrible happened in the lab. There was an accident that exposed us to the virus. I watched all of my co-workers die. I was the lone survivor.

Goth was outraged that we breached protocol. When he finally calmed down, he sent in a team outfitted with hazmat suits, to scan everything in the lab, including me. We needed to know why I was unaffected by the deadly virus, so they turned me into a human guinea pig.

I endured months of fruitless poking and testing. Every theory, no matter how wild it seemed, was considered. We followed every lead, but all were dead ends. The virus defeated us at every turn.

Through all the frustrating moments, the thing that bothered me the most was the nagging feeling I already knew the answer. It seemed to hover near me like a ghost that refused to abandon the mortal world. The answer was close at hand, yet remained elusive. It was maddening.

The breakthrough came from an unexpected source. A giant sinkhole suddenly appeared in Guatemala City, gobbling up most of a city block. Video taken from the air showed a bottomless black hole leading to some unknown Hell. I was astounded that it was a perfect circle and there appeared to be drill marks in the granite.

The news reporter read a script about the natural process that causes sink holes, but she didn't look convinced. Neither was I. The hole didn't look natural at all. It looked to me like a giant shaft had been drilled by some ancient technology and then covered up until years of rainfall once again exposed it to the world.

There was something else about it that caught my attention. I only caught a glimpse of it, but I'm certain I saw marks in the stone just before it flashed off the television.

I rushed to my computer and searched online for pictures of the sinkhole. None of them gave me a clear view of the markings, but I could see enough to confirm it wasn't my imagination. Etched in the stone was an ancient symbol similar to an Ouroboros, but instead of a snake swallowing its own tail, it depicted a snake eating a bird, and the bird simultaneously eating the snake.

The picture stirred a memory from our honeymoon. Your mother and I took a cruise down the Amazon River with nothing but the gear we could stuff into a couple of backpacks. I know it's an unusual honeymoon location, but I was drawn by some inexplicable force to the Amazon River.

At first, the boat ride sounded like an amazingly romantic adventure, but the trip did not go well. While on the river, I became ill. In desperation, your mother sought help from a lone native standing on the river bank. In the throes of fever, I saw only his kind eyes and a gold medallion around his neck. The medallion depicted a snake eating a bird, and the bird simultaneously eating the snake.

The man gave me a few sips of an herbal tea and told me to rest. As far as we could tell, there wasn't another person within miles of this location, let alone a hospital. Your mother figured I was as good as dead, but during the night the fever broke. The next day there wasn't a sore bone in my body.

What a miracle! In the middle of nowhere, we had the good fortune to stumble upon a Medicine Man, who was gracious enough to heal me. When I asked him about the medicinal tea he gave me the night before, he handed me a leaf.

"This is Great Mother," said the Medicine Man. "When darkness rides the four winds, you will return."

I figured something was lost in the translation, but I was grateful all the same. When we returned to Louisville, I stuck the leaf in a book and forgot about it. I had a new wife, a family to start, and a deadly virus to cure. I believed in science and for the next few years I was consumed with the search for a cure.

I had all but forgotten the leaf until I saw the sink hole and the carving of the snake eating bird. It reminded me of the Medicine Man's medallion and his magical cure, Great Mother.

Years later, sitting in the comfort of my own home, it seemed incredible that the sinkhole in Guatemala City could have the same strange snake eating bird symbol as the Shaman's gold medallion. I took a few minutes to ponder what it meant. Could there be some connection between the two, I wondered. If there was, I sure didn't see it.

It had been several years and I wasn't sure which book I stuck the leaf in or if I even still owned the book, but it was worth a try. As I stood in my library staring at the shelves of books, there was one that stood out above all others. I leaned a little closer and read the title on the spine. It was the classic Jules Verne book, "Journey to the Center of the Earth."

I first opened Verne's book one rainy day many years ago and learned the power of story. I could barely read at the time. In fact, like most school children, I found reading to be a tortuous affair and never imagined it could bring me pleasure. Journey to the Center of the Earth took the younger me on a magic carpet ride to a wondrous place deep inside of the Earth.

Verne stirred my imagination in ways I didn't know were possible. When I opened his book, it returned the favor by opening my mind to possibilities I never knew existed. I dreamed I would someday uncover life's mysteries.

In fact, that's why I decided to be a scientist. Science is a systematic tool for discovery and I wanted to be a discoverer when I grew up. Many years later, the sight of the old tome still stirred visions of prehistoric creatures living inside the hollow Earth. Verne's book truly held a special place in my heart.

So, it was with a trembling hand, that I reached out and took the dusty old hardback from the shelf. I didn't open it immediately. Instead, I held it in my hands and felt the weight of it. For something so light, it carried an unbelievable amount of what I like to call, "idea-weight".

I raised it to my nose and inhaled deeply. I love the smell of old books. If infinite possibilities had a smell, I imagine it would be the scent of a book. I'm not sure how long I stood there with the tip of my nose pressed against the book's cover, but when I finally returned to the present, I couldn't tell which world was more real…the library den on the Earth's firm surface or the prehistoric jungle at the center of the Earth. Imagination is a wondrous thing.

The book seemed to open itself and what I found astounded me. Buried between its pages was the leaf and it was as fresh as the day the Medicine Man handed it to me. As I pondered this great mystery, a phrase from Verne's book jumped off the page, "While there is life there is hope."

The next morning I rushed into my supervisor's office and excitedly told him the Amazon story. He was not impressed, but did take the leaf, and rather absentmindedly, mumbled something about looking into it. Months went by without a word. Each time I asked him about it, he just shrugged and told me to get back to work.

Then one day after work, two men showed up at our house. They quickly flashed identification and claimed to be Federal Agents. We were told they had a search warrant and watched helplessly as they tore our home apart.

A few personal papers and the computer were the only things they found of interest. At first we didn't know what they were looking for, but when they began questioning us about the dangerous narcotic we brought back from the Rainforest, we knew this intrusion had to do with the Shaman's leaf.

The Feds questioned us for several hours about the leaf. They wanted to know where we got it and whether we had any more. We told them the Amazon story and assured them the one leaf was all we had.

They threatened to lock us away in prison if we didn't cooperate with them. The thing is, we were cooperating and I sure didn't believe the leaf was dangerous. There was something wholesome about the Shaman's tea. I felt the goodness of it from the very first sip and there was no doubt in my mind that it cured me.

I was beginning to smell a rat, but your mother was beside herself. She begged the agents to show us mercy. She frantically tried to convince them the Shaman was just a silly old man who called the leaf "Great Mother." What a silly name for a plant she pleaded. How could we possibly know it was a dangerous drug, she asked.

They eventually left, but the aftermath was worse than all of the questioning. Our home was in shambles. More importantly, their intrusion pushed our marriage to the edge. I was shaken, but stubborn in my belief that something was not right.

The next day my supervisor summoned me to his office and told me I should be fired. He said the company did not employ drug dealers, but he was going to give me a break because I had been a loyal employee. If I was smart I would get back to work and forget it ever happened.

I was stunned. The possibility I could get fired over a leaf I brought back from the rainforest never once crossed my mind. I needed my job and planned to forget the whole thing. Then something happened that forever changed our lives.

A few weeks later, I was asked to report the latest results of our research to the Board of Directors. The meeting did not go well. We were prepared to give our presentation, but were unexpectedly told it wasn't necessary because the program had been terminated. Some of us would be reassigned. Others would be laid off. That's all we were told before being abruptly dismissed from the meeting.

I felt ill and made a detour to the executive wash room. As I sat in a stall wondering how I would support my family, Wilbur Goth and his assistant, O.J. Renfield, entered the room.

"Did you see the news today?" asked Goth.

"Yes, it's escalating," said Renfield.

"War, crime, violence, famine, disease, earthquakes, tornadoes…the end is near," said Goth.

"Next they will turn on us," said Renfield.

"If the people discover how powerful they really are then there will be no controlling them," said Goth.

"We can't let that happen," said Renfield. "We must either kill them or weaken them with illness."

"Illness and fear of death make cowards of us all," said Goth.

"Now that we have the cure, we can unleash the virus," said Renfield.

"Has a test site been chosen yet?" asked Goth.

"Several small villages in the Middle East are under consideration," said Renfield.

"Perfect," said Goth. "Just make certain it is blamed on terrorists."

"No problem," said Renfield. "The ground work has already been completed."

"Is there any progress on the development of a domestic delivery system?" asked Goth.

"Our new heartburn medication, Gutchriem, is showing great promise," answered Renfield.

"Does it effectively mask the virus?' asked Goth.

"The preliminary results are promising," answered Renfield.

"Good, I can't emphasize how important this is," said Goth. "We must have an effective means of spreading the virus to the general population that is totally fool proof," said Goth.

"Understood," said Renfield.

"Failure is not an option," said Goth.

"We will not fail," said Renfield.

"It is also critical that no one ever know we have a cure," said Goth.

"Who would have thought it," said Renfield. "A weed from the jungle wipes out viral infections."

"The damn thing is a wonder drug," said Goth. "It cures everything and restores optimal health. Hell, I bet we could live forever thanks to this little plant."

"It would wipe out the entire healthcare industry," said Renfield.

"It would destroy our business," said Mr. Goth. "We've made billions from the common cold alone."

"More importantly, we'd lose our ability to control the masses," said Renfield. "Besides, it could ruin all our plans."

"Once we eliminate the unsuitable masses, we will start all over and build our kind of society," said Goth.

"Only the chosen ones will be allowed to survive," said Renfield. "The rest will be fed to the worms."

"They must not get their hands on the cure," said Goth. "Have you had any luck finding and destroying the plants at their source?"

"No, the Amazonian Rainforest is huge," answered Renfield.

"If necessary, destroy the entire Rainforest," said Mr. Goth. "This plant grows like a weed and we want our farming operation to be the only source."

"It's already in the works," said Renfield. "We've ramped up our efforts to create a false market for rainforest products. We estimate two acres of rainforest are destroyed every second."

"Good," said Mr. Goth. "How long will it take to destroy the entire thing?"

"Thirty-five years at the current rate," said Renfield.

"Too damn long," said Goth. "How's Plan B going? Any leads from Bardough?"

"Nothing helpful," said Renfield. "All he remembers is meeting a native somewhere on the river bank. The Amazon River is four thousand miles long. That's too much riverbank to explore."

"Watch him carefully," said Mr. Goth. "Maybe he will lead us to the source. Once he does, then kill him."

CHAPTER 37

Holy crap! If this is true, then it explains why Gutchriem is making people sick. Goth is using it to deliver a bio-weapon that will murder millions of innocent people. This guy is a monster and I defended him in Court. To make matters worse, I convinced a jury Gutchriem is safe and then it put my mother in a coma. If it wasn't for me, Goth would be sitting in prison right now and Mom wouldn't be fighting for her life.

What have I done? My client is not only guilty, he is evil and should be behind bars.

My body was shaking so badly, I found it difficult to focus on my surroundings. When my eyes finally came to a rest, it was Ginny's face that I saw. Her eyes were calm, but I could see a fire smoldering just below the surface. She studied me closely.

"It has started," she said.

I nodded.

"Official corruption is wide spread," I said. "Discontent is growing. People are beginning to riot against unjust governments. It's only a matter of time before it explodes worldwide.

"The signs of decay that trigger Goth's plan to wipe us all out," she said.

"He's a psychopath," I said.

"Yes, he is," said Ginny.

"I kept him out of jail," I said.

"You couldn't have known," she said.

"No, I guess not," I said.

"The only relevant question is what are you going to do about it?" she said.

"We need to stop him," I said.

She nodded.

"How?" asked Ginny.

"We have to warn everybody," I said.

"Who would believe us?" she asked.

"You're right of course," I said. "We'll need clear and convincing evidence."

"How do we get it?" she asked.

I shrugged.

"Let's begin by talking to your dad," I said.

"So you believe he is my father?" she asked.

"It's weird how he looks like he should be your brother, but weird has become the story of my life," I said. "Yes, I believe."

"Then there's hope," said Ginny.

I smiled and said, "Yes, there's hope."

Ginny looked thoughtful and said, "Until he returns there's something I want to ask you."

"Sure, ask anything you want," I said.

"Is there an us?" asked Ginny.

I think I may have stopped breathing, so I swallowed hard to kick start it again. When I could trust myself to speak, it came from the heart.

"All I've ever wanted is to be loved...ummm...errr...to be loved by you," I said.

"Yessss!" she said and threw her arms around me.

We held each other for a long time before reluctantly separating. Ginny looked thoughtful.

"Well there won't be much for us until we resolve your legal problems," she said. "Really, Grant, you're a lovable mess."

"Yeah, I've hit a rough spot," I admitted. "The criminal charges were taken care of by the military. They shut down the murder investigation in exchange for my silence about what really happened at the Center."

"What do you think really happened?" asked Ginny.

"I only know what I saw and that was a brief flash of images," I answered. "It's sort of like subliminal pictures that were burned into my mind."

"What did you see?" she asked.

"When the shooting started, people rushed the exits, but the doors remained closed," I said.

"Were they locked from the outside?" she asked.

"It sure looked that way to me," I answered.

"What else did you see?" she asked.

"They started shaking," I answered.

Ginny's hand flew to her mouth.

"Oh my god!" exclaimed Ginny. "I saw that too. At first, I thought it was an epileptic convulsion, before I realized that might happen to an individual, but not an auditorium full of people."

"That's true," I said.

"Is there something we could have done for them?" she asked.

"Maybe, but I was focused on getting us out of there and as far away from the shooter as possible," I answered.

She clutched herself and said, "I just remembered something. There was a hiss. I heard it between the shots."

"A hiss?" I asked.

She nodded.

"Like a cat?" I asked.

"No, it was more like gas escaping from a canister," she said.

"When I awoke after the shooting, the news was on," I said. "They reported all of those people had been killed by an accidental gas leak."

"If it was a gas leak, they would have fallen asleep, wouldn't they?" she said.

I nodded.

"It seems highly unlikely it was a gas leak," I said. "Shaking is the first symptom of Gutchriem poisoning."

"All of those people couldn't have been suffering from acid reflux," she said.

"I agree, while chronic gut issues are at epidemic proportions, I doubt the entire audience was taking Gutchriem," I said.

"Do you think Goth has other ways to spread the virus?" asked Ginny.

"He's been working on it for years, so I would guess that he does," I said.

"Do you think the hiss was the sound of someone releasing the virus into the HVAC system?" she asked.

"It's possible," I answered.

"They planned to test their bio-weapon on a third world village, but I'm having a hard time imagining stone age people taking heartburn medicine," said Ginny.

"You're right," I said. "It makes sense that Goth has other delivery systems."

"Nothing about this lunatic makes much sense," said Ginny.

I pointed to the journal.

"This entry is from twenty years ago," I said. "How does a madman fly under the radar for twenty years?"

"You can hide a lot of crazy with wealth," said Ginny. "Do you know if they ever actually used it on a village?"

I shook my head.

"If they disguised it well, then it could have blended in with hundreds of other terrorist attacks," I said.

"Dad might know," said Ginny.

"Yeah, he might," I agreed.

"We need to talk to him, but while we wait for his return, let's try to come up with some way to prove Goth is killing people," said Ginny.

"I may have a lead on that, but we'll need to get back to Louisville," I said.

"What is it?" she asked.

"I had a strange conversation with Zeke Kruthers after the trial," I said.

"I'm sorry, I don't know who that is," said Ginny.

"I sometimes forget you no longer live in Louisville," I said. "He's the prosecutor who believes Goth intentionally deceived the public about the risks of Gutchriem."

Ginny shook her head.

"You lawyers," she said. "One minute you're in Court fighting tooth and nail to beat each other into submission, and in the next, you're have drinks."

I shrugged my shoulders.

"It's a job that requires professionalism, Ginny," I said. "In most towns, the legal community is small. Without civility and professional courtesy, it would be a toxic community."

"I get that, but sometimes we hide behind concepts like professionalism to justify behavior that is inherently wrong," she said.

"There's a lot of truth to that," I said.

"So, tell me about this strange conversation with Mr. Kruthers after you soundly beat him in court and set Goth free," said Ginny.

I groaned, but the look in Ginny's eyes told me her comment was not intended to be critical.

"While we were waiting for the verdict, someone provided him with an envelope filled with documents," I said.

"What documents?" she asked.

"He wouldn't say," I answered.

"Who left them?" she asked.

"He thought I did," I said.

"I assume you didn't," she said.

I shook my head.

"What did he say about the documents?" she asked.

"He said they are a game changer," I answered.

"A game changer," she said.

I nodded.

"Pathogen is somehow involved," I said.

Ginny raised an eyebrow and said, "In what way?"

"He wouldn't say," I answered.

"Geez, what did he say?" she asked.

"He said my law firm is implicated," I said.

Ginny looked alarmed.

"Are you implicated?" she asked.

"I don't see how," I said. "It has something to do with my boss, John Biggs."

"Are you talking about the co-worker who hung himself?" she asked.

I nodded.

"He killed himself after he spoke to Zeke Kruthers about the documents," I said.

"We need to know what those documents say," she said.

"I agree, but ethical considerations may prevent Zeke from telling us," I said.

"Then we need to find another way," she said.

"It would help if we knew who provided them to Zeke," I said.

"Any ideas?" she asked.

I shook my head.

"Someone who wants to take Pathogen down," I answered.

"That could be a long list," she said.

"Yep," I said. "There's more."

"What else did he say?" she asked.

"He told me to look into my father's death," I said.

"I thought it was an accident," she said.

"Yeah, me too, but now I'm not so sure," I said.

"Do you think his death has something to do with the documents?" she said.

"It's hard to say for sure, but it was the only clue he would give me," I said.

"Did he say anything else?" she asked.

"One more thing," I answered. "He said he was afraid of these people and warned me to watch my back."

"A Federal prosecutor said that?" she asked.

I nodded.

"Who's he afraid of…and why?" she murmured.

"There's something I haven't told you yet," I said.

"I'm not going to like this, am I?" she asked.

"Probably not," I said.

"Tell me," she said.

"Do you remember me telling you about the little man I bumped into outside of John's office just before I discovered his body?," I asked.

"Yes, you called him Mr. Bowtie or something else equally colorful," she said.

"Mr. Suit," I said.

"Mr. Suit," she repeated.

"It was expensive," I said.

"The suit," she said.

I nodded.

"Mr. Suit showed up at the hospital and threatened me," I said.

"What kind of threats?" she asked.

"He threatened to torture me," I answered.

Ginny inhaled sharply.

"Torture!" she said.

"They had me strapped to a bed and Sadistic Doctor was planning to run electricity through my brain," I said.

"Electroshock…I thought they stopped that years ago," she said.

I shrugged.

"Evidently not," I said.

She shuddered.

"It seems so barbaric," she said.

"I think of it as the little death, because it's just one twist of the knob below the electric chair," I said.

"Don't they at least use anesthesia?" she said.

"Sadistic Doctor never used it on me," I said.

Ginny looked appalled.

"That's…that's…torture!" she said.

"I can handle it," I said.

"Because you've been through this before," she said.

"Yes, I have," I said.

"When we were kids…after the incident with mother," she said.

I nodded.

Her eyes filled with tears.

"I'm so sorry, Grant," she said.

"Ginny, you have nothing to be sorry for," I said.

She hung her head and sobbed.

I put the journal down and went to her. She laid her head on my chest and all the years of heartache came pouring out…from both of us.

When the sobs subsided, I wiped the last of her tears with my thumb and said, "There's more."

She sighed.

"Of course there is," she said. "What else?"

"Mr. Suit thought I had something that belonged to him," I said.

"What?" she asked.

"Confidential files," I answered.

"What files?" she asked.

I shrugged.

"Do you think he's looking for the prosecutor's envelope of documents?" she asked.

"It could be anything, but that seems highly probable," I said.

"We need to talk to him," she said.

"Yes, we do," I said.

"There's one more thing," I said.

She raised any eyebrow.

"Mr. Suit was looking for your father," I said.

"Oh my God, so was Slotter," she said. "Do you think they are working for Goth?"

"Everything is pointing in that direction," I said.

"We need to talk to Dad," she said.

I nodded.

"We should talk to him when he returns," I said. "In the meantime, I'd like to finish reading his journal."

"I'll let you finish reading while I do some thinking," she said.

She tried to smile, but it was grim.

Once again, I saw the grit she used to build a multi-billion dollar company within ten years of graduating from college. I no longer carried this burden alone. Together we could succeed. With that comforting thought, I returned to her father's journal.

* * *

I had to do something to stop them. If I confronted them or went to the police, they would just deny it. Besides, the incident with the Feds reminded me that they owned the police. I hoped someone out there would listen.

Unfortunately, I had no proof. I needed to get more of the plant. It was risky. They had terrorized my family and threatened to arrest me. On the other hand, life had handed me an important task. I knew I couldn't walk away from it. My conscience wouldn't permit it.

I thought about it for days before deciding it was time to return to the rainforest and find the source of Great Mother. I figured once I had the medicine in hand, then I could figure out how to deliver it to the people. Free of illness, they will enjoy optimal health for the first time in their lives. This will end the healthcare crisis and destroy Pathogen before it destroys us. I just needed a way to slip away without their watchdogs following me.

The first wave of layoffs hit our department, but they kept me on. I needed the money, but I hated working for these people. If I quit, then I might tip them off that I was on to them. I decided to use an upcoming conference in Vegas as cover to look for the plant.

In order to keep you safe, I decided to keep the details of the plan to myself.

Besides, the Feds scared your mother and she wanted me to drop the whole thing. It led to terrible arguments whenever I tried to discuss returning to the rainforest. I didn't want to leave you, but I saw no other way. To keep you safe, I asked Robert Li to look after the two of you if anything ever happened to me.

* * *

My father!

I looked up and saw Ginny studying me. There was a strange look to her face that reminded me of a mother looking after her young. I wasn't sure what it meant, but it made me feel safe.

It was a new feeling for me and that seemed wrong somehow. How can a grown man not be intimately familiar with safety? Such a man would have spent his life in a fight or flight mode...and I am such a man.

"Your father asked my dad to watch over you," I said.

"Yes, he did," said Ginny.

"Then Dad let us both down," I said.

She shook her head.

"He did not let me down," she said.

"My dad let me down," I said.

"No, Grant," said Ginny. "Think this through."

"What do you mean?" I asked.

"They tried to kill my dad," she said.

I nodded.

Ginny waited.

"When did your father die?" she asked.

I did some quick mental math. Dad was killed by a hit-and-run driver around the same time Ginny's father left for South America. Then it hit me.

"Do you think the hit-and-run was intentional?" I asked.

Ginny didn't answer, but I detected a slight nod and asked, "Do you think they killed my dad?"

"I don't know Grant, but these people seem capable of anything," said Ginny.

They kidnapped Ginny, shot us both, tortured me, and tried to kill her father. To force a motorcycle off the road and leave a small boy's parents to die in a ditch requires a certain level of cold-heartedness that only the worst of villains have. Yes, they are capable of anything.

"Could this be what Zeke Kruthers was talking about when he suggested I investigate Dad's death?" I asked.

"It seems likely to me he was trying to point you in the direction of your own client, Wilbur Goth, and his pharmaceutical company, Pathogen," she said.

"If he's right, then Goth stole my childhood by killing Dad and turning Mom into a bed ridden paraplegic for the last twenty years," I said.

"We have to do something about Goth," said Ginny.

I nodded absent mindedly, but I was really thinking about Mom in a coma and fighting for her life once again, thanks to Goth. More anger than I ever thought I had begun to rise to the surface. Knowing there is nothing noble about anger, I tried to push it down, but it was irrepressible.

To Ginny's credit she didn't interfere. Instead she sat quietly and bore witness to the pain I had buried so deep I was no longer aware it existed. It was Great Mother that pulled me out of that hell and back into the world of the living.

"Do you think Great Mother could help Mom?" I asked.

"Yes...yes, I do," answered Ginny.

Her quiet confidence in this strange jungle plant calmed me. I exhaled slowly and decided to find a way to give it to Mom as soon as we returned to Kentucky. In the meantime, I wanted to finish her father's journal, so I continued reading where I had left off.

* * *

I changed my flight and flew into Ecuador. As soon as I arrived in Quito, I rented a jeep and drove to Manaus. It was a brutal, five day, three thousand mile journey, but I wanted to make absolutely certain they couldn't follow me. I practically lived on Yerba Mate that I drank through a silver straw.

In Manaus I chartered a small plane to tour the Amazon rainforest. I hoped by some miracle I could find the shaman who healed me. He gave me Great Mother once. Maybe he would do it again.

It was an insane plan. The rainforest is huge and it all looked the same from the air. The flight was unproductive and I was discouraged as we turned back. The only other idea I had was to recreate the river cruise we did on our honeymoon. That would take much longer and my memories of the river were not good.

I took one last look at the jungle below and wondered if I would ever find the plant. As I peered out the window, I saw a military helicopter approaching our plane. Curious, I studied it closely. As it got closer I could see there were gunmen at the open door with weapons pointed in our direction. I was about to tell the pilot about the helicopter when a rocket was fired in our direction.

CHAPTER 38

Her father's story was interrupted when a young woman entered. Like all of the Guardians, she looked to be twenty-something, but had the presence of someone much older. Most people seem to become more tolerant as they age. Being at ease with the world around them, gives them an air of dignity that can't be faked. The young woman was clearly very comfortable in her own skin.

Like the others, she was nude. As far as I could tell, there wasn't a scar or blemish anywhere on her body. She was flawless. I'm embarrassed to say that I thought the Guardians all looked alike when I first arrived, but the longer I stayed with them the easier it was to tell them apart.

It was the little differences that set them apart from each other. For instance, this woman wore her black silky hair in a long braid that she pulled over a swimmer's shoulder and let fall gently around the curve of her right breast. Just below her nipple, the braid split into three braids for about four inches and then came back together into one before finishing its descent in a curly flourish.

Smiling she said, "I'm called Coral. I was sent to fetch you to your bath."

Ginny raised an eyebrow.

"They think we stink," I said with a grin.

"Like a skunk," quipped Ginny.

Coral led us down the path leading to the bubbling springs. Along the way, we passed two women playfully fondling each other. Coral paid the giggling couple no attention. I cut my eyes to Ginny. She cast them a curious look, but said nothing about it.

Much of the community was gathered near the fountain. It is a natural formation of rock vaguely shaped like a couple entwined in an erotic embrace. Water emerged from a hot spring deep within the Earth and flowed between the couple's legs before emptying into the steaming pool.

Eric was surrounded by a group of beautiful women about twenty yards to the left of the Fountain. Camo Girl was nowhere in sight. Layah was swimming laps in the cooler water nearby. Ginny tested the hot springs with her big toe.

Nodding her approval, she said to no one in particular, "Oh, I so need this."

She was a little too eager and lost her footing on the steps leading into the pool.

It was a good thing I was following her because she fell right into my arms. Startled, she looked back and caught a glimpse of the bliss radiating from me. With a sigh, she slowly relaxed into me and stayed there a little longer than necessary.

It felt good, maybe a little too good. I was getting very turned on again. I willed it down. It refused to comply. I couldn't hide behind Ginny forever. Shit. I was screwed.

This was a growing problem that seemed to be happening when other people were watching. I never thought of myself as an exhibitionist. In fact, you might say I've been obsessed with avoiding public displays at all costs. This visible state of arousal was yet another example of the many ways my life had turned upside down over the last few days.

I figured Ginny felt my erection because her head suddenly whipped around. Her attention didn't help. I burned with a mix of embarrassment and desire. It didn't take her long to figure out my predicament and her mouth formed a mischievous smile that I'm not sure I liked. This one was going to cost me big time.

She laughed. The tension broke. The beast retreated in the face of laughter, but not completely.

The intimate moment was interrupted by a shout from Eric.

"Mr. Johnson...oh Mr. Johnson, would the four of you like to join us?" shouted Eric.

When I raised an eyebrow, Eric cut his eyes to my predicament. It's possible I may have ground my molars together in exasperation. Eric could be so sophomoric at times. Addressing my body parts as Mr. Johnson was the kind of juvenile behavior he thrived upon.

I was about to decline Mr. Subtlety's invitation, but both Ginny and Coral headed in his direction. Eric does that to women. He draws them in with some kind of powerful magnetic force of personality that has always mystified me. I let out a sigh and followed the girls.

"Where's Camo Girl?" I asked.

With a twinkle in his eye Eric said, "I think I wore the poor girl out. She's napping. By the way, her name is Anna, but I think I prefer Camo Girl. You've got to love that outrageous getup she had on. Not that it exists anymore. They burned our clothes, you know. Now that's a level of commitment to naturism I can respect."

Coral eyed Eric like he was a special treat.

"Your clothes aren't necessary," she said. "It's warm here and we have nothing to hide from each other."

Ginny chimed in.

"Besides, clothing collects odors and I'm fresh out of deodorant," she said.

"I love your natural scent," I mumbled under my breath, but Ginny heard me.

"You could have mentioned that before I sunk all the way to my chin in this delicious hot bath," said Ginny.

"I could have, but clean is good too," I said. "You're yummy with or without cooties."

Ginny's eyes widened slightly and her breath caught in her chest for just a split second, but I saw it. She started to say something, but then stopped. Finally, whatever she intended to say was replaced with a smile that began in her eyes before spreading to her lips.

"What are cooties?" asked Coral.

That started a round of laughter that brought tears to my eyes. When the laughter finally subsided, Eric leaned over and whispered something in Coral's ear.

In one smooth movement, her hand slipped into the clear water, and for the first time, I watched another man grow from his humble state of rest into an angry beast. I had no idea Eric was so well-endowed.

Coral slipped under the water and took him into her mouth. Eric grunted just before his eyes rolled back into his head. The girl must have been half fish. She was down there a long time by my reckoning. It was way longer than any normal person could have held their breath.

I'm not sure how my hand found its way between Ginny's legs, but it was there exploring the soft petals of her flesh. As if she sensed the tentativeness of my touch, she let out a soft moan and pressed herself more firmly against my hand.

Encouraged by her reaction, I slipped the tip of my forefinger just inside of her. Her moan got a little deeper. It stirred an equally deep place inside of me and I suddenly had to have her, right then. I pulled her onto my lap and plunged into her.

I wanted to get as deep as I possibly could and held nothing back. She took it. She took all of it without a whimper, without any resistance. That was a first for me. It was as if we were made to fit. This time it was my lips that allowed a moan to escape.

It was a good thing she was on top. Otherwise, I would not have lasted much longer than the initial plunge. While I had pulled her onto my lap, Ginny was now in charge and her eyes held me in a deep embrace.

Without moving, we looked deeply into each other. It was then that I really saw her for the first time. I really saw her and in that instant I ceased to exist. There was only us.

The rest of our bath time was soothing and relaxing as we basked in the afterglow of love making. I was beginning to like this communal bath a lot.

Afterwards, Ginny went for food and I returned to the journal. Gratefully, she promised to bring me something to eat. Grinning, she told me I needed to keep my strength up. I like the way her grin takes up all of her face like Wonderland's Cheshire cat. With that she sashayed off in the direction of the cooking fire.

I picked up her father's journal and continued where I left off.

* * *

Our plane was hit by the rocket. I'm pretty sure we crashed, but the only thing I can say for sure is I lost consciousness.

The last thing I remember as we tore through the tree tops was the pilot repeatedly saying, "You fired on me! You weren't supposed to fire on me."

When I came to, there was a beautiful woman leaning over me. Her hand gently caressed my cheek. Her big brown eyes sparkled with an amazing light. I had never seen anything like her and was certain she was an angel.

She spoke, but her words didn't make any sense. The only word I recognized was "Namaste," which means the creator in me honors the creator in you. So, it's possible she was speaking Sanskrit. Which was very weird considering we were in South America.

The Angel gave her head a little shake and switched to Spanish. When that didn't work, she tried several more languages in rapid succession before she settled on English.

"My name is Layah," she said. "How do you feel?"

I wiggled my toes, clinched my left hand into a tight fist, and then rolled my head from side to side. Satisfied they seemed to be in good working order, I did a full body scan. Everything seemed to be in tip top shape. In fact, I felt great. I hadn't felt that good since the shaman healed me on my honeymoon.

"I feel amazing, but that makes no sense," I answered. "Half of the airplane's wing was shot off and we went down fast. I should be dead right now."

"We saw Quetzalcoatl blasted from the sky by a helicopter and went to investigate," she said. "The crash left a path of destruction in the forest. Countless plants were wounded and more than a few were completely destroyed. We saved as many of our four legged brothers and sisters as we could."

Layah folded her hands and placed them over her heart. With bowed head she said a prayer of thanks for their sacrifice and then opened her arms wide above her head, releasing their spirit to the creator. As if on cue, a beam of sunlight cut through the dense foliage and illuminated her face. It only lasted a few breaths before the light softened and she continued her story.

"The crash site was scattered with torn and twisted metal", she said. "Foul smelling smoke rose from burning chunks of plastic plane parts. No one moved to stop the fires. Instead, we left them to cleanse this sacred place."

"You were found lying in a crumpled heap at the base of an ancient Yerba Mate tree where you had been thrown by chance upon impact. We pulled you from death just before the soldiers came. After searching the area, they once again mounted the vimana and flew away."

"Vimana?" I asked.

With a little shake of the head, she said, "I think you call them helicopters."

"Isn't vimana the name for an ancient Indian flying machine?' I asked.

"It's not quite as ancient as you might think, but yes," she said.

I had no idea why she would say they are not ancient, since the vimana were discussed in fifth century B.C. Hindu texts. That seemed pretty old to me, but I had no desire to argue with the angel and decided to change the subject.

"You saved me," I said. "Thank you."

"Yes, but you have persistent enemies," said Layah. "The soldiers came back many times, but the jungle was not friendly to them and they eventually abandoned their search."

I needed to know who was behind this and asked, "Did the pilot survive? I have a few questions I want to ask him."

She shook her head.

"No, he was beyond help," said Layah.

"His injuries must have been serious," I said.

"It's less about the extent of injury and more about timing," she said. "We can heal any harm if we catch it in time."

I decided to take a chance and asked, "With Great Mother?"

Layah nodded and said, "Get some rest. We'll talk more later."

She brushed the hair out of my eyes and chanted a strange lullaby, "He rides on the wings of a morning star. Oh, great serpent, uncover all that lies hidden below."

It felt as if electricity pulsed from her. I wanted to touch more than her finger tips, but I was a married man. A wife and child awaited my return. It was time to turn away from my unfaithful thoughts.

As I drifted off to sleep I wondered about the weird turn of events that delivered me to the exact place I needed to be. I had found the mother of all medicinal herbs!

CHAPTER 39

Ginny arrived with food and insisted I eat something. I'm not sure, but I think it was Anaconda Stew. Sometimes it's best to avoid asking too many questions.

"Do you want to talk about it?" asked Ginny.

I wasn't sure what she meant by "It," but I knew enough about women to know she wanted to talk about "It". I decided the safest course was to keep my answer simple, but broad.

"Yes, I do," I answered.

She waited patiently for more. I didn't know what to say, so I said nothing in the hopes she would speak up and tell me what was on her mind. That didn't work very well. Ginny proved to be more patient than me.

Given the onslaught of her frustratingly patient gaze, I ventured a guess she wanted to talk about our lovemaking at the Fountain. Maybe she wanted me to reassure her...to tell her that we have a future together and that I love her.

These were the thoughts that led me to say, "I don't want you to worry about what happened in the water earlier."

Ginny went completely still. I couldn't even detect the gentle rise and fall of her breath. She looked at me with cold deadpan eyes. I have to admit, it was more than a little scary seeing her like this. When she finally spoke, her voice was hard.

"That was just a fuck, Grant," she said. "Don't get your panties in a bunch."

She could have jumped up and down on my chest with six inch stilettos and it wouldn't have hurt as badly as those two sentences spoken with such coldness. I didn't know what to say. What happened in the water was more than that for me...way more.

On the other hand, a part of me was not surprised by her attitude. It is certainly a view held by my wife. I guess I had come to expect it from all women.

Me...well I wanted something more. I wanted the fairy tale. I wanted happily ever after. I wanted to be reunited with my soul mate...my twin flame. Plato once wrote that love is nothing more than the desire to be whole again. That's what I wanted...to be whole. When we made love, I was whole for the first time in my life.

Ginny is my other half, but I didn't have the skill-set to handle her rejection, so

I turned away. I must confess it took a while for my vision to clear enough to resume reading her father's journal.

***

Happy Birthday Ginny! You are ten today and I hope your day is filled with much joy and happiness. I imagine you are growing like a weed. I wish I was there to see it. I miss you more than ever.

It hasn't been easy for me to stay away. At first I was eager to return. I missed you and I was determined to put a stop to Pathogen's evil plans. Great Mother can cure the virus, but I also discovered it does much more. It restores the body to a state of optimal health. Free of the fear of illness and functioning at full capacity, people can focus on making a better life for themselves. It is a game changer and I wanted to share Great Mother with the world.

The Guardians convinced me it is not yet time. They told me that someone else was destined to bring Great Mother to the world, but I still have a role to play. Instead, they invited me to stay with them and assist in their cause. I was reluctant to abandon you and your mother. On the other hand, I knew Pathogen would kill me if I returned. It was also possible that they would harm you to get to me and that was not acceptable.

The Guardians promised they would protect you. I found it hard to imagine. They are a gentle and kind-hearted group of people who still live in the stone ages. Besides, you are my responsibility, not theirs. For days, I struggled to find a solution. The days turned into weeks and then months. Time made the decision for me.

As the months flew by, more than my body was healed. Living with these people has calmed my mind and restored my spirit. Men and women live as equals. There is no conflict between the sexes. The men do not control the village's resources. Women do not trade their bodies for security. Pleasure is shared by all. No one is exploited.

In this garden, they live as I imagine Adam and Eve lived in the Garden of Eden. They have no concept of property. If someone is hungry, then they are fed. They wear no clothes, so there are no expensive shopping sprees. No one lives in a mansion or slum. They sleep together in a shared building. There is no competition between them and no rules of the game. They do not fear each other, so there is no need for government and law. They are truly free.

There is something else you should know. There was a birth of a beautiful boy. Layah's delivery was quick and painless. The entire village witnessed his grand entry into the world. He was passed from person to person.

Each one said the same thing, "Welcome, my son."

When he was passed to me, I looked into his beautiful blue eyes and wondered how that happened in a village full of brown eyes. Then it hit me, I alone have blue eyes. Ginny darling, you have a brother.

As I read her father's journal, Ginny was as quiet as a church mouse. I tried to pretend she wasn't in the room, but failed miserably. I was fully aware of her presence, each and every minute. I felt her with all of my being. Still, it startled me when she spoke.

"I'm sorry," she said.

I wanted to tell her it was nothing, but that wasn't true and it caught in my throat. It was something to me. What happened at the Fountain was extremely important to me. The way she devalued it was painful and I had to choke back tears.

It wasn't like me to be so emotional. I was turning into someone I didn't recognize, someone I didn't know very well. Yet, somehow it felt real. I felt more authentic than I ever remember being, so I followed Ch'ing's advice and embraced the emotions churning inside of me.

When I finally pulled myself together, I managed to say in a croaking sort of way, "It was more than a fuck for me."

Ginny stared at me with the most profound amazement on her face. She looked at me like I couldn't possibly be real. Like I was a sweet dream and she would wake up any second only to find herself alone once again.

It was her turn to choke on words I never heard. It was her turn to struggle with strange new emotions. I could see the emotional symphony play out on her face and in her body language. It was complex. It was rich. It was deep. When she finally pulled herself together, her voice was soft.

"When I returned with the food, I intended to discuss dad's journal," said Ginny. "I never thought we would be having this discussion. You caught me by surprise and I guess I misread your intent. I'm sorry I upset you."

I scrambled to make sense of it. We had this beautiful experience and then everything turned upside down in the blink of an eye. We made a deep soul-confirming connection, but then abruptly disconnected when she misread my intent. I wanted to understand so we would never repeat it, but came up with nothing. It was damn frustrating.

I was completely in the dark, but then a light bulb went off. This was about all those years when she needed me the most and I wasn't there for her. She must have thought I was once again distancing myself from her. Ginny, was trying to protect herself. It was time to set the record straight.

"Ginny, I'm the one who should be apologizing," I said. "I fell in love with you when I was five years old. Not once have I stopped loving you. I'm ashamed I let your mother scare me away. If you will have me, I promise to stand by you no matter what life throws at us."

Ginny's eyebrows shot up so high it gave her wide eyes an exaggerated comical appearance. It's possible I caught her by surprise.

"Did you...did you just propose?" asked Ginny.

I swallowed hard. It all hung in the balance and there was nothing for me to do, but to speak the simple truth.

"Yes, I believe I did," I answered.

As an afterthought I added, "I think I should ask for your father's permission, don't you?"

In answer to my question, Ginny flew into my arms, but it caught me by surprise and we tumbled to the ground, where she proceeded to smother me with kisses. I didn't mind one bit.

That's exactly where Eric found us. Being Eric and all he couldn't help but joke about finding me flat on my back with Ginny in total control.

"I can't leave you kids alone for five minutes without finding the two of you rolling around in the dirt," said Eric. "What's up with that?"

Ginny broke for air and said, "We're celebrating."

"Celebrating what...the loss of Grant's virginity?" quipped Eric.

"She said yes!" I said.

"Yes...you mean the big yes...the all in capitals YES?" asked Eric.

I nodded vigorously.

"You proposed marriage to this beautiful woman?" asked Eric.

I nodded even more vigorously.

"And...and she said yes," sputtered Eric.

"Yep, can you believe it!" I exclaimed.

Eric gave each of us a hand and pulled us to our feet.

"Well it's about fucking time," said Eric. "Come here you two and give me a hug."

"Ooooh, time for what?" asked Camo Girl. "A little foursome, maybe?"

I froze. She had somehow slipped in on us. There was no way in hell I was into that. I did not want to share Ginny with anyone.

The people who know me the best came to my rescue. Both Ginny and Eric shook their heads, but it was Ginny who spoke first.

"Not with my husband, you don't," said Ginny.

Eric chimed in, "Oh, that would be like incest or something. Grant and I are brothers. There are plenty of other playmates around here."

"Husband?" asked Camo Girl.

Ginny's grin was even bigger than the wide Cheshire Cat grin she usually flashes. Her head nods were equally exaggerated.

Camo Girl rushed to Ginny and threw her arms around her. There might have been a shrill attempt at speech that accompanied the hug. Who can say what language that is, except most women seem to speak it fluently.

Eric threw his arm over my shoulders and pulled me in tight as he said in a husky tone, "Way to go, Grant."

There might have been tears in his eyes as well. Mine too, for that matter. Hell, we were all crying up a storm when Pony Tail showed up.

"What's all the fuss about?" asked Pony Tail.

These people lived very casual lives. I wasn't sure whether they would share our joy over the engagement. I shouldn't care, but they had gotten under my skin very quickly. Despite the rough start with Pony Tail, he was Ginny's brother and I wanted his blessing. It was odd, but I realized I wanted all of their blessings.

"There's going to be a wedding," said Eric.

"I love...love weddings," said Camo Girl.

"Really?" asked Eric. "You sure don't seem like the marrying type to me."

Camo Girl dropped her chin slightly and punched Eric in the arm with a hard right hand. As far as punches go, it was pretty damn respectable. Eric loves a good fight and I think her martial skill surprised him too.

"I'll have you know, mister, that I've been successfully married four times," said Camo Girl.

"Is that all?" asked Eric as he rubbed his arm. "Why at your age, you should have at least six under your belt by now."

With narrowed eyes Camo Girl said, "Funny guy…I'm only twenty four."

Eric gave his arm a little shake and said, "I can't speak to how good you are at marriage, but I can confirm you pack a respectable wallop in that right hand of yours."

"Pussy," said Camo Girl, but there was no real contempt in her voice. In fact, she was beaming with pride.

Four failed marriages by twenty four. Geez! Right on the tail of my judgmental thoughts it hit me. I'm already married. I have a wife.

"Ginny, you are glowing," said Pony Tail. "It must be your wedding we're talking about and I can tell by the look of terror on Grant's face he's the groom. We better have the wedding quickly before he loses his nerve."

Ginny's glow quickly dimmed as she cut her eyes to me. This was something that could go South very quickly if I didn't nip it in the bud. The divorce was only a formality and it shouldn't take too long to wrap up once I got back to Louisville.

"There is nothing I want more than to marry Ginny," I said.

I heard a voice behind me say, "Good. Then it's settled. We'll have the wedding tomorrow."

Lao Tzu once wrote that the Great Tao lowers the high and raises the low. I had just tumbled from the peak of happiness into the depths of despair. Okay, maybe that's a tad bit melodramatic. The fact is, I wanted to marry Ginny tomorrow, but having two wives is against the law.

On the other hand, Ginny was riding high. She rushed toward me with arms outstretched and face aglow with happiness. I raised mine to accept her embrace, but she swept right past them and threw her arms around a curvaceous Hispanic woman of undetermined age.

Unlike these gentle giants who call themselves the Guardians, this woman was maybe 5'4". Although she was the shortest person in the room, there was something about her that made her larger than life. I think maybe it was her eyes. They were filled with an ocean of wisdom.

"Marguerite," shouted Ginny. "I can't believe you're here!"

Ginny had told me about Marguerite. Once upon a time, Marguerite was Ginny's nanny, but I think she was much more to Ginny than just a babysitter. She was Ginny's lifeline. With an absent father and a bat shit crazy mother, she was more relevant than her own family. You might say Marguerite was all the support she had.

Ginny told me she had planned a reunion during her trip to Louisville, but Marguerite never showed up. Oddly, that was about the same time that my martial arts teacher, Ch'ing, disappeared. Of all the damn places for her to materialize, this remote village in the middle of the rainforest was the last I'd have guessed.

Ginny laid her head on Marguerite's shoulder and wept. I could be mistaken, but it sounded to me like Marguerite was purring as she stroked her hair. When Ginny's sobs passed, Marguerite kissed the top of her head and turned to me.

"Well, you've grown into a handsome young man," said Marguerite.

Even though she was looking at me, I figured she was talking to Pony Tail, since I had never met this woman in my life. It was difficult, but I managed to break her hypnotic gaze and cut my eyes to Pony Tail thinking he'd reply to her compliment. When he didn't, I returned my attention to her.

"Yes, Grant, I'm speaking to you," said Marguerite.

"Have we met?" I asked.

"I've been watching over you from the beginning," she answered.

"You mean, like a guardian angel or something?" I asked.

Of course, my question was intended as a joke. I followed it with a laugh so weak, it embarrassed even me. She smiled anyway and it warmed the dark corners of my being. It felt like her smile came from the heart of the Earth, as if she was born of its very core.

"Something like that," was her simple response, but that smile said so much more.

I believed her. It felt good knowing someone had been watching over me. At times it seemed like I was drifting through the days of my life without any real direction. At other times, I felt like I was getting more than my fair share of troubles. Marguerite made me feel like my life was on course after all.

"I've done the best I could under the circumstances," I said.

"It's okay, Grant," she said. "There is no need to make excuses before you've made your confession."

I couldn't imagine what she wanted me to confess. After all, I was raised Catholic and had spent my fair share of time in the confessional making up sins to confess to our parish priest. I didn't trust him with the truth and always wanted to get away from him as fast as I could.

Later, when he abruptly left the parish, no one would say why, but I overhead an adult whispering something about little Timmy Spreeng and the terrible things that awful priest made him do.

I wasn't sure what that meant, but one day he asked me to undress completely before I put on my altar boy robes. I didn't do it, because the Fat Lady said I'd be punished if I ever undressed in front of anyone again.

Afterwards, Father Pediman took me off the altar boy schedule. That was okay with me. I didn't really like how much time I was spending in church anyway. I'd much rather be in the woods and was glad to be free of his altar.

I needed to tell these people that my divorce was not yet final, but timing is everything and this reconciliation with Ginny felt fragile. Circumstances beyond my control were forcing me to deal with the unexpected consequences of my failed marriage before I was ready and I didn't like it.

I sighed. A relationship must be built on truth or it will never last. It was time to stop whining and tell these people the truth.

"I'm still married," I said.

Marguerite studied me closely and asked a question I didn't expect.

"What do you think marriage is?" asked Marguerite.

The lawyer in me spoke up and said, "It's a legal binding agreement to share one's life and worldly goods with another person."

Marguerite raised an eyebrow, but said nothing. Instead she waited for more. I felt like there was something better inside of me to give. It was something more real than the legal bullshit I had just spouted. I swallowed. Marguerite wanted more than legalese and Ginny was looking crushed by my comments.

"It's completion," I said. "Like closing a circle. Ginny completes me."

Marguerite nodded her approval.

"Dude," said Eric softly.

Camo Girl dabbed at a tear in the corner of her eye.

Pony Tail gripped my shoulder and said softly, "Yes."

Ginny closed the gap between us in two quick steps. At first I thought she was going to throw her arms around me, but she stopped just short and held me with her eyes.

I liked what I saw in Ginny's eyes and would have been content to gaze into them, but slowly she stretched a hand to my cheek and caressed it ever so lightly with the back of her finger tips. A spark of electricity crackled between us and some of the tension I had been carrying around for the last few days melted away.

Ginny's breath quickened. In anticipation of her touch, my breathing matched pace with hers. I wasn't disappointed. She curled her hand behind my neck and then pulled me into a kiss. I had never experienced anything like it. The kiss filled an ocean of loneliness with love and I knew that I would never be the same.

The sky exploded and the Earth shook. I was thinking that was some damn kiss, when Layah rushed in and pointed a finger at Camo Girl.

"The enemy is here," said Layah.

Camo Girl's eyes darted wildly about, as if she was looking for an escape route. Having found none, she puffed herself up and started to say something, when a bullet knocked her to her knees. At first she seemed confused, but then a wave of acceptance washed over her face.

Her last words were, "Victor...forgive me."

The next round of gunfire missed the mark, but we got the message. It was time to fight or flee. It was Marguerite who took charge.

"They're here," she shouted. "We need to move, now!"

CHAPTER 40

My grandmother's chickens liked to hide their eggs from time to time. As hard as she tried, she couldn't find them all and a few were left to rot in their hiding places. I once stepped on one of the bad ones and will never forget the awful smell. It took days to get rid of it. Spent gunpowder has a distinctive odor, but it smells faintly of rotten eggs.

I scanned our surroundings for signs of the enemy, but blue smoke obscured my vision. I could see enough to tell we were surrounded. The forest had become a dangerous place once again.

"There's not much time," said Marguerite. "We must move quickly."

"Who are they?" asked Eric.

"Lost souls," answered Marguerite. She pointed to a cache of weapons and added, "Grab whatever you need and follow me."

Ginny chose a blade the size of a steak knife. Eric grabbed a short spear and I had an axe. Pony Tail carried a bow and quiver of arrows. Marguerite waived off a blow gun saying she had her own defenses.

We used the heaviest smoke as cover to slip quietly past the soldiers. Marguerite led us deeper into the forest. Thinking we had made it out safely, I began to relax when she suddenly stopped and motioned us down. Ginny was following a little too closely and bumped into my back.

"Sorry," she whispered as she stepped on my foot.

The misstep cost her balance. When she tried to recover she cut me with her knife. I let out a yelp and whipped around to take the offending blade from her when I felt the sting of a bullet whizzing past my ear. I had a vision of an earless Vincent van Gogh and fought back a wave of panic.

I released the pressure on the cut and was using the bloody hand to make sure my ear was intact, when the bushes parted and a man carrying a machete two handed above his head leapt toward Ginny's back. I pushed her aside and exploded into him.

The next thing I remember were voices asking me if I was all right. I opened my eyes. I felt a hand on my bicep jiggling my arm. The voice sounded like it was coming from a tunnel.

"Grant, what happened to you?" asked Ginny.

The faces hovering above me gradually came into focus. I was flat on my back. Something was pressing into my kidneys. I smelled blood and wondered if it was mine.

"Grant?"

It was Ginny again.

There was a sharp pain in my chest. My knees felt weak. I opened my eyes.

"Where are we?" I asked.

Marguerite asked, "Do you remember what happened?"

I didn't have a clue and said, "I remember Ginny was attacked by a man with a snake tattoo. After that...nothing."

"Snake tattoo...was it wrapped around his right arm?" asked Ginny.

"Yes," I answered. "I've seen it before. The first time was one of the women who grabbed me in Manaus."

"So have I, Grant," said Ginny. "Match Breath had a tattoo like that."

We turned to Marguerite and Pony Tail for an explanation. It was Pony Tail who answered.

"Slavers," said Pony Tail.

Marguerite looked troubled and said, "That particular serpent tattoo is the brand for a secret society of slave traders who call themselves Knights of the Golden Circle."

"So Wife Beater and her group of freaks were slave traders," I said.

Pony Tail nodded.

"They are well-trained and relentless," said Pony Tail. "Once they begin a job, they never give up until their mission is accomplished. If one of them goes down, two take his place."

"What could slavers possibly want with us?" I asked.

"Match Breath planned to sell me to a brothel," said Ginny. "Maybe they had a brothel in mind for you."

"Very funny, my beautiful fiancée," I said, "but Meat Cleaver wanted to split your pretty head open, not turn you into a sex slave."

Ginny's face lit up, "You think my head is pretty?"

In answer to her question, I took her in my arms and kissed the top of her head.

Eric pointed to a pile of bodies and said, "Dude, I've never seen you fight like that. You went berserk. Coiling and striking with incredible speed. After you dispatched Meat Cleaver, you killed four more in less than a minute. What the hell got into you?"

I shrugged, "I wasn't about to let those men harm Ginny."

Eric stuck his lower lip out in an exaggerated pout, "That was pretty damn selfish, you know. You could have left one or two for me."

Eric loves a good fight and I wasn't surprised by his comment, but the rest of the group looked at me like there was something else bothering them. I had no idea what it might be, so I waited for one of them to bring it up. It was Ginny who finally broke the awkward silence.

"I think maybe we all want to know about the other...ummm...odd behavior," said Ginny.

"What odd behavior?" I asked.

"Dude, you hissed," said Eric.

"Hissed?" I asked.

They all nodded.

"There's more," said Ginny. "You stood over the bodies and flicked your tongue like a snake scenting the air," said Ginny. "It was creepy."

I was stunned. Ginny looked at me like she had just learned some terrible truth about a loved one and didn't know what to make of it.

Eric nodded and asked, "What's gotten into you?"

Marguerite looked thoughtful.

This was all news to me. I didn't remember any of it. I wanted to say something to reassure them. Instead, I stood there staring at them, feeling cold and empty.

"Afterwards, you crumbled to the ground and began shaking," said Pony Tail. "Do you have a history of seizures?"

I shook my head.

"What happened when you killed the Anaconda?" asked Marguerite.

"Not much really," I answered. "I was losing the fight. The damn thing was squeezing the life out of me and I couldn't breathe. In desperation I stabbed a finger as far as I could into the serpent's eye socket and then passed out."

"Grant, this is important," said Marguerite. "Did anything else happen before you passed out?"

"Yeah, I was consumed by white light, followed by darkness," I answered. "I think I died. At least I thought I was dead. I kept looking for Dad. I wanted him to guide me to the other side, but he never showed up. I was alone."

In barely a whisper Ginny said, "You're not alone."

Eric put his arm around me and rumpled my hair.

"Did anything happen before you saw the white light?" asked Marguerite.

At first I couldn't think of anything so I returned to the experience and played it slowly out in my mind. Then I remembered.

"There was a shock," I said. "It felt like I touched an exposed wire with my finger, but it was cold, intensely cold. The cold ran down my arm to the base of my spine. There it gathered in a pool. Something heated it, until it churned like molten lava. Then it shot up my spine. When it reached my crown it exploded into white light. I don't remember anything after that except darkness. All of this happened in the blink of an eye."

"Hurry everyone," said Marguerite. "Time is of the essence. We must see the Council immediately."

"What Council?" I asked.

She didn't answer. Motioning for us to follow, she headed deeper into the rainforest. Hoping for an answer, I cut my eyes to Ginny, but all I got from her was a shrug. There was nothing to do but follow Marguerite deeper into the rainforest.

The sounds of battle could be heard all around us. Since Marguerite was in a hurry, I figured we would move quickly through the jungle, but in stealth mode. Instead, Marguerite acted like she was on a Sunday stroll in the park and didn't have a care in the world.

Every time the gunfire drew near, I expected us to drop to the ground and survey our position, but instead we marched steadily on without changing course. Eventually the gunfire stopped and all we could hear were the voices of rainforest creatures. I liked it much better than the violence we left behind.

The rainforest is a living thing. Scientists believe they can understand it by cataloging the diverse plants and animals who call it home. That doesn't really work. The only way to understand the rainforest is to embrace the whole thing. It cannot be dissected.

Not that we could see much of it in the dark thanks to a thick canopy that blocked most of the night sky. Still, our eyes somehow adjusted to the limited light, revealing just enough of the shadowy forest that we somehow maneuvered our way through it without incident.

We hiked all night. Even though the forest floor was soft with damp leaves, it was not an easy hike in bare feet. I was grateful when we took a break just as the morning sun peeked through a gap in the leaves.

Marguerite stopped. She took a long slow deep breath and told us we were almost there.

I couldn't see it, but I heard running water. Marguerite led us to a bubbling stream where we took refreshment and renewed ourselves. After taking a long drink of water, Pony Tail fell fast asleep. Eric sat with his back to a tree and watched the sun rise through a break in the foliage. Ginny rested on a flat rock and dipped her feet in the water.

I took a few minutes to marvel at the flowers. The way they grow both on the ground and in the trees gave this place a fairy tale atmosphere that Ginny seemed to fit into perfectly. I was thinking how perfectly she fit into my life as well when I sat down next to her on the rock, but she stiffened and leaned away from me.

Not a good sign, I thought. She hadn't been the same since my killing spree. I wanted to say something that would make it all better, but nothing came to mind.

She felt so distant and I didn't know how to bridge the gap between us. To make matters worse, I was divided against myself. I knew if I didn't fix it, I was lost. I remember Ch'ing telling me that when things aren't going right all you have to do is return to your ground. I didn't know what the hell that meant, but I did feel the urge to do Tai Chi.

I stood up and stepped into the water. Facing upstream, I could see a mountain in the distance. For some reason it soothed me. Taking a deep breath, I imagined I was drawing the mountain into me. It felt good, so I did it again and again, until every cell of my body was filled with vital energy.

One morning I found Ch'ing doing the opening movement of Tai Chi, over and over again. It is a very simple posture called, "Spreading a Silk Sheet." I was about to ask why he didn't continue with the full set but he spoke first.

"If I can only get this right, then I will return to a state of balance," said Ch'ing.

I thought he was joking. Ch'ing is a Master. It's the simplest movement to learn in Tai Chi. How could such a simple repetitive exercise restore his balance? Anyway, he seemed pretty balanced to me.

On the other hand, my life was way out of balance. I wondered if Ch'ing's exercise would work for me and decided to give it a try.

I began by slowly drawing my hands up and catching the air under an imaginary silk sheet. In coordination with my rising hands, I drew air into my lungs and then used it to fill the space under the billowing sheet.

When it reached its apex, the floating sheet was spread wide above the king sized bed and my lungs were expanded to the max with oxygen rich air. Then and only then, did I slowly begin to exhale. Without air to support it, the sheet floated gently to the surface of the bed.

Not satisfied with the way it spread, I repeated the exercise over and over again. With each repetition, I softened and rounded the movement and worked to make my breath as smooth as a silkworm pulling its fragile thread.

Something strange began to happen. At times I was the sheet. At other times, I was the bed. It wasn't until I knew that the sheet, the bed, and I were the same, did I finally get it right. I felt an incredible peace spread through me.

I don't know how long I rested in this peaceful state, but the serenity was interrupted by a chill. It began in my feet and slowly crept up my legs. Hungering for the warm fuzzy feeling I just enjoyed during meditation, I ignored it, but the cold wouldn't go away. It continued its relentless march up my back. I was exposed and wished there was something to cover my nakedness.

I hate being cold. Ch'ing knew this about me, so he would teach us outdoors in the dead of winter. The first time it happened, Eric and I awoke to a heavy snow storm one morning and planned to do some sledding on Hippie Hill. We covered ourselves from head to toe in layers of warm clothing and headed out.

Ch'ing caught us on the way out the door. Seeing our heavy clothing, he sadly shook his head and announced it was time for a lesson. He sent us back into the house with instructions to remove all of our useless winter clothing.

Eric looked at me and groaned.

I whispered, "This can't be good."

We reluctantly removed our winter coats, gloves and hats, but kept our sweaters and jeans. Much to our dismay, Ch'ing insisted we remove those as well.

I did not want to take my clothes off. My mind raced as I formulated a list of excuses to avoid following Ch'ing's instructions. It wasn't so much the cold that concerned me, although that was certainly a problem. Nudity just wasn't something I did in public.

Ch'ing had been like a father to me. I loved and trusted him. The thought of disappointing him was unbearable. Still, it wasn't until I realized that I was about to disappoint myself, that I found the courage to remove my clothes and step outside. It was the hardest thing I had ever done.

Shifu found the deepest snow bank to begin class. Standing naked in the snow, it didn't take long before our teeth were chattering.

With a grin Ch'ing said, "So you boys think you're cold."

I was cold and my chattering teeth proved it.

"I bet you wish you had all those clothes right now to keep you warm," said Ch'ing.

Our heads bobbed up and down in agreement.

"There is an endless supply of heat inside of you," said Ch'ing. "I'm going to show you how to connect with it. So listen up."

Ch'ing paused for dramatic effect. When he was satisfied we were listening, he continued.

"Close your eyes," said Ch'ing. "Take a long deep breath. Then another one and another one until you begin to feel the fire in your belly."

It didn't take long before I began to feel the fire in my belly. Grasping at the warmth it provided, I let it spread throughout my body. I clung to it until I felt the first beads of sweat dripping from my forehead. It was then that Ch'ing told us to open our eyes.

Ch'ing's eyes twinkle when he's about to teach us a hard life lesson.

"You boys need to learn how to look at your naked selves," he said.

Eric looked at me and snickered. I wasn't quite so amused. Looking at naked girls is pretty much all two teenage boys ever think about, but there was nothing exciting about standing outside in the cold snow in nothing but our birthday suits.

Ch'ing rolled his eyes and said, "If you two perverts can manage to control your hormones, I will continue your lesson."

When we finally stopped giggling, Ch'ing continued.

"Right now, I bet you think I'm talking about your physical bodies," he said.

Of course that's what we thought he meant by naked selves and nodded in unison.

"Noooo, not at all," said Ch'ing. "So, if it's not the obvious, then what do you think I might be talking about?"

When we didn't answer, Ch'ing pointed to Eric and asked, "Eric, what's left when you eliminate the obvious?"

Eric hated answering questions in class and usually responded with a wise crack. This was no different.

"Umm, are you talking about my stash of girlie magazines?" asked Eric.

"Always the irreverent one, aren't you, Eric?" said Ch'ing. "I'm talking about your authentic selves."

He paused and studied us closely before continuing.

"There I go again using big words with lots of syllables," said Ch'ing. "If you pay attention, you boys might learn something yet. I'm not talking about your skin. What is real about each of you is beneath your skin."

Once again he waited and watched.

"The only way to see your naked body is to strip away all the layers of clothing," said Ch'ing. "Well guess what? Your real selves are covered with layers of bullshit and lies. The only way to see it is to strip away the layers of self-deception. Let me warn you boys. It takes tremendous courage."

"The shivering you were doing earlier didn't have anything to do with today's temperature," said Ch'ing. "You were shivering because you're just scared little boys right now. If you want to grow into the men I know you can become, then you must have the guts to be honest with yourselves and strip away the stories you tell yourselves about yourselves. Do you understand?"

I figured I was pretty honest. About the only thing I lied about was what I was really doing for all that time in the bathroom. Touching myself several times a day wasn't something I could easily talk about. Especially since it was plain ole' Ginny I thought about when I was doing it.

Ch'ing continued his lesson, "Today, I'm going to give you the tools you need. It will be up to you to know when to use them."

Ch'ing gave us a conspiratorial look and lowered his voice, "I bet you didn't know there are a bunch of crazy monks in the Himalayas who sit naked in the snow during meditation. The mountain wind can be brutal up there. They have nothing but their inner fire to warm themselves. As if being naked isn't enough, they spread wet cloth across their backs to dry. They measure their skill by the number of towels they can dry and the size of the puddle created from the snow they melt."

Eric and I looked at each other. Now this was some cool shit. He had our undivided attention and we were hanging on every word.

With his typical dramatic flair, Ch'ing waited patiently until we asked, "How do they do that?"

He grinned. "Well I'm glad you asked. I'm going to teach you how to do it. One day you will come face to face with your naked self. When you do, you will feel cold even though it's warm out. Don't be fooled. Your shivers are fear, nothing more. The truth can be scary as hell."

As I stood there shivering in the middle of the stream, I knew what I needed to do. It was time to be honest with myself. For some reason, I was afraid to open my eyes. Thinking of the monks sitting in the snow, I began the mediation Ch'ing taught us so long ago.

The warmth was comforting. When I was ready, I opened my eyes. I was staring into a pool of water. The reflection was unfocused at first. When it cleared, I nearly fell backwards. It wasn't me I saw reflected in the water. It was the Anaconda and its mouth was wide open to attack.

I couldn't move. It was as if my legs were buried beneath me. There was nothing I could do but continue the meditation. I stoked the inner fire to a blaze. The Anaconda wasn't daunted, but it didn't attack either. It waited. Then I knew what I had to do. I wrapped my arms around it and hugged.

Now I understood. Something happened when I jabbed my finger into its brain. I felt a jolt of electricity. Something passed from the great reptile to me. It awoke something inside of me. It drove me to satisfy my base needs, first and foremost. Kill or be killed. Eat or starve. Fuck or forever die. The cold blooded reptile was inside of me and I accepted it.

My peace returned. I was drifting in a void where I felt nothing, heard nothing, saw nothing and thought nothing. I don't know how long I was there, but it was interrupted by a beautiful sound…it was laughter. It was a good sound. I was drawn to it. I followed it to the source. It was the sound of joy. It was my joy. The laughter came from a deep place inside of me.

When I thought I was all but laughed out, I opened my eyes. Something had shifted. I was the mountain, the stream, and the rainforest. A hand touched my arm. Without looking, I knew it was Ginny. Nothing was said. Nothing needed to be said. What needed to be said was communicated by the touch. All was well between us.

It was then I heard the distinctive sound of a gun bolt loading a fresh round into the chamber. We had been discovered.

CHAPTER 41

It wasn't just one soldier, it was a whole squad, and that was a lot of damn guns in our faces. The Stone Age battle axe I carried all night was now propped against a tree three paces away. Not that it would have made much difference anyway. Its range is a bit shorter than the squad's M4A1 automatic weapons.

I didn't like the way they were looking at Ginny and had a sinking feeling this wasn't going to end well. These men looked like they had been in the bush too long and they were accustomed to taking what they wanted, especially when it came to women. This naturism thing has a few drawbacks.

The only hope I had was the possibility the rest of our group hadn't been discovered and they would somehow slip in behind the soldiers. If that happened, then we might have a slim chance of surviving the impending battle. Whether we got help or not, I planned to fight to the death before I let them harm Ginny.

They were dressed in uflage pattern pants, shirts and vests loaded with pockets. Their heads were covered with matching patrol caps, but their combat boots were tan. None of the uniforms had any identifying patches that I could see.

I guess the money they saved on patches went into their guns. The rifles were the latest military issue automatic weapons loaded with a variety of special operations modifications. Things like aiming lasers, illuminators, and grenade launchers. These guys were serious about their guns.

I was about to ask them what they wanted, when Ginny spoke.

"What are you doing?" she demanded.

No one answered, so Ginny tried again.

"You men work for me," she said.

There was no response.

"Philippe, lower that weapon and explain yourself," ordered Ginny.

He must have been the short guy on the right flank because his eyes showed the first signs of doubt as he looked to see what the rest of the squad was going to do.

Ginny took advantage of this weakness and said, "Raul, tell Philippe to lower his weapon."

Raul must have been the guy standing next to Philippe, because he opened his mouth to comply with Ginny's order, but was interrupted by the sound of an approaching helicopter and then snapped it shut again. His face was conflicted, but the last thing I saw flash cross it just before it went stone blank again was sheer terror.

The progress Ginny made softening them was wiped away in an instant. Each soldier, without exception, went hard and cold. They feared whoever was in the whirly bird more than her.

There was nothing to do but wait, but the wait didn't last long. The Apache attack helicopter is fast and it was on the ground within minutes. I didn't think the soldiers faces could get any more grim, but when the helicopter engine shut down, they proved me wrong.

I wasn't sure what to expect, but when the door opened I sure wasn't expecting to see a flamboyant pipsqueak hit the ground with a bounce. He was a tiny man at 5'2" and 110 pounds, who dressed like a flamer, with lime green yoga pants and an orange blouse, opened wide to the navel. Hanging between his pierced nipples was a black onyx necklace. The final touch to his unusual fashion statement was a dab of eye liner applied to the lips and at the corners of his eyes.

Ch'ing taught me to never underestimate people, but this guy did not fit my idea of what a villain should look like. I have to confess, I felt cheated. Still, he made a grand entrance and I couldn't help but wonder who the hell he was.

The little fop strutted over to us like an aggressive bantam rooster with his chest all puffed out. He thought he was something special, but I wasn't seeing it. He stopped a couple of paces in front of us and looked me up and down. Actually, it was more down than up and it made me uncomfortable that he stared so openly at my junk.

"Victor, what the hell are you doing?" demanded Ginny.

Victor reluctantly turned his attention to Ginny and said with a sigh, "Why isn't it obvious, I'm staging a coup?"

"A coup...I don't understand," said Ginny.

"Don't be a bore," said Victor. "You're smarter than that."

I wasn't about to let him insult Ginny and asked, "Do I know you?"

"My name is Victor Branco," he answered.

Victor Branco was Ginny's head of security and I had a few questions I wanted to ask him.

"Why did you hire me to guard, Padma?" I asked.

"Oh, is that the best you've got?" he asked with an exaggerated yawn. "I'm disappointed in you, my yummy hunk. I was expecting something more probing from you than that. If you must know, I was following orders."

"On whose orders?" I asked.

"Oh...well...now that's the question, isn't it?" he replied.

"You're not going to tell me, are you?" I asked.

Victor shook his head and added, "Nope."

"I'm the one who signs your pay check, Victor," said Ginny. "It wasn't my orders."

"You again," said Victor with a sigh. "I love being the one to tell you this, but you're such a small player on this game board, my bitch of an ex-boss."

Ginny's eyes blazed and her face flushed red, but her voice was cold, very cold, as she said, "Ex is right you little prick."

Victor smirked, "Oh dear…little prick she says. You know so little about me, you arrogant bitch. I may be short of stature, but I'm hung like a donkey. Would you care to see it?"

It was me he was looking at when he asked the question, but I sure as hell wasn't taking that bait.

"I'll pass," I said. "I have one of my own, but I would like to know how you found us in the middle of this vast jungle?"

Victor looked genuinely disappointed. I thought maybe he might press the point, but instead he let out a little bark. At least it sounded like a bark, but you know how it is when something happens that is too incongruent to believe. First we do a double take and then reinvent what happened. I decided it was a snort laugh and not a bark at all.

"Oh, that was easy," said Victor. "I'm her chief of security and one of her most trusted employees. I have complete access to her. I just replaced that locket she wears around her neck with a tracking device."

"Locket," I said.

"Yes…yes…the one with your picture in it that she never takes off," he said.

"Tracking device…picture," I said.

"I've been following her movements for years," he said

I cut my eyes to Ginny, hoping for some explanation about the locket. Looking embarrassed, she avoided my gaze and instead focused her attention on Victor.

"Why would you follow me?" asked Ginny.

"I've been waiting for you to lead us to your father," he said.

"What do you want with my father?" asked Ginny.

"It's not what I want," answered Victor. "It's what my employer wants."

"And, you're not going to tell us who that is," I said.

He shook his head.

"It doesn't matter," I said. "I know who you work for."

"Nice try, but you don't know shit," said Victor.

"Wilbur Goth, Pathogen's psycho CEO, thinks Bill Bardough can lead him to a special healing plant," I said. "The real question is why you betrayed Ginny for that piece of shit."

Victor rubbed the back of his neck with his left hand and let out a long hissing breath. He looked at me and then at Ginny. He shook his head and then turned to the helicopter pilot and waived him toward us.

The pilot hustled over and Victor whispered something to him. The pilot sprinted back to the helicopter, rummaged around inside for something and then returned with a satellite phone that he handed to Victor.

Victor punched in a number and said, "I have them, but there's something you should know. They know more than we realized."

He paused and listened before saying, "They know who you are and what you want."

He listened for a bit and then hung up.

"Kill 'em," he said.

Philippe turned to Victor, "Sir…"

Ginny stretched a desperate hand toward the soldiers, "Don't do this. I beg you."

Everyone froze.

Victor exploded, "That was an ORDER!"

The soldiers refocused with grim determination. Whatever hold Victor had over them was bigger than anything Ginny could surmount. These men were going to kill us.

That's pretty much when all hell broke loose. Of all the people to save us, I never expected it to be the slavers. A band of men with the tell-tale tattoo around their biceps sprang from the bushes and attacked the soldiers with machetes.

We used the diversion to sprint for cover. While we escaped Victor and the squad, we stumbled onto a second group of soldiers holding Eric and the others hostage. Fortunately, we had flanked them and as they tried to turn toward us, Eric sprang into action with Marguerite and Pony Tail right behind him.

This time I felt the serpent inside of me and we fought as one to destroy our enemies. Only one of the soldiers managed to slip away. Once we finished with his mates, we fled back into the rainforest.

CHAPTER 42

Marguerite led us upstream toward the mountain. When we came to white water cascading around huge boulders covered in lime green moss, we left the stream to make our way through the thick undergrowth. It was a trail I would not have attempted to blaze on my own, but thanks to Marguerite's leadership we wove our way through it with effortless grace.

When we finally broke through the brush, the character of the forest changed. The trees got bigger, way bigger in fact. I didn't recognize the variety, but they were comparable to the California sequoia in size.

At first I thought these massive trees had brown and black stripes, but when I got a closer look I saw that it was an optical illusion caused by deep grooves in the bark. The ruts were deep and wide, maybe the length of my forearm. Their branches drooped like a weeping willow as if these trees wanted to claim all of the light their space offered.

They also housed a particularly ugly variety of vultures. The sight of these scavengers was a bad sign. I figured, all we needed were skull and crossbones to complete the message we weren't welcome here.

Marguerite ignored the vultures and led us through a natural arch surrounded by a misty haze. I had seen many such arches in the Daniel Boone National Forest, but this one was much taller and more narrow than those in the mountains of Eastern Kentucky.

Beyond the arch, we rapidly gained elevation. As we climbed the mist thickened into a heavy fog making visibility on the narrow mountain trail difficult and treacherous.

One misstep could mean a fall of several hundred feet. While I do not generally fear heights, the risk of a deadly fall was enough to make me hyper vigilant about where I stepped. Unfortunately, the pursuit pressured us to push forward as quickly as possible.

Gunfire popped behind us. Our pursuers had not give up and it sounded like they were gaining ground. Despite our cautiousness, Ginny seemed to have the most trouble. When we heard voices behind us she slipped on loose rock. I caught her in the nick of time or she would have fallen to her death.

Despite the fog we managed to make our way without getting killed. Bullets kicked up dust at our feet making trail visibility even more challenging. When we were nearly to the top, the trail ended at a rock outcropping. To make matters worse, Marguerite circled to the right of it and disappeared into the face of the mountain. In unison, we all turned to Pony Tail in hopes of an explanation.

He shrugged.

"I've never been here before," said Pony Tail.

Ginny's curiosity got the best of her. She cautiously approached the spot where Marguerite disappeared. Just in case, I followed close behind to make sure she stayed safe. There was a shallow crevice too small to fit into. Ginny began to feel around with her hands. Her arm disappeared into the shadows. She turned around and grinned at us.

"It's an illusion," she said. "The shadows hide a cave entrance."

To see better, I moved a little closer. Sure enough, I saw an arched opening that was clearly man made. There were markings on the stone. At first, it appeared to be ornate decoration. I studied it more closely and saw it was a single word, "Unity." Actually, it wasn't written in English at all and I'm not exactly certain how I knew what it said, I just did.

"We better hurry," said Pony Tail. "The pursuit is closing fast."

We slipped inside and found Marguerite waiting for us. I expected a dark cavern, but instead the arched doorway opened into a well-lit passageway. As far as I could tell, there was no visible source of light. The floor and the walls were lined with polished stone.

Ginny voiced my thoughts.

"This isn't a cave," she said. "What is this place?"

Pony Tail's voice was filled with awe as he replied, "The Temple of the Gods."

"We're inside an ancient pyramid," said Marguerite.

"Is it Mayan?" I asked.

"No, it's much older," answered Marguerite. "Come, follow me."

She led us down a corridor that opened into a large area the size of a city block. At the center of the room was a huge hole in the floor. You could have dropped an office building into it. Marguerite walked in the direction of the hole and then fell.

"Marguerite!" shouted Ginny.

I was stunned and should have paid closer attention to Ginny. She dashed after Marguerite and disappeared into the cavernous pit. A high-pitched scream echoed throughout the cavern. My stomach flipped and acid burned its way to the back of my throat. There was no time for despair. I couldn't lose her now and rushed toward the spot where she disappeared.

There I found Marguerite and Ginny waiting for us on the steps of a spiraling staircase. Up close, the hole looked like a giant well. It was perfectly symmetrical. Like the passageway, the walls were polished smooth. I didn't see any sign of the bottom. The damn thing seemed to go on forever.

Eric threw his arm over my shoulder.

"Dude, you screamed like a little girl," said Eric.

I didn't realize I was the source of the scream, but it didn't surprise me. I thought I'd lost Ginny. I took her hands and squeezed gently.

"I'm sorry I scared you," she said.

If my hands had been free I would have used them to wipe the tears from my eyes. Instead, I let them run their course unimpeded and contented myself with the knowledge that Ginny was unharmed.

It was Marguerite who broke the spell.

"Hurry," she said.

Marguerite led us in a counter clockwise descent into the bottomless pit. Deeper and deeper we went into the belly of the Earth. I kept thinking it would end soon, but she marched on. The descent was so long, I began to imagine we were headed straight to hell and expected the temperature to rise as we approached the Earth's core, but it remained constant.

I was looking into the pit for signs of fire and brimstone when Marguerite made a sharp turn to the right. It was another passageway. Before I stepped into it, I took one last look at the hole. There was no sign of the bottom. I couldn't help but wonder where the hell it went.

At the end of the long passageway was an arched doorway leading into an eight sided chamber. At its center was a pool of water. On each face of the octagon sat an empty throne marked with a trigram of the I Ching.

The I Ching is an ancient Chinese text that is usually translated as the Book of Changes. It is typically thought of as a book of divinity or fortune telling. Ch'ing once told me that trying to use it to predict the future misses the mark. He said it is a blueprint of life and nothing more. Geez, as if understanding life is nothing. Ch'ing is such a master of understatement.

My eyes were drawn to the pool of water. There was the outline of a symbol the Taoist call The Grand Terminus. Most westerners call it the yin-yang symbol. It is a reminder that opposites must exist in a balanced state. When you deny one or the other, then nature will work to restore balance.

We are not what other people want us to be. When we accept ourselves as we are, then we can move through life's changes until balance is restored. Then and only then can we live an authentic life. Living life on our own terms is the great end.

My thoughts were interrupted by footsteps coming from the hallway we had just exited. Pony Tail spun around and dropped to a crouch. Eric slipped over and took a position on the opposite side of the archway.

Pony Tail growled in a low voice, "Our enemies have followed us into this sacred place."

Ginny dug her nails into my upper arm. I can't be certain, but I think she drew blood. She leaned toward me and whispered.

"What do we do now, Grant?"

"We fight," I answered.

"Let 'em come," snarled Eric.

All eyes were fixed on the archway. The footsteps suddenly stopped and the passage beyond the archway grew silent. There was nothing to do, but wait and breathe. I took a long slow breath and waited with Ginny at my side.

None of us had weapons. They had been taken by Victor's men. We had no choice but to face the enemy with bare hands, strong hearts, and our wits.

It wasn't as bad as it seemed. Guns gain you an advantage when there is distance between you and your enemy. In close quarters, the advantage is lost. Besides, the ultimate weapon in any fight is the mind. The man with the greater will to survive usually does.

It came at us fast and high. I couldn't quite make it out, but was thinking it looked vaguely familiar when I heard a squawk.

"Aaawk," squawked Bird. "Do not fear! It is I, Ponce de Leon."

Bird landed softly on my shoulder and rubbed the back of his head on my cheek. I was lost for words. Bird never shows me affection.

"It's you, Bird," I mumbled.

"Aaawk, damn right baby," said Bird. "It doesn't get any better than this."

Bird turned his attention to Ginny.

"Aaawk, hey there sexy girl," he said.

Ginny purred, "Oh Bird."

Bird moved to Ginny's shoulder and gave her a rub on the cheek.

With a lecherous bird beak grin he squawked, "Aaawk, naked gooood and you wear it so well."

Ginny looked startled and took a quick look down at herself. Before she could respond Bird hopped to Marguerite's shoulder. She reached up and stroked his feathers. It was Bird's turn to purr.

"It's been too long Ponce," said Marguerite. "I've missed you."

Bird was uncharacteristically quiet.

"Can't that old fool keep up with you?" asked Marguerite.

Bird's dramatic entrance had completely distracted us from the footsteps. When we returned our attention to the archway, we found Padma standing there looking the part of a Christmas elf in his red robe and green cowboy boots.

Padma's smile was sweet and his eyes twinkled. For just an instant, I thought he might actually be Santa.

"Old fool!" said Padma. "Is that any way to speak to someone of my stature?"

Marguerite laughed as she pointed at his round belly.

"Your stature has grown substantially since we last saw each other," said Marguerite. "You've added another half a Padma to your already prominent self."

Padma giggled like a school girl.

"There just isn't enough of me to go around," said Padma.

Marguerite spread her arms wide.

"Come give me a proper greeting, dearest," said Marguerite.

Padma strolled over and wrapped her up in a big ole bear hug. When they finished, he did the same with the rest of us. I wanted to ask him about his disappearance, but he spoke first.

"There will be time for questions later," said Padma. "I must make a few preparations before Council begins. Please make yourselves comfortable."

After Padma left, Marguerite took a seat on one of the thrones. I glanced at the markings at her feet and saw it was the symbol for Earth. Bird flew over and perched on one of the thrones. It was marked Wind.

Curious about the yin-yang symbol in the pool, I walked over to get a closer look. Ginny followed me. Pony Tail and Eric remained posted at the doorway like a couple of palace guards.

The water was crystal clear. There was no bottom in sight. The symbol seemed to float on the surface. It was also slowly rotating counter clockwise. There was writing engraved around the edge of the pool. I followed the lettering and read, "From This Pool Springs Eternal Life."

I was about to share it with Ginny when she stepped into the water. What the hell! My stomach flipped and I lunged for her but it was too late. Instead of sinking, she walked across the water and came to a rest at the center.

Standing on the yin-yang symbol, she beckoned me to come to her. There must be stepping stones. I looked at the path she took and saw no sign of them. I wanted to join her, but I didn't know how the hell she did it.

A thought popped into my head, "Suspend reason. Trust her."

I took a deep breath and gazed into Ginny's eyes. What I saw was unconditional love. I allowed it to push the doubt aside. Choosing trust, I stepped into the water.

Never once taking my eyes off of her, I walked across the surface of the pool and joined Ginny at the center. Standing face to face, she took both of my hands into her own. All awareness of our surroundings disappeared. We stood silent and never once wavered.

I have no idea how long we stood there wrapped in love. Gradually, the chamber reappeared. I was surprised to see all eight of the thrones filled and damned if Padma didn't rest comfortably in one of the seats. I was even more surprised to see Marguerite and Bird still seated. However, nothing matched the shock of seeing Ch'ing.

"Ch'ing", I whispered.

Shifu had disappeared without a trace from his home. The house had been ransacked. Eric and I didn't have a clue what happened to him and feared the worst. I thought we had lost him. Of all the places for Ch'ing to turn up, I never expected it to be deep in the belly of the Earth.

I caught Eric's eye and we nodded to each other. A wave of gratitude spread through me.

A round woman with a kind face and smooth skin a shade lighter than rich cocoa began the discussion.

"It is time," she said. "Long ago there was a break in the circle. A prophesy followed. An era of suffering will spread across the Earth like a pestilence. People will lose themselves. They will know only fear and violence. Many lies will be told to them to mask their illness. When all hope is lost, two acting as one will rise to the top and heal them."

A giant of a man pointed toward us and said in a deep baritone voice, "Eve are you satisfied they are the ones?"

All eyes turned to us. I wanted to ask Ch'ing what the hell was going on, but something in his expression stopped me. There was nothing to do but wait.

A beautiful young woman with waves of golden hair responded in an angelic voice, "I am not convinced."

To my surprise Eve's seat was marked with the trigram representing Heaven. It is the symbol for creativity, but it also represents the risks of being head strong.

"The water accepted them," said Marguerite.

"He stands in the feminine and she stands in the masculine," said Ch'ing.

I glanced down. The light half of the yin-yang symbol represents masculine energy. Ginny was standing within it. The dark half represents the feminine counterpart and there I stood.

Padma added, "More importantly, they stand as one."

Eve wasn't about to concede and said, "There remains one more test."

Ch'ing slumped in his seat. Marguerite stiffened. They looked very concerned. This can't be good. I was surprised to hear Bird speak without his usual squawk.

"Please don't do this Eve," said Bird.

Eve may have been the most petite among them, but at this moment she seemed to tower over the others.

Smelling victory she said, "What's the matter Ponce? Are you afraid your pets won't survive it?"

What did she mean…survive it? The test must be dangerous. The thought of losing Ginny was unbearable. I opened my mouth to protest, but was interrupted by a shout from Bird.

"I'm not afraid," said Bird. "It's just…"

He in turn was interrupted by the Giant's booming voice, "Eve, you have gone too far this time."

Eve looked pleased with herself. I doubt she agreed she had gone too far at all.

In a soothing tone Layah said, "Relax everyone. Eve, I see no reason to put them to the test. All we need is someone capable of bringing Great Mother to market."

The Prophesy Lady said, "It will be no easy task to bring this medicine to the world. They will face resistance on many fronts. It will be extremely dangerous. We need to know if they have what it takes to accomplish this task. I agree with Eve. They must face the final test."

Eve moved in for the kill.

"Listen to Delphoria," said Eve. "Billions of dollars are at stake. This medicine will make us all very rich."

Rich…is this all about the money? They have the ability to heal and all they think about is getting rich. Great Mother can end the world's suffering. My God, what we could accomplish if we solved the health care crisis. We could move into a Golden Age. Exploiting the world's suffering is just more of the same. Shame on them.

That's when it occurred to me that if I turned my back on the Council, then I might never be able to give the medicine to my mother. I had a moment of self-doubt. If I did what they wanted, then I could save my mother. I thought about Pathogen's evil plans and it occurred to me that to fight the rich and powerful I needed to be rich and powerful too.

It was tempting, very tempting.

I turned away from the Council and focused all of my attention on Ginny. Her eyes were filled with tears. In those tears I found myself. The course was clear. Together we spoke, two voices as one.

"No," we said. "We will not do this for you. This medicine cannot be sold. We will not profit from the suffering of others. Great Mother must be given freely to everyone."

There was a long stretch of silence. I figured we had failed the test. They would probably throw us out and that would be the end of it.

It was Eve who finally spoke up.

"Congratulations," she said. "You have passed the final test."

"A new era begins," said the Giant.

"It is time for the two of you to spread Great Mother to the four corners of the world," said Ch'ing.

The Council members rose from their thrones and began to dance. It was a dance of joy.

It took a moment, but then I understood. The final test was the lure of unimaginable wealth. At the edge of the pool was a small plant in a simple earthen pot. They had given us Great Mother.

The plant drew us across the surface of the water, and we were almost to it, when gun fire exploded in the chamber. I forgot Great Mother and pulled Ginny to safety. Once we were both flat on the ground, I surveyed the room. Eric and Pony Tail stood with their arms in the air. Behind each of them stood a soldier with a weapon jammed into the center of their backs.

Victor pointed a gun toward the plant and said, "I'll take that."

The weird thing was the Council members were still dancing around their thrones. It was as if they hadn't heard the gun fire. Victor was stammering and sputtering indignantly at their odd behavior. When his patience finally ran out, he turned the gun on them.

"You freaks need to stop that weird shit and die with some damn dignity," screamed Victor.

At that very instant, the light went out and the chamber became pitch black. I heard Ch'ing's voice close to my ear.

"It is time to leave," said Ch'ing. "Take my hand."

CHAPTER 43

They say your senses heighten when one is lost. It went pitch black right after Victor threatened to shoot everybody, so maybe fear had something to do with it as well. Whatever the explanation might be, I heard a symphony of heartbeat and breathe, accompanied by the tap and shuffle of dancing feet playing in the darkness.

"Turn on the damn lights," shouted Victor.

"It is time to leave," whispered Ch'ing.

Victor blocked the only entrance to the chamber. Since he was armed with an automatic weapon, it didn't seem possible we could get past him. Ch'ing is like a father to me and I trust him with my life. If he says it's time to leave, then he has a way out. I was ready, but wasn't going anywhere without Ginny.

Victor was once Ginny's most trusted employee. The traitor now works for the pharmaceutical giant, Pathogen. He tracked us across continents and into the belly of the Earth. Thanks to the miracles of modern technology, not even a secret chamber hidden far below a lost pyramid is enough to keep him at bay.

He plans to kill us and I'm not sure why he didn't do it when he had the chance. Instead, he opted to profane this sacred place with gunfire. He's a jerk all right, but Victor's need for a dramatic entrance has cost him the kill…so far.

We dove for cover when he blasted off a round, but other than the cover of darkness, there isn't much to hide behind. Council chambers is an eight sided room carved out of stone. On each face sits a marble throne. In the center is a pool of clear water that has no bottom the eye can see.

The dancing feet belong to an ancient council. They are a hodgepodge of the strangest characters you have ever laid eyes upon and they have an even stranger agenda. Just before Victor made his dramatic appearance, they delivered a powerful new medicine to Ginny and I on the condition we freely spread it across the world.

There's just one problem. Victor's new boss, Wilbur Goth, C.E.O. of Pathogen, wants the medicine for himself and he will do anything to stop us. It was Goth who ordered Victor to kill us.

My name is Grant Li. Up until a few days ago I had a promising legal career ahead of me, but now I'm an unemployed attorney. In my first big case, I defended Goth against charges that he intentionally deceived the public about the risks of Gutchriem, an acid-reflux medicine that is believed to be killing people. I won the case, but now there is new evidence that Gutchriem is laced with a deadly virus.

Ginny Bardough is a childhood friend and my one true love. Up until a few days ago, it had been years since we had last seen each other. Our reunion has not been easy. So far, we've had to overcome huge obstacles, including our present situation with Victor. If we get out of this alive, I plan to marry her as soon as my divorce is final.

She was lying next to me at the edge of the pool. Not exactly touching, but close enough I could feel strands of her hair tickling my shoulder. The polished stone floor was just shy of slippery and surprisingly warm. The scent of gunpowder quickly gave way to a stream of air that smelled as fresh as the blue sky after a summer squall.

Ch'ing is usually relaxed, but I sensed urgency in his whisper, "Take my hand."

"I have enough lead to cover every square inch of this God forsaken hole in the Earth," shouted Victor. "If you don't turn the lights back on like I said, then I'm going to start shooting and I won't stop until every last living thing in here is dead."

I led a lunatic into this sacred place and I knew I should do something about the danger I put everyone in, but Ch'ing is right. It's time to flee. We need to get home with the medicine. Mom is trapped inside a coma and the nursing home is about to evict her. We also need to stop Pathogen from using a dangerous virus against innocent people.

"Aaawk, bring the babe with you," squawked Bird in a voice loud enough to wake the dead.

Bird is a Macaw I inherited from Dad. It turns out he is more than he seems. He claims his real name is Juan Ponce de León, and I'm starting to believe him, since he is one of the mucky-mucks on the council of elders.

Ginny inched a little closer.

"Give me your hand," I whispered.

She didn't hesitate. Once her hand was firmly in mine, we rose together as quietly as we could. Despite our best efforts, we made enough noise that a stealthy escape was out of the question.

I turned to Ch'ing and whispered, "We're ready. Let's go."

Whether he heard me is hard to say since the room erupted into a second round of gunfire that sent us back peddling. When my heel caught on something hard, I instinctively looked down to see what it could be and caught a glimpse of Ginny's face in the gun flash.

I thought the shadows were playing tricks on me until I smelled blood mixed with the gun smoke. I'm not sure if the searing pain I felt was from a bullet or the heartache of seeing blood splattered across Ginny's face. Either way, it hurt like hell.

As I fell backwards I could not help but wonder what might have been had I not spent a lifetime avoiding Ginny. I tried to let her go, but she had me in a death grip and pulled with all her might.

Her effort was heroic, but it was not enough. The momentum from the fall, coupled with the dead weight of my body carried us both into the water. I fought it at first. I fought like the dickens for the life we could have together, but the powerful current sucked us down into a spiraling whirlpool of liquid death.

When I had nothing left and the fight was lost, fear began to creep into the corners of my mind. I didn't like it one bit. I might not win the fight against the current, but fear is a product of my mind and therefore, it is something I can control. Instead of fear, I chose to fill my mind with peace.

Once I stopped fighting the whirlpool, I began to notice how it good it felt...like I was wrapped in a liquid cocoon. It was not warm, nor was it cold. It was the perfect temperature, like the womb. It was weird time to think of the womb. At first, I thought it was the beginning of a life review, or could just as easily have been my imagination, but somehow I am certain I could remember the time in my mother's womb.

It was pure bliss until I saw Ginny's desperate face close to mine. I reached for her just as everything began to fade out. The last thing I remember was her lips mashing mine while her tongue forced my mouth open. It was if she was trying to breathe life into me, or then again, maybe it was just a goodbye kiss.

After that, there was nothing until I awoke alone on a tropical beach that sparkled in the sunlight like a field of tiny diamonds. Sand usually makes me feel dirty and has an annoying way of creeping into unwanted places, so when I visit the beach I try to minimize contact with it.

I usually carry a beach chair with me rather than sit on a towel, but for some strange reason I felt an overwhelming urge to roll among these sparkling lights, so that's exactly what I did, rolling haphazardly like a Texas tumbleweed along water's edge.

When I finally rolled to a stop and allowed myself to relax into the sand, it felt like a thousand tiny hands massaged away the old and left me tingling fresh, as if I had just shed an old skin and replaced it with a shiny new me. The diamond beach shredded the false and left a virgin field where a more authentic me could flourish.

There was something special about this place. It was rich and full of infinite possibilities and I was determined to choose among them with the greatest care. Inhaling deeply, I filled my lungs with fresh air and allowed it to nourish the seedlings of change.

It was good to be alive. Allowing the joy to spread into my arms and legs, I stretched them wide and began sweeping sand angels. A nearby sea turtle paused in her nest making, gave me a long frank assessment and then dismissed me as an amateur.

Sea turtles get big, but this girl looked like she had swallowed enough steroids to compete in a bodybuilding contest. She was eighteen feet long and more than twice the size of any sea turtle I had ever seen.

The Ancients revered the tortoise and legend has it that Taoist longevity practices evolved from observations of its slow movements. Energy cultivation begins with conservation. Chi is not something you should waste. Given everything I had survived lately, I was starting to feel immortal.

I had survived a knife fight with an ex-special forces war hero, got shot in the back, grappled an anaconda with monstrous teeth and went berserker on a machete carrying psycho intent on doing Ginny harm. I don't know how many guns had been pointed in my face before I was flushed down the drain of a lost South American pyramid and landed on this beach.

By all reckoning, I should be dead, and the presence of the sea turtle added to the sense this was part of some personal vision of an afterlife. In the ultimate battle, the tortoise is the Dark Warrior of the North who emerges from the water and escapes the clutches of the Grim Reaper.

Yet, here I was making sand angels next to the mother of all sea turtles. Her presence was no accident. If I had learned nothing else from Ch'ing, the one thing he taught me was to pay attention and never assume events are accidental. The Universe gladly delivers the message we most need to hear. All we have to do is pay attention and the way will become clear.

I took a slow deep breath and focused on a pinpoint of light at the still point of my being. It is from this vantage point that each of us co-creates life with all conscious beings. The stillness expanded until it filled me with emptiness. When I couldn't contain it any longer, peace spilled into the world around me, as it should, since we are all in this together.

When I finally opened my eyes, the sun was overhead and I stared directly into it. For some odd reason, the light didn't hurt my eyes. The teaching that the sun's light will blind us is supported by a lifetime of pain whenever we get too big of a dose. For this reason, I was torn between letting the light in or snapping the lids shut.

This light was softer than usual and it cast a coral tint to the skyline. That would normally mean the day was nearly over, but the sun was straight above so I figured it was high noon.

On the distant horizon, a large bird caught a current of rising air to gain elevation. As it spiraled upward, I caught a glimpse of a long tail. Maybe it was a trick of the light, but it was not a bird's tail exactly. Instead, it looked as if belonged to a monkey, but with a fin at the end molded into the shape of a four-faced spearhead.

The bird's cry was haunting, as if the beast was searching for a lost love. Then again, perhaps I was projecting my own feelings onto it. Ginny was still alive. I could feel it and it was time to find her.

CHAPTER 44

The pyramid had spat me onto a remote beach at the edge of the Amazon Rainforest. The funny thing is, when we were climbing to the top, there was only forest as far as the eye could see. Therefore, I am pretty damn sure the pyramid was not anywhere near the ocean.

I scanned the horizon for the megalithic structure, but all I could see was forest. It was nowhere in sight. There were no mountains. There was no one on the beach in either direction. Ginny and I were pulled into the whirlpool together, so she had to be somewhere nearby.

As I stood to brush the sand off, the turtle abruptly withdrew into her shell. I was surprised to discover there wasn't a single grain clinging to me. It didn't make a bit of sense. I searched every nook and cranny, especially my bare bottom, and couldn't find a one. Sand always clings to me, but not this stuff. It was weird.

I took another gander at the beach. Other than the sparkle, it looked ordinary. I thought maybe I should scoop a handful and inspect it a little closer. When I bent over, I felt a gust of wind across my back and figured a storm was rolling in because the light dimmed and I heard a clap of thunder.

If it wasn't for the piercing scream I may have missed what really happened. It startled me enough that I fell backwards and landed on my bare ass. The bird's tail whipped across my shoulder, and then with one last flick, took a shot at my face. It barely missed taking an eye, but the burning sting on my shoulder told me I had not escaped unscathed.

I got my first look at the bird up close. In the muted sunlight, its iridescent feathers shined blue black with a touch of red. I desperately wanted it to be an Andean Condor, but it looked more like a Pterodactyl.

While the Condor has a vulture's face, this bird's head was shaped more like a raven's with a long snout. The nose reminded me of the river dolphin I had seen a few days ago on the Amazon River. However, unlike the dolphin, which has a huge forehead housing an equally huge brain, this bird had little or no forehead, and most likely, a brain no bigger than a walnut.

Unlike its tiny brain, the beast had an expansive thirty-foot wingspan. That's two or three times bigger than a Condor. I had to admit to myself, the case for it being a Condor had a hole or two. Still, there was no way it could be an extinct prehistoric dinosaur, so I ignored what my eyes told me and chose to believe the fiction I created for myself to explain the impossible.

I must admit that my faith in this conclusion was shaken considerably when I tried to rub the sting out of my shoulder and felt a skewer sized barb protruding from it. Even though it was the exact spot the bird's tail had swatted me, I convinced myself I picked it up while rolling in the sand.

When I grabbed hold and yanked the barb, it tore a chunk of flesh out of me. The wound hurt like hell. It felt like fire was spreading outward from the wound and I feared there might be some kind of poison in it. To make matters worse, the damn Thunderbird was banking to the right and on its way back for another pass at me.

I'm pretty sure those claws would shred a person's flesh in minutes. I needed to find cover fast, but the tree line was at least forty yards away. During my football playing days, a forty-yard dash was nothing, but thanks to ten years behind a desk, I'd grown softer. Besides, my career ended with a badly torn hamstring that never quite healed properly. Hobbled by the injury, it was not going to be an easy sprint across the soft sand.

The sky rumbled with another low growl from the Thunderbird who was coming in fast over the water. Habits are funny things and dropping to a three-point stance to begin my sprint is no different. At the sound of a ghostly whistle on a hot August gridiron, I exploded out of the stance and huffed my way to the tree line.

I almost made it before I felt the beast's hot breath on the back of my neck. Instead of risking it, I dropped to the ground like a short stop diving for a hard grounder breaking for left field, snagged a handful of sand, and with a twist worthy of an Olympic diver, flung it directly into the bird's yellow eyes.

Thunderbird screamed in outrage and stretched its claws for my throat. I was as good as dead, but a tiny grain of sand turned the tide. The yellow eyes blinked once, then twice, before the beast began furiously shaking its empty head.

Were the head goes the body follows. The beast wobbled in mid-flight before crashing on top of me. The damn thing's breath smelled like a landfill. I pushed hard against the bird to escape the foul smell, but it was heavier than it looked.

The shock of the crash was quickly wearing off and I knew if I didn't kill it soon, then it would kill me. I fought desperately to free myself, but the giant bird countered every move I made. When it slipped a claw the size of a butcher knife within a razor's edge of my throat, I knew it was over for me.

The Pterodactyl threw its head back and let out a victory cry that sent a chill coursing through me. I gave one last frantic push that had little effect on the beast, but left me physically spent. Still, I refused to surrender, and was frantically searching for a way to save my sorry ass, when a pair of hands appeared out of nowhere and covered Thunderbird's eyes.

Blinded and confused the Thunderbird whipped its tail in an attempt to dislodge the unexpected attacker straddling its back. The barb slapped against flesh just before fingers dug deep into the bird's eyes and then twisted until I heard the satisfying crack of a broken neck.

When I finally managed to dig myself out from underneath, I saw Ginny lying next to the Thunderbird looking small and frail. Her hands were lying limp at her sides…the hands that saved me. Ginny killed this monster. I couldn't imagine where she found the strength.

I checked her pulse. She was alive. I examined her for injuries and found none other than a barb in her shoulder that I pulled free. Thanks to the Pterodactyl's tail, we had matching shoulder injuries, but as best I could tell, she was otherwise injury free.

An overwhelming sense of gratitude spread through me like warm honey. I held her tight and relished the sweetness of life. When her eyes opened, I added a few happy tears to the mix.

The Sea Turtle give us a long appraising look. A wave of respect radiated from the old girl that was surprisingly satisfying. I resisted the temptation to pound my chest and grunt, "Tarzan…Jane."

"How do you feel?" I asked.

She titled her head at an odd angle and gave me a strange look. It was such a peculiar mannerism…something you might see small bird do.

"There was a blinding light and a jolt of electricity just before I blacked out," she said.

I had a similar experience a couple of days earlier during a life and death battle with a giant anaconda. Somehow I acquired the spirit of the great serpent, and in my case, the experience was followed by strange side effects that only show up in battle. I wondered if Ginny had acquired Thunderbird's spirit.

"Do you feel anything odd or unusual?" I asked.

She shook her head.

"Can I get you anything?" I asked.

"Water," she answered.

There was an ocean of it, but salt water is not drinkable. Ginny saw me looking toward the surf and nodded.

"The ocean is all the water I've seen since I awoke on this beach," I said.

"It's okay, help me up," she said.

We walked to the water's edge. Ginny sank to her knees and then sat back on her calves. I expected her to scoop a handful and taste it first, but she didn't. Instead, she looked in all directions, before leaning forward at the waist and lapping water directly from the ocean. Once her mouth was full, she sat up straight, leaned her head back and then swallowed.

"I've had enough of the beach for one day," I said. "What about you?"

She nodded.

"Let's seek shelter in the forest," I said.

The forest is like a second home. The deeper I hike into the backcountry, the more profound a peace comes over me, but for some reason I froze at the edge of the tree line. It was too quiet. There were no sounds of life and I found the profound silence unnerving. Many people think silence is simply a function of not talking, but it is much more than that.

Absolute silence is very rare. Life is noisy. The world is an orchestra of sound that fills our days with the music of ordinary life. Even when the world sleeps, our chattering thoughts are there to pick up the slack. Absolute silence is the absence of life and so it sounds like death.

The only sounds I heard in these woods were my own thoughts. Something was wrong.

CHAPTER 45

Saying all forests look alike is similar to saying all puppies look alike. It is an unnecessarily narrow view of the world around us. When you look closely, then it is possible to bear witness to the beautiful diversity of life.

As we stood at the edge of the forest, I knew that generalization was not going to be problem, because it was like none I had ever seen before. For example, the tree trunks were charred black, as if they had survived a great holocaust.

In addition to the odd color, the trees were unusually tall and thin. Redwoods have some girth to compensate for the extreme height. These trees appeared taller than redwoods and were considerably thinner. It was if someone had grabbed the branches and stretched them beyond their intended height. I would have thought a good wind would have flattened them like a pancake long ago.

Since there were no low hanging branches, you would expect there to be a lot of undergrowth, but there was not any at all. The forest floor looked to be a soft bed of reddish moss. It was not fire engine red, just a subtle hint of rose tint that the rays of sun light shining through the branches highlighted.

Speaking of which, the rays of sun light cut through the branches at multiple angles. It did not make any sense to me. Sunbeams normally come from a single direction. How could the sun be radiating from multiple directions all at once? The forest felt wrong.

Something else bothered me about this place. It was too damn quiet, but I could feel someone's eyes on me. There was someone out there. I knew it.

As we teetered on the edge, trying to decide whether to enter the forest or not, gunshots shattered the silence and the bullets tore at our feet. Victor was running hard along the tree line. He stretched his gun out in front as if the extra length of his arm was all he needed for the shots to reach their mark. The bastard followed us into the well and came out on the same beach as us. He is tenacious. I'll give him that.

"Victor's here," I shouted. "Follow me."

There was nowhere to go, but into the forest. Guided only by our primal instincts to survive, we cut as straight a path as we could moving deeper into the woods and away from the gunman. We ran hard and fast, intent only on saving our lives and didn't pause until we came to a stream.

Ginny pointed upstream and said, "We split up. You head that way and I'll go the opposite before circling back and flanking him."

It was a good plan. I knew we couldn't just keep running. Eventually, Victor would catch up and put a bullet in both of us. We had to turn the tables. It was time for us to hunt Victor.

I pulled her to me and poured everything I had into the kiss of all kisses. It was ferocious and tender all at once, but not nearly long enough.

"We can take him," I said.

"I love you, Grant," said Ginny.

"And I you," I said.

Once we broke our embrace, I shifted to stealth mode and moved quietly upstream. The water was lukewarm and the bottom of the stream was level. I could have used it to hide tracks, but it was more difficult to stay silent, so I left the stream after a short distance and hiked along the soft moss covered bank. After a quarter of a mile, I circled back.

I figured Victor for a city boy. If I was right, he was out of his comfort zone and it would give us a small advantage. When my instincts told me he was nearby I slowed the pace, stopping every few steps to listen for any sound that would give his location away.

Just when I started to lose patience with the silence, I heard Ginny scream. I abandoned the plan and ran in the direction of her voice. I was not paying much attention to the surroundings and it proved to be a mistake.

"Freeze motherfucker," said Victor.

Victor Branco is a flamboyant pipsqueak and why Ginny chose him as her chief of security is beyond me. A security chief should look like he can protect something. This man was 5'2" and 110 pounds.

He wore lime green yoga pants and an orange blouse, opened to the waist. A black onyx hummingbird dangled between matching nipple piercings. His eyes gleamed victorious behind heavy mascara.

"I don't have time for this shit," I said.

"You go that right," he snarled. "You are out of time pretty boy."

"Ginny is in danger," I said. "If you ever cared for her, you will step aside."

He ran the tip of his tongue over black lips.

"Unless you want to take a bullet up your ass you'll do as I say," said Victor.

I did not like this little fop. Nor did I have the patience to manage his Napoleon complex. I knew I could snap him like a twig, if I could only get my hands on him, but first I had to find a way to close the gap without taking a bullet.

As I considered the problem, Victor offered a solution, but I did not like it much.

"Bend over and grab your ankles pretty boy," said Victor.

The hunger in his eyes was unmistakable.

"I don't think so," I said. "Ginny needs my help and I'm going after her. You'll have to shoot me in the back."

Before I could move, he ripped off a round of gunfire that shredded the plants at my feet. None of the bullets hit me, but I got the message loud and clear.

"That's the only warning you'll get," snarled Victor. "Bend over."

I needed to disarm this little fop before I could help Ginny and that sure as hell wasn't going to happen unless he got a lot closer. I had an idea, but it was dangerous. I knew he expected me to turn around and show him my ass. Instead, I continued to face him, but lowered my eyes in submission and then bent forward to grab my ankles.

"Easy does it," I said. "I'm unarmed."

"Do exactly as I say or you're a dead man," he said.

I kept my eyes down and waited for Victor to come to me. Instead, he didn't budge. This wasn't going as planned and I was about to shift to an even more dangerous Plan B, when he spoke.

"If you move a muscle, I'll shoot you," said Victor.

He waited another breath or two and then moved cautiously toward me. I waited. Given the limited field of vision, his feet were the first things I saw and they gave me a chill because I had seen Victor's sandals once before on Tiny's killer.

Tiny was the head of the Dragon Gate Motorcycle Club, but also worked part time as a security guard at the Center. He was brutally stabbed the night Padma planned to reveal to the world the secret to living a happy life.

I had arrived at the Center to guard Padma when I discovered Tiny in a pool of blood. The killer, disguised as a monk, viciously attacked me and then fled the scene of the crime.

As I stared at Victor's feet, I realized it wasn't just the sandals that gave him away. Although they are beautifully crafted and made of distinctive Italian leather, it is what they reveal about his feet that is more telling. Victor has six toes and so did Tiny's killer.

Victor leveled the gun barrel at my head. He was close, maybe close enough, but I waited for him to take one more step before I acted. Of course, that is exactly when Victor decided to stop. Maybe he sensed something was wrong. It's hard to say.

The tip of the barrel disappeared. I cautiously allowed my eyes to follow in the same direction. Victor was using it to scratch a spot along the jaw line. It was then that I sprang for his throat, but he was fast with the trigger. Maybe too fast, because blood trickled down the side of his face just as I slammed a fist into his chest and drove it upwards as far as it would go.

I felt the satisfying crunch of bone as his knees buckled and he folded into the blow, but Victor wasn't done. He managed to soften the impact by rolling at the last minute and then used the momentum of the turn to smash the gunstock into the side of my face.

My head filled with stars and I came close to passing out. I had underestimated Victor. The fop was surprisingly tough.

He moved in for the kill, bloodlust in his eyes. I took a half step back, more as a deception than a retreat. That was all the encouragement he needed. Thinking I was done, he acted rashly and used the gunstock once again to deliver his homerun blow, a hard uppercut.

Side stepping the blow at the very last instant, I continued its arc and added energy of my own. The maneuver worked. The edge of the gunstock caught him between the eyes and split his skull wide open.

Wanting to finish it, I drove the gunstock downward toward his toes, as I imagined splitting his body in half like a gruesome cartoon character. Victor collapsed into heap at my feet. He died the way he lived, violently.

Even though he was traitor and tried to hurt everyone I cared about, I took a moment to send him off on his next journey. Victor's journey took him to dark places, but he still deserved compassion. He was a pawn in a bigger game. Despite our differences, we are all brothers and sisters at the end of the day.

I considered taking the gun with me, but it was a tainted weapon, used for dark purposes. I left it with Victor's body and turned to resume the pursuit of Ginny, but was shocked to find her standing next to a giant.

They were both nude, but she appeared unharmed. I'm not sure why the giant was naked, but Ginny and I didn't have much choice in the matter.

Lost in the vastness of the Amazon Rainforest, an indigenous people calling themselves the Guardians came to our rescue. At first, I thought it was pure chance, but only a fool would attribute to chance the amazing synergy of events that came together in such a seamless fashion. Clearly, there are forces at play that are beyond my understanding.

The Guardians live a natural lifestyle, free of the confines of clothing and the beliefs we hold so dear about sexuality. One of the first things they did was throw our clothes into the fire. I was uncomfortable at first, but now it isn't a big deal since nudity has become a way of life for us in this strange new world.

If you had known me before, you might find it rather shocking that I have become some sort of hippie naturist, since I was once the biggest prude that ever walked the planet. Transformation can be a funny thing. If it has taught me anything, it's that nothing, absolutely nothing, is set in stone.

Ginny's head was bowed, but not in submission. Instead, her eyes were open as wide as they would go as she stared at the ape's monstrous feet. They were about three feet long and two feet wide. The foot hair was limited to the long tuffs at the first knuckle.

While the giant wasn't as big as King Kong, he had to be at least seventeen feet tall. The top of Ginny's head was slightly above his knees.

Unlike Kong, this guy looked more man than ape. He had thick orange hair, similar to an Orangutan's, flowing down his back in unruly wavelets. A matching Santa beard spread nearly as far to the left and right as it did south of his broad chin. The rest of his unclothed body was covered in orange hair, but no more so than any other hairy guy. His skin was pink. I'm not talking about your average white guy kind of pink. This guy was really pink. Although it wasn't quite hot pink, it was damn close.

I consider myself a levelheaded attorney and am proud to say have never suffered from hallucinations, nor have I heard imaginary voices echoing inside of my head. The giant could easily have been a cartoon character born of the creative imagination of a comic book cartoonist, but the sting in my shoulder served as a reminder this isn't a fairy tale and the things I've seen since my arrival are very dangerous.

When faced with the absurd, the only thing to do is to laugh and that is exactly what I did. It was a great belly laugh that rolled past the tonsils, along the length of the tongue and out into the world around me.

The giant cocked his head ever so slightly as if he was listening to a piece of music and wanted to give his ear a chance to catch it all. When my laughter subsided, he surprised me with a show of huge fangs that could rip a man to shreds in the blink of an eye.

I took this as a warning and vowed to show him a more neutral face. Under no circumstances would I allow him harm Ginny. I needed to find a way to free her, and if martial arts have taught me anything, I've learned that size doesn't mean much in a real fight if you're willing to do whatever is necessary to win.

I have a habit of assigning nicknames to strangers, but they are not always original. I was undecided about the giant. I couldn't seem to make up my mind between King Kong and Bigfoot.

The beast looked displeased. When he opened his mouth I expected to hear a growl, but instead he spoke in an exaggerated British accent.

"Do you make a habit of leaving destruction in your wake?" he said.

It was a shock hearing English spoken by someone who looked more animal than man. Besides, everybody knows apes can't talk. It was then that I knew for sure all of this was an elaborate nightmare and all I had to do was pinch myself awake.

So, that's exactly what I did. I pinched myself hard, and when that didn't work, I willed myself to wake up.

"No, you're not dreaming," he said. "It never ceases to amaze me how you people refuse to believe what is right in front of you."

"What are you?" I asked.

With a sad shake of the head, he said, "I find both King Kong and Bigfoot offensive."

"How did you know…I meant…errr…what are you called?" I said.

"You meant both, but I am called, Nephilim," he answered.

"Isn't that from the old testament?" asked Ginny.

It was the first words she had spoken and I was glad she sounded like herself, strong and confident.

"Yes, but they got it wrong," he said.

"Then you're not an offspring of the gods and the daughters of men?" she asked.

Nephilim crinkled his nose in distaste.

"That is the imaginings of a primitive mind," he answered.

"Let me get this straight," I said. "You're saying you are from the Old Testament?"

"That book is not very old to me," answered Nephilim. "They got it wrong."

"Moses got it wrong?" I asked.

"Moses didn't write the book of Genesis," answered Nephilim.

"How old are you?" asked Ginny.

"This is a place without time," he answered.

"Are we dead?" asked Ginny.

"What do you think?" he asked.

"I feel alive, don't you Grant?" she asked.

"Yes, I feel alive, but this place is surreal," I answered.

"You are not supposed to be here," he said.

"You've got that right," I said. "Now that I've found Ginny, we'll be headed home."

"Come with me," said Nephilim.

I shook my head. I didn't want to go anywhere with this beast and cut my eyes to the automatic rifle laying at Victor's feet. A bullet could solve all of our problems.

"You do not know where you are or how to get home," said Nephilim. "You need me to show you the way out of this place."

He had a point. We fell into a deep well and ended up in this strange land. What's more, I have to get home in time to stop the unspeakable, but I don't know the way. Yes, he's right. We need him.

"That's only half of it," said Nephilim. "If you shoot me in the back, then who is the beast, me or you?"

CHAPTER 46

Nephilim didn't wait to see if I went for the gun. Maybe it was because he was a mind reader and knew I wouldn't harm a man who posed no threat to us. Instead, he just walked away, leaving little doubt that we were free to do as we pleased.

I pulled Ginny into my arms and whispered, "Are you okay?"

Her only response was to squeeze tighter. The questions could wait. We held each other until our pulse beat as one. She gave me one last squeeze and then hand in hand we followed Nephilim into an uncertain future.

He stopped every couple of minutes to wait for us to catch up, as if we were small children or something. Things have gotten weird lately, but this turn of events was beyond weird.

Ginny was unusually quiet. This went on for a half hour before either of us spoke.

"There was blood," I said.

Ginny took my hand and turned me to face her. The love in her eyes was all I needed to give my racing thoughts some rest.

She brushed her fingertips across my chest and whispered, "I think it was your blood."

"Another miracle," I said.

"I'll never be surprised again by a miracle healing," she said.

"Did you use the plant to heal me?" I asked.

She nodded.

"The kiss?" I asked.

"I stuffed a leaf in my mouth when I realized we wouldn't likely resurface," she answered.

"Did you save the rest of the plant?" I asked.

She shook her head and said, "It was lost in the water."

"Do you know how we ended up on a tropical beach?" I asked.

She shook her head.

"The whirlpool was strong," she said. "I fought it at first. When I could fight it no more, I used the last of my energy to deliver the medicine with a kiss before surrendering to death. That's all I remember until I awoke on the beach."

I nodded.

"There's something else," she said.

I waited patiently for her to tell me, but I already knew what she was going to say.

"I saw something," said Ginny.

She looked into my eyes. I nodded.

"You saw it too?" she asked.

"Yes," I answered.

"It was the face of God, wasn't it?" she asked.

I nodded.

"What did God look like?" asked Nephilim.

He stood facing us with hands on hips and a twinkle radiating from sky blue eyes. For the first time I saw his intelligence and humor. From that point forward, he was no longer a great beast to me.

"There are no words that come even close," said Ginny.

Her response was exactly what I felt and it reminded me of the opening line of Lao Tzu's *Tao Te Ching*.

"The Tao that can be spoken is not the true Tao," I said.

Nephilim raised an eyebrow.

I jabbed my thumb in Ginny's direction and said with a crooked smile, "What she said. It's best we don't confuse the real deal with lame descriptions."

He nodded and winked. It took me back a bit, since Uncle Jim uses the same expression when I figure something out for myself.

"Look around you," said Nephilim with a broad sweep of his arm.

It was an invitation rather than an order, but we complied all the same.

"What do you see?" he asked.

It was a cornucopia of color. Before us was a valley dominated by a hot pink lake situated at the foot of a great mountain range. The sky shimmered like the Aurora Borealis on a cold Alaskan night. The forest behind us spread as far as the eye could see like an emerald and ebony ocean. The beach we washed up on just a short time ago was nowhere in sight.

"This place is weird," I answered. "It's as if the scenes keep shifting every few minutes."

"Minutes?" asked Nephilim.

"We've been hiking less than an hour and the ocean is nowhere in sight," I said. "From this high point we should still be able to see it."

"You'd think," said Ginny. "This place is magical...so other worldly. I've never seen anything like it."

"Other worldly you say...have you seen the entire world?" asked Nephilim.

I shook my head.

"Of course not, but I've seen a bunch of it," answered Ginny.

"Do you even know what the world is?" asked Nephilim.

I had no idea what he was asking. Ginny must have been drawing a blank as well, because she stood there with a look as blank as my own thoughts.

"It is creation incarnate," he said.

When we didn't say anything in response, he added, "A construct of mind."

"Then all of this is just our imagination," I said. "Like some sort of dream, or something."

"Does a place exist even though you have never seen it?" asked Nephilim.

"Yes, of course," answered Ginny.

"Did you know of this place before you arrived?" he asked.

We shook our heads.

"You see it ...smell it...hear it with your own senses?" he asked.

"Yes, yes," answered Ginny.

"Do you doubt this place exists?" he asked.

"No," I answered.

"Then it's more than your imagination," said Nephilim.

We nodded.

"Are your minds, the only mind?" he asked.

We shook our heads. I sure had not expected this philosophical discussion. The big guy stroked his whiskers for a moment as he carefully considered his next words.

"You have indeed seen the face of God," he said. "Try not to forget."

Without another word, he lumbered off toward the pink lake.

Once we got to its shore, I could see that that the water was clear and plants with broad pink leaves flourished below the surface. That solved one mystery in this land of mysteries.

Just as I was finally beginning to feel optimistic that other such oddities would prove to have logical explanations as well, I saw big dark eyes peering through the underwater foliage. There was such deep intelligence in them that without thinking I gave a small wave in greeting.

"Who are you waving at?" asked Ginny.

"There's someone in there," I answered.

"In the water?" she asked.

I pulled Ginny in close and guided her gaze with a pointed finger to the dim outline of a face in the water. It winked and then disappeared.

I felt an overwhelming sense of loss and desperately wanted to see those soulful eyes once again. Taking Ginny by the hand I led us to water's edge and would have taken the next step into the water had Nephilim not prevented it.

"You are forbidden," he said.

As strong as the pull to follow the eyes in the water felt to us, it wasn't nearly as strong as Nephilim's command, so with a heavy heart we turned to the giant. His expression was intense, but not so much angry, as willful, like a carnival hypnotist intent on mesmerizing his gullible targets.

"Forbidden!" said Ginny. "We are not children to be commanded by you."

"You are not making this any easier," he said.

"Why don't you tell us what you are up to?" I said.

"You wouldn't understand," he said.

Ginny folded her arms across her chest and said, "Try us, buster."

Nephilim glared at us. When that didn't work, he showed his fangs.

"We refuse to take another step until you tell us where we are," said Ginny.

He let out a long sigh before saying, "Agartha."

"Yeah right, this is the mythical land in the center of the Earth?" I scoffed.

"I don't really expect you to believe me, but what about your own senses," he said with an expansive wave of the arm. "Do you believe them?"

"That would explain a lot," said Ginny.

"Surely you don't believe this guy," I said.

Ginny pointed at Nephilim and said, "How do you explain his size?"

"There has to be a logical explanation," I said.

"More logical than calling a giant a giant, instead of a big person, or some other politically correct euphemism?" asked Ginny.

"If you will please follow me, there is more to show you before you leave," he said.

I looked at Ginny and shrugged, "What do we have to lose?"

CHAPTER 47

We climbed high into the mountains and after an hour of hiking saw a city in the distance like none I had ever seen before. Most cities are like a plate of spaghetti randomly thrown on the wall to see what sticks. From the vantage of the mountaintop, the design of the entire city was visible, and clearly, nothing was left to chance.

In fact, it had a distinctive shape that took me by surprise. For whatever reason, the planners had designed the city as a circle within a circle with eight gates leading to the center.

"The eight gates," I murmured.

After a hit and run driver robbed me of my parents, I was lost in sadness. Ch'ing told me it is okay to be sad because sadness is one of the eight gates of change and someday I would stand at all eight gates. Much later, I learned Baguazhang, a Taoist martial art that uses the eight gates of change to transform your life.

There was more to the city than the eight gates. Many of the futuristic buildings were designed as inverted glass bowls standing on tall delicate stems filled with a swirling rainbow of colored gas. It was a vision of a distant city in a far off galaxy that could only have been created by a science fiction writer with ample imagination.

In sharp contrast to the otherworldly buildings scattered across the cityscape, other multi-faceted structures sent towers and spires high into the sky. Some were conical shapes reaching for heaven, much like you'd see on a medieval cathedral, but others were capped with brightly painted onion domes reminiscent of St. Petersburg, Russia. I couldn't help but imagine them filled with Cossacks and Czars kneeling in prayer.

"Look at those spires," said Ginny. "They remind me of Istanbul, but Turkey is half a world away. What city is this?" asked Ginny.

"Shambala," said Nephilim.

"That's a fable taught to Tibetan children, no different than the Santa Claus myth in the west," said Ginny.

"Who says Santa isn't real?" asked Nephilim.

"Next you'll be telling us there really is a Santa's workshop in the north pole," said Ginny.

Nephilim pointed off in a direction beyond the mountains and said, "Yes, in the pole."

I was thinking this guy had a few screws loose and we needed to get to an airport as soon as possible. Since Ginny had an office in Manaus, we could gather some clothes and fly out of there.

"How far is Manaus from here?" I asked.

"It depends on the route you take," said Nephilim.

In the last few days I had learned a few things about circuitous routes when I followed Ginny south from Louisville to Manaus. I was shanghaied by a pack of freaks, who took me deep into the Amazon Rainforest. Since then I have been hopelessly lost in its two million square miles of jungle.

My thoughts were interrupted by a voice whispering on the wind, "Look what the cat drug in."

Ginny leaned in with a whisper of her own.

"Do you hear that?" she asked.

Her question eliminated any hope of pretending it was just my imagination playing tricks on me. We looked around and confirmed there was no one nearby.

"The stuff of fairy tales," answered the tree boughs.

"They're not very heroic, if you ask me," said the wind. "They don't have a clue where they are, do they?"

I nodded. They were right about that.

"Hush," said Nephilim. "Show some respect for a change."

I wasn't sure if he was talking to us or the voices on the wind. Either way, he was clearly annoyed by the turn of events.

"They may be lost, but it didn't prevent them from bringing death along for the ride," whispered the tree boughs.

"And destruction," agreed the wind.

"Two lay dead," whispered the tree boughs.

"Send a crew to clean the mess," said Nephilim.

"They belong to Kali," whispered the wind.

"Perhaps darkness should clean her own mess," agreed the tree boughs.

"Agartha is home to us all," said Nephilim. "You can't escape your duty by blaming others. Besides, Kali's solution for destruction is to bring more destruction."

"Yes, she loves to change things up whenever possible," said the wind.

"No one can calm her wrath, except maybe Shiva," said the tree boughs.

"Dancing on his naked body seems to mollify her," agreed the wind.

"Together they bring balance to the creative and destructive process," said the tree boughs.

"What of these two...they're pretty damn scrawny don't you think?" asked the wind.

A glaring light hit me right between the eyes and even though I tried to shield it with my hand, it seemed to penetrate to the darkest depths of my being. It felt both intrusive and orgasmic at the same time.

"You'd think they'd send someone more impressive then these two," scoffed the tree boughs.

"The Prophesy should be fulfilled by a man and woman who look the part, don't you think?" asked the wind.

"Yeah, someone bigger than life," answered the tree boughs.

In one smooth motion, Nephilim raised his arms overhead from the sides and brought his palms together in a thunderous clap.

"Enough," he bellowed.

"All right…all right, no need to get your panties in a bunch," grumbled the wind and tree boughs in unison.

"Panties?" said Nephilim. "You two have been eavesdropping on the surface again."

"Do you make a habit of shouting down the wind?" asked Ginny.

In response to Ginny's question, Nephilim made a peculiar hand movement and the wind died.

"You can't stay here," said Nephilim. "You have a task to complete and must return to the surface. "

He had to be talking about Great Mother, the healing plant given to us by Ch'ing and the other members of Council, but how did this ape-man know about that?

"What do you know of our task?" asked Ginny.

"You have been entrusted with a sacred duty," answered Nephilim. "It is one that will change the world as we know it."

"Are you talking about the healing plant?" I asked.

"It was lost in the whirlpool," said Ginny.

"That is only the beginning," answered Nephilim. "Your destiny is much greater than that."

"What do you mean…return to the surface?" asked Ginny. "The sky is above us and we stand on the solid ground."

"Haven't you figured it out yet?" asked Nephilim.

"The water… it must have something to do with the well we fell into," murmured Ginny.

Nephilim waited expectantly. I had an image of Alice tumbling down the rabbit hole. Like Lewis Carroll's classic allegory, we found ourselves in a strange land…a world so surreal it couldn't possibly be real. Surely, it was just a bad dream. I mean, we were talking to Bigfoot for God's sake.

As old Scrooge once blamed a ghostly vision on a bit of undigested meat, I wanted this weirdness to have a logical explanation, but try as I might, couldn't come up with one.

"All will be revealed soon enough," said Nephilim. "Follow me."

The hairy giant disappeared into the large mouth of a poorly lit cave. I would have sworn on my mother's life that it was not there before.

I looked at Ginny. She looked at me. We didn't say a word, but it was clear that neither of us wanted to follow him. I was about to suggest we explore the city instead when a deafening roar electrified the hair on the backs of our necks and caused my stomach to lurch into a graceless back flip that sputtered and crashed somewhere near midpoint.

At first, I thought Nephilim was bellowing from inside the cave, but a subtle change in the light caught my attention. I am not sure what I expected to see, but nothing could have prepared me for the beast crouched on the ledge above us. Most of the creature blended into the surrounding stone. On the other hand, maybe it was the stone. If it wasn't for the pearly whites, I might have missed it.

It took a moment to register the size of the teeth since they were unlike anything I had ever seen before. I thought maybe my eyes were playing tricks until the beast raised itself to a crouch.

Curved canines finally revealed themselves in their entirety. They were at least two feet long and sharpened to a razor's edge. A bead of saliva the size of a plum rolled along the edge of the left scimitar and came to a tenuous rest at the tip where it hung precariously for a moment before finally giving way to gravity and splattering in the dust at our feet.

I instinctively raised my arm across Ginny's chest as a bar to the huge cat and took a slow step backwards. It was a mistake. The saber tooth giant let out a deafening roar and sprung toward us. Without thinking, I rolled to the right, but Ginny went left and lofted herself onto the big cat's back. I was fast, but the cat was faster. It adjusted mid-air and dropped a paw the size of coffee table onto my chest.

A single claw the size of a bowie knife targeted my eye. It twitched ever so subtlety, as if it had a mind of its own and was eager to deliver a gruesome strike. The other three legs surrounded me a like the furry bars of a freaky S&M cage.

To add insult to injury, he had a pink erection the size of Louisville Slugger leveled at my bottom. I did not like the direction this was headed and was prepared to swing that bat somewhere else, if I could. Any direction away from me would do.

Saber Kitty panted in my face, expelling short bursts of hot breath smelling faintly of its last supper. At any moment, I expected to feel its fangs ripping into me, but Ginny had it by whiskers, holding them firmly like a horses reins.

The cat was not happy with Ginny, but growled its displeasure at me. In response, Ginny tugged ever so slightly to the right and Saber Kitty's head turned. It was Mexican standoff and I wasn't sure it was going to turn out well.

"Don't eat our guests, Fluffy," said a surprisingly gentle voice.

With one exception, she was the most beautiful women I had ever laid eyes upon. I say woman, but I can't say for certain how old she was. At first, I thought she was in her twenties, but for some unknown reason I was suddenly convinced she was a teenager.

That didn't last long before I was certain it was a trick of the light and she was a well preserved forty…then sixty. This shifting went on and on until I was utterly confused and fully convinced age is a clever trickster.

Most folks have something that doesn't quite measure up with the rest of themselves. You might say their halves don't match. This girl-woman was different. As far as I could tell, she was perfectly proportionate. Nothing was out of balance and there was something particularly soothing about her physical symmetry. I decided she was an Angel.

Unlike Nephilim, she was normal size, but on the tall side at 5'10". She was soft and round in all the right places, but tight and long in others. Her hair was blond, almost albino white, with matching bright blue eyes and skin that glowed with radiant good health. Her only adornment was a white orchid tied around her left wrist.

"He won't hurt you," said the Angel. "He's really very sweet once you get to know him. Aren't you Fluff?"

The big cat purred in agreement.

Ginny released Fluffy's whiskers and scratched him behind the ears just before dismounting. His purrs got louder. With a surprising nimbleness, he released me from saber tooth prison and proceeded to give himself a bath with a tongue the size of beach towel.

"I am honored to stand before the Living Grand Terminus," said Angel.

I had no idea why she would call us the Living Grand Terminus. Taoists call the Yin-Yang symbol the Grand Terminus. It depicts black and white spooning each other in a circle. Neither white nor black exists exclusive of the other. White exists within black and black within white.

Imagine the two dimensional symbol as a globe spinning through space. It spins so fast that you can't really tell where white begins and black ends. In fact, it spins fast enough that you can't distinguish between white or black. All you see is a sphere hurling through space.

The Grand Terminus is a reminder that opposites are just different sides of the same coin. Duality is an illusion. Unification is the true nature of things.

"The big end to what?" asked Ginny.

"It is written that the Living Grand Terminus will usher in the next age of the world," said the Angel.

Ginny cut her eyes to me and asked, "Is that a Taoist thing?"

"The Grand Terminus is a Taoist concept, but I'm not familiar with this concept of the Living Grand Terminus," I answered.

The Angel smiled and said, "You won't find this in your Taoist Cannon or any other book, for that matter. You must look to the Akashic Records."

"You mean the air?" asked Ginny.

"You have a problem with the air?" asked the wind.

"She wouldn't live long without breath," said the tree boughs.

"Or, be so pretty," said the wind.

Akasha is Sanskrit for air. You could also think of it as life force or Chi. The experiences of all living beings on Earth are recorded in the Akashic Records. Think of the Earth as a living being and the Akashic Records are the Earth's mind or memory bank. Since we are of the Earth, we have the ability to connect with the Earth's mind, but because we live in a dark age, it is a forgotten skill.

"Our fate is not a dream painted across a distant horizon by some higher power," I said to the Angel.

"You have the opportunity to restore your integrity," said the Angel.

"Are you suggesting I'm a liar?" I asked.

"Is it possible you have forgotten who you really are?" she asked.

"We are just regular people," said Ginny. "I want to marry this man and raise a family with him. What makes you think we will change the world?"

"Yeah, what she said," mocked the wind.

The Angel swept her arm toward the cave entrance and said, "Don't take my word for it. Your destiny awaits you. See for yourself."

A warm light radiated from the cave. I was reminded of near-death survivors who report seeing a light at the end of a long tunnel. Without exception, they say they are drawn to the light. I took Ginny's hand, gave the Angel and Fluffy one last look, and we walked hand in hand into the light.

CHAPTER 48

Before life was abruptly altered by a hit and run driver, one of my fondest memories was a family trip to Mammoth Cave. While famous as the world's longest cave system, what I remember most is holding Dad's hand as we peered into the "Bottomless Pit."

"You see that, Grant?" asked Dad.

I wasn't sure what he wanted me to see since there was nothing but darkness in that pit. Dad gave my hand a squeeze. Sometimes the little things reassure us the most.

"There's nothing there," I said.

"Are you sure of that?" he asked.

Curious, I took a closer look. The park ranger told a small group of tourist how it was formed by natural forces, but I didn't believe him. I knew without a doubt that giants dug the pit.

Pointing into the darkness, I said, "Giants dug it."

Raising an eyebrow, he replied, "Well now, that was said with confidence. What evidence do you have to support your hypothesis?"

"Grandma's well," I answered.

He raised an eyebrow and waited for more.

A few weeks earlier, I watched a crew of men drill a new well for grandma. The old one dried up and she insisted on digging a new one rather than connecting to the municipal water source. Turning up her nose in distaste, she said people should trust their senses more than the government and that anyone with clear sinuses could tell that city water is full of nastiness.

I pointed to the drill marks in the rock below, and said, "Those marks look like the ones they made drilling grandma's well.

Dad nodded and asked, "What about the giants?"

"It's a giant sized hole," I answered. "Only giants need to make one that big...so they don't bump their heads."

With the innocence of a child, I believed giants were real. Who could have guessed that many years later I would actually encounter one?

Stepping into a cave is like returning to the womb, but in this instance, the inside was more like a 1950's set for a bad science fiction movie. I wanted to ask Nephilim about this strange futuristic place, but he refused to answer any questions, and instead, motioned us to hurry as if our lives depended upon it. I gave up trying to interrogate him and contented myself to observe the surroundings firsthand.

Nephilim led us through a network of bewildering hallways that glowed softly with a muted red light. It did little to put us at ease. Instead, it stirred troubling thoughts of hellfire and brimstone.

The flooring operated like a moving sidewalk, but at a speed, I couldn't begin to guess. It was mostly smooth and level, but at times, it seemed more like an escalator moving on both vertical and horizontal planes through round doors that opened of their own accord with a zipping sound reminiscent of a starship.

There are occasions when time plays tricks on us and this was one of them. On the one hand, it seemed like we had only been in the underground passageway for a few minutes, but on the other hand a part of me knew it had been much longer. How long I could not say for certain, but it all ended abruptly when the sidewalk sent us tumbling down a rocky hillside and into a shallow pool of water with a splash.

Ginny groaned.

"Are you injured?" I asked.

"I'm bruised but otherwise uninjured," grumbled Ginny.

"What is that that rotten egg smell?" I asked with distaste.

"I think it's sulfur," answered Ginny.

"Oh great…we'll never get rid of the stink," I said.

It was pitch black in the cave and judging by the sounds coming from somewhere in the darkness, we had bigger problems than the bad smell.

"Do you hear that?" whispered Ginny.

I nodded, before realizing it was pitch black and she couldn't see me.

"It's getting closer," I whispered.

"What do you think it is?" she whispered.

I was trying to track it, but her whispers were echoing in the cave.

"Shhh," I said.

"Don't you shush me," she said a little too loudly.

Labored breathing echoed off the stonewalls of the cave. One minute it seemed to be getting closer to us and in the next, it receded into the darkness. It was difficult to tell whether it was an aggressive beast or something more shy and tentative.

"What do you think it could be?" I asked.

"My money is on a pervert," answered Ginny.

A small flame appeared in the vast darkness. We had a glimpse of a face, but it quickly disappeared when the flame blazed into an inferno. The burst of light stabbed at our eyes, like painful little daggers.

"That I am," said the flames.

When our eyes finally adjusted to the explosion of light, we saw a two-foot torch held by a man who couldn't have been more than two and half feet tall. The dwarf had wild hair, intense eyes, and a frizzy beard that lay across a belly so round, he looked pregnant.

This tiny man with a big voice and even bigger attitude was completely naked. Normally I would say that qualifies him as some kind of pervert, but of course Ginny and I had been walking around naked for days.

"Aren't you the cutest little thing?" said Ginny.

I thought it was a bit condescending of her to say that to him. Even by dwarf standards, he was small. Still, she said it with such warmth and sincerity that I hoped he would let it pass.

The dwarf glared back at her with eyes so grey I thought maybe they were only reflecting the color of his beard. It was a tense moment, but since I did not see any weapons, I was sure I could take him, being a badass martial arts master and all, if I do say so myself.

"Yes, I am sweets," purred the dwarf in a surprisingly seductive voice. "I may be small, but I'm all man."

"I can see that," said Ginny with genuine respect.

The appraising look in the dwarf's eyes was unmistakable. Ginny is a beautiful woman. Tall and athletic, her flawless legs lead the eye upward toward a tight little behind. She has broad swimmer shoulders that contrast perfectly with her slim waist and hips.

Her dark brown hair falls gracefully in soft wavelets onto shoulders highlighted with a cluster of brown freckles. The remainder of her skin is smooth and olive toned. Ginny's eyes sparkle with abundant life. Even though I have known her as long as I can remember, I find their color difficult to pinpoint. They are an unusual shade of blue or green that can best described as the color of a tropical sea.

The rest of Ginny's face is equally magnificent. She has an aristocratic high-bridged nose set between wide cheekbones that narrow into a high forehead. It's a beautiful face enhanced with the flush of radiant good health. I certainly understood why the dwarf might find her attractive, but a wave of jealously was a harsh reminder that Ginny was my fiancée and not for him.

I was about to go cave man on the cave dwarf when he spoke up and said, "Sorry, toots but you are off limits."

"Damn right," I muttered.

With a shake of his head the dwarf said, "Still a guy has a right to express his appreciation for such a booty-luscious hot tamale, don't you think?"

"Booty-luscious hot tamale…what kind of comment is that to make about a man's fiancée?" I demanded.

The dwarf gave me a knowing look and said, "Don't you agree with the assessment?"

I opened my mouth to deliver the perfect comeback, but a cold stare from Ginny stopped me cold. When she was fully satisfied I got the message, she returned her attention to the dwarf.

"I wasn't offering you anything and what do you mean, I'm off limits?" asked Ginny.

"A ban has been placed on the two of you," answered the dwarf.

Ginny pinched her brow and pressed the little man for a more satisfactory answer, "What do you mean by a ban?"

The dwarf's eyes shifted from right to left and then back again. His demeanor became less friendly and a lot more cagy. He cleared his throat as if to prepare himself for a big speech, but then stopped himself and said nothing.

Ginny was having none of it. She stood tall and firm, hands on hips, like a mother who had cornered a small child that she was not about to set free until she got her answers. It was a look of unrelenting determination. However, the dwarf looked formidable, and it might turn out to be a Mexican standoff, but my money was on Ginny. She is accustomed to getting what she wants.

"The two of you are acting as one to change the course of events," said the dwarf. "No matter how charming or how hard they try, no one can come between you."

Ginny let out a long sigh.

"Let me introduce myself," said the dwarf. "My name is Mudwick. I will be your guide for the remainder of your journey through the maize and to the surface."

Since we were hopelessly lost in this strange place, a guide would be helpful, but I wasn't convinced he could be trusted.

"Our last guide dumped us into this sulfur pit," I said.

"Where is Nephilim?" asked Ginny.

"You are where you are supposed to be," answered Mudwick. "Nephilim has completed his mission. Now it is my job to take you where you will be."

"Where might that be?" asked Ginny.

"To your life and to the lives of all you care for," answered Mudwick.

I thought of my sick mother and the lost medicine she so desperately needs before they kick her to the curb. This journey could have turned out much differently if the medicine had made it out of the well. Now, I saw dark days ahead of us.

"Where are we?" asked Ginny.

Mudwick made a grand sweep of the torch-bearing arm and said, "Welcome to the heart."

His gesture drew our attention to the cavern around us. In sharp contrast to the foul stench, the cave was a wonderland of exotic beauty.

The Earth, in all of her magnificent diversity, makes certain that those with senses wide open are filled to the brim with awe. The cavern did not disappoint. I was deep within the belly of Mother Earth and the depth of her beauty filled me with awe.

If you are like most people, it is easy to dismiss the underground world as nothing but dirt and rock. Although there was plenty of that in the cave, there was so much more. If you hope to understand what we experienced, then you must first abandon the notion that all dirt and rock look alike. Nothing can be further from the truth.

They say Eskimos have many different words for snow. That's not surprising. When you open your senses to a world of snow then you can't help but experience all of its diversity. If you want to communicate clearly about your experience, then you will dig deep for a variety of words or phrases to accurately describe it. The dirt and rock around us requires some digging as well.

Maybe it was the way the fire light danced on the walls of the cave, but I saw colors that I never knew existed. It was as if the cavern had a rainbow of its own painted from a pallet that was new to me. Primary colors were taken by the artist and transformed into something unique. The best I can do is to say it was painted by Mother Nature with unusual shades of red, orange, yellow, blue and green.

Stalactites hung from the ceiling in patterns reminiscent of the musical score for a complex symphony, each point a note evoking a deep emotional response. It left me wondering if Mozart had not studied it before writing his musical score, note perfect.

The cavern itself was round with high domed ceiling. I would estimate it to be three hundred feet in diameter and the ceiling no more than sixty feet high. There were dark passages leading in four directions. I saw no sign of the futuristic sidewalks that had brought us to this place or of Nephilim.

"You are to follow me," said Mudwick. "Come."

Left to our own devices, we had a twenty-five per cent chance of taking a passage that led us back into the light of day. Without Mudwick, we would be grouping our way blindly in the dark. I searched his grey eyes for any signs of treachery.

Having found none, I took Ginny's hand in mine and said, "Do you trust him?" Ginny nodded.

"Our lives are ours to live," I said to Mudwick. "We follow no one but ourselves. However, your guidance to the surface would be appreciated."

"Then we must hurry," he said. "Time is running short."

I expected him to lead us into one of the four dark passages, but he didn't. Instead, he walked quickly to the center of the chamber where everything below his shoulders disappeared. He looked back at us expectantly. As far as I could see, there was nothing there. We hesitated. He motioned for us to follow.

"What do you think?" asked Ginny.

"Everything about this place is odd," I said. "So going down to return to the surface makes about as much sense as anything else we've encountered."

Ginny grinned from ear to ear and said, "That's the spirit. There's no point in having this adventure make any sense."

Her grin was contagious and on that note, we followed the dwarf down into a dark pit with a light heart and even lighter step.

Sometimes the truth is counter-intuitive. That usually happens when our assumptions are based upon beliefs that are disconnected from reality. Likewise, we sometimes find ourselves lost when our sense of direction lets us down. We get turned around and left should be right, and up is down.

Ch'ing once told me the universe sends us these things to keep us humble. Things like tripping in front of a group of martial artists at the ceremony to recognize you as a Master. Sometimes the truth is counter-intuitive. That usually happens when our assumptions are based upon beliefs that are disconnected from reality. Likewise, we sometimes find ourselves lost when our sense of direction lets us down. We get turned around and left should be right, and up is down.

"Lighten up," Ch'ing would say. "Nobody is paying attention to you anyway."

Mudwick led us deep into the belly of the Earth. Along the way we wadded across streams, climbed over giant boulders, that turned out to be precious stones, and crawled on our bellies through the mud in passages so tight, I'd have sworn that there was no way in hell we could have fit through them, but we did.

It forced us to face our claustrophobia and the fear of unseen things hiding in the dark. It was a mind-altering journey into our dark selves. I don't want you to think it was all dark, because it wasn't. There were caverns filled with stars and others with strings of white twinkling lights reminiscent of Christmas.

There was much beauty in the underworld, the likes of which we have never witnessed before. Places as different as a mountain and an ocean. My favorite was a cavern filled with giant crystals.

"What is this place?" asked Ginny.

"Some call it the House of Crystals, but I prefer Moment of Truth," answered Mudwick.

"Why?" I asked.

Mudwick held the torch up to a large quartz crystal and said, "Look for yourself."

We stood hand in hand and gazed into the crystal. To my utter amazement, I saw our reflection shift from the people I know us to be to a pterodactyl and anaconda, then to an angel and a devil, to a snake eating bird that once again shifted into a Yin-Yang symbol, a phoenix and a dragon, and finally back to our regular faces. The cycle repeated faster, then faster yet again until I no longer knew for sure who we are.

"The snake eating bird," murmured Ginny.

This symbol was familiar to us. It is similar to an ouroboros, which depicts a snake swallowing its own tail. However, this symbol is different. A snake swallowing a bird and the bird swallowing a snake form a circle.

"Now you know why I like to call this place Moment of Truth," said Mudwick.

There were times during this journey I had a feeling Mudwick was taking the long route just to take the measure of our characters. The thing is, it didn't bother me much because I was with Ginny and we were both healthy and alive.

The only time I became annoyed with him was when I thought of the nursing home. At those times, all I wanted was to get our asses back home soon.

Mudwick's sense of urgency shifted radically. He rushed us forward through a long narrow tunnel, urging us to move quickly, as if we were running late for an important appointment, but our progress didn't last long before Ginny let out a howl and stopped dead in her tracks. At first I thought she had seen something that frightened her, but she dropped to the ground and grabbed her foot. There might have been a curse or two escape her lips.

"Are you okay, Ginny?" I asked.

Her only answer was more cursing as she gently massaged her big toe.

"It's best to watch where you put your feet," said Mudwick.

Ginny glared at him.

Mudwick shifted from foot to foot looking like an impatient child overdue for a bathroom break.

Ginny ignored his discomfort.

"We must hurry," said Mudwick.

"Enough!" said Ginny. "Where are we, Mudwick?"

Mudwick opened his mouth to answer her question, but must have seen something in her expression that caused him to snap it shut. Instead, he tugged at his beard while weighing his options.

I was less interested in where we were and more concerned about getting home as soon as possible. The clock was ticking and I still didn't have a solution for my mother's nursing home. I was beginning to think we'd never get out of this cave.

I took a step toward Mudwick and demanded, "How much longer are you going to drag us through the mud?"

"The end is the beginning," said Mudwick.

"Mudwick," growled Ginny. "Where are we?"

He glanced over his shoulder in the general direction we'd been heading before exhaling sharply.

"Well, if you must know, we are in a remote area of a place you call Mammoth Cave," he said.

It was Ginny's turn to drop her jaw.

When she finally found words, all she said was, "You mean we're in Kentucky?"

"Yes, yes," he said.

"How can that be?" she said.

He sighed.

"Please explain," said Ginny.

"If you must know, Mammoth Cave is one of the main connectors between the surface and Inner Earth," he said.

"Inner Earth?" said Ginny.

"The Earth is not solid," said Mudwick.

"Not solid?" said Ginny.

"You mean it's hollow, " I asked.

"Yes, that's exactly what I mean," said Mudwick.

"And we've been somewhere on the inside of it?' asked Ginny.

"Yes, Agartha," answered Mudwick.

"Agartha?" I asked.

He nodded.

"You said Mammoth Cave is one of the connectors to Inner Earth," said Ginny. "What are the others?"

Mudwick sighed and with the patience of an adult teaching a small child the most fundamental lesson, said, "Well, you already know about the Amazon Rainforest. There are others, but the main ones are the two poles and Sovereign's Refuge."

"I've heard that name before," I said.

"Me too," said Ginny.

I raised an eyebrow.

"From Marguerite," she said.

I nodded.

"Ch'ing has also mentioned Sovereign's Refuge," I said.

"Where is it, Mudwick?" asked Ginny.

"In the Himalayas," he answered.

"It's what Ch'ing called his monastery, but he never said anything about a portal to the underworld," I said.

"I know this is difficult to wrap your heads around, but it hasn't been that long ago since your ancestors thought the Earth was flat," said Mudwick.

"This is crazy," I said.

"That's what everybody said when Pythagoras first proposed that the Earth is a ball spinning through space," said Mudwick.

"Pythagoras...you mean Galileo don't you?" I asked.

"Actually, Galileo correctly theorized that the Earth moves around the Sun," said Mudwick.

"How do you know this?" I asked.

"How do you not?" answered Mudwick.

"What does this have to do with the Earth being hollow?" asked Ginny.

"A solid Earth is only a theory," said Mudwick.

We stared at him blankly.

"Like many theories, it's someone's best guess to explain something they don't understand, but in this instance it's dead wrong," said Mudwick.

"Why should we believe you?" I asked.

"Don't trust me, trust your own senses and powers of reason," said Mudwick.

"It would explain a lot about what we've been through since we fell in the well," said Ginny.

She was right of course. We had just experienced some pretty weird shit that didn't make a bit of sense unless we changed the way we looked at it. Still, it was a hard pill to swallow and I was about to tell Mudwick why he was crazy when he pointed to a narrow crack between two rocks that I didn't think we could possibly squeeze through.

Catching his drift, Ginny shook her head and said, "Well, that's not ever going to happen."

Mudwick never missed a beat before he clapped his hands and said, "Enough! In here, hurry, hurry, my friends."

Ginny opened her mouth to object, but seeing the look of absolute conviction in Mudwick's face, shook her head and looked at the rock crevice once again. It didn't take long before she shook her head and looked to me for a decision. Since he hadn't failed us yet, I shook off a wave of claustrophobia and led Ginny into the tight crevice. While it was indeed a tight fit, it was shorter than I thought it would be. Pushing forward, I slipped through a narrow crack between two boulders and fell with a splash into the middle of a stream.

The sun was just breaking over the horizon. It was dawn and we had made it to the surface at last.

CHAPTER 49

Ginny's bare leg rested halfway in the stream, where the clear water worked its magic washing away the mud and grim, the only evidence of our strange journey below the surface of the Earth. Even though the sun was low in the sky and to our backs, her eyes blinked rapidly in an effort to adjust to the change in light.

Mudwick was nowhere in sight. That came as no real surprise to me. Folks might have trouble accepting such a sight. Naked dwarves aren't something you see every day, except maybe on a fringe web site.

Speaking of naked, unless, we are near the Guardian's village, Ginny and I will need to find something to cover ourselves. If necessary, we might fashion a loincloth out of leaves, like Adam and Eve after the fall.

Once we adjusted to the light, Ginny's eyes found mine. They were filled with such love that I felt a strange peace wash over me. I wasn't alone anymore. All the years of loneliness rinsed away with the mud.

I reached out to Ginny with the intention of rinsing the rest of the dirt from her body, but instead we wrapped ourselves in each other's arms and held tight. It only took a few breaths before we fell into a synchronized rhythm of breath and pulse. I had never experienced anything like it before. It was if we were the same person and any idea of separation was a big fat lie.

It seemed as if we stayed that way for a very long time. Then again, it may have only been a minute or two. I only came back to myself when she let out a strange moan that sounded less like a person and more like the cry of a cat in heat.

Afterwards we sat in the middle of the stream and bathed each other. The rays of light from the morning sun cut through the branches of the deciduous trees lining the bank of the stream. It was a warm morning, but the cool water raised goose bumps on our skin as it cleansed our pours and healed our wounds.

All of my senses were engaged. The air was heavy with the sweet fragrance of honeysuckle offset by a trace of pungent that I think might have come from a skunk's passing during the night. Somehow, the two harmonized into an unexpectedly beautiful duet of scent. It was by far the most sensual experience of my life.

When we finished our bath, we retreated to a patch of soft grass under the branches of a massive poplar tree where we curled up together and fell into a deep sleep. I am the luckiest man in the world was the last thought I had before I drifted off.

I don't know how long we slept before a barking dog woke us, but the sun had changed sides and now filled the sky with shades of pink. According to Ch'ing, at the end of each day, the immortals gather in the coral colored clouds to party. He promised I would see them when my heart is ready. I never watch a sunset without hoping for a glimpse of my dad.

As I lay there with Ginny watching day's end, I noticed that a splash of the color was moving in an unexpected way. It was if the fabric of the sky was torn and something miraculous would spill through any second now.

"Aaawk, would you look at the naked love bugs laying there in the weeds," squawked Bird.

"Bird!" squealed Ginny. "I have missed you."

"Aaawk, I'm glad one of you has some manners," squawked Bird. "I missed you too Angel! Welcome to the better species. What about you Pekerwood...are you going to say hello, or what?"

Bird is all about respect.

"Hey Ponce," I said grumpily.

"Aaawk, that's Mr. de Leon to you Peckerwood," said Bird.

I sighed. Not very manly of me, but Bird has always been difficult.

"Aaawk, are you going to just lay there or are you going to get up and fulfill your destiny," squawked Bird. "It's time!"

Damn, it was time to take responsibility for losing the plant that could cure the world of all its ills, so I said, "About that destiny thing...umm...we kind of..."

Despite my best intentions, I was struggling to make the confession. Bird has a way of making me feel like a small child. Gratefully, Ginny came to my rescue.

"We lost it," said Ginny.

Bird cocked his head slightly to the left and gave us a long appraising look.

"Aaawk, don't tell me you finally lost your virginity," squawked Bird.

"We lost the plant," I said.

Bird raised himself to his full height of eighteen inches, beat his wings against a rainbow colored chest, and then began grooming himself like a common house cat.

"I think he took that pretty well, don't you think?" said Ginny.

"It could have been worse," I said.

"Aaawk, when you two are finished talking about me as if I'm not here, tell me what that is next to you," said Bird.

I looked at Ginny and said, "The most beautiful woman in the world."

"Awe, do you really think that?" purred Ginny.

"Why yes I do," I answered.

Ginny threw her arms around me and sobbed on my shoulder. They were tears of joy, but I soothed her with gentle strokes all the same.

When her sobs subsided, Bird squawked, "Aaawk, if we are finished with the tender moment, take a look and tell me what's on your other side, Peckerwood."

To our utter amazement, the potted seedling was sitting in the soft grass next to us.

In our darkest hour, when all hope is lost, the most amazing miracles take place. Even though these miracles may save our sorry asses from certain disaster, we do not always notice because we have learned to dismiss them as coincidences. On top of that, they can be subtle little devils, pretending to be ordinary events. When blessed with a miracle, it is not a bad idea to acknowledge it and then express our gratitude.

I looked at the plant, then at Bird. There is no way he could have carried it to us, so my inclination was to ask a bunch of questions. The lawyer in me wanted to get to the bottom of it, but I resisted. Instead, I stopped myself from being distracted by the how of the miracle, took a breath and then expressed my deepest gratitude.

"Thank you, Bird," I said.

"Aaawk, while you two were partying in Agartha, someone had to lug this damn thing home," squawked Bird.

"How did you know we were in Agartha?" I asked.

"Aaawk, other than watching you fall into the portal?" asked Bird with his usual level of sarcasm.

"You mean the well?" I asked.

Bird has an annoying habit of ignoring questions about the obvious. Instead, he preened a red feather.

"What can you tell us about Agartha?" asked Ginny.

Bird looked up from the feather now polished to a sheen and squawked, "Aaawk, it's better than Vegas, baby."

"You've been to Agartha?" asked Ginny.

"Aaawk, what's with the inquisition?" complained Bird.

"Is it really in the center of the Earth?" I asked.

"Aaawk, weren't you there?" answered Bird.

"It's just a metaphor for the equator, right?" I asked.

Bird shot me a disgusted look followed by more preening.

"Just one more question, Bird," I said.

"Aaawk, no more questions," said bird. "It's time to get your lazy asses moving and start the revolution."

With those kind words of encouragement, he flew off. His parting words had something to do with the birds and bees.

"You'd think he would have helped us find our way out of this rainforest before he flew off to harass every feathered female in the jungle," said Ginny.

"I guess we'll have to blaze our own trail," I said.

"It doesn't make sense to begin our journey at twilight," said Ginny. "It will be night soon and we'll never find our way out of this jungle stumbling around in the darkness. Thanks to the cave, I've had a belly full of dark places."

I had to defer to Ginny. After years of searching for her father, she was familiar with the Amazon Rainforest. On the other hand, I had been stumbling around the jungle, hopelessly lost from the beginning. Now that we were out of the cave, it made more sense to wait until daylight to travel.

"Do you know the way home?" I asked.

Smiling she said, "North."

"You're so bad," I said as I gave her ribs a tickle.

For some strange reason, I didn't really feel lost. Since my arrival in the

Amazon Rainforest, I had stayed completely centered in the present moment. Partly because there were so many extraordinary things to see and experience, but it was more than that. I somehow felt like I belonged to the jungle.

Still, I had important business to take care of at home and in a sudden shift, desperately wanted to get us back to Louisville as soon as possible. In addition to taking care of Mom, there was the business of getting a divorce from Cynthia so I could marry Ginny.

There was a lot to do and not much time, but for now, the prospect of curling up with my lover on this stream bank was very appealing.

"You are right," I said. "It wouldn't make much sense to venture into the jungle at dark without a guide, but I would like to climb this river bank and see what's on the other side. Then we can develop a plan of action for tomorrow. Would you like to join me?"

Ginny peered up the bank and then back at me.

A playful smile danced on her lips, but all she said was, "Yes, let's go take a look before it gets dark. Once we get back, I'm sure we can find something to occupy our attention for the rest of the night."

With the promise of a passionate night, we walked hand in hand up the steep bank. When I slipped on a moss-covered rock near the top, Ginny pulled me close. The fire in my lower belly flared hot, but the kiss that followed was tender. As delicious as it was, it did little to satisfy our hunger. I desperately wanted her and judging by her reaction, she felt the same.

I hesitated, so Ginny took matters into her own hands and that's all it took for us to once again loose ourselves in the joy of the other. Our lovemaking was intense. Our hunger brought out the animal lust in us. We alternated between rough sex and tender love. There were moments when I couldn't tell where one extreme began and the other ended. In the end, we lay in tangled heap of sweat and panting breath.

As we mellowed into afterglow, it was Ginny who saw it first and said, "Grant, isn't that your Uncle Jim's backyard?"

CHAPTER 50

We were home. I should have immediately recognized the creek when we squirted from the belly of the Earth, but I had other things on my mind. Besides, I assumed we were still in South America. I don't know how we managed to get from Brazil to Kentucky via the underworld, but we did, thanks to the help of a very strange cast of characters.

Uncle Jim lives in a red brick two story that backs up to Harrods Creek. While his conservative neighbors might see an occasional deer or squirrel on their well-tended lawns, I would bet Ginny and I are the first nudist.

We stood hand in hand with Agartha behind us and Uncle Jim's signature 1970's style barbeque pit straight ahead. A half dozen Adirondack chairs painted in hippie shades of pink, purple and lime green faced outward from the gnarly trunk of an ancient oak that is home to a bug zapper suspended from the lowest hanging branch.

Sadly, it was the distinctive sound of the zapper's murderous work that gave us the first irrefutable proof we were home and this wasn't some mirage or other trick of the mind.

"I have a strong desire to click my heels together and chant, there is no place like home," I said.

Ginny snort-laughed, which made me love her all the more.

"Such a beautiful dork," I said lovingly.

She squeezed my hand and quipped, "This coming from a naked man who secretly wishes he had a pair of magical ruby slippers to carry him home."

I gave her my best pouting face and said, "It isn't much of an adventure without flying monkeys and a green faced witch. We was robbed, I tell you."

The snort-laugh returned and didn't stop for several minutes. I figured she was releasing pent up tension, because it wasn't that funny by any definition of humor. Still, it's good when a man can make the woman he loves laugh.

Laughter releases endorphins into an otherwise beleaguered body. Fortunately, all those good people looking out for our best interest haven't quite figured out how to make this natural high illegal, but I'm sure they're working on it. As far as I'm concerned, endorphins rank right up there with a good night's sleep and great sex on the bliss list.

Eric and I showed up for Kung Fu during a fit of teenage grumpiness a few years back, so Ch'ing adapted the day's lesson plan to include Laughter Yoga. Like most of the useful things he taught us, it's a simple practice. You just fake laugh until it becomes the real thing.

By some strange alchemy faking it actually works. Within a few minutes, our spirits lifted and we began to see humor in everything. To Ch'ing's credit, he opened a door into a world filled with light-heartedness and didn't close it again like some adults might. Instead, he allowed us to laugh and cut-up until our hearts were full and the mirth morphed into contentment.

Laughter is indeed contagious and I enthusiastically joined Ginny until we both had tears of joy flowing down our grubby cheeks. Somewhere toward the end of our fit of laughter, another voice joined in. It originated deep in the belly and I knew it well. Ch'ing slipped from the shadows and joined our bubbling well of laughter.

"Ch'ing!" I shouted.

He responded with a bow in the formal manner of our martial tradition. The left hand stretches forward before circling back to the center of the chest. Along the arc of the circle, the palm addresses all four directions. It is something we rarely do other than at the beginning and ending of a class.

I returned the bow, noticing in the corner of my eye that Ginny matched my movements. I made a mental note to ask if she learned the greeting from her teacher, Marguerite, or if she had just picked it up on the spot.

Even though I have known Ch'ing most of my life, in many respects he is still a mystery to me. Other than a monastery in Tibet, he never speaks of his past. Although, he once lived as a monk, he didn't look like one. He was wearing black slacks, Gucci loafers, and a t-shirt that read, "Immortality Is Only Kinky the First Time."

I had seen that shirt once before. Street vendors were selling it outside of the Kentucky Center the day Padma Ganesha spoke at a lecture series hosted by Ginny's company, Emerald Allure, called "Ideas to Change the World."

As far as I know, Ch'ing did not attend the conference. Around that time, he disappeared without a trace and then later reappeared in a South American pyramid as a member of a mysterious Council that entrusted us to spread Great Mother across the Earth.

"Did you two enjoy your journey through the inner Earth?" said Ch'ing with a lopsided grin.

"It was an amazing experience," answered Ginny.

"Awe Ginny," said Ch'ing warmly. "You look radiant this morning. What is your secret?"

I don't know how he does it, but Ch'ing seemed to know about our recent love making. His innuendo caused Ginny to blush, but she quickly recovered her composure and answered him.

"Clean living," she said.

Ch'ing laughed all the way down to his toes. A rich heartwarming sound that filled me to the brim like comfort food.

"It's next to Godliness, my dear," said Ch'ing.

He winked at me and added, "You keep it up. It's good medicine."

Ginny was glowing. There are moments when everything seems perfect and nothing is impossible. This was one of those moments for me.

"I plan to," was all I said.

"Now that each of you has acquired your animal spirit, you are ready for the work ahead," said Ch'ing.

"You must be talking about our battles with the giant Anaconda and the Pterodactyl," I said.

Ch'ing nodded and said, "Like all epic battles they transfer untold power to the victors."

"About this animal spirit thing," Ginny said. "We saw some pretty weird shit in the…umm…the Crystal Cave."

"I bet that diminutive rascal called the place Moment of Truth just before you got a glimpse of your authentic selves?" said Ch'ing with a twinkle in his eye.

"Yep, he really likes to stage drama, doesn't he?" asked Ginny.

"He's a frustrated carnival hawker," said Ch'ing.

"Was it real…what we saw in the crystal?" I asked.

"It depends," said Ch'ing. "What did you see, Grant?"

"Ginny was angelic," I said. "Me, well I was a devil."

"Is that that the best you can do?" asked Ch'ing.

"There was talk of a prophecy…two acting as one," said Ginny.

"Ginny and I restore balance to primal forces…forces once in opposition," I said.

"Except?" asked Ch'ing.

"Except there is only one primal force," answered Ginny.

"Good and evil…angel and devil acting in opposition to each other is an illusion," I said.

"So you have evolved into what?" asked Ch'ing.

"We are the living Grand Terminus…the Snake Eating Bird Eating Snake," we said with one voice.

Ch'ing looked at us and said, "Yes, you are."

"Can we ask you a few questions about Great Mother?" asked Ginny.

"Of course," said Ch'ing. "What do you want to know?"

"Does it require an environment like the Amazon Rainforest to grow?" asked Ginny.

"No, Great Mother thrives under the harshest of conditions," answered Ch'ing.

"Does it really cure any illness or injury?" I asked.

"It restores optimal health," answered Ch'ing.

"Will it extend a person's life span?" asked Ginny.

"Yes," answered Ch'ing.

"How long?" asked Ginny.

Ch'ing spread his arms as wide as they would go and grinned nearly as far.

"Damn," I said. "How can that be possible?"

"What most people call aging is really untreated illness," answered Ch'ing.

"How old are you?" I asked.

Ch'ing shrugged.

"This sounds amazing," said Ginny. "Why has it been kept a secret?"

"There are forces that want to suppress Great Mother and they will do everything they can to stop you," answered Ch'ing.

"Are we in danger?" asked Ginny.

"The gravest," answered Ch'ing.

Another voice chimed in.

"Oh, we are going to have so much fun, don't you think?" said Eric.

Eric is my best friend, and as you can see, he loves a good fight. Ch'ing began training us when we were snotty nosed eight year olds who could hardly focus on more than running the streets barefooted.

For most martial artist, the dojo provides a positive outlet for aggression. Once it is out of our system, we become staunch advocates for peaceful solutions. Eric of course is the exception to the rule. The man really enjoys a good fight and can't seem to get enough of it.

He is tall, lean, and well proportioned. I'm a couple of inches shorter than Eric and more muscular. His blond hair and blue-eyed Viking good looks drive chicks crazy. My brown eyes and dark skin speak to a much different ancestry.

I am related to U.S. Grant on Mom's side, but her father was African-American. My ancestry gets even more interesting when you look at Dad's side of the family. He was Chinese and loved to brag about his ancestor, Li Ching-Yun, a famous internal martial artist who lived a ridiculously long life. One of Dad's prized possessions was a yellowed New York Times article reporting Master Li's death at age 256. Dad was known to produce it with a dramatic flair as irrefutable evidence of his ancestor's impossibly long life.

This very interesting bloodline explains my somewhat exotic, foreign look, but I must admit that as the world shrinks, it is getting increasingly more difficult to define exotic.

Eric was dressed in Bermuda shorts, olive drab flip-flops, and a black Haulover Beach tee shirt that in pink lettering read, "Clothing Optional or Nothing." Even though the setting sun was dipping close to the horizon, he was wearing dark Ray Bans. Maybe the glasses helped with the glare from his final accessory, a lounge lizard gold chain wrapped snugly around a muscular neck tanned to perfection.

"So, what's the plan?" asked Eric. "I mean for healing the world and kicking some serious ass."

"Before we save the world I need a hot bath and massage," said Ginny.

"Fortunately, I'm a skilled masseuse," said Eric with a lascivious grin.

I did not like the sound of that one bit and for the first time in my life, I distrusted Eric. He was my best friend in all, but the thought of him putting his hands on her triggered ugly feelings. Jealousy can ruin a perfectly good friendship, not to mention a brand new engagement.

"Your hands are not getting anywhere near me, Mister," said Ginny.

I let out an audible exhalation. All eyes turned to me. As much as I wanted to pretend I wasn't getting all worked up with jealousy, I knew I couldn't fool this crowd. Sometimes, a simple acknowledgment of a dark truth is all it takes to be rid of it, so I shrugged an apology.

"I'm so busted," I said. "When it comes to Ginny, I expect you to keep your hands to yourself, my friend."

Eric winked. It was either an acceptance of my lame apology for not trusting him or one of his own. Since we were such close friends, I don't think there is much difference between the two.

"I don't know whether I should be offended or flattered," said Ginny.

"If in doubt, I suggest you take the high road and see Grant's awkwardly jealous moment as flattery," said Ch'ing.

"All right…all ready, I'll keep my hands to myself," said Eric. "Can you at least tell me what happened to the two of you? I mean, you fell into the water and didn't resurface. That usually means you wash up on some distant shore, bloated and pretty much deader than a door knob."

I was about to give Eric a quick summary, but Ginny spoke up and said, "After waiting heartbroken all of these years, with nothing to do but pray that one day Grant would come back to me…come back to me because he's all I ever wanted, the only guy I ever loved…"

Ginny said all of that in one breath, as fast as she could get it out, like she needed to unburden herself before she lost her courage, but it was too much and she broke down with a sob. I moved to comfort her, but she held a hand up to stop me, so I let her be.

After she regained her composure, she continued, but the tone had changed. The new voice was charged with resolve.

"The traitor…ummm…Victor's bullet hit Grant square in the chest," said Ginny.

Her face was hard and her voice filled with venom as she spoke of Victor, who was once her most trusted employee. She paused, took a calming breath and then continued.

"I wasn't about to let him die and tried to keep him from falling into the water, but I only had the use of one hand since I grabbed Great Mother with the other," said Ginny. "I needed that medicine to heal his gunshot wound."

Ginny tried to hold back a sob, but it refused to comply. She took a moment and then continued.

"We were pulled downward by a whirlpool," said Ginny. "I held my breath as long as I could, but knew I wasn't going to last much longer, so I desperately pinched a couple of leaves from the plant, stuffed them into my mouth and used a goodbye kiss to push the medicine between Grant's lips. My last thought was a prayer for him…and by some miracle, the last thing I saw was the face of God. "

"God?" asked Eric.

Ginny nodded.

"What does God look like?" asked Eric.

"Love," answered Ginny.

"Love?" asked Eric.

"Yep, that's about right," I answered.

"You saw it too?' asked Eric.

I shrugged.

"When I came to, I was on the most beautiful beach I had ever seen," said Ginny.

"All beaches are beautiful," said Eric.

"Maybe so," I said. "But this beach looked like a tapestry of stars glistening in the sun."

"Stars?" asked Eric.

Ginny nodded before continuing, "I heard something moving in the forest. Hoping it might be Grant, I went to investigate."

"Aaawk, I bet it wasn't the Peckerwood, was it?" asked Bird.

"No, it wasn't," answered Ginny.

"Aaawk, give it up toots," said Bird. "Who was it then?"

"Not who, but what," answered Ginny.

"Aaawk, now we're getting somewhere," squawked Bird.

"What was it?" asked Eric.

"I'm not exactly sure," answered Ginny. "My best guess is a komodo dragon, but there's more."

"What do you mean more?" asked Eric.

"The dragon walked upright," answered Ginny.

"No way, dude," said Eric. "You mean like a basilisk lizard."

"Aaawk, what's so special about a lizard that runs across the water?" demanded Bird. "Have you ever seen me…"

"That's enough Bird," said Ch'ing. "Put your self-aggrandizement to rest and let her finish her story."

"Thank you Ch'ing," said Ginny.

"Humph…self-aggrandizement…" grumbled Bird.

"There's plenty more," said Ginny. "Would you like me to continue?"

Everyone nodded yes, except for Bird, whose beak was buried under his wing. I can't say for sure what was going on in there, but he was mercifully quiet for a change.

"The dragon spoke to me," said Ginny.

"Awe, now you're just pulling my leg," said Eric.

"Aaawk, what did ole' lizard face have to say?" asked Bird.

"He welcomed me to Agartha," answered Ginny.

"Agartha," said Eric. "You mean the place inside the hollow Earth the fruitcake fringe talk about?"

"Do you think Admiral Byrd was a fruitcake?" asked Uncle Jim.

"What does a long dead admiral have to do with the myth of a hollow Earth?" asked Eric.

"He discovered it when he was searching for the North Pole," answered Uncle Jim.

"Of all people, I would think you would see how silly that is," said Eric.

"It doesn't get more credible than an eye witness report from Admiral Byrd," said Uncle Jim.

"Aaawk, what else did my cold blooded friend have to say," squawked Bird.

"He told me I was lucky he found me because there were some very bad people who wanted to hurt me," answered Ginny.

"Did he say who?" asked Uncle Jim.

"No, but he said he would protect me and…" Ginny trailed off looking a little embarrassed.

We waited.

"That I should call him God," continued Ginny.

"God?" asked Eric. "The komodo dragon said he was God?"

Ginny nodded.

"You sure about that?" asked Eric.

Ginny nodded yet again.

"Is this the same God you saw in the water?" asked Eric.

Ginny shook her head.

"Grant, did you see the komodo dragon?" asked Eric.

"No, I washed up on a different part of the beach," I answered.

"So you can't confirm Ginny's tale about a taking dragon?" asked Eric.

I shook my head and added, "I had my own problems."

"What kind of problems?" asked Eric.

"I was attacked by a pterodactyl," I answered.

"The flying dinosaur?" asked Eric.

I nodded.

"You don't really expect us to believe you were attacked by a pterodactyl, do you?" said Eric.

I shrugged.

Eric turned to Ch'ing and asked, "Does Great Mother cause hallucinations?"

Ch'ing shook his head.

"Are they having some kind of psychotic break?" asked Eric.

"Open your mind, Eric," answered Ch'ing.

"Damn, I missed all the fun," said Eric. "I knew I should have followed you and Victor into the water, but Ch'ing stopped me."

I gave Ch'ing a questioning look.

"It wasn't Eric's time," said Ch'ing.

Eric was pouting so Ch'ing added, "Don't worry Eric, there is a great battle ahead that is tailor made for you."

"Just don't leave me out again," said Eric.

I was about to reassure Eric that he could join in all the reindeer games, but before I got the words out, he quickly added, "There's no way in hell that a komodo dragon was really God. Ch'ing, the dragon isn't God, is it?"

"That's a complicated subject best left for another day," answered Ch'ing.

That was an unexpected answer and I wanted to press Ch'ing to explain it, but Uncle Jim interrupted.

"I have hot cornbread and molasses," said Uncle Jim. "Are you going to stand out here all night or come inside for dinner?"

"I'm starving," said Ginny. "We'll be right in."

"While you're at it, put on some damn clothes, would you?" said Uncle Jim.

"Aaawk, what's the matter, haven't you ever seen a naked girl before," squawked Bird.

"When then hell did you two turn into a couple of damn heathens?" said Uncle Jim.

It was good to be home.

CHAPTER 51

Since Uncle Jim refused to serve us without clothes, I took about ninety seconds to throw on a pair of navy blue gym shorts and a white t-shirt. Ginny wore a newer version of the same cotton shorts and one of my white dress shirts with the sleeves rolled to the elbow. I was comfortable. She was adorable.

Uncle Jim was wearing a pair of faded army surplus pants cut off at the knees, a concert t-shirt so beat up I couldn't tell who the band was, and house slippers. I like to tease him from time to time about his old man slippers, but it usually ends up in a friendly tussle to see who can get the other in a headlock and deliver a ceremonial scalping.

Ch'ing taught me well, but the United States Marine Corps taught Uncle Jim how to fight for his life. When I lose, which is most of the time, I complain he uses dirty tactics. He just shakes his head and tells me that's loser talk. If a man resorts to violence, then he damn well better be prepared to win at any costs.

These days Uncle Jim divides his time between mastering the art of southern cooking and exploring the world. He likes to point out that Uncle Sam was kind enough to send him to some very exotic places, but unfortunately, they kept him busy with work.

Work details are not open to discussion. He delivers a curt response to any question about his time in a Special Forces unit.

"Uncle Sam guards its secrets," he says. "There are questions you should never ask, even in jest."

His travels these days are for him. He goes where he wants and does what he wants, when he wants. He is fond of looking me in the eye to make sure I'm listening before delivering his responsibility speech.

"A man should never blame others for his shitty circumstances," says Uncle Jim. "If he wants to call himself free, then he must take full responsibility for his life."

When he cooks his kitchen is a model of efficiency. Responsibility and efficiency may well be the two most important guiding principles in his life.

"Proper timing is the key to any task worth performing," says Uncle Jim. "If half the meal is cold when it is set on the table, then the cook has failed to time the meal properly."

For this reason, not much distracts him when he is wearing an apron, but on this occasion, he greeted us with warmth and sincerity. Of course, the warm fuzzies only lasted a moment before he returned to the job of preparing fried catfish, skillet potatoes, mixed field greens and cornbread.

Now this food is delicious, but I don't want you to get the idea Uncle Jim isn't health conscious. Why there was also green iced tea, and one of my favorites, berries mixed with walnuts, raw honey and almond extract.

Bird was perched in his usual spot on top of the icebox. He was uncharacteristically quiet, spending most of the time preening feathers and taking thirty-second NASA naps.

Ginny looked around the table at my ragtag family and exhaled slowly before saying, "God I love this."

These are my people, but home doesn't quite feel the same anymore. I now have new people in the heart of the Amazon Rainforest who also nurture me. In a very short span of time, it has become a place to call home as well. Home has expanded and it feels right.

I squeezed Ginny's hand and dove into a plate of food big enough to feed three. We hadn't eaten for quite a while. How long is difficult to say, since time got weird for a while, but I had some catching up to do for sure.

Uncle Jim was glowing like an over attentive mother hell-bent on keeping her family well fed and healthy.

"Now that's what I call eating," he said. "Do you want another serving? I made plenty."

He was telling the truth about the amount of food he had prepared, but I was stuffed to the gills and declined his offer. He looked like he might argue with me about it, but Ginny came to the rescue.

"I could use a little more catfish," she said.

Judging by the size of the serving heaped on her plate, I suspect they had a different idea about the meaning of a little more, but Ginny never said a word. Instead, she tore into the food like a lumberjack. I guess she was hungry too.

When everyone had finished eating, I told the rest of our story about the underworld. There was a lot of back and forth with Eric and Uncle Jim about the strange cast of characters we encountered, but Ch'ing and Bird were strangely quiet on the subject. I suspected they knew much more about this strange world than they were willing to reveal.

Uncle Jim had a bunch of questions about our time with the Guardians, especially details about Ginny's brother, who healed his injuries and promised to restore his missing eye. He lost it a few years back in a rock climbing accident and has since worn an eye patch that he now massages every time Pony Tail's name is mentioned.

After dinner, everyone but Bird pitched in with the cleanup so it was finished in no time. After the last plate was dried and put away, I pulled Uncle Jim to the side.

"How's Mom?" I asked.

His normally smooth brow crinkled into four deep lines and his grey eyes steeled. The set of his jaw told me he had to bite back a few harsh words. I counted two breaths before he spoke.

"Those bastards," was all he said between clinched teeth.

"I got a call from them a few days ago," I said.

"You don't have to tell me," he said.

"We need to get her out of there," I said.

He nodded.

One of the most difficult things we ever did was put Mom in a nursing home. It's been tough, both emotionally and financially. There's no insurance to cover it and paying for long-term care out of my own pocket has been challenging. I fell behind on her bill, so now they are evicting her at the end of the month.

I thought I would sell her house to pay off the bill, but Cynthia is fighting it. She doesn't have a legal-leg to stand on, but she can tie the sale up long enough in divorce court that it will be too late to save Mom.

I demanded a raise from my law firm, but they laid me off instead. I can't borrow the money, because Cynthia has ruined our credit. At this point, I'm out of options.

Finding the money to pay her bill is only part of the problem. The doctors said her broken back will never heal and she is destined to be a paraplegic for the rest of her life. One of the dangerous risks to her condition are the random occasions she loses the ability to breathe on her own and requires a respirator. To make matters worse, she had an adverse reaction to her medication and is in a coma.

Something has to change, because Mom deserves a better life. Her condition is life threatening and I don't know whether Great Mother can heal her or not, but I have to give it a shot.

"The first thing I want to do now that we are back from South America is get Mom out of that place and try to heal her with Great Mother," I said.

Considering how excited he was about the healing power of Great Mother, I expected Uncle Jim to support my plans, but he surprised me. His eyes darted toward Ch'ing, then to Eric and back to me. I can't remember a time when I thought Uncle Jim was being shifty, but I sure felt it then.

"I don't think that's a good idea, Grant," said Uncle Jim.

"Why is that?" I asked.

He pointed to the potted plant sitting on the counter and said, "All you got there is one tiny seedling and it's meant for bigger things than what you're planning to do with it."

I knew Uncle Jim was right and I could ruin everything, but a wave of emotion overrode all reason.

"You don't seem to understand," I shouted. "They are going to throw her into the gutter at the end of the month. I will not let that happen."

Uncle Jim's eyes flared, but then the fire went out and they filled with tears instead. It was the first time I've seen him cry and the rawness of it deflected my anger.

"We will not let any harm come to her," he said between sobs. "I promise."

I did something radical and took two steps forward until we stood toe to toe. He didn't look up, but instead, kept his head down as if that would somehow hide his tears. I reached out and hugged the tough old marine while he wept on my shoulder.

Not once had I stopped to consider how this affected him.

"We'll figure something out," I said in a soothing tone.

"We need to get the crop established as soon as possible," I said. "Does anyone have any ideas?"

"If you're going to be farmers you'll need land," said Eric.

"A place with a good vibe and clean soil," said Ginny.

"I'm broke," I said.

"No, you're not," said Ginny. "We have plenty of money."

"I don't think you understand," I said.

"Grant, what is mine is yours," said Ginny.

"Thank you, but that feels wrong," I said.

"Why is that, Grant?" asked Ginny.

"It makes me feel like a gold digger, or something," I answered.

"Are you planning to marry me for my money?" asked Ginny.

"Oh, God no, the thought never crossed my mind," I said. "I've loved you since we were snotty nosed little kids. I wouldn't care if you didn't have two nickels to rub together."

"Then let's use the money I have to do some good," said Ginny.

"Once we have an established crop, then we will use it to heal your mother," said Uncle Jim.

"I have no idea how to do that," I said.

"Me either," said Uncle Jim. "To play it safe, let's use an experienced healer, like Ponytail, to administer the medicine."

"Now that is settled, are you interested in an organic farm in Goshen?" asked Eric.

Goshen is a mix of horse farms and residential subdivisions encroaching on the agricultural way of life.

Ginny looked at me and I nodded.

"Tell me about it," she said.

"There is only eighty-five acres, but the land is rich and mostly level," he said. "Other than five acres of heavy woods on the southern perimeter, the rest is tillable land. The fields were sown with bluegrass earlier this spring."

"Aaawk, maybe I'm color blind, but it has never looked blue to me," said Bird.

We all nodded our agreement. There is quite a bit of poetic license with the whole bluegrass thing.

"Is there anything else you can tell us about the place?" asked Ginny.

"Let's see, there is a two story farmhouse, painted white with a white porch swing hanging from the wrap-around porch," said Eric. "It has a barn with eight stalls, a large greenhouse and indoor hydroponics."

I raised an eyebrow.

"What did they use the indoor hydroponics for?" asked Ginny.

"The prior owner used the popularity of organic food as a cover for his marijuana operation," answered Eric. "When the DEA busted him, they tried to seize the farm, but his family had strong political connections and while they could not keep the drug dealer out of jail, they did save the farm."

"Ginny, you want a place with a good vibe and clean soil, so how do feel about a farm that was used to grow weed?" I asked.

"It's legal in California and many other states are following the trend to legalize it," said Ginny.

"There is growing evidence weed is both safe and effective medicine," I said.

"Well, it's still illegal in Kentucky and the farm's history has pushed the selling price well below market," said Eric.

"Is it available for a quick sale?" asked Ginny.

"If you have cash you could close the deal in a few hours," said Eric.

"What's the asking price?" asked Ginny.

"$1,300,000.00," answered Eric.

"What's wrong with it?" she asked.

"Other than the drug history, not a thing," said Eric.

"That seems low to me, but I'm accustomed to California prices" said Ginny.

"When can we look at it?" I asked.

"It's dark now, but we can swing by at first light, if you want," said Eric."

CHAPTER 52

We fell in love with the place and closed the sale the next day. Normally, a real estate transaction is time consuming because of the lending process. Thanks to Ginny's cash, a lender was not required, so we had a deed and keys within a few hours of our first viewing.

Since Pathogen was looking for us, the first thing I did was set up a series of shell corporations to hide our activities. I knew Goth would eventually find us, but we only needed to buy enough time to jump-start the enterprise.

We planned to avoid contact with the neighbors, not because we are anti-social, but because our lives were in danger and we didn't want to reveal our location to the bad guys. More importantly, we wanted to settle into our new life together without unnecessary distractions.

Since things rarely go as planned, our isolation didn't last long. We spent the first night in a nest made with old blankets and sleeping bags. The next morning as we were having coffee in the kitchen and discussing our planting strategy, we were interrupted by loud banging at the back door.

"Who could it be at 6:00 a.m.?" whispered Ginny.

I shrugged.

She looked at me in the strangest way. There was a tear in her eye that told me something was afoot.

"Are you okay?" I asked.

She nodded and rose from her seat. I expected her to answer the door, but instead she brushed the morning hair back from me forehead and kissed me.

"I got a glimpse of our future in that shrug," she said.

"I don't understand," I said. "Was it a bad thing?"

She shook her head.

"No it's something you see old married couples do all the time," she said. "I want us to have a long and happy marriage together. If we're lucky, then one day we'll be an old married couple too."

I held her tight until our early morning visitor pounded on the door a second time. With a growl I released my future bride and stomped to the door. The unwelcomed visitor must have heard the footsteps because the banging stopped just as I yanked the door open.

I'm not sure what I expected, but the door's beat down came from a tiny blue haired grandmother with matching blue eyes, who couldn't have been more that 4'10". She wore a sky blue jogging suit and pristine white sneakers.

"Can I help you?" I asked.

She peered at me with such intensity; I almost forgot who was doing the interrupting. When she finished her evaluation of me, her attention shifted to Ginny. I thought for moment she had something to say about Ginny's bare left hand, but she moved on. It wasn't until she finished sizing us up did she finally speak.

"I'm Delores Boone," she said in a deep voice that suggested she might be a heavy smoker.

Resisting the temptation to bark at her, I asked politely, "What can we do for you Delores?"

"I want you to get your drug dealing asses out of my neighborhood before I call the police and have you sent away like the last fucking drug dealer who lived here," she said in a voice loud enough for anyone within a quarter mile to hear.

"Drug dealers…I…don't understand," I stammered.

She shook a bony blue veined finger with a stained nail in my face and said, "You've been warned."

Without another word, she turned on her heel, and stomped off. Despite the shock, I noticed a hitch in her movements. I am not a doctor, but it looked like she was favoring her left hip. I figured her restricted range of motion was most likely caused by arthritis and I knew just what to give her, but it wasn't time yet, and besides, the old bat just threatened us.

"What do you make of that?" asked Ginny.

"If she calls the police, then we will need to move our launch date up before Pathogen finds us," I answered.

"We have nothing to launch yet," said Ginny.

"I know we're not ready," I said. "Success depends on our ability to reach the greatest number of people at once."

"That number would be zero at the moment," said Ginny.

"Yea, we're getting way ahead of ourselves here, but we may have to do something," I said. "As tiny as that old bat might be, I've got a feeling she is formidable and we sure as hell don't need another enemy stirring up trouble."

Ginny cleared her throat and gave me one of those looks as she said, "Old bat?"

"You're right, that was rude of me," I said.

"How do we turn Delores into an ally?" asked Ginny.

"She walks with a slight hitch," I answered.

Ginny's eyes lit up.

"We win her over with the gift of healing," she said.

"Let's give her something she desperately wants," I said.

"I like it!" exclaimed Ginny.

"If it works, then we might be able to make her the face of our Great Mother campaign," I said.

"A new lease on life for arthritic grandmother's the world over," said Ginny.

"They would be hard pressed to try to take that away, don't you think?" I asked.

Ginny had a twinkle in her eye when she said, "You are particularly sexy when your genius comes out."

We giggled like naughty teenagers as we made our way to the bedroom in the back of the house. You have to love the honeymoon phase of a relationship, but a harsh voice echoing in the hall spoiled the mood.

"Crap," I groaned.

"Why are your pants chanting bah humbugs?" asked Ginny.

"Umm, it's a new ringtone," I answered

"Really…and who put a lump of coal in your Christmas stocking?" she asked.

"It's a bill collector calling about Mom's nursing home account," I said.

"Interesting choice of ringtones," she said with a raised eyebrow.

I nodded.

"Are you going to answer it?" she asked.

It was the sixth call in the last twenty-four hours. I needed to deal with this and can be fearless when I'm advocating for a client, but sometimes fall short when it comes to facing my own shit as evidenced by the churning in my gut.

I wanted to answer the call in a manly deep voice, but it didn't work out that way.

"Umm…hell…hello," I croaked.

"Mr. Grant Li, we have been trying to reach you over the telephone about your delinquent account," said a woman in an accent that told me she was from India.

I started to say, "Yea…about that," but she interrupted me.

"We most regret to inform you that your mother's room has been reassigned," she said.

"Reassigned…I don't understand," I said.

I knew exactly what she meant, but stalled for time in the hopes of pulling a rabbit out of my hat. I didn't want to discuss this within ear shot of Ginny and turned to ask her if I could have a few minutes of privacy, but she was nowhere in sight.

Letting out a long sigh of relief, I waited for the caller to provide more information about Mom, but she had stopped talking.

"You must be mistaken," I said. "We have until the end of the month."

She didn't respond.

"Hello," I said. "Are you still there?"

Silence.

The nursing home's actions were forcing me to act now and I figured I had two choices. One was to borrow money from Ginny to pay them off right now, but it embarrassed me and I felt like a loser even considering it.

The other option was to slip past Pathogen's spies and give Mom the medicine. If it worked, then we could walk out of there together. That would really be something, but a stab of conscience reminded me that I had agreed to wait until we had an established crop.

My thoughts were interrupted by a shout from Ginny.

"Grant!"

It sounded like it was coming from out back near the greenhouse, so I rushed out to see what the fuss was all about. As I neared the building, I could see her standing inside. Her back was to me and she was staring at the table where we had put Great Mother.

I felt a wave of fear because I couldn't see the seedling. Did Goth steal it during the night?

As I bolted into the greenhouse, she stepped aside and pointed at a plant that must have been four feet tall. My worst fear had come true. Someone took the seedling, but why would they replace it with this other plant. How could anyone ever think we would be tricked into believing this was the same plant? It was too ridiculous to consider.

"What happened to Great Mother?" I asked.

"She grew," said Ginny.

"That's impossible," I said.

"You can see for yourself," she said

"The seedling wasn't more than four inches tall last night, so this can't be the same plant," I said.

She handed me her cell phone.

"Yeah, that's what I thought too, but look at this," she said.

It was a picture of the seedling.

"All this does is prove my point," I said.

"Look more closely," she said.

I'm no botanist, but the leaves looked similar. I turned my attention to the simple red clay pot. There were faint markings around the rim. I zoomed in and saw that a snake eating bird was etched into the clay. I bent down and peered at the pot in front of me and realized it was the same pot.

"How can...how can this be?" I asked.

"I searched the internet to see if there are any other fast growing plants," said Ginny.

"What did you find?" I asked.

"Bamboo can grow up to three feet a day," she said.

"Bamboo?" I said.

She nodded.

"Do you know what this means?" she asked.

"This plant is the Great Mother seedling that we were given yesterday," I said.

Ginny smiled.

"What else?" she asked.

"This isn't going to take as long as we feared," I said.

"And?" she asked.

"Mom...it means...it means we don't have to wait to give it to Mom," I said.

Ginny's smile grew until it took up her whole face.

I threw my arms around her and squeezed as tight as I could without hurting her. She squeezed back even harder. It felt good like a deep tissue massage. We hugged each other for several minutes, squeezing out all of the fear and replacing it with love.

"As soon as my brother returns, we can ask him to heal her," said Ginny.

"Umm...about that," I said. "That call I got earlier from the nursing home...umm...they've reassigned her room. We need to do something now."

"We don't know what we're doing," said Ginny. "What if we do more harm than good?"

"Maybe Ch'ing will know," I said.

"While you call him, I'll try to reach Marguerite," said Ginny. "Maybe one of them can help us."

Neither answered their phones. We were running out of options.

"Without proper medical care, Mom's life is at risk," I said.

"Let's pinch off a small piece of leaf and make her a tea," suggested Ginny.

"She's in a coma, so she won't be able to drink it," I said.

"Does she have an IV?" asked Ginny.

I nodded.

"Last time I saw her, she did," I answered.

"We could add the tea to her IV, a syringe at a time until she awakens," suggested Ginny.

"Do you think it's safe?" I asked.

"I don't know, Grant, but it has worked miracles for us," answered Ginny.

"Let's make the tea and take it to the nursing home," I said. "Once we're there, we can assess the situation and make a decision then."

"If you don't mind, I would like to stay and do some research," said Ginny. "I want to get up to speed on agricultural techniques. We need to get this plant in the ground as soon as possible."

I made the tea and then rushed to the nursing home hoping this plan would work. I consider myself a generally positive person, but the minute I walked into Shady Days I knew something was wrong.

It began with the receptionist, Ginger. Without fail, I smile, wave and say hello when I'm there for visits. In return, she tells me how Mom is doing and I then ask if she needs anything. It has been our little ritual for years.

I did my usual thing, but Ginger pretended to study a piece of paper from her desk. I stopped in my tracks and turned to make sure she was okay, but Ginger picked up the telephone and spoke to someone in hushed tones while casting a furtive glance in my direction.

Trying to shake off the growing sense of unease, I headed down the hall toward my mother's room. I saw Roxanne headed my way, but when she saw me she abruptly stopped and slipped through a doorway on her left.

When I got to the door, I noticed the nameplate said it was a custodial closet. I thought about knocking, but the prospect of confronting Roxanne was distasteful and a growing panic pushed me onward to mother's room instead.

It wasn't much further and only took less than a minute. Her door was closed, so I knocked before entering. I'm not sure why I did that, other than respect for her, since Mom wasn't capable of answering. As I feared, the room was empty.

It took every ounce of will power to keep from rushing out in a panic. Instead, I stood at the foot of her empty bed and took a few minutes to take a calming breath or two. When I finally felt relaxed, I considered the possible explanations for her absence. Unfortunately, none of them seemed plausible since this had never happened before.

I was just about to head out to the administrator's office when the door opened and a man came in with a mop and bucket. He studied me closely, but said nothing.

"Where is my mother?" I asked.

He shook his head.

"Did they move her to another room?" I asked.

He shook his head a second time.

"What happened to her?" I asked

He stopped mopping and said, "They lost her."

Losing someone you love is never easy, but how does a coma patient just disappear. It was too impossible to consider seriously. Mop Guy had to be pulling my leg.

He appeared to be in his late fifties, with a potbelly and more salt than pepper in the remnants of a head of hair. He was wearing white cotton, except for the shoes. They were glossy black patent leather with rubber soles.

The odd thing was the suntan. People who work indoors rarely have suntans. You might occasionally see them with a Monday morning burn, but rarely a tan. Then I noticed something else odd. His clothes still had packaging creases, so they had to be brand new. None of this added up, but when I saw he was making awkward mopping sweeps with a dry mop and wore a gold Rolex watch, I knew this guy wasn't a janitor.

"You're not really a janitor, are you?" I asked.

He froze. Slowly his head lifted and the instant I saw his eyes I knew an attack was coming. Mop Guy simultaneously kicked the empty bucket toward my ankles and flipped the mop directly into my eyes.

Both were diversions. He quickly closed the gap and threw a hard uppercut intended for my solar plexus. If the punch had landed, it would have knocked the air out and left me helpless. Instead, I caught the mop and redirected it in a tight curve that swept around his hip and then smashed upward into his groin.

He let out a loud groan and grabbed his junk to protect it from further blows. While he was preoccupied, I swept his weighted foot and took him to the ground, face first. Positioning myself with a view of the door, I jammed a knee into his lower back, and cranked his right wrist up his spine as high as it would go.

I know it hurt like hell, but he did not scream. Instead, he let out a sharp grunt and then began to breathe deeply. The guy was clearly a pro and I doubted he would tell me anything, but I asked anyway.

"Who do you work for?" I said in a low hard voice.

He said nothing. I checked his pockets. They were empty. I cranked the arm a little higher and heard a bone crack. Another grunt was his only reaction.

"Who took my mother?" I asked.

More silence. I was not sure what to do next. Torture is not my thing. All I wanted was find my mother. Voices outside the door forced a decision. Just before they opened the door, I released him.

On my way out I said, "The janitor slipped on the wet floor and hurt himself."

I quickly headed for the exit, but then decided to change directions and confront the administrative director. I figured Mop Guy did not work at Shady Days, but would backup my cover story to buy himself time to get out of the building.

Alexi Minted was sitting at her desk when I barged in. Even though she cannot be more than thirty-eight, her retro afro looked like it was styled in the late sixties. Other than the hair, she was all 21st century style with a sharp grey business suit, white blouse, and designer glasses.

"Mr. Li, you're just the man I wanted to see," she said.

"I want to talk to you about my mother," I said.

"There are a few discharge papers that still need to be signed," she said.

"Discharge?" I asked.

"We missed a couple of them, with the rush and all," she said. "You know the government…they love to bury us with paper."

"I don't understand," I said. "I wasn't here earlier."

"Of course you weren't," she said. "It was your friend, Eric Cotungin."

"Eric checked my mother out?" I asked.

"Yes…yes," she said.

"When?" I asked.

"It was a couple of hours ago," she answered.

"Did he say where he was taking her?" I asked.

Alexi's brow pinched.

She cleared her throat and asked, "You don't know?"

I shook my head.

"Ummm…he had a power of attorney from you," she said.

I shook my head.

The panic in her eyes made it clear she was more worried about a lawsuit, than mother. She cut her eyes to the file in front of her and began rifling through the paperwork.

"It was signed by you," she said.

I had the feeling she was rehearsing her defense for a judge. She found it and triumphantly pushed it across the desk to me.

I looked at it. It was not my signature and shook my head.

"Try comparing the signature with something in the file you know I signed," I said.

She didn't bother.

Instead she tried to apologize, "Ummm…I'm a…ummm…I'm a…"

I cut her apology off and asked, "Did he say where they were going?" I asked again.

"Ummm…let me look," she said.

While Alexi rifled through the paperwork, I wondered why Eric would he do such a thing.

"Here it is," said Alexi. "She's headed to a lab run by Pathogen. I think he mentioned something about an experimental treatment."

CHAPTER 53

When nothing makes any sense, return to base and regroup. The drive back to the farm was a blur of meaningless unfocused images and thoughts. I do remember thinking just before the wreck that I needed to fix the broken spring nipping at my behind.

Ginny bought a new truck for use on the farm, but I'm partial to Dad's. Despite the frequent repairs, the old girl still gets me where I need to go. At least she does on most days.

I didn't see the crotch rocket until it locked its brakes and swerved to avoid a mirage up ahead in the road. The last image as I ditched the old Ford was a streak of black on the highway. It came with the smell of burnt rubber riding a cloud of smoke. As a fellow biker, I said a quick prayer for the dumb ass on the motorcycle just before I blacked-out.

It's hard to say how long I was out, but when I finally opened my eyes the sun was high above the Ohio River bridges and the Belle of Louisville, loaded with the matinee cruisers, paddled upstream. I was sitting in the passenger seat of a Jaguar that smelled as if it was just off the showroom floor. I don't know how it got there, but dad's truck was parked a few spaces away.

I didn't recognize the car, but I knew the place. We were on the bank of the Ohio River at Cox Park. The boat ramp was empty except for a solitary fisherman fighting the strong current to get his bass boat onto a trailer. I imagined he was headed home to a cold cut sandwich and chips rather than fried fish. Few are brave enough to eat the fish pulled from the river.

Next to me sat a pudgy man dressed in an expensive blue suit. In contrast to the fine clothes, Mr. Suit's face was covered with surgical tape used to reset a broken nose. Despite the swelling and heavy bruising, I recognized him as the asshole who strapped me to a table in the mental health ward and threatened to torture me to get something I didn't have. Eric busted in and shattered the guy's face as we made our escape.

"Glad to see you're finally awake, Mr. Li," he said.

I didn't think for a minute it was a coincidence that he has shown up right after Mom disappeared from the nursing home. Still, I was having a hard time imagining why Eric was now in league with the likes of this scum.

Since Mr. Suit is the best lead I have to find Mom, I set aside my feelings of betrayal and planned to do whatever it takes to get him to talk, beginning with slamming that broken nose on the steering wheel to remind him who's in charge. The plan changed when I heard the unmistakable sound of a hammer pulling back and felt cold steel pressed into the back of my head, just below the hairline.

I sighed and slowly raised a hand to pinch the bridge of my nose in hopes of softening a massive headache.

A deep voice growled from the back seat, "Easy."

I decided to let the headache run its course and dropped my hands.

"What do you want?" I asked.

"I want to make you a very rich man," said Mr. Suit.

That was the last thing I expected to hear.

"We both know that's bullshit," I said. "You don't give a damn about me."

"I'd just as soon kill you, but you have something my employer will pay a lot of money for," he said.

"The evidence against Pathogen?" I asked.

He gave me cold hard stare down.

"You've read the memos?" he asked.

The cold steel pressed a little harder.

"No, but it's the only thing that makes any sense," I said.

He sighed.

"That's a part of it, but you've managed to acquire something else he has wanted for years," said Mr. Suit.

"My devilish good looks?" I asked.

Mr. Suit sighed.

"You're not James Bond, so don't insult us with your childish humor," he said. "He wants exclusive rights to the medicine you brought from the rainforest."

"It's a wild plant," I said. "How do you own mother nature?"

"Really?" he said. "You're a lawyer. We use smoke and mirrors. What else is the law but that?"

"Use a legal fiction," I muttered.

"All property law is a legal fiction," said Mr. Suit.

"What exactly are you proposing?" I asked.

"We pretend you hold the patent rights to the plant and you sell them to my employer," he said.

"What does your employer plan to do with Great Mother?" I asked.

"Is that what you call it…how quaint," he said.

"It's what they call it in the Amazon Rainforest," I said. "What are you going to do with the medicine?"

"Why, get filthy rich, of course," he answered.

"More bullshit," I said. "Pathogen is already filthy rich. This medicine will put you out of business."

"I've been authorized to offer you one billion dollars," said Mr. Suit. "You can buy yourself an island, or mountain, or whatever else your heart desires with that kind of money."

I wish I could tell you that I told him to shove it, but I didn't. The truth is, I was stunned by the obscene amount of money and couldn't help but think about the lifestyle it would provide. When I was finally able to speak, I didn't say what I knew needed to be said without any hesitation. Instead, I stalled for time.

"I don't know what to say," I said.

"The correct response is, I accept," said Mr. Suit.

I swallowed hard.

"I...I...umm..." I stammered.

"Do you accept, yes or no?" asked Mr. Suit.

I opened and then closed my mouth several times, without a sound escaping.

"A simple yes will suffice," he said.

A billion dollars is a lot of damn money, and I didn't trust myself to speak. So, I locked my lips and stared at the driftwood floating down the river like lost souls that had hit rock bottom. After a few minutes of this stalemate, Mr. Suit changed tactics.

"I tell you what, Mr. Li," he began. "You have Mr. Goth's private cell, call him when you come to your senses and are ready to make a better life for yourself."

With the smuggest of looks, Mr. Suit reached across and opened the car door to dismiss me.

"Don't delay too long, Mr. Li," he said. "Circumstances can change and generous offers can be revoked."

I looked into his cold arrogant eyes and asked, "What's your name?"

He shook a finger and dismissed me with a subtle movement of the eyes toward the open door.

I climbed out of the Jaguar without saying another word and headed for dad's pickup.

When I started her up, I heard a voice repeating, "A billion dollars...a billion dollars..."

An engine backfire from the old Ford sent a puff of blue smoke in the direction of the Jaguar just as it drove off with an air of imperial elegance and entitlement. I pointed the truck in the opposite direction.

At first, I thought the vibration might be a flat tire, but then I realized it was my hands shaking hard on the steering wheel. Plenty was happening and it was coming hard and fast.

Meditation has taught me to focus on a simple task, like breathing, and let everything else fall away. The task was to get home safely and not lead any bad guys to our sanctuary. Fortunately, our new home isn't far from the river park. I shifted attention back and forth between the lines on the road and closely watching the rearview mirror to make certain no one was following.

It went pretty well, except I nearly missed the turn off. The old farmhouse sits off the road a good piece and is far enough back, that you cannot see it from the road. The privacy it offers is one of the things we like most about the place. As I rounded the last curve in the long gravel drive from the highway, I saw Eric's car sitting in front of the house.

Eric is brash. His choices do not always make sense at first, but he has always been a good friend to me. I like to think I have the ability to see the good in every situation. As I parked the truck next to Eric's car, I made up my mind that he must have had a good reason for what he did and I was damn well going to be open to it.

Despite my good intentions, I stormed into the house ready to demand an explanation, but instead of my best friend, I found his wife, Kinsey, sobbing on Ginny's shoulder.

She and Eric have been together since freshman year. Kinsey is tall and thin. Her only soft parts are the C-cups she picked up in New York during a modeling stint and a heart of pure gold that she's had as long as I've known her.

Strands of damp strawberry blond hair clung to her cheeks. For an instant, there was a glimmer of hope in her puffy eyes until she realized it was only me standing in the doorway. I didn't take it personally when they quickly filled with despair and she returned to the comfort of Ginny's shoulder.

"Umm…is everything okay?" I asked.

Kinsey shook her head without looking up. I shifted attention to Ginny, who had a wild-eyed look that left me wondering what this was all about. Instead of answering my question, she stood there stroking the back of Kinsey's head as if it was the most important thing at the moment.

As I stood in the foyer of that old farmhouse watching the love of my life comfort my best friend's wife, I wondered how my life had become such a mix of horrible and wonderful. The drama was getting old. I desperately needed happily ever after, but it sure wasn't coming on this day.

"Any chance you can fill me in on what's going on?" I asked hopefully.

Kinsey's sobbing subsided. Dabbing her eyes with a tissue, she sat up straight and squared her shoulders. It looked like she was about to speak, but instead she took a ragged breath, and then another one. When she finally managed to get it out, her voice was low, almost a whisper.

"It's Eric," said Kinsey.

My stomach turned and a mantra began running in my head, "What the fuck…what the fuck…what the fuck…"

Her voice got a little stronger, "He's lost his way."

"What do you mean, he's lost his way?" I asked.

"He disappears for long periods of time," she said.

I was tempted to say something harsh like, what do you expect from this crazy open-marriage crap, but held my tongue. Despite their conservative upbringing, they chose a life of debauchery. While they claim all of the kinky behavior strengthens their marriage, I have a hard time believing it.

"When I ask Eric where he's been, he gets vague and defensive," said Kinsey. "I thought he might be seeing someone, but we tell each other everything and always share."

"So you think it might be something else?" I asked.

Kinsey nodded.

"Do you have any idea what it might be?" asked Ginny.

"A large deposit was recently made to our account," answered Kinsey.

"Is that unusual?" asked Ginny.

"It's the largest I've ever seen," answered Kinsey.

"How much was it?" I asked.

"One and half million dollars," she said.

"Damn!" I said. "Why is that a bad thing?"

"I didn't recognize the source of the funds," she said.

"What did Eric say about it?" asked Ginny.

"We have a new client who pays well and should just be grateful for it," answered Kinsey.

"That doesn't sound like Eric," I said.

Kinsey nodded grimly.

"Don't you run the accounts department?" asked Ginny.

It's no secret that Kinsey is the brains behind their successful business. After graduating with honors from a tough business program, Kinsey set out to build a first rate business with Eric, who was working as a bouncer in a biker bar. Thanks to her shrewd marketing skills, their security company grew rapidly.

"Yes I interface with all of our clients, but have never dealt with this company," answered Kinsey.

"Who is it?" I asked.

"NWO Lab," she said.

'It sounds familiar," I said.

"I had to look them up," she said. "NWO is an acronym for New World Order."

"Interesting…there are people who believe that a group of rich bankers are running a worldwide shadow government called the New World Order," said Ginny.

"I don't know anything about that, but I did do some more digging because of the huge sum of money involved," said Kinsey.

"Did you discover anything of interest?" asked Ginny.

"NWO Lab is a subsidiary of Pathogen," answered Kinsey.

"Pathogen!" said Ginny. "You were paid one and half million dollars by Pathogen! For what?"

Kinsey shrugged.

"Did you ask Eric?" asked Ginny.

Kinsey's eyes filled with tears.

"I haven't seen him for two days," she said.

"We saw him at Uncle Jim's last night," said Ginny.

"He was there?" asked Kinsey.

We both nodded.

"Did he say anything about where he's been?" asked Kinsey.

"He was in South America with us," I said. "Have you seen him since he got home?"

She nodded.

"That's when it all started," said Kinsey. "He's been off key ever since he got back."

"Eric has always had a touch of tone deafness, but it gets worse," I said.

"How can it get worse than this?" asked Kinsey.

"I just came from the nursing home," I said.

"Oh, I almost forgot," said Ginny. "Did you give your mom the tea?"

I shook my head.

"Why not?" asked Ginny.

"She's missing," I said.

"What do you mean she's missing?" said Ginny.

"Eric signed her out of the facility," I said.

"Eric!" said Kinsey. "How could he even do that?"

"He used a fake power of attorney," I said.

"Why would he do that?" asked Ginny.

I shrugged.

"Where did he take her?" asked Ginny.

"To a Pathogen lab for experimental treatment," I answered.

"Do you think it's the same lab," asked Ginny.

I nodded. There wasn't much value in sugar coating the grim reality of Eric's treacherous behavior.

"Umm…Grant, there's something else you need to know," said Ginny.

I didn't like the sound of that at all. So far, our first day back home had turned out to be a real bummer.

"It can't get any worse than this, can it?" I said.

Ginny's expression was grim.

"The seedling is missing," she said.

"Yeah, I know, it's hard to call it a seedling since it's growing like crazy," I said.

She shook her head.

"It's not in the greenhouse were we left it," said Ginny.

"It didn't just get up and walk away," I said.

"I think someone took it," said Ginny.

"Took it?" I said.

She nodded.

"Who would do that?" I asked.

"You know the answer to that," said Ginny.

Eric was the prime suspect in my mind, but I pressed my lips tight and said nothing.

Kinsey started praying softly between the sobs, "Please God…please God…"

When I couldn't handle Kinsey's sobs any longer without surrendering to my own growing panic, I turned toward the door with the intention of going out for some fresh air, but found Ginny blocking my path. She looked worried.

I tried to shift my gaze to the door, but she locked her eyes onto mine and refused to let them go without a fight. For the first time, I didn't want her to see me and tried my best to disappear.

Finally, she asked the question I was dreading, "What aren't you telling me, Grant?"

I told myself and then I told her I was just worried about Mom, but that was just a damn lie and we both knew it, because I didn't tell Ginny about Pathogen's offer to buy Great Mother.

CHAPTER 54

Eric betrayed us. He kidnapped Mom, and then delivered her, along with the seedling, to Pathogen. It was a painful blow and I did what I always do after a setback, I adjusted the plan and then focused on achieving the goal.

The plan was to give Mom the medicine as soon as the crop was stable. Our only plant was gone and Mom no longer had access to a ventilator. I gave up on the plan to give her the medicine and just focused on the need to find her before her lungs collapsed.

Besides, who knows what Pathogen would do to her. Most likely, Goth would try to leverage her to get what he wanted from me. Except I no longer had what he wanted. Once Goth is certain he no longer needs her, then Mom's prospects of survival get significantly worse. I needed to find her and time was running short.

The first task was to locate NOW Lab. Hopefully, Mom would be there. Kinsey wasn't much help. Her company files listed a post office box as the lab's mailing address, so I searched the internet instead.

NWO Lab's website is nothing more than a slick marketing brochure and doesn't reveal anything useful, like the company's physical location. It did provide a phone number, but it connects to an elaborate system of menus and never to a live person. The only way to communicate with them is via email. Maybe I'm old-school in my thinking, but it seems to me a reputable company should have basic contact information available on their website.

I searched the Kentucky Secretary of State's corporate records and learned NOW Lab maintains an office on East Jefferson Street. The area is a mix of ghetto and expanding healthcare facilities. Crime is so bad that medical staff park in a garage connected by secured overhead tunnels to the surrounding medical complex.

The other thing I learned from the public records sent a chill up my spine. Wilbur Goth is listed as the company President and he is hell-bent on stopping us by any means possible, including murder. Goth sent Victor to kill us in Brazil and that bastard was crazy enough to follow us into a whirlpool of liquid death just to make the kill.

These people are crazy dangerous, so I can't send anyone else to the lab. It had to be me, and even though I planned to go alone, I wasn't without help. Kinsey pulled herself together and set up a stakeout of Pathogen's corporate offices. Ginny was in a mood and would only tell us she had some business that needed her attention.

As I headed west on US 42, there was time to mull everything over. I couldn't help but think there was something about all of this that didn't stack up right, but I couldn't put a finger on it.

When I got into Prospect, I turned onto River Road and took the scenic drive along the Ohio River into downtown Louisville. The only boat on the river was an empty coal barge pushing upstream toward Cincinnati.

At Waterfront Park, I cut over to Butchertown, drove past the old meat packing plant and then hung a left onto Jefferson Street. Even though it was the middle of a hot and humid summer, the first person I saw was a homeless woman bundled in layers of dirty clothes pushing a banged up old grocery cart that was loosely packed with her worldly possessions.

She turned in my direction and I caught a glimpse of her dark vacant eyes set deep into a face stretched tight by hunger and illness. She seemed lost and forgotten like the empty buildings she shuffled past on her journey through desperation.

The lab was located in a nondescript brick four-story box. I had driven past it many times without paying it any mind. There were no windows and the only thing that identified it as a business was a 6" x 10" bronze plaque hanging at eye level that announced NOW Lab in two inch lettering.

I checked the door and found it securely locked. There was no doorbell or knocker that I could see. I raised a knuckle, but thought better of it, and decided instead, to walk around and see if there was another entrance to the building.

The left side of the lab was attached to the adjoining building, an abandoned three story that smelled of squatter piss and shit. A grey sidewalk led around the right side, but an eight-foot iron gate at the corner barred the way.

I would have to go around the block and come up the alley if I wanted to try the rear of the building, but given the security gate, I figured the rear was equally well secured. So instead, I went back to the front door and rapped on it.

No one answered. I tried again, but still no answer. Thinking three might be a charm, I banged hard with the palm of my hand. Just as I was about to give up and leave, the door creaked open about four inches and then stopped.

I waited, but nothing else happened.

"Hello, is there anyone there?" I said.

No one answered.

I pushed the door and was surprised how heavy it felt. It inched forward, so I pressed against it as hard as I could, but the extra effort didn't make a bit of difference. The door moved at its own pace, as if it had a mind of its own. When it finally opened enough for me to squeeze through, it stopped. I did what anybody in my shoes would do, I made myself as small as I could and squeezed inside.

The only light came from the open door, but it was enough to tell me the place was empty. At least I thought it was empty until I heard a creaking floorboard somewhere upstairs. I held my breath and listened, but heard nothing else.

I used the flashlight app on my phone to cast light into the dark corners of the front room. There was nothing I could see other than a heavy layer of dust disturbed by three sets of footprints. The smaller prints were made by bare feet.

This is not what I expected to find here. I could turn around and leave, but this was the only lead we had and I feared time was running short. There was nothing to do but follow the tracks and see where they lead, so that's exactly what I did.

No matter how hard I tried to move like a silent ninja, the floor creaked with each step I took. Since stealth was out of the question, I decided to try a different tactic and called out.

"It's okay," I said. "You can come out of the shadows."

I waited for an answer, but heard nothing other than a slight echo. The footprints led up a narrow staircase. There were none leading down. As far as I could see, the dust was undisturbed elsewhere. I added my own prints to the mix as I crept slowly up the steps.

The tracks stopped at the top of the stairs. The floor was clean of dust and polished to a brilliant sheen. This wasn't making any sense, so I paused and listened for any sound that would tell me where to look next.

At first, the place was as quiet as a mausoleum, but then I heard a muffled moan. At least, I think I heard it. It was so faint that I second-guessed myself thinking it might be my imagination.

There was a door to my left that was slightly ajar. A beam of light escaped through the crack. I slowly pushed it open and was flooded with blinding light from a large floor to ceiling east facing window. I caught a glimpse of office furnishings and something far more chilling just as I shielded my eyes from the painful light.

It was a woman tied to a side chair. She was barefooted and dressed in a pale nightgown. Her back was to me, so I didn't see her face. I heard footsteps and a door opened and then slammed shut. I was torn in two directions and the moment of indecision cost me big time.

The only warning of the blow to the back of my head was the faint rustle of fabric. I'm not sure how long I was out, but I awoke on the front stoop. I tried the door, but it wouldn't budge an inch.

My phone, car keys and wallet were missing, but the thief did leave me with a headache. Dad's truck was no longer parked at the curb. I hurried down the alley, hoping to stop any escape out the back, but saw no one. There was a ground level door that was locked tight. Cast iron stairs painted black led to a second story door that was also locked. I nearly lost my footing and fell from the second story landing thanks to a wave of dizziness. I was out of ideas and needed rest, so I decided to call it quits for the day. There was nothing to do but to walk to the interstate ramp and hitchhike home.

Standing at the curb with my thumb out gave me a lot of time to think since no one seemed interested in giving me a lift. Who was the woman and why didn't they just leave me inside after the robbery? I was out cold, so they could have easily escaped. It didn't make sense to drag me outside and risk getting caught, unless there was still something inside they didn't want me to see. I needed to get back inside that building.

I was just thinking about going back and pounding on the door, when a bleary-eyed nurse coming off a double shift rolled down her window and said, "Bad neighborhood to be hitchhiking. Where you headed?"

"I'm not sure," I answered.

"Join the club," she said.

"I'm ummm…"

"There's blood on your collar," she said.

I felt the back of my head. It was still damp, so I hadn't been unconscious too long.

"Somebody robbed me," I said.

"Did you call the police?" she asked.

"They took my mobile," I answered.

"You want to use mine?" she asked.

I shook my head.

"I'm a nurse," she said. "I can help with that cut."

"I've had worse," I said.

"Do you have a headache?" she asked.

I felt a wave of dizziness and threw up.

"Could be a concussion," she said.

I wiped my mouth with the back of my hand and tried my best to focus on her face.

"Where is home?' she asked.

"Goshen," I answered.

"Hop in," she said. "I'm headed to River Bluff."

She was driving a late model Honda Civic that proudly announced it was a Hybrid. Other than a car seat covered in baby vomit, the back seat was full of fast food wrappers and a half empty box of diapers. The front seat was only slightly cleaner.

I climbed into the passenger seat and said, "You're taking a big risk picking up a stranger."

"You look harmless to me," she said.

"Thanks, but that's the last thing a man wants to hear from a beautiful woman," I said.

She looked at me long and hard like I might be full of shit before saying, "Let me see that cut."

The nurse in her took charge. She turned me enough to see the back of my head, pressed the area around it, and grunted.

"Yeah, you need stitches," she said. "I better take you to the ER,"

"No, thanks, just take me home," I said.

"Suit yourself," she said. "Can't say I blame you since hospitals are where people go to die."

"I'm Grant," I said.

"Like the dead President?" she asked.

I nodded.

"They call me Lindsey," she said.

She chattered the rest of the way about her job at the hospital. It was mostly negative. I had a lot on my mind and just listened with an occasional grunt thrown in for good measure.

I figured Lindsey would drop me at her turn off from US 42, but she drove past it. I may have tensed a little and started to say something, but she beat me to it.

"Relax, there's no need for you to walk the rest of the way in your condition," she said.

"Thanks," was all I said.

"Besides, I have a sick child at home and no one to talk to," she said.

Her hands clinched the wheel a little too tight. Lindsey wasn't wearing a ring, but I noticed slight change in color where a ring had been recently.

"Is the illness serious?" I asked.

"I'm a mother," she said. "Any illness is serious."

"What does the doctor say?" I asked.

"I work every day, side by side, with a bunch of overeducated doctors and not one of those assholes knows what's wrong with her," she said.

"Take the next right," I said. "It's the gravel drive in the middle of that patch of woods."

"I see it," said Lindsey.

"Have you tried alternative medicine?" I asked.

"At this point, I'd try anything," she answered.

"You can park anywhere in front of the house," I said.

Ginny and Kinsey were sitting on the porch enjoying a glass of lemonade.

"Nice place," she said.

"Thanks, you want a glass of lemonade?" I asked.

As an answer to my question, she asked, "Do you have anything stronger?"

"I'm sure we do," I said. "Let me introduce you and then I'll see what I can rustle up."

"I can introduce myself," she said. "I'll take a closer look at your noggin once I have that drink in hand."

Ginny tensed when I leaned in to kiss her and asked, "Any luck?"

I shook my head and then left the girls to get to know each other while I poured a generous two fingers of our best bourbon. After recapping the bottle, I stood at the kitchen sink and looked out over our new farm. It was beautiful land, but the crop was missing. We had planned to make cuttings and root them in water before moving them from the greenhouse. First, we had to find the missing plant or there would be nothing to grow.

It had not been a good day. I felt another headache coming on and absent-mindedly reached for the bourbon glass and took a sip. I nearly spit the liquid out, but my body wouldn't allow it, and instead, gulped the drink like hungry newborn.

I'm no fool. I knew right off it wasn't bourbon and took a closer look at the glass. The damn thing was full of water and new roots from a small cutting sticking about an inch over the rim. Ginny must have made the first cutting before the plant was stolen.

The bourbon was still sitting on the counter, undisturbed. I had picked up the wrong glass. Damn if there wasn't hope after all. Feeling much better, I took our guest her drink and was happy to find the girls in high spirits.

"Is bourbon okay?" I asked Lindsey.

"Are you kidding me," she answered. "Last time I checked Goshen is a part of Kentucky."

That set the girls off on a round of laughter. When it subsided, Ginny spotted the blood on my collar.

"Honey, what have you done to yourself?" asked Ginny.

"He went and got himself clobbered," said Lindsey. "Since this hard-head refused to go to the ER, maybe I'll stitch it without using anesthesia. Come here and let me get a closer look in this light."

"I feel fine...even great," I said.

"Yea right" she said. "He was throwing up on the side of road when I picked him up. Let's add concussion to the diagnosis."

I winked at Ginny and took a seat next to Lindsey. She took a sip of bourbon before leaning in for a closer look.

"What the fuck," she said. "It's healed already. How could that be?"

CHAPTER 55

After explaining everything to Lindsey, we sent her home with a small vial of the root water for her sick child. Before she left she pulled Kinsey aside. I'm not sure what she said to her, but whatever it was, it worked like a charm. Kinsey got her swagger back.

Insisting we let the pros take over the search for Eric and Mom, Kinsey sent a team to NWO Lab, but the entire building was empty when they got there.

"That's all right, Grant," said Kinsey. "If it were easy, then anybody could do it."

"What are you going to do now?" I asked.

Kinsey opened her laptop and said, "I'm about to do what any loving wife would do under the circumstances. I'm hacking into Eric's GPS. One way or another, I'm going to find my prodigal husband and bring his sorry ass home so I can kick the shit out of it."

In the meantime, Ginny and I had an important job of our own. Considering we only had one little plant and neither of us were gardeners, let alone farmers, spreading Great Mother to the world seemed like a daunting task. We gave ourselves a crash course in organic farming, but as it turned out, our worries about losing the crop proved unwarranted.

Since the cutting had an extensive set of roots, we moved it to the greenhouse. Once in dirt, it took off and grew at a scary fast rate. We worked overtime making new cuttings and within days, the green house was overflowing with seedlings that we moved to the freshly plowed fields.

To our utter amazement, wherever there was disturbed soil, and we had plenty of it thanks to Ginny and the new tractor, Great Mother appeared and flourished. Plowing the fields became one of her favorite tasks. She took to calling it Zen time and fiercely resisted any offer of help. Wearing nothing but a straw hat to keep the freckles at bay, she reminded me of a twenty-first century Lady Godiva streaking through the fields on her John Deere tractor.

We soon had eighty acres of healthy plants, but there are seven and a half billion people in the world. How would we ever serve all of them? We needed help.

I went looking for Ginny to discuss the problem and found her in the kitchen baking. It smelled wonderful. We follow an 80-20 guideline for our meals. Eighty percent of our meals consist of organic fruits, vegetables, nuts and seeds. The other twenty percent is everything else.

We do our best to manage the twenty percent so that we don't fill ourselves with high calorie junk food. Since we do enjoy baked goods, Ginny will often experiment with new recipes that minimizes white sugar, white flour and saturated fats. I could tell by the smell that the cake in the oven contained all of those ingredients.

"What are we having?" I asked.

"Sorry lover, but it's not for us," said Ginny.

"Rats, whoever is getting that mouthwatering cake is lucky," I said.

My face must have shown more disappointment then I intended, because Ginny patted me on the cheek and promised an even better dessert. That perked me up.

"Who's it for?" I asked.

"Our neighbor, Delores Boone," she answered.

"Did you bake any drugs into it?" I asked.

"Just a little Great Mother mixed in with the zucchini," she said with a grin. "I'll also be serving a rare exotic tea from the Amazon Rainforest with the zucchini bread."

"It might backfire if she starts feeling too good," I said.

Ginny frowned as she said, "Yes, I thought of that. Too much change, too fast, might upset her. People like her have spent a lifetime with their various aches and pains. They wear them like an old pair jeans."

"When is she coming?" I asked.

Of course that is the exact moment I heard the sound of Delores' trademark knock. There were three quick raps, followed by one whole breath cycle and then hard pounding that lasted until I opened the door. Our neighbor does not have much patience.

"Took you long enough, didn't it," barked Delores.

There was plenty I wanted to say to her, but instead, I just bit my lip and smiled. I may have bit it a little too hard, because I tasted blood. Just as I was thinking I needed a big slice of that cake to go with the blood, she pushed me aside and walked into our kitchen.

Ginny wiped her hands on an apron before extending a welcoming hand to Delores as she said, "Hello, I'm Ginny Bardough and this is my...fiancée..."

"I know who you are," snapped Delores.

I looked at Ginny and shrugged.

"Welcome to our home," I said through clenched teeth.

"I've been here before," said Delores.

Ginny smiled and said, "Oh, did you know..."

Delores cut her off, "I've known the drug dealer's family for years. My family has been here since the Lewis and Clark expedition."

"Was your family part of the expedition?" I asked.

Her face softened just a tad as she said, "We sent Charles, but he didn't make it back. They buried him in Iowa."

"I don't remember a Boone being in the expedition," I said.

"There wasn't a Boone in the expedition," said Delores. "That is my dead husband's name. My maiden name is Floyd. Sergeant Charles Floyd was a part of the expedition. He kept a journal you know. You have to admire a man who has the good sense to record his experiences for posterity."

I found it interesting she was more proud of her connection to an obscure member of the Lewis and Clark expedition than Kentucky's most famous native, Daniel Boone.

"A journal...humm...I'd like to read it sometime," I said. "You wouldn't happen to have a copy would you?"

Delores peered over the top of her glasses. For the first time she looked at me as if I might be a civilized human being.

"As a matter of fact, I do have a copy that I might lend you," said Delores.

"Thank you," I said with sincerity. "I'm a bit of a history buff and adventurer. One of my particular interests is the Lewis and Clark expedition because of its connection to this area. How did Charles die?"

"No one knows for sure, but we think his appendix busted," she answered.

"If they buried him in Iowa, then it was early in the expedition," I said.

"Yes, just a few months," she said sadly. "He was only twenty-two."

"What a shame...a young man cut down at the onset of the adventure of a lifetime," said Ginny.

"Amen to that sister," said Delores with eyes bloodshot with tears.

"I can only imagine how wild and primitive it was then," said Ginny.

Delores eyes flashed as she said, "It was raw the way it's supposed to be. Civilization is built on a foundation of lies."

It was then I knew she was a kindred spirit. Ginny caught her breath and I knew she had seen it too.

"Medicine was pretty primitive, back then," said Ginny.

"It still is," said Delores. "Those crooked bastards know nothing about healing. All they care about is emptying my pocketbook."

"You got that right," said Ginny. "It's a multi-trillion dollar industry and most treatments aren't cures...they only manage symptoms."

Delores shook her head and grunted, "Humph...a girl might as well live with the pain and keep her hard earned dollars. Except most people can't handle pain. They're such a bunch of puss..err...bunch of whiners, if you ask me."

"Wouldn't it be something if the cure grew like a weed in our own back yards?" asked Ginny as she handed Delores a slice of zucchini bread and a cup of herbal tea.

It looked and smelled wonderful. Delores nodded absent-mindedly, but her focus was on the food. She took a small bite of the cake, chewed slowly, and swallowed. At first, I wasn't sure whether she liked it or not because she didn't react one way or the other. Instead, she just sat there with the strangest expression.

Finally, her fork descended for a second bite. This one was considerably larger. She stuffed it into her mouth and chewed a little faster this time. Once she swallowed it, a small smile began to form at the corner of her mouth. She cut her eyes to Ginny, gave her a small nod of approval and then enthusiastically tore into the rest of it.

Not once did she pause to look up from the plate or to speak. Not until every crumb had been consumed and washed down with the last drop of tea, did she finally push herself away from the plate and speak.

"There was something wonderful in that recipe that I can't put a finger on," said Delores.

Ginny nodded.

"Oh, I must have your recipe," gushed Delores.

Ginny had hooked her, now we needed to reel her in.

"Of course you can have the recipe," said Ginny. "The secret ingredient is an herb Grant and I brought back from the Amazon Rainforest."

Delores's skin was looking remarkably less pasty and far pinker. Her blue eyes twinkled with life and energy. She sat a little straighter and her voice sounded years younger when she spoke next.

"You two have been to the Amazon Rainforest!" exclaimed Delores.

"Yes, it was my first trip, but Ginny has been many times," I said.

"Tell me all about it," said Delores.

Ginny flashed Delores a radiant smile and closed the deal.

"The Rainforest is beautiful, exotic and vast," said Ginny. "The natives have their own medicine…an ancient medicine. They call the herb Great Mother and they honor it as the medicine of all medicines because it heals them. How did it make you feel?"

Delores titled her head slightly while she performed a quick survey of herself. She opened and closed her hands and peered at them as if something was puzzling her. Then she abruptly stood up and walked around the room. Her limp was gone. Her face lit up and she started dancing a little jig in the middle of our kitchen.

"I feel amazing!" she said. "Does it wear off?"

Ginny matched her smile and said, "We've both used it to recover from serious injuries. It hasn't worn off yet. Once you're healed, you're healed."

"Yahoo!" shouted Delores.

Her face darkened.

"I have something to say," she said.

We waited.

"I took the potted plant from your greenhouse and turned it over to the authorities," she said.

"You did what?" I said.

"Why would you do that?" asked Ginny.

"I thought you were drug dealers and didn't want you here," she said.

"Do you still feel that way?" asked Ginny.

"Oh, you're drug dealers all right," said Delores.

"Not exactly," I said. "We're not pushing this medicine on anybody. We plan to give it away."

"You are going to give this away?" she asked.

We nodded in unison.

Delores wiped a tear from her eye.

"I want to help," she said.

Ginny gave Delores a hug and said, "We would be honored."

Delores had transformed before our very eyes into a radiantly beautiful woman glowing with good health.

"Go look in the mirror," suggested Ginny. "There's one in the bathroom down the hall."

As Delores skipped off to the bathroom, she was humming a happy little tune. I'm pretty sure it was a 1970's disco hit about dancing. It made me want to dance and that is exactly what Ginny and I did while Delores was admiring her new youthful appearance in the mirror.

"Do you know what this means?" said Ginny.

"Yep, Eric didn't steal the plant for Pathogen," I answered.

CHAPTER 56

Folks tend not to value things without a big price tag. Free just seems cheap and worthless to them. The bigger the price tag, the better they like the product even though it is not a bit better.

Giving it away might not be as easy as we thought. If people refuse to use the medicine because they believe it's useless, then the plan will fail. We needed to find a way to establish its value. That's exactly what I was discussing with Ginny a few days after Delores's transformation.

"We can't claim it's a medicine," I said to Ginny.

"But it is," said Ginny.

"Yes, but if we do that, then we will spend years tied up in red tape with the FDA," I said.

Ginny thought about it for a few minutes and the said, "This is a grassroots movement. What if we rely on word of mouth?"

"I like it," I said. "Let's start looking for ways to create buzz."

The best way to create a buzz is to deliver the message to the neighborhood gossips, since they know everyone and love to talk. Delores was a no-brainer for this task. She gave a seedling to all of her friends and family with strict instructions to plant it in every available inch of their property and to share it with all of their friends and family. Over the next couple of months, Great Mother spread like wildfire.

The plant spread so fast, our only concern was it might be too fast. At first, we worried that Great Mother might be one of those invasive species that chokes out everything else, but fortunately, she plays well with the other plants, growing peacefully side by side with them. In fact, rather than diminishing them, they seem far healthier and vibrant than they were before her introduction.

Despite the rocky start, we were right to trust Delores. She became a great friend, a fierce advocate of the plant and a regular around the farm. The only thing that concerned us about her was the way she took to calling herself a drug dealer.

"If you're going to be a drug dealer," said Delores. "Then you damn well better be a good one."

"You ever met one of those people who vilify gays all their life, until one day, they are themselves exposed as being gay," said Ginny with a good-natured smile to soften the rub.

Delores laughed so hard, I think she may have wet her pants, judging by the strange expression that suddenly came over her. To her credit, she shook it off, and went back to slapping her thighs and laughing all the way from her lower belly.

When she finally caught her breath, she managed to say with a twinkle in her eye, "So are you saying I'm one of those hypocritical bastards when it comes to drugs?"

We nodded our heads in unison, which started another round of laughter. The one thing you can say about Delores is she really does not need any softening before you deliver a harsh truth. This woman likes being difficult. In fact, the only time I saw her get annoyed with Ginny was the time she called Delores sweet. That really pissed her off and she didn't speak to Ginny for a couple of days.

Thanks to Delores's boundless enthusiasm and the fact that she knew damn near everyone in the County, Great Mother spread like a wildfire across Goshen and into the surrounding areas. People were beginning to share stories of their miraculous healings and when those stories spread to social media, Great Mother went viral.

Word was spreading faster than we had ever thought possible and then it happened. The one thing we feared. The one thing we knew was coming. The storm began.

The first reported deaths appeared on a conservative cable news channel. The sour faced news anchor urged viewers to see a doctor immediately if they had any exposure to a new drug believed to be responsible for the deaths of four people in Kentucky. A picture of Great Mother flashed across the screen for added emphasis.

"Oh my God!" said Ginny.

My initial reaction to the news report was horror, but something, maybe it was the lawyer in me, smelled a rat. The story was dramatic, but it did not provide any significant details. Lawyers are trained to challenge unsupported statements offered as fact. It's a good thing too, because very often they prove to be untrue.

If Great Mother was killing people, we needed to pull the plug on it. On the other hand, if the story was a lie, then we needed to find a way to expose the lie.

"This is bad," I said.

Ginny pulled her eyes away from the television and said, "You're not buying this either, are you?"

I shook my head.

"We need to get to the bottom of it…and fast," I said.

"Who do think is behind it?" asked Ginny.

"Goth," I answered.

Ginny nodded.

"Let's see if we can get more information and then we'll develop a response," I said.

Someone knocked at the front door, just as both of our cell phones went off. I sometimes take pleasure in ignoring the techno-tyrant. In this instance, I preferred to give my attention to someone who has made more of an effort than looking me up in their contacts folder, and therefore, let my phone ring while I gave the person at the door my undivided attention. On the other hand, Ginny checked her text message.

"Grant, don't answer it!" she shouted.

It was too late. The door was open. I don't know what I expected, but it sure as hell wasn't an angry mob with torches and pitchforks. Okay, maybe I exaggerate just a little. There were no torches and pitchforks, but there was an angry mob. It sure didn't take long for our neighbors to descend on the house and pepper us with questions.

"How could you do this?" whined a chubby man with thinning dark hair who looked to be in his early forties.

"You poisoned us!" said a teenage girl.

"You're going to rot in jail for this," said an old farmer carrying a shovel.

Of course, that is just a random sampling. They said much more, oh so much more.

I was known at the law firm as the Jedi Master because I have the strange ability to calm people during an emotional outburst. As I stood in front of this angry mob, the calming force escaped me. Instead, I was tongue-tied.

Ginny appeared next to me in the doorway, and together, we stepped out onto the porch to face them. The crowd grew quiet. No one moved a muscle. Worry replaced anger. These people feared for their lives.

"I guess you have heard the news reports," said Ginny.

They nodded their heads in unison. No one spoke.

"You are worried for yourselves and for your loved ones," she said.

More nods. The mother pulled her gurgling baby a little closer.

"Did any of you take Great Mother?" she asked.

The all nodded their heads.

"Are any of you sick?" Ginny asked.

No one spoke up. A few shook their heads.

"Do you feel better or worse?" she asked.

A hand went up in the back of the crowd and a woman's voice said, "We are better."

"What's your name?" asked Ginny.

A mother with a baby on her hip came forward. She was wearing scrubs and had a stethoscope around her neck that her little boy would make a grab for and she would pull it out of reach at the last minute. I recognized her immediately as the nurse who gave me a ride home.

"Hello everyone," she said. "My name is Lindsey...Lindsey Graft."

"Hello Lindsey," said Ginny. "What is your baby's name?"

"This is Michael," answered Lindsey.

"He's beautiful," said Ginny.

Lindsey glowed as she pulled Michael just a wee bit closer to her breast.

"Did you use Great Mother?" asked Ginny.

"Yes, I did," she answered.

"Did it help?" asked Ginny.

Lindsey stared back at us as if she wanted to see inside of our hearts before she spoke.

"We respect your privacy, and if you'd rather not, then that is okay, but would you mind sharing your story?" asked Ginny.

"I don't mind sharing it with these people," answered Lindsey with a broad sweep of her arm. "Michael is six months old. I wanted the full experience of childbirth so I refused drugs. It was a difficult birth. I was in labor for twenty hours."

Lindsey paused and took a deep breath before resuming her story.

"When Michael finally came into this world, my life changed. There were complications for both of us, but his were far more serious. He wouldn't stop crying. I mean, he literally cried twenty-four hours a day."

Lindsey kissed Michael.

"Michael saw just about every specialist in town," said Lindsey. "I couldn't get a straight answer out of any of them. They tried to pass it off as colic. I'm a nurse and mother. I knew it was bullshit."

"Finally, I snapped," she said. "Of course, they called my angry outburst a psychotic break and wanted to put me on drugs. I refused the drugs, because I have child to care for."

"It went from bad to worse when Michael stopped eating," said Lindsey. "He was losing weight fast and slipping away from me. I was desperate. That's when I heard about Great Mother. I had nothing to lose."

"Did you give some to Michael?" asked Ginny.

Lindsey nodded. A cooing Michael stretched his arms toward his mother's neck. She took his tiny hand in hers and kissed the palm before laying it to rest on her sternum. The little guy's fingers opened and closed like a kitten kneading its mother's fur. Michael radiated good health.

"What happened then?" asked Ginny.

"Michael stopped crying," answered Lindsey. "He started eating again. As you can see for yourself, he couldn't be healthier. I got my son back thanks to Great Mother."

A middle-aged woman shouted, "Amen!"

The crowd nodded.

"How long ago did you use Great Mother?" asked Ginny.

"It's been a couple of months," answered Lindsey.

"Has Michael had any more symptoms?" asked Ginny.

"Not a one," answered Lindsey.

"Has Michael seen a doctor since he was healed?" asked Ginny.

"No, and I won't go back," she said. "They cured nothing, but thanks to all of the medical bills, I'm on the verge of bankruptcy. If it wasn't for the double shifts I've been working, I would have lost everything."

"Those greedy bastards," shouted the farmer with the shovel.

"Have any of you not been healed by Great Mother?" shouted Ginny.

The crowd was silent.

"Does anyone not feel better since you took Great Mother?" asked Ginny.

They shook their heads.

"Do any of you personally know anyone who has been harmed by Great Mother?" asked Ginny.

No one came forward.

"Neither do we," said Ginny.

"We are heartbroken over the news reports, but they don't make any sense to us," I said.

"Maybe those people died from some other cause," said a teenage boy with curly red hair hanging in this face.

"I bet it's all lies," said a thin woman with thick glasses pushed on top of her head.

"Has anyone ever read the warning label on a prescription bottle," said an elderly man with little or no hair.

"We all have," shouted a young man in blue jeans and work boots. "That shit is poison."

"I stopped reading them," said a blue haired frumpy lady wearing a cotton dress. "They are full of side effects that sound even worse than the sickness they are treating."

The farmer with the shovel spat on the ground and said, "None of it cures anything. It controls symptoms or pain as if they want to drug us into submission."

"That's right," shouted the middle-aged man with thinning dark hair. "They always tell you that you will need to take the medication for the rest of your life. It sounds to me like they are creating lifelong customers, instead of cured patients."

"Folks, we don't know yet if Great Mother has hurt anybody," I said. "Let's wait and see before we jump to any conclusions."

"I don't believe it did," said Lindsey. "And even if it were true, I would still use it because I know it saved my son's life."

It is time to come out of the shadows.

CHAPTER 57

It isn't just a healthcare crisis we're having, it is a much bigger problem. Access to affordable and effective healthcare is indeed a huge problem, but there is more to it than that. The leaders we trust and rely upon for protection are lying to us. Truth needs a voice.

The success stories were pouring in, but we knew it wasn't enough. The safety of Great Mother was paramount to us. We needed strong scientific evidence to combat the criticism we knew was coming. Ginny hired Lindsey away from the hospital to head a group of independent scientist who would study the effects of Great Mother on the human organism.

We weren't finished. We needed a voice in Washington. As it turns out, Delores knows a lot of movers and shakers on the political scene. She was the best choice to be our lobbyist. We tried to hire her, but she told us in no uncertain terms she was richer than we could possibly imagine, and while she would indeed lobby for Great Mother, she insisted we give her salary to Lindsey.

Meanwhile, the topic of discussion on conservative talk shows was the growing problem of deaths caused by illegal drugs. While they did not specifically mention Great Mother, they periodically flashed a picture of the plant on the screen during their shows.

Kinsey sent a team of investigators from her security company to gather more information on the deaths, but ran smack into a stonewall. The reporter refused to discuss his sources. He wouldn't say who had died. He even refused to reveal the date of death. He repeatedly told our investigators that his information came from a respected and reliable source. No one at Conservative TV would discuss the details of the four deaths.

It was time to try a different tactic, so I called Detective Rose Bloom at Louisville Metro Police. Uncle Jim and Rose were inseparable when I was growing up. Like many couples, they found it difficult to sustain their relationship through the tough times and grew apart.

I hated to see that happen, since Rose was like a second mother to me. If there was anybody on the police force I could trust, it was her. Instead of speaking over the telephone, she offered to visit us at the farm. While I was looking forward to seeing her, she never failed to mention Uncle Jim. Clearly, she still had feelings for him and I never knew what to say to her.

I braced myself for a tense visit, but was astonished to see Rose behind the wheel of Dad's old truck and Uncle Jim sitting next to her.

"You found Dad's truck!" I said.

"Yep, and we're glad to see you too," said Uncle Jim.

"Where'd you find her?" I asked.

Uncle Jim pulled Rose close and said, "Once I eliminated my stupidity, she was right in front of me."

Rose leaned in and kissed Uncle Jim on the cheek.

"That's sweet, dear, but I think he's talking about his truck," said Rose.

I nodded.

"She was abandoned in a back-alley off Lytle Street," said Rose.

"Portland is a rough neighborhood, so I'm surprised she wasn't stripped bare," I said.

"She's pretty bare already," said Rose.

"Not much to strip there, even in the poorest of neighborhoods," said Uncle Jim.

"What are you saying?" I said.

Uncle Jim opened his mouth to answer, but Rose quashed his snarky comment with a poke to the ribs. Instead, she flashed a hand full of bling.

"We're getting married," she said.

Her engagement ring caught the light just right, sending a ray of hope into my day.

"How long...when did...when?" I stammered.

"While you were crawling around in the jungle, we were renewing our relationship," said Uncle Jim.

"We wanted to make sure it was going to stick this time, before we told anyone," said Rose.

"I think she means, until she got a ring," said Uncle Jim.

Rose punched his arm playfully. Uncle Jim radiated happiness. It finally registered in my thick skull that they were once again a loving couple.

"It's about time," I said. "You guys belong together."

I pulled them into a group hug. Bird landed on Rose's shoulder and wrapped the happy couple in his wings.

"Aaawk, let's add some color to this love-in," squawked Bird.

"Awe, Bird, I've missed you so much," said Rose.

The tip of one of Bird's feathers dropped low and slipped under Rose's top.

"Mind your feathers, you lecherous old fool," said Uncle Jim.

"Aaawk, natural and magnificent!" said Bird.

It's hard to tell if Bird meant his feathers or Rose's boobs.

"I'm so happy for you," I said.

Ginny slipped up behind me and said, "We're having a wedding! That's the kind of happy news we need to hear more of around here."

While the girls shared their happy tears, the guys pretended we didn't have red puffy eyes too.

"Aaawk, speaking of news, I hear the Peckerwood is knocking off poor unsuspecting sick people," squawked Bird. "This one is a real serial killer, if you ask me. Rose, I hope you brought your cuffs."

"I guess you have seen the news," I said.

They nodded.

"Rose, do you know anything about an investigation into drug related deaths?"

"I'm not aware of any," she answered.

"If the news reports are correct and there is an ongoing investigation, who do you think would be conducting it?" I asked.

"If it was a controlled substance, then our narcotic detectives would investigate, but there have been no drug related deaths in Louisville," answered Rose.

"What if the death was caused by something other than a controlled substance?" I asked.

"Do you mean something like food poisoning?" she asked.

I nodded.

"In most cases, it would be the health department, but in some instances the federal government gets involved, but it's hard to say which agency," she answered. "Most likely the FDA, but depending on the facts, Department of Agriculture or even the CDC might get involved."

"Have you ever personally dealt with any of those agencies," I asked.

Rose shook her head.

"Aaawk, stop with the institutional acronyms," squawked Bird. "It's giving me a headache. Are there any live people in those shallowed halls who can discuss the bogus news reports with Peckerwood?"

"You probably meant to say hallowed halls," I said.

"Aaawk, I never misspeak," said Bird.

"We can't find anyone who will give us any details about the four deaths," I said.

"I can get you names of someone to ask for at each of those agencies, but I can't promise they will know anything about it," said Rose.

"That's a start," said Ginny.

"Someone has to know something about the deaths," I said.

"You'd think," said Ginny.

"Even if they do know something about the deaths, there is no guarantee they will even talk to you," said Rose.

"If they don't then we will need to keep looking until we find someone who will talk," I said.

"Talk or not, it will be impossible to prove Great Mother didn't harm those four people without an autopsy," said Rose.

"Surely they have done an autopsy," said Ginny.

"Probably, but Goth has a shit load of money," I said. "He could have bribed someone to tamper with the results."

"It's beginning to look like they are setting us up for certain failure," said Ginny.

"If we try to prove as a general matter that Great Mother has never harmed anyone, we will get caught up in an endless debate," I said.

"That's right, you can't prove a negative and if you try you will forever be chasing your own tail," said Rose. "You need to take a different approach to this problem."

"Aaawk, listen to her Peckerwood," squawked Bird. "This is the woman who pulled a Jack Ruby on that butch ex-soldier with the mass murderer name."

On national television, Jack Ruby shot Lee Harvey Oswald at point blank range. Oswald was under arrest for the assassination of President Kennedy. Likewise, Rose shot Kim Slotter while she was in police custody for kidnapping and attempted murder.

I'm not sure exactly sure how Rose managed to stay out of prison. Except, this military goon whisked Slotter off in a helicopter. Afterwards, they played the national security card and offered me immunity for two murders I didn't commit in exchange for silence about what really happened at the Center. The authorities were using a gas leak cover story to explain all of those deaths at the Center and they were worried I would expose their lie.

Rose took it personal because her daughter was one of the victims at the Center. Since Slotter was the prime suspect, she shot her. Bird was not much for subtly. He prefers to lance an infected wound and there is something to be said for his approach.

"You are always stirring up shit, my little feathered friend," said Rose.

"Aaawk, did she just call me little?" squawked Bird. "I have you know that I'm in the upper seventy percentile."

Rose opened her mouth to speak, but Bird cut her off, saying, "Aaawk, you like guns. Just take a gander at these, Officer Bloom. You might as well arrest me now for carrying a concealed deadly weapon."

We endured an eternity, or at least sixty seconds, of body builder poses, because if we didn't, Bird was known to get a little testy. If I've learned nothing else in my twenty-eight years, I know to avoid upsetting Bird. He can get difficult and a difficult Bird is not something you want to be around for very long.

"Oh, Bird you are magnificent," gushed Ginny.

We all agreed with Ginny and complimented his huge muscles. We encouraged Rose to cuff him immediately for the safety of everyone. It worked because Bird stopped posing, but he grew suspicious and searched our faces for any hint of insincerity. I'm pretty sure he knew our praise was faked, but his ego got the best of him and he accepted it all the same.

With the Bird problem resolved for the moment, Rose said, "I'm sure all of you want to know how I managed to stay out of jail for shooting Slotter, but the price tag of my freedom is silence."

"Given the chance, everyone in this room would have shot Slotter for what she did," Ginny said.

"Damn right," agreed Uncle Jim.

Rose cut her eyes to Uncle Jim.

"That bitch hurt everybody I care about," she said.

Uncle Jim moved a little closer to her, but kept quiet. His silence may have something to do with his red puffy eyes, but that's not something you generally talk about with a tough old marine.

"I'm not surprised they want to muzzle you," I said. "They came to me in the hospital and tried to buy my silence, too."

"These are powerful people who know how to control public opinion," said

Rose.

"I don't believe Great Mother killed anyone, but if they convince the public it is dangerous, then they will be able to ban it," said Uncle Jim.

"We need to expose these false news reports," said Ginny.

"Do you have any ideas how we can get to the bottom of it?" I asked.

"You can sue them for defamation and take their depositions," said Uncle Jim.

"It's too slow to be effective," I said. "The reporters will file motions with the Court to protect their sources and then tie us up for years with appeals."

"If we have evidence of a crime, then we can get a search warrant," said Rose.

"I can set up surveillance of the reporter and see if anything shakes out," said Uncle Jim.

Uncle Jim spent his military career in intelligence. If anyone could dig something up on the reporter, then it would be him.

"That's a good idea, Uncle Jim," I said.

"I can poke around and see who is handling the police investigation of the deaths," said Rose.

"Thanks Rose," said Ginny.

"Then we'll get started right away," said Uncle Jim.

"I need your help with something else," I said.

"What is it, son?" asked Uncle Jim.

"There's no easy way to say this, so I'm going to just spit it out," I said.

I lost my nerve and didn't finish. I hadn't told Uncle Jim about Mom because I was afraid of what he'd do to Eric. Whereas, I planned to kick Eric's ass when we found him, Uncle Jim might do something worse than that.

"Aaawk, spit it out Peckerwood," squawked Bird.

"Ummm…" was all I managed to get out.

"What the hell is this?" demanded Uncle Jim.

"Stay calm everyone," said Ginny. "I think Grant is trying to tell you his mom is missing."

"Missing?" said Uncle Jim.

"Eric, checked her out of the nursing home," said Ginny.

"Why the hell would Eric pull a stunt like this?" asked Uncle Jim.

"We don't know," said Ginny.

Uncle Jim goes very still when he is angry. The only tell is a twitch along his jaw line. When both sides of his face are twitching, like now, then you know he has gone ballistic.

"Calm down, dear," said Rose. "There has to be some logical explanation for Eric's strange behavior."

I wanted to hug Rose for saying that, but for the life of me, I couldn't figure out what Eric's reasons might be.

"It gets worse," I said.

"I know…she needs constant medical supervision," said Uncle Jim. "That dumbass has put her life at risk. How does it get worse than that?"

"We think he may have turned her over to Pathogen," I said.

"If one hair on my sister's head is harmed, I'll kill that motherfucker," said Uncle Jim.

CHAPTER 58

A law school buddy with a talent for languages works for the Central Intelligence Agency. Since Jake was also an ex-Navy SEALs, it didn't come as a great surprise he chose to be spy rather than spending his life in the courtroom. The last I heard, he was somewhere in the Middle East fighting terrorism, so Jake was the last person I expected to get a call from.

"You know I can still kick your ass, Grant," said the voice over the phone.

I recognized Jake's voice instantly. Besides, the ass kicking debate was the only thing that kept the two of us sane during law school. Jake is like Eric, he likes to fight, so we spent a lot of time in the gym kicking the shit out of each other.

"You might land a punch if we were surrounded by water, Frogman," I said.

"Yeah, you swim like a kitten, you little pussy," he said with a good-natured laugh.

Jake Blitzer ran cross-country in high school. I played football. In the pecking order of high school jocks, a runner is low on the cool list. They do not ordinarily insult football players, but we were long out of high school and Jake had his own level of cool. He was also a certifiable badass, who served god and country, and I was proud to call him a friend.

You'd think the SEALs Team program would recruit big macho football players, but they don't. Instead, they seek smart, mentally tough young men, with lots of stamina. These recruits have proven on their cross-country teams that they can run through injuries and go the distance, every time, without fail.

"If God wanted us to swim, then he would have given us fins and gills," I said. "It is unnatural to strap an oxygen tank to your back and swim with the little fishes in the deep blue sea."

"I think you mean, swim with the sharks, like the badasses we were meant to be," he said with a laugh.

"Only until a fun-loving dolphin shows up," I said. "Then the sharks run for the hills...or wherever cowards go down under."

"All right...enough of that from you my land loving friend," laughed Jake.

"So, what's up, buddy...to what do I owe the pleasure of your insults?" I asked.

"We need to have a beer and catch up," said Jake.

"I'd love to Jake, but I'm up to my ears in some deep shit," I said.

"Umm…Grant, we NEED to catch up," said Jake with a little more urgency.

You don't have hit me over the head with a baseball bat to get my attention. Jake needed to talk to me about something important and he didn't want to do it over the phone.

"Sure, buddy…where did you have in mind?" I asked.

"Someplace lively…and very loud," he answered.

"Gotcha…how about Ed's Tavern in thirty?" I asked.

The favorite watering hole of the boating community is located on the bank of the Ohio River at the mouth of Harrods Creek. Hungry and thirsty after a day on the water, boaters stop in for fish sandwiches and cold beer. Sitting under colorful umbrellas, they rub elbows with bikers out for a scenic ride along River Road. The mix of black leather and bikinis makes for an interesting evening of people watching.

Since I decided to ride Dad's old Harley, I showed up in faded jeans, beat up old cowboy boots, white t-shirt and a farmer tan. The Frogman was wearing flip-flops, Bermuda shorts, and a Dive Cayman Islands t-shirt. His right arm was covered in new ink. It appeared to be a group of naked sirens tempting a blindfolded Hercules.

Jake is 6'2" with dark hair and six-pack abs. Every chick in the place, young and old, turned and watched as he walked by. The guy defines tall, dark and handsome. However, the ladies were wasting their time since he is also gay.

Many women have tried their best to turn him, but to no avail. Jake loves men. He is particularly attracted to soft and pudgy teddy bears. The more hair they have covering their bodies, the more he loves them. They are the same guys that most chicks wouldn't bother to give a second look.

"Dude, there's something different about you," said Jake.

"Same old me," I said with a grin.

"No seriously…let me see…I've got it," he exclaimed with a flamboyant flourish of the hand. "You're in love. Grant finally found his soul mate."

"You're right for the most part," I said. "I am in love and it is my soul mate, but I've known her since pre-school. I was kind of a dick to her all through school, but she never faltered."

"Well…are you going to tell me her name or do I have to guess," said Jake.

"Do you remember Ginny Bardough?" I asked.

"I knew it…I knew it…I knew it!" shouted Jake.

The happy hour crowd was loud, but Jake was louder. A dozen or more heads turned in our direction.

"I take it that is a big fat yes," I said.

Jake tapped his forehead with his forefinger and said, "I have a special sense. I know things and I've always known you had a thing for Ginny. This is huge…huge, I tell you."

"Really, ESP powers?" I said. "I knew the SEALs training was out there, but Dude, you're not telling me the United States Navy taught you to read minds."

"Ginny Bardough…it's about time my friend," said Jake.

I'm pretty sure those were tears I saw welling up in his big brown eyes. Jake may be a certified badass, but he has a heart as big as Texas.

"You are seriously messed up," I said with a shake of the head. "I wouldn't change a thing about you, even if I could."

"Thanks Grant," said Jake. "That means a lot to me. I love and respect you, which is why I'm here."

His voice dropped to just above a whisper on that last sentence. I knew for sure something was up when his eyes darted from side to side, as if, the joint was full of cold war spies.

"What's up with the cloak and dagger...don't you get enough of that at work?" I asked.

"Your name has popped up as a person of interest on the domestic terrorism watch list," whispered Jake.

"Watch list...you've got to be shitting me," I said. "I'm no terrorist."

"I know that, but you've made some powerful enemies and they're coming for you," whispered Jake.

"Let 'em come," I said. "Have you ever known me to run from a fight?"

"Hell no, but you can't face this one on your own!" said Jake.

"I'm preparing for one hell of a fight," I said. "Can I count you in?"

"I don't know what you've gotten yourself into, my friend, but I can be your eyes and ears on the ground," he said.

"This is big Jake," I said. "Not all enemies of freedom wear uniforms and wave flags. We are going to change everything about healthcare as we know it."

"Folks don't like change much," said Jake.

"Most like change that improves their lives, just not change the hurts them," I said.

"There are seven and half billion people in the world," said Jake. "What improves one life might harm another."

"That's generally true, but everybody wants good health," I said.

Jake nodded.

"So, why don't we have it?" I asked.

"Because the world is filled with sickness and disease," he said.

I nodded and asked, "But does it have to be like that?"

"Dude, you're talking about something that is inevitable, like taxes and death," said Jake.

"Maybe those things aren't inevitable," I said.

"Now you sound like an idealistic sophomore who smoked too much weed," said Jake.

"Here's a fact for you...healthcare is a four hundred trillion dollar a year industry," I said.

Jake stared at me cold and hard. I wasn't sure what he was thinking, so I continued.

"Medical bills are one of the leading causes of bankruptcy," I said.

"Somebody you love gets sick, what are you going to do?" asked Jake.

There was something in Jake's face that told me he knew all of this already. He wasn't just talking. He was experiencing it himself.

"Oh shit, is somebody you care about sick?" I asked.

Jake stared at his untouched beer. When he looked up again, his eyes were puffy.

"It's Zeke…he has…has testicular cancer," said Jake with sob.

I took his hands in mine and just sat with him for the longest time.

"His insurance isn't worth shit and the money is gone," said Jake. "The asshole doctors refuse to treat him unless he can pay for it…not that it helps anyway."

"I'm sorry, Jake," I said. "Have you looked into the alternatives?"

"They are all a bunch of arrogant bastards," he said. "When you mention alternative treatments, they make you feel like an idiot, as if desperation is making you a sucker that would fall for anything."

"Medicine has a virtual monopoly on treatment protocols," I said. "There are no significant alternatives, so the industry can charge desperate patients whatever they want and get away with it. While doctors are buying vacation homes, their patients are losing the only homes they have."

"I wish we had an alternative for Zeke," sobbed Jake. "We are at the end of our rope."

"Jake, don't give up hope," I said. "We have a medicine from the Amazon Rainforest that heals illnesses with no side effects, unless you want to call optimal health a side effect."

"You're joking, aren't you?" asked Jake.

"Not joking," I answered."

"What does it cost?" asked Jake.

"That's the best part, my friend, it's free and grows like a weed," I answered.

Jake looked at me with a combination of shock and awe.

"I'm going to give you a plant," I said. "Stick it in the dirt and watch it grow and spread. Make Zeke tea from its leaves and watch him heal."

Jake got up from his seat, walked around the table, and then kissed me right on the mouth.

"I'm in buddy, but I will need a different point of contact," he said. "You are being watched and we can't meet again until this is over. We have to be low key."

It was just a reflex, but I wiped my mouth with the back of my hand.

"You call what you just did low key?" I asked.

"Umm…sorry about that," he said. "I know you're straight and besides, I'm in love. It didn't mean nothing."

"I've never been kissed by a guy before," I said. "It's kind of weird."

Jake flashed me his best shit-eating grin and said, "Yeah, I know…good shit right."

"Let's get back to what you and I do best…which is fighting," I said. "This could get ugly. I learned long ago about the dangers of getting between a hungry dog and its food bowl. The bad guys may try to scorch the Earth, rather than give up their revenue stream. You and Zeke could end up in the line of fire."

"What do people like me and Zeke have to lose, anyway?" said Jake.

"By the way, do you know anything about Pathogen running a bio-weapons program?" I asked.

"Pathogen…are you talking about the pharmaceutical company?" he asked.

I nodded.

"No, do you think that has something to do with your medicine from South America?" he asked.

"Yes, I do," I answered.

A long thin hiss escaped through Jake's lips.

"Do you think your jungle juice could effectively neutralize their bio-weapon?" he asked.

It was my turn to look around and make sure no one was listening, before answering with a nod.

"Holy shit!" he said.

"Yeah, holy shit," I repeated.

"If that's true, then the stakes are high," he said.

"Lives can be lost," I said.

"Lives can be saved," he said.

I nodded.

"We'll fight the bastards to the bitter end and win," said Jake. "You know I don't like to lose."

"Not an option," I said.

"You got that right," he said.

"Umm…there's one other thing," I said.

"What's that my friend?" he asked.

"Eric is missing and I could use some help finding him," I said.

"Eric is MIA…are you sure he didn't just run off with a skirt," said Jake.

"In a way he did, he took Mom with him," I said.

"Geez, isn't she bad sick?" asked Jake.

I nodded.

"Something bad has happened to them," I said. "I can feel it. Anything you can do to help find them would be appreciated."

Jake cut his eyes to the right, then to the left, before lowering his voice to a whisper.

"You now have the unofficial resources of the CIA at your disposal," said Jake. "If they can be found, then we'll find them. Now, how do I get my hands on that medicine for Zeke."

CHAPTER 59

Ginny and I are early risers. We like to sit outside and sip morning coffee. Taking inspiration from the festive culture of Manaus, Brazil, we painted the cast iron furniture orange and added a lime green umbrella. Bright colors are surprisingly comforting to us, so we constantly look for opportunities to put more color into our lives.

I inhaled the rich aroma of freshly brewed coffee. We use only dark roast coffee beans that we grind ourselves and distilled water. Our little distiller makes a gallon of fresh water every few hours. It was something Ginny insisted we do.

When I tried to convince her that municipal water is clean and safe she said, "Grant, you call this water clean but it has fluoride and other chemicals in it."

"Well yes, but they are part of cleaning process," I responded.

"The cleaning process you are talking about is a killing process," she said. "Those chemicals are anti-life. Since we are living beings, we don't need to put anything in our bodies that destroys life."

I saw the logic of it, but was not convinced until she showed me the waste product from a gallon of distilled water. It was two tablespoons of nasty yellow liquid chemicals. It smelled like chlorine and other toxins I couldn't identify. I didn't want to touch it, let alone drink it.

So now, we distill all of our drinking water. Besides, it makes for a more delicious cup of coffee when you eliminate the chlorine taste.

The morning after I met with Jake was no different. We sat quietly listening to a symphony of bird song as we sipped our coffee. Ginny chimed in with the birds. It was something she has been doing since we got back from the underworld.

I thought she was just mimicking them and jokingly asked, "What are you birds singing about?"

"We are thanking the creator for this beautiful day," she said.

Feeling the truth of it, I took another sip of hot coffee. Ginny likes to load her cup with spices, but I take mine black. It varies each morning, but she usually includes raw honey, turmeric, cocoa, cayenne, and cinnamon. At first, I thought it was a strange combination, but must admit it tastes delicious.

A grey squirrel sitting in a willow tree fussed at a nearby robin. I wondered what the argument was about and considered asking Ginny, until I saw their babies chasing each other through the treetops. We have seen a couple of red-tailed hawks hanging around lately that would seem to be a greater threat. I guess, a mother's job is to protect her youngins against any threat, real or imagined.

"Smells good...do you have a cup of that for me?" said a vaguely familiar voice from behind us.

Ginny was sitting at an angle where she could see the intruder from the corner of her eye I wasn't particularly concerned because our neighbors stop by unannounced all of the time, but when Ginny's eyes opened wide and she gasped, I knew something was up.

That is when I realized the voice belonged to Kim Slotter, the psycho ex-special forces chick who kidnapped Ginny and then tried to kill everybody I care about. This woman is dangerous and I was not about to let her hurt Ginny again. I leapt out of the chair, twisted in midair, and then came down awkwardly on my left foot. It sent me tumbling face first into the mulch.

"Damn, that was ugly," said Slotter.

"I'll show you ugly," I growled.

I was up fast and almost on her when a missile spraying a trail of hot liquid whizzed past my ear and bounced off Slotter's eyebrow. If it had been just a half-inch lower, she might have lost an eye. As it was the cup cut a one inch gash just above the eyebrow and the brown liquid blinded her long enough for me to lay into her with a ferocity I didn't know I had. We had tangled before, but I think the intensity of the attack surprised her as much as it did me.

Before she could get her hands all the way up to protect herself, I caught her left arm with my right, used her resistance to turn her and circled to her back. Hooking her chin with my left hand, I tilted her head backward. Once her balance was broken, I owned her. A simple twist would break her neck.

Sometime during the scramble, Ginny flew out of her chair and pressed the narrow end of a spoon to the soft spot in Slotter's throat, just above the breastbone. I am also certain I heard Ginny cry out during the scuffle in a voice that reminded me of the Pterodactyl. It played like a duet with the hiss that escaped my own lips.

"You can kill me and I probably deserve it," gasped Slotter. "But...but believe it or not, I'm one of the good guys."

"The hell you are," growled Ginny.

"I work for military intelligence," she said.

"Bullshit," I said.

"Why should we believe anything that comes out your mouth?" asked Ginny.

"I was on a mission and you got caught in the cross-fire," she said.

Ginny glared at Slotter. There may have been some unresolved anger she was working thorough. Who could blame her? Slotter put a bullet in her head. Whether she was telling the truth or not, Slotter shot Ginny between the eyes. If it were not for the healing powers of Great Mother, Ginny would not be alive.

"Mission my ass," we said in unison.

If the situation had not been so tense, then we might have giggled, pointed our fingers at each other and shouted "Jinx". It is something we've been doing since we were little kids.

Synchronicity is one of those beautiful things that happen when two people are meant to be together. As far as I'm concerned, Slotter was not meant to be a part of our lives.

"Please let me explain," she pleaded. "We need your help."

"Who is we...your partner, Victor, is dead," I said coldly.

"Victor was a corporate spy working for Pathogen," said Slotter.

"So are you," said Ginny.

"I am a spy, but I work for Uncle Sam," said Slotter.

The problem with being a spy is all of the lies you must tell to survive. You eventually become the lies and who you were before the lies, disappears. Once exposed as a liar, it is damn near impossible to restore your credibility. As far as I'm concerned, Slotter has no credibility and I didn't see any upside to trusting her.

However, I did want to learn as much as I could from her, so I asked, "What kind of mission are you on?"

"It's classified," she answered.

"Then you're dead," I said.

"In about twenty minutes a federal judge will sign a search warrant and then federal agents will tear this place apart," said Slotter.

After my conversation with Jake, I knew this was coming, but did not expect it so fast.

"Which Judge?" I asked.

"It's a sneak and peak warrant coming from the Foreign Intelligence Surveillance Court," she answered.

A sneak and peak warrant gives police the right to sneak into our home when we are not here, search it, take pictures and remove our property without telling us.

"We are Americans and we haven't broken any laws, so why would you do this to us?" asked Ginny.

"First off, I didn't do this to you," answered Slotter. "Secondly, since 9-11 these warrants are issued all of the time for the flimsiest of reasons."

"If you didn't do this, then who did?" asked Ginny.

"I think you know the answer to that already," answered Slotter.

It had to be Wilbur Goth, the head of Pathogen. He is rich and powerful enough to get a Judge to do his bidding. Goth sees Great Mother as a threat and wants to destroy the plant. His thugs failed to stop the spread of the plant with violence, so now he is sending something even scarier after us, the Government.

"That would be Pathogen, but I still don't understand how these people can just come into our homes without our permission," said Ginny.

"The Patriot Act grants broad powers to the government to fight terrorism," answered Slotter.

"But...but...we're not terrorist and Pathogen is not the government," said Ginny.

"Welcome to the new land of the free and the home of the brave," said Slotter.

"Why should we trust you?" I asked,

"You shouldn't," answered Slotter. "I wouldn't if I was you, but your enemies will destroy you without my help."

"Why would we accept your help?" said Ginny. "You leave dead bodies in your wake."

"I didn't kill those people at the Center," said Slotter. "I was trying to stop it."

"Like you stopped Tiny," said Ginny.

"I didn't kill the security guard," said Slotter.

"Umm…she's telling the truth about that," I said. "Victor killed Tiny."

Ginny cut her eyes to me.

"What made you change your mind?" she said.

"Victor wore the same sandals as the killer," I said.

We all looked at Slotter's boots. Ginny didn't look convinced, shoes can be changed.

"There's more," I said. "The killer had six toes.

Slotter shook her head.

"I can remove my boots, if you want," she said.

"Victor had six toes," I said.

Ginny growled in frustration.

"Had?" asked Slotter.

We shrugged.

"If we decide to accept your offer, what do you want in return?" asked Ginny.

Slotter looked at Ginny and said, "We need to speak to your father?"

Ginny took a big step back and shook her head.

"Why do you need to speak with him?" I asked.

"It's classified," she answered.

I released her and said, "You're done here. We don't need, nor do we want your help."

Slotter exhaled and gave me a long hard searching look before taking a cell phone from her pocket and making a call on speaker.

"Yes," said a vaguely familiar voice over the speaker.

"I am with both of them, Colonel," she said.

Now I remembered the voice. The police brought me in for questioning after the massacre at the Center. I was given a series of medical tests and interrogated by men and women from the CDC, Homeland Security, Louisville Metro Police, and the military. A marine colonel was the last interview, and by far, the most intense.

While everyone else asked questions about the deaths at the Center, the only thing the Colonel was interested in discovering was the whereabouts of Kim Slotter. He tried to provoke me and may have succeeded, except my attorney intervened. Later, when Rose shot Slotter the Colonel whisked her away in a military helicopter.

"Are they willing to help?" asked the Colonel.

"No sir," answered Slotter.

"What do you need to persuade them?" asked the Colonel.

"I need permission to give them access to classified information," answered Slotter.

"Granted," said the Colonel.

"Thank you sir," said Slotter.

"Captain," said the Colonel.

"Yes, sir," said Slotter.

"Failure is not an option," said the Colonel.

"Understood, sir," said Slotter.

Slotter ended the call, swiped the screen, waited for about twenty seconds, before handing her smartphone to us. There was an open document with a seal from the National Security Agency at the top. It was marked CLASSIFIED in large red letters. It took us about twenty minutes to read the entire document.

When we finished reading, we took a deep breath and handed the phone back to Slotter. The document described an event that occurred fifteen years earlier in a small village in Egypt. Every man, woman and child was found dead as the result of a mysterious illness. The dead numbered in the hundreds.

The only clue came from a scrap of paper left in the central building of the village. It read: We breath the air, but our bodies refuse it. Everyone is suffocating. Pain in every face. Death comes fast. Why has Allah forsaken us?

"Oh my god!" said Ginny.

I was stunned. Ginny's father overhead the CEO of Pathogen, Wilbur Goth, planning to test the bio-weapon in a third world village. It looks like they carried out their plan.

"We believe those people at the Center died from the same illness," said Slotter.

"Oh my God," said Ginny.

"Did anyone survive?" I asked.

Slotter shook her head and answered, "None we know of."

"This is similar to the Center," I said.

Slotter nodded grimly.

"It gets worse," said Slotter. "There are seven other villages at various locations around the world where this has occurred."

After what Slotter did to Ginny, I should kill her, but the horror of these mass murders changed everything. It put it all in perspective for me. Pathogen was the enemy, not Kim Slotter. They must be stopped and to hell with their billion dollars.

"Is there a pattern?" asked Ginny.

"If there is one, we can't find it," answered Slotter. "The event at the Center was the first to occur in the United States."

"Has the cause of the illness been identified?" I asked.

"No," said Slotter.

"Do you have any clues?" I asked.

She looked at Ginny and said, "Your father worked at Pathogen. If he is still alive, then we need to talk to him."

I looked to Ginny for direction. She hesitated.

"About what?" said a familiar voice.

Ginny's father had seemingly appeared out of thin air.

CHAPTER 60

Bill Bardough is tall, muscular and very blond. He was wearing crisp white cotton slacks and matching shirt that contrasted with his golden tan. The first time I saw him in the jungle, he looked like a big Viking. Today, he looked more like a runway model.

Twenty years ago, he disappeared into the Amazon Rainforest while searching for a cure for Pathogen's deadly virus. The pharmaceutical giant sent men into the forest to stop him. They managed to find him and shoot his airplane down, but Bill survived with the help of a group of natives who miraculously had the very cure he was searching for.

We found him years later still living in the jungle with the natives who had saved him, but before he could answer any of our questions about his life over the last twenty years, he left on a secret mission. The last place we expected to see him again was in our own backyard.

Ginny rushed to him and threw her arms around his neck. There was a little girl innocence to her behavior that touched me deeply. It was if this grown woman became a child again whenever her father was around. Of course, it makes perfect sense when you consider how much time they lost. She suffered through years of heartache and loneliness.

"Daddy!" she shouted.

"There's my lil' froggy," he said.

"I missed you," said Ginny.

Her father stroked her wavy black hair and whispered soothing nonsensical sounds in her ear.

"The two of you look like you're the same age," said Slotter. "How could you possibly be her father?"

Bill is in his late forties or early fifties, but looks twenty-something. It's as if he took a dip in the Fountain of Youth and came out fresh and new.

"Aren't you the woman who put a bullet in my daughter's head?" asked Bill.

"I was…was playing a role in an undercover operation that went sideways really fast," she stammered.

"You kidnapped her," said Bill.

"We needed to find you," said Slotter.

"You held my child at gunpoint," he said.

"I pointed a gun at her, but…but it was never supposed to go off like that," said Slotter.

"You are a trained fighter and that is the best explanation you can give us," said Bill. "This is my daughter. Explain why I shouldn't put a bullet in your forehead as you did hers."

Slotter's hands were shaking badly. Her toughness was crumbling. For a moment, she looked like she might make a run for it, but then unexpectedly she bowed her head in submission. I didn't think I would ever see her do that.

"I can't…I can't explain how…how it happened," she said. "I don't understand it, but I take full responsibility for my actions."

The remorse was genuine and her admission of guilt was unexpected. I began to wonder if we could really be fighting for the same cause after all. What Slotter said next finally convinced me.

"A small minority within the government, believe that the greatest threat facing humanity is the pharmaceutical giant, Pathogen, and its CEO, Wilbur Goth," said Slotter.

"And why is that?" asked Bill.

"They have a virtual monopoly on pharmaceuticals," answered Slotter. "While their stock is publicly traded, the company is controlled by a handful of stockholders. The wealth they have amassed is unprecedented and their influence is growing."

"Wealth alone is no reason to be concerned," said Bill. "What other reasons do you have?"

"There is growing evidence that Wilbur Goth suffers from paranoia," she answered.

"What is he afraid of?" asked Bill.

"Everybody…umm…well…he believes the biblical end time is near and the masses will soon rise up."

"Many people share that belief, what is different about Wilbur Goth?" asked Bill.

"We believe he is trying to keep people dependent on his drugs," answered Slotter.

"What do you mean?" asked Bill.

"There are exceptions, but much of modern healthcare is focused on symptom management, rather than cure," said Slotter. "This is accomplished with costly and addictive drugs. The rising use of pain medication is one example."

"That is all true, but very general information," said Bill. "Do you have any specific evidence against Wilbur Goth and Pathogen?"

"Nothing strong enough to stop them," said Slotter. "We believe they are behind the deaths of several thousand people around the world."

"How are they responsible?" asked Bill.

"We believe they have developed a dangerous virus," she answered.

"They are a healthcare company," said Bill. "Why would they murder large groups of people by spreading disease?"

"Create a demand for their products," answered Slotter.

"You mentioned a small minority in the government," said Bill. "Who else believes these things?"

"I'm not going to expose them until I know where you stand,' said Slotter.

"What is it you want from me?" asked Bill.

"You worked for Pathogen, correct?" asked Slotter.

"Yes, I did," answered Bill.

"You worked on a team looking for a cure for a deadly virus, is that correct?" asked Slotter.

"That's correct," answered Bill.

"Every member of that team is dead, except for you," said Slotter.

"Dead...I didn't know they were all dead, but I know they want me dead," said Bill.

"Why?" asked Slotter.

"Because I discovered the cure for their virus," answered Bill.

"Shouldn't a pharmaceutical company be pleased you found a cure?" asked Slotter.

"You would think," answered Bill.

"What else aren't you telling me?" asked Slotter.

"Ask these two," answered Bill pointing in our direction.

"The cure for this virus does much more," I said.

"Like what?" asked Slotter.

"It cures any injury or illness," answered Ginny.

"Any illness...so that explains how you survived a gunshot to the head," said Slotter.

"Yes, Great Mother saved my life," said Ginny.

"Great Mother?" asked Slotter.

"That's what they call it in the Rainforest," answered Ginny

"There's more," I said.

"More than it cures everything?" asked Slotter.

The three of us nodded. I wasn't sure if I could trust Slotter with my latest suspicions about the plant.

"It spreads like a weed," I said.

"Then anybody can grow it," said Slotter.

"Anybody...anywhere," I said.

"It will put Pathogen out of business," said Ginny.

"And change the world as we know it," said Bill.

"Do you have proof that Pathogen created this virus?" asked Slotter.

"Men like Goth always plan for plausible denial," said Bill. "They use the judicial system to avoid responsibility rather than seek justice. It takes a lot of proof to bring them to their knees and we're working on it."

"Do you have any proof that they tested it on people?" asked Slotter.

"We have useful information to share," said Bill. "Are you willing to work together?"

Slotter nodded.

"Yes, we need to work together," said Slotter. "Pathogen must be stopped."

"What I have to share will put your life at risk," said Bill. "Are you prepared to do that?"

Slotter's eyes narrowed.

"I'm a soldier," she said. "Risking my life is part of the job description."

Bill studied her closely before making a decision.

"All right then, but I'm not prepared to put my daughter greater danger," said Bill. "Do you mind if we speak privately?"

The question was directed more at Ginny, than Slotter, and she did not look happy about it. She searched her Dad's face for some explanation for being left out, but he revealed nothing. Then she looked at Slotter, who offered nothing but a noncommittal shrug. Finally, Ginny looked at me. I agreed with her father and didn't want her placed in any unnecessary danger, so I nodded my consent in the hopes she would agree to respect her father's wish. Ginny sighed and turned back to her father.

"As long as it's understood, that we have a few questions of our own that we expect you to answer once you're finished," said Ginny.

Both Bill and Slotter nodded in agreement before slipping off for another hour to compare notes. Ginny and I warmed our coffee and then settled in to wait for them to finish. When they returned, Slotter looked grim, but determined.

"I have a lot work to do, but I will keep my promise and answer your questions first," said Slotter.

"Did you have anything to do with my mother's disappearance from the nursing home?" I asked.

She shook her head.

"Will you help me find her?" I asked.

"Yes, tell me what happened," said Slotter.

I filled her in on the details of Eric's odd behavior and our efforts to find them.

"Why would Pathogen want your mother?" asked Slotter.

"As leverage," I said. "To force me to give them exclusive rights to Great Mother," I said.

"There's a couple of problems with that theory," said Slotter. "Did you get a ransom note?"

I shook my head.

"Then why do you believe they are holding her as leverage against you?" asked Slotter.

Ginny and Bill were watching me closely.

"Within an hour of Mom's disappearance, they made me an offer," I said.

"What offer?" asked Ginny.

"They offered me a lot of money for the exclusive rights to Great Mother," I said.

"How much money?" asked Ginny.

"Err...a billion dollars," I said.

"You're just now telling me this!" said Ginny.

"This doesn't make any sense," said Slotter. "How can you give them exclusive rights to something you don't own?"

"I can't and wouldn't if I could," I said.

"Then how?" asked Slotter.

"Pathogen has very good lawyers," I said.

"How can you own the earth or sky?" asked Bill.

"You can't, but we pretend anyway that you can," I said.

"I don't follow," said Ginny.

"All property rights are a legal fiction…meaning, it's just something we made up to minimize disputes that can lead to bloodshed," I said.

"Great Mother is a living thing, how do you own a plant?" asked Ginny.

"How do you own another human being?" I said.

"Slavery is an abomination," said Ginny.

"Yes, it is and yet it continues to exist even today in both overt and disguised forms," I said.

"Pathogen wanted to destroy Great Mother at its source, but retain some for themselves," said Bill. "Then they could use the virus as a weapon to kill who they wanted."

"Goth planned to use Great Mother to keep himself and his loyal minions alive after the release of the virus," said Slotter."

"Victor failed to accomplish that task," I said.

"Now that Great Mother has spread like wildfire, how can Pathogen control it?" asked Ginny.

"They will need new strategies, both legal and political, to suppress Great Mother," said Bill.

"The warrant to search your farm is only the beginning," said Slotter.

"This could get ugly," I said. "I have a friend from law school who works for the CIA. He told me that my name has appeared on a watch list," I said.

"What do you mean…watch list?" asked Ginny.

"For domestic terrorism," I answered.

"Somebody wants to discredit us really badly," said Ginny.

I nodded and said, "If we don't do something about this, we could end up in prison."

"Yes, but I wouldn't discount their willingness to resort to violence," said Bill.

"Like killing Eric and Mom, if they are no longer of any use to them," I said.

The expressions on the faces around me were grim.

"Then we need to find them before it's too late," I said.

None of us had the heart to admit that it might already be too late.

"Have you considered there might be a connection between your missing truck and their whereabouts?" asked Slotter.

I smacked my forehead.

"It disappeared from Pathogen's lab and then reappeared in Portland," I said.

"Exactly, let's begin our search in the area where the truck was found," said Slotter.

"Rose can tell us exactly where it was found," I said.

"Ummm… she tried to kill me," said Slotter. "I'm not one of her favorite people right now."

"I'll explain everything to her," I said. "We need to work together if we expect to save Mom."

"Don't forget Eric," said Ginny.

I was still unsure about Eric's role in all of this, but since he is my best friend, he deserves the benefit of the doubt.

"I have resources we can use once I know more about the truck," said Slotter.

"Be careful about who you trust. Goth's wealth reaches into a lot of pockets."

She slipped off without another word about Goth or Pathogen, but she did take a Great Mother seedling with her.

I turned my attention to Bill.

"As long as I can remember, I have loved Ginny," I said.

He nodded.

"The worst thing I ever did was turn away from her," I said.

There was no judgment in his eyes, only compassion.

"There will always be reasons to abandon the ones we love," said Bill.

"There were reasons I did what I did, but none of them were good enough," I said. "With your permission, I will make her my wife and I promise that I will never turn my back on her again."

"I believe that Plato was right," said Bill. "We are only half of ourselves and our primary mission in life is to find the other half. Only then can we learn life's true lesson of love."

"Ginny, is that to me," I said.

"Yes, I can see it," said Bill. "You have my blessing."

I reached out to shake his hand, but Bill took my hand and pulled me into a hug. Not to be left out of our moment of joy, Ginny piled on.

Bird arrived out of nowhere, landed on my broad shoulder and whispered, if you can call his squawk that, "Aaawk, not bad, Peckerwood, not bad at all."

When we finally untangled ourselves, Bill asked, "Is there anything else you wanted to ask?"

"Was my father involved in this mess?" I asked.

"Yes, he also worked at Pathogen," said Bill.

"On the same project?" I asked.

Bill shook his head.

"No, he was working on a different project," answered Bill.

"Did Dad know about the virus," I said.

"Yes, he did," answered Bill.

"Did he also know about Great Mother?" I asked.

Bill nodded.

"Before I left for the rainforest, I told him everything and asked him to watch over Ginny for me," said Bill.

"Was the motorcycle crash an accident?" I asked.

"I'm sorry, Grant, I may have unintentionally put him in the line of fire," answered Bill.

"So, Goth did this to my family," I said.

Bill nodded.

I tried to wipe the tears from eyes, but they refused to be held back.

He placed his hand on my shoulder and squeezed.

"Our families have already paid a high price in this fight and it isn't over," said Bill.

"Then we will finish it," said Ginny.

"Yes, we will," said Bill.

We spent the rest of the day together. The quiet family time was a much-needed break from all of the drama we had been through lately. Before leaving at sundown on yet another secret mission, he returned the journal to Ginny. It contains twenty years of entries that he wrote while he was away from home.

We read the early passages in the rainforest, but events prevented us from finishing it. The journal helps us understand the enormity of the threat we face, but to Ginny it is much more. The journal is a way for her to connect with her father across space and time. To her, it is a great treasure.

Bill's parting words to me were, "Grant, I want you to know that I am proud to call you son."

CHAPTER 61

The first objective of all living organisms is to tend to the basic requirements of life. The most basic of the basics is nourishing food, clean water and fresh air. We must have them to survive. Without them, we grow ill and die. Since life clings to life, nourishing our bodies, minds and spirits is hard-wired into all of us. First light nourishes my spirit.

There's a spot on our wraparound porch where I've positioned an old rocker to watch the sun rise. Each morning I take a perch with a steaming mug of dark roast and usher in the new day with our dog at my feet.

I call him ours, but we don't really know who he belongs to. One evening at sundown, Ginny found a stray German Shepard sitting on our back porch covered in ticks and blood. The left ear was shredded and she found a few other scars as she rummaged through his fur in search of bloodsucking parasites.

There were no tags and the neighbors didn't recognize him, so we left food out and gave him the run of the farm. When he wasn't begging for attention, he was usually seen sneaking off with something in his mouth. I could never quite make out what it was and tried to follow him a few times to get a closer look, but he always found a way to slip away from me. It was as if he disappeared into thin air. Ginny found it amusing and took to calling him, Packie.

Ginny didn't waste any time filling Kinsey in on Slotter's offer to use military intelligence to find Mom and Eric. Kinsey had long since taken ownership of the project, but the toll was high. I don't think she had slept longer than an hour or two at a time since Eric's disappearance.

While she was suspicious of Slotter, her involvement gave her new hope and reinvigorated her. Besides, she couldn't argue with the insight Slotter had about the truck and immediately rolled up her sleeves and began looking for a link between Pathogen and Portland.

Slotter was telling the truth about the search warrant. Just as the birds began their morning songfest, the first of the black SUVs hit the gravel drive leading into the farm.

Thanks to tinted glass, I couldn't see the drivers. Packie greeted the intruders with a low growl that sounded far more menacing than loud barking. He circled each vehicle, stopping only to piss on their tires. Their response was no response, as if they were trying to stare us down.

The stare down was starting to seem silly to me, so I joined Packie with a low growl of my own. He titled his head in my direction and smiled one of those tongue lagging dog smiles as if he was happy to see I had finally joined his little growling party.

All four doors of all six vehicles opened simultaneously. Then, like synchronized swimmers, twenty-four legs covered with black polyester, stretched straight out of the door at an ninety-degree angle, and set the heels of black combat boots on the gravel. Again, they paused. Packie winked. I was starting to think the synchronized swimmer analogy was way to accurate given the seriousness of the situation.

Ginny joined us on the porch with breakfast treats. Packie got a ham bone fit for a king and she handed me a thick slice of cinnamon toast. It was something my mother made for me as a kid. One morning just after we moved into the farm, I was sitting on the porch remembering my favorite breakfast, when to my utter amazement, Ginny walked out the door with a huge chunk of toast for me. After all these years, she remembered.

She nodded toward the SUV's and said, "We should be filming this shit, because no one will ever believe it."

"This is the third or fourth move they've executed in perfect synchronicity," I said.

As I spoke, twenty-four men emerged head first from the vehicles and came to attention. All of them wore the same dark ray bans, white polo shirts, and side arms. They were roughly the same height, weight, and all had dark hair cut short around the ears.

"Sad…very sad," said Ginny shaking her head.

Packie thumped his tail on the hardwood porch.

"I wonder if they realize how this regimented lifestyle robs them of their true nature," I mused.

"Unlikely," she said.

"I wonder how long it will take before they wake up," I said.

"It's hard to say," said Ginny. "Some of them may have to hit rock bottom first."

I did not see a leader in the group. It was almost as if an unseen wizard was controlling them remotely. Simultaneously, all twenty-four men raised their right hand to their right ear leading me to believe they were listening for orders.

"So many…I wonder why they sent so many," said Ginny.

"Wait there's more," I said.

The final person to emerge from the motorcade was a red headed woman, dressed in a man's black suit, white shirt, black necktie and black wingtip loafers. She wore no make-up that I could see and her hair was pulled severely back into a tight matronly bun. There was a decidedly butch air to her, as if she was more of a man on the inside, than a woman.

To add to the gender confusion, her mannerisms were masculine. She radiated masculinity. She was a man in charge…a man with a mission. Using crisp hand signals, the men fell into formation behind her and they headed our way.

"She looks like an undertaker," said Ginny.

"Or, a man in black on the hunt for a rogue alien," I said.

"This should be interesting," said Ginny.

They came to a stop at the foot of the porch. The Undertaker gave us a frank appraisal. Her eyes lingered on Ginny. Without any sign of embarrassment, she stared openly at her tits, before returning her gaze to Ginny's eyes.

When she did not get the invitation she hoped for from Ginny, she turned her attention to me. I had no interest in being one of her subs and I certainly wasn't interested in her sexually, so she didn't waste any time on me.

Packie didn't like her or her posse much and had not stopped growling since they moved toward the house.

"You better muzzle him or else I will take care of him myself," she said.

"Don't you dare touch him," said Ginny in a tone of voice that made it clear she meant it.

Like most bullies, The Undertaker was a coward deep down and I saw her true nature flash across her face for just an instant, before she recovered and restored the "I'm The Bitch In Charge" persona she wore as a professional mask. She knew we all saw the truth and I could tell it pissed her off.

"Step out of the way, I have a warrant to search this place," she said.

"Let me see your identification," I demanded.

She made an impatient move toward the door and we blocked her way. Ginny pulled her smartphone out of her pocket and began to film the encounter.

"These vehicles are unmarked," I said. "None of you are wearing any identifying clothing and you ignored my request to identify yourself. That would qualify you as trespassers and this as a home invasion. Show me your identification and the warrant."

She made a movement toward Ginny's camera. I immediately took a half step in her direction and Packie dialed up the growl. In unison, the subs placed their hands on their side arms.

"I'm streaming this video live," said Ginny calmly.

The Undertaker grunted in frustration, but abandoned her plan to snatch the smartphone and instead stretched her hand behind her without taking her eyes off the camera. The sub standing immediately behind her retrieved a folded sheet of paper from his pocket that he laid into her waiting palm.

Withholding information is one form of bully behavior. She did not want to hand the document over, but the live stream video forced her hand.

"This piece of paper purports to be a warrant signed by Judge Kimberly Freeman," I said. "Wait here while I call Kim to verify the authenticity of the document. She won't be happy that I'm calling so early, but you can explain to her why you showed up here at 6:45 a.m. with a small army in unmarked vehicles and refused to identify yourself. Whoever you are, I wouldn't want to be you right now."

When I turned toward the door The Undertaker said in a higher, slightly shrill voice, "Wait!"

I paused, but said nothing. Ginny continued to film. Packie continued growling.

"I am Special Agent Gloria Neuday," she said. "Hold your call until 9:00 a.m.

to give the Judge time to arrive at the courthouse. We will return after lunch. Is 2:00 p.m. acceptable?"

"Hand me your card," said Ginny. "We will call you to schedule a time for you to search our home after Grant speaks to the Judge."

Special Agent Neuday retrieved a business card from one of her subs and politely handed it to Ginny. In unison, all twenty-four subs marched back to their fleet of black SUV vehicles and left quietly.

"Do you really know Judge Freeman?" asked Ginny.

I shook my head.

"I didn't think so," said Ginny. "Nice job changing the tone of the discussion."

"It's a trick Ch'ing taught me," I said with a grin. "When someone gets aggressive with you, take their force and fold it back against them tenfold. Were you really streaming live?"

Ginny shook her head.

"She tried to intimidate us by showing up at dawn with a search warrant and a small army," said Ginny. "The chance I was broadcasting her actions to the world gave her something to think about."

"You have to love the power of transparency," I said. "She thought she had the upper hand, so we turned her strengths into weaknesses."

"Her arrogance caused her to overreach," said Ginny.

"It's easy to unbalance someone who overreaches," I said.

"You can't fight effectively when you're off balance," said Ginny.

"It makes all the difference between winning and losing," I said.

"We're going to win, aren't we?' asked Ginny.

I took her in my arms and kissed her.

The screen door opened, but didn't close. I looked up and saw Kinsey with her head out the door. The dark circles under her eyes bore witness to another sleepless night.

"When you two are finished making out like a couple of teenagers, then I need to show you something," said Kinsey.

"What is it?" asked Ginny.

"You need to see this for yourself," said Kinsey.

"Did you find them?" I asked.

She answered with a pained expression and a nearly imperceptible shake of the head. Asking Kinsey for updates on the search for Mom and Eric had become a painful experience. I thought she was too close to the investigation to be effective, which is one of the reasons I've been adding others to the team. Ginny agreed, but she felt Kinsey needed to stay involved for her own peace of mind.

We followed her inside. The television was on, but the volume was turned down so that it was barely audible. Conservative TV had an image of Great Mother on the screen. A news ticker that read, Doomsday Cult linked to drug deaths in Kentucky, scrolled across the bottom.

"If the doomsday cult lie isn't bad enough, listen to this craziness," said Kinsey.

She turned the volume up so that we could hear it.

"The doomsday cult in Kentucky has been connected to Padma Ganesha, who is believed to be a religious extremist responsible for violent terrorist deaths across the globe."

"Padma...terrorist..." I mumbled.

"Padma is a man of peace," said Ginny. "Why would anybody think he's a terrorist?"

"It seems ridiculous to us, but this fake news is believed by millions of people," said Kinsey.

"Why are they doing this?" asked Ginny.

"They are shaping public opinion to deflect attention from their own behavior," I said.

"That's right, if anybody is a doomsday cult responsible for deaths all over the world it's Goth and his drug dealing company," said Ginny.

"Aaawk, do I detect a note of bitterness in that statement?" squawked Bird.

"Lies are a bitter pill to swallow, especially when they are about you and your friends," said Kinsey.

Packie's tail thumped the floor. Ginny reached down and scratched him behind the ears. His tail thumped faster as if it was trying to keep time with his bliss.

"This is really bad PR," said Ginny. "We need to get out in front of this."

"What do you have in mind?" asked Kinsey.

"We need to find a way to broadcast the truth," she said.

"The problem isn't just Conservative TV," said Kinsey. "Rich companies, like Pathogen, control the media with their advertising dollars, and in some instances, actually own them outright."

"We'll find a way," said Ginny.

"In the meantime, I want to discuss this search warrant with Filmore," I said. "Maybe we can get it recalled."

"I'm headed into Portland to investigate a suspicious building," said Kinsey.

"I think I'll plow a field," said Ginny. "There's nothing like sitting on a tractor to clear a girl's head."

CHAPTER 62

Laurence Filmore is my eccentric, but formidable attorney. While I consider myself to be a very good lawyer, only a fool represents himself, and the Admiral recently got me out of a jam with the police over a couple of murders I sure as hell did not commit.

After a stellar career in the navy, the Admiral shifted to law and is considered by many to be the best lawyer that has ever been. In the span of a single sentence, he is capable of commanding one moment and seducing the next. He is truly an attorney's attorney and I was lucky to call him my own. If anybody could get a search warrant recalled, it would be him.

I didn't want to discuss this over the phone and getting in to see him on short notice would be a challenge. His secretary is like the grandmother I never had. Given the chance, I'm pretty sure she would spoil me rotten. The two of us conspired to wrangle a few minutes with the Admiral between hearings.

The Jefferson County Judicial Center is ten floors of courtrooms where many of life's battles are resolved by an elected Judge rather than bloodshed. I took the elevator to the seventh floor and waited within view of the mahogany doors leading to the courtroom.

There were five other people waiting nearby, all of them with their eyes glued to their smartphones. I prefer people-watching rather than surfing the net and filled the time assigning people nicknames and guessing their story.

When the doors to the courtroom swung open, I rose from my seat expecting the Admiral, but was shocked to see one of Goth's lackeys instead. Mr. Suit is a butterball of a man that I keep running into, but it's never a pleasant encounter.

He froze in his tracks when he saw me. From the look on his face, he was as shocked as I was. He took a quick peek over his shoulder before cutting his eyes toward the elevators. I guess he decided that fleeing to the elevators wasn't in his best interest, because he steeled himself and walked straight to me.

"I have to say, Mr. Li, that I'm disappointed in you," said Mr. Suit.

"And why is that?" I asked.

"I never took you for a fool," he answered.

"You don't know me," I said.

"I know you turned your back on a life of ease and comfort," he said.

"The best blades never come from a forge of ease and comfort," I answered.

"You will need more than a sharp edge if you hope to survive the storm that's coming," he said.

"Is that a threat?" I asked.

"You've chosen the wrong side, but it is not too late to take the money," he said. "Do not be a fool, Mr. Li. We know your little girlfriend has some resources of her own, but a billion dollars is a lot of money."

The courtroom door opened once again and the Admiral strolled out. He is a tall man, at least four inches taller than my six feet, with a full head of white hair that drapes his proud face like a lion's mane. While in his early sixties, as far as I can tell, the man does not have an ounce of fat on him anywhere.

Without another word, Mr. Suit turned and headed to the elevators. The Admiral's face lit up when he saw me and I walked over to greet him.

He took my hand in his big paw and said, "Grant, it is so good to see you."

"It's good to see you too, Admiral," I said.

"I wish you'd stop calling me that," he said.

I grinned and shrugged.

He looked at my farmer tan and sighed.

"Rumor has it you've been taking some time off after your big trial," he said.

"I was placed on administrative leave after John's death," I said.

The Admiral studied me with piercing blue eyes that seem to reflect the oceans he has known.

"Their loss is my gain," he said. "Come work for me."

"I've committed to something else and I need to see it through," I said.

"Am I bidding against another firm for the City's best young talent or are you just playing hard to get?" he asked.

I shook my head.

"Neither," I said. "There's not another firm in the country I'd choose over you. I've got some things to take care of first."

"Don't wait too long before you get back into the mix," said the Admiral.

"Right now, I need your help," I said.

"Not another murder investigation, I hope," he said.

"No, but I think I better do a conflict check first," I said.

"A conflict check...what's this about?" said the Admiral.

"Who is that man who just walked out of the courtroom ahead of you?" I asked.

"You don't know," said the Admiral.

I shook my head.

"You were just talking to him," he said.

I nodded.

"His name is Renfield," said the Admiral. "He works for your client, Wilbur Goth."

"Is he your client?" I asked.

"No, he was here on the case called ahead of mine," he answered.

"Do you represent Wilbur Goth or Pathogen?" I asked.

"No, but you do," he answered.

"Not anymore," I said.

"What the hell is going on, Grant?" demanded the Admiral.

"Judge Freeman has issued a search warrant of our home," I answered.

"On what probable cause?" he asked.

"Someone has placed us on a terrorist watch list," I said.

"Homeland security?" he asked.

I shrugged.

"It's a sneak and peak warrant," I said.

"And you think Wilbur Goth and Pathogen are behind it?" he asked.

"Yes," I answered.

"What are you involved in?" asked the Admiral.

I gave the Admiral a quick synopsis of recent events.

"Can you get the warrant recalled?" I asked.

"I can try," he said. "This one could be tricky."

"Thanks Admiral, we need all the help we can get right now," I said.

"Son, you are headed into a real shit storm," he said. "I'll see what I can do, but right now I have a motion that will be heard in a few minutes two floors up."

When I stepped outside of the building, the first thing I noticed was a significant drop in temperature. We were finally getting a welcome break from the heat wave that had melted the city for weeks. A stiff breeze cleared the sky of the unhealthy smog that had lain heavy upon us. It was blue for the first time in a long while, but dotted with scattered clouds that had black hearts ringed in white. It was a strange sight that left me with an uneasy feeling.

When I got home, Ginny was frantic. She flew past without seeing me. Her focus was inward as she tore through the house, randomly grabbing things in her path and then tossing them aside. She searched here and there, under and over, without any thought of the mess she was making and it was a spectacular mess. The house was a complete wreck.

I stood in the doorway watching and not daring to enter the fray. At some point, it would be necessary to engage, but the timing was critical. I figured I needed to wait for a crack to appear in her temporary madness.

She finally froze dead in her tracks. I was tempted to say something, but then I noticed that while her body may have come to a rest, the eyes were still wild. They darted from me, to the left and right, and then back again. This went through several cycles, but with each one, it slowed as she finally began to pull herself from the dark place and into the present moment.

She let out a long slow exhale and said, "It's gone."

When I didn't get more clarification, I asked, "What's gone, darling?"

My voice seemed to startle her for a moment, but then recognition took hold and she said, "Someone has taken it."

"What are you looking for?" I asked. "Maybe I can help you find it."

"It's not here," she said. "They came while we were gone. The bastards came into our house and they took it."

"Who are you talking about?" I asked.

"That sneaky bitch waited for us to leave and then invaded our home," she said.

"Are you taking about Special Agent Neuday?" I asked.

Ginny nodded.

"Damn, the Admiral didn't get the warrant recalled," I said.

"She was supposed to make an appointment," said Ginny.

"The sneak and peak warrant authorizes them to search our home when we are not here," I said. "I was hoping my attorney could stop it."

She must have taken something during the search, but I couldn't imagine what, since we had nothing to hide.

"What did they take Ginny?" I asked.

"His journal," she said with a sob. "That bitch took daddy's journal."

Life threatening situations force us to draw upon internal resources we never knew we had. Of course, there is no guarantee we will survive them, so most of us prefer to find a way to harness those resources without putting our necks in a noose.

I pulled Ginny close to me and held her tight until her breathing slowed to match mine. We must have stood like that in the middle of the small living room for five or so minutes, before she finally began to relax into me.

Now that she was calmer, we sank to the floor; our eyes glued together forming an unbreakable bond. With breath moving in and out in unison and the mirrors to our souls connected, we lost our individual selves.

When we find love, we find ourselves, and the light that radiates from our newly opened heart is like beacon to the rest of the world. Without self to obscure our vision, a soft golden light gathered around us and began to move. It rose up our backs and then down the center, first slowly then at its true speed, the speed of light.

At first, it was only a faint haze, but then it took the shape of an egg. I wasn't sure what to make of it until I realized it was a protective shield that deflects all forms of abuse from the outside world and returns it to the source.

Seek to understand and embrace change. Most of us resist change. That is because we leave change to chance. Whether we know it or not, we create our lives. The more we focus on the life we want, the more relaxed we become about change.

It was time for us to stop reacting to the manipulations of others and to focus on the outcome we desired. We choose to live in a world where we were all healthy, happy and loved.

CHAPTER 63

When things get tough, you never know for sure who will face the challenge and who will run. Sometimes an ally emerges from the most unlikely places, while a trusted team member quits the field. Courage, like other matters of the heart, is a mystery.

Uncle Jim showed up at our house a few hours after Ginny discovered the journal was missing.

"Grant, the shit is hitting the fan," said Uncle Jim.

"Which pile are you referring to?" I asked.

He lifted his eye patch and winked with the missing eye socket. It isn't pretty and first timers can find it a bit shocking. Me on the other hand, well, I've seen him do it hundreds of times and am numb to it. Still, he only does it when there is something big afoot, so I perked up.

"There's been another report on Conservative TV," he said.

"I don't believe anything on that network," I said. "How the hell can you keep watching it?"

"Awe shucks, conservatives aren't so bad," he said. "If you hippies would just listen up, you might learn a thing or two."

"Yea, right," I grumbled.

He handed me a thumb drive and said, "You might change your mind after you see this."

Conservative TV is without a doubt the most conservative news channel on cable television and has been a thorn in our side since we returned from the Amazon Rainforest with Great Mother. This is the channel that first reported the devastating news of an outbreak of drug related deaths caused by Great Mother. They were also the first to call us terrorists.

I popped the thumb drive into a tablet and opened the only file in the directory. It was a video file labeled "goodshit." I immediately recognized the face on the screen.

Claudia Smurk is an unlikely television star. She is short, rail thin and looks more like a crack whore than a movie star. Don't underestimate her. Prior to her television show, she won the best actor award for her role as a desperate single mom who would do anything to feed and protect her five young children.

Her latest success came as the host of a program called, "Ramin' the Scammers." Claudia uses a team of investigative reporters to expose scams. They have gone after some of the largest companies in the world and won. People love to see the high and mighty exposed, so the show has built a large and loyal audience.

She has developed a lot of credibility because her investigations are thorough and the facts are unimpeachable. Once Claudia sinks her claws into you, she does not let go until she has shaken the truth out. For such a tiny woman, she scares the shit out of scammers. I admired her commitment to making the world a better place.

As the video began, I thought Claudia looked different. She did not look like her usual haunted self. It was if she had evicted her demons and the real Claudia stood before the camera. When she began to speak, her voice came out steady and strong instead of the usual sharp tongue she uses to shred the bad guys to pieces.

"Over the last few years, I've gotten lots of advice about my appearance," began Claudia. "I didn't ask for it. Some of you gave it out of kindness and others are just haters. I want all of you to know, that I was listening, but there was not enough makeup to hide the dark circles under my eyes. Still, I tried anyway, but once skin cancer spreads to places like the liver, lungs and lymph nodes, it is a death sentence."

Claudia took a deep breath while the monitors flashed a series of very unflattering pictures of her without makeup. She looked like she was at death's door.

"These photographs were taken over the last few years," said Claudia. "As you can see for yourself, I was in a bad way and desperately saw every specialist who was willing to see me."

The monitors scrolled through a list of the names and qualifications of the physicians she had seen. Many work at leading hospitals and clinics around the country. A few are international.

"Between the headaches and the fatigue it became increasingly more difficult to work," she said. "I never thought poisoning myself with radiation and chemotherapy was a good idea, but I listened to my doctors and did it anyway."

She opened her medical records to the audience. Page after page gave witness to her ordeal. The conclusions were always the same…her cancer was relentlessly spreading.

"I was mad as hell and wanted to blame somebody, so I focused like a laser beam on the latest healthcare craze," said Claudia.

This time the monitors flashed through a series of images of Great Mother with titles like, "New Dangers from Invasive Species" and "Drug Deaths." They were followed by pictures of Ginny with titles like, "Fashion Queen Advocates Snake Oil Cure." The images of me had titles like, "Mental Health Patient" or "Troubled Lawyer." The images of Padma identified him as a "Known International Terrorist" and "Sex Addict."

"Medical fraud is arguably the biggest scam of our era," said Claudia. "Everyday people are duped into fake treatments that benefit no one other than greedy people willing to exploit human suffering."

The screen behind her flashed images of suffering people. Intermittently, the words "Medical Fraud" flashed across the screen while she spoke. It was a powerful display. It was gut wrenching. Claudia was in her groove.

"The doctors gave me a few months to live and I was determined to go out with a loud bang doing what I love," she said.

Tears began streaming down her cheeks. She didn't wipe them away, but instead, let them flow as visible proof of her pain. I had never seen her demonstrate so much compassion for the human condition. It was raw. It was the real deal.

"I was determined to expose the scammers," she said between sobs. "So, I searched for the victims of this strange plant from the Amazon Rainforest. I wanted to bring them here so you could hear their stories firsthand."

The screen flashed beautiful images of the vibrant life in the emerald forest. There were pictures of exotic plants and flowers. She showed us images of amazing animals in all of their splendid diversity. Finally, there were pictures of indigenous peoples, proud and free.

"As hard as I tried," she confessed. "I was unable to crack their stories. Without exception, each and every person who claimed to have taken Great Mother told amazing stories of healing."

This time she flashed images of smiling faces of regular people from all walks-of-life. This was the longest image break of them all. Face after face flashed across the screen of people giving testimony to their good health by virtue of their radiant smiles.

"People had died and I wasn't buying these stories," said Claudia. "I requested copies of the investigative files, but no one seemed to know who was in charge of the investigation. Days were wasted in this frustrating search, and in the end, I got nothing from the government."

Claudia paused and stared directly into the eyes of the audience. Then she raised her empty hands in front of herself and held them there without speaking for several breath cycles.

"I couldn't even get a copy of a single death certificate," she said plaintively. "I have to admit, it was frustrating. I was convinced it was my destiny to end this great fraud. The only course of action left to me was to use the plant myself...to be a human guinea pig in a well-documented test to prove it is all a lie."

"The film you are about to see was shot ten days ago," said Claudia.

The scene changed from the studio to a laboratory. Claudia wore a hospital gown and sat at the end of examination table. The door opened and a man wearing a lab coat walked into the room.

"This is Doctor Raymond Flitz," said Claudia to the camera. "He has agreed to give me a physical and to oversee the experiment."

He checked her pulse and blood pressure. Using a pocket scope he peered into her eyes, ears, and throat. Finally, he listened to her heart with the stethoscope hanging around his neck.

She turned her back to the camera and pulled her shirt up, exposing her wasted body. The area across the broadest part of her back was covered with sores. Some were dark and angry; others were reddish and open, as if the skin was being eaten away by a voracious parasite. She was sickly thin. The sight of her protruding ribs reminded me of the photographs of prisoners who slowly starved to death in concentration camps.

"Like many of you, I struggle with an illness that I couldn't seem to shake," said Claudia. "Despite catching it early and enduring several rounds of chemo, the cancer spread. I am a dying woman."

When he finished the physical examination, Claudia asked, "So doctor, am I good to go?"

"Your blood pressure is too high and your heart has an irregular beat," he said.

"Can we proceed with the experiment?" asked Claudia.

"For the record, I strongly object to this and will not be held responsible for what happens," he said.

"As you requested, I signed the legal waivers absolving you of responsibility," said Claudia. "Other than your legal concerns, are there any medical reasons we cannot proceed?"

"This treatment has not been approved by the FDA," said Dr. Flitz. "There are reported deaths linked to this plant. So yes, there are medical reasons not to proceed."

Claudia's face flared red with anger. She glared at the physician without wavering. It was a test of wills and the physician didn't have a chance. After a thirty second stare down he relented.

"My objections have been recorded," he said. "You can now proceed with this ridiculously dangerous plan."

The camera panned to the counter to the right. A potted plant was sitting on the counter next to an electric teapot. The camera zoomed in to show that the plant was Great Mother.

A nurse wearing protective surgical gloves took a pair of scissors and snipped three or four leaves that she dropped into a coffee mug. After pouring hot water over the leaves, the nurse handed the mug to Claudia, who took it tentatively, as if she was afraid of it.

She held the mug in both hands and stared into it. I could see a bit of steam swirling upward, and watched curiously, as Claudia slowly bent over it and took a deep breath. She hovered there for several breath cycles before lifting her head and staring into the camera again. Her expression was a mixture of surprise and peacefulness.

She held the mug up as if she was making a toast and said, "I'm dying and have nothing to lose."

Claudia began with a small tentative sip of the hot drink. I could clearly see she was swirling it around in her mouth as if she was giving herself one last chance to abort the experiment. Finally, she made a decision and swallowed. Once again, she waited to see what would happen next.

After a minute or so, she took another drink. This one was much bigger. The cup parted from her lips about a half-inch and then suddenly she began gulping the rest of the drink. Only after the last of it was gone, did she set the mug down, but not before licking every drop from her lips.

Her pale face began to flush with color. She ran her fingertips through her limp hair and began fluffing it. Then she stretched her arms high overhead and titled her head back as she let out a series of strong cleansing breaths. She dropped arms to her sides with a loud slapping sound and looked into the camera with clear eyes that sparkled.

"Still not dead," she said. "As a matter of fact, I feel better than I have in a long time. Doctor, would you check my vitals?"

Dr. Flitz went through the same routine as earlier, but he paused while taking her blood pressure, readjusted the cuff of the sphygmomanometer, and then took it a second time. Shaking his head, he shifted his focus away from her blood pressure and then listened to her heart. He paused and then with greater urgency moved the stethoscope around her chest as he listened to her heartbeat.

"Is there something wrong, doctor?" asked Claudia.

"Umm…well…not exactly," he said.

"What do you mean, not exactly?" she asked.

"Umm…well…your blood pressure is normal and your heart is beating regularly," he said.

"Well that's an improvement," she said. "My blood pressure has been high for years and I've had an irregular heart beat since I was in my teens."

"I don't understand how this could happen," he said.

"I need a nap," said Claudia with a yawn. "Is that okay?"

"Uh…oh sure," said Dr. Flitz absent-mindedly.

The last we see of Claudia before the scene switches back to the studio is her curled up on the exam table with her eyes closing shut.

"That was ten days ago," said Claudia. "I want to show you something."

She turned and lifted her shirt to expose her back to the audience. The camera zoomed in. Her skin was pink and healthy. All visible signs of the cancer were gone.

"I just got a biopsy report back," she said. "My cancer is in remission."

Her biopsy report flashed across the screen. She turned and lifted the potted plant from the lab video. The camera zoomed in to Great Mother.

"I am cured," she said. "This South American plant that grows like a weed has…"

The video cut out mid-sentence.

CHAPTER 64

Claudia's miracle cure went viral on social media and quickly became the most viewed video in the history of the internet. Great Mother became an overnight sensation and our website was flooded with requests for seedlings.

Stories about Great Mother's benefits were spreading like a wild fire. Much like Claudia's video, everyone wanted to share their personal healing experience and it became the number one topic in social media.

When computers and smart phones started freezing up, they said the cause was high demand for Claudia's video cure. Later, people began to grumble when searches for Claudia's video were re-directed to a FDA page about the agency's investigation into Amazoniamagna related deaths. Amazoniamagna was the new name they gave to Great Mother, as if they could control the medicine by renaming it.

It did not work. When they canceled Claudia's popular show the discussion shifted to conspiracy theories. The public usually has a short attention span, so you would think people would quickly lose interest, but something different happened. They got mad and fought back.

Social media was blocking all discussion of Great Mother, so the first act of rebellion was a mass exodus from social media. The rebellion went old school and took to the streets. Impromptu showings of the video popped up everyone. Reminiscent of the 1960's, they took to calling them "happenings."

The blatant censorship created an urban legend. Claudia had a huge following and word of her video spread across the land the old fashion way, by word of mouth. Sports bars played it instead of the game. It was everywhere. Things were going pretty well despite the censorship, until they weren't anymore.

As it often does, it started with an uninvited guest knocking at the door. Our friends know we spend a lot of time either in the kitchen or out back, so they know to come to the back door. Using the front door is a dead giveaway you are not one of our people.

I was in kitchen making a salad of field greens for lunch, so Ginny answered the door. When I heard the voice, I knew immediately who it was, and my beautiful day took a dark turn. My wife had found us.

"Hello, I'm Cynthia Li," said my wife in that dismissive voice I so hated. When Ginny didn't respond, she added, "I'm Grant's wife."

"I know who you are," said Ginny coldly.

There was an awkward silence before Cynthia finally asked, "Is he here?"

"Aren't you going to introduce your little friend there?" asked Ginny.

"Ummm…this is Candida…my errr…my friend's name is Candida," said Cynthia.

I had never heard Cynthia sound off-balanced before. She normally bullies her way through life, oblivious to the people around her.

"We're here to speak with her husband, not you," said Candida.

"Interesting," said Ginny. "Did your mother know she was naming you after a yeast infection?"

"It's a stage name," blurted Cynthia.

"Oh, you're a performer," said Ginny.

"A dancer,' said Cynthia.

'A dancer," repeated Ginny. "Where do you dance?"

'I'm retired," said Candida.

"Retired," repeated Ginny. "Late thirties is awfully young to be doing nothing."

"I'm not in my late thirties!" said Candida. "I'm only twenty-two."

"Oh, it must be the morning light that's making you look so much older," said Ginny.

Candida started to say, "Cindi, do I look…"

However, Cynthia interrupted her, "No, babe, you don't look…"

"What do you do to earn a living now that you are too old to dance?" asked Ginny.

"I'm not too…" said Candida.

"That's why we're here," interrupted Cynthia.

"Are you looking for a job?" asked Ginny. "We need help spreading the manure," said Ginny. "We're organic, you know."

"Umm…no…we're here to discuss the divorce settlement," said Candida.

"It doesn't pay well…actually it doesn't pay at all, but it is for a good cause," said Ginny.

"I don't need a job," growled Candida. "We want to discuss the financial terms of the divorce."

"Oh, are you getting a divorce, too?" asked Ginny.

"No, I'm not," said Candida.

"We want in on Great Mother," interrupted Cynthia.

"I'm not sure it can fix what you suffer from, but it's worth a try," said Ginny.

"We're not sick," said Cynthia.

"This is going to make her husband really rich," said Candida. "I only want what she's got coming to her."

"You want what's coming to her?" asked Ginny.

"Umm…I mean she wants it," said Candida.

"Don't play word games with us," snarled Cynthia. "If Grant wants me to sign the divorce papers, then he needs to pay me my fair share."

"That shouldn't be a problem at all since we freely give Great Mother away," said Ginny.

I had moved from the kitchen into the living room and now stood behind Ginny. Cynthia had a retro eighties rocker thing going. Her hair had been bleached albino white with blue highlights added back. She cut her hair at different lengths and then spiked it in random directions reminiscent of the early girl bands.

Cynthia tied a large pink bow on the left side of her head and wore matching leggings. The pink was contrasted by a black three layered short skirt with grey lace. She wore a pink athletic bra underneath a sheer yellow top with a couple of strands of pink Mardi Gras beads layered on top.

In sharp contrast to Cynthia's little girl outfit, Candida wore a men's black button down shirt, black pleated slacks with cuffs, and black wing tips. I was surprised to see Candida was dressed as the top, since Cynthia was such a control freak, but as I watched them interact with each other, the clothes didn't really jive with the energy between them.

"Is that right, Grant?" barked Cynthia.

My response was calm, "Yes, I think she wants what's coming to you?"

Candida clutched at Cynthia as she said shrilly, "I do not!"

Cynthia peeled Candida's hand from her arm and said, "Are you really so stupid that you would give this medicine away for free?"

"Are you really so greedy that you think you can profit from something like this?" asked Ginny.

"Oh Jesus," said Cynthia. "You finally found someone as stupid as you, Grant."

"I'm not sure how smart I am, since I married you, Cynthia, but I know one thing for certain, Ginny is brilliant," I said.

"I want what's mine and I damn well will get it," she said.

"I've given you everything," I said. "The only thing I have left are the credit cards you maxed out, but you can have those to, if you want them."

"There's more...there's always more," said Cynthia.

"I have nothing left to give you," I said. "Thanks to you, we are on the verge of bankruptcy and if you keep pushing, then you'll lose the things you have."

"Bullshit, Grant, you are sitting on a gold mine," she said.

"Great Mother is not for sale," Ginny said.

"You haven't heard the last of this," said Cynthia. "Since you and your slut have proven incapable of running this business, my lawyer will be filing a motion with the Court to appoint a receiver to run it for us."

CHAPTER 65

A covered porch is one of those relics of the past that we have whole-heartedly embraced. With the promise of shade and fresh air, it pulls us from the inside of the old farmhouse and out into the world each day, where for the most part, we just sit quietly and bear witness to the happenings around us.

On this day, we were sitting on the front porch discussing our strategy to find Mom, when Packie came flying around the corner of the house barking at an unseen intruder. His early warnings are never wrong and this was no different. A black Cadillac came barreling down our drive, leaving a trail of gravel dust similar to a streak of contrails pushing a jet across the sky.

The classic luxury car belonged to Laurence Filmore, otherwise known as the Admiral. Having him show up unannounced at our home could not be a good thing. When I first met him, he was teaching at my law school. While Filmore has a reputation for teaching in clothing more suited for a beach than the halls of justice, he must have just come from court, because he was wearing expensive blue suit pants, a crisp white shirt with sleeves rolled half way up the forearm, and a red power tie. We shushed Packie and rose to greet him.

"Admiral, it is always a pleasure to see you," I said warmly. "Welcome to our home."

Packie sat respectfully at Filmore's feet and waited expectantly for a pat on the head. The Admiral did not let him down and if I didn't know better, I would swear the dog purred at his touch.

"Hello, Grant," said the Admiral as he stretched a big paw toward me.

I took his hand and gave it a firm shake. His eyes were warm and revealed nothing of the reasons that brought him to our door.

"This is Ginny," I said with a turn of the hand toward my fiancée.

The Admiral gave her a long appraising look before saying, "It's an honor to meet the girl who has opened Grant's heart."

Ginny's neutral expression shifted to a soft glow as she said, "I gave Grant my heart when I was five years old, but it took him a few years to accept it."

"He's not very smart, is he?" asked the Admiral with crooked grin.

Ginny cut her mischief-filled eyes to me as she said, "Well, you are his

371

Professor, but I must admit he has his moments."

"Aaawk, are you here to get Peckerwood out of another jam, Counselor?" squawked Bird.

I do not know how he does that. We had not seen Bird in days and suddenly he appears out of thin air. What makes it even odder, is how much it seemed to startle Packie, since no one sneaks up on him, other than Bird.

"Did that bird just formulate a coherent question on his own?" asked Filmore.

"Aaawk, yes and I recite poetry too," squawked Bird. "Do you want to hear some?"

Bird did not wait for an answer from Filmore to his last question and instead answered it himself, "Yes, of course you do. Here is one of my favorites. There was once a girl from Nantucket..."

"That's enough Bird," said Ginny sternly.

Filmore raised an eyebrow at Bird, but otherwise declined to engage the outrageous macaw in conversation. Instead, he turned his attention back to Ginny. It is hard to say for sure what goes on behind his inscrutable countenance, but if I were a gambler, then I would bet he was evaluating her character as a future witness.

"The shit is about to hit the fan," he said to Ginny. "Are you up for it?"

"I've been dodging flying shit my entire life," said Ginny. "Tell me why you think this is any different."

"Aaawk, who are you calling flying shit?" demanded Bird.

The Admiral ignored Bird's question.

"It will get personal," he said. "In fact, you can bet on it."

"By personal do you mean they are going to say mean things about me," she said.

He nodded.

"Things like...my clothing line corrupts the youth of America and I should do everyone a favor by following Socrates' lead and drink a cup of hemlock," she said.

"Nice touch comparing yourself to Socrates," said Filmore. "What else?"

"Thank you," said Ginny. "What else...I enjoy sex with my married fiancée and therefore should be publicly branded with a scarlet letter to protect the innocent village boys."

"The Scarlet Letter is a nice analogy," said Filmore. "The narrow minded Puritans forced Hester Prynne to wear a public symbol of her adultery, while her lover, the town minister, went unpunished."

"That's right," said Ginny. "Hester was guilty as hell, but Nathanial Hawthorne used the story to challenge assumptions about sex and gender roles.

"Should sex be a crime?" asked Filmore.

"That's the question all right," said Ginny with an exaggerated sweet smile. "The answer to your rhetorical question is, hell no."

"Rhetoric aside, in this instance, our hypocritical modern day Puritans are coming after both of you," said Filmore.

"My wife was here yesterday making threats," I said. "I'm assuming your visit has something to do with that."

Filmore did not respond. Instead, he gave us his best courtroom poker face.

"She was with her lesbian lover," I said. "Surely you don't view her as a puritanical threat."

"Grant, haven't you figured out that the loudest puritanical prudes, are often the biggest freaks behind closed doors?" asked Ginny.

"She filed court pleadings asserting that you are incompetent to handle your own affairs," said Filmore.

"That's ridiculous," I said.

"Her affidavit asserts that you have mishandled marital funds and are heavily in debt," he said.

"She has spent every nickel we have and then some!" I said.

"She claims you haven't paid your bills in months," he said.

I thought about the stack of unpaid bills sitting on the coffee table in my shabby little apartment above a hookah bar. I looked at Ginny. Her face was full of concern. It did not help. Instead of feeling better, her compassion made me feel like a loser.

"Between her spending and Mom's medical bills...I'm...I'm...and losing my job...I'm dead broke...umm...I'm living...I've been living off of credit cards and they are nearly maxed out," I said.

Filmore turned his attention to Ginny and said, "This is where it starts to get really ugly."

"Let me guess," said Ginny. "She says Grant is living with a slut whore who has muddled his mind and is stealing his money."

"Pretty damn close," said Filmore grimly.

"Ginny doesn't need my money," I said.

They both looked at me as if I had lost my mind.

"Aaawk, steal from the poor and give to the rich," squawked Bird.

"I've given Cynthia everything," I said. "What else can my greedy wife possibly squeeze out of me?"

"Your freedom for one," said the Admiral.

"Aaawk, back to the slammer where you can make new friends and influence people, Peckerwood," squawked bird.

"My freedom!" I exclaimed. "That makes no sense. This is a divorce, not a criminal case."

"Well, yes, but she's says you have a history of untreated mental illness and is requesting a mental inquest," he said.

Professor Filmore once stood before a class of eager want-to-be lawyers and told us to never...never plead a client not guilty by reason of insanity. If successful, then the client loses virtually all civil liberties and can be locked up in a mental institution where a doctor, and not a judge or jury, determines his fate. These hospitals are worse than any prison and few people ever escape them. Once they go in, then most criminal patients are in for the rest of their lives.

I knew he was telling the truth because I had been in one of those places. I was five years old, maybe six, and Ginny's mother had caught us with our pants down. We were just curious children, but she reacted with rage, beating Ginny and threatening me.

I did not sleep for weeks. Exhaustion sent me over the edge, so they sent me to a hospital for treatment. The electroshock administered by a sadistic doctor was much worse than the nightmares caused by the Ginny's mother.

Bird landed softly on my shoulder. I really expected him to rub this latest turn of events in, but instead he rubbed the side of his beak against my cheek.

"What history of mental illness?" asked Ginny.

"Well, for starters, she has a sworn affidavit from Dr. Denise Laitrel, who treated Grant, both as a child and an adult."

Ginny searched my face. I figured she was looking for a denial, but I knew it was true. I was not feeling well. Her face was unfocused and I felt very hot. I am sure the only thing that kept me from retching was Bird's beak gently rubbing along my jaw line.

"I never heard of her," said Ginny. "Who is she Grant?"

"Sadistic Doctor," I muttered.

Ginny's eyes opened a little wider as she repeated, "Sadistic Doctor?"

"She's a psychiatrist," said Filmore.

"What does this psychiatrist say in her affidavit?" asked Ginny.

Filmore looked grimmer than I have ever seen him as he said, "She says that Grant is subject to violent outbursts triggered by psychotic delusions and that his treatment was terminated before it was completed."

"That's insane!" said Ginny. "What delusions?"

"It's a long list, but at the top are things like him fighting battles with giant snakes and flying dinosaurs," said Filmore.

"I was there," said Ginny.

"You saw him fight a giant snake?" asked Filmore.

"Well, not exactly," answered Ginny.

"Did you see him fight a pterodactyl?" he asked.

"It was about to kill him so I jumped on its back and broke its neck," said Ginny.

Filmore looked at me. I nodded. He turned to Ginny and studied her with renewed interest. He must have seen what he wanted, because he nodded.

"There's much more detail about his alleged delusions and there are several more affidavits detailing his violent behavior," said Filmore.

"Grant isn't violent," said Ginny.

"Jonathan Wiemp, M.D. swears otherwise," said Filmore.

"Dr. Wiemp was holding me against my will," said Ginny.

"He says Grant viciously attacked a hospital employee," said Filmore.

"Oh that..." said Ginny in a defeated tone.

"Dr. Wiemp ordered a security guard to take me to the psych ward," I said. "I was defending myself."

"Did you point gun in a security guard's face?" asked Filmore.

"Yes," I answered.

"Were you about to squeeze the trigger," asked Filmore.

I stared back at him blankly, knowing the answer was yes, but refused to say it aloud. Ginny was the only thing that kept me from pulling that trigger.

Filmore shook his head as he said, "These sworn statements establish a prima facie case that you require medical attention for a mental illness that creates an imminent danger of substantial physical harm to yourself and others. The Judge was prepared to execute the warrant for your commitment."

I interrupted him, "I am not going back to that hospital."

"We will clear this up," said Ginny in a firm and confident voice, "but there's something I don't understand about this. Yesterday, Grant's wife said she wanted money. How does this help her accomplish that?"

"If Grant is hospitalized, then she will control all of the assets," said Filmore. "At best, she only gets half in a divorce."

"I have given her everything," I said. "There is nothing left for her to control except Great Mother."

"We are committed to giving this cure to the world free of charge," said Ginny

"Is there an outstanding offer on the table to buy it from you," said Filmore.

"Damn," said Ginny.

"Ummm...I was offered a billion dollars to sell it to Pathogen," I said.

The Admiral's eyebrows shot up as high as they could possibly reach.

"We don't have much time to prepare," said Filmore. "The hearing is tomorrow morning."

"So soon!" said Ginny.

"I was only able to convince the Judge to delay a decision by giving him my personal assurances that Grant would not harm himself or anyone else prior to the hearing," said Filmore.

The tears in Ginny's eyes damn near broke my heart.

CHAPTER 66

Sleep was impossible. I tried every trick I knew before finally slipping out of bed around 1:00 a.m. to avoid disturbing Ginny. During the Goth trial, I found it helpful to work for an hour or two when I couldn't sleep. Doing something constructive calms my worries. Once I let go of the worry, I can then grab a few early morning winks before court. It is not ideal, but its better then tossing and turning all night.

I sat at the kitchen table and sipped a glass of water while scribbling notes on a dog-eared yellow pad. This practice helps liberate churning thoughts so that I can finally get some peace. I also find it useful to write down the worst-case scenario. Once reduced to a few sentences on paper, it feels less ominous.

The biggest thing I feared was losing Ginny. The reality of my failed marriage had arrived center stage in all of its ugliness. Cynthia was showing her ass to everyone and it reflected poorly on me. If she had not moved her lover into the house, then I would still be with her, desperately trying to find solutions to our problems. I wondered what that says about me as relationship material. It sure doesn't reflect well that I would settle for a marriage like that.

After Filmore grilled us for hours, Ginny went straight to bed and fell into a deep sleep. I did not have a chance to discuss the day's developments with her and was feeling insecure. On the one hand, I knew Ginny truly loved me and that she was committed for better or worse. Unfortunately, Cynthia was making a strong case to have me locked away in a mental hospital. If she succeeds and the divorce doesn't go through, then marrying Ginny will be impossible.

As it turned out, I stayed up the rest of the night and spent it examining my life. It occurred to me that I did indeed suffer from delusions, but not the kind that Cynthia hoped to use against me. These delusions are even more insidious because the hide behind the weight of cultural normality.

The most widespread delusion in our culture is something that is at the very root of our legal system. This delusion is something we call guilt. I realized in the wee hours of the night that I have spent a great deal of time blaming others for the problems in my life.

I blamed the hit-and-run driver who stole my parents and left me an orphan. I blamed Ginny's mom for driving us apart and robbing us of the joy and love we could have had together for the last twenty years. I blamed Cynthia for...well for, being her greedy self and trying to have me committed to a mental institution so she could take Great Mother from us. As far as I could see, nothing good has ever come from all of this blame. In fact, it has carried me once again to the steps of a mental hospital.

Two paths lay before me. One led to a padded cell and the other led to freedom. Years ago, blaming others led to a breakdown that put me in the hateful hands of Sadistic Doctor. If I continue blaming other people for my circumstances, then I will end up on her table once again. I need a new strategy for living, or risk losing everything.

The path to mastery is a very simple one, stop blaming other people for my problems. There is only one path to freedom and that is to take full responsibility for my life. If I do this, then I will live the life I choose for myself, without fail. I was ready to take control of my life.

By sunrise, I had a completely new attitude about life. Of course, I couldn't wait to share these new insights with Ginny, but when she came down for coffee her pinched brow and scowl warned me it wasn't time. Squaring my shoulders, I headed to court with an absolute sense of self-confidence about the direction I was headed.

We met Filmore outside of the Courtroom. He took one look into my eyes and a slow smile spread across his face. He said nothing. Instead, he patted me on the back and we headed inside where we took a seat at counsel's table.

Cynthia arrived a few minutes later with her attorney. Candida was nowhere in sight. Cynthia was dressed for Sunday church services in a navy blue dress and sensible pumps. Her hair color had been restored to its natural mousy brown shade and was pulled back severely into a tight bun. Her makeup was hardly noticeable, just the right touch to highlight her strengths, but not enough to make her look cheap.

Cynthia's attorney is a well-known divorce lawyer, Sandra Kingsport. Sandra only represents wealthy women in high profile divorce proceedings. She is short, no more than 5'2", but seems to be much taller. The grey streaks in her witchy black hair are uncolored. She wears them like Cruella De Vil as a physical reminder she is vicious in the courtroom and never loses. Filmore has a comparable reputation, but he is a criminal defense lawyer.

The proceeding pitted two of the very best attorneys against each other. While they have never crossed swords before and only knew the other by reputation, neither was the slightest bit intimidated. It was going to be an interesting morning.

In recent years the trend is toward female Family Court judges, however, Judge Thomas Kruthers was male and had been on the bench for over thirty years. You might say he wrote the book on the new Family Court system and is known to be a huge advocate for family values. Ginny's presence in the courtroom could prove problematic.

Judge Kruthers is tall, thin, stooped and has sharp hawkish nose. He is well past the age for retirement, but continues to work because he believes idle hands are the devil's workshop. I couldn't help but notice that his eyes lingered on me as he entered the courtroom.

We resumed our seats as he opened the case file and read the contents. When he finished reading, he took another long hard look at me and then at Ginny. Ms. Kingsport cleared her throat to speak, but Judge Kruthers held a hand up to stop her.

"I've read the file and this case has all the markings of a potential spectacle," said the Judge. "I will not permit my courtroom to be turned into a media circus, is that understood Ms. Kingsport?"

Ginny's attorney nodded.

Judge Kruthers turned his attention to the Admiral.

"Mr. Filmore?" asked the Judge.

"Understood, your Honor," said the Admiral.

"Have you read this petition, Mr. Li?" asked Judge Kruthers.

"Yes sir," I answered.

"How does it make you feel?" he asked.

"A little sad sir," I answered.

"Does it also make you angry?" asked Judge Kruthers.

"No sir," I answered.

"Did you recently travel to South America?" asked Judge Kruthers.

"Yes sir," I answered.

"Did you return with a plant?" asked Judge Kruthers.

"Not exactly, sir," I answered.

"What do you mean?" he asked.

"A seedling was given to us in South America, but we left it behind," I answered.

"Was it a seedling of the plant called Great Mother?" asked Judge Kruthers.

"Yes, sir," I answered.

"Did you obtain another seedling after your return to Louisville?" he asked.

"Yes, we did," I answered.

"How did you come into possession of the plant?" he asked.

"I'm not sure, sir," I said.

Judge Kruthers raised an eyebrow and waited.

"It somehow followed us home," I said with a shrug.

Cynthia snorted and began whispering with her attorney.

"A plant followed you," said Judge Kruthers. "You do understand, Mr. Li, that your wife asserts that you are mentally incompetent?"

"It's a figure of speech, your Honor," I answered. "I have no idea how it came to be here in Kentucky."

"Regardless of how it got here, do you distribute seedlings to others?" he asked.

"Yes sir," I answered.

"Do you sell them for profit?" he asked.

"No sir," I answered.

"Is it true that Pathogen has offered you a billion dollars for the plant?" asked Judge Kruthers.

"Yes, sir," I answered.

My answer set off another round of whispering between Cynthia and her attorney. Ginny, on the other hand, went deathly still.

"Do you also understand Mr. Li that your wife claims this is a marital asset?"

asked the Judge.

"I understand that is her claim?" I said.

"Have you accepted the offer?" he asked.

"No sir," I answered.

"Then you rejected it?" he asked.

"Ummm...no sir," I answered.

"Do you intend to accept Pathogen's offer?" he asked.

Everyone in the room froze, including Cynthia. I knew that the answer would seal my fate. If I do not sell the plant, I will be sent back to the psych ward and Sadistic Doctor will resume her electroshock treatments. If I say yes and accept Pathogen's offer, then I have betrayed everyone I care about and will most certainly loose the love of my life.

"Mr. Li?" said the Judge.

"Yes sir," I said.

Ginny gasped and Cynthia let out an odd sound that I couldn't quite identify.

"You intend to sell," said the Judge.

"Oh, no sir," I answered.

Cynthia said, "What I tell you...he has lost his fucking mind."

Judge Kruthers frowned at Cynthia and said, "One more outburst like that and I will hold you in contempt of this Court."

He turned his attention back to me and asked, "I can see from your file that you are financially insolvent," said Judge Kruthers.

"Yes, I am flat broke," I admitted.

"Surely you realize that's a lot of money, Mr. Li," he said. "Why would you not accept Pathogen's offer?"

"This medicine is a gift," I answered. "It was not only given to me and Ginny, but to you and to everyone else. It is like the air we breathe. We promised the men and women who entrusted it to our care that we would share it freely with everyone. I intend to honor that promise."

"Pathogen is a world-wide pharmaceutical giant, surly they have a better distribution system than you," said the Judge.

"I don't know what Pathogen intends to do with Great Mother, but I seriously doubt they will give it away for free," I said.

The judge turned his attention to Cynthia and said, "Mrs. Li, how long have you lived in Kentucky?"

"All my life," answered Cynthia.

"Has it been more than sixty days since you last had marital relations with your husband?" asked Judge Kruthers.

"You mean sex?" asked Cynthia.

"Yes, Mrs. Li," said the Judge. "I mean sex."

"I stopped having sex with him over a year ago," said Cynthia.

"Are you pregnant?" asked the Judge.

"No," said Cynthia.

"Is your marriage irretrievably broken?" asked the Judge.

"I'm not sure I understand the question," answered Cynthia.

"Is there any chance the two of you will patch things up?" asked the Judge.

"None," answered Cynthia.

"Have you divided the marital assets and debts to your satisfaction?" asked Judge Kruthers.

"Your honor, may I..." interrupted Cynthia's attorney, but for the second time in ten minutes, Judge Kruthers raised a hand to quiet her.

"Mrs. Li, are you satisfied with the division of property?" asked the Judge.

Cynthia shook her head and said, "No, I'm not satisfied."

Judge Kruthers took a second look at the paperwork and said, "According to the paperwork filed with the Court, you will receive all of the marital assets and Mr. Li will assume the debts, is that correct?"

"Yes," answered Cynthia.

"Are there other assets that have not been disclosed?" asked the Judge.

"For starters, I want the house," said Cynthia.

"Are you talking about the house where you currently reside?" asked the Judge.

"Yes, I am," said Cynthia.

Judge Kruthers rifled through the file.

"I see here that title to that real estate is in the names of Mr. Li's parents," said the Judge. "Are they still alive?"

"His father is dead and the mother is practically a vegetable," said Cynthia.

"She's alive?" asked the Judge.

"Barely," answered Cynthia.

"Is there any other real estate?" asked the Judge.

"The farm in Goshen," answered Cynthia.

He looked through the file before saying, "I don't see a farm in Goshen listed here."

Cynthia pointed to Ginny and said, "It's where he lives with that slut."

The Judge frowned at Cynthia and then turned his attention to me.

"Mr. Li, is this correct?" asked the Judge.

"It is not correct that Ginny is a slut and I find it offensive that she would call her that," I answered.

"Yes, it is offensive," agreed the Judge. "Do you own real estate in Goshen?"

"No sir," I answered.

"Do you currently reside in Goshen?" asked the Judge.

"Yes sir," I answered.

"Who owns the real estate where you reside?" asked the Judge.

"The foundation we set up to distribute Great Mother," I answered.

"Where did the funding for the foundation come from?" asked the Judge.

"Ginny, provided it from her personal savings," I said.

The Judge looked at Ginny and said, "I'll get to you in a moment."

He turned his attention back to Cynthia. She looked pleased. I knew her well enough that I could almost hear her thoughts and what she was thinking about Ginny wasn't kind.

"Mrs. Li, is there any other real estate?" asked the Judge.

"No," answered Cynthia.

"It says here that you will receive the Mercedes, is that correct?" asked the Judge.

Cynthia nodded.

"You will have to speak up," said the Judge.

"Yes, I get the Benz," said Cynthia.

"Is there any money in the bank accounts?" asked the Judge.

"No," said Cynthia.

"Are there any other assets that have not been disclosed?" asked the Judge.

"Your honor," interrupted Sandra Kingsport.

"Ms. Kingsport, if you interrupt me again I will hold you in contempt of court," said Judge Kruthers.

Ms. Kingsport set her jaw, but nodded to the Judge. I doubt she is accustomed to being dressed down by the Court.

"Yes, the rights to the medicine Grant brought back from South America," answered Cynthia.

"Are you referring to the plant Mr. Li testified about earlier?" asked the Judge.

"Yes, I am," answered Cynthia.

"Do you believe this plant is a marital asset?" asked the Judge.

"Yes, it is," answered Cynthia.

"Why do you believe that?" asked the Judge.

Sandra Kingsport opened her mouth to speak, but thought better of it when the Judge glared at her.

"Because if Grant won't sell it, then Pathogen has offered to buy it from me," answered Cynthia.

"The only way you can do that is to have sole control over the plant by having Mr. Li declared incompetent, isn't that right?" he asked.

"Yes, that's what my attorney told me," answered Cynthia.

Sandra Kingsport slumped a little deeper into her seat.

"If I commit your husband to a mental hospital then you will be free to sell Great Mother to Pathogen, is that correct?" asked the Judge.

"That's the plan," said Cynthia.

The Judge gave Cynthia a long hard stare before cutting his eyes to her attorney. Ms. Kinsgport reminded me of a deer caught in the headlights of four thousand pounds of speeding death.

"Mrs. Li, have you witnessed any behavior that would lead you to believe your husband is mentally ill?" asked the Judge.

"He wants to turn down a billion dollars," answered Cynthia.

"Other than that, Mrs. Li," said the Judge. "Is there anything else to support your claim Mr. Li is mentally ill?"

"He thinks he met giants and dwarves in the underworld," answered Cynthia.

"Is this something he told you personally?" asked the Judge.

"I heard it," answered Cynthia.

"Is there any behavior you personally witnessed that supports your claim he is mentally ill?" asked Judge Kruthers.

"Grant doesn't like sex," said Cynthia. "I mean look at me. I'm hot and we only had sex maybe a half-dozen times during our marriage, but I could tell he didn't like it."

Judge Kruthers took a long hard look at Cynthia over the top of his glasses. Like most judges, he has a good poker face, but I noted a touch of distaste in his eyes.

"Anything else, Mrs. Li?" he asked.

"Isn't that enough?" asked Cynthia.

"I'll be the judge of that, Mrs. Li," he answered. "If I grant your petition and appoint you guardian, will you sell Great Mother to Pathogen?"

"Yes," answered Cynthia.

"Did you tell your husband about your plan?" asked the Judge.

Cynthia shook her head ever so slightly.

"You'll have to speak up, Mrs. Li," said the Judge.

"No, I did not," said Cynthia.

"Why not?" asked the Judge.

"Because…because, he's crazy and that slut he's living with will try to steal it from me," answered Cynthia.

"Why do you think that?" asked the Judge.

"That gold digger is living with a married man," answered Cynthia.

The judge turned his attention to Ginny and asked, "Are you Virginia Bardough?"

"Yes, sir," answered Ginny.

"Were you with Mr. Li in South America?" asked the Judge.

"Yes, I was," answered Ginny.

"Is he telling the truth about the plant?" asked the Judge.

"Yes sir," answered Ginny.

"Have you sold the plant to anyone?" asked the Judge.

"No, we have not," answered Ginny.

"Have you given it freely to anyone who wanted it?" asked the Judge.

"Yes sir," answered Ginny.

"Have you witnessed any erratic behavior that causes you concern for Mr. Li's ability to handle his affairs?" asked the Judge.

"No sir," answered Ginny.

"You will have my decision within ten days," said the Judge.

We rose as Judge Kruthers exited the courtroom.

"What the hell just happened?" demanded Cynthia.

"Not now," said her attorney.

"What do you mean, not now?" demanded Cynthia.

"The Judge just took your divorce proof," answered her attorney.

"What the hell does that mean?" said Cynthia.

"It means he can dissolve your marriage at any time," answered her attorney.

"What the fuck!" said Cynthia. "I don't want a divorce, I want the fucking money."

"You need to calm down," said Ms. Kingsport.

"This isn't what we planned," shouted Cynthia. "I paid you to get that loser of a husband locked safely away in a padded cell."

Her attorney started to say, "Ms. Li, I hardly…"

Cynthia interrupted her, "Did you hear that crazy shit he was spouting? He wants to help people by giving away a billion dollars worth of medicine…unfuckingbelievable."

"For the last time, we will discuss this later," answered her attorney.

"You work for me and you will discuss this right now," shouted Cynthia.

Sandra Kingsport peered over the top of her glasses at Cynthia before saying,

"Please have your new attorney give me a call, Mrs. Li and I will fill him in on your case."

"You can't quit you fucking bitch, because I'm firing you," shouted Cynthia as Ms. Kingsport walked out of the courtroom.

When the door shut behind her attorney, Cynthia turned toward me and scowled, "Well Grant, I see you managed to stay out of the loony bin for now by bribing the Judge. When this is all over, I'm going to have both of you disbarred."

The proceedings in family court are routinely videotaped and there is a red light at the center of the Judge's bench that shows everyone in the courtroom when the videotape is running. Normally, the Judge turns it off before he leaves the courtroom, but I guess he forgot it in this instance because it was still recording.

CHAPTER 67

The honeymoon phase of a relationship is full of hope, but the warm fuzzy feelings can only be sustained with a high degree of acceptance and trust. Communication is critical. Ginny saw the ugly truth of my life with Cynthia and we needed to talk about it, but she was moody and distant.

For some reason folks tend to be more accepting in the beginning of a relationship, but once it gets better established, the criticism demon shows up. Cynthia and I never got past it. I was determined to do better with Ginny, but her moodiness inflamed my fears.

One of the things I attribute my success as a trial lawyer to is a commitment to following instincts. It was up to me to patch this up with Ginny and my gut told me it needed to be done now.

I found her sitting in the middle of a field of Great Mother. It was a beautiful day. The sky was clear and the air was warm, but not too hot. Ginny's hair was pulled back into a ponytail, but a few stray strands danced with the light breeze. She was dressed in grey cotton gym shorts, a Fund for the Arts t-shirt, and cheap hot pink flip-flops that looked like they came from the dollar store.

She sat cross-legged, back straight, chin dropped slightly, and eyes closed. It did not seem right to interrupt her meditation. I considered turning back, but the prospect of sitting with her was far more attractive.

Dropping to a seated position across from her, I settled into the present moment and forgot my worries for the time being. Great Mother has a unique scent that smells like a drop of sunshine. I let it move through me like a sunrise illuminating all of the dark places with healing light.

When I opened my eyes, it was with a renewed spirit that I said, "Ginny, we need to talk."

"There's something I need to say to you," said Ginny.

I figured she was about to give me a blast of shit and would have preferred to head it off but I graciously said, "You first."

"Communication is critical to the success of any relationship, don't you agree?" she asked.

Resisting the impulse to swallow hard, I said, "Yes, I do."

"I'm glad you agree," said Ginny. "I have a confession to make."

"A confession," I said.

"I have followed your every movement for years," said Ginny.

It was not what I expected to hear and mumbled, "You did what?"

"I have shamelessly stalked you," answered Ginny.

"Stalked me," was my brilliant response.

Ginny nodded before continuing, "I knew about your problems with Cynthia and I secretly wished your marriage would fail."

"You knew," I said.

"Yes, I knew about her spending problems and the strain it created on your marriage, especially considering the cost of keeping your mother in a nursing home," said Ginny.

"My mother," I repeated.

"I could have offered to help at any time, but I didn't," she said.

"Help...how?" I asked. "I don't understand."

"I could have paid your mother's nursing home bill," she said.

"But it wasn't..." I said.

Tears streamed down her face.

"It's all my fault that your mother is in danger," she said. "Oh Grant, I've been a terrible friend."

I was oddly pleased to learn she cared enough to follow my life for all these years, but Ginny was not to be blamed for my problems. I wanted to reassure her and opened my mouth with the intention of vehemently denying she had been a bad friend, when our conversation was interrupted by the clanging of the old dinner bell hanging between two posts at the edge of the field.

In an earlier era, the dinner bell called the farmhands to the table, where they gathered for food and conversation. I had seen it hanging there like a relic from bygone days, but had no idea the thing still worked. There was something about its tone that inspired reverence in me.

Delores stood next to the bell, pulling with one hand and waving us toward the house with the other. She wore a big floppy sun hat made of straw and decorated haphazardly with colorful ribbons. Other than the straw hat, she was dressed exclusively in white cotton. Her shirt was several sizes too big and the sleeves were rolled to the elbow. Other than the last few inches above the knees, her shirttail covered most of her shorts. The outfit was completed with white cotton tennis shoes that looked like they had been recently bleached.

"It looks important," I said.

"We can finish this later," said Ginny. "Let's go see what she wants."

As soon as we got within earshot I could hear Delores repeating, "Those mother fuckers, those mother fuckers..."

She led us into our own house as if it were hers, still repeating her mantra, grabbed the television remote and tuned the flat panel to Conservative TV. The President and a first year Congresswoman from South Carolina, Ellen Prusten, were holding a press conference on the steps of the FDA.

The Food and Drug Administration was created in 1906 by Congress to protect the public from dangerous food and drugs. Over the years its supervisory powers have expanded to include things like condoms and cell phones.

The FDA spends a staggering amount of money, four and half billion dollars a year, to run a vast organization with a physical presence in all fifty states and many foreign countries. The eyes and ears of the organization is the Office of Regulatory Affairs. This small army of investigators makes certain that nothing goes inside of our bodies without its prior approval.

A balding overweight man wearing an inexpensive navy blue suit, white shirt and red tie stepped in front of the microphone. The monitor identified him as, Stanley Jacobs, FDA Associate Commissioner. After nervously clearing his throat, he began speaking with a sharp New England accent.

"Good morning," he began. "Let's get right to it. I'm in charge of an investigation into the deaths of four people in Kentucky. The investigation confirms all four of these people consumed Amazoniamagna prior to their deaths. The post mortem autopsies revealed alarming changes to critical biological systems in all four of the deceased that warrants further study."

With that brief statement, he stepped away from the podium, but he did not get far before the stunned press began shouting questions.

"What are their names?" asked a woman in the front row.

"Dr. Jacobs, can you tell us the cause of the death?" shouted a man next to her.

"Can you give us more details about these changes you mentioned?" asked someone from the rear.

The questions went unanswered, but the white house press secretary quickly replaced him at the podium and the clamoring died down.

"We will release more information as it becomes available," said the press secretary. "The President will make a brief statement and then Congresswoman Sarah Prusten will give a statement regarding a collaborative new bill that is being introduced today. Ladies and gentlemen, the President of the United States."

President, David Shultz, took office a year earlier after a stunning victory over the Republican front-runner. Most experts believed the country was not ready for a Jewish president, fearing that it would incite a wave of terrorist attacks from radical Islamic groups like Isis. A physician by trade, he was a Washington outsider and the country was ready for change.

"This country, and indeed the entire world, is faced with a threat the likes of which has never before been seen," began President Shultz. "If left unchecked it will prove the undoing of us all. In times of great crises, we are called upon to take decisive action or perish. Make no mistake about it; this is the worst national crisis we have ever faced and I am working with Congress to meet this threat. We will stand together."

The President waved Sarah Prusten to the microphone while saying, "Congresswoman Prusten will provide you with the details of the new bill we are proposing. We must not fail."

Like President Shultz, Sarah Prusten is a physician who won her seat in a surprising win over an incumbent with years of political experience. She was forty-something, medium height, with a hawkish nose, and witchy black hair pulled severely back into a tight bun. Unlike most professional women, she did not wear a suit, but instead opted for evening gowns, usually black, and high heels.

"Congress can no longer continue to ignore the growing scientific evidence that Amazoniamagna has a dangerously high risk for abuse," said the Congresswoman.

"The likelihood of psychological or physical dependence is unparalleled. Think of it as heroin on steroids."

After looking around the crowd she continued, "New legislation will be introduced into Congress later today to classify Amazoniamagna as a Schedule I controlled substance and to impose stiff criminal penalties for its use or possession."

"The new law will provide strong weapons to prosecutors in their fight against drug crime," she said. "For use or possession of Amazoniamagna the penalty would be twenty years to life and a mandatory fine of $25,000,000.00 and/or seizure of all assets."

"Any person who has knowledge of its use or possession and fails to report it to the DEA or other law enforcement agency, will face similar penalties," she said with emphasis.

"This drug is the biggest threat of our generation," she said. "It cannot be permitted to destroy everything we have built and it will be dealt with severely.

Refusing to answer questions, she left the stage.

CHAPTER 68

They want to criminalize a plant that never hurt a soul. How do you make one of nature's children a crime? You might as well call yourself a crime. Their propaganda machine was working full-time to convince the world that Great Mother is dangerous when in fact she is the exact opposite.

Propaganda is the systematic use of misleading information to manipulate public opinion. Edward Bernays is considered the father of modern propaganda. Using the work of his uncle, Sigmund Freud, he developed techniques to exploit the subconscious desires of the public. They work so well that Adolf Hitler used them to build the Third Reich and wage a world war. Incredibly, it is legal.

"This is some evil shit," said Delores.

It looked like she was about to spit on our living room floor to show her disgust, but caught herself just in time.

"What is evil?" asked Kinsey.

I turned to find Kinsey standing behind us butt naked. She and Eric have been nudist since they discovered Haulover Beach in Miami.

"Do we need to turn the thermostat down?" asked Delores.

Kinsey looked down at her nipples and said with a wink, "No, thank you, I'm good."

Delores reached for the glasses dangling from a chain around her neck, sat them on the bridge of her nose, and then looked over the top at Ginny.

"Are the three of you into that kinky shit?" asked Delores.

"We're as square as they come, but the people we lived with in the Amazon Rainforest didn't wear clothes either and we picked up the practice," said Ginny.

Delores cut her eyes in my direction and I nodded.

"After a while, you stop noticing," I said.

"Nudity stops being a sexual thing and becomes as natural as short sleeves on a hot summer day," said Ginny.

"I once visited a topless beach in the south of France, so I get it," said Delores.

"My husband and I have an open marriage that has nothing to do with us also being nudist," said Kinsey.

Delores looked like she had something to say about that, but Kinsey broke into a sob. Ginny went to comfort her friend. To Delores' credit, she held her tongue. There is nothing like sadness to put things like propriety into perspective.

"Her husband disappeared," I said. "That's why she is staying here."

"Another woman?" asked Delores.

"Sort of," I answered.

Delores raised an eyebrow so I added, "He checked my mother out of the nursing home and the two of them have vanished."

"You put your mother in a nursing home?" snapped Delores.

"My Uncle Jim did," I answered. "I was only eight at the time. She was in a motorcycle wreck. It killed my dad and left her a paraplegic."

Delores' hand flew to her mouth as she said, "Oh my, so young to have lost your parents."

"It explains a lot about me," I said.

"Did he take her for the cure?" asked Delores.

I shrugged.

Kinsey wiped her tears with the back of her hand as she said, "Eric loves Grant and wouldn't do anything to hurt his mother, but he doesn't have the medicine to give her."

Delores asked the question we were all afraid to voice, "Then why did he take her?"

Kinsey resumed her sobbing on Ginny's shoulder.

"We don't know," I answered.

"When we find her, then we need to give her the cure," said Delores.

I nodded.

"If there is still a cure to give," said Delores pointing to the television. "What are we going to do about these mother fuckers?"

"As corrupt as it is, it's still a representative form of government," said Ginny.

"I guess you mean to say that these mother fuckers still work for us," said Delores.

Ginny nodded.

"We need to remind them of that simple fact," said Delores.

"How do we do that?" asked Kinsey.

"We use their weapons against them," I said.

"And what might that be?" asked Delores.

"Propaganda," answered Ginny.

"We turn public opinion against them," I said.

"I don't know, that's such a dirty business," said Kinsey. "Do we really want to stoop to their level?"

"Damn right, without public support the bastards have no job security," said Delores.

"We make sure they are voted to the curb," said Ginny.

Delores gave us her best villainous laugh, "Mwahahahaahhaha... I like it! We attack those lying, cheating bastards with the truth."

"Do you mean we spread the truth about them or about Great Mother?" asked Kinsey.

"I was thinking both, but mostly we focus on Great Mother," said Delores. "We strip away all of the bullshit and show everybody the naked truth."

We looked at Kinsey standing butt naked in front of three clothed people and then followed Delores lead with a villainous group laugh, "Mwahahahaahhaha…"

When the laughter finally died down, I could feel the calming effects of the endorphins. There is nothing better than a good belly laugh to cut tension.

"Anyone have any ideas where to begin?" I asked.

"We should begin with a full-on media blitz," said Delores.

"I could call my public relations team," said Ginny.

"You have a public relations team," I asked.

"Well, duh…she makes her living from a best-selling line of clothing," said Kinsey.

Ginny shrugged.

It never occurred to me that Ginny might have a public relations team, but it makes sense. She works diligently to change worldwide attitudes about women and their role in society. That takes some serious skill and delicate public relations.

"What clothing line?" asked Delores.

"Emerald Allure," answered Ginny.

"Omg, you're that Ginny?" asked Delores.

"One in the same," answered Kinsey.

"I love that shit," said Delores. "Hell, your passion line almost saved my fourth marriage. Or was it the fifth?"

"Delores threw her arms around Ginny saying, "Who cares! I have met the master."

"When the two of you are finished with your private moment, what do you say we get started with our campaign strategy," said Kinsey.

"Right, our media blitz," said Delores. "Where do you want to begin?"

"Let's organize everyone who has benefited from Great Mother," I said.

"They can share their stories with the world," said Delores.

"I love it," said Ginny. "We can create a podcast and publish a collection of stories. We'll call it the Revenge of the Herd."

"That's right," I said. "The one thing they fear the most is the herd instinct of the people."

"Right, but we don't herd anyone," said Kinsey. "Let's make this a real democracy and collaborate with them. We'll call ourselves the Herd and draw on everyone's talents against the men who so desperately want to control us with lies."

"Fear the herd," said Ginny.

"Fear the herd," we chanted.

When the chanting subsided, Delores took Kinsey's hand and said, "I can help you find that husband of yours."

Kinsey blinked a couple of times and then swallowed hard, before finally whispering, "How?"

"I got a guy," she answered.

"A guy," said Kinsey.

"He's the best," said Delores. "If anybody can find your man, he can."

Kinsey gave Delores a big hug and tearfully thanked her. It was an interesting site. Delores is tiny and the top of her head came to rest just below Kinsey's boobs. While it was a warm hug, I have my doubts how nonsexual it was for Delores since I am sure I saw her hand linger on Kinsey's ass for just a beat or two longer than platonic would allow.

"Aaawk, girl on girl," squawked Bird.

Delores jumped out of her skin, the mood lost for the moment. While the rest of us have gotten use to Bird's random appearances, I do not know how he gets into the house like that. We had not seen him since before court and then he just appears unexpectedly.

"What the hell!" said Delores.

"Aaawk, don't stop on my account," said Bird. "I like watching midget sex."

"Did that bird just call me a midget?" asked Delores.

"Aaawk, come give us a hug, Toots," squawked Bird. "You're just the right size for me."

"That would be, Ms. Toots, to you," said Delores. "Show some respect, would you."

"Aaawk, alright, alright, but if you ever decide to switch sides, I'm the guy for you," said Bird.

"Humph, I think it's time for me to make a few calls," said Delores.

Delores left the same way she arrives, abruptly. She is a natural town crier and we knew we could count on her to spread the word.

"Aaawk, so what is this I hear about your husband stealing vegetables from the nursing home," squawked Bird.

Cynthia gasped and then fled to the spare bedroom.

"You can be a real dick sometimes, Bird," said Ginny as she followed Kinsey.

"Aaawk, what…what did I say?" pleaded Bird.

"Dude…" I said with a shake of the head.

"Aaawk, before you judge too harshly, where's that sword Ch'ing gave you?" asked Bird.

The only thing of value I had left in this world was a dusty antique sword. With a twinkle in his eye, Ch'ing told me it was older than the hills, and a priceless piece of junk when he gave it to me. It was with the rest of my things I left in my old apartment.

"It's in my apartment," I said.

"Aaawk, you best get that sword before they do," said Bird.

I wanted to know who they are, but Bird suddenly turned into a dumb animal and refused to answer any questions. My gut told me he was right about the sword. I had to get it and my instincts told me I needed to do it now.

CHAPTER 69

Before I moved out of the house, Cynthia had already moved her lover in. It is not quite as bad as it sounds. She told me Candida was an old friend who had hit on some hard times and needed a place to stay for a few days. I became suspicious when a few days turned into a few weeks.

My gut told me there was something off about Candida, but I gave Cynthia the benefit of the doubt. Our marriage was in a shambles and I was trying my best to work it out. When I caught the two of them in our bed, it confirmed my growing suspicions. Afterwards, I did not waste any time moving out of the house and into a small apartment above a hookah bar in the hippie part of town.

The Highlands has been through many changes over the years. It was once the premier Louisville suburb, but by the 1960's it was run down and shabby. Unemployed hippies moved in because of the cheap rent and never left. Today they are stockbrokers, accountants, and physicians. They have utilized their spike in income to restore most of the old houses to their former glory.

Despite the revitalization of the neighborhood, the shops along Bardstown Road still have a decidedly hippie feel to them. Four-star restaurants rub elbows with crystal shops and hookah bars.

As I topped the last of the heavily worn steps, I paused outside of the door. Something was wrong. My stomach was churning and I thought I might have to throw up. Taking a couple of cleansing breaths, I waited it out.

When the nausea passed, I tried to unlock the door, but the key didn't work. At first, I thought it had something to do with my shaking hands, so I steadied the right with the left and tried again. It didn't help. Frustrated, I banged my forehead against the door.

It must have been louder than I thought because a neighbor stuck her head out and said, "The police came around a few weeks ago asking questions about you."

She was young, maybe nineteen or twenty, wearing heavy makeup in a failed attempt to hide her acne. Her left nostril was pierced with a shamrock stud that matched a small tattoo on her neck. Her hair was dyed coal black and cut boy short.

She wore a red flannel shirt like a nightgown. It was mostly open, except for the top two buttons exposing a flat belly and red laced panties worn low on her hips. I could see she had a boyishly flat chest to go with the belly and was clean-shaven except for her skinny legs. They were covered in a fine mist of reddish blond down from the knee down.

We had crossed paths many times on the stairs and even though we had introduced ourselves, I could never seem to remember her name, so I nicknamed her Shamrocks, but later shortened it to Shams.

"What did they want?" I asked.

"Not much," she said in a lazy drawl. "They asked if you had many visitors."

"Anything else?' I asked.

"You having legal problems?" she asked.

Since it was none of her business, I ignored her question.

"It ain't the first time the police came for you," she said. "I was here when the fascist pigs took you away."

I waited.

"Was it drugs?" asked Shams.

"Why do you think that?" I asked.

"You were in there with that crack whore and later her drug dealing husband showed up here looking for you," she answered.

"What makes you think he is a drug dealer?" I asked.

"I may not be a fancy pants lawyer like you, but I ain't stupid," said Shams.

"No you're not," I said in a calming voice.

"I lied to the cops," she said.

"What do you say to them?" I asked.

"I didn't tell them nothing," she said. "I didn't like 'em much. Detectives, I think, since they wasn't wearing no uniforms."

"Umm…thanks," I said.

"Harry came by after that," said Shams.

I didn't know who Harry was so I raised an eyebrow at her.

"He's our landlord," she said. "Anyways, he posted an eviction notice on the door."

I looked at the door. There was no notice. I felt sick again. They usually clean a place out following an eviction and the sword might be gone.

Shams stuck her head out a little further and looked at the door as she said, "It was there yesterday."

"Well thanks again," I said.

"Harry said you stirred up a hornet's nest and he wants no part of it," she said.

I was drawing a big blank on Harry, so I said, "Maybe I should talk to him. Do you have his number?"

"You want to come inside while I look for it?" she asked.

It was an innocent enough question, except Shams cut her eyes to my pants and lingered there long enough to make it clear she was interested in more than phone numbers.

"I'm in a hurry…umm…maybe some other time," I said.

"Yeah, sure," she said. "Are you gay?"

"Umm…no," I said. "Why do you ask?"

"I've never seen a guy as pretty as you turn down so much pussy, unless he was gay," she said.

"I'm engaged," I said.

Shams smirked, "What does that have to do with you getting laid?"

It was time to end this conversation and said, "Thanks for the information."

I wanted to get out of there as fast as I could and in my rush I bumped into the document clerk from my old law office, Gaia.

"Oh it's you," said Shams to Gaia.

"Jennifer, don't you look pretty today," said Gaia. "Are you expecting company?"

So much for Shams. It's funny how someone's name can be both on the tip of your tongue and yet remain so elusive you just know there is no way in hell you will ever remember it. That is until you hear someone else speak it and then you wonder why you had forgotten it in the first place. That is how I felt about Jennifer's name, especially since she was my next-door neighbor.

Jennifer was looking a little grumpy as she said, "I guess I'll grab that number for you."

"Thanks," I said.

Jennifer disappeared into her apartment, the door closing behind her with such finality I doubted I would ever see the number.

Gaia was dressed in blue jeans and a t-shirt that read, "Forest Will Save You." Her long black hair hung in two braids; one down her back, and a second smaller braid with big attitude curled around her left cheekbone and came to a stop within an inch of the corner of her mouth. The attitude braid included bits and pieces of Lapis Lazuli matching her lively blue eyes.

"Mr. Li," said Gaia with a crooked smile.

"Hello Gaia," I said. "How do you know Jennifer?"

"We're neighbors," answered Gaia.

"Do you live in this building now?" I asked.

Gaia gave me an odd look and said, "There's something you need to know."

I waited for her to continue but she just stood there in front of me, calm and unassuming. It can be a bit unnerving, but I was accustomed to it, although I had not seen anyone do it since I left the jungle behind.

"Come inside, I'll explain everything," said Gaia.

She slipped a key into the lock and opened the door to my apartment. I followed her inside. Gaia nodded in the direction of the couch and went to get us a beer. I'm not sure what I expected, but the damn place hadn't changed a bit.

The larger of the two rooms is divided by a Formica counter top into a kitchen and living room. The initials of a prior tenant are carved into the Formica and judging by the burn marks, it was once used as an ash tray.

Two mismatched thrift store bar stools line the bar. One was solid enough, but the other is a menace and I keep meaning to throw it out before someone gets hurt.

Other than a half-eaten pizza and an empty tequila bottle that had been setting there for several weeks, the apartment was neat enough. The stack of unopened mail lying in a pile of dust at the end of a beat up old coffee table had grown considerably in the last few weeks.

At the end of the counter is an open door leading into a small windowless bedroom. On the floor is a king sized mattress that takes up most of the room. I had not slept there in several weeks, but it looked exactly the way I remembered leaving it.

I was relieved to see the sword was still standing in the corner of the room. I didn't give a shit about the stack of mail, but the sword was a different matter. It felt like an old friend. My eyes were drawn to its strange markings. The script was similar to the markings on the door to the pyramid in South America. I studied it closely. Humm, I thought, "Freedom Balances on the Edge."

While I'm not trained in ancient languages, I've been able to read them since the battle with a giant anaconda. It attacked me outside of the Guardian's village. In a desperate attempt to survive suffocation, I jammed my thumbs through its eye sockets and deep into its brain.

The maneuver saved my life, but I suffered a strange electric shock that knocked me unconscious. Since then, some very strange things have been happening to me. For example, when a machete carrying mad man attacked Ginny, I went berserk and killed him.

I do not remember anything about the fight, but the witnesses say I hissed when I attacked him. Eric said he has never seen me fight like that…coiling and striking like a serpent. Afterwards, I stood over the dead man and flicked my tongue. I know it's creepy, but imagine if it was you they were describing.

Seeing Gaia here was unsettling. Even more confusing was her apparent ownership of the apartment. Even though nothing had changed much, it clearly no longer belonged to me. Since I did not want to forget the sword, I gathered it into my arms and was still clutching it when Gaia returned with our drink.

I had plenty of questions, but sipped the beer and waited for an explanation. She relaxed into the overstuffed chair and studied me. When she finally spoke it raised new questions and answered none.

"What do you know about your parent's motorcycle crash?" asked Gaia.

"How did you…what do you know about my parents?" I asked.

"Your father was working at Pathogen when he was killed," said Gaia.

When you are a normal eight-year-old boy, you do not really pay much attention to your dad's line of work. Work is just something that takes him away from you. It is a time thief, but not as big of a thief as death. Ginny's father told me there was a connection between Dad's work at Pathogen and his death.

"What do you know about Dad's death?" I asked.

"It wasn't an accident," said Gaia. "He was forced off the road by one of Wilbur Goth's men."

"Goth?" I asked.

She nodded.

"What's his name…the man who did this?" I asked.

"He goes by the name of Renfield," she said.

I went completely still. My breath and heart rate slowed. I did not even blink. I just sat perfectly still and watched Gaia so closely I could see the pulse in her neck. It was warm in the apartment and a tiny bead of sweat trickled down her cheek.

"It is good you have embraced the serpent's power," said Gaia.

I had not spoken to anyone about it except for a few friends in the Amazon Rainforest.

"Who are you?" I asked.

She answered with a question, "How's my father?"

Gaia's blue eyes twinkled with amusement, as if she was dealing with someone a bit slow on the uptake. You do not see blue eyes on a Hispanic woman very often. In fact, I had only seen it once, on Pony Tail and he was half Viking.

Finally, I got it. The resemblance was uncanny. On top of that, she had a self-possessed presence about her. It was the same as the Guardians.

"You're with the Guardians, aren't you?" I asked.

"Yes, and what else?" she asked.

I continued, "You're Pony Tail's sister."

Gaia squealed with delight, "Pony Tail!? That's what you call my brother?"

"The blue eyes must mean Bill Bardough is your father," I said. "Oh, my god, you're Ginny's sister."

"Yes, and Layah is my mother," she said.

"That means you're practically my sister," I said.

She nodded vigorously. My sister was sitting across from me...my sister. I had siblings. My family was growing. Gaia flew out of the chair and into my arms. The force knocked me flat on my back, but neither of us cared. A sister...I had a new sister.

"Grant, I have a present for you," said Gaia. "See that large envelope. Now is a good time to open it."

"What is this?" I asked.

"Resolution," she answered.

"Did you also give a copy to the federal prosecutor, Zeke Kruthers?" I asked.

Gaia shook her head, "The first time I saw these papers was in John Biggs' office after he killed himself."

"What were you doing in there?" I said.

"I heard Helen scream and went to help," she answered.

"She walked in as I was helping him down from the chandelier," I said.

"I saw you running away," said Gaia. "Why did you do that?"

"Damn if know," I answered honestly. "It was cowardly and nearly cost me my freedom. I have a feeling I haven't heard the last of it either."

"When you ran, so did Helen," said Gaia. "I found her fleeing to the ladies room. Once I made sure she was okay, I went to check on Mr. Biggs. It was too late for him, but when I caught sight of Dad's name on the paperwork lying on his desk, I couldn't resist having a look. After seeing what it was, I gathered it up into the envelope and left with it before the police came."

"Why are you giving it to me?" I asked.

"You'll know what to do with it," she said.

"What are you doing here in my old apartment?" I asked.

"Waiting for you," answered Gaia.

"It's no accident you were working at my law firm, is it?" I asked.

"I was sent there to guard you," she said.

"Guard me!" I said.

She nodded.

"From what?" I asked.

"The evil that would use and then destroy you," answered Gaia.

CHAPTER 70

It was time to close the chapter on the shitty little apartment above the hookah bar. Gaia assured me Ginny didn't know about her and insisted we surprise her with the news. After gathering all of my earthly possessions into two garbage bags, I loaded Gaia and the sword into Dad's rusted-out old pickup and headed home to the farm.

Before we left, I used my smartphone to photograph the documents and upload them to the cloud. I also emailed them to the only journalist I trusted, Claudia Smurk, with a message to expose the bastards when the time is right. As an afterthought, I copied all of my contacts on the email. As a final measure, I texted the documents to both Kim Slotter, at military intelligence, and Jake Blitzer with the CIA.

We were only a few blocks away from the apartment, when I noticed a black SUV behind us. I made a few random turns to confirm we were being followed. Bardstown Road is a busy street with plenty of witnesses. The middle of traffic seemed like as good of a place as any to confront a stalker.

"Hold on!" I said to Gaia and then slammed on the brakes.

The old truck was a tank and I figured the newer vehicle would crash into us and do enough damage to disable it, but the driver of the SUV had better reflexes than I expected. Even though it thumped into the rear end of the old pickup truck, it did manage to stop in time to avoid doing any damage.

So much for driving off and leaving a disabled vehicle in our wake, I thought. It was no big deal, since I was sick of running from these bastards anyway. If Ch'ing taught me nothing else, he taught me to end a conflict swiftly and decisively. If possible, end it long before the first punch.

"Stay here," I said to Gaia.

I jumped out of the truck and marched back to the SUV. Catching the driver side door as it began to open, I helped it along a bit. Gaia didn't follow instructions, but then again she was raised by the Guardians. They are undoubtedly the fiercest warriors I've ever seen. She took position next to the passenger door and waited.

"You!" I said.

"Don't get your panties in a bunch," said the driver.

I am not exactly sure whom I expected to see, but it sure wasn't Slotter. There was a time when I thought she was our enemy, but I'm not so sure. She is a military intelligence officer investigating Pathogen. Slotter was not dressed like a soldier. Instead, she was wearing a men's dark business suit, crisp white shirt, olive drab tie, and sunglasses.

"Why are you following me?" I asked.

"Anybody that drives as badly as you needs someone to keep an eye on them," she said with a smirk.

"I'm tired of people following me," I said.

"You're on center stage, get use to it," said Slotter.

"I don't need more protection, I got her," I said pointing to Gaia.

"Can she fight?" asked Slotter.

"I'll have you on your back in less than three seconds," said Gaia.

"Well, I guess that makes you my type," said Slotter.

"When you two stop flirting, maybe you can tell me why you're really here," I said.

"Let's wait until we get back to the farm," said Slotter. "That is where we are headed isn't it?"

"Did you get my text?" I asked.

Slotter cut her eyes to Gaia and asked, "Can we trust her?"

"Where do you think I got the documents?" I asked.

Slotter pulled her sunglasses down a notch and peered over the top at Gaia.

In return, Gaia pointed a finger at Slotter and asked, "More importantly, can she be trusted?"

"She put a bullet in your sister's head, so I sure as hell don't trust her, but I think your dad might," I said.

Slotter pointed at Gaia and said, "Dad…sister? Hummm…when I marry sweet cheeks here, you and I will be family, Dragon Boy. Just think about that for a minute before you try to kick my ass and fail yet once again."

"Don't you think you ought to ask a girl first, before you go and announce an engagement," said Gaia. "Besides we don't believe in marriage where I come from."

Slotter gave Gaia a long frank look. I guess she liked what she saw because a slow smile spread across her face. Given the way Gaia returned her smile, I would say the interest was mutual.

"There ain't no damn damage," shouted the driver waiting impatiently behind the SUV. "Move 'em out of the way."

We had been shouting over the honking horns long enough, I waved Gaia toward the truck. She took another long look at Slotter and shook her head.

"I think I'll keep a close eye on the enemy," she said.

"Suit yourself," I said.

"That's my girl," said Slotter.

The rest of the drive was uneventful, so I had time to think. If I'm not careful, it is easy to focus too much on the obstacles life throws my way and not nearly enough on my goals. I find that when I think more about who I want to be and what I want to do with my life, the happier I am. The quiet ride gave me time to think about all the crazy turns life had taken. I was beginning to think that maybe I had been given one hell of a big shit sandwich, when I pulled up to the farm.

Ginny was waiting for me with Uncle Jim, Rose, and Jake. I was surprised to see the federal prosecutor, Zeke Kruthers, waiting with my friends and family and hoped he wasn't delivering bad news. The last I'd heard from him was the day of the Goth trial when he tried to warn me about Pathogen and my boss, John Biggs. Whatever it was that he knew about them may have caused John to kill himself.

Slotter and Gaia rolled in behind me, followed by a cloud of gravel dust. Packie trotted up, tail wagging, and greeted me with all of the love that a loyal dog brings to the relationship. My beautiful fiancée rose from her rocking chair and slipped in next to Packie. Sandwiched between them, I was smothered with love.

All of the doubt fell away in an instant. I knew in that moment that the people I love are good people and that I am truly blessed.

"Welcome home, darling," said Ginny. "We have guests."

Ginny gave Slotter a cold hard look before saying to her, "We can't seem to get rid of you."

Slotter shrugged, "I have a job to do, but now that I've met your sister, you might be seeing even more of me."

"Sister?" said Ginny.

Gaia opened her mouth to speak, but Ginny held a finger to her lips to stop her. She studied every inch of Gaia. A slow smile spread across her face as she opened her arms to embrace her new sister. Ginny's broad smile shifted to tears in the blink of an eye.

"Our home is now your home," sobbed Ginny.

"Thank you sister," said Gaia. "Being away from the Guardians has been difficult, but your kindness helps wash the loneliness away. I am called Gaia, but you can call me sister if you will."

"Everyone, please welcome my sister, Gaia," said Ginny.

The group migrated to the yard to greet us with hugs and well wishes. I stuck my hand out to shake Zeke's, but was shocked when he pulled me into a warm hug instead.

"Thank you for saving my life," he whispered.

"Saving your life?" I asked.

Jake slapped me on the shoulder and said, "Damn right that Great Mother is good shit."

"I had no idea you were Jake's Zeke," I said. "I never put the two of you together when he told me he had found the love of his life. Are you cancer free?"

His blood shot eyes were filled with happy tears as he vigorously nodded his head. Who would have known? A few months ago, Zeke and I were on the opposite sides of the table, battling against each other in Federal Court over the culpability of Wilbur Goth and now look at us. As it turns out, I won, but he was right about Goth's guilt.

"Another happy customer," said Uncle Jim.

There was something different about Uncle Jim that I couldn't quite put my finger on. His hair was the same. I didn't see any changes in his clothing, since he was wearing his usual faded blue jeans, well-worn cowboy boots, and a black Harley t-shirt.

"Well, for such a high powered lawyer you sure don't have the best powers of observation," said Uncle Jim with a crooked grin.

I looked to Rose for help, but I could tell from the wicked twinkle in her eye that she planned to let me dangle in the wind.

"Aaawk, he's blind as a bat," squawked Bird.

Bird was always giving me a hard time and at first I figured it was more of the same, but when everyone started laughing at his comment as if it was the funniest thing they'd ever heard, I knew I was missing something so obvious that I must be blind.

"Aaawk, you might as well cover those eyes of yours with patches for all the good they do you," said Bird.

Geez, he wasn't going to give it a rest, I thought, and that comment about patches was seriously insensitive. Uncle Jim fell a few years back rock climbing in the Red River Gorge. He lost an eye and gained a limp, but he was lucky to be alive. He wore that eye patch like a proud pirate.

"Oh shit," I said. "You...where's...Uncle Jim you have two eyes!"

"Damn right I do," he said with a laugh.

"I don't understand, how is this possible?" I asked.

"Pony Tail kept his promise and cured me with that weed you got growing all over the place," said Uncle Jim.

"Are you serious, Great Mother can be used to replace a missing eye?" I asked.

"Aaawk, we told you this was the good shit," squawked Bird. "Nobody listens to Bird. Maybe they'll listen to them."

Bird nodded toward a convoy of cars and trucks of all sizes and shapes turning off the highway onto our gravel drive. It wasn't just a few, it was thousands and they kept pouring in until there was no place for them to park and then they just stopped on the highway and walked the rest of the way in.

No one spoke. You'd think with all of those people that someone would have something to say, but not a soul uttered a word. They gathered in a half circle around us, standing tall and still like the Queen's Guard outside Buckingham Palace.

Claudia Smurk and her film crew, laden with video equipment, poured out of an unmarked white paneled rapist van parked near Dad's old truck. They didn't waste any time getting set up. Once they were finished, Claudia took the microphone, looked into the camera and began speaking.

"Hello, I'm Claudia Smurk and we are streaming live from the home of Grant Li and Ginny Bardough in Goshen, Kentucky," she said in a strong broadcaster's voice.

Claudia swept her arm around the farm and the cameras panned out to show the world the pastoral beauty of the Bluegrass State. Of course, instead of bluegrass and racehorses, they saw Great Mother thriving in fields once used to grow tobacco.

"We have with us several thousand people who have something they want to say to the President and to anyone else who thinks they have the right treat adults like children," said Claudia.

Again, she swept her arm wide, but this time it was in the direction of the people who had gathered at our farm. The camera crew followed her gesture and recorded the many faces standing vigil before us. I too followed her gesture. It was a diverse crowd of proud men and women of all races.

"These men and women have gathered here this day to share their personal stories of healing," said Claudia. "I won't put words in their mouths. Instead, I will let them tell you in their own words what Great Mother has done for them."

Having said that, she did something most celebrities find hard to do, she handed the microphone to the nearest person and then gracefully stepped out of the spotlight.

It was an elderly man who looked to be in his late eighties or early nineties. The thing that struck me the most was the way he stood tall and straight without any sign of a stoop. He looked straight into the camera and with the voice of a man in his prime, began to speak.

"My name is George Fineagan," he said. "Mr. President and ladies and gentlemen of Congress, it is important that each of you remember who you work for. You serve at the will of the people and we are the people, not you."

George paused while the crowd cheered. It was first sound they had made since they arrived. The applause lasted a full minute and only died down when George smiled and raised his hand.

"It would serve you well to listen to what we have to say about your proposal to ban Great Mother," said George.

Again the crowd roared. George waited with the patience of the elderly who have lived through much and learned that nature has its own agenda.

"A few weeks ago, I awoke on my kitchen floor," said George. "I don't know what happened or how long I lay there, but I crawled to a phone and dialed 9-1-1."

"EMS rushed me the hospital where I was seen by an army of doctors who tested me for all kinds of things that I really didn't understand," continued George. "What I do understand is I was ashen, weak, and near death."

"I try to be a trusting man, but it isn't easy sometimes," said George.

"Amen to that brother," shouted someone from the crowd.

"You see, my doctor prescribed thirteen different medications for a wide variety of ailments," said George. "It was crazy trying to take all of those pills on schedule, but I did my best."

George paused and looked out into the crowd. I followed his eyes and saw heads nodding their understanding.

"I only began to recover when they finally altered my medications," said George. "I asked every one of those doctors who saw me in the hospital if my problems were caused by the medications."

George paused again. You could hear a pin drop.

"What do you think they told me?" he asked the crowd.

"Nothing," shouted a woman in the front row.

"They didn't answer your question, did they?" asked someone else.

"That's right, they didn't," said George. "Not one of those doctors was willing to admit that the medications nearly killed me."

The crowd grumbled.

"I have always placed my trust in modern medical science and believed them when they told me that alternative medicine is dangerous," said George. "I bet a lot of you did the same."

Many people in the crowed nodded in agreement.

"Do you know what I learned when I was at death's door?" asked George.

Someone shouted, "You can't trust someone who doesn't tell you the truth."

"That's right," said George. "You can't trust a liar, but when your life is on the line, it is plain stupid to listen to them."

"They're criminals," shouted a middle-aged woman.

"Something ought to be done about it," shouted another woman.

"That medication poisoned me and no one would admit it," said George. "I would still be taking that poison if it wasn't for my daughter. As soon as she got me out of that hospital, she told me about an amazing new cure and I listened."

"Are you listening Mr. President?" asked George. "Are you listening ladies and gentlemen of Congress? Great Mother cured my daughter and it cured me. I don't take any medications. I have a whole new life, thanks to this plant and it's free."

The crowd roared.

"Just in case anybody has any questions about the truth of what I have said, a copy of my complete medical record will be posted to Claudia's blog under my name," said George. "Read it for yourself."

George passed the microphone and the next story began. When that one was finished, the microphone was handed to the next person, and then to the next in a seamless stream of revelation. Thousands of witnesses testified in favor of Great Mother and the world listened.

CHAPTER 71

Even though the sky was clear as far as we could see, the perky weather girl on Conservative TV warned everyone that a storm was coming. She predicted high winds and possible tornados. With a smile that stretched from ear to ear, she warned everyone in our area to take cover. The Cured were camped all over our farm, as well as surrounding farms, and showed no signs of taking the weather girl's advice.

Weather prediction is a strange kind of voodoo. No matter how many times they get it dead wrong, they just keep making their predications as if they know what they are talking about.

It's a funny thing, this matter of saying something as if it was the absolute truth. Sometimes, it actually works. What we think and say has power, whether based on an objective reality or not. In a sense, it becomes a self-fulfilling prophesy. So, Ch'ing always warned us to be careful what we think and say. It might just come true.

Jake found me sitting with Uncle Jim and Slotter. I mostly just listened while the two of them told war stories. For two people who had tried to kill each other recently, they sure were bonding well.

"Did you know that Zeke's father is a judge?" asked Jake.

"No, I didn't," I said politely as I wondered what he was getting at.

"Yep, his last name is Kruthers," said Jake eyeing me closely.

A lot has happened lately and I may have been slow on the uptake, but I couldn't help but think that name was familiar. Then it hit me. The man presiding over my divorce is Judge Thomas Kruthers.

"Why are you telling me this?" I asked.

"You have more friends than you realize, Grant," said Jake.

I looked around at all of the people who had showed up in support of Great Mother and nodded.

"A shit storm is breaking as we speak," said Jake. "The FDA, backed by the CDC and USDA, are coming after you," said Jake.

"What about the FTC and CIA?" I asked with a grin.

Jake returned the grin and said, "Be strong, you have formidable assets."

"You're a good friend, Jake," I said.

Slotter poked me in the ribs and said, "Don't worry, Grant, we don't intend to let you lose this fight."

Delores stormed into our personal space with her usual diplomacy and demanded, "Where's Kinsey?"

"Last I saw her, she was inside," said Uncle Jim.

"What's up?" I asked.

"My guy found him," she said.

It took me a minute to register she was talking about Eric and demanded, "Where is he?"

"Kinsey first," she said. "We owe her that."

I didn't like it much, but nodded in agreement. Besides, I wasn't ready to set Uncle Jim off before I had a chance to confront Eric.

He looked like he was about to chime in, so I turned to Slotter and asked, "Are the documents I sent you helpful in your investigation?"

Her eyes danced with more happiness than I'd ever seen in them as she said, "Helpful! Damn right they're helpful. I'd kiss you, if you if you were my type."

"Can we trust the people you work for?" I asked.

"Probably, but I have built in safeguards anyway," she said. "Never enter a fight without contingency plans."

"Did somebody mention a fight?" said a familiar voice.

It was my prodigal best friend, Eric. I did what any good friend would do and broke his nose.

"Shit, what did you go and do that for?" said Eric as he worked to reset his nose.

"You got a lot of explaining to do," I answered.

"Me…why the hell did you hit me?" he asked.

"Where have you been?" I demanded.

"You've got no right to be like this considering you left us," said Eric.

"What are you talking about…I didn't leave you anywhere," I said.

"I heard you calling out," he said.

This was not going as planned. I took a deep breath.

"What are you talking about?" I asked.

"We were tied up…prisoners," he said. "I was beginning to think no one would come for us and then I heard a door open and you called out."

Then it hit me.

"The empty lab," I said.

"I heard a thump and then someone drug a body down the stairs," he said.

"She had her back to me," I said.

"They moved us after that," he said. "It was a dark place. There were rats."

"I was so close," I said.

"You let them get the drop on you," he said.

"Why did you check Mom out of the nursing home?" I asked.

"I became suspicious when a new client paid us a huge retainer, so I checked up on them," he said.

"Let me guess, it was one of Pathogen's subsidiaries, NWO Labs," I said.

He nodded.

"I knew you were in a financial jam and needed money to pay your mom's bill, so I hatched a plan to surprise you," he said.

"Surprise me?" I asked.

"Yep, I paid her bill and got her out of that place," he said. "I loaded her into an ambulance and gave her a dose of Great Mother. Then everything went black. When I woke up, I was hogtied, gagged and blindfolded."

"Hogtied," I said.

He shrugged.

"I'm not sure how long I was like that before I heard your voice," he said. "At first I thought it was my imagination, but I clung to because it was the first shred of hope I'd had since I woke up."

"Who did this to you?" I said.

"I never saw a face, but I heard the name Renfield once," he answered.

"Renfield!" I said.

"Yeah, just like Dracula's creepy little helper," he said.

I couldn't believe that Mr. Suit's name was once again connected to something bad happening to the people I care about.

I think Eric misunderstood my response because he shrugged and said, "I had a lot a time to think about it."

"Where's Mom?" I asked.

It was a woman who answered, "Standing behind you."

Mom hasn't spoken a word in twenty years. Nor has she stood on her own two feet, for that matter. What kind of person would play such a cruel joke, I wondered. I intended to kick some ass, but first, I turned ever so slowly to see who was behind me.

"Grant, is that really you?" said Mom.

She was standing there with her arms open and tears streaming down her cheeks. I didn't know whether I should trust my senses or not. Many nights, I dreamed she had stirred from her long sleep, only to awaken the next morning to the harsh reality that she was still bedridden.

"Mom…Mom, is that really you?" I asked.

Since I seemed incapable of moving, she gathered me in her arms. It was my turn to cry and cry I did. I let it out. Every bit of sadness, anger, and fear held inside for so long, came out. Yes, I was unashamed of my pain and I let it out…all of it.

"There…there…my son," was all she said, but it was all I needed to hear.

When I finished crying, I felt Eric's hand on my shoulder petting me gently as if I was a puppy or something.

"There's much we need to discuss," said Mom. "But first, I want to see my future daughter in-law and speak to my brother."

Mom held Ginny's hands while she searched her face.

"Do you love my son?" she asked.

"Truly," answered Ginny.

"Will you stand by him no matter what?" asked Mom.

"I will never falter," answered Ginny.

Mom's smile began in her eyes where all true smiles begin, and then she pulled Ginny in for a warm hug.

"I believe you," said Mom.

After she left with Uncle Jim, I apologized to Eric for busting his nose up and then sent him inside to make amends with his wife, Kinsey.

I was wondering how my life had brought me to this place when Claudia tapped me on the shoulder and said, "I got the documents and it looks like we'll be using them soon."

"Why, what's up?" I asked.

"There's breaking news that the FDA is demanding a recall of Great Mother," answered Claudia.

"How do you recall something that grows wild and free like a weed?" I asked.

"Damned if I know, but you should prepare a response anyway," she said. "Everything these people have built is crumbling. Like any cornered animal, they are more dangerous now, than ever."

"They just keep coming and coming in waves, don't they?" I asked, with a shake of the head.

"We all have a role to play in this unfolding drama and it is time for you and Ginny to step up," said Claudia as she walked off to talk to a cute guy who had just finished telling his story on the live feed.

Since the weather girl was predicting a storm, I thought it might be a good idea to unload my things from the back of the truck. As I lifted one of the bags, a pair of navy blue suit pants fell to the ground. When I gathered them up, I remembered I last wore them the day John killed himself.

I wanted to say that's when it all began, but I knew it began long ago when I was just a kid. Back then, our parents found themselves mixed up in an ugly mess and they didn't fare too well. I resolved we would do better.

A wad of paper fell from the pants pocket to the ground. As I bent to pick it up, I remembered finding it in John's office after he killed himself. It occurred to me I had never read it, so I unfolded it and began to read. I read it a second time and then a third before I called the number. As much as I tried, my hands wouldn't stop shaking.

***

A war was brewing. No matter how hard good people work to avoid conflict, it is part of the human condition. You might even say, it is nature's way, and if you doubt it, then ask the antelope what it thinks of the lion tearing at its hindquarter.

The FDA was using social media to deliver its propaganda. While their posts claimed Great Mother was killing people, we had yet to see any evidence the plant is harmful to anything other than pathogenic influences.

Meanwhile, Claudia streamed personal stories of healing and hope told by the Cured. Like George, each one of them posted their personal medical records as evidence of the truth of their assertions. Some followed Claudia's example and posted videos to substantiate their stories. A few were time lapsed film tracking the healing process.

It was powerful stuff and public opinion was shifting in favor of Great Mother. More and more of the sick were abandoning their treatment plans and taking Great Mother instead. Hospitals were beginning to look like ghost towns complete with dust bunnies tumbling down the empty hallways. There were even a few turncoat doctors promoting Great Mother. The healthcare industry was desperate and they pushed Congress to act.

A call from your lawyer is rarely a good thing. I figured Filmore was calling with news about the divorce, but I was wrong.

"Grant, put Virginia on the speaker," said the Admiral. "This involves her too."

Virginia? I blinked not once, but twice. Filmore is an astute student of human nature and I'm pretty sure he caught on right away that I didn't know my fiancée's proper first name. Well, I knew it, but I wasn't accustomed to using it.

"I am of course referring to your beautiful fiancée, Ginny," he said. "A woman, who by the way, I'm not completely convinced you deserve. The jury is still out on that one."

"Oh, Ginny," I mumbled lamely.

"Grant, the speaker…we don't have much time," said the Admiral with a tone of exaggerated patience.

We were sitting out back on the patio catching up on recent events. Our home had become a public place with people camped in every possible nook and cranny. By some unspoken rule, the Cured never violated our private time on the patio.

"It's the Admiral," I said to Ginny.

"Oh, is everything okay?" she asked.

"I don't know," I answered. "He wants to speak to both of us. Do you mind if I put it on speaker?"

Ginny nodded, "It must be important. Let's find out what he wants, darling."

"We're both here, Admiral," I said.

"I sure wish you'd call me something other than Admiral," said Filmore.

"Aye aye sir," I said.

The Admiral groaned, "The things I have to put up with."

"Do you have news?" asked Ginny.

"The two of you have been subpoenaed to appear before a Congressional Subcommittee," said Filmore.

"What's this about?" asked Ginny.

"Congress is investigating the FDA's recall of Great Mother," said Filmore.

"When?" I asked.

"Tomorrow morning," he answered.

"That doesn't leave much time to make travel arrangements," said Ginny.

"I've already booked a flight," said Filmore.

CHAPTER 72

Ginny and I were up at dawn preparing for our trip to Washington, when Uncle Jim stuck his head in the door and said, "You'll want to see this."

We followed him outside where we found my mother in front of the cameras with microphone in hand.

Ginny gripped my arm, "Oh my God, it's the medallion."

The sun's first light reflected off a gold medallion dangling from Mom's neck. It depicted a snake eating a bird and the bird simultaneously eating the snake.

"I was once married to a wonderful man," began my mother. "We have a son who you might know. His name is Grant Li. He and his fiancée, Ginny Bardough, brought Great Mother to the world."

The crowd cheered.

"On my husband's birthday, an unmarked van forced us into a ditch," she continued. "He was killed instantly and I've been bedridden for the last twenty years.

She looked so sad.

"None of the doctors believed I would recover and if it wasn't for the love and faith of my son, it would have been over for me long ago," she said. "Like many of you, my life and good health was restored thanks to a plant that once only existed deep in the Amazon Rainforest."

She paused and looked directly into the camera.

"The police called it an accident, but it was intentional," she said. "My name is Heather Li. I know who did this to my family and I know why you did it."

She paused. The early risers didn't move a muscle.

"Your time is up," she said. "We are coming for you!"

Mom passed the microphone to a young woman with a child in hand. The little boy looked to be two or three. Mom kissed the top of the child's baldhead and then she disappeared into the crowd.

Ginny dabbed at her eyes and said, "They killed your father, Grant. I'm so sorry."

"She just put a target on her back," I said.

"Why would she do that?' asked Ginny.

"To divert attention from us," I said.

"That was brave of her...and smart," said Ginny.

I looked deeply into Ginny's eyes and asked, "Are you ready for this?"

She caressed my cheek and said, "With you at my side, of course I'm ready."

I felt more peaceful going into this fight than I've ever felt in my life.

I pulled her close and whispered, "I love you, Ginny."

She hugged me tight and said, "I love you too, Grant. I'm so glad to have you back in my life. Now, let's get moving. We have a job to do and we don't want to miss our flight, darling."

Eric drove us to the airport. No one spoke until we arrived at the gate.

"Uncle Jim is guarding your mother," said Eric. "It's my job to get you to the Capital safely."

We nodded. There was no one we trusted more than Eric to protect our back.

As we waited at the gate I had time to reflect on the mess we were in. Illness has an insidious way of turning us into cowards. We allow healthcare workers to treat us rudely, even though we are paying customers. Hell, they work for us, don't they? After the staff pushes us around, then we meekly stand before a physician and accept any bullshit treatment plan they offer, even though they adamantly refuse to guarantee success.

Later, they bombard us with incomprehensible billing statements whether they actually helped us or not. We wonder why insurance doesn't cover these bills, but don't really understand the policy, so we call the insurance company hoping to get some answers, but instead spend hours battling an endless electronic voice system that ultimately leaves us on hold forever. Eventually, we just pay the medical bill without question, even though we have to dip into the children's college fund to do it.

It is helpful to remember that we heal ourselves. Most of modern medicine does not cure illness, but instead only treats symptoms and pain. For an illness like cancer, the treating physician strings out the treatment until the patient is no longer financially capable of paying for it. Once the money dries up, then the doctor terminates the ineffective treatment, leaving the sick person feeling like it was somehow their fault they didn't get better.

Healthcare law favors the industry and is heavily stacked against the sick patient. There is even a growing body of law that requires people to get medical treatment, even if they don't want it, whether it works or not.

A regulation is by definition a limit on freedom, but it is more than that. It is also the power to destroy. The House Subcommittee on Health controls all regulations related to healthcare in America, including biomedical research and development. This gives them the power to destroy Great Mother.

The healthcare industry is a multi-trillion dollar industry. Approving a new medicine, especially one that only manages symptoms, rather than cures, can make someone very rich. Since the subcommittee controls which medicines reach the public, members of the committee are very powerful. Like it or not, whether people will be allowed to use Great Mother is in the hands of these rule makers.

We met Filmore at the airport and used the extra time created by the early check-in to prepare for the hearing.

"What should we expect once we get to the Capital?" asked Ginny.

"The members of the committee will spend a lot of time reading from prepared statements," said Filmore.

"Will there be questions?" asked Ginny.

"Yes, but often it will sound more like a speech than a real question," said Filmore.

"Are you expecting television coverage?" I asked.

"Yes, if you consider C-span television coverage," answered Filmore. "Sometimes, mainstream press is present. This will likely be one of those times, but we'll see."

"Is there anything we should be concerned about?" asked Ginny.

"Representative Ellen Prusten is a member of the House Subcommittee on Health," answered Filmore.

"Isn't she the sponsor of the bill to criminalize Great Mother," I said.

Filmore nodded and said, "This is more than an inquiry into the FDA recall."

"I'm assuming there will be a lot of grandstanding about the people killed by Great Mother," I said.

"You can count on it," said Filmore.

"Eric, what has your investigation come up with?" asked Ginny.

Eric shook his head.

"Not a damn thing," answered Eric. "It's frustrating as hell, but I'm not alone. According to Rose, the police have nothing. Slotter is mad as hell because the CDC is giving military intelligence the cold shoulder. Hell, even with the CIA's resources, Jake can't get any information about these deaths. None of us believe it ever happened."

"Keep in mind that the subcommittee has authority over the CDC," said Filmore.

Ginny's phone rang and she slipped off to take the call.

"Do they control the FDA too?" I asked.

"Yes," answered Filmore.

"Is there a legal basis for the FDA's recall?" I asked Filmore.

"None," answered Filmore.

Ginny returned from her call and said, "The Department of Agriculture has blacklisted Great Mother."

"What does that mean?" asked Eric.

"They classified it as a noxious weed and ordered us to destroy all of it," said Ginny.

"That's crazy!" said Eric. "Why?"

"According to the USDA, it is an invasive species that jeopardizes existing eco-systems," she answered.

"They want us to destroy a miracle cure," said Eric.

"Don't you dare do it," said an old man standing nearby.

He was medium height, had a full head of silver hair cropped short, and was dressed completely in white. The clothing looked expensive and fit him perfectly. He returned our stunned gazes with eyes so blue they looked like he plucked them from the sky.

"That's what I said, but was told they would impose stiff civil and criminal penalties," said Ginny.

The glint in his eyes seemed to turn up a notch or two as he asked, "Will they?"

We turned to Filmore and asked, "Can they do this?"

"I'll have my law clerk research it during the flight," he said.

We turned back to the man in white to ask him what he knew about all of this, but he had vanished. This was followed by a scene between Filmore and Eric at the security gate when Eric stepped ahead of us pulling a ticket from his hip pocket.

"What are you doing?" demanded Filmore.

"I'm going with," said Eric with his best shit-eating grin plastered across his face.

"Why?" asked Filmore.

"I'm security," said Eric.

"We have a SEALs Team waiting for us in Washington," said Filmore. "We don't need additional security."

Eric took a step toward Filmore, which was about a step too close into anyone's personal space. Filmore was accustomed to issuing orders and having them followed. Eric was used to ignoring orders. The Admiral glared at Eric, but he stood his ground.

Filmore is tough, but I've never know Eric to back down from anyone and it was Filmore who backed down.

"Suit yourself," he said.

We boarded our flight. Filmore had purchased first class tickets for us. I had never flown first class in my life and said so. It seemed to me that we were on a mission for the people and should travel coach with them.

"It only costs a little more to go first class," said Filmore. "Why would you ever want to settle for less?"

"What's the matter, dude...don't you believe you deserve the very best of everything?" asked Eric.

The last trip I took to Washington was over a year ago to attend a meeting on behalf of my former client, Pathogen. Even though I flew coach, I have to admit I was puffed-up with importance. This time, I sat in first class and felt less important...humble even.

If we don't find our own validation, then life will constantly push us up and down like mercury in a cheap thermometer. The ground is self-esteem. A person has to like himself. It begins there.

Ginny seemed restless in the seat next to me. She was preoccupied with something. I resisted the temptation to storm in on a big white horse and make it better. She would share, if and when, she wanted to share.

After the pilot announced we had reached cruising altitude Ginny whispered in my ear, "I have a tradition I would like to honor on this trip."

The whisper was intriguing and I must admit that some crazy things whisked through my head in the span of a few seconds.

"What is it?" I asked.

"I always visit Mount Vernon when I'm in Washington," she answered.

"Jefferson's home?" I asked.

She poked me in the ribs and said, "George Washington's silly."

"Oh, umm...right," I said lamely.

"Can we go?" asked Ginny.

"Of course, darling," I answered.

"Thank you for being a good sport about my nerdy tendencies," she said.

"I think your inner nerd is adorable," I said.

She exhaled the pent up tension, laid her head on my shoulder and fell fast asleep. Some people can sleep on a flight, no matter how short. Others find it to be nearly impossible. I fall somewhere in the middle. In this instance, I spent the flight wide-awake and feeling grateful that Ginny was in my life.

The Washington traffic was crazy. The roads were jam packed with pickup trucks heading in our direction. I figured there was a farmer's convention in town.

Filmore arranged a car for us, if you want to call it that. It was a black mini-bus with dark tinted windows. A detail of Navy SEALs acted as our escort. I guess an Admiral has the resources to mobilize the SEALs, if necessary. It seemed over the top, but for the first time I felt we might be in danger.

They weren't dressed like soldiers, but they sure looked like fighters. A fighter knows another fighter. We just do. I don't enter into fights lightly, if it can be avoided. Eric is a different story. He likes to fight. On more than one occasion, I have trusted him to protect my back in a bar filled with bikers hopped up on drugs and whiskey.

It doesn't matter how tough you think you are, someone is tougher. You may want to put all of your faith in your training, but you best remember that there is someone out there who is better trained. One other thing to think about…they may not look like central casting's version of a badass. Wimpy Clark Kent was Superman in disguise.

"How many times you do BUDS?" asked Eric.

BUDS is Navy SEALs basic training that all SEALs team members must complete. It is brutal and all but a few drop out. Many SEALs have to wait and try again later before they complete the course.

"I'm a Miller Lite man," said the driver.

"Oh, what about you, Shotgun?" asked Eric.

"I don't care much for beer," he said.

Eric went completely still. It's a ten minute drive from Ronald Regan National Airport to Capitol Hill, but that was more than enough time for Eric to decide the SEALs were fakes. Oh, they were fighters, they just weren't Navy SEALs.

A lot of would be tough guys pretend to be ex-special forces. We've seen it before, but didn't confirm in this instance until the driver passed our exit and crossed the Anacostia River. We were officially headed in the opposite direction of Capitol Hill.

"Capitol Hill is in the other direction," said Eric.

The fake SEALs remained silent. In addition to the driver and the man-riding shotgun, there were two more in the rear seat of the bus. Filmore wasn't in the vehicle. He told us he had Navy business to tend to and would meet us outside of the committee room. It was beginning to look like the Admiral had betrayed us.

When we were kids, Eric and I had developed a set of signals using subtle eye movement to communicate with each other during a kidnapping, because like all ten-year-old boys, we knew beyond a shadow of doubt that one day they would come in handy. Eighteen years later Eric was using them to tell me to take out the two fake SEALs in the back, while he dispatched the ones up front.

That might have been an option in an unrealistic action film, but as we sped down the Interstate toward crime scene number two, I wasn't about to risk Ginny's life in a car crash. Besides, I wanted to find out where they were taking us before we kicked their asses.

The tension in the van was thick. Ginny changed to the seat behind the driver. She winked at Mr. Shotgun and then leaned toward the driver. Mr. Shotgun started to say something, but Ginny beat him to it.

"Last time I was D.C. we had to detour around a bunch of construction," she said. "It took us way out of our way and made me late for a meeting. Don't you hate when that happens?"

The driver let out a visible sigh of relief and said, "Yes, ma'am."

"We have some time to kill before our meeting," said Ginny. "How long do you think this will take?"

"I can't say for sure, Ma'am," answered the driver.

Eric pleaded with his eyes to kick some ass. I declined. He signaled his disappointment. I smiled in return. His eyes gave up and turned their attention to the freeway traffic. The bitterness they held was duly noted.

The driver exited at Pennsylvania Avenue and headed south a block to Minnesota Avenue where he turned left. We traveled a few blocks to the rotary where we spun off to circle Fort Circle Park. I thought he might be looking for a parking place to access the park, but instead he turned down an alley next to the Baptist church and parked at the base of a blue water tower.

We sat there for a less than a minute when a late model Mercedes pulled in behind us. I heard steps outside of the bus and someone walked past the window. The door to the bus opened and a woman stepped in. She was blond, middle aged, and dressed with casual elegance. In her hands was an unmarked Redwell file folder.

"Mr. Li," she said.

"Yes," I said.

"This might be helpful," she said.

I started to get up but she signaled for me to remain seated. Instead, she handed the folder over and turned to leave, but paused at the bottom step and looked back.

"Good luck today," she said.

"Thank you," I said.

The driver closed the door behind her and turned to Eric.

"We tell that Miller Lite joke to all of the SEALs team groupies," he said.

"I thought you were imposters," said Eric.

"It took me two tries to get through BUDS," said the driver. "It was the hardest thing I've ever done in my life."

"Same here," said a voice from the back.

"These other two clowns did it in one," said the driver.

"Sorry, I've been a real dick," said Eric. "When your tour is finished and you're looking for a job in the private sector, look me up."

"We know who you are," said the voice in the back. "Thanks for not making us kick your ass."

"Highly unlikely," said Eric with a grin.

"Name's Grekowski," said the driver.

Eric shook his hand and then we all introduced ourselves.

CHAPTER 73

It was a quick drive to Capitol Hill. The driver used a security pass to park in the garage and then led us to the committee meeting room. I've been in some courtrooms that inspire that same kind of respect and awe you might feel when entering a cathedral. The committee room did not possess that level of stateliness. Instead, it felt institutional and devoid of any real grandeur.

Blue drapes and a small flag hung on the wall behind a long curved bench with fourteen overstuffed leather chairs. Name plates with party affiliation were set in front of each seat. Two other shorter benches separated the main one from the witness table. The witness table had three settings, each with a microphone, empty glass and water bottle.

"Are you nervous?" asked Ginny.

I gave her hand a reassuring squeezing and said, "Not at all."

"There's something different about you, Grant," said Ginny.

"This is the first of many battles to come," I said.

"I'm glad it has begun," said Ginny.

"Me too, darling," I replied.

"Let's kick some ass," said Ginny.

"Yes dear," I replied with a grin.

The room was filling fast with spectators. We found seats in the front row reserved for witnesses. Several video cameras marked with network and cable logos were set up in an area reserved for the press. I was surprised to see several well-known journalists sitting near the cameras.

A door to the right opened and the committee members entered the room. Accustomed to courtrooms, I expected the crowd to rise in respect, but it didn't. In fact, no one paid them much mind.

There was one woman on the subcommittee, first year Congresswoman from South Carolina, Ellen Prusten. The rest of the members were white males. All but one was overweight and graying. Without exception, the most prominent thing they wore was a serious face, as if it somehow enhanced their importance.

The Chairman dropped a gavel to silence the crowd. On second thought, maybe he did it for show, since the crowd was already quiet. He adjusted the microphone, cleared his throat, and then surveyed the crowd. His eyes lingered on Ginny an extra beat or two before moving to the press. He gave the reporter from Conservative TV a slight nod of recognition and then began speaking.

"I see we have a full house," said the Chairman. "Welcome to the Health Subcommittee emergency hearing on the need to regulate an invasive species of plant commonly known as Great Mother in order to protect the public safety of American citizens. Before we begin, I'd like to welcome Ms. Prusten of the great state of South Carolina."

Representative Prusten was sitting on the far left in the second chair from the end. She raised her head from the stack of notes in front of her, pushed her glasses to the top of her head, and then squinted in the Chairman's general direction.

"The written opening statements will be made a part of the record," said the Chairman.

He glanced at his notes and then cleared his throat before resuming.

"A dangerous plant was smuggled into the United States," said the Chairman. "This plant is a particularly invasive species that is spreading like a wild fire. If left unchecked, it will choke out our native species, taking over the fields where we grow the food we put on our tables. Widespread food shortages are inevitable."

"This plant also threatens the health and vitality of our people," continued the Chairman. "Already there have been four confirmed deaths in Kentucky and we fear more to come. To compound the problem, con men have tricked the gullible into believing that this plant will somehow heal them. Make no mistake about it, there is absolutely no scientific evidence to support these claims. God fearing Americans are risking their lives as a result of lies told by snake oil hucksters. It is our duty to protect ourselves from this insidious threat. If left unchecked, it will destroy the very fabric of our healthcare system."

"Our first witness is Harold Feelmin, Assistant Director of the United States Agriculture Department," said the Chairman. "Dr. Feelmin is the leading expert in this country on invasive plant species. Will you please take a seat at the witness table and introduce yourself, Doctor?"

Harold Feelmin was short, round, and bald. He was dressed in an ill fitted grey suit that appeared to be made of wool. Judging by the stream of sweat pouring from his brow, it was much too heavy a fabric for a muggy Indian Summer day. It's also possible that the banker's box he lugged to the table had something to do with his overheated state.

He heaved the box onto the table, but miscalculated and sent a glass tumbling to the floor where it shattered into jagged pieces of glass.

"Oh shit!" he said loud enough for everyone in the room to hear.

There were a few snickers from the audience, but the Chairman silenced them with a glare worthy of a jaded high school teacher. Dr. Feelmin moved to clean the mess, but was stopped by the Chairman.

"Dr. Feelmin, if you will take a seat we will have someone clean that mess at our first recess," said the Chairman.

He took a couple of more steps in the direction of the glass, blinked, and then ran his hand over the top of his head.

"What's that?" asked Dr. Feelmin.

"Please have a seat, Doctor," said the Chairman.

"Oh…yes…yes…of course," said Doctor Feelmin.

He settled into the seat on the left, opened the box and retrieved a three-inch stack of paper that he placed on the corner of the table, making sure that the edge aligned perfectly with the edge of the table. Once he was satisfied, he reached into the box and retrieved a second stack of paper that he placed next to the first. Using his left hand, he measured three fingers to adjust the stack.

The Chairman interrupted his adjustments, "Are you familiar with Great Mother?"

The Doctor looked up from his task and said, "I hardly think you need to bring my mother into this."

The Chairman quashed a second round of snickers with a chop of the hand that stopped just short of hitting the bench. He cut his eyes to the gavel and let out a small sigh. He placed his hand over the microphone and whispered to Congressman John Bliel, a Republican from Tennessee, sitting to his right. Bliel glanced at his notes and then whispered a response.

"I believe the scientific name for Great Mother is Amazoniamagna," said the Chairman. "Are you familiar with it?"

"Why yes sir, I am," said the Doctor.

"Is the plant native to the United States?" asked the Chairman.

"No sir," answered the Doctor.

"When was it brought to this country?" asked the Chairman.

"We aren't certain, but we believe a few months ago," answered the Doctor.

"Were the necessary permits obtained prior to bringing it into the country?" asked the Chairman.

"No sir," answered the Doctor.

"In plain English, can you tell us what an invasive plant is?" asked the Chairman.

"It is an aggressive plant that chokes out native species," said the Doctor.

"Even crops?" asked the Chairman.

"Yes sir," answered the Doctor.

"Is Amazoniamagna an invasive plant?" asked the Chairman.

"Yes sir," answered the Doctor.

"How long will it take to choke out our native species?" asked the Chairman.

"Nobody can say for sure," answered the Doctor.

"Do you have an estimate?" asked the Chairman.

"Yes sir," answered the Doctor.

"Can you tell us what it is?" asked the Chairman.

"What, what is?" asked the Doctor.

"What is your estimate for how long it will take Great Mother…er… Amazoniamagna to choke out our native species?" asked the Chairman.

"At its current rate of growth, less than a year," answered the Doctor.

"Is there a way to stop it?" asked the Chairman.

"Destroy every last plant," said the Doctor.

"Every plant?" asked the Chairman.

"Without fail…every damn one of them," said the Doctor.

"Anyone else on the committee have any questions?" asked the Chairman.

One of the men cleared his throat as if he was about to speak, but the

Chairman cast him a slightly softer version of the same look he gave the crowd when they snickered. The man sunk a lower in his seat and shook his head.

"Since there are no other questions, you are excused Doctor," said the Chairman.

Somebody's phone went off. The Chairman glared at the audience until it stopped.

"Please make sure your cell phones are turned off," said the Chairman.

I pulled the mobile from my pocket and noticed that I had just missed a call from the Admiral. As much as I wanted to know what happened to him, I complied with the Chairman's order and shut it off.

"Our next witness is Dr. Darlene Hibbs, Deputy Director of Center for Disease Control," said the Chairman.

Dr. Feelmin cast a backward glance in the general direction of the sensible shoes pounding their way across the marble floor. Dr. Hibbs wore an equally sensible blue suit and crisp white blouse. Her salt and pepper hair was pulled back into a tight bun held firmly in place by invisible ties. There wasn't a single frill that I could see. This woman was sensible.

Dr. Feelmin rushed to pack his box, but it wasn't fast enough for Dr. Hibbs. She cast him a disapproving look and then seated herself at the center of the table.

He dropped the lid on the box, mumbled "bitch" loud enough for the rest of us to hear, and then tried to stand and lift the box at the same time. That didn't work out well for him because it sent the water bottle tumbling to the middle of the broken glass.

The Chairman got out ahead of the snickers this time and glared at the audience before anyone had a chance to voice his feelings at the doctor's expense. The doctor fled the room without making an effort to retrieve the water bottle.

"Dr. Hibbs, tell us what you do at the Center for Disease Control and Prevention?" said the Chairman.

"I head a department that investigates foreign threats to health," answered Dr. Hibbs.

"Does that include threats from terrorists?" asked the Chairman.

"Yes, in addition to responding to deliberate attacks to health, we also have a bio surveillance role?" answered Dr. Hibbs.

"In other words, it's your job to keep America safe from biological attacks," said the Chairman.

"Yes, you could put it that way," said Dr. Hibbs.

"Is Amazoniamagna a threat to health?" asked the Chairman.

"Yes sir," answered the Doctor.

"In layman's terms, can you tell us why?" asked the Chairman.

"Well, we are working furiously to build a scientific case against it, but at this time, we can say for certain that Amazoniamagna poses the greatest threat to health we have ever seen," answered the doctor.

"Is this a deadly threat?" asked the Chairman.

"Yes, it is," answered Dr. Hibbs.

"Do you have a solution to the threat?" asked the Chairman.

"Yes, it must be eradicated," answered the doctor.

"By eradicate, do you mean we must destroy every last plant?" asked the

Chairman.

"Yes, that is exactly what I mean," answered Dr. Hibbs.

"Thank you doctor," said the Chairman. "That's all the questions I have. Does anyone else on the Committee have any questions?"

Not one of the committee members moved a muscle. It made them look like cardboard caricatures of themselves. I wondered when they last had a thought of their own they weren't afraid to share.

The Chairman nodded his head in approval.

"If no one has any questions, then we will ask our next witness, Stanley Jacobs, Associate Commissioner of the Food and Drug Administration, to come forward and take a seat at the witness table," said the Chairman.

Dr. Jacobs appeared to be wearing the same rumpled blue suit and red tie worn during the recent press conference with the President and Representative Prusten. He shook hands with Dr. Hibbs as she left the table and then took her seat.

"Dr. Jacobs I'm going to cut to the chase here," said the Chairman. "You're investigating the death of four people in Kentucky, is that correct?"

"That's correct," answered Dr. Jacobs.

"All four of those people had consumed Amazoniamagna prior to their deaths, is that correct?" asked the Chairman.

"That's correct," answered Dr. Jacobs.

"Have you taken any steps to protect the American people from this plant?" asked the Chairman.

"We are pushing for new legislation to criminalize Amazoniamagna," answered Dr. Jacobs.

"Anything else?" asked the Chairman.

"We have issued a recall notice for Amazoniamagna," answered Dr. Jacobs.

"Who did you issue it to?" asked the Chairman.

"The importers, Grant Li and Virginia Bardough," answered Dr. Jacobs.

"Have they complied?" asked the Chairman.

"No sir," he answered.

"Do their actions put public health at risk?" asked the Chairman.

"Yes sir," answered Dr. Jacobs.

"If there are no further questions, then I will call for a thirty minute recess at this time," said the Chairman as he dropped his gavel. Without waiting for a response from the committee, he arose and immediately left the room.

CHAPTER 74

It doesn't take a genius to see that we were being set up. To make matters worse, our lawyer was missing in action. We did the only thing we could do under these circumstances when we took each other's hand and walked out of the room with our heads held high.

The press was waiting for us with bright lights and a barrage of questions. I was tempted to duck into a small conference room across the hall, but Ginny squeezed my hand and lead us boldly into the limelight.

"We want to thank you for giving Great Mother a voice," said Ginny.

The reporter from Conservative TV pinched her brow and demanded, "How do you respond to the reports that Great Mother is a gateway drug?"

"Great Mother is a gateway to optimal health," said Ginny.

"Why did you really smuggle this plant into the country?" asked a young blond.

"We didn't smuggle it into the country, but I'm glad it's here," I answered. "If it weren't for the plant my mother would still be a prisoner of her own bed, unable to care for her most basic needs."

"Have there been any more deaths?" shouted someone from the back row.

"We can't find any proof that Great Mother has killed anyone," I answered.

"You are all very competent journalists," said Ginny. "Have any of you uncovered any proof that Great Mother has killed anyone?"

Their collective heads shook from side to side...even the reporter's from Conservative TV.

"In my experience, Great Mother saves lives," I said.

Ginny looked into the cameras and said, "If anyone out there has reliable information that Great Mother has caused any harm, then please come forward. The world needs to know the truth."

The doors to the committee room flew open and a burly man with a conservative buzz cut interrupted the news conference.

"I'm sorry folks, but the committee is ready to proceed with the hearing," he said.

"It's been less than ten minutes," said one of the reporters.

"Yeah, they said thirty minutes," complained another.

"The Chairman has called the meeting to order and these two are the next witnesses," he said.

"Our attorney hasn't arrived yet," said Ginny.

I reached into my pocket and turned my phone on.

"I need to return a call from my attorney," I said.

"There's no time for a call," he said. "Please come with me."

Ginny looked to me for direction, so I nodded confidently toward the door. I added a reassuring squeeze to her hand and we headed inside to answer questions from members of Congress about Great Mother.

Rather than wait for an invitation from the Chairman, we headed straight to the witness table and had a seat. The Chairman glared at us.

"Now that Grant Li and Virginia Bardough have finally joined us, we can proceed with this hearing," said the Chairman.

There was a long pause from the Chairman as if he expected an apology from us, but we calmly returned his gaze while remaining silent. He cleared his throat. We didn't take the bait.

"Well then, we will turn this portion of the hearing over to Representative Prusten," said the Chairman.

"Thank you Mr. Chairman," said Ms. Prusten.

She began to roll up her sleeves. It was such an obvious cliché, Ginny couldn't resist unbuttoning the two top buttons of her blouse. It worked as I imagined she intended, since all eyes shifted to Ginny's cleavage and away from Ms. Prusten's forearms.

Representative Prusten glared at Ginny and said, "Make no mistake about it, I have made it my personal mission to protect the public from liars who would exploit the sick."

"We agree that exploiting human suffering for personal gain is evil," said Ginny.

Representative Prusten clenched and unclenched her fists, as if she was squeezing a small rubber ball to relieve stress. I doubt the Congresswoman even realized she was doing it.

"Is it true you ignored the recall notice?" demanded Ms. Prusten.

"It is an impossible request," I answered.

She raised an eyebrow and said, "Can you explain why it is impossible?"

"It's like trying to recall the sunrise," answered Ginny.

"That's very poetic, but people's lives are at risk," scoffed Representative Prusten.

"How are they at risk?" I asked.

"I'm asking the questions," she said.

"It's a simple question," I said. "Are you refusing to answer it?"

Representative Prusten looked directly into the cameras and said, "Four people are dead, how many more must die before we stop this insanity?"

"Those four people died when their car was struck by a drunk driver," I said. "Surely you don't blame Great Mother."

The Chairman slammed his gavel to silence the buzz from the audience.

"Humph…we must be talking about different people," said Ms. Prusten.

"Then who are you talking about?" asked Ginny.

"I'm in charge here, not you," said Ms. Prusten.

"You answer to ordinary people like us," said Ginny.

"The people need to be protected and I will protect them whether they want it or not," said Ms. Prusten.

"We are not children to be protected by the likes of you," we said in unison.

"We'll see about that," said Ms. Prusten. "You have made outrageous claims about the benefits of Great Mother that simply are not supported by science."

"Are you certain of that?" asked Ginny.

Looking unsure of herself Ms. Prusten asked, "Have you performed scientific studies on Great Mother…err… Amazoniamagna?"

"No, we have not," I answered.

Ms. Prusten allowed herself a small smile and then plowed in for the kill, "Then you have no evidence to support the assertion that this plant has the slightest medical benefit."

"But we do," we said.

She cast a wary eye at the file folder on the table in front of us, but we made no move to open it.

"If you do indeed have such evidence, then way have you not produced it?" she asked.

"Because it was hidden from the public," I answered.

"That's ridiculous, why would you hide it?" she scoffed.

"We didn't," answered Ginny.

"But you just said you did," complained the Congresswoman.

"It wasn't us who hid it," we said.

"Why would anyone hide it?" she demanded.

"That's a good question that we all want an answer to," said Ginny.

"Stop playing games with me," said Ms. Prusten. "If you have such evidence, then produce it now."

As if on cue, the cell phones in the room began chiming and everyone dug into their pockets and purses for them.

The Chairman slammed his gavel once again and barked, "All electronic devices must be turned off this instant."

Everyone froze, but when the committee members began whispering to each other, phones in hand, everyone went back to checking their own. Well, everyone except Ms. Prusten and the Chairman checked their phones. Instead, they glared at us with undisguised hatred.

"I can clear this room if need be," shouted the Chairman.

Representative Bliel leaned in, whispered to the Chairman, and then showed him his phone. The Chairman's face went white at first, but the color came back with a vengeance, rising quickly from the neck.

With a trembling hand, he reached for his gavel, but not before the doors to the committee room flew open and Zeke stormed in with two burly US Marshalls.

"Ellen Prusten," said Zeke.

"Yes, who are you?" she asked.

"I am Assistant United States Attorney, Zeke Kruthers," he answered.

"Why are you interrupting the interrogation of these two con artists?" demanded Ms. Prusten.

"I have a warrant for your arrest," said Zeke.

"What possible warrant can you have for her arrest?" asked the Chairman.

"Fraud, among other things," answered Zeke.

"There must be some mistake," she said. "I'm a member of the United States Congress."

"I assure you that there is no mistake," said Zeke. "During your long employment at Pathogen you conducted many experiments that prove Great Mother cures every human illness thrown at it and you suppressed all of these results."

"How could you possibly know that…those studies are proprietary trade secrets of Pathogen and any information you have about them could only have been obtained illegally," she said. "I will have you arrested for theft."

Zeke smiled a crooked smile and sent the burliest of the two US Marshalls to her seat at the bench with handcuffs in hand.

"Good luck with that, Representative Prusten," said Zeke.

"Well, if that's all you have, Mr. Kruthers," said the Chairman.

"There is one more matter to attend to, Mr. Chairman," said Zeke.

The Chairman shifted in his seat and then mindfully laid the gavel back onto the bench next to the ornate sound block.

"Yes…yes…what is it?" asked the Chairman.

"Have you seen the news report, Mr. Chairman?" asked Zeke.

"Son, I've seen many news reports in my lifetime," said the Chairman. "Few of them get it right."

"This one is special and it's going viral as we speak," said Zeke.

Representative Biler once again offered his phone to the Chairman, but he impatiently waved him off.

"What does mass murder half way around the world have to do with me?" asked the Chairman.

"You worked for Pathogen, did you not?" asked Zeke.

"Yes…yes…many years ago," said the Chairman.

"What did you do for them?" asked Zeke.

The Chairman ran his hand through his thinning hair, exhaled slowly, and then focused all of his attention on Zeke.

"I don't know what that has to do with anything, I've faithfully served this country for twenty years," said the Chairman.

"You were a Vice-President at Pathogen, were you not?" asked Zeke.

"Yes, I was," answered the Chairman.

"You were head of research and development," said Zeke.

The Chairman hesitated and then nodded his assent.

"You took a special interest in viruses, did you not?" asked Zeke.

"Like all healthcare workers, we were on the frontlines in the fight against viral infection," answered the Chairman.

"Does that fight include the development of a virus for use as a bio-weapon?" asked Zeke.

The Chairman rose from his seat and said, "I have given my life to public service and will not sit here and suffer through your outrageous insinuations."

Zeke sent the remaining United States Marshall to the bench and said, "I have a warrant for your arrest."

"Son, you don't survive in politics as long as I have without making friends who must come to your aid in a time of need," said the Chairman.

"I do not doubt you have friends in Washington, but how many friends do you have in Egypt and the seven other countries where you wiped out entire villages with your virus?" asked Zeke.

The Marshall cuffed the Chairman, and then together with Ms. Prusten, they took the walk of shame down the aisle and then out the mahogany doors with the shiny brass hardware.

My phone went off, yet again. This time it was a text message from the Admiral.

"It's from the Admiral," I said. "My divorce is final, so I can finally make an honest woman of you."

Ginny threw her arms around me and I kissed her while the audience cheered and clapped their approval.

"If we hurry, darling, we can spend the rest of the day at Mount Vernon," said Ginny.

# # #

Thank you for reading *Great Mother*. Won't you please take a moment to leave a book review?

Peace out,

Robert

COMING SOON!

Sovereigns' Refuge

OTHER BOOKS BY ROBERT GRANT

Naked Tao
Nostrum Conspiracy
UnderBelly

ABOUT ROBERT GRANT

Among Robert Grant's many interests are martial arts. He comes from a long line of Taoists, who left their sheltered lives in a mountain monastery to wander a world filled with raw beauty. These wandering monks have a long tradition of telling stories that both entertain and teach. Robert promised his Shifu he would keep the tradition of storytelling alive and began developing a story idea about a lawyer who discovers his client is behind a conspiracy that will hurt millions of people. The choices he makes could hurt the people he loves most or lead to love, redemption, and a worthy life purpose. It is an easy fast read with subtle depth and easy humor. The result is a first-rate thriller with a mystical twist that will have you laughing one minute and crying the next. Come, open a book and travel to places you never knew existed.

CONNECT WITH ROBERT GRANT

Thank you for reading *Great Mother*. Please tell your friends and family about my work. I am busy writing the next book. If you would like to receive updates on the book launch, book cover contests, and coupons for book pre-orders, then drop me a note at Robert@NTPublishingCompany.com. Lastly, I want to invite you to come and hang out with me.

Send your mail messages to: Robert@NTPublishingCompany.com

Follow me on Twitter: https://twitter.com/nakedtao

Like my Facebook page: http://www.facebook.com/AuthorRobertGrant

Follow me on Google Plus: https://www.google.com/+RobertGrantNakedTao

Follow my blog at: http://www.ntpublishingcompany.com

Welcome to our family and please remember to leave a review of *Great Mother*. This book is also available as an eBook at most online retailers.

Peace out,
Robert